OXFORD ENGLISH NOVELS
General Editor: HERBERT DAVIS

THE
SPIRITUAL QUIXOTE

S Wale del,   C.Grignion Sc,

RICHARD GRAVES

THE

Spiritual Quixote

OR

THE SUMMER'S RAMBLE OF
MR. GEOFFRY WILDGOOSE

A COMIC ROMANCE

Edited with an Introduction by
CLARENCE TRACY

LONDON
OXFORD UNIVERSITY PRESS
NEW YORK   TORONTO
1967

Oxford University Press, Ely House, London W.1

GLASGOW NEW YORK TORONTO MELBOURNE WELLINGTON
CAPE TOWN SALISBURY IBADAN NAIROBI LUSAKA ADDIS ABABA
BOMBAY CALCUTTA MADRAS KARACHI LAHORE DACCA
KUALA LUMPUR HONG KONG TOKYO

PRINTED IN GREAT BRITAIN

CONTENTS

INTRODUCTION   XV

NOTE ON THE TEXT   xxiv

BIBLIOGRAPHY   xxv

A CHRONOLOGY OF RICHARD GRAVES   xxvi

THE SPIRITUAL QUIXOTE

Dedication of the Second Edition   1

A Prefatory Anecdote   2

Postscript   5

Advertisement   6

The Author's Dedication   7

Introduction   8

VOLUME ONE

BOOK I

   I. *The Education and juvenile Pursuits of Mr. Wildgoose*   13

  II. *A Dispute with the Vicar*   15

 III. *The serious Consequences of it*   16

 IV. *Mr. Wildgoose enters upon a new Course of Studies*   18

   V. *Adopts a new System of Religion*   20

 VI. *Preliminaries with the fastidious Reader*   21

 VII. *What sort of Man Jeremiah Tugwell was*   22

VIII. *Sketch of Mr. Wildgoose's Theological System*   25

 IX. *He commences Orator*   26

   X. *A peculiar Species of Ecclesiastical Discipline*   28

 XI. *Mr. Wildgoose takes an extraordinary Resolution*   29

BOOK II

I. *Original of Methodism. Mr. Wildgoose's Resolution to visit the Society at Bristol* 30

II. *Communicates his Intentions to Tugwell* 32

III. *Jerry's affected Scruples* 35

IV. *Essay on Quixotism* 39

V. *Mr. Wildgoose and his Friend Tugwell sally forth in Quest of Spiritual Adventures* 42

VI. *Tugwell meets with a perilous Adventure* 44

VII. *The natural Effects of Hunger and Fatigue* 46

VIII. *Character of Mrs. Wildgoose. And the Perplexity occasioned by the Elopement of Mr. Wildgoose and Tugwell* 47

IX. *Proceed towards Dover's-hill Revel* 50

X. *Mr. Wildgoose's first Harangue* 52

XI. *Armigerorum Laudes; or, a Panegyric on Esquires, both ancient and modern* 56

XII. *Mr. Wildgoose's hospitable Reception at the House of an orthodox Clergyman; and the Event of a Dispute between them* 58

XIII. *What happened at the Parson's Habitation* 61

XIV. *Night-thoughts: Of Ghosts and Goblins. They meet with an uncommon Adventure* 64

XV. *The Event of Mr. Wildgoose's second Harangue* 67

BOOK III

I. *Mr. Wildgoose's Reception at the Bell at Gloucester, the Birthplace of Mr. Whitfield* 69

II. *An hospitable Barber accommodates Mr. Wildgoose with a Lodging, and a Place to preach in* 70

III. *At Gloucester* 72

IV. *Our Itinerant's Popularity increases* 75

V. *Mr. Wildgoose's Success with the Ladies* 77

VI. *The History of Miss Townsend* 79

VII. *Miss Townsend's Story continued* 81

VIII. *Miss Townsend's Story continued* 83

IX. *Miss Townsend's Story continued* 85

X. *Miss Townsend's Story continued* 86

XI. *Miss Townsend's Story continued* 87

XII. *Miss Townsend's Story continued* 89

XIII. *Miss Townsend's Story continued* 91

XIV. *Miss Townsend's Story continued* 93

XV. *Miss Townsend's Story continued* 94

XVI. *Miss Townsend's Story continued* 96

XVII. *Miss Townsend's Story concluded* 97

XVIII. *The Effects of Miss Townsend's Narration* 98

XIX. *A Dissertation on Periwigs* 100

XX. *The Farewell-Harangue is attended with a disastrous Circumstance* 104

BOOK IV

I. *The Pilgrims set out for Bath* 106

II. *The Tinker's Tale* 109

III. *Their comfortable Reception at Park-corner, near Lord Bathurst's Woods* 111

IV. *Spiritual Advice* 114

V. *A Stranger, of a Peculiar Character, arrives* 115

VI. *Some Account of the Virtuoso* 119

VII. *An Hurley-burley in the Modern Taste* 120

VIII. *The Mistress of an Inn not easily to be converted* 122

IX. *The Travellers pursue their Journey* 123

X. *A Knight-errant of a peculiar Kind. Compassion for dumb Creatures* 124

XI. *The polite Philosopher* 127

XII. *A singular Mansion* 130

XIII. *Mr. Graham's Story* 131

XIV. *Mr. Graham's Story continued* 133

XV. *Mr. Graham's Way of Life* 136

BOOK V

I. *The two Pilgrims arrive at Bath* 138

II. *Popular Reports sometimes a little erroneous* 141

III. *Landlord alters his Tone. A Female Saint* 142

IV. *Wildgoose attends a Bath Meeting* 143

V. *He harangues on the Parade* 144

VI. *A Digression on Message-Cards* 146

VII. *Tête à Tête* 148

VIII. *Mrs. Booby's Story* 149

IX. *Mrs. Booby's Story continued* 150

X. *Mrs. Booby's Story concluded. Wildgoose's Opinion of the Marriage-Contract. Description of a Bath Life* 152

XI. *A Scene in genteel Life. Enter Mrs. Bardolph, Miss Trufle, and Mr. Rouvell. Their Characters* 158

XII. *Various Chit-chat* 161

XIII. *Story of Calomel and Lady Riot* 164

XIV. *Universities defended, &c.* 166

XV. *Tricks among Servants. News from Mrs. Sarsenet* 169

XVI. *A serious Conversation with Mr. Rouvell* 171

XVII. *Lady Sherwood's Character and present Situation* 173

XVIII. *A learned Conversation, not essential to the Story* 175

XIX. *Learned Account of the Bath Waters. Mr. Wildgoose and his Friend take their Leave of that City* 179

VOLUME TWO

BOOK VI

I. *Mr. Wildgoose meets an old Friend* 183

II. *Description of Mr. Rivers's House, and some Account of his present Situation* 185

III. *The History of Mr. Rivers and Charlotte Woodville* 187

IV. *Mr. Rivers's Story continued* 189

V. *Mr. Rivers's Story continued* 191

VI. *Mr. Rivers's Story continued* 193

VII. *Mr. Rivers's Story continued* 195

VIII. *Mr. Rivers's Story continued* 198

IX. *Mr. Rivers's Story continued* 199

X. *Mr. Rivers's Story continued* 202

XI. *Mr. Rivers's Story continued*   203

XII. *Mr. Rivers's Story continued*   205

XIII. *Mr. Rivers's Story continued*   207

XIV. *Mr. Rivers's Story continued*   212

XV. *Mr. Rivers's Story continued*   215

XVI. *Mr. Rivers's Story continued*   217

XVII. *Mr. Rivers's Story continued*   220

XVIII. *Mr. Rivers's Story concluded*   221

XIX. *Mr. Wildgoose questions Mr. Rivers on Religion*   224

XX. *Comforts of Matrimony*   226

XXI. *They arrive at Bristol*   227

BOOK VII

I. *Mr. Wildgoose's Interview with Mr. Whitfield*   229

II. *Hears Mr. Whitfield at Kingswood*   233

III. *Evening's Entertainment*   235

IV. *Wildgoose mounts the Rostrum. An unexpected Incident*   236

V. *Gloucester Journal*   238

VI. *Triumphs of Faith*   240

VII. *Theatrical Entertainments. A new Project for their Regulation* 243

VIII. *A ridiculous Distress. Advantages of the Sacerdotal Habit*   246

IX. *Modern Prophecies. Effects of Wildgoose's Eloquence*   248

X. *Effusions of Self-importance. Wildgoose meets with a Repulse* 252

XI. *Mr. Wildgoose becomes a great Casuist*   255

XII. *Some unexpected Incidents*   258

XIII. *Event of their Voyage*   260

BOOK VIII

I. *The Pilgrims arrive at Cardiff*   263

II. *Adventures in the Inn at Cardiff*   266

III. *Mr. Wildgoose holds forth to a Welsh Audience*   268

IV. *An unlucky Mistake*   269

V. *An Apparition*   271

VI. *Their Reception by the Parson of Newport*   273

VII.	*An agreeable Solitude. An Holy Family, in the Flemish Style*	274
VIII.	*Ecclesiastical Pride in the Diocese of Landaff*	277
IX.	*Mr. Wildgoose collects an Audience*	279
X.	*Miracles and slight Persecutions*	281
XI.	*Reception at Monmouth*	283
XII.	*A Stranger introduced to our Hero*	284
XIII.	*The Adventures of Captain Johnson*	286
XIV.	*The Adventures of Captain Johnson continued*	287
XV.	*The Adventures of Captain Johnson continued*	289
XVI.	*The Adventures of Captain Johnson concluded*	291
XVII.	*A Temporary Conversion*	293
XVIII.	*A warm Breakfast, followed by a cold Collation*	295
XIX.	*A seasonable Relief*	297
XX.	*The Pilgrims taken up upon Suspicion*	299
XXI.	*A Justice, and a Justice of the Peace*	301
XXII.	*A Friend in Need is a Friend indeed*	302
XXIII.	*The real Highwayman produced. Tugwell escapes a Gaol, and gets a Dinner*	305
XXIV.	*Man of Ross*	308
XXV.	*Forest of Dean. Equality of Mankind*	309
XXVI.	*Perils amongst false Brethren*	311
XXVII.	*At Gloucester*	314
XXVIII.	*The Pilgrims kindly treated by Mrs. Whitfield*	315
XXIX.	*They set out for the North*	316

VOLUME THREE

BOOK IX

I.	*Good Effects of Mr. Wildgoose's Labours*	319
II.	*The Hotel at Tewksbury*	320
III.	*The Life of a Stroller. Criticisms on Shakespear*	321
IV.	*State of Religion at Worcester*	324
V.	*An unexpected Rencounter*	325
VI.	*A just Character of Lady L—n, from a discarded Servant*	327

VII. *A Sketch of the Leasowes, and of the Character of the worthy Possessor of that Place*   329

VIII. *A Practical Lecture against the Vanities of this World*   331

IX. *A Discourse on Idolatry*   332

X. *Slight Persecutions*   333

XI. *A Glimpse of Miss Townsend*   335

XII. *Meet with a seasonable Invitation*   337

XIII. *Some Account of this Stranger*   339

XIV. *The Life of a dying Man*   340

XV. *A Remedy for Want of Appetite*   342

XVI. *History of a Long-liver, and other Chit-chat*   343

XVII. *Rules for Health*   345

XVIII. *A new System of Education*   347

XIX. *Account of the little fat Rector*   349

XX. *Further Account of the little fat Rector*   350

XXI. *Set out for Ashbourn, near the Peak*   352

BOOK X

I. *A Phænomenon*   354

II. *A modest Plea*   355

III. *The Generosity of a Quack*   356

IV. *Ecce autem alterum!*   357

V. *An affecting Scene. Tugwell in Jeopardy*   359

VI. *A judicious Magistrate*   360

VII. *They set forth towards the High-Peak*   362

VIII. *Fall in with a musical Party*   363

IX. *Characters of Sir William and Lady Forester*   365

X. *Character of Colonel Rappee*   367

XI. *A Conversation on Religion and other Subjects*   368

XII. *A Scene in the Nursery*   372

XIII. *Family Prayers; followed by Repartees*   373

XIV. *A Morning Conversation on the Back Stairs*   375

XV. *On the Expediency of a regular Ordination*   376

XVI. *A Lecture in the Servants Hall*   378

XVII. *Lady Forester's Morning Engagement* 380

XVIII. *A Scene more agreeable than the last* 381

XIX. *A slight Alarm* 383

XX. *The Lawfulness of eating a good Dinner* 384

XXI. *Protestant Nunneries. The disconsolate Widow* 386

XXII. *Frailty not confined to Females* 389

XXIII. *Wonders of the Peak* 391

XXIV. *View of a Lead-mine* 393

XXV. *Beauties of Nature* 396

XXVI. *Narrative of a licentious Amour* 397

XXVII. *The Narrative continued* 398

XXVIII. *Its fatal Event* 400

XXIX. *A Remedy against Suicide* 402

XXX. *Love triumphant over Sensuality* 403

XXXI. *More nocturnal Perils* 405

BOOK XI

I. *The two Pilgrims decamp without Beat of Drum* 407

II. *A learned Inn-keeper. Wildgoose meets an old Acquaintance* 409

III. *The last Efforts of expiring Vanity* 411

IV. *A Parody on the Speech of Jaques, in Shakespear's As you
like it* 413

V. *Trifling Difficulties* 415

VI. *Tugwell is under a Necessity of drinking Strong-beer instead
of Small* 416

VII. *The fortunate Isabella* 419

VIII. *Further Account of Isabella* 420

IX. *A curious Inscription* 423

X. *Mr. Wildgoose makes a new Acquaintance* 424

XI. *At Warwick* 426

XII. *Olympic Honours* 427

XIII. *Mr. Wildgoose's Farewell Sermon* 428

XIV. *Work for the Doctor* 429

XV. *An old Gentleman in Black arrives* 431

XVI. *Character of Dr. Greville*   432

XVII. *Dr. Greville and Mr. Wildgoose*   434

XVIII. *At Dr. Greville's*   435

XIX. *Mrs. Mahoney's Intelligence canvassed*   438

XX. *Mr. Wildgoose retires to Rest*   439

BOOK XII

I. *The Inn at Warwick*   441

II. *Kitchen-stuff*   443

III. *At Dr. Greville's*   444

IV. *At Mr. Townsend's*   446

V. *At Doctor Greville's*   448

VI. *An Interview*   453

VII. *Mrs. Mahoney's Story finished*   454

VIII. *At Dr. Greville's*   456

IX. *An Invitation to Mr. Townsend's*   457

X. *At Stratford upon Avon*   458

XI. *More Lumber yet; a Wife and two Children*   460

XII. *A Plan for Reformation*   461

XIII. *The same Subject continued*   462

XIV. *Mr. Wildgoose's Reception at Home*   464

XV. *Jerry Tugwell's Reception at Home*   466

XVI. *The grand Point settled*   467

XVII. *Modern Taste, and that of our Ancestors*   469

XVIII. *Other Matters adjusted*   470

Conclusion   472

NOTES   475

A LIST OF PRINCIPAL VARIANTS   499

INTRODUCTION

As the Reverend Mr. Graves, rector of Claverton, himself admitted, *The Spiritual Quixote* originated 'in a pique'. An itinerant preacher had intruded into his parish, bringing with him 'a large congregation, and preached and sang psalms in a large old house', until the rector found his church 'almost deserted'.[1] He promptly drove out the interloper, who was a journeyman-shoemaker and had neglected to take out a licence, and, in due time, sat down to compose a satire on Methodism. But pique is not the tone of this genial novel. If Graves had hugged his grievance from 1757,[2] when he began to write, down to 1773, when he published, he would have far exceeded the record of the gentleman mentioned in one of Walton's biographies who remained in prison 'very angry for three years'. How hot Graves's anger ever was and how long it lasted I do not know; but his novel is a happy book, expressing common sense and sincere piety, and showing a zest for life in a multiplicity of incident and character drawn from the riches of his own experience. The underlying satiric purpose, though never quite forgotten, is constantly being suspended to enable its author to share a joke or an experience with his readers. If he began it in pique, it is only fair to add that he also said he completed it because it amused him to do so.

Even to call his book a satire is to suggest unfair comparisons with the great satires of Voltaire, Butler, and Swift. Graves himself gave it the more modest description of 'comic romance'. He does link it with the tradition of Cervantes, and his indebtednesses to *Don Quixote* are too obvious to need enumeration. But as soon as one makes this comparison, one is aware of the disparity between the two writers not only in ability but also in the nature of their comic conceptions. Don Quixote is a romantic obsessed with a hopelessly lost cause: the age of chivalry had long been dead and the Don brings his creator's ridicule down on his head because

[1] Cf. C. J. Hill, *The Literary Career of Richard Graves* (Northampton, Massachusetts, 1934-5), p. 24, and *The Public Characters of 1799-1800* (1799), p. 395.

[2] Hill, p. 17. Even this date may be late. On p. 327 Graves calls Lyttleton, who became Lord Lyttleton in 1756, 'Sir George L ——— n'.

B

he refused to face this fact. But Geoffry Wildgoose was trying to revive true Christianity, which the Reverend Richard Graves was very far indeed from thinking dead; he ridiculed only the means adopted by the Methodists for propagating it. His views were moderate and conciliatory and are expressed by several characters in the novel: Mrs. Wildgoose, for example, in one of the early chapters speaks for Graves when she says: 'If the clergy would but do their duty, as her poor father did, and as the canons of the church required, there would be no necessity for these extraordinary proceedings.'[1] Dr. Greville, Mr. Graham, and others make the same point almost too abundantly clear. John Wesley himself might have endorsed the sentiment, and Christopher Collop, Graves's authorial persona, was suspected of favouring the Methodists in his heart.

Graves's view of eighteenth-century Methodism may have been one-sided, but to look at it through the eyes of a thoroughly good and sensible man like him is a healthy corrective to what we have been told so often about the eighteenth-century Church by Whig historians and pious Victorians. Through him we are able to see the movement as it must have appeared to thousands of ordinary educated people in his time, the 'good sort of people' whom Whitefield and Wesley scorned. Wesley, who makes one dramatic appearance in the novel, Graves treated with considerable respect, but Whitefield shows up as a firebrand and a hypocrite. More striking are Graves's descriptions of the 'new birth', which must have come from observation as well as from a close study of the journals of both Wesley and Whitefield. When undergoing the new birth the Methodist rank and file uttered loud and bitter cries, threw themselves on the floor frothing at the mouth, and lost consciousness. Little children were 'pricked through and through with the power of the word' and went home from sermons speechless with terror. All of these things were considered by the Methodists to be manifestations of divine grace. The journals of both leaders are full of accounts like this one:

Forty or fifty of those who were seeking salvation, desired leave to spend the night together, at the society-room, in prayer and giving thanks. Before ten I left them and lay down. . . . Between two and three in the morning I was waked, and desired to come down stairs. I immediately heard such a confused noise, as if a number of men were all putting to the sword. It

[1] p. 20.

increased when I came into the room and began to pray. One whom I particularly observed to be roaring aloud for pain was J. . . . W. . . ., who had been always 'till then very sure, that 'none cried out but hypocrites'; So had Mrs. S. . . . ms also. But she too now cried to God with a loud and bitter cry. It was not long, before God heard from his holy place. He spake, and all our souls were comforted. He bruised Satan under our feet, and sorrow and sighing fled away.[1]

Graves transferred that incident to his novel, subtly omitting the marks of Wesley's wonder at the power of God in the hearts of men, and substituting satire on religious hysteria:

But, about two in the morning, Mr. Wildgoose was waked by a confused noise, as if a number of men were putting to the sword. He went up into the Society-room, where the people had worked themselves up to such a pitch of religious phrenzy, that some were fallen prostrate upon the floor, screaming, and roaring, and beating their breasts, in agonies of remorse for their former wicked lives; others were singing hymns, leaping and exulting in extasies of joy, that their sins were forgiven them.[2]

Graves's attitude is not only marked by common sense, but is likely to be congenial to a modern reader more aware than either Wesley or Whitefield were of the psychic dangers inherent in the nervous tensions and emotional orgasms induced by these preachers. We are quite prepared to see the irony in Wildgoose's remark: 'People are never nearer to the Kingdom of Heaven than when they are mad . . .'.[3]

In general, Graves's indictment of the Methodists runs as follows: that they were righteous overmuch, that they neglected their humbler duties in order to watch and pray and preach (as Wildgoose thoughtlessly deserted his mother when he commenced itinerant), that they sold salvation too cheaply (Whitefield was accused of inducing his followers to become saints 'upon easy terms', faith alone being required of them), that they stirred up mass hysteria, and that they reintroduced superstitions into a society that had been freed from them (as when Wesley used a Christianized version of the *sortes Virgilianae*). Graves was no seer, and his criticisms do not tell the whole truth about Methodism,

[1] John Wesley's Journal for 11 Aug. 1740.
[2] p. 294.
[3] p. 295.

but they do show that the opposition to it was not inspired, as is so often suggested, merely by intolerance and vested interest.[1]

The gently comic tone of Graves's book is particularly indicated in the fact that Wildgoose was subjected only to minor persecutions, and to none of the terrible catastrophes encountered by the characters in *Candide*. Early in the novel he announced his intention of going to preach to the miners at Wednesbury, where he might well have been stoned, scourged with wires, or sawn asunder, because at Wednesbury the Methodists had had to face their worst persecutions: their houses had been wrecked and looted and many of them had suffered grievous bodily hurt. If in his starry-eyed innocence Wildgoose had gone there, the novel would have been given a much more bitter tone. But instead Graves sent him off on what turns out to be mainly a sight-seeing tour of the Peak country. Like any eighteenth-century tourist, he visited gentlemen's seats, admired prospects, and exclaimed at precipices and waterfalls. In the end, when he attempted to preach at the Warwick races, he was knocked on the head with a decanter and sent to bed for a day on account of shock. Even this mild persecution was a blessing in disguise, because it brought him back to his senses and the Church of England. Wildgoose's obsession, in other words, unlike Don Quixote's, is not incurable and the novel ends in reconciliation.

To some readers of these later chapters Graves may seem to have abdicated his satiric mission, padding out his book with popular but irrelevant episodes instead. But a strong undercurrent of irony is pointed up by these digressions and is Graves's chief means of conveying his message. The blow on the head may have been the efficient cause of Wildgoose's return to sanity, but the sanity to which he returned is partly composed of love of the country, of wonder at God's creation, and of happy conformity to the age-long tradition of English life. Love of God, Graves seems to be saying, implies a love of what God made, and the fault in the Methodists is that they turn their backs on the world that God made, finding it full of sin, and deny themselves both illegitimate and legitimate

[1] Graves's criticisms are similar to those made by William Warburton, Bishop of Gloucester, in his *Doctrine of Grace* (1750). Graves's reading of this book may have inspired his novel, for he referred to it (p. 4 and note 2) and he used many of the same quotations from Wesley's journal that Warburton used. Moreover Warburton twice referred to Cervantes in this connexion, likening the Methodist preachers to Don Quixote and Sancho Pancho [*sic*]. See pp. 322 and 381 n.

pleasures, expecting perfection in an imperfect world. All about them the sun shines on the grass in the meadows, the fish swim in the streams, the huntsman's horn echoes across the hills, and good ale is on tap in the inn—calling men out of themselves, if only they would hear the call. This is the artistic purpose of the sightseeing digressions, to be a symbol of a more healthy and less introspective way of life. We are reminded of this right from the start. Graves never wrote better prose than in the exquisite description of the Vale of Evesham as the two pilgrims saw it on their first setting out:

> The sun had now begun to exhale the dews of the morning; which, being thinly dispersed through the air, gave a charming freshness to every object that rose to their view. There was an extensive prospect of the rich vale of Evesham, bounded at a distance by the Malvern hills. The towers and spires, which rose amongst the tufted trees, were strongly illuminated by the sloping rays of the sun; and the whole scene was enlivened by the music of the birds; the responsive notes of the thrushes from the neighbouring haw-thorns, and the thrilling strains of the sky-lark, who, as she soared towards the heavens, seemed to be chanting forth her matins to the great Creator of the universe.[1]

Wildgoose, it is true, was touched momentarily by the sight and broke out into a quotation from Milton. But within a page he was nagging at the faithful Jerry for smoking his pipe: 'Thou art not content with the heavenly manna of meditation,' he says to him, 'but still lustest after the garlic and flesh-pots of Egypt.' The message of nature is not heard by him until much later, and then largely subconsciously; but it is heard by the reader throughout.

The Spiritual Quixote is a classic, if a minor one, because its author delivered himself completely in it, expressing the freshness and charm of his personality as well as his magnanimity and under-standing. His other published works, almost all of which are of later date, fall short of it in these qualities, for Graves was not a man of powerful imagination. His success was achieved through recollection and self-expression, and this can be done fully only once.

Much indeed of his material came out of his own experience only slightly transmogrified in the process. Jerry Tugwell is a true rustic type, faithfully observed and truly represented, one of the most convincing louts in eighteenth-century fiction. His model could not have been hard to find among the Claverton yokels. Geoffry

[1] pp. 42–43.

Wildgoose, the Don Quixote to whom Jerry plays Sancho Panza, owes at least a few of his lineaments to Charles Caspar Graves, the author's brother, who became a Methodist. Among his minor characters the reader will quickly recognize a few real persons, like William Shenstone and Lady Lyttleton. At other times he will merely be told by the author in a footnote that such and such is a 'real fact', and often, though he is told nothing at all, he will suspect that a character has been modelled on some friend of Graves's. Sir William and Lady Forester, for example, who figure largely in the chapters devoted to the Peak, have all the characteristics of real rather than fictional people, and in 1831 W. J. Croker produced a 'key' in which among others Sir William was identified with William Fitzherbert of Tissington, Graves's employer for three years in his early career.[1] But the identification is by no means certain. Other allusions are even more elusive. For example, in the light-hearted mock-heroics that open Chapter IV of Book I, the 'parson of F[rox]field,' on the Bath road, who 'no longer threw his oyster-shell into the street . . . but supped in his garden upon codlins and cream', must have been one of the author's friends. The vicar of Froxfield in 1773 was a certain Thomas Hill,[2] and that a personal allusion was intended is probably also indicated by Graves's withdrawing the name of the parish in the edition of 1774, Hill having died in the meanwhile. I have been able to find out nothing more about him, and because of the loss of most of Graves's private papers this as well as many of his other personal allusions remains matter for conjecture.

The most remarkable of the personal material that Graves used in this novel, however, is the autobiography that went into the interpolated stories of Mr. Graham and Mr. Rivers, which are based on scapegrace chapters of his own youth. Thanks to the work of Dr. C. J. Hill, whose monograph on the *Literary Career of Richard Graves* is the only systematic study ever made of his life and work, I am able to show in the notes of this edition the extent to which Graves here told his own story.

His literary model is Fielding's comic epic in prose. He imitates Fielding's buoyant intrusiveness in his narrative, his mock heroics, his interpolated anecdotes, his teeming tapestry of characters from the lower and the lower-middle classes. He also largely shares

[1] Boswell's *Life of Johnson*, ed. W. J. Croker (1831), iv. 524 (Appendix 5).
[2] Thomas Phillipps, *Wiltshire Institutions*, ii. 86.

Fielding's point of view, his lack of prudery, and his respect for healthy, robust living.

He also shows the influence of Sterne in packing his pages with learned and obscure quotations. For example, the list of biblical commentators given in the first paragraph of his introduction was probably put together puckishly from the most obscure names he could recall from his Oxford days, and many of his poetical quotations are from the works of minor writers. These may have been better known to his contemporaries than to us, but the second epigraph on the title-page of his third volume, for example—'Humour without a moral is buffoonry', which comes from No. 9 of a short-lived and seldom-remembered periodical called the *Lay Monk*—can scarcely have been a household word even then. Moreover he impishly refers to the Bishop of Gloucester's solemn polemic *The Doctrine of Grace* in such a way as to give the unsuspecting reader the impression that it was a work of 'exquisite humour'. These things and many others like them were no doubt jokes and much relished by contemporary educated readers, and the euphoric inaccuracy of many of his citations must similarly be put down to whimsey rather than irresponsibility. Eager as he was to supply ample documentation for his indictment of Methodism by quoting the very words of the leaders of the movement over and over again, and fair as many of these quotations are, some of his footnotes are misleading and a few of his 'quotations' have eluded repeated search. But he could easily have defended himself by declaring that he had written a comic romance, not a doctoral dissertation.

Graves, indeed, was the true amateur, who went in for authorship only in later life when he had achieved some leisure. Though published when he was nearly fifty-eight, *The Spiritual Quixote* (1773)[1] was his first book except for a thin collection of epigrams eight years earlier. It must have been moderately successful, for a second edition, embellished with a new frontispiece in each volume, was called for before the end of the same year, though dated 1774. In it some stylistic errors were corrected, some inconsistencies eliminated, and a few passages toned down that must have given offence to primmer Christians. For example, in Chapter II of Book II, Jerry, when asked by Wildgoose if he had ever been guilty of worshipping idols, said in the first edition:

[1] An edition in 1772 is sometimes referred to, but must be a ghost.

'No, no! thank God, I never *troubles* my head about them. I *says* my prayers, and *worships* the Father, the Son, and the Holy Ghost; but there is no great harm in that; for they are all the same, as a body may say.' But in the edition of 1774 his second sentence was put into a form more acceptable to tender Protestant ears: 'I *goes* to church on Sundays and holydays, and *worships* the twelve Apostles, and *sich* like; but I never pray to the Virgin Mary, or worship images, as the *Papishes* do.' And in the next page, when Jerry was asked if he had ever taken the name of God in vain, he replied in his own inimitable vernacular: 'No . . . I hope not; God be friends, I never was guilty of that.' In the second edition his blasphemy was turned into piety: 'God be praised!' A few more changes of the same kind were made in the third edition (1783), which was described as 'A New Edition, Corrected and Improved', but the author added a sentence to his preface in defence of his original readings: 'As for the frequent allusions to Scripture, the author is sorry that the truth of his principal character, not only justifies, but makes such allusions necessary; and the charge of prophaneness will fall upon the journals from whence those expressions are taken, and not upon the author of this history.' In view of this defence, the subjoined footnote is inconsistent: 'Many of these scripture expressions are omitted in this edition.' In fact, not many omissions were made. However, the capital letters, italics, and quotation marks with which the scriptural quotations had been indicated were removed, so that the weaker brethren might unsuspecting read them and not be offended. There is a suspicion in my mind that the responsibility for doing this and for inserting the footnote I have just quoted was the printer's. Though in one of his later essays Graves professed horror at impieties and the unnecessary use of sacred names, I think that his printer had gone further in cleaning up the text of *The Spiritual Quixote* than the author intended. In 1792 a fourth edition appeared.[1] This is not the whole of the bibliographical history. In 1774 there was a Dublin reprint, and there were reprints in London and America during the first decades of the nineteenth century, as well as translations into German and Dutch. Altogether, for the first major literary venture

---

[1] Dr. Hill thought that the fourth edition was a fake, consisting of remainder copies of the third dressed up in a new title-page. But though the two editions appear to be virtually identical, the press numbers are entirely different. Consequently the fourth edition must have come from a fresh setting of type.

of an ageing country parson, it was a success. Though never widely acclaimed as one of the great novels, it has drawn praise from critics as discerning as Charles Whibley and Havelock Ellis, to say nothing of an anonymous special writer in *The Times Literary Supplement* in 1922, and it was reprinted handsomely in 1926. 'A comic master-piece,' noted Ellis, 'in its own way among the best of English novels.'[1]

C. T.

[1] *Nineteenth Century*, lxxvii (1915), 848.

NOTE ON THE TEXT

THE present edition is based on the first edition (1773), but many obvious misprints have been corrected and the revisions and additions made in later editions during the author's lifetime have been incorporated, except for bowdlerizations. Those have been excluded in favour of the readings of the first edition, on the ground that the author meant what he said in defence of the latter. The reader should also be warned that Graves never made more than a shadowy distinction between a direct and an indirect quotation, using quotation marks for both and slipping insensibly from one into the other, and that no attempt has been made here to correct him.

The Dedication and the three full-page illustrations were added to the novel for the first time in the second edition (1774), from which they have been copied for this edition.

BIBLIOGRAPHY

W. H. Hutton, *Burford Papers* (1905).

Havelock Ellis, 'Richard Graves and *The Spiritual Quixote*', *Nineteenth Century*, lxxvii (1915), 848–60.

Anon. *Times Literary Supplement*, 11 May 1922.

Charles Whibley, Introduction to *The Spiritual Quixote*, 2 vols. (1926).

Charles Jarvis Hill, *The Literary Career of Richard Graves* (Northampton: Massachusetts, 1935).

A CHRONOLOGY OF
RICHARD GRAVES

Age

1715 (4 May)   Born in Mickleton, Gloucestershire

——   Early schooling in Mickleton under William Smith, curate of the parish

c. 1728   Sent to school in Abingdon · · · · · · · · · · · · · · 13

1732 (7 Nov.)   Matriculated at Pembroke College, Oxford · · · 17

——   At some time in the 1730's or early 1740's, jilted Utrecia Smith, daughter of his first schoolmaster. See *The Spiritual Quixote*, IV, cc. 13-14

1736   B.A. · 21

1736   Elected to fellowship at All Souls College, Oxford · · 21

1740   M.A. · 25

1741   Entered household of William Fitzherbert of Tissington, Derbyshire, as companion and probably curate of the parish. See *The Spiritual Quixote*, X, cc. 9-31 · · · · · · · · · · · · 26

1744   Erected urn in memory of Utrecia Smith in Mickleton churchyard · 29

1744   Became curate of a parish near Reading, probably Aldworth, and boarded with one of the churchwardens, Edward Bartholomew, whose 15-year-old daughter Lucy he married secretly. See *The Spiritual Quixote*, VI, cc. 2-18 · · · · 29

1747   Birth of Richard Graves, his first child · · · · · · · · · 32

1749   Birth of Morgan Graves, his second child · · · · · · · · 34

1749   Became rector of Claverton, Somerset, near Bath, where he resided until his death. Conducted a boarding-school in the rectory for a number of years · · · · · · · · · · · · · · · 34

1750   Birth of Danvers Graves, his third child · · · · · · · · · 35

c. 1757   Composition of *The Spiritual Quixote* begun · · · · · 42

1763   Became vicar of Kilmarsden (a plurality) · · · · · · · · 48

1765   Birth of Lucilla Anna Maria, his fourth child · · · · · · 50

1765   *The Festoon*, a collection of epigrams (dated 1766) · · 50

1770   Birth of John Charles Edward, his fifth child · · · · · · 55

		Age
1773 (13 Mar.)	*The Spiritual Quixote*	57
1773	*The Love of Order* (a poem)	58
1774	*The Progress of Gallantry* (a poem)	59
1774	*Galateo* (translation in prose)	59
1776	*Euphrosyne*, Vol. I (poems)	61
1777	Mrs. Graves died	62
1779	*Columella, or the Distressed Anchoret* (novel)	64
1780	*Euphrosyne*, Vol. II (poems)	65
1784	*Fleurettes* (poetical translations)	69
1785	*Eugenius* (novel)	70
1786	*Lucubrations* (essays and poems)	71
1787	*A Letter from a Father to his Son* (prose)	72
1788	*Recollection of William Shenstone* (prose memoir)	73
1789	*The Rout* (poem)	74
1789	*The Heir Apparent* (prose translation)	74
1790	*Plexippus* (novel)	75
1793	*Hiero* (prose translation)	78
1793	*The Reveries of Solitude* (essays and poems)	78
1794	*The Coalition* (comedy)	79
1795	*The Farmer's Son* (poem)	80
1799	*Sermons*	84
1801	*Senilities* (essays and poems)	86
1804	*The Invalid* (essays and poems)	89
1804 (23 Nov.)	Died	89
1805	*The Triflers* (essays and poems)	

[Dedication of the Second Edition, 1774]

TO

EDWARD SEYMOUR, Esq.[1]

SIR,

THOUGH the author of this work seems to have been actuated by ambitious motives, in dedicating it to a person in so eminent a station under his late Majesty; yet, as the editor has no views of that kind, he begs leave to inscribe this second edition to you, Sir; as a friend, with whose amiable qualities he has long been acquainted; and whose future conduct in life, he is convinced, will do credit to your illustrious ancestors. I am, with much affection and esteem,

SIR,

Your obliged humble servant,

THE EDITOR

October 12, 1773

A PREFATORY ANECDOTE

By the EDITOR

GOING lately into the shop of a little Upholsterer, not far from the celebrated haunt of the Muses called Grub-street, I observed him with a bunch of small keys in his hand; with one of which he had just opened a black leather port-folio, or travelling letter-case. The poor man shaking his head with an air of disappointment, I enquired into the cause of his chagrin; upon which he gave me the following account.

'Some years ago,' says he, 'a jolly plump Gentleman, with a very serious countenance, came to lodge at my house, and rented an apartment up three pair of stairs backwards. It is not usual,' continues he, 'to give any long credit to lodgers of that kind. But the Gentleman in question looked like a very honest man. (By his dress, indeed, I should have taken him for a Country Clergyman; but that he never drank ale or smoked tobacco.) I was unwilling, therefore, after the first week, to give him the trouble of a weekly payment; so had let his rent run on for near six weeks: at which time, one Friday morning, before any one was stirring, he suddenly decamped; leaving nothing behind him, but an old Bible, an old pair of shoes, and an old grizzled periwig. I did not think it worth while to advertise my lodger. I made enquiries after him at the Coffee-house however which he frequented, and at the Chop-house where he dined; but have heard nothing of him to this day.'

The Upholsterer, it seems, was in hopes, that this Letter-case (which, upon removing the bed-stead, he had found thrust over the tester) might have contained a bank-bill, or something of value. But, to his utter confusion, he found nothing in it, except the manuscript of the following History; which he considered as waste paper, and, prophetically of its fate perhaps, said, 'it was good for nothing but to line trunks and band-boxes.'

Upon casting my eyes, however, over two or three different pages, I thought it might suit the taste of the present age: in which also the subject appeared by no means unseasonable. I therefore offered the honest man an equivalent for his six weeks rent; and, after drinking half a pint of mountain together at the next tavern, we finished our contract.

Upon examining my purchase, I found the following rough-draught of the Author's Preface; which, notwithstanding the sagacious Upholsterer's argument to the contrary, makes it probable that the history was written by a Clergyman.

'The APOLOGY

OR

A WORD to the WISE

'THE first Romance that we read of (called The Loves of Theagenes and Chariclea) was written by Heliodorus,[1] a Thracian Bishop. The Prelate was called before a Synod for this indecorum; and having his choice given him, either to suppress his Romance, or to quit his preferment, he is said to have preferred the literary fame of that juvenile performance to the revenues of a bishoprick.

'But, though the good man may be blamed for his conduct, I think the Synod were too severe in their censure: for I can see no more harm in a Fable of this kind (if properly conducted) than in any other either mythological or parabolical representation of the truth. Nay, I am convinced that Don Quixote or Gil Blas, Clarissa or Sir Charles Grandison, will furnish more hints for correcting the follies and regulating the morals of young persons, and impress them more forcibly on their minds, than volumes of severe precepts seriously delivered and dogmatically inforced.

'The following narrative was intended to expose a species of folly, which has frequently disturbed the tranquillity of this nation. The Author indeed by no means considers Ridicule as a proper test of Religious opinions. But they are the practices of their itinerant preachers, rather than the general principles of the people in question, which he thinks exceptionable. And the following work is so far from ridiculing Religion (as perhaps may be objected), that, he flatters himself, it has a direct tendency to prevent Religion becoming ridiculous, by the absurd conduct of such irregular Teachers of it. And he does not see how the honour of God is any more concerned in an attempt to expose the ill-judged zeal of a frantic Enthusiast, than the authority of the King would be in our laughing at the absurdities of some pragmatical Country Justice or a Petty Constable.

C

'As for the frequent allusions to Scripture, the author is sorry that the truth of his principal character, not only justifies, but makes such allusions necessary; and the charge of prophaneness will fall upon the Journals from whence those expressions are taken, and not upon the author of this history.'[1]—Thus far the Author.

In a blank leaf, next to the title-page, I found an odd instance of the Author's peculiar turn: for he had there written this whimsical parody upon Shakespear's whimsical Epitaph;

> Reader! for goodness sake, forbear
> To change one word that's written here.
> Bless'd be the man that spares my scribbling;
> But, curs'd be he that would be nibbling.

Accordingly, as I found the language tolerably correct, and the whole piece as highly finished as this species of writing is thought to deserve, I have given it to the publick, just as I found it; though I cannot but think that the Author might have heightened the ridicule of his principal character, by making more use of some modern Journals: which has since been done, on a different occasion, with exquisite humour, by one of the first writers[2] of the age for genius and learning.

Now, what became of the Author of this History; (whether he was picked up by those foes to indigent merit, the Bum-bailiffs; or those friends to bashful courage, a Press-gang;) it is impossible, in this particular, to gratify the Reader's curiosity. But, from his Landlord's account, it seems probable, that, having some scruple about publishing this work, he left it, as the ostrich does her eggs, to take its chance: or perhaps made use of this innocent stratagem; that, if ever by any accident, his piece should see the light, he might engage the attention of the publick to a subject which he thought of importance: and by his mysterious and sudden departure would insinuate, that he had put a voluntary period to his own life. For, I cannot but think, that instead of an Editor's informing the world, that a work was produced, either amidst an hurry of business, or in retirement; in a fit of sickness, or on a journey; by a youth under twenty, or by a Lady; or the like uninteresting circumstances; it would be more likely to rouse the curiosity of mankind, to assure them, that it was written by a man that had either hanged or drowned himself.

POSTSCRIPT

AFTER the above ludicrous defiance of the Criticks, I could not but smile at the following memorandum; which partly accounts for the Author's not giving his work to the publick, according to his first intention.

'*N.B.* Having written the following Tale for my winter-evenings amusement; when a *weakness in my eyes* would not permit me to read: and being conscious that I have transgressed, in several instances, the strict rules of epopœa; I was deterred from publishing it by a sett of *censorious Christians*, lately started up, called *Reviewers*; who will not suffer a man to nod in his elbow-chair, without giving him a jog; nor to talk nonsense, without contradicting or ridiculing him.'

ADVERTISEMENT

Since the Preface was printed off, happening to mention this adventure with the Upholsterer, as also the Cypher at the end of the following Dedication, to a Gloucestershire Squire, he lifted up his hands; and, in a strain of alliteration, cried out, 'Cot's life! my old friend and crony! that comical Cur, Christopher Collop!—commonly called—the comely Curate of Cotswold! he was always scribbling; and, I remember, about ten years ago, took a walk to London (as he always walked to keep down his *fat*), with an intent to publish something, as his friends imagined: but he would never discover the event of that journey.'

'What is remarkable, however,' (added the Squire) 'if Kit were really the author of a thing of this kind, is, that, although he did not approve of the Methodists rambling about the country, as many of them do; yet he was suspected to *favour* them in his heart; and continued so to do, to the day of his death.'

THE AUTHOR'S DEDICATION

TO

MONSIEUR PATTYPAN, Pastry-Cook to
His most sacred Majesty KING GEORGE II

SIR,

THOUGH a stranger to your person, I am no stranger to your ingenuity and your profound skill in your profession. I have often amused myself with some of those elegant *compositions* with which you daily *entertain* the publick. I have long been acquainted with the *virtues* of your diet-bread; am a great friend to your *wigs*;[1] and think myself under great obligations to your admirable *puffs*.

As I am convinced therefore you will make a *proper* use of my works; will do justice to their merit, and *cover* their defects: that, by the well-known goodness of your *taste*, you will *preserve* them from the attacks of the *sourest* criticks; and, by the *sweetness* of your disposition, defend them against their *bitterest* enemies: if you are not over-stocked with waste-paper by my brethren of the quill, I beg leave to dedicate these few sheets to your service; and am, Sir,

Your devoted humble Servant,

𝕏 𝕏

THE INTRODUCTION

EVERY Barber and blind Fidler[1] is acquainted with the false delicacy of Politian and Peter Bembo; who would never read the Bible (the Vulgate translation of it, I suppose) for fear of corrupting their style. Now, though I would not be so unreasonable, as to expect the gentle Reader of this trifling History to have read his Bible, much less all the numerous Commentators upon it: to have perused the profound treatises of John Burstamantius upon the Sacred Animals, or Laurentius Codomannus upon the Scripture-chronology; to have studied Quistorpius's Annotations, or the learned labours of Copenstenius, Stumpius, Conrade, Goclenius, and the like:[2] yet, in order to relish many parts of this narration, and to enter into the humour which is sometimes aimed at; I think it absolutely necessary that a man should have some smattering in the Religion of his country: some tincture of that education which prevailed in England in the reign of Queen Elizabeth; I mean, that he should have been taught his Catechism in his infancy; or, at least, the Creed, the Lord's Prayer, and the Ten Commandments, in the vulgar tongue: nay, that he should have dipped into the Bible sometimes; or, at least, should have occasionally conversed with those that have. For, as the Hero of this Romance sallies forth in order to revive the practice of, what he imagines to be, true Christianity; it is impossible that a person of a mere modern education (of which the doctrines of Christianity seldom make the least part) should comprehend the Writer's intention.

But, as I would wish, for the sake of the Bookseller, to have my work as universally interesting as possible, such a person may yet perhaps find some little amusement; especially if he has a taste for regular Journals or Books of Travels; where we frequently attend the adventurer with great patience from stage to stage: though perhaps we meet with nothing more material, than the distance of one place from another; the provisions the traveller finds at his Inn; the 'number of aldermen that govern, or the number of bells that entertain,' a borough town; or the like diverting particulars.

The Reader will likewise meet with several trifling incidents from real life; which, however, the Author flatters himself, are so far disguised by an alteration of the circumstances of place and time, as to prevent a particular application—unless where a particular application was intended.

VOLUME ONE

... Amusement reigns
Man's great Demand.
YOUNG[1]

Romances are almost the only Vehicles of Instruction that can be administered to a refined and voluptuous People.
ROUSSEAU[2]

THE
SPIRITUAL QUIXOTE

BOOK I

CHAPTER I

The Education and juvenile Pursuits of Mr. Wildgoose

IN a sequestered village, whose Gothic spire (though hardly discernible in a map of the world) makes a picturesque appearance under the Cotswold hills, the family of the Wildgooses had been settled for many generations. The only surviving heir to their freehold estate, which, next to that of the squire, was the most considerable in the parish, was Mr. Geoffry Wildgoose, the subject of the following history. They had had another son indeed, who died in his infancy: and also a daughter: but as she married young, contrary to her parents' approbation, and became the mother of many children, she, for that reason, made but a small figure in the annals of the family.

Mr. Geoffry Wildgoose received the first rudiments of his education at a little free-school by the side of the church-yard; from whence he was removed, at a proper age, to a considerable grammar-school: and having, by the time he was seventeen, gained as much classical knowledge as is usually taught in those seminaries, the master greatly extolled his parts and genius. His father therefore, whose veneration for learning rose in proportion to his own want of it, thinking his son might augment his fortune by some learned profession, sent him to finish his studies in the university of Oxford. Young Wildgoose applied himself to the sciences with great assiduity. And, though he had been prevailed on to make one or two excursions to London, and had taken a glimpse of the fashionable world: had seen Quin in his meridian at Drury-lane;

and Garrick in his dawn at Goodman's-fields:[1] had shewn his face
at the Bedford coffee-house, and even eat a jelly with Betty Careless
in Covent-Garden[2]—notwithstanding these youthful sallies, young
Wildgoose went through the business of the college with diligence
and regularity. And having in his person and behaviour something
naturally agreeable, an openness of countenance and a simplicity
of manners; he gained the love and esteem of his acquaintance,
which were pretty numerous, and of the genteeler sort of young
people in the university. But, soon after he had been created senior
soph, by the solemn imposition of Aristotle upon his head (which
solemnity he made a pretence for drawing upon the old gentleman
for ten guineas extraordinary), and when he was just aspiring to
the high dignity and honourable privileges of a bachelor in arts,
he was recalled to his native seat by the death of his father.

Old Mr. Wildgoose had always shewn a great affection for his
son. But the necessary expences of an university education appearing to him the height of extravagance; according to the opinion he
now entertained of his son Geoffry, he was afraid his estate would
be squandered away, the moment he was laid in his grave. Besides,
as it had been freed from a considerable incumbrance by Mrs.
Wildgoose's fortune (who was the daughter of a wealthy clergyman), and as it had been greatly augmented by her good œconomy
and his own frugality, he left a great part of his fortune in Mrs. Wildgoose's power. As Mr. Geoffry however was the only son, and was
conscious of being the darling of his mother; this circumstance
gave him no kind of uneasiness. And though his father had intended
him for some learned profession (as was observed); yet, being now
his own master; and the natural aversion which most young people
have to confinement falling in with his mother's inclination to keep
her son always with her; he dwelt at home for some years: a comfort
to his mother in her decline of life; a conversable companion to the
neighbouring gentlemen; an oracle amongst the farmers; and a wag
amongst the gossips at every christening and festival entertainment.

Mr. Wildgoose's chief employment was to manage to the best
advantage that part of his mother's estate which she kept in her
hands. This however, with the assistance of an old servant, gave
him little trouble; and left him at liberty to amuse himself, either in
company or in the common recreations of the country; or, what was
more to his taste, in reading history, poetry, and, in short, most of

the best authors in the English language. He frequently walked out indeed with his grey-hound, or with his spaniel and gun: but the one was rather for a companion, and the other for shew, than for any great pleasure which he took either in coursing or shooting. In this obscurity Mr. Wildgoose had probably spent his life, and joined the undistinguished list of his deceased ancestors; but for the following contemptible incident.

CHAPTER II

A Dispute with the Vicar

CHRISTMAS being still observed amongst the lower sort of people as a solemn festival, Wildgoose had been invited by a substantial farmer, at that season, to spend a sociable evening with Mr. Powell, the vicar of the parish, and other company. Mr. Wildgoose, though a sensible man, used frequently to entertain his illiterate companions, and excite their admiration, with some academical paradoxes: and was fond of exhibiting his dexterity in managing an argument, on the most trifling occasions, in all the forms of mood and figure, agreeably to the rules of Aristotle or Locke.

In the course of this evening's conversation there arose a dispute between Wildgoose and the vicar, in which, according to the letter of the law, Wildgoose perhaps had the right side of the question.

There had lately been a new window-tax imposed, which, amongst the middling sort of people, was a frequent subject of complaint. Wildgoose, it seems, since his retreat into the country, had been improving the old mansion-house, by opening a glass-door into the garden. The question was, whether this door ought to be taxed as a window, or not; as the overseer, supported by the vicar, seemed to think it ought. Wildgoose insisted upon it, 'that, however a sett of country-justices (who seldom were great logicians) might determine, a door was not a window: that it was essentially distinguished from it, by its name, its structure, its use, and what not.'

The vicar, instead of answering him merely in a serious way, turned his reasoning into ridicule; with some humour, and, perhaps, with some solidity. He said, 'that as a glass door conveyed light, it answered the end of a window; and ought to be taxed as such: that its being used as a door, did not destroy the use of it as a window: and, that the name of a thing did not alter its nature. In short, says the vicar, you may as well argue, that a pudding and a dumplin are essentially distinguished, as that a glass door and a glass window are so.'

As a pun or a ludicrous expression has frequently more weight with the vulgar, than the most solid argument, the doctor by his raillery turned the laugh against his antagonist, and put him to an aukward silence. The conversation however was soon changed; and the company continued their mirth and good humour. But this defeat sunk deeper into Wildgoose's bosom than one would easily imagine, and was attended with considerable consequences, which greatly affected the future conduct of his life.

CHAPTER III

The serious Consequences of it

SOME of the most important events in history, if traced to their original, have sprung from the most trifling causes. The murder of Cæsar in the capitol was chiefly owing to his not rising from his seat, when the senate tendered him some particular honours. The negotiations with the pope for dissolving Henry the VIIIth's marriage (which brought on the Reformation) are said to have been interrupted by the earl of Wiltshire's dog biting his holiness's toe, when he put it out to be kissed by that ambassador. And, not to multiply instances in so plain a case, the duchess of Marlborough's spilling a bason of water on Mrs. Masham's gown, in Queen Anne's reign, brought in the Tory ministry, and gave a new turn to the affairs of Europe.

Thus, to descend from these heroic examples, the greatest revolution in Mr. Wildgoose's life sprang from a frivolous dispute; in which he was apparently so slenderly interested.

To account for his resentment on this occasion, however, we must observe, that every man acts a kind of subaltern part in conversation. And he, who is an inferior or a common man in one company, may be a captain or a leading orator in another. There are few persons of so mean a capacity, or so despicable accomplishments, as not to have a circle of acquaintance, who reverence their opinions, and amongst whom they are heard with attention, and utter their decisions with a kind of oracular authority. This was the case with Mr. Wildgoose. In company with any of the neighbouring gentlemen, his superiors, he was modest, and patient of contradiction: but in an assembly of yeomen, he was in his glory; in his very kingdom. By ridiculing his opinions therefore, and diminishing his consequence amongst his own subjects, Mr. Powell was guilty of a kind of high treason; which Wildgoose could not easily forgive.

Time however might have worn off this unreasonable disgust against the vicar, if Mr. Wildgoose had not gone to church the next Sunday; whilst the impression was strong upon his imagination. He had always been remarkably decent in his behaviour at the public worship: and not only made his responses with an audible voice; but generally, leaning over the pew, accompanied the minister through both the lessons, with a Latin Bible, which he had brought with him from the university. At the same time, however, Mr. Geoffry was shrewdly suspected to have been guilty of some slight offences against the rules of chastity with his mother's maid. And though, in general, he might not be worse than his neighbours: yet he probably did not surpass them so much in his private character, as he did in his external deportment at church.

Now it happened unfortunately, that the doctor was haranguing that day upon the sin of hypocrisy; which, one would think, is a subject the least liable to a particular application by the hypocrite himself: for what knave or debauchee would be encumbered with the mask of piety, unless he flattered himself, that it concealed his real character, and screened him from the attacks of public censure? It is to be feared, however, that Mr. Wildgoose was conscious to himself of some slight failings, inconsistent with his sanctified appearance; and was too nearly concerned in the subject of the parson's discourse, not to make a particular application. And whether he suspected Mr. Powell to have pried into his secrets; or whether, as he was piqued against the vicar, he thought the resentment was mutual; whatever was the cause, he from that time avoided his company, and determined for the future to absent himself entirely from church.

As he could not, without exposing his weakness, give any reasons for this alteration in his conduct; he by degrees grew shy of the rest of his acquaintance; and sunk insensibly into a gloomy, unaccountable kind of misanthropy. Mrs. Wildgoose, who was fond of her son, became very uneasy on his account, but could not guess at the cause of his malady. She was always pressing him to go more abroad, and visit his neighbours. Nay, she got Mr. Powell, the vicar, himself (who was really a good-natured man, and, with his wife, often drank tea at Mrs. Wildgoose's) to talk to her son on the subject. Mr. Geoffry pleaded lowness of spirits; and a disrelish for company; and said, with some sullenness, 'that he chose to be alone.' In short, he found out so many excuses from time to time, that at last it was looked upon as his way, his humour, to be always alone; and Mrs. Wildgoose desisted from her maternal expostulations.

CHAPTER IV

Mr. Wildgoose enters upon a new Course of Studies

BUTTERED toast for breakfast now became unseasonable, and gave way to sage and bread and butter. Lamb and sallad ceased to be a Sunday's dinner, or part of the second course, and was an obvious dish at every table. The parson of F-field[1] no longer threw his oyster-shell into the street, ambitiously luxurious! but supped in his garden upon codlins and cream, or a bit of soft cheese and a cucumber. In other words, the spring was far advanced—when Mr. Wildgoose was, one day, sitting in his old-fashioned parlour; and, in an indolent posture, ruminating upon such trifles as usually employ a disgusted mind: the windows were shaded with an overgrown laurel; and the solemn vibrations of an old clock from its sable trunk, with the distant sound of a doleful ditty which the servant whistled as he was digging in the garden, concurred to increase his melancholy.

He roll'd his eyes, that witness'd huge dismay;[2]

and surveyed, over and over again, every picture and every part of the hereditary furniture of the mansion-house; which had been so familiar to his eyes from his very infancy. At last, he happened to

fix them on an old forlorn quarto, that lay upon a lofty shelf,
covered with dust, and tinged with smoke, an inch within the
margin. Something prompted him to look into it; which, starting
from his elbow chair, he immediately put in execution. He found
it to contain a miscellaneous collection of godly discourses, upon
predestination; election, and reprobation; justification by faith;
grace and free-will, and the like controverted points of divinity:
the productions of those self-taught teachers and self-called pastors
of the church, in the time of Cromwell's usurpation. As his usual
studies had been very insipid to him, since he was become thus
a prey to melancholy, and out of humour with himself, the vicar,
and all the neighbourhood, this crude trash happened to suit Mr.
Geoffry's vitiated palate: especially as these writings abounded
with bitter invectives against the regular clergy, and the established
church: and with sentences of reprobation upon all mankind,
except a few choice spirits, called the Elect.

Mr. Wildgoose read over this curious volume in an indolent
manner; which rather amused, than pleased him; and bewildered,
rather than instructed him. He was so far from being cloyed however with this crabbed food, that he found his appetite increase by
indulgence. And, recollecting that there was a closet in the house,
which had been locked up ever since the death of his grand-mother
(who was a rigid Nonconformist), thither he instantly resorts; and
finds it stored with a variety of authors of the same stamp: some
Presbyterian, some Independent, some Anabaptist, some Fifth-
monarchy men: the works of that swarm of sectaries in the last
century; all differing somewhat in their principles, but all agreeing
in their inveteracy against the Church of England.

This was no unpleasant food for Wildgoose's disorder. For,
having conceived so great a prejudice against the vicar of the parish,
he gladly embraced any system, that seemed to thwart his usual
doctrine. In short, in half a year's time, he had gone through the
whole library of godly discourses; the Marrow of Divinity, Crumbs
of Comfort, and Honey-combs for the Elect, The Spiritual Eye-
salves and Cordials for the Saints, and Shoves for heavy-ars'd
Christians;[1] and was forced, at last, to take up with an old tattered
folio of Foxe's Martyrology; and another of Master Clark's Lives
of famous Men: amongst others, that of Mr. Carter of Norwich;
who (the history informs us) was a mighty lover of Norfolk-
dumplins.

D

CHAPTER V

Adopts a new System of Religion

THE Puritanical principles, which he had thus imbibed, prepared Mr. Wildgoose to relish the doctrines of the Methodists; which began, about this time, to spread in every corner of the kingdom. And he was much pleased with the journals of their proceedings; two or three of which he had accidentally met with, and which made no slight impression on his imagination. Such a multifarious body of divinity indeed quite unsettled Mr. Geoffry's mind; and filled his head with such a farraginous medley of opinions, as almost turned his brain. It produced at least, to speak candidly of the matter, that sort of phrenzy, which we ascribe to enthusiasts in music, poetry, or painting; or in any other art or science; whose imaginations are so entirely possessed by those ideas, as to make them talk and act like madmen, in the sober eye of merely rational people.

But, to compleat poor Geoffry's religious phrenzy, some straggling itinerant had lately penetrated into that neighbourhood; and held-forth once or twice a-week at a market-town, a few miles from the village where Wildgoose lived. These nocturnal meetings he now frequently attended: at first, without his mother's knowledge, or that of any of his neighbours; and when she discovered it, by his frequent absence, she thought it more prudent to connive at his whimsies, than aggravate them by opposition.

A pious inclination to retail the doctrines, which he heard at those meetings, as well as the natural propensity which men have to propagate their own opinions, concurring with the prejudice which Mr. Wildgoose had conceived against the parson of the parish, strongly urged him to give vent to that fund of spiritual knowledge, which (like the volatile bee) he had been the whole summer in gleaning from those flowers of rhetoric and from those flourishing orators above-mentioned.

He would now and then venture to defend the cause of the Methodists, before his mother: but she would never hear him with patience on the subject. She said, 'If the clergy would but do their duty, as her poor father did, and as the canons of the church required, there would be no necessity for these extraordinary proceedings. And if they neglected their duty, complaint should be

made to their lawful superiors. Her own father (she said) was a very
good man. And, whatever little shew of piety these upstart preachers
might raise amongst their followers, by the novelty of the thing;
she was sure her father did more real good in his sphere, by a regular
discharge of his duty in an extensive parish. That he instructed the
ignorant, and reproved the vicious: that he catechized the children,
visited the sick, and (as far as his circumstances would permit)
relieved the poor: and that not only his own parish, but the whole
neighbourhood were the better, for his instructions and his
example, to this day.'

As Mrs. Wildgoose was so zealous an advocate for the church,
Mr. Geoffry forbore to display his sentiments any further in her
presence: though he took an opportunity, now and then, of
privately insinuating his notions into the maid, who, being young,
was more attentive and more pliant than the man, whom age and
habit had rendered stubborn and averse to speculation. In other
respects, as Wildgoose had long since deserted his old companions
amongst the creditable part of the neighbourhood, he was under a
necessity, at present, of keeping 'silence from (what he thought)
such good words,' though it was no small pain and grief to him.

CHAPTER VI

Preliminaries with the fastidious Reader

MR. WILDGOOSE, being impatient of any longer confinement,
began after some time to creep out in the dusk of the evening, and
join the sober assembly of labourers and mechanics under an old
elm, at the cottage-gate of an honest sociable cobler; where the
news of the parish, or the weather of the ensuing day, the badness
of the times, or the scarcity of money, and other matters of general
concern, were adjusted with great wisdom and penetration.

As Jeremiah Tugwell (which was the name of this cobler) will
bear a considerable part in this history, the polite reader will not
be offended with a slight sketch of his person and character.

Here however it may be necessary, once for all, to settle preliminaries with such readers, as are possessed with the modern
tapino-phoby, or dread of every thing that is low, either in writing

or in conversation. For as people in high life are less prone to that excess of zeal or religious enthusiasm, which gave occasion to the following tale, than people in a less elevated sphere, the author could not, consistently with probability, introduce him so frequently amongst the former, as amongst the latter.

I have sometimes been tempted to think, however, that high and low are by no means necessarily confined to the different ranks and stations in life; and have even suspected (though I do not presume to have penetrated into the very 'sanctum sanctorum' of high life) that there may be as much low wit and as many practical jokes going on over a bottle of burgundy at the Star and Garter, or at Arthur's; as over a pot of porter at the Robinhood Society.[1] It seems at least probable, that as we sometimes find very low wit employed upon the highest subjects; so there is room for high humour (if the author had abilities) upon the lowest subjects.

If the reader however has otherwise determined it; if he is of opinion, that every representation of nature, that does not relate to the great world, is to be exploded as contemptible stuff; he will certainly repent of having read thus far; and I would exhort him, by all means, to return in peace to his card-assembly or to his chocolate-house, and pursue so low a subject no further.

For the sake however of the less critical customer; the 'fat, sleek-headed' guest; who, like a prudent traveller in a stage-coach, instead of affecting to be more squeamish than his companions, is resolved to be pleased with whatever is set before him, we will proceed in our narration.

CHAPTER VII

What sort of Man Jeremiah Tugwell was

COME! then, thou goddess Fame, if haply thou canst steal a moment from high life; from trumpeting forth the praises of the great artist of the golden-boot in Berkley-square,[2] and I do not blasphemously invoke thy power to record the humbler virtues of a rural craftsman; come to my aid! and bestow one blast in honour of the fidelity, courage, wit, and humour of the renowned Jeremiah Tugwell.

Jeremiah Tugwell then, or Tagwell, or Tackwell (for, learning having been at a low ebb in the family, the orthography is somewhat dubious: nay, a conceited fellow in the village, who pretended to etymology, said it ought to be written Tugwool, and that wool was put for sheep, and sheep for mutton (by a synecdoche): so that the true meaning of the name, according to his conceit, was Tug-mutton. But I value at a nut-shell these fanciful etymologies; which endeavour to elicite a significative meaning from every family name; the originals of which are infinitely uncertain; and our conjectures about them are often as far from the truth, as the interpretation of dreams by an old midwife).[1] Tugwell then was a thickset little fellow, near fifty; but of a strong constitution and hale complexion. And though age and accidents had made considerable depredations on his person; had turned the colour of his bushy locks; had made bald the crown of his head, and robbed him of most of his grinders; yet these strokes of time had only given him a more picturesque appearance: and one solitary tooth in his upper mandible, when any thing excited his mirth, gave an inexpressibly droll and joyous air to his physiognomy.

As to his character, Jerry had a tolerable share of natural sense: but, having somewhat of a speculative turn, and being fond of books, he too much disregarded the common maxims of prudence; and passed amongst his more provident, though really less sagacious, neighbours, for an half-witted fellow. By which means, though Jerry was really a tolerable hand, a more popular operator having started up, he had lost most of his custom as a shoe-maker, and was dwindled into a mere mender of shoes, or, what is vulgarly called, a cobler. He still worked for Mrs. Wildgoose's family, however; who had always made it a point of conscience, not wantonly to change their tradesmen; from any imaginary want of skill in an old man, whose honesty and desire to oblige them were unquestionable.

Though Jerry was fond of books, it was chiefly those of the fabulous kind; which dealt in the marvellous and the romantic. As he did not trouble himself about the niceties of chronology or geography, Jerry was particularly fond of 'the Seven Champions of Christendom,' who are said by the historian to have sprung up soon after the destruction of Troy; that is, about some thousand years before Christ was born: and one of them to have ridden on horse-back from Sicily, through Cappadocia, Tartary, the Island of

Cyprus, &c. the direct road to Jerusalem. Tugwell was possessed
also of the old edition of Mandeville's Travels; who is the author
alluded to by Shakespear, as speaking 'of antres vast and deserts
idle; and of men whose heads do grow beneath their shoulders.'[1]
Jerry delighted to talk of Prester John, of the Holy-land, and of the
wandering Jew; 'that cursed shoe-maker,' who thrust our Saviour
out of the judgement-hall; for which he is condemned to a vagabond life, till Christ comes in judgement; whose real existence
Jerry as firmly believed, as any part of the Gospel.[2]

He had also some smattering in astronomy; though he had not
yet embraced the Newtonian system: he could point out Charles's
wain and the polar star; and could give as good an account of the
'Northern lights' as most other philosophers: yet Jerry strenuously
denied their appearance in England before the beheading of the
rebel lords in the year fifteen.[3]

For, as to his political principles, Tugwell was suspected, like
some of his neighbours, to be strongly attached to the Stuart family:
though this attachment seemed to have no other foundation, than
a compassion for the distressed: and never shewed itself but in an
harmless pun once a year:[4] in wearing a sprig of rue and thyme on
the Eleventh of June (the accession of his late Majesty), as the
Tenth was honoured with a white rose.

As for Jerry's moral character, his justice, temperance, and
fortitude, they will sufficiently appear in the course of this
history.

Tugwell had no family but his wife Dorothy, his dog Snap, and
a tabby cat. His only son Joseph, having violated the chastity of the
Justice's maid (who was known to be common to all men), rather
than marry her, listed for a soldier; and was supposed to be dead
in America.

Jerry and his spouse were more equally yoked than Jobson and
Nell in the farce;[5] though in the present instance the female
prerogative rather preponderated: by a proper exercise of which,
notwithstanding his censorious neighbours thought Jerry cursedly
hen-pecked, Dorothy contrived to convince him, that he had the
best wife in Christendom.

CHAPTER VIII

Sketch of Mr. Wildgoose's Theological System

'No more of Jeremiah Tugwell! for heaven's sake;' says the
delicate reader, whose patience has hitherto been unexhausted.
I shall only add therefore, that as Tugwell's name was liable to
puns, and capable of significant applications; so the situation of his
stall, within view of the street, exposed him to the familiar saluta-
tion of those that passed by. And, as every one had something to say
to Jerry, so Jerry had something to say to every one: and this gave
a sort of petulant dicacity to his repartees, by no means agreeable
to the natural civility of his disposition.

The reader will observe likewise, that Tugwell's profound knowledge of books had infected his language: which was frequently
interlarded with hard words, not always applied or pronounced
with the utmost propriety.

Such then were the circumstances, person, and character of
Jeremiah Tugwell, at whose cottage-gate Mr. Wildgoose made the
first essay towards propagating the doctrines which he had lately
adopted.

He took occasion first to lament the great decay of Christian
piety (which with regard to his present audience was probably
a complaint but too justly founded). He then began to insinuate,
'That the present doctrine and discipline of the church were the
chief causes of this degeneracy: That, for his part, he had attended
the public worship, as others did, merely because it was the custom
of the country; but that he had always found it a tedious piece of
lip-labour, without the least edification: That as for the parson's
preaching, it might serve just to keep up some little appearance of
religion amongst us; and perhaps might prevent some people from
being quite so bad, as they would otherwise be; but could never
reform one sinner; nor "make men wise unto salvation." Besides,
says he, if we could live a good moral life, and practise all the good
works which the doctor so earnestly recommends; all this would
be little to the purpose. Faith in Christ, says he, is all in all. We
must be cloathed with the splendid robes of his righteousness,
instead of the "filthy rags of our own works." In short, (continues
Wildgoose) we must be assured, that we are in the number of the
elect, and have the seal of adoption (the impression of which, he

hinted, none but a few choice spirits like himself were acquainted with); and if our name were thus once up (according to his doctrine), we might lie a-bed, and give ourselves no further trouble.'

With this, and a great deal more to the same purpose, Mr. Geoffry entertained his little circle under the great elm at Tugwell's gate: and though they were not capable of distinguishing nicely between his doctrine and what they heard at church; yet being delivered to them in a more familiar manner, and by a new teacher, and in a new place, it made a considerable impression upon them; and brought them punctually the next evening to their usual rendezvous. But, as the report of Mr. Wildgoose's appearing amongst them soon increased the number of this little assembly, and also as the evenings began now to be pretty cool, he thought it proper to adjourn to Tugwell's chimney-corner. Besides, Mr. Wildgoose was sufficiently sensible of the difference between mere talking, and preaching in a fanatical manner. Where nothing was intended but informing the understanding, the former alone might answer the end: but where the passions were to be moved and the affections engaged, a more vehement action (approaching to gesticulation), a greater earnestness, and more impassioned tone of voice, were to be made use of: which an orator upon a level with the crowd and in the open street could by no means exert to the best advantage.

CHAPTER IX

He commences Orator

MR. WILDGOOSE therefore now borrowed a stool of Dame Tugwell; and, exalting himself above his audience, harangued them in the true gospel tone and style of address. To shew them the necessity of the new birth and of a divine faith, he began to describe, in heightened colours, the universal depravity of human nature. He confessed, 'that for his part, he had violated every precept of the moral law, as contained in the ten commandments.' And, in the heat of his oratory, (with eyes fixed and foaming mouth) he insisted upon it, 'that he had blasphemed God, and cursed the king: that he had dishonoured his father and his mother: that he had mur-thered his brother.'—Here the company stared, as it was well known, that he never had but one brother, who died of the chin-cough.—He declared, 'that he had defiled his neighbour's wife; that he had robbed upon the high-way—'

'Stop! stop! master, (cries Tugwell, who could hold no longer) why sure you are beside yourself—I believe your Worship is as honest a gentleman as any in the county—'

'Ah! Jerry, replies Wildgoose (correcting himself) I have not perhaps been actually guilty of those enormous transgressions: but every unregenerate man is daily guilty of them virtually, as we say; inasmuch as he has the seeds of corruption in his heart: and it is only by the grace of God, that he is restrained from putting them in execution.'

In this style Mr. Wildgoose usually addressed his little audience: and though he had really a classical taste; and, on common subjects, an elegance of expression; yet, by confining himself so long to the puritanical writings above-mentioned, and those of the Metho-dists, he had strongly imbibed their manner: and his language on religious topics abounded with that strange jargon of those pious people, which chiefly consists in applying the quaint Hebraisms of the Old Testament; and the peculiar expressions of the primitive apostles to their own situations, and every trifling occurrence of modern life.

Thus, in allusion to the sacred unction, he would tell them, 'that God anointed (that is, greased) the wheels of his soul;' and blas-phemously makes him act as a surgeon and apothecary, 'purging him with hyssop, healing his putrid sores, and binding up his broken bones.' Sometimes God is a Grub-street writer; and 'writes bitter things against him.' And he always speaks of himself, as an apostle and evangelist; 'that few could resist the power with which he spoke;'[1] and that 'he spake as one having authority, and not as the scribes;' that is, common country parsons.

As Mr. Geoffry was sometimes rather prolix in his discourses, Tugwell would put him in mind, that talking was dry work. He therefore frequently enforced his arguments, with a flaggon of good ale from his mother's cellar; which afforded great comfort to his thirsty audience; cemented their friendship, and contributed not a little to convince them, that they were in 'the right way.' And to keep Dame Tugwell in good-humour (who was sovereign in that mansion), and to make her some recompence for the use of her house, Mr. Geoffry ordered her to come daily to his mother's kitchen: where, together with her broth or pot-liquor, he contrived to slip something more substantial into Dorothy's pipkin.

CHAPTER X

A peculiar Species of Ecclesiastical Discipline

BY this kind of management, Mr. Wildgoose's audience greatly increased, and became almost as numerous as Mr. Powell's, the vicar's, at church. For though Mr. Powell did his duty in the parish with sufficient care, and, as Jerry used to say, was 'a pretty man in a pulpit;' there was a peculiarity in his conduct, which made him many secret enemies, and which deserves to be recorded.

Mr. Powell was a man of great benevolence; but being a Cambro-Briton, (of the Ap-hoels of Brecknockshire) he was subject to a national impetuosity of temper: and being endued with great bodily strength and proportionable courage, if any of his parishioners were notoriously guilty of swearing, drinking, or any other scandalous vice, he would address them in this manner: 'Look you, my friends; your drunkenness and profaneness are an open insult upon the laws of that great King, whom I have the honour to serve; and an affront to me, who bear his commission. As I have often admonished you therefore against swearing and drinking, and you still persist in the same course; I give you fair warning once more; that the next time I hear or see any thing of this kind, I will drub you most confoundedly.' This method had so good an effect; that as they knew he had strength and courage to put his threats in execution, he was very seldom under any necessity of doing so.

Those, however, who were thus kept in awe, though they could not but reverence Mr. Powell's character, rather feared than loved him; and were glad to listen to any doctrine which they thought was in opposition to the vicar's. But to return from this digression.

CHAPTER XI

Mr. Wildgoose takes an extraordinary Resolution

BY haranguing so frequently upon the same topicks, Mr. Wildgoose began to talk very fluently: and from attending to the applauses of his little audience, and observing the effect of his oratory upon them, he began to entertain no mean opinion of his own eloquence, and to aspire after a more extensive fame. Nay, he thought himself false to his trust, thus to bury 'his talent in a napkin;' to hide his 'candle under a bushel' and not to let his 'light shine before men,' for the benefit of his fellow-creatures.

Besides, from reading the accounts of God's dealings with several of his saints; particularly with John Bunyan; who, in his youth, had been greatly addicted to the diabolical diversions of ringing bells, dancing at may-poles, and other profane amusements (as he himself informs us):[1] yet in his advanced age, was thought worthy, for his pious labours in God's vine-yard, to be sent to Newgate: from perusing these, I say, and the Acts of our modern Apostles, contained in their Journals above-mentioned; Mr. Wildgoose was ambitious of emulating their spiritual adventures, and even burnt with zeal to imitate them in their sufferings; and wished for nothing so much as to be persecuted for the sake of his religion. The suffering for one's opinions gives a man an air of consequence in his own eyes; as it supposes him to think for himself; and to be distinguished from the herd of mankind, who live and die unregarded; content with the hereditary notions of their unthinking ancestors.

Mr. Geoffry Wildgoose therefore, having no longer any pleasure in the society of his more creditable neighbours; nor in his wonted amusements, since his fancy became entirely possessed with these enthusiastic ideas; determined to leave the management of his mother's estate to their old servant Stephen; and, like a true 'Spiritual Quixote,' to abandon his dwelling: and, in imitation of Mr. Whitfield[2] and his associates, to use his earnest endeavours, to revive the practice of primitive piety and the doctrines of the Reformation, by turning missionary; and publishing his religious notions in every part of the kingdom.

BOOK II

CHAPTER I

*Original of Methodism. Mr. Wildgoose's
Resolution to visit the Society at Bristol*

WHEN the learned Humphry Prideaux (as the story goes) offered
his Life of Mahomet to the bookseller; he was desired to leave the
copy with him, a few days, for his perusal.[1] The bookseller, who
had not the learning or taste of a modern artist, having consulted
with his learned Garreteers, who were highly pleased with the
performance, told the Doctor at his return; 'Well; Mr. What's-
your-name, (says he) I have perused your manuscript: I do not
know what to say to it; I believe, I shall venture to print it: the
thing is well enough; but—I could wish there were a little more
humour in it.'

Now though the courteous reader should be as fond of humour,
as this facetious bookseller was; yet if, in travelling through a flat
country, he should now and then meet with a picturesque prospect,
sometimes with a bit of galloping ground, and sometimes with a
droll object upon the road, he must patiently submit to jog on some
parts of the way, without any thing to entertain or amuse him;
for such probably will be the fate of the gentle reader of this
various history.

About this time, the sect of the Methodists (as was before
observed) began to spread into most parts of the nation: though
perhaps it is doing them too much credit, and at the same time an
act of injustice, to call them a sect; as I know of few novel opinions
which they maintain, except that of the lawfulness of preaching
without a legal call; and of assembling in conventicles or in the open
fields in direct opposition to the laws of the land.

A late writer[2] does Mr. Whitfield the honour of being the first
author of Methodism; whom he also calls a fellow of Pembroke
college in Oxford. But as Mr. Whitfield disclaims all worldly

grandeur; and with great humility assures us, that (like the blessed Founder of our religion) he was born in an inn:[1] so, like him, (I am persuaded) he will confess, 'that he came not to be ministered unto, but to minister.' For he was really a servitor, and not a fellow, of that learned society. Neither was Mr. Whitfield concerned in the first institution of Methodism; though he has since made so shining a figure amongst them. For, some years[2] before he came to the University, Mr. John Wesley, fellow of Lincoln-college, his brother Charles, a student of Christ-church, Mr. Clayton of Brazen-nose, and two or three more young gentlemen, (with a very laudable intention) agreed to spend two or three evenings in a week together, in reading history or other entertaining and instructive books; instead of drinking, which (at that time) was too much in vogue among the young people of the University. The Sunday evenings they appropriated to religious authors: which soon convinced them of the great neglect of practical religion in that place, as well as in other parts of the kingdom. In consequence of these convictions, they formed themselves into a little society; and raised a small fund for charitable uses: to relieve the necessitous, buy medicines for the sick, and to disperse books amongst the ignorant. They agreed also to go occasionally, and visit the prisoners in the castle; who, at that time, were much neglected. And, that they might have the more leisure for these charitable offices, without breaking in too much upon the business of their colleges, they were obliged to fix stated hours for these employments, and their other religious exercises: to which they were directed by Mr. Nelson's 'Practice of devotion.'[3] This strict regularity and Methodical conduct, after some time, acquired them the name of Methodists: though not without allusion probably to an ancient school of Physicians of that denomination.

Mr. Wesley however, I am convinced, had no thoughts, at that time, of separating from the Established Church, (the most essential of whose doctrines he has generally adhered to) much less of robbing the community of so many useful mechanics: who, with a view of raising themselves above their fellow-plebeians, without any other apparatus than a long cravat and a demure pertness of countenance, together with a little common-place jargon (picked up at their weekly assemblies), forsake their lawful callings, and commence reformers and teachers of their brethren. But 'the beginning of strife is as the letting out of water:'[4] and if one man may break through the established order of society, another has the same right to do it; which must end at last in utter confusion.

These people then had several societies at this time, in London, Bristol, and in most of the considerable towns in England. But as Bristol was the nearest to the place of Mr. Wildgoose's habitation; and he saw, by the news-papers, that Mr. Whitfield, at this time, made that his principal residence; he resolved to visit the society in that city, and confer with them upon the subject of the cause in which he was now a volunteer; and to take instructions for the better discharge of the mission, to which, he flattered himself, he had a divine call.

CHAPTER II

Communicates his Intentions to Tugwell

MR. WILDGOOSE, having determined to go on a pilgrimage to Bristol, after some deliberation, communicated his intention to his foresaid honest neighbour, Jeremiah Tugwell, but under a strict injunction of the greatest secresy. And, as he thought it would be more agreeable to have a companion in his travels, finding him alone in his stall, he began to sound Jerry upon that subject.

Mr. Wildgoose esteemed Tugwell, and Tugwell fancied himself, a true convert to his religious system. For, hearing him harangue so often upon the same subject, Jerry had learnt, whenever Mr. Wildgoose talked to him upon that head, to echo back most of his expressions, with an appearance of a sincere conviction. If Mr. Wildgoose lamented the sad decay of Christian piety; Tugwell would shake his head, and clinch it with a more vehement exclamation against the wickedness of the age. If Wildgoose asserted the preference of faith to works; 'Yes, yes, cries Jerry, faith's all; our good works are no better than "filthy rags," in the sight of God.'

And as Jerry's passions were naturally tame and moderate, he was not often guilty either of swearing or drinking; the most common foibles of men in his rank of life.

As to the former, however, Jerry might rather be called a Demi-juror, than a Non-juror: as, instead of the usual profane execrations, he would content himself with some softening modifications of them. Instead of the shocking exclamation of 'G-d damn you!' Jerry would use, 'G-d mend you, or convert you!' Instead of 'Od's blood, od's wounds, or pox take you;' Jerry was content with 'Odsbodikins, odszounterkins, pok-i-cat take you,' and the like. And even these castrated imprecations Jerry seldom used, even in the paroxysms of his wrath, without a decent salvo; as, 'God forgive me for swearing;' or 'I was going to say,' and the like. Which however answered the purpose of venting his rage, and at the same time secured him from the imputation of impiety and profaneness.

As to drinking, Tugwell's greatest temptation was from the Angel, in his neighbourhood; I mean, the sign of the Angel, where he longed to be tippling with the sociable part of his acquaintance. But as there is no law in England against the wife's 'wearing that emblem of sovereignty, the breeches,' Dorothy kept the cash; and by that means kept Jerry within tolerable bounds, unless when he could secrete a tester for some bye-jobb; on which occasions he would sometimes elope and take his fill. But since Mr. Wildgoose had made use of his cottage for their nightly assemblies, this supplied the place of other less innocent amusements. So that Tugwell flattered himself, he was a true convert to religion; that he had made a great progress in the road to heaven, and was qualified to teach others the way.

But, to prepare Tugwell for a proper assistant in his mission, Mr. Wildgoose took this opportunity of examining him upon some of the distinguishing doctrines which he had of late been inculcating.

Wildgoose asked Jerry therefore, 'whether he had a true sense of his fallen condition, and that he was a wicked sinner, and had broken every commandment of the moral law. For, unless he was convinced of sin, he said, he could not hope for pardon.

'Tell me, therefore, Jerry, says Wildgoose, have you ever broke the first or second commandment; or have you ever been guilty of worshipping idols?'—'*Idols!* says Jerry, why yes, to be sure, I have been very *idle* sometimes, that's *sartain*; especially at Christmas and Whitsuntide, and *sich* good times, as one may say!'—'Pshaw! (says Wildgoose) you mistake me, Jerry; I mean, did you ever worship more gods than one, or any false gods, as the Jews and Heathens did?'—'Oh! says Jerry; what! Bel and the Dragon, and Nebuchadnezzar, and *sich* like: No, no! thank God, I never *troubles* my head about them. I *says* my prayers, and *worships* the Father, the Son, and the Holy Ghost; but there is no great harm in that; for they are all the same, as a body may say.'

'Well, Jerry; but you may have been guilty of idolatry, by setting up idols in your heart, and loving any thing more than God.'

'Ah! says Jerry, God forgive me! to be sure, I formerly loved nine-pins and cudgel-playing, better than going to church and saying my prayers.'

'Well then, Jerry, thou hast broken the first and second commandment. Now for the third—Didst thou never take the name of God in vain?'

'No, says Jerry, I hope not; God be friends, I never was guilty of that—though to be sure, when a body is in a passion, a body may use a bad word, now and then, such as, Pock-i-cat take you, Od's bobs, Odsbodikins, and the like—But there is no harm in that'—

'Why, says Wildgoose, if you think them bad words, there is harm in them, and they are very wicked: and if you do not, they are very ridiculous. Do you know, Jerry, that many of those words are corruptions, either of the most tremendous oaths, or of the most shocking execrations? "Pock-i-cat take you," is only a corruption of "The pox of God take you!" "Odsbobs" (as you call it) means "As sure as God's above us!" and "Zounterkins," (which you frequently use) is a corruption of God's wounds, and is a most shocking oath, as swearing by the precious wounds of our Redeemer. In short, Jerry, the only way to avoid the guilt of profane swearing, is to use the greatest simplicity of speech; to let your Yea be yea, and your Nay nay, as our great Master directs.'

Tugwell stared at this exposition of his unmeaning gibberish; but Wildgoose proceeded in his examination.

'In the next place, Jerry, have you never profaned the sabbath, by doing your ordinary work on the Lord's day?'

'No, says Jerry, except paring turnips, now and then, and boiling the pot; which we han't time to do always on working-days—And I remember, I once sate up till Sunday morning, to finish a pair of shoes against Easter.'

'Well, Jerry, (continues Wildgoose) if I were to examine you through the whole decalogue, I am afraid there is not one of the moral precepts, but what thou hast transgressed, either in thought, word, or deed. For, as the tenth commandment is intended to guard against the breach of the rest; if you have not actually been guilty, you may intentionally, even by coveting your neighbour's house, your neighbour's wife, or any thing that is his.'

'Nay, says Jerry, as for coveting my neighbour's wife; no body can accuse me of that; for, thank God, I have the best wife in England.'

Just as Jerry was saying this, Dorothy, who had listened for some time, and did not hear the noise of the hammer, called out, with no very harmonious voice, 'Why don't you mind your work? Don't you know those shoes must all be finished against Whitsunday?'

The dread of Dorothy's displeasure, therefore, put a stop to Mr. Wildgoose's scrutiny for the present; and so they parted, but in the evening resumed their deliberations.

As Jerry then had no family to provide for, but his wife Dorothy, who could support herself by her own industry, and (as he suspected) had already made a purse for herself, he wanted but little persuasion to come into Mr. Wildgoose's proposal; especially as the course of his studies had given him a romantic turn, and a strong inclination for travelling; although his situation in life had never permitted him to indulge that propensity. Besides, as Jerry made a sort of merit of accompanying Mr. Wildgoose, he did not doubt but he would, some time or other, recompence him for his trouble. Tugwell therefore told Mr. Wildgoose, 'that he should be very proud to bear him company, if he was resolved to go. But, please your Worship—' Jerry was here going to propose some artful scruples, which will be related in the next chapter.

CHAPTER III

Jerry's affected Scruples

TUGWELL assured Mr. Wildgoose 'he should be very proud to accompany him to the Land's end, if occasion were; for that he always loved travelling. But, Master, (says he) what must we do for money to pay for our lodgings, and to provide necessaries upon the road? For as Madam is not to know of our going, belike your Worship's purse will soon be *dis*hausted.'—'Oh! as for that, (says Wildgoose) you may make yourself easy—The labourer is worthy

E

of his hire. Those to whom we impart our spiritual things, will abundantly supply us with those carnal conveniencies, which you are so anxious about; at least, Providence will infallibly provide for those that rely upon him: and I have as good security for the necessaries of life in God's promises, as if I had millions in the Bank of England.

'Was not Elijah fed as well by ravens, dost thou think, as he would have been from the king's table? And did not he sleep as sweetly under a juniper-tree, as he would have done upon a bed of state?'

'Yes, yes, (says Jerry) that is very true; but then that was in the Holy Land; where belike it is much warmer than it is in this country. And then mayhap there were no inns nor ale-houses in those days; nor any thing to be got for love or money, in the wilderness where Elijah travelled: so that he was obliged to trust to Providence, as a body may say.—However, folks were not so hardhearted in those days; but were more given to *hostility*, than they are now.'—'Hospitality, I suppose you mean, says Wildgoose.'—'Well, well, that is all one, replies Tugwell; but I am no Oxford scholar, that's *sartain*;' (which was all that Jerry thought requisite to make him as wise as his master.)—'But howsomever, now-a-days, if a poor man does but ask for a cup of drink upon the road, he's taken for a thief or a *bugabond*. Instead of giving a man any thing to eat, they will only give one good advice, "Why don't you get to your own parish?" says one: "Why don't you work? says another, and not beg?" "Here are so many idle fellows about the country," says another. And then it's good luck, if the house-dog be not set upon one; and one gets off without a torn skirt! I should like well enough to travel amongst your Turks and *Hometans* (as Thomas Coryat, the Somersetshire man, did)[1] where a man may lay down his knap-sack in an evening, and lodge in a sort of alms-house or *carry-fancy*, as the book calls it, and no body ask any questions: but there's no travelling in a Christian country, without a little money in one's pocket.'

'Well, says Wildgoose, if that be all, I could take money enough, to provide us necessaries upon the road. But I greatly question, whether it be lawful, for a preacher of the Gospel to take any thought for the things of this life: the first apostles (you know) were forbid to take, "either purse or scrip, or to have two coats a-piece".'—'Well, says Tugwell, I believe we shall have but one

coat between us; as your Worship will hardly walk in a greatcoat
this summer time; and mine is but a waistcoat, and make the best of
it!'—'Why, I suppose, the only intention of those particular
expressions (replies Wildgoose) is, that we should not distrust
Providence—but should give good Christians an opportunity of
displaying their charity and benevolence.'

'Well but, Master, continues Tugwell, what must we do for
clean linen, as a body may say? For your Worship belike has been
used to shift you twice a week: and I, most commonly, *puts* on
a clean neckcloth every Sunday, and sometimes a clean shirt. Now
I have a thought (if so be it is not contrary to Scripture) to take my
wallet over my shoulder; and that would hold some clean linen,
and a crust of bread and cheese, sometimes. For we may happen
to lose our way upon Cotswold; and that's but a heathenish sort
of a country at best.'

'Why, to be sure, Jerry, replies Mr. Wildgoose, we ought to take
all prudent means for our subsistence, and not expect Providence
to feed and cloath us by a constant miracle, as he did the children
of Israel in the wilderness.'—'No, no, says Tugwell, to be sure,
their meat dropt into their mouths, as a body may say; and their
shoes never waxed old, in their forty years travels; and yet, I
believe, they trampt it on foot all the way.'

'Well, says Wildgoose, I do not recollect, that either Mr. Wesley
or Mr. Whitfield ever make any mention in their Journals, that
they took either money or clean shirts with them, nor whether they
thought it lawful or unlawful to use any precaution of this kind.
But, let me see, you have got a brown jug at home, I think, Jerry;
have you not?'—'That I have, Master; and it will hold two quarts,
good measure.'—'Well, well! you must know then that Mr. Whitfield and his friends have revived a custom of deciding doubtful
points, by lot. He does not tell us indeed, the manner of doing
this. But I know, the method amongst the ancients was to write
down the two questions upon scraps of paper, and shake them in
an urn or pitcher, and leave the determination to Providence.'—
'Why, says Jerry, if that be all, one may put those same papers into
an old hat: or, why cannot one toss up an halfpenny, heads or tails,
as boys do: but then, methinks, it may happen wrong sometimes:
and what is lawful at one time may be unlawful at another, just as
it turns up trump.'—'Why you must observe, Jerry, this method
is only to determine particular facts, or whether one should act so

or so, on any particular occasion; and this sure we may leave to
the decision of Providence.

'But however, Jerry, without any more dispute on the matter,
we may be sure of this, that whilst we are honestly employed in
promoting the glory of God, and the good of mankind, he will
never suffer us to want what is necessary for our support. "Seek
ye first the kingdom of God, and his righteousness, and all other
necessary things shall be added unto you." ' A text of scripture,
how absurdly soever applied, was always decisive with Tugwell.
And he was now worked up to a pitch of Spiritual Quixotism;
and grew impatient to set out, and begged Mr. Wildgoose to name
a day for their departure towards Bristol.

Wildgoose told him, 'that as Whitsuntide was at hand; and as
great irregularities were practised amongst the common people
upon those festivals, at wakes and revels, and other ungodly
meetings: particularly at a heathenish assembly of that kind, on
the Cotswold-hills, called Dover's meeting:[1] he had thoughts of
making that in their road to Bristol.'—'Ah! (says Tugwell) I have
been many a time at Dover's meeting, and won an hat there, at
cudgel-playing, when I was a young man: and they say, there is to
be good sport there this year.' —'Ah! Jerry, replies Wildgoose,
dost thou call that sport, where so many poor souls are devoted
to destruction, by drinking, swearing, and all kinds of debauchery?
These wakes or revels are the Devil's strong-holds, whence he
issues forth, and takes captive the poor deluded people at his
pleasure: however, I am determined to bear my testimony against
them, by preaching to our brethren, and warning them of their
danger, "whether they will hear, or whether they will forbear."
And so, we'll resolve to set out next Thursday morning; which
I think is the day when that meeting is always held.'

Tugwell said, 'He would be ready to attend his Worship at break
of day, if he could give Dorothy the slip. But (says he) there is
another thing which I had forgot, how does your Worship design
to travel; on foot or on horse-back?'—'Why, Jerry, says Wildgoose,
didst thou ever hear that the Apostles rode on horse-back? No;
St. Peter himself never thought of any such thing, (much less of
riding in a coach or post-chaise, as many of his successors have
done,) but performed all his journeys on foot, as I intend to do.'—
'Well, well, Master, says Tugwell, I do not speak upon my own
account: for I never have been on horse-back, since I was twelve

years old; when I used to ride the Squire's horses to water sometimes, along with old Thomas Heartwell, the coachman.

'Well, Master Geoffry, I will be ready to attend your Worship
on foot or on horse-back; by land or by sea; whenever you please:'
and so they parted for the present; each to make what little preparation he thought necessary for such an expedition.

CHAPTER IV

Essay on Quixotism

THOUGH the profession of chivalry has been exhibited to us by
Cervantes, as an object of ridicule; we must not imagine that it was
in itself, and in its original, really ridiculous. Knight-errantry took
its rise from true heroism, and the most generous principles of
honour and publick spirit.[1] The most celebrated heroes of antiquity
were in reality knights-errant: who wandered about, to subdue
monsters or to deliver men from oppression; to protect the innocent, or chastise the insolent; and, in short, to redress those
grievances which were not sufficiently provided against by established laws, in the ruder ages of the world.

The absurdity which we laugh at in the celebrated Don Quixote
is, his attempting to revive that profession, when the more perfect
regulations of civil society had rendered it, not only unnecessary,
but unlawful.

By poring incessantly over the legendary tales of romance, his
ideas of things were so strangely perverted, and his imagination
possessed with such frantic notions, that he thought himself
obliged in honour to sally forth, and submit to voluntary hardships; in quest of adventures which he was not likely to meet
with; and to redress grievances which no longer existed: or in
which, under a regular government, he had no right to interfere.

Thus he not only mistook wind-mills for giants, and an harmless
flock of sheep for an army of Pagans; but challenged an honest
farmer to mortal combat for correcting his own servant, and set at
liberty some prisoners who by legal authority had been condemned
to the galleys.

The like absurd imagination had possessed our Spiritual

Quixote. There was a time, when Providence, for wise reasons, thought fit to delegate men, invested with extraordinary powers, to publish some important truths to mankind; to warn them of approaching calamities; to combat the superstitious opinions, or to reform the immoral practices, which had prevailed in the world to an enormous degree.

In this sense, Patriarchs and Prophets, Apostles and Evangelists, and even St. Paul himself, might be styled Spiritual Knights-errant: though they had divine commissions to take the profession upon them, for the most important ends.

And even our primitive reformers had both reason and scripture so evidently on their side; and the errors of Popery were become so flagrant and intolerable; that they seem justified in breaking through the restraints of human establishments, by the palpable necessity of the occasion.

But our modern itinerant reformers, by the mere force of imagination, have conjured up the powers of darkness in an enlightened age. They are acting in defiance of human laws, without any apparent necessity, or any divine commission. They are planting the Gospel in a Christian country: they are combating the shadow of Popery, where the Protestant religion is established; and declaiming against good works, in an age which they usually represent as abounding in every evil work.

But there is another species, or rather a slighter degree of Quixotism, which proceeds merely from the mimetic disposition of mankind, and is perhaps more common in the world than is generally imagined; what I mean is, a desire of imitating any great personage, whom we read of in history, in their dress, their manner of life, their most indifferent actions, or their most trifling peculiarities: especially of those who, by living in some distant age of the world, have acquired a kind of venerable heroism to their character. And there are few people, I believe, so severely rational, as not to have some slight tincture of this harmless frailty, or, as the wise men of the world would call it, this ridiculous affectation.

Indeed, life itself would be insipid; nor could human-nature support itself upon merely rational pleasures: did not fancy enlarge our sphere of enjoyment; not only by giving an additional gloss to the most substantial objects; but also by stamping an imaginary value upon the most trifling: which by that means, whilst the novelty lasts, frequently become the source of the most exquisite delight.

I remember a gentleman of the House of Commons, a man of great learning and fine taste; who, having been particularly conversant in the English history and antiquities, and whose fondness for the paintings of Vandyke had given him a relish for the dress of our ancient nobility, indulged himself (when at his country seat) in the humour of wearing shoe-strings, instead of shoe-buckles; and a collar-band, instead of a neck-cloth; and in several other antiquated customs: which he would gravely defend by arguments of convenience and propriety.

I also knew a man in the University, who, having read at how great a price the earthen lamp of Epictetus was sold after his death, and flattering himself that the implements of his lucubrations might be valued as curiosities by posterity; determined to renounce the use of candles (as a modern invention) and (like that philosopher) to study by a lamp: which, to his utter confusion, he happened to over-turn, and spilled a considerable quantity of oil upon an handsome folio, which he had borrowed of his tutor.

Nay, a whimsical gentleman, within my memory, took it into his head, that, instead of a night-cap, he would sleep (like the ancient heroes) in an iron helmet, which adorned his hall; till one night it unfortunately fell off his head, and demolished his chamber-pot.

Thus Mr. Wildgoose, in imitation of our primitive Reformers, and those other worthies in the frontispieces of those books of the last century with which he had been lately conversant, who wore their own hair according to the fashion of the times: that he might resemble those venerable men, even in his external appearance, Mr. Wildgoose, I say, since his retreat from the world, had suffered his own hair to grow for some months: though perhaps there might also be something of convenience in this at first, to avoid the impertinence of his officious barber; who, whilst he was working the lather into his stubbed hair, would take upon him to insinuate some sociable advice into his patient, which was more irksome to Mr. Wildgoose in his present gloomy situation, even than the rough instruments and heavy hand of this rustic operator. This alone therefore would have been a sufficient reason for his omitting to be shaved, and nourishing his own hair: which, though it was now thick enough to keep him warm, yet as it did not extend below his ears, he made but an uncouth appearance to those who had been used to see him in a decent periwig. But to proceed in our story.

CHAPTER V

*Mr. Wildgoose and his Friend Tugwell sally forth
in Quest of Spiritual Adventures*

EARLY on Thursday morning then, in the Whitsun-week,
Mr. Geoffry Wildgoose forsook his downy bed; and rejecting that
artificial covering of the head, called a peruke, just smoothed his
locks with his fingers, put on a plain blue coat, with a black plush
waistcoat and breeches, and, with a few guineas in his pocket,
issued forth in quest of spiritual adventures.

The harmless red-breast, with his solitary note, began to break
in upon the stillness of the dawn; and, from the sweet-briar that
grew round the lattice, to interrupt the gentle slumbers of Jeremiah
Tugwell, when Mr. Wildgoose arrived under his window; and,
by the signal agreed upon, summoned him to the place of rendezvous. Jerry soon appeared at the cottage-gate, in his short
jerkin, (being somewhat between a coat and a waist-coat) his jelly-
bag linen cap upon his head, with his oaken staff under his arm,
and his wallet on his shoulder.

Wildgoose delivered to him a couple of shirts, a small Bible,
and two or three pious manuals, which were to be the companions
of his pilgrimage. Tugwell however (who was a happy composition
of flesh and spirit) having some regard to the body as well as the
soul, had the precaution, which Wildgoose wanted, to thrust
privately into his wallet a good luncheon of brown bread, and some
Gloucestershire cheese; which clandestine conduct it is not
recorded that Wildgoose ever thought proper to resent.

The sun had hardly appeared above the horizon, when the two
pilgrims turned their backs upon their native village, making what
speed they could towards the Cotswold-hills; to avoid meeting
any of their neighbours, whose curiosity might retard them in their
progress.

In about two hours, they reached the brow of the hill; when
Mr. Wildgoose, making an halt, to take breath, looked round
upon the country below them. The sun had now begun to exhale
the dews of the morning; which, being thinly dispersed through
the air, gave a charming freshness to every object that rose to their
view. There was an extensive prospect of the rich vale of Evesham,
bounded at a distance by the Malvern hills. The towers and spires,

which rose amongst the tufted trees, were strongly illuminated
by the sloping rays of the sun; and the whole scene was enlivened by the music of the birds; the responsive notes of the
thrushes from the neighbouring haw-thorns, and the thrilling
strains of the sky-lark, who, as she soared towards the heavens,
seemed to be chanting forth her matins to the great Creator of
the universe.

Wildgoose was touched with a kind of sympathy: and a ray of
true devotion darting into his soul, he broke out in the words of
Milton, with whom he had been much conversant—

> These are thy glorious works, Parent of good,
> Almighty! Thine this universal frame,
> Thus wondrous fair; Thyself how wondrous then?
> Unspeakable! who sit'st above these heavens,
> To us invisible, or dimly seen
> In these thy works; yet these declare
> Thy goodness beyond thought, and power divine.[1]

After a little pause, 'Jerry,' says he, (addressing himself to Tugwell) 'I am always charmed with this fine prospect, though I have
viewed it so many hundred times.'—'Yes,' (says Jerry, who was
slipt behind his master) 'one may see—a number of miles here—
that's *sartain*.'—'I don't think the beauty of a prospect depends
upon the number of miles one may see,' says Wildgoose, 'but upon
the number and distinctness of the objects, and the richness of the
country.'—'Why, yes,' says Tugwell, 'to be sure—the vale—is
rich land—and most of it—worth forty shilling an acre—but then
—it's plaguy dirty—in the winter.—'

As Tugwell was going on, Mr. Wildgoose turned about, and
found that the breaks in his speech were owing to the regular whiffs
which he took at his pipe. For whilst Wildgoose was engaged in
contemplation and soliloquy, Jerry had been employed in striking
fire to some touch-wood, which he always carried in his tobacco-
box for that purpose: and had just lighted, and was puffing with
violent efforts, his short pipe. 'Ah! Jerry,' says Wildgoose, 'I find
thou art not yet weaned from the vanities of this world—Thou art
not content with the heavenly manna of meditation, but still
lustest after the garlic and flesh-pots of Egypt.'—'Why then,
Master Wildgoose, is it any sin to take an harmless pipe of tobacco?
I don't think smoking now and then is contrary either to the law or
the gospel.'—'Jerry,' (says Wildgoose) 'I don't think smoking

tobacco absolutely sinful: for to the good, all things are good, if it be received with thanksgiving.'—'Then, belike, one ought to say grace over a pipe of tobacco?' says Jerry.—'I don't say that,' replies Wildgoose; 'but I'll venture to say, that one ought not to take any sort of pleasure, for which one cannot return God thanks. In short, Jerry, I am afraid thou hast got such an habit of tickling thy palate with something strong, that thou canst not easily do without it; for which reason thou oughtest to break it off at once.'— Jerry, who was a little nettled at being interrupted in what he thought so innocent an enjoyment, cried out, 'Well, well, I *loves* a pipe; and, thank God, can afford to buy an halfpenny-worth of tobacco: and I would not leave it off, if the Bishop himself, or even Mr. Whitefield, were to preach against it. In short, Master, if smoking a dry pipe¹ be a sin, God send us some good liquor! which is all that I'll say about the matter.'

Wildgoose shook his head, and began to fear that Tugwell was only half a convert: but thought it was best not to exasperate his fellow-traveller, or discourage him by too much severity at their first setting out; he therefore dropped the dispute, and trudged on at a round rate, for some time.

CHAPTER VI

Tugwell meets with a perilous Adventure

THE two friends now proceeded on their journey; Mr. Wildgoose occasionally inculcating some wholesome doctrine into his disciple, and Tugwell fumigating the air with the incense of his tobacco.

They had travelled near two miles without any occurrence worth recording; when, on a sudden, they heard at a distance the chearful cry of a pack of hounds, accompanied with the music of French-horns. As they trudged on, the sound approached still nearer and nearer; and at last they were surprized with the appearance, not of four or five fox-hunters, as might be expected; but of four-score or an hundred horse-men, upon full speed. The case was, Lord B— of Nottinghamshire had taken a seat upon the Cotswold-hills, for buck-hunting; and had that morning turned out a fine stag—

which the hounds had pursued with great eagerness—and probably over-run the scent: for, coming to a wall, they were now at a stand; and gave the whole company an opportunity of coming to a rendezvous.

I have observed, there is hardly a man amongst the vulgar people, but affects to be a sportsman, and that would not think it as great a disgrace to be thought a coward or deficient in courage—as void of taste or ignorant of the terms peculiar to the manly exercise of hunting.

Accordingly Tugwell, though his sedentary occupation had permitted him to be but little conversant with field-sports, or the pleasures of the chace, yet was ambitious of being thought a sportsman; and, seeing the dogs at a stand, lagged behind Mr. Wildgoose (who walked on wrapped in meditation) to wait the event. At last, in the midst of a furze-brake, Tugwell spied the head of some animal; which his imagination immediately represented as the branching horns of the stag. And now, fired with ambition, and making sure of the applauses of the whole field, Jerry waved his hat over his head; and, with the utmost vociferation, in the fox-hunters' language, cries out, 'Tallio! Tallio! Tallio!'[1] The huntsman understood him, and immediately drew off the dogs towards his bawling monitor; when, to his great vexation and Tugwell's utter confusion, up starts a swinging jack-ass; whose long ears Jerry mistook for the horns of the stag. The jack-ass, with his hideous braying, put to flight the huntsman's courser: who, however, was wheeling round to reward Tugwell for his intelligence with the discipline of a horse-whip. And many of the gentlemen being now come up, and disappointed of their sport; and suspecting that Jerry had done it out of fun, were surrounding him in great wrath, and threatened to be the death of him. Poor Tugwell threw himself upon his knees; and with one hand flourishing his staff to guard his head, he extended the other to sue for mercy: but expected every moment to fall a sacrifice to the rage of the vociferous stag-hunters. At last, one of the gentlemen, who saw these affairs in a less important light, turned it off with a joke, and dismissed him, in the polite phrase, (being a mixture of real compassion and affected profaneness)— 'D-mn the fellow; let the poor devil go about his business.'

Tugwell took them at their word, and gathering up his steps with great agility, and without looking behind him, soon joined his

friend Wildgoose: who, wrapt in contemplation, was advanced
a considerable way before him; having not given the least attention
to what was going on—but upon Jerry's relating to him his danger,
and his escape from it, Wildgoose immediately started from his
reverie; and, in the first transports of his zeal for his friend, was
determined to attack these sons of Nimrod with the thunder of his
eloquence. But, luckily for them, they were by this time gone off
many furlongs in pursuit of their game, and out of the reach of
Wildgoose's rebukes.

He therefore contented himself with sending a pious ejaculation
after them; and with reprimanding Tugwell for his officious impertinence: recommending to him a more simple and uniform
conduct for the future; and not to entangle himself again in the vain
amusements of a carnal and wicked generation.

CHAPTER VII

The natural Effects of Hunger and Fatigue

THE two pilgrims had now almost reached the plain called Dover's-
hill, where the revel was to be held: but as the sport did not begin
till the afternoon, and the sun now began to wax troublesome, Jerry
proposed resting under an oak, that cast an inviting shade near the
side of a wall; and opening his wallet, he produced a large fragment
of a brown loaf, and cheese in proportion, the reviving odour of
which put Wildgoose in mind of his breakfast: for hitherto he had
not bestowed a thought upon that article, nor on the means of
procuring it.

'Now, Master,' (quoth Tugwell) 'if we had trusted to Providence,
and I had not brought some bread and cheese in my wallet, what
would your Worship have done for a breakfast?'—'Hold thy
prophane tongue!' replies Wildgoose: 'this is not a difficulty which
requires the interposition of Providence. But whenever that is the
case, I am certain of his assistance: and God often makes those his
instruments to bring about his gracious designs, who intend
nothing but their own pleasure, as I suppose thou didst, Jerry, in
bringing thy bread and cheese in thy wallet.'

After making an hearty, though dry breakfast (for his precaution did not extend so far as to provide drink as well as food) Jerry's spirits having been exhausted by his early rising, long walk, and the consternation he had been in from the huntsman's whip, he threw himself at length upon the turf; and was soon got into a world of his own, snoring most profoundly.

Mr. Wildgoose at first pulled out one of his little manuals, and began to read: but he being likewise a little fatigued, soon yielded to the demands of nature, and followed his fellow-traveller's example: where we shall leave them to their repose a little, whilst we enquire what effect their departure had upon Mrs. Wildgoose and Dame Tugwell, whom they left at home.

CHAPTER VIII

Character of Mrs. Wildgoose. And the Perplexity occasioned by the Elopement of Mr. Wildgoose and Tugwell

MRS. WILDGOOSE was a woman—that wore a white-hood—and breakfasted upon sage-tea—which particularities, and the principles that gave rise to them, were the distinguishing strokes of her character. For, in every instance, Mrs. Wildgoose (like a sensible woman) preferred convenience to shew; and always sacrificed any present pleasure to the future ease and happiness of her life. Accordingly, in contempt of modern fashions, and to guard against the tooth-ach, she continued the venerable sarsenet hood, which was the mark of gentility in the days of her youth: and she drank sage-tea, rather than indulge herself in the delicious flavour of hyson or congo, at the expence of her health; which she found affected by that more agreeable beverege.

Mrs. Wildgoose had a truly maternal fondness for her son; and was disappointed in not having him as a constant companion at her meals, and her hours of leisure from her domestic business. But as she was sensible that he was at present under a wrong influence, she forbore to exasperate his malady by opposition or teazing expostulations. She was no stranger (as we observed) to her son's frequenting Tugwell's house, to the company he kept there, nor to the manner in which he entertained them; had heard of his attending the Methodist's meeting at ——; and had frequently intended to consult with Mr. Powell, the vicar, on that subject. But though she was afraid this religious cast of mind was rather the effect of melancholy than of any rational conviction; yet she thought it was the most innocent turn his disorder could take; the dram-bottle or other vicious indulgences being too frequently the sad refuge of such unsociable mortals in their solitudes. And as his motions had of late been so very irregular—and he frequently walked out at the garden-gate very early into the fields with his grey-hound, and breakfasted at his own hours, she took no notice of his absence this particular morning.

But Dame Tugwell, though Jerry had been often as early as this at the labours of the strap, and was frequently whistling and singing, to the disturbance of his neighbours, before sunrising— yet she regularly summoned him at eight o'clock, from his little stall near the house, to partake with her of a warm breakfast; but not finding him this morning at his station (if I may use that expression for want of a better) she had made diligent enquiry amongst her neighbours without success. At last, it came into her head, that Mr. Wildgoose and he had been more frequently together of late, than they ever used to be before. She, without much hesitation, therefore, repairs to Mrs. Wildgoose's, to enquire if he had been there this morning. Upon being answered in the negative, and also informed, that Mr. Wildgoose had not been seen that day (though it was now much later than he had ever been absent before) both she and Mrs. Wildgoose began to be greatly alarmed.—'I will be hanged now' (says Dame Tugwell) 'if these two have not some *figary* in their brain:[1] I have observed his Worship and our Jerry always whispering and laying their heads together of late: and whenever I came near them, they were as mute as a fish forsooth. For my part, I never liked all this preaching and praying: there is no occasion for it; is there now, Madam Wildgoose? If a body does but *keep one's church*, and does one's best to live, and pays every one his own, I do not see what else is required of us.'—(This she said as knowing Mrs. Wildgoose's opinion of the matter.) 'But what crotchet can be got into their heads now?' continued Dorothy. 'Master Wildgoose has been so *malancolly* of late, to be sure he would not go to such a place as Dover's meeting: for, else, our Jerry has been talking of the *sport* there two or three times within this day or two—but what should Jerry do there now, unless he puts in for the silver spoon, that is to be grinned for? However, I shall hear

of him, if he is thereabout—and I will lock up his best waist-coat
for the future—and make him know, he shall not run about spending his money at this rate without my leave.'

Mrs. Wildgoose, as soon as the volubility of Dame Tugwell
would permit, desired her 'to make herself easy about her husband;
that, if he was gone with her son, she would pay him for his trouble,
and be answerable for his coming to any harm.'—'No! God
forbid!' (quoth Dorothy) 'for I am but a poor helpless woman,
you know, Madam, since my poor Joseph went for a soldier; and
now if my husband should leave me too, what will become of me?
Times are so hard, and money so scarce—and I can earn but one
poor eighteen-pence a week—and that is but a small matter to
keep a body, you know, Madam—' Dorothy was running on, like
the flyer of a jack,[1] when Mrs. Wildgoose desired her to be pacified,
ordered her some victuals, and left her.

When Mrs. Wildgoose was alone, however, she began to be very
seriously alarmed for her son. She could not possibly guess what
project he was engaged in. She was at first inclined to send her old
servant to Dover's-hill, which Dame Tugwell had mentioned, that
she might be satisfied whether he were gone thither or not: but
immediately rejected that design; as she was convinced young
Wildgoose, in his present state of mind, would not appear at a
publick meeting of that kind.

Whilst she was in this perplexity, Mr. Powell, the clergyman of
the parish, came in, as he frequently did in the morning: who being
informed of the affair, immediately said, 'he should not be at all
surprized to hear that Mr. Geoffry was gone somewhere or other,
after these Methodists: for he was well assured, he had been preaching up their puritanical notions amongst his neighbours for this
half year; that he had lent two or three of their Journals about the
parish, and had frequently attended an itinerant preacher at ——
(though it had been kept a secret from Mrs. Wildgoose, as he
imagined). I have often had a mind to talk to Mr. Geoffry on this
subject' (continued the vicar)—'but you know, Madam, he has of
late avoided me; and indeed there is no reasoning with people who
refer you to their own inward feelings; which you can no more
deny, than they can prove: and who take for sacred the wildest
suggestions of their own fancy.'

Mrs. Wildgoose knew what Mr. Powell said to be very true, and
could not tell what to think of the matter—but as her son's conduct

had for some time been so unaccountable, she thought it in vain
to form any conjectures about it; so waited with patience for his
return, which she expected every hour. But in that poor Mrs.
Wildgoose was greatly disappointed.

CHAPTER IX

Proceed towards Dover's-hill Revel

THE two fellow-travellers were left, under a spreading oak, taking
a comfortable nap together. Wildgoose's high spirits, however,
would not suffer him to doze long: but having roused his companion, they were now moving on towards the scene of action,
refreshed from the fatigues of the morning: which refreshment
proved by no means unseasonable in the sequel.

Mr. Wildgoose, being intent upon his adventurous undertaking,
that of preaching for the first time to a mob of holiday clowns at a
revel, moved on in profound silence. And though he did not think
any premeditation necessary, as he depended upon some supernatural power to give him utterance—yet he could not forbear
anticipating, in some measure, the incidents which he should
probably meet with on this occasion—nor avoid recollecting how
ingeniously Mr. Whitfield spiritualized every circumstance attending his ministration.

Thus when he was to preach from the starting-post at Northampton, for instance, 'He took occasion to speak home to their
souls, concerning our spiritual race.'[1] And from the windmill at
Bedford—'He exhorted them not to be carried about by every
wind of doctrine;'[2] and the like. So Wildgoose was devising with
himself how to allegorize the different athletic exercises, which
were usually practised on these occasions, and apply them to the
best advantage.

To the wrestlers, he intended to preach up the necessity of
struggling against flesh and blood; against the world and the Devil;
and also frequently to *wrestle* with God in prayer; as Mr. Whitfield
so often did.

The cudgel-players, he thought, he might aptly enough exhort
to *bruise* and '*break the head* of that old red serpent' the Devil, as

St. Austin calls him: and to *guard* themselves against every *attack* of their spiritual antagonists—and the like.

They proceeded therefore in silent meditation for some time; till at length Tugwell took the liberty to expostulate a little with his master upon the subject. 'Please your Worship', says he, 'I have been thinking about this same preachment of ours, which we are now going about—since we are almost got to the place, methinks my heart begins to fail me a little. To be sure, it does one's heart good to hear your Worship preach—and talk about justification— and *prestination* and *reperbation*, and—and—generation, and *sich* like—in our chimney corner—in an evening: for then, as one may say, we have nothing else to do; and nobody to contradict us. But here, when folks are got together—to make merry; that is, to break heads—and to kick shins, and *sich* as that; methinks, they will hardly have time to hear us preach: and mayhap, they may only laugh at us, for talking about religion at *sich* a time as this—or belike may pelt us with dirt or horse-dung—and *sich* as that.'

'Ah! Jerry,' says Wildgoose, 'have not I told thee, how Mr. Whitfield has preached to twenty thousand people at a time, upon Kennington Common—where (as he assures us himself) he was frequently attended by fourscore coaches, and numbers of horses; and yet all was hushed, the moment he began to speak—their hearts were melted;[1] they would have plucked out their eyes, and have given them to him; they crowded about him, hugged, and were even eager to salute him![2] But be that as it may, Jerry; I am determined to discharge my duty; and should think myself happy to suffer in so glorious a cause.—The true Saints have often most ardently thirsted after contumelies, derisions, and other instances of persecution.'—'Well, well! Master, God's will be done!' says Tugwell; 'I did but speak—not that I am afraid of any one, for my part; nor would not turn my back to the best man in Gloster-shire.'—'Well, do not be too confident, neither, Jerry; remember the violent professions of St. Peter: and yet he was found deficient in the time of danger.—We must trust in the Lord, and take the sword of the spirit; but if we confide to our own strength, and to *carnal* weapons, we may find ourselves deserted in the day of temptation.'

F

CHAPTER X

Mr. Wildgoose's first Harangue

THEY now approached the place of rendezvous, where the revel was held; which was a large plain on the Cotswold-hills. Their ears were saluted with a confused noise of drums, trumpets, and whistle-pipes: not those martial sounds, however, which are heard in the field of battle; but such as those harmless instruments emit, with which children amuse themselves in a country fair. There was a great number of swains in their holiday-cloaths, with their belts and silk handkerchiefs; and nymphs in straw hats and tawdry ribbands, flaunting, ogling, and coquetting (in their rustic way) with as much alacrity, as any of the gay flutterers in the Mall.

A ring was formed about the wrestlers and cudgel-players, by the substantial farmers on their long-tailed steeds, and two or three forlorn coaches [were] sauntering about with their vapourish possessors: who crept out from their neighbouring seats—to contemplate the humours of these aukward rustics, and waste an hour of their tedious month in the *country*; where (as a great modern observes) '*small matters serve for amusement.*'[1]

Wildgoose and his friend Jerry, making but a small figure in this numerous assembly, were at a loss how to draw the attention of the multitude. As they had made a dry breakfast, and had drunk nothing the whole day, Jerry asked his master, 'Whether it were any sin, to call for a pint of ale, at *sich* a time as this?' So, with Wildgoose's consent, they went to one of the booths, and were refreshing themselves with the foresaid potation; when the company began to divide; and proclamation was made, that a holland shift, which was adorned with ribbands, and displayed on a pole, was going to be run for; and six young women began to exhibit themselves before the whole assembly, in a dress hardly reconcileable to the rules of decency.

'Nice people have been observed to have the grossest ideas.' And perhaps such chaste men have the most unchaste conceptions of things. Be that as it will; Wildgoose no sooner perceived that mysterious veil of modesty, the holland smock, thus rudely exposed to public view, and these young women prepared to engage in so loose a diversion, than he found his wonted zeal revive; and mounting upon an inverted hamper, near the booth, he beckoned to the mob, crying out,

'For Christ's sake, my Christian brethren, if you have any regard to the *health* of your souls, shun, as you would the *plague*, these anti-christian recreations; which are utterly inconsistent with the holiness *prescribed* in the Gospel, and are *poison* to your future expectations.'

The people, seeing a man of a tolerable appearance thus exalted above the crowd, and preparing to harangue, began to stare, and to enquire of each other what he would be at! As they heard imperfectly the word *health*, and more words of a medicinal tendency, the prevailing opinion was, that a mountebank was going to dispense his medicines, for the benefit of mankind: and Tugwell's wallet was supposed to contain the sovereign packet of the learned Doctor. Mr. Wildgoose however soon undeceived them, by addressing the crowd in the apostolical style; though he had not yet acquired the true *bon ton* or Gospel lingo of Mr. Whitfield and his associates.

'Men, brethren, and fellow-Christians! You are here assembled to keep holiday; that is, to sacrifice to the Devil: to perform the most agreeable service, which you could possibly devise, to that enemy of mankind.

'This festival is called Whitsuntide, and was appointed to commemorate the most solemn event recorded in the annals of our religion; namely, the effusion of the Holy Spirit upon the primitive apostles. But, instead of being filled with the Holy Spirit, as the apostles were, you are filling yourselves with spirituous liquors and strong drink: with the spirits of geneva; with English spirits, and foreign spirits, and what not?

'Oh! my brethren, consider what you are about: is this renouncing the Devil and all his works? Is this despising the pomps and vanities of this wicked world, and resisting the sinful lusts of the flesh? The very purpose and intent of this ungodly meeting is directly opposite to your most solemn vow at your baptism. Instead of guarding yourselves against the attacks of your spiritual adversary; instead of bruising the head of that old serpent, the Devil; you are breaking one another's heads with cudgels and quarterstaffs; instead of wrestling against flesh and blood, you are wrestling with and supplanting one another. So far from renouncing the pomps and vanities of this wicked world, you are

running for holland smocks; and making provision for the lusts
of the flesh.

'Ah! my dear country-women; you that are so solicitous for
these terrestrial garments; these garments spotted by the flesh! let
me beseech you to labour after the celestial robes, the spiritual
decorations and saint-like ornaments of piety, meekness, and
chastity: and not to set your hearts upon such profane trappings
as pink ribbands and holland smocks.

'Indeed, what use will you make of these tawdry shifts, should
you gain the prize? I blush to answer such a question. They may
make a poor SHIFT, like the fig-leaves of Eve, to cover the nakedness
of your bodies; as our good works do the nakedness of our souls.
But unless you are cloathed with a better righteousness than your
own, you will hereafter be stripped bare, and be exposed to the
derision of men and angels—'

From the secret connection which this subject had with generation, Mr. Wildgoose was insensibly sliding into the nature of
regeneration, and the new-birth; and was going to explain some
of the most mysterious doctrines of Christianity to these unruly
disciples: when a good orthodox publican, thinking his craft was in
danger, cried out, 'Come, come, what's that to the purpose; lift
up the smock! Come, my maids! stand ready for the sport!'

He was seconded by a shrewd young carter, (with a silk handkerchief about his neck) who could not but laugh at the familiarity of
Wildgoose's comparisons: and thinking also that this harangue
would spoil the diversion, which they were now intent upon, he
threw the rind of an orange at the orator's head. Another leveled
a piece of horse-dung (with an unlucky dexterity) exactly into
Tugwell's mouth, as he stood listening with a conceited attention
to his master's eloquence. Their example was followed by a great
part of the company; who, as Jerry had foretold, began to bombard
them so furiously with clods of dirt and horse-dung, that Mr. Wildgoose was soon forced to dismount from the top of his hamper.
And one of them, tilting up the form on which Tugwell was exalted,
laid him sprawling in the moisture, occasioned by the staling of
horses, or spilling of the liquor; where he lay wallowing for some
time, being saluted with several bumps and jostles in contrary directions; which prevented his emerging from the slippery soil.

In short, Wildgoose thought it adviseable to preserve himself
for a more favourable opportunity: wherefore, lifting up and

disengaging his fellow-labourer, they drew off from the field of battle, amidst the loud scoffs and exulting shouts of the unthinking multitude; Wildgoose only expressing his compassion for them, by a significant shake of the head, and crying out, 'Poor souls! they know not what they do.' And Jerry, when he was got pretty well out of their reach, bawled out, 'Ay! ay! *parsecute* on—*parsecute* on— *parsecute—parsecute!* You have the best of it in this world; but we shall be even with you in the next.'

Thus unsuccessfully ended Wildgoose's first effort towards reforming the world: which, however, so far from discouraging him, only excited his zeal: and he thought himself extremely happy in being counted worthy even of so slight a persecution; and desired Jerry not to be disheartened, for that they should meet with better success, when God should think fit to incline the hearts of his people to listen to their admonitions.

Tugwell (who was a little disconcerted by the bad success of their first attempt) answered, 'that he did not doubt but God would bring every thing about in his own good time; but (says he) perhaps the time is not yet come.' And having a great desire (though he did not care to speak out) to return to his own chimney-corner, said, 'Suppose, Master, we were to go and try first what we can do with the men in the vale. And now, I don't think there was any body at Dover's-hill that knew us: for I did not see one soul of our town, and I know they are all busy in hay-harvest: so that we might slip home again at night, and nobody be ever the wiser.'

'Why, Jerry,' (says Wildgoose, with some warmth) 'dost thou think me such an apostate? what! to turn back, as soon as I have put my hand to the plough? No, Jerry, you may do as you please; but I will this night make the best of my way towards Gloucester, where Mr. Whitfield was born, and first preached the word; and I make no doubt but I shall there find a little flock at least ready to receive me.'

This gentle rebuke had its effect upon Jerry; and he found his spirit of travelling begin to revive. He told his master, therefore, 'he scorned to forsake him;' and said, 'when he had washed his face, which was a little sullied by his fall, he should not value what had happened, of a rush. But,' adds he, 'if it were to do again, I would have had one bout with the cowardly dog, who tilted up the form.'

Wildgoose exhorted his friend to Christian patience, and to return good for evil; and so they trudged on for some miles, without any other adventure.

CHAPTER XI

Armigerorum Laudes; *or, a Panegyric on Esquires, both ancient and modern*

'WHOSE house is that,' (said I to some labourers on the London road) 'with a little cupola on the top, and an enormous length of Chinese rails before it?'—'Squire Shapely's, the Londoner's,' says one of the labourers.—'Yes,' (says another, with an arch leer) 'he was a London Taylor; but has got a little money, and has built a fine house; and is now a Justice o' peace, and a *Squire*.'—Such is the style and title, taste and oeconomy of your London Esquire.

A country 'Squire is a gentleman in a remote province; who resides constantly at the mansion-house of his ancestors, which he keeps in tolerable repair—makes a new pair of gates, and builds a summer-house at the corner of his garden. Relying upon his silver spurs and a tight boot, he makes one attempt towards gaining a rich heiress: but not succeeding, he marries his maid, gets an heir to his estate, dies, and is forgotten.

He visits the metropolis once in his life-time; and takes up his quarters at the Ram in Smithfield—goes to visit his old aunt, from whom he has great expectations: who, for the credit of the family, makes him put on a sword, which gets between his legs, and almost oversets him. He therefore walks through Fleet-street in his boots; a sharper jostles him into the kennel—another snatches his whip from under his arm, under pretence of revenging the affront, and makes clear off with it—gives five and six-pence for a pair of buck-skin gloves, double-stitched; returns into the country, with a terrible idea of the extravagance and tricks of the town—and (though a constant dupe to the knavish cunning of his tenants, and the exorbitant gains of a country shop-keeper) detests every thing that bears the name of London, except 'the London Evening-Post,' and the London carrier that brings him down a barrel of oysters at Christmas. Now this sort of man is your country Esquire.[1]

From these instances, I infer, that Esquires are of various kinds; and that an Esquire, in the modern sense of the word, is a being, in his definition, his existence, and his oeconomy, totally distinct from the Squires of antiquity. The race of Squires, whose utility to the world in general, and to us diminutive authors in particular, I wish to celebrate, were, in their original, *Armigeri*, or *Scutiferi*;

that is, armour-bearers to some ancient heroe; and from thence transferred into modern tales and romances, in which every Knight has his Esquire. Such was Automedon to Achilles, the faithful Achates to Æneas, Sancho Panza to Don Quixote, and Ralpho to Hudibras. Now, as the Squires of the heroic ages performed those inferior offices of life, which were beneath the dignity of the heroe himself; drove his chariot, bridled his horse, or ran on errands, and the like: so in mock heroics, or familiar romance, the Squire is frequently the vehicle of low humour; or the subject of such practical jokes, as would too much degrade the solemnity of the Knight-errant himself. Thus Sancho Panza is tossed in a blanket; whilst good epic rib-roastings, and heroic knocks on the pate, are reserved for the noble Don, his master.

And as poetry and romance is, or ought to be, an imitation of real life; the like subordination of character is frequently to be met with in company, and the conversation of the world. An Esquire, in this view, is a gentleman of an easy submissive temper, of moderated appetites, and patient of injuries; who acts an under-part in life, and serves as a kind of shield to protect, or a foil to set off, the principal character.

Every person of any distinction is accordingly surrounded by his proper satellites or attendants of this kind. My Lord has his Dangler, who secures him a proper deference amongst strangers, by setting the example himself. The Bishop has his Chaplain, who, at loo or all-fours, lets his Lordship name the trump. Nay, every Squire in the modern sense of the word has a Squire in the ancient sense, who attends him on all occasions, in the shape of an hunting Parson, a nominal Captain, or a pacific Lawyer; who shields him from the vehemence of his brother Justice's wit; or acts the dwarf in understanding, whenever his Worship is disposed to shine or to be witty himself; or explains his jokes, or defends his paradoxes, as the occasion happens to require.

I might proceed to shew the same convenient subordination of character, in every rank of life; but this would be too great a digression from my purpose, which was, only to shew the utility of this race of men, in works of this kind; and to intreat the reader to consider the Squire as a lawful representative of the Knight, or rather as a *Merry Andrew* to our Spiritual *Quack*; and that, if Tugwell is not only 'witty in himself,' but 'the cause that wit is in other men' (as Falstaff says)[1] —if he utters a facetious thing, or

receives a kick on the breech; let it be placed to account, as so much
wit and humour in the author; which he could, with the same ease,
though not with the same propriety, have transferred to Wildgoose
himself, his principal character.—

But to proceed in our history.

CHAPTER XII

*Mr. Wildgoose's hospitable Reception at the House of an
orthodox Clergyman; and the Event of a Dispute between them*

THE two pilgrims had now proceeded near seven miles from the
place of their luckless atchievement; Wildgoose rejoicing that he
was counted worthy to suffer for religion (as he thought it), and
Tugwell consoling himself with the hopes of better success for the
future; when they arrived at an obscure village on the side of the
hills, a little before sun-set. They were directed to a neat publick
house, by a small sign—whose device it required some skill in
hieroglyphics to decypher. The painter had probably intended it
for the Red Lyon; but some ambiguity, which arose from an
injudicious mixture of the lights and shades, gave it rather the
appearance of a Shoulder of Mutton.—When they entered the
house, they found it pre-occupied by a very sober party; consisting
of an Exciseman, a Grazier, the Parson of the parish, and a Mole-
catcher.

Mr. Wildgoose inquired of the landlord, 'whether he could
furnish them with a bed?' Instead of answering his question, the
landlord (according to custom) asked him, 'which way they were
travelling?' This not being to the present purpose, Wildgoose
desired an answer to his first question. Mine host told him, 'theirs
was but a by-place, and no great thoroughfare, and that they had
seldom any body lie there: but, however, when his Dame came
home (which she certainly would do before midnight, as she was
only gone to a merry-making in the next parish), he would see
about it; and he did not doubt but they could contrive to lodge
them; though,' says he, 'we have but one room, where I and my
wife lie; but then we have two beds in it.—Well, but what will you
please to drink, Sir?' continued my landlord.

Our travellers being a little disconcerted at this account of my host's accommodations, Wildgoose enquired, 'How far it was to Gloucester?'—'To Gloucester, Sir? Why, you are out of your way to Gloucester, but *howsomever* we call it twelve miles; and, I believe, it is pretty good measure: do not you think it is, Master Pottle?' This was the name of the honest Clergyman; to whom mine host appealed, by way of commencing a conversation between him and the travellers; as talking together is generally an introduction to drinking together, which it was his interest to promote. But Mr. Pottle, being conscious of the impropriety of his present situation, and that he must appear in a low light to a stranger of a tolerable figure as Wildgoose was, affected to have no connexion with the company; but to be employed in some useful meditation. Instead of regarding my landlord's appeal therefore, he assumed all the dignity he was possessed of, inflated his cheeks, and puffed out whole volumes of smoke, which being reverberated by the low roof, he soon filled the house with the fumes of his tobacco.

As the Doctor did not vouchsafe them an answer, Wildgoose had now given his attention to a common subject of dispute, which was carrying on between the Grazier and the Exciseman—the former of whom had asserted, 'That if a man happened to buy an horse, which was *touched in the wind*, or had any other concealed defect; it was no harm to put him off again, without discovering his faults.'—As this dispute bore some relation to the precepts of religion, and seemed to concern Wildgoose, who had taken upon him the office of reforming pernicious principles and corrupt practices; he could not forbear interposing. And having been formerly a smart logician (as was observed in the beginning of this history); after expressing his concern, that such a practice should bear a dispute in a Christian country; he said, 'that most controversies were perplexed for want of settling precisely the question in debate, and keeping strictly to the terms. He begged leave therefore to reduce the dispute to the following argument, or syllogistical form, as it is called;

All cheating is sinful:

The putting off an unsound horse for a sound one is cheating: Therefore,

The putting off an unsound horse for a sound one is certainly sinful.'[1]

Here the Doctor, taking the pipe from his mouth, could not

forbear putting in his verdict. 'Oh! ho! Sir,' says he, 'I find you have been bred at the University. *Negatur minor:* I deny your second proposition, "That putting off an unsound horse, *in a fair*, is properly cheating, in the *popular* sense of the word." '—'Look you there now,' says Wildgoose; 'this is the common method of disputing: you beg the question—and have also changed the terms of the proposition upon us; and put words into the premises, which have nothing to do with the conclusion. If we were to be governed by popular opinions and popular practices, we should soon have no more honesty amongst us than we have religion.'—'Religion!' says Pottle; 'why, to be sure, it is a very profligate age that we live in; and the world is over-run with infidelity, heresy, and enthusiasm; and the Church never was in so much danger from Atheists and Sectaries as at this day.'

'Sir,' says Wildgoose, 'I apprehend the church's greatest danger is from the careless lives and degenerate principles of its own members.'—'Come, come,' replies Pottle, 'we will not dispute about religion in this place. And, as I am afraid my landlord cannot very commodiously lodge you; rather than you should be distressed, you shall be welcome to such a bed as I can give you, at my house.'

Though Wildgoose recollected what had passed between him and the Parson of his own parish; and was a little apprehensive of being involved in some controversy with a person whose profession would probably lead him to combat his present opinions, and discourage him from the undertaking in which he was now engaged; yet he could not refuse so kind an offer, especially as it was now too late for them to think of going further that night. He therefore thanked the Doctor for his great civility; and, attended by his trusty friend, accompanied him to the parsonage-house.

As they were going out of the house, my landlord's curiosity prompted him to whisper Tugwell, and ask him, 'Whether he and his fellow-travellers did not deal in corks? Or perhaps,' says he, in a low voice, 'you have some *run*[1] goods in your wallet, to dispose of.'—'No, no,' replied Tugwell, 'my master is no such person as you take him for: he is a gentleman that is heir to three or four hundred pounds a year, and scorns to sell any thing. But, no matter for that: I shall not tell our private matters to every fool that asks me. No, no, I understand travelling better than that comes to.'

CHAPTER XIII

What happened at the Parson's Habitation

MR. POTTLE had now brought his two guests to his own house; and, sending Tugwell into the kitchen, took Wildgoose into a tolerably neat parlour. His elbow-chair stood ready for his reception; and his Tunbridge-ware tobacco-dish, with some scraps of paper folded up for the use of his pipe, were placed upon the table. There were several old news-papers lying in the window, and a single picture of Cardinal Fleury hung over the chimney-piece.

Mr. Pottle was an hale man, of about five and fifty; was a batchelor; and all his domesticks were, an elderly house-keeper and a manservant about his own age. His character will sufficiently appear from the evening's conversation.

Pottle had a cloth laid for himself and Mr. Wildgoose, who eat pretty heartily of a cold shoulder of mutton and cucumbers; and Tugwell was very happy in the kitchen, with a jug of good liquor, and the remains of what came out of the parlour.

After supper, Pottle filled his pipe, and began to beat about and investigate what scheme Mr. Wildgoose was engaged in; what was his business at Gloucester; and how he came to travel on foot. As Wildgoose despaired of converting a man of his years and profession, whose principles were probably settled for life, he was at first a little upon the reserve, and evaded the hints Pottle had thrown out in regard to the intention of his journey.

Pottle then began to make some apology for being seen in an ale-house; and, that his guest might not suspect it was his usual custom, he said, 'as the parsonage-house was so far from the church, he had gone thither to wait for the funeral of a poor man, that died three miles off, in an hamlet belonging to his parish. But,' says he, 'they know my method; that if they do not come by six o'clock, I would sooner leave the corpse in the church-yard all night, than bury it. And so, I suppose, they have deferred it till to-morrow.'

'Why,' replies Wildgoose, 'I believe, the poor country people are very troublesome upon these occasions: but their ignorance is rather to be pitied, than blamed. They fancy it a mark of respect to their deceased friends, to keep them above ground as long as possible.'—'Yes,' says Pottle, 'and don't care what inconvenience they put us to, for the sake of their ridiculous humour; which *can* be of no service to the dead.'—'Why, to be sure,' says Wildgoose, 'it is of no great consequence, what becomes of the *bodies* of the deceased. But yet, I think, one should condescend a little to the scruples, and even to the weaknesses of our brethren, in indifferent things, especially if our doing otherwise may probably prejudice them against us, and prevent our being of service to them in their more important concerns. I own, if I were a clergyman, I should consider myself, in some measure, as the servant of the public; and think myself obliged to bear with their humours, in some degree, rather than forfeit the good opinion of my parishioners.'

'Sir,' replies Pottle, with some warmth, 'whatever opinion a parcel of ignorant country bumpkins may have of me, I'll never submit to their unreasonable prejudices and superstitions. A pack of rascals! the more you humour them, the more they will impose upon you. If they have any thing to complain of, let them complain to the Bishop; but I'll do my duty as to the *cure of souls*, and let them go and be hang'd!'

'Pray, Sir,' says Wildgoose, '(if I may take the freedom) what do you mean by the cure of souls?'—'By the cure of souls? Why, I mean, burying the dead—baptizing children, and marrying— and—and—reading prayers, and preaching—and the like.'— 'Why, as to burying and marrying,' replies Wildgoose, 'those functions seem rather to belong to the care of the body, than to the cure of souls. And as for preaching (though I don't doubt, Sir, but your doctrine is an exception) yet, from what I have observed from the generality of preaching, whatever becomes of our souls, Christianity cannot long subsist amongst us, unless it should please God to send some better labourers into his vineyard.'

Upon this, Pottle flew into a perilous passion; took the pipe from his mouth, started up from his chair; and, advancing towards Wildgoose, 'Sir,' says he, 'what! do you affront me in my own house? I am afraid you are a Presbyterian; or, what is worse, one of these Methodists, that ramble about the country, unsettling people's minds, and prejudicing them against their proper pastors —a pack of rascals! who are a reproach to toleration.—But, S-S-S-Sir,' says he—Though Pottle was eloquent enough in his pulpit, where nobody contradicted him; yet, having naturally some impediment in his speech, it shewed itself upon the least opposition. Being therefore in great wrath with Wildgoose, his choler almost choked him, and he could hardly utter his indignation

intelligibly. But, cocking up his tobacco-stopper on his little finger
—'I'd have you to know, Sir,' says he, 'the ch-ch-ch-church has
po-po-power—I say, the ch-church has po-power to pu-pu-pu-
punish such r-r-r-rascals—I say, the ch-ch-church has po-
power—' Just as he was uttering these words, and was retreating
backwards from Wildgoose, who was got up to pacify him, he
happened to tread in a smoking-box filled with leaves, and fell
flat upon his back—bawling out and reiterating, 'The church has
power,' so loud, and in so angry a tone, that Pottle's man (who,
together with his house-keeper and Tugwell, came to listen) threw
open the parlour-door; and seeing Wildgoose standing over his
master (whose wig was tumbled off in the fall) and endeavouring to
assist him in getting up; the man mistook his intention, and
imagined it was the posture of a triumphant combatant. He therefore runs up to him, and with great violence gave Wildgoose a blow
under the left jaw. Tugwell, seeing his master thus rudely treated,
attacks Pottle's man in his turn. The old house-keeper fell upon
Tugwell, tooth and nail, crying out, in an exalted key, 'I thought
they were a couple of *casuistical*, *tyrannical*[1] rascals; and would
not have had my master harbour such vagabonds. After filling his
belly with the best in the house, to knock a gentleman down!
a *dis-gratitude*, *villantry* fellow!'

The house-keeper's voice, being a sort of unison to the barking
of a dog, alarmed an old spaniel that lay sleeping in the chimney-
corner; who began yelping round the combatants with great
fierceness, and completed the tumultuous uproar.

Pottle however had now raised himself, and with Wildgoose
was endeavouring to part Tugwell and his man Jonathan, who were
the only parties that continued the fray. Pottle also explained the
affair to the old house-keeper; told her, 'the stranger was in no
fault as to his fall; but,' says he, 'I am afraid we have taken a couple
of wolves in sheeps-cloathing into our house.'

Wildgoose likewise, perceiving he had forfeited the good opinion
of his host, could not bear the thoughts of remaining all night under
his roof. He therefore bade Tugwell follow him; and making the
best apology the circumstances would bear, to Mr. Pottle, for the
trouble he had occasioned in his family, and thanking him for his
kind entertainment, marched out of the house, without any interruption from his reverend host.

CHAPTER XIV

Night-thoughts: Of Ghosts and Goblins.
They meet with an uncommon Adventure

THE character and conduct of this very orthodox Divine contributed not a little to convince Mr. Wildgoose of the necessity of some reformation in the church; and confirmed him in his resolution of prosecuting with all diligence his romantic[1] undertaking.

The moon shining very bright, and there being but little night at that time of the year, the two pilgrims pursued their journey, taking the first road they could find which pointed towards Gloucester. They had travelled near a mile, and were now got into a very dark lane (by the side of a wood) that led down the hill on which the village stood. The gloominess of the scene, and the stillness of the night, in a strange place, raised in Tugwell some ideas of terror, which (notwithstanding his personal valour in rencounters and at fist-i-cuffs) he had in his youth been greatly subject to. And though he pretended now to be above these childish fears, yet he stuck very close to his master; and, with an affected bravery, began to fish out Wildgoose's opinion about ghosts and apparitions.

'Some folks now,' quoth Jerry, 'would be almost afraid to walk by themselves, in such a dark lane, at this time of night. But I don't suppose there is any *sich* things as spirits now-a-days—do you think there are, Master Wildgoose?'—'Any such thing as spirits, Jerry? Why I believe there are no more walk by night, than there are by day: and I am *partly* of the same opinion with a great man, who says, "That goblins and spirits have really no more to do with darkness than with light;" and accounts for our terror on these occasions from what he calls "the association of ideas".'[2]—'Yes, yes,' says Tugwell, 'I remember the *sociation* in the time of the rebellion;[3] our Squire would not *sociate*.'—'No, no, Jerry, what I mean, is the joining things together in our fancy; so that when a child is told, by his nurse, of ghosts appearing by night, he shall never be able to separate the notion of spirits from that of darkness, as long as he lives.

'But though this may account for that particular kind of terror, yet certainly the sense of our being off our guard, when alone in the dark, and ignorant what enemies we may be exposed to, must necessarily make us apprehensive of danger upon those occasions. So that, let a man have never so clear an head to separate ideas; yet, I think, it almost impossible to be equally calm and easy in darkness and solitude, as we are in the open daylight.'

Tugwell was as still as a mouse during this discourse of Wild-goose, though he did not understand a word that was said.

'As for there being any such thing as spirits in one sense,' continued Wildgoose, 'no one that is not an Atheist can deny this: but though perhaps, before the times of Christianity, Providence might think it necessary more frequently to interpose, by permitting the visible appearance of superior beings, upon *important occasions*; and though I am convinced the Devil has still as real an influence over the souls of men as he had then; yet you may take it for granted, Jerry, that every story which you ever heard of their visible appearance, is an imposture, and, if more nearly inquired into, may be accounted for from natural means; taking its rise, either from the interested designs or terrified imaginations of wicked or weak people.—I myself remember, when I first went to the University, I lived in a large chamber, hung with green baize; the bed was placed in a sort of recess, separated from the dining-room by two large folding doors, which were thrown open, when I went to bed, to make it more airy. I happened once to wake about midnight: and, it being star-light, saw, on the further side of the room, a tall figure in white, near six feet high. It seemed to have a square cap on its shoulders, but was without an head.'—'Lord have mercy upon us!' (says Tugwell, laying hold on Wildgoose's skirt) 'yes, without a head! So my grandmother used to say, that ghosts commonly do appear without a head.'—'Well,' continues Wild-goose, 'though I used to laugh at things of this kind, I could not account for this dreadful phænomenon. The more I stared at it, the more I was convinced it was something real. After lying some time, and mustering up my courage, I leaped out of bed, determined to unravel the mystery—when lo! I embraced in my arms, a white surplice, which a scholar of the house, having left [it] in my room after evening prayers, had hung upon a brass peg, over which I had suspended my square cap, such as they wear in the University.'— 'Yes, yes, your *trenchard*[1] caps, I have heard of them,' says Tugwell.

'Thus, I am convinced, would every story of apparitions have ended,' says Wildgoose; 'if the scared spectator had had resolution enough to examine it to the bottom.'—

'Why, to be sure,' says Tugwell, 'apparitions are not so common now-a-days as they were in former times. But I remember, when I was a boy, father had been to fetch the midwife upon your grandfather's mare, old White-foot. She was as good a servant as ever went upon four legs. Your grandfather bought her of old Simon Perkins.'—'Well,' says Wildgoose, 'proceed with your tale.'—'It was a very dark night,' continues Jerry; 'and father was riding by a lone uninhabited house, at the end of a close lane, as this may be, when he saw *strange* lights in every window. And when he came into the middle of the lane, vast balls of fire rolled along under his horse's feet: and then the Squire's lady, who died in child-bed, drove along in her coach and six, with her child in her arms; and—and—the coach-man (it is *sartain* true) the coach-man was without a head—and—.'—As Jerry was going on with his terrible story, bounce came his foot against something; and down he tumbled a—se over head; bawling out, 'Lord have mercy upon me! I have tumbled over a coffin!'—'Blockhead!' cries Wildgoose, 'why, thou wilt talk so long about ghosts, till thou art frightened at thy own shadow.' Jerry however (strange as it was) happened to be in the right: and the reader will easily guess at the cause of such a shocking indecency: it was the very corpse which Parson Pottle had been waiting for, of a poor man who died at the extremity of his parish; and his surviving friends, willing to take a decent leave of the deceased, had continued drinking till after six o'clock; when bringing him to the bottom of this hill, and recollecting that Mr. Pottle would certainly not perform the last office that night, they had left the coffin there, to the terror of poor Tugwell and the astonishment of his friend.[1]

They were now come into the open plain again, and travelled a good pace till towards break of day; and Tugwell pretended to know, by the course of the stars, that it was near three o'clock; and, as his zeal was not quite so active as his master's, he began to complain of fatigue and want of sleep. They therefore made towards a barn, a little out of the road; which being locked, they were forced to repose themselves upon some straw under a shed, where however they slept soundly for some hours; and rising greatly refreshed about eight o'clock, proceeded on their journey; Jerry, according to custom, reminding his master to lay in a good breakfast at the first public house upon the road.

CHAPTER XV

The Event of Mr. Wildgoose's second Harangue

In the afternoon, when they were got within a few miles of Gloucester, at a genteel house near the end of a village, they saw almost the whole parish assembled in the court, to see a set of morrice-dancers: who, (this holiday-time) dressed up in bells and ribbands, were performing for the entertainment of the family, and of some company that had dined there. Wildgoose thought this a proper opportunity of displaying his eloquence, and communicated his intention to his fellow-traveller. But he, having not so soon forgot the ill success of their yesterday's adventure, would have dissuaded Wildgoose from making a second attempt at so unseasonable a juncture; and said, moreover, 'that, for his part, he loved to see people merry at *sich* a time as this:' but Wildgoose soon silenced his scruples; and he being by this time sufficiently convinced of his master's obstinacy, immediately got amongst the morrice-dancers, and acquainted them with his intention. As they were no strangers to itinerant orators in that country, they suspended their diversion for a while, and got round the preacher; who, by this time, was mounted upon some steps, and began to hold forth, with great vehemence, against all festival amusements, as contrary to the serious spirit of the Gospel; and particularly against those irregularities which were practised at revels and Whitsunales. This doctrine, being rather ill-timed, was not much relished by a great part of the audience, who soon began to be impatient of the interruption which was given to their entertainment.

Those who are acquainted with this sort of *morrice-dance*[1] (which is still practised in several parts of England) must know that they are usually attended with one character called the 'Tom Fool:' who, like the clown in the pantomime, seems to be a burlesque upon all the rest. His fool's cap has a fox's tail depending like a ramillie whig;[2] and instead of the small bells which the others wear on their legs, he has a great sheep-bell hung to his back-side.

Whilst the company therefore were all attentive to the preacher, this buffoon contrived to slip the fool's cap upon Tugwell's head, and to fix the sheep-bell to his rump. Which Jerry no sooner perceived, than his choler arose, and spitting in his hands, and clenching his fists, he gave the Tom-fool a swinging blow in the face. The

G

Fool, having more wit than courage, endeavoured to escape amongst the croud. Tugwell pursued him in great rage, with the sheep-bell at his tail; the ridiculous sound of which, forming a sort of contrast to the wrath in Jerry's countenance, caused a great deal of loud mirth amongst the company.

Wildgoose, now finding it to no purpose to continue his harangue, assisted in extricating Tugwell from the throng, who had now formed a ring round him and the Jack-pudding:[1] and reprimanding him for his want of Christian meekness, he bade him follow him, and 'shake off the dust from their feet,'[2] according to the language of our modern Apostles, when they would decently extricate themselves from any uncommon difficulty. They now therefore pursued their journey, without any further molestation.

Wildgoose told Jerry, 'they had hitherto indeed met with but unchristian-like usage;' but comforted him with the assurance of meeting with a more friendly reception, when they should arrive at the Bell at Gloucester (where Mr. Whitfield was born); 'for,' says he, 'where a true Gospel-spirit prevails, the genuine fruits of it are, Peace, Joy, Brotherly Love, and Christian Charity.' Jerry replied, 'that a cup of good ale would be the greatest *joy* to him at present; for that he was very dry.' Wildgoose however would not take the hint, nor stop till they arrived (early in the evening) at the ancient city of Gloucester.

BOOK III

Mr. Wildgoose's Reception at the Bell at Gloucester, the Birth-place of Mr. Whitfield

IT had been the custom of Mr. Wildgoose, in any little excursions which he had formerly made, whenever he came into any city or considerable town, to enquire (like other travellers) into the trade and manufactures of the place; or what curiosities, of art or nature, were worthy of a stranger's notice. But, in the present situation of his mind, he had lost all relish for things of that kind: instead therefore of making any observation upon the situation, buildings, or antiquities of Gloucester; or being in the least struck with the beauty of its cathedral, and the remarkable lightness of its Gothic tower; Mr. Wildgoose considered it in no other light than as the birthplace of Mr. Whitfield, and immediately enquired for the Bell-Inn.

When they arrived under the gate-way, the travellers addressed themselves to a waiter (who was carrying a dish of Scotch-collops into a parlour across the court) and asked, 'Whether they could have any lodgings there?' He, surveying them with a contemptuous air, did not vouchsafe them an answer.

They then applied to a sort of scullion, who was doing some drudgery near the kitchen. She, seeing two people about her own level (as she thought), spoke to the cook, who, after some muttering expostulations, went to her mistress behind the bar, and asked her, 'whether she would lodge two foot-passengers.' Mrs. Whitfield,[1] being engaged with company, rose up with some reluctance, and came to the window of the bar; where spying two such dusty figures, her usual politeness to strangers forsook her.—'Hey-day!' quoth she, 'lodgings indeed! yes, to be sure; because Squire Fielding, forsooth, in that romancing book of his, pretends that Tom Jones was harboured here, we shall be pestered with all the trampers that pass the road.'

Wildgoose was thunder-struck at this unchristian-like reception.
But Tugwell, who, on the first appearance of so fine a lady, had
stood with his hat off, now replaced it on his head; and repeating
her words, '*Trampers* indeed!—I would have you to know,' says
he, 'his Worship could have rode upon as good a gelding as any
one in the county; and could have mounted me too, for that
matter; if it were not more like good Christians to travel on foot.
But I thought folks that keep an ale-house were obliged to take
in all comers.'—'Keep an ale-house! you sawcy jack-an-apes!' says
Mrs. Whitfield, who had not much Christian meekness—'you
have mistaken the house; you should have gone to the Bird in
Hand, in Tripe-Lane. There perhaps you would find rest for
travellers, such as you.'—'Well, well, Dame,' says Tugwell, 'there
is no harm done; if you won't lodge us, I suppose there are others
that will, and be glad of our custom. Trampers indeed! I think
Mr. Whitfield might have preached you into better manners.'

CHAPTER II

An hospitable Barber accommodates Mr. Wildgoose with a Lodging, and a Place to preach in

THE two pilgrims were a little disconcerted at this mortifying
reception, and at a loss how to proceed. And though Wildgoose
had of late affected to despise all worldly distinctions, and to make
light of external respect, the consequence of them; yet he was a little
shocked at this unforeseen effect of his voluntary humiliation, and
almost began to wish that he had travelled in a manner more suitable to his station in life.

As they were deliberating what course to take, Wildgoose espied
a Barber's pole; and reflecting, that perhaps Mrs. Whitfield, being
ignorant of his enlightened heart, might be scandalized at the
frowsy appearance of the outward man, resolved to get rid of his
beard, have his hair refreshed, and his cravat a little decently
adjusted. He therefore entered the shop; where the case was quite
reversed. The honest Barber, whose less affluent circumstances
inspired more gentle manners, and made him civil to the meanest
customer, received them with great affability and apparent

benevolence; and, with a voluble tongue, as he was preparing his razor, ran over the heat of the weather, dustiness of the roads, and other general topicks, which those artists have ready at hand, for the entertainment of their customers, and to divert their attention from the pain which often attends the operation under the most skilful performer.

Whilst Wildgoose was doing penance under the instrument of this ingenious Tonsor, he took the opportunity of consulting him about a lodging for himself and fellow-traveller; and informed him what treatment he had met with at the Bell. This Tugwell confirmed, with some expressions of resentment; assuring the Barber, 'that his master could afford to pay for whatever he called for; and did not want to spunge upon any one. We know the custom at such houses,' continues he; ' 'tis *touch pot*, *touch penny*—we only want money's-worth for our money.'

The Barber, encouraged by these overtures of familiarity, took the liberty in his turn to enquire, 'which way they came; whither they were travelling; what stay they should make at Gloucester; and, if he might be so bold, what branch of business Mr. Wildgoose was engaged in?' Wildgoose, from the fulness of his heart, soon let the Barber into the nature of his calling; and that he intended to employ the talent of preaching, which had been intrusted to him, for the good of the poor inhabitants of that city. The Barber replied, 'that Mr. Whitfield, to be sure, had preached there frequently with good success; and had left a few scattered disciples amongst them: but,' says he, 'the Shoe-maker's wife often goes in ragged shoes.'— 'That is an old saying, and a true one, to my knowledge,' cries Tugwell.—'Well,' says the Barber, 'I was going to observe, that although there had been a Society begun here by Mr. Whitfield, yet since he went to Georgia, and has been in so great request in London, Bristol, and other parts of England, the people of Gloucester are not much the better for having had so great a Prophet born amongst them.

'As for lodgings,' continued the Barber, 'our house is large enough, for that matter; though it is a little out of repair—and, as I have a wife and a family of children, we are a little streightened for beds: however, perhaps my wife will endeavour to accommodate you.'—Wildgoose replied, 'that he was very easily accommodated in that respect, for he had determined not to pamper the flesh; and would submit to any hardships for the good of his

brethren.—But,' says he, 'what must we do for a room to assemble
in?'—'Why as for that,' returned the Barber, 'we have a sort of old
dining-room, which will exactly suit your purpose; though there
is no furniture in it, but a few broken chairs, and an old cyder-cask
or two, which will not be much in the way.' In short, the Barber
informed his wife of the affair; who having peeped at them through
the kitchen door, and formed an opinion of them no ways injurious
to their honesty, they soon came to an agreement; and the two
pilgrims took up their residence at this friendly Barber's.

CHAPTER III

At Gloucester

THE Barber's shop in a country town has been (time out of mind)
the grand office of intelligence: partly from the leisure and loqua-
city of that race of men; and partly (as was hinted before) from the
peculiar nature of the connection which is formed between the
Agent and the *Patient*, during the act of shaving, in which nothing
but news or other general topicks can prudently be the subject of
their conversation. The arrival of a stranger, therefore, of so extraordinary a character as that of Mr. Wildgoose, could not long be
a secret amongst the lower class of Plebeians; especially as the
Barber, in order to bring more custom to his shop, took care to let
every one know, that a stranger of good fortune was to hold forth
there that very evening; for so Wildgoose had determined, if he
could raise any thing of an audience; being impatient to impart
some spiritual advice to his poor country-men: whom, notwithstanding the residence of their good Bishop, Dean, and a whole
College of learned Prebends amongst them, he considered 'as
sheep not having a shepherd.'[1]

He was attended the first night only by a few mean persons, who
either came accidentally to the shop, or who had been invited by
the Barber's wife from amongst her nearest neighbours. But the
fame of this extraordinary Preacher being spread abroad, by each
of these, in their several circles of acquaintance; before the next
evening it had reached the remotest parts of the city; and had
brought together not only the straggling disciples of Mr. Whitfield,

but also the idle and the curious of every denomination, most of whom bestowed no small encomiums upon the youthful Orator. This success encouraged Wildgoose to make a longer stay in Gloucester, than he had at first intended; so that in a week's time it became a sort of fashion to hear him; and he was attended by people of all ranks and degrees—from the sauntering old batchelor and antiquated virgin, who lived upon their annuities and their card-money—to the pennyless porter who ran on errands, and the second-hand sempstress who got her bread by reconciling old rags and making pin-cushions.

'Let a man preach like an angel in his own church,' (as Mr. Wesley justly observes) 'no one regards him: but as soon as one comes unto them, and says, "Lo! yonder is a man preaching upon a mountain!" the multitude flocks out to hear him. It is the un-commonness of the thing,' says he, 'that especially recommends field-preaching.'

The same may be said with regard to Mr. Wildgoose's success in his conventicle at Gloucester. If the Sexton had given out, on a Saturday night, that a stranger was to preach the next day at the cathedral, it might perhaps have brought those to church, who happened not to have upon their hands any more agreeable Sun-day's amusements. But when it was proclaimed, that a traveller was to preach at the Barber's upon a cyder-cask, leaning over the top of an old cheese-press (which was all the pulpit which the Barber's lumber-room could supply), immediately the house was crowded with attendants from every quarter of the city.

But it must be remembered likewise, that Mr. Wildgoose, not-withstanding the present uncouth appearance of his short hair, had something naturally agreeable in his countenance, and also a very musical tone of voice: and though, in the vehemence of his harangues, he had a wildness in his looks, proceeding from the enthusiastic zeal which possessed his imagination, yet that very circumstance gave a more pathetic force to his eloquence. And he himself appearing so much in earnest, and affected with the sub-ject, it had a proportionable effect upon his audience.

He usually began his discourse with lamenting the universal corruption of mankind, and with a lively representation of the dreadful consequences to be apprehended from the justice of God: and instead of speaking of Hell and Damnation in the refined terms and elegant circumlocutions of modern Divines (as a place not proper to be mentioned to a polite audience);[1] he ran perhaps into the contrary extreme, by too gross and minute a detail of particulars: which, however, though it might render his descriptions more ridiculous than terrible, to sensible people; yet it had its effect upon the bulk of his audience, and engaged their most earnest attention.

When he had sufficiently terrified them by the denunciation of eternal torments, he shifted the scene, and melted them into tears by the tenderest descriptions of the mercy and compassion of God, and the fondest expressions of love from the great Shepherd of their souls.

And having been so deeply read in the Puritanical writings of the last century, and their lineal descendants the Methodists of these times, he had thoroughly imbibed their manner and style of eloquence, which consists chiefly in a figurative application of the most luscious expressions and sensual ideas to spiritual subjects; and which have been observed frequently to captivate the hearts of the most profligate, and lull them into a strong persuasion, at least, that they have received lively foretastes of the joys of Heaven; when they have really been soothing their fancies with the luxurious recollection of their former sensual indulgences.

Thus did Mr. Wildgoose adapt his metaphors to the various characters and failings of his different hearers. For the lewd and lascivious, he abounded with amorous expressions, and talked much in the nuptial style.—'Their souls were espoused to Christ: he shall carry the dear lambs in his bosom, and entertain them with sweet kisses from his *lily lips*—more sweet than the sweet-smelling myrrh: he shall embrace them, and fill them with ravishing delights.'[2] This sort of language particularly charmed the female devotees.

For the thirsty soul and luxurious epicure, he had 'streams of joy and rivers of pleasure: feasts of fat things—milk, honey, marrow and fatness,' and all the most savoury—ideas to express the comforts of a spiritual life.

To the covetous and ambitious, he talked of nothing but 'of hidden treasures; gold, silver, jewels, and precious stones: kingdoms, crowns and sceptres,' and every thing that could captivate a worldly imagination.[3]

In short, by this soothing eloquence, and the earnestness of his manner, Wildgoose softened those hearts, which, for some years, had resisted the admonitions of friends, and the suggestions of conscience; and made many converts to religion: at least he made them so as long as the brightness of those similies continued to glow in their imaginations. But, their affections only being moved, and their understandings not enlightened, nor their reason convinced, too many of them soon relapsed into their former dissolute courses.

There was a buxom Widow, however, amongst his disciples, who, enjoying an handsome house only for her widowhood, and being therefore cut off from *iteration* of *nuptials*,[1] had allowed herself some variety in her amours: but she was now touched to the quick; and determined for the future to keep constant to an half-pay Officer, who lodged in her first floor.

And a drunken Pettyfogger, who had been engaged in several dirty litigations, resolved hereafter to be more sober in his conduct; and also never to undertake any litigious suit—unless he were sure of being well paid for his trouble.

Nay, an inveterate Miser felt such a lively compunction, that he formed, upon the spot, a solemn resolution to distribute amongst the poor all his old cloaths, which had been hoarded in his wardrobe from the very days of his courtship: and so far persevered in his charitable design, as to give away, the very next morning, an old waistcoat—that was too little for him; and two pair of shoes—that pinched his corns: and even added a codicil to his will, by which he ordered a suspicious moidore, which had been refused by his banker, to be given in charity on the day of his funeral.

CHAPTER IV

Our Itinerant's Popularity increases

THE fame of Mr. Wildgoose's eloquence being thus spread through the city, Mrs. Whitfield was amongst the first whose curiosity led them to make part of his audience. She soon discovered him and his fellow-labourer to be the individual *Trampers*, whom she had treated with so little ceremony at the Bell; and finding they were bound on a pilgrimage to her brother-in-law and the Society at Bristol, she took an opportunity of making some apology for her

incivility; and told Wildgoose, 'that, as he could have but indifferent accommodations at his present lodgings, he was very welcome
to a bed at the Bell, whilst he stayed in Gloucester.' But though
Mr. Wildgoose was ready enough to overlook the personal slight
which had been put upon him; he thought there was something
meritorious in his present state of humiliation. He therefore
thanked Mrs. Whitfield for her kindness, but chose to continue
where he was.

One evening, when Wildgoose was deeply engaged in haranguing
to a full house, an ordinary fellow, in a silver-laced hat, came into
the room; and, squeezing through the crowd, gave a letter to one
of the company, who handed it to Tugwell, who was sitting on the
head of a cask under his master, and officiated as a sort of clerk.
He watched his opportunity till Wildgoose made a pause, and then
presented the letter. As soon as he began to look on the direction,
the man that brought it (who was no other than the Gloucester
Journal-man) calls out, 'Read it, Master, read it; it brings you some
news of your poor mother.' Wildgoose, renouncing all family-
connections, and disregarding whatever concerned himself,
stretched out his hand, and cried out, 'Behold my mother, my
sister, and my brother!'[1] and immediately went on with his discourse.

The case was, that, although there were none of their towns-
men at his first preachment on Dover's-hill; yet there were many
that knew him by sight, notwithstanding he was disguised in his
own hair: and the story had soon spread to Mrs. Wildgoose's ears.
The odd turn which her son's melancholy had taken, we may be
sure, must greatly affect a fond parent; and it had really thrown
Mrs. Wildgoose into a fit of sickness. Mr. Powell, therefore, the
Vicar of the parish, having been informed by the Journal-man, that
an itinerant Preacher of some fortune (as was given out) had been
shewing off at Gloucester, soon guessed, from the description of
him and his attendant, that it was his good neighbour Mr. Wildgoose; and so dispatched a letter by him, on his return, to acquaint
Wildgoose with the effect his extravagant whim had had upon his
worthy mother. But Enthusiasm is deaf to the calls of Nature; nay,
esteems it meritorious to trample upon all the relative duties of life.
Men of this cast think nothing of any importance, but what corre-
sponds with the chimerical notions which have possessed their
fancies.

Wildgoose therefore paid no other regard to the Doctor's intelligence, than writing a short letter to his mother; in which he expressed his concern for her illness, but said, 'he was not at his own disposal; and could not, in conscience, live in carnal ease and security, when the spiritual harvest was so great, and the true labourers so few. In short,' says he in conclusion, 'woe be unto me, if I preach not the Gospel!'

CHAPTER V

Mr. Wildgoose's Success with the Ladies

'If chance some blooming nymph, with locks of gold,
The brilliant lustre sparkling in her eye,
Shading her lovely cheeks with hat of straw,
Or silken bonnet green of glossy hue,
Enters the shop of learned Bibliopole,
That vends his ware at Tunbridge or at Bath,
Retailing modern trash to saunt'ring beaux—'

SHOULD any of my amiable country-women, I say, smit with the love of novelty, carry home this trifling volume from some Circulating-library; and throwing herself negligently upon her settee or sopha—or even on the feet of her truckle-bed—have patience to attend two such odd fellows thus far; she will probably be disgusted that she has not been entertained with a single love-tale, which are generally looked upon as essential to works of this kind; and not only make a principal part of every episode, but are usually interwoven with the body of the fable. But I would have them consider the peculiar character of our Hero; which is not (at first sight) at all friendly to the softer passions. If they can prevail on themselves however to attend him a few pages further, they may perhaps discover some slight symptoms of an affection, not entirely of the seraphic or platonic kind.

There was amongst Mr. Wildgoose's female votaries one Mrs. Sarsenet, a Millener; who notwithstanding she supported an infirm mother and a lame sister by her industry, yet, from the severity of Mr. Wildgoose's doctrine, had conceived some scruples about the innocence, or even the lawfulness, of her profession. She therefore desired Mr. Wildgoose to drink a dish of tea with her; and took that opportunity of consulting him as a Casuist upon the subject. Upon considering the affair with some deliberation, Wildgoose told her, 'that, although some branches of the trade, as it was often practised, might *accidentally* promote vice; yet as some part of the female dress was not only *decent*, but even necessary in this cold climate; and as the trade had not *directly* any bad tendency; he could not look upon it as absolutely sinful. However,' says he, 'it greatly concerns you, not to countenance the ladies that deal with you, in any vain ornaments or wanton attire; but to discourage any thing of that kind, even against your own interest, as much as you decently can.' The reader will find, in the sequel, that Mrs. Sarsenet carried this doctrine rather to an extreme, and to the prejudice of her temporal interest and that of her family.

We must not imagine, however, that this grave matron was a proper object of desire to a religious enthusiast. There was with this Millener a young lady, who seemed not to be in the capacity of an apprentice, but rather as some friend upon a visit to Mrs. Sarsenet, and who had something in her manner and appearance above her present situation. A nice critic might perhaps dispute her title to the character of a perfect beauty: but she had a sprightliness in her air, and a piercing brilliancy in her eyes, which, joined to the gloss of youth, could not fail to attract the particular regard of Mr. Wildgoose, and made him very assiduous in directing his pious precepts to so fair a disciple. Whenever he said any thing to which he expected a particular attention, he applied himself to Miss Townsend (by a kind of instinct) for her approbation. But though this young nymph seemed well enough pleased when Mr. Wildgoose talked to her upon indifferent subjects, she was inclined rather to disapprove of, and even to railly, the severity of many of his opinions. Nay, in one of his visits, which he repeated pretty often, she took upon her to ask Wildgoose, 'how he could be so cruel, as not to visit his poor mother; who, she found, was ill and desired to see him? For,' says she, with a sigh and down-cast look, 'Heaven will never prosper disrespect to a parent!' Miss Townsend's earnestness upon this subject excited Wildgoose's curiosity; and, with a more gallant air than usual, he desired to know 'why she looked so very dismal upon the occasion?' After a little pause and a few blushes, she replied, 'that the greatest misfortune of her

life, and her present unhappy situation, was owing to her disrespect to a worthy, and, in general, a very kind father.'—'Pray,
what misfortunes can so young a lady as you are have experienced?'
says Wildgoose; 'for you don't seem yet to be above sixteen!'—
Miss Townsend seemed in confusion at having discovered so much
of her own affairs: but Mrs. Sarsenet told her, 'She need not be
afraid of talking freely to so *good* a man as Mr. Wildgoose; who
would never make any wrong use of her confidence; and might
probably give her some spiritual consolation, which would make
her more easy under this little calamity, which her own indiscretion, or rather *my folly*,' says she, 'has brought upon you.'

Mr. Wildgoose wishing it might be in his power to give her any
assistance, and intreating her to gratify his impatience to be
acquainted with her story, Miss Townsend dropped a tear; then,
pulling up her spirits, gave the following account of herself.

CHAPTER VI

The History of Miss Townsend

'MY father (as Mrs. Sarsenet knows) has a *small* estate on the
borders of ——shire, where he now lives.'—'No,' says Mrs. Sarsenet, 'I know that Mr. Townsend has a very *considerable* estate,
which has been in the family for many generations.'—'Well,'
says Miss Townsend, 'I don't know what it is; but ——shire is
my native place. My poor mother has been dead about a twelvemonth, to my inexpressible misfortune, and that of the whole
family. She left behind her me and two sisters, one a few years
older, the other considerably younger, than myself. Whilst my
mother lived, we saw a great deal of genteel company; and she took
care to have us instructed at home in all the usual accomplishments
of our sex. But, soon after her death, my father sent us all three
(though two of us were almost grown up, and my eldest sister
capable of managing his house) to a country boarding-school, to the
astonishment of the whole neighbourhood. We soon found, however, that my father's intention was, to make way for another
house-keeper, to whom he had taken an unaccountable fancy. This
was an Irish woman, whom I shall call the *widow* Townsend; as she

came into the neighbourhood, about half a year before my mother's death, in the character of an officer's wife, one Captain Townsend, who had made a small fortune in America, and called himself a relation of ours: but he dying soon after, this woman took lodgings in a small market-town, at a little distance from my father's; and, as she did not appear to be left in very affluent circumstances, she made no scruple, I believe, of undertaking the management of my father's family, in the capacity of an house-keeper.

'The widow Townsend, as I said, is an Irishwoman, and about forty; not handsome; but has something in her manner, which attracts the regard of the gentlemen, as much as it disgusts the generality of our sex: my poor mother (as Mrs. Sarsenet well knows) could never bear her. She is a woman of no sort of conversation, and yet my father now makes a constant companion of her; and we have no reason to doubt, that, after a decent time, he will make her our step-mother: in which case, though I should think it my duty to shew her all the respect which is due to my father's wife; yet, at present, I own, I could not bring my stubborn heart to submit with tolerable decency to the many mortifications I daily met with from a woman in her situation.

'For, you must know, at Christmas last, my father thought it proper to permit my eldest sister and me to leave school, and return home again; as it must appear to every one, that we were banished for no other reason than to make way for a woman in her ambiguous situation—though I believe she had another view in having my sister at home, which I will explain to you hereafter.

'The widow Townsend affected, at first, to treat us with great civility, and even apparent affection; and used great art to make us rest satisfied under the authority which she had acquired. She indulged us in several little instances and articles of finery; in which, I believe, my own mother would have thought it improper to have gratified us. These things won my sister's heart; and it would be affectation in me, to say that I was not pleased with my gold watch and other trinkets, which she had persuaded my father to procure us. But still I could not bear to be obliged to a woman, whom I considered as having an improper influence over my father, for what I imagined I might reasonably have expected from the great affection he had formerly shewn me in particular; in whose favour, I flattered myself, he had always discovered some little partiality.

'For my father, you must know, was always a very bookish, and is, I believe, a very learned man; and is reckoned a great Antiquary and Virtuoso. I flattered myself, therefore, that he was particularly pleased with the taste I discovered for reading, preferably to every other amusement: to humour which taste, he himself had contributed, by turning me loose into one corner of his library, which contained a collection of books made by an old maiden aunt of ours; and consisted of Dryden's plays, and all the dramatic works of the last age; novels, and romances of every kind.'

'I am afraid then,' says Wildgoose, 'you had not many religious books put into your hands by your good father?'

'No,' says Miss Townsend; 'but I had a few by my good mother, which I made a point of reading every Sunday; such as Tillotson's Sermons, the Whole Duty of Man, and the like.'

'Why,' replies Wildgoose, 'you might as well have read the Seven Champions or Jack the Giant-killer, as either the Whole Duty of Man or Tillotson, who knew no more of Christianity than Mahomet.'[1]

'Well,' says Miss Townsend, 'I am not a judge of those things; but will go on with my story.'

CHAPTER VII

Miss Townsend's Story continued

'My taste for reading,' continued Miss Townsend, 'not only rendered me the object of my sister's jealousy (who never looked in a book), but made me less agreeable to the widow Townsend; and has been, I am afraid, the principal cause of my present unhappy situation.

'For this woman (you must know) though she affects to be a great œconomist, yet (like most of the Irish ladies) is never compleatly happy, but at the card-table: and as I was unpolite, or rather impolitic, enough constantly to declare my aversion to cards; this gave her frequent occasions to represent me to my father, as one that regarded nothing but my own gratification; "which, she said, was a very bad symptom in a young person." And, what is surprizing, she had brought my father, (who was formerly never easy out of his study) to make one at quadrille or piquet, every evening. And my sister, who had rather do any thing than read, or work at her needle, was always happy in being of the party.

'The widow Townsend having so far succeeded, as to make my father less pleased with my favourite amusements; as it was her interest to have no rival in his affection, she began, by degrees, farther to insinuate, "that it would be much more to my credit, if I would apply more carefully to my needle;" in which article she represented me as very defective: and even hinted, "that another year's schooling would be greatly to my advantage:" though Mrs. Sarsenet, I believe, is far from making any complaint of that kind. In short, my father began, by degrees, not only to reprimand me, whenever he found me with a book in my hand; but daily discovered, on every occasion, less fondness for me than he had formerly shewn. This encouraged Mrs. Townsend to treat me with less ceremony; and as for my sister, she not only became reserved to me, in order to recommend herself more effectually to our gouvernante; but began to consider me as a troublesome rival in another affair, which I will now explain to you.

'My sister (you must know) had a very considerable fortune (near seven thousand pounds) left her by a great aunt, independently of my father; and this she will have in her own power, the day she is eighteen; which will be within these six weeks. This, I am inclined to think, was Mrs. Townsend's chief motive for bringing her brother (one Captain Mahony, as she calls him) into the neighbourhood, and introducing him into our family; where he comes almost every day, and frequently stays there for a week together: he is a Lieutenant, I believe, in a marching regiment, though upon half-pay. He is about thirty; a tolerably good person, and dresses very genteely; but conceited and ignorant. Yet, as very seldom any other gentleman came to the house (nor indeed much company of any kind since this woman has been there), this coxcomb contrived to make some impression, I believe, upon my sister's heart. And because he would sometimes condescend to direct his nonsense to me (either to conceal his designs upon my sister, or to raise her jealousy), she, by degrees, began to consider me as her rival, and of course as an obstacle to her wishes; and to treat me accordingly.

'In short, this behaviour of my sister, the insults I daily met with from the widow Townsend, and the coldness with which my dear father began to treat me, made my situation at home extremely disagreeable.

'But, completely to ruin me in the widow Townsend's good opinion, and of course in my father's favour, was a friendly letter which I happened to receive from my good Mrs. Sarsenet here; who, having a particular regard for my late mother (they having been school-fellows at Chelsea), and hearing that this woman (to whom she knew my poor mother had a particular dislike) was come to keep my father's house; she had written to me upon the subject; and, with more honesty than prudence perhaps, had declared her real sentiments of the matter: which letter the widow Townsend (I believe, by my sister's means) unluckily got a sight of; and from that time grew so inveterate against me, that (presuming upon the influence she had over my father) she insisted upon my being sent to school again with my little sister Quintilla, or somewhere out of the house; otherwise she herself was determined to leave him.'

CHAPTER VIII

Miss Townsend's Story continued

'BEING now continually exposed to the widow Townsend's forbidding looks and reproaches; as also to the neglect of my dear father, and the ill-natured treatment of my sister, who would not suffer me quietly to enjoy the only relief which I sought, that of reading alone in my closet; but above all, the apprehension of being sent to school again, at my age—all these things put together provoked me beyond all patience.

'My romances furnished me with innumerable instances of this kind of domestic persecution; which generally terminated in the elopement of the innocent sufferer, her unexpected success in life, and her triumphant return.

'In short, I had an high idea of the grandeur and politeness of London; and saw several instances even of the lower sort of people, who, having been sent for by rich relations or taken into good services, came down more polite and entirely different sort of creatures from those which I generally conversed with.

H

'I last month therefore formed a most romantic scheme, for seeing the world, and going to London by myself. In order to this, I determined to get to Oxford, and out from thence in the stage-coach, and endeavour to find out a particular friend and distant relation of my mama's, who, I knew, lodged somewhere in West-minster; and who had spent a good part of the last summer before my mother's death with us in the country, and used frequently to invite me to London; or, if I should not find her out; having twenty guineas, given me at different times by a god-mother, in my own possession, I thought, with œconomy, I could subsist for some time; and had some vague ideas of introducing myself into good company, or, perhaps, even of making my fortune, as other distressed or persecuted damsels had done.

'As I had no confidante in my own family, I communicated my intentions to a woman in the neighbourhood, who had been my mother's maid, and was now married to a man, who, in my mother's time, had been our coachman; both of them were favourites of my mother's, and of course were not so with the widow Townsend. The poor woman at first dissuaded me from pursuing so strange a resolution; but when she found me bent upon it, and knew how disagreeably I lived at home, the man consented to carry me behind him (on an horse which he kept to lett) the next night to Oxford, as I had desired; without considering the probable consequences of so imprudent a step.

'As my sister was engaged almost every evening at cards with my father and the widow Townsend, I took those opportunities at least of sitting up in my closet to read; and my sister frequently went to bed without making any enquiries after me; so that I easily eluded any immediate search, and escaped to the house appointed.

'Not to trouble you with too many particulars; having packed up an handsome brocaded suit of cloathes, two silk night-gowns, with some pretty good linen and my money, I got safe, with my luggage, to Oxford, and met with a place in the coach, which set out the next morning for London.'

CHAPTER IX

Miss Townsend's Story continued

'THERE was amongst the passengers, a well-looking elderly gentle-man; of good fortune (as I had reason to think by his generous behaviour to me, and by a genteel footman behind the coach). He was a little surprized, I believe, at the first sight of so young a person, tolerably well dressed, and going such a journey quite alone. He, by degrees, began to sift out my situation in life, and what expedition I was now engaged in. His humanity, and a desire to serve me, rather than mere curiosity, seemed to be the motives for his enquiries. When we came to dinner, and I happened to be left alone with him, I soon communicated my whimsical project to this gentleman. He was vastly surprized, and expressed great concern both for me and for my father; whom he found to be almost the only person that I was sorry to have left behind me.

'He asked me, "how I could think of supporting myself for any time, in so expensive a place as London was?" I told him the state of my finances; and that, if I could not find out my late mother's friend in Westminster, I proposed lodging in some cheap part of the suburbs. He smiled at my simplicity; and began to describe to me the extreme danger such a young person, as I was, exposed myself to, in so romantic an enterprize; the wickedness of the world in general, and of the town in particular; and in short, ventured to foretell my inevitable ruin; which he painted in such strong colours, that I burst into tears, and begged him to advise me what method to pursue. "What!" says he, "Madam? why, as soon as we arrive in town, give me leave to take another place for you, the next day, in this same coach; and return again to your friends in the country."

'I was a little staggered at this proposal; and could not bear the thoughts of exposing myself to the resentment of my father, the insults of Mrs. Townsend, and the ridicule of my sister. But when we came to London, and I saw the vast hurry and extent of that metropolis, my heart began to fail me; and, in the evening especi-ally, when we reached the inn in Holbourn, and the gentleman had bid them send the chamber-maid to shew me to my bed-chamber; in came a bold ill-looking fellow, who called himself the Chamber-lain. "There, Madam," says the old gentleman, "you see who is to wait on you to bed to-night, and to lace your stays in the morning: this is the attendance which a young lady must generally expect at the inns in London."

'I was now struck with all the horrors of my situation; and therefore told the gentleman, "I should gladly accept of his kind offer; and would beg him to take a place for me against the next morning:" which he very politely did, and insisted upon treating me with the earnest[1] which he had paid for the coach. I was ashamed to accept of such a favour from a stranger; but he desired me to say no more about it. I took my leave of him that evening, without being able to discover his name; though I found, by several circumstances, that he lived in Herefordshire.'

CHAPTER X

Miss Townsend's Story continued

'BEING thoroughly fatigued with my journey, I slept soundly till the morning; when I was called, I suppose, by the chamberlain; but was so drowsy, that I knew not what answer I gave him, when he told me "the passengers were all in the coach, and just setting out." However, he insisted upon it afterwards, that I said, "I could not get up, if they went without me." In short, about nine o'clock, I was waked by the mistress of the house; who, having heard that I was a very young woman, without any attendants, came to satisfy her curiosity, and to enquire into my intentions. The woman was civil enough; and when I expressed my surprize at the coach's being gone without me, and my distress what course to take, she said, "as I was come to London merely out of curiosity, and was now obliged to stay till the next coaches went out, she would shew me something of the town, if I would give her leave."

'I told her, "I had a relation in Westminster, whom I would now try to find out."—She asked me, "What street her house was in?" —"She has no house," says I; "but I know she lodges somewhere in Westminster; and, as she is a lady of a large acquaintance, though small fortune, I dare say, I shall easily find her out." The woman laughed at my ignorance of the town, and said, "I might as well look for a needle in a bundle of hay."

'She then took me down to breakfast with her, behind the bar; where I spent most part of that day, she not being at leisure to attend me abroad. In the afternoon, a neighbour of hers, who had a small house in one of the adjacent courts, came to drink tea with her. The woman of the house being frequently called away into the bar; I was left alone with Mrs. Skelton (which was the name of the other woman). After enquiring into my motives for coming to London, and finding I had no friends or acquaintance there, she offered to take me to her house, as a boarder; and to bring me acquainted with every thing that was worth seeing in London. To reconcile me to her proposal, she soon discovered, that she was my country-woman; and said, "she had relations in that part of England." In short, I was so well pleased with the apparent friend-ship of this woman; and, for the reasons above-mentioned, found so little inclination to return to my friends in the country; that I began to be very well pleased with the coach's going without me, and leaving me in London.

'I then acquainted the woman at the inn with Mrs. Skelton's offer. She said, "I could not lodge with a better sort of woman; that she had known her for some years; and she was a clever,[1] sensible person; and kept the *best of company*;" ranking herself, I suppose, in that number. I therefore paid my bill at the inn, took my leave of the mistress of it, and accompanied Mrs. Skelton to her house.

'I am now astonished at my simplicity; but was quite ignorant of the world: and indeed, after my first imprudent step, what other scheme could I pursue? I soon found, however, that the world in reality was very different from what it appeared in poetry and romance.'

CHAPTER XI

Miss Townsend's Story continued

'MRS. SKELTON affected to have taken a great liking to me; and the next morning performed her promise of shewing me the town. That she might do this in the most compendious manner, the first place she took me to was the top of Saint Paul's, where indeed I was struck with astonishment at the appearance of that vast metropolis.

'After dragging me on to the Tower, she made me take a coach to bring us back to Holbourn. By the way, however, she stopped at a millener's near Saint Paul's, and equipped me with, what she thought, a more fashionable cap, and other things which she thought necessary; but without putting me to any great expence. When we came home, she helped me to adjust my dress, according to her own taste; and told me, "the gentleman who lodged in her first floor would dine with us. He is a gentleman of very large fortune, I assure you," says she, "and perhaps may fall in love with you. He is rather too old for you," continued she; "but I know several young ladies, who would be very happy in such an opportunity of setting their caps at him, I can tell you."

'Well; at dinner this fine gentleman appeared, dressed in blue and gold. He seemed to be about fifty, and was agreeable enough in his person: but what gave me a sort of liking to him was, that he put me much in mind of my own father. Nay, finding how entirely unacquainted I was with the town, he very kindly cautioned me against the artifices of the people I should probably meet with; and told me, "if I made any stay in London, he would introduce me to some of the female part of his own family."

'The next morning Mr. Blackman (which was the gentleman's name) breakfasted with us; and, though he was engaged to dine with some gentlemen of Lincoln's-Inn, he said, "he hoped to be at home again with us in the evening." At the same time he told Mrs. Skelton, "that there was a very good play to be acted that night; and asked her, if she did not intend to go?" She pretended to make a scruple of leaving me alone; on purpose, I suppose, to give him an opportunity of offering each of us tickets for the play; which he immediately did.

'Accordingly to the play we went, and sat in one of the side galleries. There happened to sit next to us, a young lady most splendidly dressed; who, I found, was an acquaintance of Mrs. Skelton's. She talked a great deal, and even in the most interesting parts of the play; and seemed to ridicule every thing that was grave or decent. She was particularly merry upon a country gentleman and his wife, as we judged them to be, who sat together in one of the side-boxes; and said, "it was astonishing to her, how any woman could think of burying herself with an husband in the country; to sit nodding at each other, whole winter evenings, on each side the parlour fire, with nothing to amuse them but a formal visit

once a week from some unfashionable creatures like themselves.
In short, (says she) I'd rather be a mistress to a tradesman in town,
than the wife of any country Squire in England." I was greatly
shocked, instead of being diverted, with this lady's conversation,
and began to wish myself in some other place; but I was highly
offended at hearing Mrs. Skelton ask her, "when she should have
the honour of seeing her in Holbourn?" To which she answered,
"She would do herself that honour very soon."

'When we returned from the play, we found an elegant supper
ordered from the tavern by the old gentleman, who was waiting for
us with great patience in the parlour. After supper, Mr. Blackman
and Mrs. Skelton drank several glasses together; and the latter
would have forced me to pledge them: but Mr. Blackman desired
"I would drink no more than was quite agreeable to me, as probably
I had never been used to any thing strong." In short, as there was
something of a paternal tenderness in the behaviour of Mr. Blackman; so it inspired me with sentiments of quite a filial love and
respect. And I lived near a fortnight in the house, quite agreeably;
Mr. Blackman and Mrs. Skelton treating me like a daughter for
whom they had a great affection; always contriving something to
amuse and entertain me.'

CHAPTER XII

Miss Townsend's Story continued

'ONE morning Mrs. Skelton asked me, "whether I should like to
take a voyage by water? for," said she, "I want to make a visit to an
acquaintance as far as Chelsea. We shall have another lady and
gentleman of our party, which will be more agreeable, and lessen
the expence of our voyage." I told her, "I should be very glad of
such a jaunt; as I had never been upon the river, and was very fond
of water." She wished Mr. Blackman could go with us; "but,"
said she, "he has so many grand acquaintance, it is hardly probable
that he will be disengaged." Upon her mentioning it to him at
breakfast, however, he replied "that he would meet us, if possible,
about twelve o'clock, at the water-side."

'When we came to the place appointed, I was surprized to see, not only Mr. Blackman, but the lady whom we had met at the play, attended by another gentleman. He was a genteel, or rather a shewy man, of about forty. He addressed us with an air of familiarity, and affectation of gaiety, which to me was very disgusting; though he was what some people would reckon a chearful companion and an handsome man.

'Mr. Blackman had provided a covered boat, and furnished it with biscuits, almonds and raisins, and a bottle of white-wine; the former, I suppose, for mine, and the latter for Mrs. Skelton's entertainment. As the other gentleman and lady, whom I took to be husband and wife, were very fond of each other, Mr. Blackman was particular in his behaviour to me, and took a great deal of pains to gain my attention to every thing which he said. But nothing attracted my notice so much as the fine prospect on each side of the river, which he pointed out to me, and explained; from the grand dome of Saint Paul's to the venerable Gothic piles of Westminster-Abbey and the palace of Lambeth, with the rural objects which present themselves gradually till we reached the noble hospital of Chelsea, whither we were bound.

'When we arrived at the end of our voyage, Mr. Blackman went immediately out of the boat, and said, "he would bespeak a room for us at a little sort of tavern close to the water:" for I soon found that this visit of Mrs. Skelton's was only a pretence; and that we were to dine at this house, at these gentlemen's expence.

'There was something in this which did not quite please me. But my inexperience, or rather my entire ignorance of the arts of mankind, prevented me from suspecting any ill design. After dinner, Mrs. Skelton said, "she would just step a door or two further, to call upon her friend, with whom she had some particular business:" and charged Mr. Blackman "to take care of her daughter," as she affected to call me.

'Soon after Mrs. Skelton was gone, the other gentleman and lady said, "they would take a walk in the garden, and return to us immediately." I stared a little; but, as they were strangers to me, and I had no inclination to cultivate an intimacy with the lady, I made no overtures to accompany her; especially as I supposed them to be man and wife. And as I had never seen any thing in Mr. Blackman's behaviour at all exceptionable, I was not uneasy at being left alone with him.

'After they had been gone a few minutes, I went up to the

window, which had a fine prospect of the Thames: and Mr.
Blackman, following me, opened a door near the window, and told
me, "I might have a better prospect in the next room"——'

Here Miss Townsend blushed and made a pause—then turned
pale, and seemed unwilling to proceed in her story. Mrs. Sarsenet,
who had heard it more than once, made an excuse for her, but desired
'she would go on; otherwise Mr. Wildgoose might suspect she had
been guilty of something which she had reason to be ashamed of.'

'That I have,' (says Miss Townsend) 'of the whole series of my
folly; though, I thank God, I have nothing to accuse myself of, but my
unparalleled indiscretion. However, I have great reason to be thankful to Providence, for preserving me from the probable effects of it.'

'Why,' (says Wildgoose) 'Providence rarely deserts us, even in
those misfortunes which are the consequence of our own inadver-
tency; if we humbly apply for assistance, and sincerely endeavour
to retrieve any false step as soon as we become sensible of it, and
do not presumptuously persist in a wrong course of action, against
the suggestions of his Holy Spirit.

'But, come, Madam; I must beg to hear the sequel of this adventure; since you have interested me in your escape from the critical
situation in which you have described yourself at the window,
where you were left alone with this fine gentleman.'

CHAPTER XIII

Miss Townsend's Story continued

'WELL, Sir; Mr. Blackman came up to me, as I told you, and
opened a door near the window, and told me, "there was a better
prospect from that room." Seeing it was a bed-chamber, I started
back; but he laid hold on my arm, pulled me in by force, and shut
the door.

'I had read in poetry of Fawns and Satyrs; in romances of dis-
courteous Knights and Savages; but had no conception that a man
of so respectable an appearance, in a brigadeer wig[1] and grave habit,
that looked more like a Justice of peace or High sheriff than a
debauched rake, could be guilty of any rudeness or indecent
behaviour.

'I cried out, with all my force; and said, "I would sooner die, than remain with him alone." I struggled, and at last got to the sash; but found it was screwed down. I continued calling out with great violence, and made all the noise I could, but to no purpose. This vile man continued his detestable importunity; and I despaired of any assistance—when I was providentially relieved by a pretty loud rapping at the outer door. Upon his opening it, the waiter introduced a very genteel modest-looking woman, and a pretty girl about ten years old. On seeing me and Mr. Blackman, who were both strangers to her, she drew back, and made an apology for her mistake. The waiter told us, "the lady had enquired for one Mr. Andrews; and insisted upon it, that he came with the company in our boat."

'Mr. Blackman reprimanded him for his impertinent intrusion: but I begged him to inform me where the other gentleman and ladies were; and upon my going out upon the stair-case, I met Mrs. Skelton coming up. I complained of her leaving me alone with Mr. Blackman, and told her how brutishly he had behaved. She affected great surprize and indignation; and, upon coming into the room, "Lord!" says she, "Mr. Blackman, I did not think you could be guilty of any thing so rude to this young lady! Why, sure, your love for her, which you mentioned, has turned your head; but I will never suffer her to be injured, whilst she is under my protection."

'Thus this vile woman endeavoured to persuade me that she was unconcerned in his villainy; but I began to have a very bad opinion of her, and to wish myself out of her hands.

'Though the fright I had been in raised my courage; yet I now found my spirits flag to such a degree, that I was hardly kept from fainting; but a little water, which Mrs. Skelton gave me, soon brought me to myself again.

'Mr. Blackman pretended he was only in jest; and was sorry he had frightened me: and hoped I would forgive him an innocent frolick. But how monstrous is vice, especially in an elderly man! This gentleman, whom I had before regarded with a filial love and esteem, I could not now behold without detestation. Age ought in general to be treated with so much reverence and respect, that I do not love to hear the two words *old villain* or *old fool* united; yet I could not separate the ideas in my mind, whenever I beheld this man for the future. But, as I was determined to make my escape the first opportunity, I dissembled my resentment as well as I could; and returned with Mr. Blackman and Mrs. Skelton, leaving the rest of the company to themselves.

'The gentleman and lady that came with us never returned after they left the room. But, as we were going out of the house, we heard a great disturbance in a parlour below-stairs; and, by what I could collect, the lady, who came so providentially to my relief, was the real wife of that other gentleman who had been of our party: and, having long suspected her husband's connection with the creature whom we had met at the play, had, by means of a faithful servant, traced out his intended jaunt for this particular day: and, with more passion perhaps than prudence, came to reproach him with his conduct: and, in order to make the greater impression upon him, had taken her eldest daughter, to be witness to his imprudence; who, I afterwards found, was squandering away upon this strumpet a good fortune, which his unhappy wife had brought him, and with which he had hitherto carried on a genteel trade in the city.'

CHAPTER XIV

Miss Townsend's Story continued

'In the evening, when I was going to bed, I asked the maid, who assisted me to undress, what sort of a man that was who lodged in the first floor. She seemed at first a little reserved: but, upon my giving some hints of his rude behaviour, she smiled, and shook her head; as if she knew more than she dared to express.

'When I told her, "I was determined to quit my lodgings, if not the town of London, the next day;" she asked me, "where my cloaths were?" I replied, "in the chest of drawers:" but, upon looking there, I found they were removed into Mrs. Skelton's room; and the maid whispered to me, "that I should find some difficulty in getting at them."—"Lord! (said I) and there's the little leather trunk gone, in which is the chief part of my money!" The girl then told me, "I had better say nothing about removing the next day; but, (says she) if you are determined to go, your things are in a dark press, in my mistress's room: and I will watch my opportunity some time to-morrow, to get your little trunk at least, if not your cloaths; and will myself accompany you the next night following; for I live here little better than a slave. But my mistress owes me a quarter's wages, which however I don't regard; for I am determined to go and live in the country again, where I was born.

' "But, for God's sake, Madam," (continues she) "don't let my mistress know what I have said; for she would contrive, right or wrong, to send me to Bridewell." I assured her of my secrecy; which promise it was so much my interest to observe.

'Having met with a sort of friend and confidante, I was a little easier in my mind; and resolved to behave with chearfulness the next day, the better to conceal my intended escape.

'In the afternoon, the lady who sate next us at the play, and had been of our party to Chelsea, came to drink tea with us. On her affecting an astonishment at our returning without them, Mrs. Skelton, with unparalleled assurance, told her, "that the poor young lady which she had taken under her protection (meaning me) was terribly frightened yesterday, by a gentleman that offered some rudeness to her." She began to railly me most unmercifully; and said, "it was a sign that I came lately out of the country; for that those things must be expected to happen to such a fine girl as I was (so she chose to express herself), if I went much into the polite world. But, child," (says she) "I would have you make the most of your charms; and get a good settlement, as I have done; and then you would never wish to see the country again."

'As she ran on in this style, she took occasion to adjust a diamond solitaire which she wore, and displayed to the best advantage three or four handsome rings. But I was not so ignorant as to be dazzled by such splendid trifles; or not to despise the creature, who, I had reason to believe, had purchased these by the sacrifice of her virtue and innocence.'

CHAPTER XV

Miss Townsend's Story continued

'WELL,' continued Miss Townsend, 'at length night came; and the maid informed me, "she had secured all my things, except one silk night-gown, which her mistress had not hung up with the rest; and she did not care to search after, for fear of being discovered."

I told her, "I should be glad to leave that, as some recompence for near a fortnight's board; for, however wicked Mrs. Skelton's intentions might be, I could not bear to be guilty of any act of injustice, that I was not obliged to for my own preservation."

'We were forced to wait till near two o'clock, before the maid had seen her mistress and Mr. Blackman safe to bed; for after he came home, they sat up for near an hour in close debate; and the maid assured me, "they were laying some other plot for my destruction."

'When we came down to the street-door, the maid shaking her head, "Ah!" says she, "it is as I feared; the key is gone." I was thunder-struck at this news; but she said, "she knew a trick worth two of that." And, bidding me follow her, we came down into the kitchen, from which she opened a door into the area (as I think they call it); and bringing a pair of steps, which were made use of about the kitchen, we clambered up to the balustrades, and got into the court; narrowly escaping the watch, who had just cried, "past two o'clock." In short, after several frights and alarms, we got clear of the town; and, about sun-rising, found ourselves beyond Hammersmith, I think, upon the western road.

'As my dress was rather too good for a foot-passenger, the girl proposed to rest that day (in some house near the road), to prevent suspicion; and so take our chance of some carriage that might pass by.

'I had hitherto been under such anxiety for fear of being pursued (though I was not conscious of having injured any one), that I had had no time to reflect, or to form any scheme; so complied with the girl's proposal. Accordingly we stopped at a little public house, where we reposed ourselves, and spent the remainder of that day, not without a mixture of joy and anxiety.

'Whilst we were here, the maid let me into the true character of Mrs. Skelton; who, I found, made a practice of seducing young people; and that the fine lady, whom we had met at the play, was an unhappy creature, who had been drawn in to prostitute her youth and beauty to Mr. Blackman, for Mrs. Skelton's advantage: though she was now kept by that tradesman, who (as has been mentioned) had almost ruined himself to support her extravagance: that the gentleman who lodged with her was really a man of good family, and considerable fortune; but who spent it all in the gratification of his own humour and vicious appetites; dividing his whole life between his tavern companions and his mistresses, with a variety of whom this vile woman was well paid for supplying him. So that I found that I had great reason to bless myself for this escape.'

Wildgoose said, 'that Providence, for wise ends, permitted such monsters to fulfill the measure of their iniquities; but that they ought to be punished, he thought, by human laws: that a double tax, however, would be the least return such useless wretches could make to the publick, for the protection they enjoyed.'

CHAPTER XVI

Miss Townsend's Story continued

'WELL,' continues Miss Townsend, 'we lay the next night at the same house: but the people, I suppose, entertaining no very favourable opinion of our characters, took care to lodge us over a little room distinct from the rest of the family.

'As we had had no sleep the preceding night, we went early to bed; and I never waked till seven o'clock the next morning; when, to my surprize, I missed my bed-fellow; and also, upon looking round the room, I found she had eased me of a good part of my luggage; particularly the little trunk, which contained my money, and the silk night-gown in which I had escaped.—My brocaded suit of cloaths however, and one silk and another cotton night-gown, were left me; and I luckily had four guineas and some silver, and my watch, in my pockets; which, according to custom, I had laid under my pillow.

'I had now seen enough of the world, to satisfy my curiosity; and had paid dear for about ten days experience. The loss of my cloaths and money was the least of my misfortune. I had certainly forfeited my father's favour; should expose myself to the ridicule and reproaches of my sister and Mrs. Townsend, and probably to the censures of the whole neighbourhood, if I ventured thither. To go back to town, where I had not one friend or acquaintance that I knew where to find, was to run into inevitable destruction. I immediately determined, therefore, to find out my good friend Mrs. Sarsenet here; who, having been an old school-fellow likewise of my mama's (though, by the misfortunes of her family, in less affluent circumstances), and having been for a month at our house about two years since, and shewed a particular fondness for me, I considered as the only friend I could apply to in my present distress; though, I am now sensible, it has given the widow Townsend an handle for irritating my father still more against me; on account of the letter, which I before mentioned she had seen, in which Mrs. Sarsenet expressed herself with some freedom in regard to Mrs. Townsend's character. In short, having enquired whether any carriage went that road to Gloucester, I was informed, that a Gloucester waggon would pass by the house that day; which it accordingly did: and meeting with an elderly woman and her daughter, who were travelling into some part of Wales by the same conveyance, I took my place, and got safe to Mrs. Sarsenet, without any disagreeable event.'

CHAPTER XVII

Miss Townsend's Story concluded

'MRS. SARSENET was kind enough to write to my father, and acquaint him with the whole progress of my rash adventure; and to assure him, "that I was thoroughly sensible of my folly; and that I was desirous to throw myself at his feet, and ask his forgiveness."

'I sent at the same time to the poor woman who had assisted me in my flight, to know what effect my elopement had had on my poor father.—She wrote me word, "that he was almost distracted at the first news of it; that it made a great disturbance in the family, as was naturally to be expected; but that the widow Townsend found means to pacify my father, by some false suggestion or other; and my sister had persuaded them that I was certainly gone to a relation's of ours near Warwick (as I had really talked about them to my sister); and that my father's first journey in quest of me was thither: but, not getting any intelligence of me there, somebody told him, "that I had been seen two or three times of late at the Coachman's house above-mentioned." Upon which, he went and threatened to send them both to gaol, unless they discovered where they had concealed me. Having extorted the secret from them, he went immediately to Oxford (where I had taken coach), and traced me to the inn in London; but, the woman there being afraid, I suppose, to discover into what hands she had recommended me, insisted upon it, "that I had returned in the same coach I came up in." My father went to Mrs. Calvert's (the lady in Westminster whom I wished to find out), and, not hearing any thing of me, was returned into the country, where he was quite melancholy, till he received Mrs. Sarsenet's letter.—What effect that had upon him, we are yet to learn: but, as it is now above a fortnight since he must have received it, I am afraid the widow Townsend will not permit him to make any farther enquiries after me: so here I am, an exile from home, and an incumbrance to poor Mrs. Sarsenet: and I do not know what return it will ever be in my power to make for the trouble I have given her.'—To this Mrs. Sarsenet made a complaisant reply, which the Author cannot recollect.

CHAPTER XVIII

The Effects of Miss Townsend's Narration

I T is a vulgar maxim, 'that a pretty woman should rather be seen than heard.' And indeed, when a fair lady seems to talk merely for the sake of talking; or with a direct intention to attract admirers, she seldom prepossesses a stranger in her favour. But as Miss Townsend's story had interested Wildgoose sufficiently to raise his compassion; there is an easy transition from pity to love; and it is far from certain, that he did not begin to feel something of that mere human passion for this young lady. But, being desirous of acting in character, he observed, 'that, to be sure, nothing but a prior obligation which we are under to obey our heavenly Father can justify our disobedience to an earthly parent: and although he by no means approved of Miss Townsend's leaving her father upon so slight a provocation; yet, as Providence frequently produces good out of evil, and makes even our own indiscretions concur with his gracious design of promoting our felicity; perhaps, Madam, (says he) you may be directed hither to receive instruction, in the way of salvation, even from the meanest of God's servants; and I may perhaps be made an happy instrument of your *conversion*.'

Miss Townsend, though a well-disposed girl, did not much relish

Wildgoose's enthusiastic notions, or nice distinctions in divinity. But, as his person was very agreeable, and they had learned from Tugwell that he was heir to a pretty good fortune, she had conceived no contemptible opinion of him; and listened with great attention, whenever he talked upon common subjects.

I would not insinuate that Miss Townsend was of a mercenary temper (for she really was not). But though fortune alone, where the person is disagreeable, has seldom any considerable influence over the affections of a young girl: yet, I believe, in conjunction with other circumstances, it operates insensibly upon their fancies, and contributes to make the person possessed of it more agreeable than he would otherwise appear; as the want of fortune frequently prevents their seeing those perfections in a man, which he is really possessed of.

Miss Townsend, however, instead of answering Wildgoose in a serious way, turned the discourse; and began raillying him upon his external appearance. 'Lord! Mr. Wildgoose,' says she, 'what makes you go about in that frightful hair of yours? I wonder you do not wear a wig, as other gentlemen do.'[1]—'Madam,' replies Wildgoose, 'I should be sorry if any part of my dress were to prejudice any one against me; much less would I willingly raise a disgust in so pretty a lady against my person. But pray, Madam, why don't you like my hair?'—'Oh! frightful!' says she, ' 'tis so *ungenteel*; so *unlike other people!*'—'Why, as for other people,' replies Wildgoose, 'I should chuse to be unlike a great part of the world, in their vain fashions and idle customs. But as to its being *ungenteel*, I am sorry any thing should be thought so, that is natural, convenient, and (I think) becoming. If you do not think so, young lady, I am afraid it is owing to mere prejudice and the force of custom.'—'*Custom!*' (says Miss Townsend) 'why, custom or fashion is every thing, in regard to dress.'—'I own, it has too great a force,' replies Wildgoose; 'and I dare say, for that reason only, you think this great hoop of yours very *genteel*, and very *becoming*: and yet, in the opinion of many people of the best taste, nothing can be more monstrous, or more unnatural, than hoop-petticoats are: and, I dare say, we shall live to see these Gothic ornaments banished from the world.'[2]—'What! hoops go out of fashion? Lord! what a creature should I be without my hoop!'

'Well, Madam,' says Wildgoose, 'as I should be sorry to differ from you in the least trifle, and not endeavour to comply with every

I

one in matters of indifference, I wish I could bring you, and all mankind, to my way of thinking, in this article of wearing one's own hair: for, you must know, the honest Barber, where I lodge, had a great dispute with me last night upon that very subject: and almost insisted upon making me a fine flowing white wig, as, he said, he had done for Mr. Whitfield; who, he assured me, was of opinion, that nothing contributed more to the conversion of sinners, than a good periwig; as it gave a dignity to our appearance, and prepossessed people in favour of our preaching.'

'Why,' says Mrs. Sarsenet, 'there may be some truth in that observation.'

'Well,' continues Wildgoose, 'it was in vain for me to plead the examples of Patriarchs, Prophets, Apostles, and Reformers. The poor Barber (for the credit of his trade) said, "if there were no wigs in those days, there were certainly Barbers, by David's allusion to the chief instrument of their art, 'With lies thou cuttest like a sharp razor.' " '[1]

'Well,' says Mrs. Sarsenet, who was apt to raise scruples upon the most trifling occasions, 'but do you really make a serious affair of this? I should be glad to be set right upon the lawfulness of using art about one's person, and especially as to false hair: as many of my customers are as faulty in that respect as the gentlemen; and, I believe, I sell as many wigs, or *têtes*, as any Barber in town.'

Wildgoose then, accustomed of late to harangue upon all occasions, proceeded upon this important subject in the following manner.

CHAPTER XIX

A Dissertation on Periwigs

'THE use of false hair, Madam, by particular people, for particular reasons, is, I believe, very ancient in the world. Vain persons of both sexes, either to conceal some natural defect, or to improve (as they imagined) their natural charms, have, in all ages, had recourse to these artificial decorations. Xenophon (a Greek writer) mentions the use of them amongst the Medes.[2] And some Commentators are of opinion, that the hair of her head, with which Mary

Magdalene wiped our Saviour's feet, was really a *tête*, or a set of false curls; which she might employ in that manner, to express her detestation of the wanton and dissolute life which she had formerly led. It is certain, however, that these unnatural ornaments were esteemed infamous in those more early times, by all good and sensible people. Julius Cæsar, though he is said to have been particularly pleased with the laurels decreed him by the Senate, because they concealed the baldness of his temples; yet that great man, I believe, would have been highly offended, if his Barber had proposed a sett of false curls for that purpose—though it is confessed, that the Emperor Otho, many years after, wore a periwig; as he also is reproached with carrying a looking-glass amongst his baggage in his military expeditions.

'The first mention which I remember to be made of periwigs, in our English history, is in the account of Prince Charles and the Duke of Buckingham's appearing in disguise at a ball at Paris, in their way to Madrid.[1] But that was evidently a masquerade-dress, as they wore false beards for the same purpose: which also was done by the Players in Shakespeare's time. Wigs were but little, if at all, used in England till the Restoration of Charles the Second; and then chiefly by persons of distinction. These indeed by degrees were imitated by the Beaux and Fops of the age. Yet it was some time before the fashion extended itself to the graver professions, of Law, Physic, and Divinity. But, when once it had the sanction of those venerable bodies, it was not long, we may suppose, before it spread amongst all ranks and degrees of men in the nation.

'At first, however, some resemblance of Nature was observed in these contrivances of Art; and a periwig was only a more complete head of hair, suited to the complexion, and fitted as exactly as possible to the forehead and temples, of the person who wore it. But of late years, any man, that has a mind to look more considerable or more wise than his neighbours, goes to a Barber's, and purchases fifty shillings-worth of false hair (white, black, or grey) and hangs it upon his head, without the least regard to his complexion, his age, his person, or his station in life. And certainly, if an inhabitant of the Cape of Good Hope were to behold the stiff horse-hair buckles, or the tied wigs, of our Lawyers, Physicians, Tradesmen, or Divines, they would appear as barbarous and extraordinary to them, as the sheep's tripes and chitterlins about the neck of a Hottentot do to us.'

Miss Townsend and Mrs. Sarsenet forced a smile, at Wildgoose's vehemence and far-fetched comparison. But he, correcting himself, went on.

'I am ashamed,' says he, 'to dwell so long upon the absurdity of our modern periwigs in point of taste. But, as Miss Townsend objected to the *gentility* of my own locks; and as the chief intent of hair, considered as ornamental, seems to be to give a softness to the features, by rising in an easy manner from the forehead, and falling loosely down upon the parts which it was designed to cover; I own, I had rather see the worst head of natural hair, than the most accurate wig that ever adorned a Barber's block. And as a good taste in other articles of dress seems to prevail in the world, I should not be surprized to see periwigs again banished from the genteel part of mankind, to our poor labourers and mechanics, to whom it may be sometimes convenient to be freed from the incumbrance of a long or bushy head of hair.

'But,' continued Wildgoose, 'I have a particular and more important objection to those supplemental locks, from the bad influence they certainly have upon the moral and religious conduct of too many in this age.'

'As how? for goodness sake!' cries Miss Townsend.

'Why, Madam,' says Wildgoose, 'perhaps there never was a period that furnished so many instances of unseasonable gaiety, or so great a number of old debauchees, as the age we live in. You yourself have met with one instance, in the short course of your ramble. Now, I have often conceived, how strange soever you may think it, that this was owing in a great measure to the use of periwigs; that is, to the great ease with which the gentlemen of this generation may conceal the effects of old age, and exchange their grey locks for those which are expressive of youth and vigour. It was certainly the kind intention of Providence, to remind us of the approach of age and infirmity, by the several symptoms of wrinkled foreheads, decaying teeth, and grey hairs. Now, when a man of a debauched and dissolute mind is almost worn out in the service of his lusts and sensual appetites, he puts on a fine flowing Adonis or white periwig (and perhaps a set of false teeth); surveys himself in the glass, and immediately forgets his real age; commences beau again in the winter of his days; and, if he cannot prevail on any modest woman to accept of him as an husband, he has probably recourse to some mercenary wretch, who squanders away his money, ruins his health, and exposes him to the ridicule of his very servants and dependents; and, what is worse, to the eternal displeasure of his offended Creator.'

'Bless me!' cries Miss Townsend, 'why you have given us quite a sermon upon periwigs. I really never apprehended there was so much sin, though there might be a great deal of folly, under the wig of a beau. But you will persuade one to believe, that (in a literal sense) "the hairs of our head are all *numbered*;" and that it is unlawful either to increase or diminish them on any account.

'Indeed I myself was imposed upon by an old gentleman in a solemn wig: and, on the contrary, I heard lately of an old Baronet, that fell in love with a young lady of small fortune (at some public place) for her beautiful *brown locks*. He married her on a sudden, but was greatly disappointed upon seeing her wig or *tête* the next morning thrown carelessly upon her toilette; and her Ladyship appearing at breakfast in very bright *red hair*; which was a colour the old gentleman happened to have a particular aversion to.'

'Well, Madam,' replied Wildgoose, 'then I hope I have almost made you a convert to my opinion, and reconciled you to the natural ornaments of the human face; though you were so lately disgusted at my appearance.'—'Why, really,' says she, 'whatever may be naturally beautiful; yet custom, as I said before, makes one like or dislike things, as the fashion varies.'

'But, Madam, if painting the face were as much the fashion in England as it is in France, could you think it lawful for a good Christian to comply with such a fashion, or to make use of such meretricious decorations?' 'Lord!' says Miss Townsend, 'you use so many hard words; you may call one names, for aught I know, and we not understand you. But, I think, we have had more than enough upon this foolish subject.'

Wildgoose therefore made an apology for his impertinence, and took his leave for the present. And, having been now near a fortnight at Gloucester, the next night he made a farewell-harangue to his usual audience; appointed Mrs. Sarsenet a sort of Deaconess, and Mr. Keen the Barber a Ruler, of the little synagogue, with instructions to assemble the brethren occasionally, and exhort them to perseverance; and left Gloucester the next day, after promising to visit them again in his return from Bristol.

CHAPTER XX

The Farewell-Harangue is attended with a disastrous Circumstance

WHEN Wildgoose came to take his leave of Mrs. Sarsenet, she happened to be gone out; and he found nobody in the shop but Miss Townsend. After a short conversation with her on the subject of religion (on which head she never seemed to relish his doctrine), Wildgoose said, 'he hoped to have the pleasure of hearing of her sometimes, by the hands of Mrs. Sarsenet.' Miss Townsend answered, 'she did not know how long she might stay at Gloucester: but,' fetching an involuntary sigh, which was immediately succeeded by a blush, she owned, 'she should be always glad to hear of Mr. Wildgoose, especially when he was returned to his disconsolate mother.' Wildgoose replied, 'that he had written to his mother, and given her the reasons for his conduct; but must leave it to Heaven to dispose of him as it should think fit.' Then, taking Miss Townsend's hand, and pressing it to his lips, he took his leave, with a deep sigh and a very expressive silence.

At Wildgoose's farewell harangue, there was a piece of fun played off, which, as it was attended with serious consequences to the poor Barber, ought not to be here omitted.

Under the same roof with the said Artist, and in part of the same ruinous mansion, there dwelt an honest Publican, to whose craft the pious Conventicle at Mr. Keen's was by no means favourable. The Publican therefore gladly connived at, or rather aided and assisted, an unlucky project of his son and some prentices, to disturb at least, if not put a stop to, this dangerous assembly. The ancient dining-room, in which they met, had a communication with each part of the house: but the common door had been stopped up, by agreement, for some years. This, however, the lads contrived to open; and from thence, early in the morning, had carefully laid a train of gun-powder by the side of the wall, as far as the tub upon which Tugwell usually seated himself near his Master; and at proper intervals had bestowed squibs and crackers, with balls of wild-fire: and into the tub they had conveyed a considerable quantity of that infernal composition.[1]

Having thus laid their plot, they waited with as much impatience for their time of meeting, as Guy Fawkes and his associates did for the meeting of the Parliament on the fifth of November. At length the evening came; and whilst Wildgoose was in the most pathetic part of his discourse, dealing about his judgement of wrath and indignation, fire and brimstone with great zeal and vehement gesticulations, they set fire to their train; which, corresponding with the heated imaginations of the audience, had its proper effect; and threw them into the utmost consternation. The Saints and Sinners fled promiscuously, without waiting for the benediction. The tub, on which Tugwell was perched, burst into a thousand pieces, with so loud a report, and such violent force, that, if Jerry's prudence had not prevailed over his fortitude, and prompted him to make his escape amongst the foremost of the company, he would probably have been sent to Heaven, before his time, in a chariot of fire. A poor decrepit old woman, however, in her crowned hat, who, on account of her deafness, was seated near the Preacher, was terribly battered and burnt by the bursting of the barrel: which, of itself, was a sufficient reason for Mr. Keen's getting a warrant, and carrying the Publican before the Mayor; who, unless he had found sufficient bail, and given security to indemnify the old woman for her burns and bruises, would have committed him to the Castle. The Publican, however, took an opportunity of revenging himself sufficiently upon his pious neighbour; which will be related in its proper place.

BOOK IV

CHAPTER I

The Pilgrims set out for Bath

MR. WILDGOOSE, during his stay at Gloucester, having heard that there was a considerable Society of godly people established at Bath, was resolved to visit that place in his way to Bristol. And being likewise informed that there was, at this time, a race at Cirencester; he was inclined to make another effort at one of those public meetings, and attack the Devil, a second time, in one of his strong holds; and resolved therefore to take his route by that place and Tetbury, and so to Bath.

Accordingly they set out pretty early in the morning, and about eight o'clock reached Birdlip-hill.

Wildgoose, being a little thoughtful on parting with his Christian brethren; and a sort of melancholy likewise succeeding in his mind, to the innocent sprightliness of Miss Townsend; but little conversation passed between the two Pilgrims. Tugwell, however, took the liberty to remind his Master of his mother's illness; and said, 'it was a little hard-hearted in him, not to write her a letter, *howsomever*; that he himself should not mind the loss of his son so much, if he could but hear from him now and then, that he might know whether he was alive or not: he hoped, therefore, that Mr. Wildgoose would write to Madam, and let her know *as how* they should be at home again very speedily.' Wildgoose replied, with some degree of peevishness, 'that he *had* written to his mother; but as to their returning home again, that was according as Mr. Whitfield should dispose of him, and according to the success of his labours in the Gospel. In short,' says he, 'hast thou forgot our great Master's declaration, "Whosoever loves father or mother more than me, is not worthy of me"?'—Jerry stood corrected, and so trudged on without farther reply.

They now proceeded for several miles, without meeting with any adventure: and Wildgoose might as well have thought of preaching the Gospel in the desarts of Arabia, as on the Cotswold hills. He would have been like the Preacher, whose discourses generally produced such a solitude in his church, that he was facetiously called, 'the voice of one crying in the wilderness or desart,' *Vox clamantis in deserto.*

Indeed the fame of Cirencester races operated so strongly, that it had drawn every man, woman, and child, for ten miles round, that could either borrow an horse, or walk on foot, into its vortex; so that they did not meet a living creature, unless a London waggon might be called so, upon the high road.

In the afternoon, however, they saw a pompous equipage, with a numerous attendance, come whirling along the road, amidst a cloud of dust. It was a landeau, or open coach, with six horses, and four or five out-riders in most flaming liveries. They came upon them so suddenly, that Wildgoose had hardly time to get out of the road; and one of the footmen gave Tugwell an hearty cut with his whip, to quicken his pace, and clear the way.

The principal figure in this gay party was a young fellow, whom, on a sudden glance, Wildgoose immediately recollected to have been an intimate acquaintance in the University. He had unexpectedly arrived at an immense fortune; was just married; and was conducting his bride, with some other company, to his country house in ——shire. He would hardly have reconnoitred[1] Wildgoose, however, in his short hair and his present uncouth appearance, if he had vouchsafed a look upon two such dusty objects as he and his fellow-traveller now were. The whole company consisted of three ladies and two gentlemen; who were laughing and talking, in all the gaiety and wanton levity of unthinking youth. Wildgoose, however, was so far from envying them, that he only lamented their unhappiness, 'that, notwithstanding their splendid appearance and seeming felicity, they had not yet been blessed with the illumination of the Spirit, as he flattered himself he and his humble companion had happily been.'

This scene was hardly shifted, when, as a contrast to the splendor of it, they espied a poor Tinker and his Trull, sitting calmly on a shady bank, under an hedge, a little out of the road. Tugwell enquired of the Tinker, 'how far it was to Cirencester.' Instead of giving a direct answer to his question, the Tinker told him, 'he would be too late for the sport; for that the horses were to start at three o'clock, and that this was the last day of the race.' The first part of this intelligence damped Tugwell's spirits; as the latter made Wildgoose waver in his resolution of going that way. He then asked the Tinker, 'whether there was not a nearer way to Tetbury than through Cirencester?'—'Yes,' says he, 'by some miles. If you keep the right-hand road at the next turning, it will bring you to a public house, called Park-corner, where there is good ale and civil usage.'

As the Tinker and his Doxy were regaling themselves with a bacon-bone, which they had got at a neighbouring farm-house, it put Tugwell in mind of what he had stored in his wallet: and Wildgoose, considering it as an act of humiliation, and that he might probably make a meal and make a convert at the same time, complied with Jerry's request, to join this happy couple, and refresh themselves with what Mrs. Whitfield had furnished him at Gloucester, where, besides a substantial slice or two of a round of beef, he had laid in an old French-flask, filled with some good ale or strong beer. They therefore, with a proper apology, took their seat upon the bank; Wildgoose next the Tinker, and Tugwell by his Trull.

They were hardly seated, when Wildgoose (in his way) asked the Tinker, 'why he chose to lead such an idle, vagabond life, as those of his profession generally did?'—'Yes,' says Tugwell, 'it is like a travelling Cobler, that goes about, and takes the meat out of the mouth of an honest workman, that is to live by his trade.' 'Hey! what the devil!' (says the Tinker) 'the Pot calls the Kettle Black a-se! Why I suppose thou art a Pedlar, as well as myself: sure, all trades must live.'—'Yes,' says Wildgoose, 'very true: but I wonder any one should chuse to live in such an unsettled way, if it is in his power to avoid it.'—'Aye,' says the Tinker, 'but those that cannot live at home, must seek their fortune abroad. It is better to pick a bone under a hedge, than to rot in a gaol; as perhaps I might have done, if I had stayed at home.'—'How so?' says Tugwell, 'What! I suppose you owed money, and had none to pay?'—'Yes,' replies the Tinker; 'I was ruined by a piece of good fortune: or rather, by trusting more to the smiles of fortune, than to my own industry.'— 'That is no uncommon case,' says Wildgoose; 'but how did that come to pass?' To which the Tinker replied, as in the following chapter.

CHAPTER II

The Tinker's Tale

'I WAS settled in a very flourishing trade, as a Brazier, in a large town in the West of England; in which I employed a great many hands: and my wife and I lived happily together. A distant relation, dying without children, left five thousand pounds betwixt me, my three brothers, and a sister; which, one would have thought, might easily have been divided between us, without the assistance of a Lawyer. But, as we were to pay an old aunt an annuity for her life, of twenty pounds half yearly, this part of the will being *ambitiously* expressed'[1]—'*Ambiguously*, I suppose you mean,' says Wildgoose. —'I mean' (says the Tinker) 'what the Lawyer told us, that it was impossible to know, as the will was worded, whether it meant twenty pounds or forty pounds a year; though every one knew the intention of my kinsman was, to leave her only twenty pounds a year in the whole; and the Lawyer that made the will had probably expressed it so, on purpose to make work for the Tinker (as the saying is). Well; we were advised to put the affair into Chancery, *in an amicable way*, as they call it; which, as they told us, would be a trifling expence, and would soon be determined. But my sister and one of my brothers dying in the mean time, and leaving children, we were forced to have Bills of Revivor (I think they call them) one after another: so that, by some means or other, we could never get a decree to settle this affair under seven years. When that was done, our Lawyer told us, the business would now soon be ended; for that there was nothing more to do, but to settle the account before a Master in Chancery; which, one would think, might have been easily done. But we soon found, that not a few years were required to settle an account, which any School-master, or indeed any School-boy, might have settled in a few hours.

'But I should have told you before, that, after a decent mourning for the death of my kinsman, I had invited some of my friends to a tavern, to partake of my joy, for the legacy which he had left me. I also thought it unnecessary to make myself any longer a slave to my business; and the respect, with which I found myself treated by the waiters and tapsters, at the public houses which I frequented, made me fond of repeating my visits at those places of rendezvous.

'My poor wife saw the absurdity of my conduct; and, whenever I came home elated with liquor, would reproach me for my folly in no very gentle terms. In short, home began to be disagreeable to me, and I was never easy out of a public house; so that, by neglecting my business, and spending considerable sums at the tavern, by the time our law-suit was ended, I found myself more in debt than the share of my legacy which the law had left me amounted to; for, instead of one thousand pounds apiece, it did not turn out above five hundred. Her vexation on this account was the death of my poor wife; and though I held up my head a year or two longer, my landlord at last seized upon my stock, for rent; and I was forced to abscond, and leave my three children upon the parish, and to fly my country.[1] And thus, by my own folly, and the iniquity of a Court of Equity, from a topping Tradesman, I am become a travelling Tinker, at your service.'

Though Tugwell had been cramming in his cold beef, during the Tinker's narration; yet he shook his head at the conclusion of it, and said, 'that the Law was a bottomless pit, as the Exciseman used to say.'

Wildgoose observed, 'that those forms in Law, which were sometimes so oppressive to individuals, were the greatest security, in general, of justice and of property.'—'That is true, Master,' says Tugwell. 'But come, let us drink, and drive care away,' quoth Jerry. He then put the flask to his mouth, and tossed off one half of it: then, clapping his hand upon the young woman's knee; who was a handsome black girl (black, I mean, from the sooty contact of her Paramour, for naturally she was as fair as the Venus of Corregio)—Tugwell, I say, squeezing her knee, with a waggish air, bid the lady pledge him. But the Tinker's dog, who lay at his mistress's feet, not approving of Jerry's familiarity, starts up, and snaps at his fingers: in return for which, he gave the dog a kick in the guts. This rouzed the Tinker's choler, already provoked at Tugwell's amorous freedom with his Doxy; and he gave him a click in the mazard. Tugwell had not been used tamely to receive a kick or a cuff: he therefore gave the Tinker a rejoinder; which would have brought on a regular boxing-match, had not Wildgoose on one side, and Trulla on the other, interposed, and put a stop to farther hostilities. The Tinker, however, sacked up his budget, and his companion her bundle, and went growling off, with hearty curses both upon Tugwell and his Master, for intruding upon them

and interrupting their tranquillity. Such was the event of Wildgoose's benevolent intention of converting this itinerant Copper-
smith and his female companion; which Tugwell called, 'casting
their pearls before swine;' though his own indiscretion alone and
carnal waggery had defeated his Master's purpose, and deprived
him of an opportunity of giving them any spiritual instruction.

Our two Pilgrims finished their repast, took a short nap to refresh
themselves, and then proceeded on their journey; leaving the
Cirencester road, and bending their course towards Park-corner:
but the shades of night overtook them, before they reached their
intended quarters.

CHAPTER III

Their comfortable Reception at Park-corner, near Lord Bathurst's Woods

'BLESSED be the man that first invented Warming-pans!' said
an old gentleman, with whom I passed the Alps, upon coming to
a comfortable inn on Mount St. Bernard. And 'blessed be that good
Christian who first found out Chimney-corners!' (said Tugwell
to himself) upon spying the distant light of the inn to which
they had been directed. 'Nothing is more comfortable,' continued
Jerry, 'than a pipe of tobacco in a chimney-corner, after wandring
about in a dark night and in a strange country, as we have done.
And if I can but meet with a bit of soft cheese and a radish, to close
the orifice of the stomach (as the Exciseman used to say), I shall be
as happy as the Great Mogul.'

Tugwell was consoling himself with these savoury ideas, when,
about nine o'clock, they approached Park-corner. But lo! instead
of this snug scene which Jerry had formed in his imagination, they
found the inn so crowded with company from Cirencester races,
that they were forced to sit drinking out at the door (it being a warm
evening); and the stables also were so full, that there were near
twenty horses standing round the sign-post.

It was in vain for foot-passengers to expect any kind of lodgings
upon such an occasion; and it was even with difficulty that they
got any sort of refreshment. Tugwell began to complain of great

fatigue, and to lament their distress: but Wildgoose, attentive to nothing so much as the conversion of sinners, cried out, in a strain of exultation, 'Now for it, Jerry! this is an unexpected opportunity! let us take possession of the Devil's strong hold; we will make his kingdom shake,[1] I'll warrant you!'

Having said this, in the warmth of his zeal, without any more ceremony, he mounted the horse-block contiguous to the sign-post, and began to harangue with such vehemence, that he soon drew together all the company about the house, and though some mocked, yet others were very attentive; for, as many of them lived at no great distance from Gloucester, they had heard of Wildgoose's fame, and were glad of an opportunity of gratifying their curiosity at so easy a rate.

But, after a little time, some of them began to regret the leaving their pipes and their punch-bowls; others were provoked at being interrupted in the midst of their songs and catches; and could not forbear renewing their melody at every period of Wildgoose's discourse: which he perceiving, after some time, addressed them in the apostolical strain, 'If any is merry, let him sing Psalms;' and ordered Tugwell to give out the hundredth Psalm. But the people of the house, thinking their craft was in danger, and that preaching and singing of Psalms interrupted more profitable business, were not much pleased with these proceedings. They connived, therefore, at a proposal of the Hostler; who, climbing up the sign-post, which was not much illuminated, discharged a bucket of water upon the heads of the two Pilgrims; which raised a great uproar, threw all into confusion, and effectually cooled their devotion.

They were now certainly in very evil plight; almost wet to the skin, and thoroughly tired; nor likely to get any bed, or any comfortable accommodations, at Park-corner; and they were assured, there was no other house upon the road nearer than Tetbury, which was six or seven miles. In the midst of this distress, however, a gentleman's servant in a green coat and black cap, with some dog-couples by his side, having observed that Wildgoose had a watch in his pocket (which he consulted about the hour of the night), and that he had otherwise the appearance of a gentleman, thought he might safely invite him and his companion to his habitation. This was part of an old Gothic building, about a mile within lord Bathurst's fine woods, which extended for five or six miles to the west of Cirencester, and are cut into glades and avenues; most of which are terminated by towers or spires, or some other striking objects, agreeably to the magnificent taste of that worthy Nobleman.

Upon the Keeper's offering them such accommodations as his house would afford, the travellers, we may be sure, having no choice, were glad to accept of so unexpected an invitation. They accompanied their honest guide, therefore, who was then going to his castle, together with a Groom of my Lord's, who had stayed out beyond his time, and intended to lie at the house in the wood till the morning.

The gloomy darkness and solemn silence of the woods, through which they were conducted by mere strangers, filled Tugwell with terrible apprehensions; which were greatly aggravated, upon their approach to the house, by the loud barkings of some wolf-dogs, pointers, and southern hounds, and the like; which, echoing from the ruinous walls, revived in Tugwell's imagination his danger from the adventure of the buck-hunters; but when they came still nearer, the canking of some Spanish geese, the gobling of turkeys, and the noise of other uncommon fowls, which are kept there, threw poor Jerry into the utmost consternation. He was soon freed from this alarm, however, on being conducted into a chearful kitchen; where the Keeper's wife was expecting the return of her husband by a good fire. Being informed of the distress from which his benevolence had freed the travellers, she received them with tolerable civility; desired them to come to the fire, and dry themselves—and entertained them with as much hospitality as their circumstances would allow of.

The Keeper had but one spare bed, which Tugwell could not be prevailed upon to partake with his Master; but took up his lodgings with the Groom in the hay-loft: and Wildgoose, making it a point of conscience, not to indulge himself in the softness of a down-bed, when his fellow-labourer fared so coarsly, wrapt himself up in the coverlet, and lay down upon the floor. So, though they were both thoroughly tired, through the complaisance of the one, and the quixotism of the other, a very good feather-bed remained useless and un-occupied. Wildgoose, however, slept tolerably well on the floor; and Tugwell would have slept better in the hay-loft, had not the Groom, who chose to lie in his boots and spurs, given Jerry now and then an involuntary titillation.

CHAPTER IV

Spiritual Advice

IN the morning, as soon as the Keeper arose, he prepared them a good breakfast of toast and ale; and, as his wife was dressing a sucking child by the fire, she expressed some concern, that Mr. Wildgoose had had so bad a lodging, and was forced to lie upon the floor all night, as she found he had done. Wildgoose, recollecting Mr. Whitfield's method of allegorizing upon such occasions, shook his head, and, turning towards Tugwell, in allusion to the child at the breast, 'Ah!' says he, 'I sweetly leaned on my Saviour's bosom; and *sucked out* of the *breasts* of his consolation; and I can truly say, the banner of his love was spread over me the whole night.'[1]

The poor woman, a stranger to this pious jargon, stared at him with astonishment, to hear a jolly[2] man, as Wildgoose was, talk of sucking at the breast: which Tugwell observing, and imagining he could explain his Master's meaning, 'Yes, yes,' (says he) 'his Worship only talks in the way of Christian discourse, look-ye! that is, (as a body may say) his Worship took a good swinging nap, and had a comfortable night's rest.' Wildgoose did not reflect upon the improbability of his audience's not comprehending his allegorical meaning; but thought the least he could do, in return for their kindness, was to impart some spiritual advice to his host and family.

After a few observations therefore upon the laudable nature of hospitality, and putting them in mind, 'that, in the primitive times, some had entertained angels, without suspecting any thing of the matter;' he proceeded to assure them, 'that in such cases (as that of Rahab the Harlot for instance) it was her *faith*, and not her kindness to the Jewish spies, that was so acceptable to God. In short,' says he, 'though it is a very commendable thing to entertain strangers in distress, as you have done us; yet you must be very cautious not to place the least *merit* in this, or in any other good work which you can possibly perform. For we must be saved by Faith alone, without works.'

'Faith and troth, Master,' replies the Keeper, (little used to religious speculations) 'I never thought about *merit*, or any such thing. I did as I would be done by. Our ale is but poor indeed; but,

such as it is, you are as welcome to it as a King: and I don't desire
a farthing for my trouble.

'However, Master, I don't know what you mean by being *saved*
without *work*. But I am sure all the *faith* in the world, without *work*,
would not *save* me from starving. It is true,' continues he, 'I live
in my Lord's house here, rent-free; but never a man in the country
works harder to support his family, than I do. And if you chuse to
take a turn here in the woods, I will shew you some serpentine
walks, which *I advised* my Lord to let me cut out this last week;' in
which, indeed, the honest man probably took more pride than my
Lord himself did.

Wildgoose, therefore, having given his hostess half a crown for
her trouble (which she did not at all expect from such guests), took
his leave, and accompanied the Keeper into the woods.

CHAPTER V

A Stranger, of a peculiar Character, arrives

As the Keeper and his guests were in the amphitheatre before the
Gothic house, there arrived a tall elderly gentleman (with his
servant), whose curiosity had brought him to see the place. 'Well,'
says he, to a country fellow, who had been his guide, 'where are
these *turpentine* walks, which you told me of?' Then, alighting
from his horse, and surveying the structure, which represents the
ruin of a castle, over-grown with ivy; 'Aye,' says he, 'a very ancient
place! Probably one of the *castra æstiva*, or summer camps, of the
Romans; some appendage to Cirencester, I suppose, which was one
of the *castra hyberna*, or winter stations, of the Roman legions. The
castle itself was probably built during the Barons wars, in the reign
of Henry the Third, or of King John.'—'Aha! look ye there now,'
says the Keeper, smiling; 'so several gentlemen have thought. But,
Sir, I assure you, it was built by my present Lord, but a few years
ago; and his Lordship used to say, he could have *built* it as *old* again,
if he had had a mind.'—'Built by my present Lord!' cries the
gentleman with a frown; 'and were there no ruins of a castle here
before?'—'Not that I ever heard of,' replies the Keeper.—'Well,
for my part,' says the stranger, 'I don't at all approve of these

K

deceptions: which must necessarily mislead future antiquaries, and introduce great confusion into the English history. I don't wonder' (continues the stranger, turning towards Wildgoose) 'that any gentleman should wish to have his woods or gardens adorned with these venerable Gothic structures; as they strike the imagination with vast pleasure, both by the greatness of the object, and also by giving us a melancholy idea of their past grandeur and magnificence. But for a man to *build* a *ruin*, or to erect a modern house in the style of our Gothic ancestors—appears to me the same absurdity, and must be attended with the same inconvenience to posterity, as that which many people have of late run into, of having their pictures drawn in the habits of Vandyke or Sir Peter Lely; or that of our modern mint-masters, of representing our English Heroes in Roman armour and the dresses of antiquity. For though I myself have a great veneration for the Roman customs, yet this foolish practice, I think, destroys one considerable use of Pictures and Medals; that of conveying to posterity the habits and customs of the age we live in.'

'I find, Sir,' says Wildgoose, 'you are a connoisseur in these things; and, I suppose, have a taste for antiquities.'—'Sir,' replies the gentleman, 'I have some little taste that way; and took Cirencester in my road to Gloucester, not to see the races, I assure you, but to enquire after some of those ꝶoman coins which are found there in great abundance.'

As the Antiquary was talking, he pulled out his *sudarium*, or pocket handkerchief, to wipe his face, when two or three silver and copper medals (which he had met with at Cirencester) dropped out of his pocket: which he picked up, and began explaining them to Wildgoose and the company: upon which, Wildgoose observed, 'that the study of Medals was a curious study; but he could never be convinced of the utility of it.'—'The *utility* of it!' (replies the Virtuoso, with some vivacity) 'why as to that, I'll only refer you to Mr. Addison's Dialogues upon that subject; to which, I think, nothing can be added.

'But people often run themselves into difficulties,' (continued he) 'and lay themselves open to their antagonists, by resting their cause upon a wrong plea: every thing must be proved *useful*, forsooth! whereas I think it sufficient if some things are proved *agreeable* and entertaining. Why has not the imagination or fancy a right to be gratified, as well as the passions or appetites, in a subordinate degree, and under the directions of reason?

'If I were to dispute with a Methodist about luxury in food, or about the necessity of fasting and mortification; I should not think myself obliged to prove, that every thing we usually eat, was absolutely *necessary* to support life.'

'Sir,' says Wildgoose, interrupting him, 'I never heard that the Methodists laid any stress upon those legal observances of fasting or distinction of meats, but eat and drank just as other people do.'—'Probably they may,' replies the Virtuoso, 'notwithstanding their mortified pretensions. At least (from what I know of their self-denial) they are the last people with whom I would trust a wife or a daughter.

'But, however, suppose I were disputing, I say, with any super-stitious person upon the subject of luxury in eating and drinking, I should say, that bread and cheese (for instance) was an hearty, wholesome food; and the staff of life (as the saying is). But I should think it a sufficient defence of the lawfulness of eating cheese-cake or custard, by saying that it was *agreeable*. Thus we may say, of several arts and sciences; of Law, Physic, and Divinity; that they are necessary for the subsistence of society: but for Poetry, Paint-ing, Sculpture, and the like, I think it enough, if they are allowed to be ornamental, and to contribute to the recreation of man-kind.

'In short, Sir, if History, Chronology, and several other branches of polite literature, are allowed to be of any use to the world, the knowledge of Medals must also be allowed to have its share of merit; as instrumental in illustrating and confirming several par-ticulars in those sciences.'

'Why, Sir,' replies Wildgoose, 'I must confess myself to be one of those, who think only one branch of knowledge at all necessary or worth our pursuit: and that is, the knowledge of our fallen state, and of our redemption, as revealed in the Bible.'

The Antiquary stared at first with some astonishment at Wild-goose's declaration. But soon guessing at his religious turn, 'Well,' says he, 'to carry the matter still farther then, we could not under-stand the Bible (at least several expressions in it) without the assist-ance of this study.

'The history of the Jews, from the time of the Maccabees to the birth of Christ, was all obscurity and confusion; till Monsieur

Vaillant, from a collection of Greek Medals, had given the world a complete series of the Syro-Macedonian Kings.[1]

'And the title of EVERGETES, or Benefactor, which is found on the coins of the Antiochus's and the Ptolomey's, very well explains what is meant by the Gentile Kings being called *Benefactors*; which the Commentators, I think, made but bungling work of before.

'The Tribute-money, with Cæsar's Image and Superscription, was a Roman *Penny* or Denarius: and the Two-Pence, which the Good Samaritan is supposed to have given the Landlord for his care of the wounded Traveller, were two of those Denarii; or about *fifteen* pence of our money. These things, perhaps, might have been known, from a slight acquaintance with the collateral histories of those times: but still it is a satisfaction to see the very Coins which were then current, and which are preserved in the cabinets of the curious.'

'Ah!' says Wildgoose, 'I want no commentaries, nor any assistance, to understand the Scriptures. When God has once revealed himself to a man, every expression speaks comfort to his soul; and he can *feel* the truth of it, without any teaching or instruction. Neither do I doubt that, although all other helps should be lost, Providence would preserve the knowledge of the Scriptures in his *Church* to the world's end. I don't mean the established or *visible* Church (which, I am afraid, has departed from its own doctrines); but the *invisible* Church or Society of true Christians; by whatever denomination they are distinguished.'

As Wildgoose was launching beyond the comprehension of the Virtuoso, and they were now come into a beautiful avenue, which terminated upon a *visible* Church, the gentleman turned the discourse to the beauty of the prospect; and they being now come near the Tetbury road, Wildgoose took his leave, and, together with his trusty companion, proceeded on his journey towards Bath.

CHAPTER VI

Some Account of the Virtuoso

As soon as they were got out of sight of the Antiquary, Tugwell began to open. 'Od'slife!' quoth he, 'this is a desperate man for the *Romans*—I suppose he's one of your *Papishes*. I never heard of such a whimsical gentleman since I was born. His *sarvant* says, he almost starved one or two of his children, by breeding them up in the Roman way; for he would never let them eat till sun-set; and would never suffer his little boy to wear a hat, because the Romans, belike, went bare-headed. He makes his children, instead of shoes and stockings, wear leathern buskins, like Joseph and his brethren in the Bible.

'And his man says, he would have had the body of his eldest son, who died, burnt to ashes, because the Romans did so; but his wife would not consent to it. Nay, he threatens to put his daughters to death, if they marry without his consent, as the old Romans, he says, used to do.

'His man says, if the Gardener happens to dig up a piece of an old cream-pot, he'll lock it up in his cupboard, and call it a piece of Roman crockery-ware, such as they used to put the ashes of the dead in. And he says, they came ten miles out of their way to see this old castle and other curiosities.'

'Did you ask where he came from?' (says Wildgoose.) 'Yes,' replies Jerry, ' 'tis one Squire Townsend, and he comes out of ——shire.' Wildgoose's heart immediately rose to his mouth, and his colour changed; for he was now convinced it was Miss Townsend's father with whom he had been talking; and he wondered at his own stupidity in not discovering this before.

It instantly occurred to him, that Mr. Townsend was going to Gloucester in quest of his daughter; and he fancied he might have said many things to him in her favour, if he had known who he was: though, it is ten to one, he could have said nothing upon the occasion, but what would have been improper, and have done more harm than good.

Though Tugwell (as was observed) had some smattering of history himself; yet, as the Antiquary did not touch upon any of those legendary subjects with which Jerry had been chiefly conversant, such as the Travels of Joseph of Arimathea—the History

of Glastonbury Thorn—or any romantic accounts of the Holy
Land, and the like, he had thought it rather a dry discourse; and
beginning *to spit six-pences*¹ (as his saying was), he gave hints to
Mr. Wildgoose to stop at the first public-house they should come
to. But there was none till they came to Tetbury; where they went
into a second-rate inn, for fear of meeting with the same insults
which they had received at the Bell at Gloucester.

CHAPTER VII

An Hurley-burley in the Modern Taste

WILDGOOSE having been thoroughly fatigued the preceding day,
and not slept very soundly upon the floor at night; having also
breakfasted upon toast and ale (which he was not much used to);
he found himself drowsy and somewhat indisposed: he desired
therefore to go into a back parlour; and, getting an arm-chair,
took a comfortable nap, whilst Tugwell was smoking his pipe in
the chimney-corner.

When Wildgoose waked, he desired to have some little matter
got ready for his dinner. My Landlady had a daughter-in-law (a
pretty girl about eighteen), who officiated as Waiter, and went into
the parlour to lay the cloth. As our Preacher always found a particular propensity to exercise his talent on the young and handsome;
he could not forbear catechizing this fair maid, as she came backwards and forwards into the room, about the state of her soul. The
poor girl, conscious of her ignorance in the principles of religion,
blushed, and seemed distressed what answer to make; and, having
placed the spoon and pepper-box on one side of the table, and the
knife and fork in parallel lines on the other, would have made her
escape from so disagreeable a persecution. But Wildgoose, finding
his rhetoric had not force enough to detain her, laid hold on her
apron, and desired her 'to hear what he had to say; which,' he
assured her, 'was for her good: nay, that nothing could be more so:
that it was better than all the beauty in the world, and of more
value than thousands of gold and silver: that he himself was the
servant of God; and that he should be very happy, if he could
prevail upon her to love *him* above all things.'

Just at that instant Mrs. Tantrum, the Landlady, came into the parlour, having both hands filled with Wildgoose's dinner. She herself, though now as coarse as Pontius Pilate's Cook-maid, yet having been handsome in her youth, and being still amorously inclined, watched her daughter-in-law with a suspicious, or rather with a jealous eye. Seeing the stranger therefore thus engaged about her apron, and hearing the words, 'Beauty,' 'Love,' 'Gold and Silver,' she immediately concluded, that he was in *love* with her *beauty*, and was bribing her with gold and silver to her ruin. Mine Hostess then, being equally a stranger to Christian meekness and to delicacy, vented her rage, without much ceremony, first upon Mr. Wildgoose. Then (setting down the dishes which she had brought in, and falling foul upon the poor girl with her brawny fists) 'you saucy slut,' says she, 'have not I charged you, often enough, never to listen to any *foot*-passengers! but to leave the room, if ever they pretended to trouble their *heeds* about you? and here you stand with your brazen face—' As she was going on, scolding, and thumping her daughter's shoulders, Wildgoose thought himself obliged, as he had been the cause of the girl's stay, to explain his motives, and to rescue her from the consequences of it. His interposition, however, would of itself have made Mrs. Tantrum more outrageous. But Wildgoose, having rebuked her for her passion with some asperity, and having also in the scuffle unfortunately torn my Landlady's gown, this added to her fury, and gave her an opportunity, which she wanted, of venting her rage more effectually upon the ill-fated Pilgrim.

There is a certain farinaceous composition, which, from its being frequently used by our ancestors as an *extempore* supplement to a scanty dinner, has obtained the appellation of an *hasty pudding*. It is composed of flour and milk boiled together; and, being spread into a round shallow dish, and interspersed with dabs of butter, and brown sugar fortuitously strewed over it, give one no bad idea of a map of the sun, spotted about according to the modern hypothesis.[1]

A dish of this wholesome food, smoking hot, mine hostess had brought in one hand, and a plate of bacon and eggs in the other. And, upon Wildgoose's presumptuously interposing between her and her daughter (as has been related), Mrs. Tantrum's fury was infinitely augmented; and, snatching up the dish, she discharged the hasty pudding full in Wildgoose's face; which, with the oiled butter and melted sugar, ran down to the skirts of his plush-waistcoat, and made no very cleanly appearance.

Tugwell, hearing the uproar, was now come into the room; and, seeing Mrs. Tantrum in the condition of a tigress robbed of her whelps, attempted to lay hold of her arms, and prevent any farther efforts of her fury: but she, snatching up the other dish, of bacon and eggs, gave Jerry as warm a salute as she had done his master. And one of the poached eggs bursting in his face, and mixing with the greasy contents of the frying-pan, poor Jerry was in a worse plight even than his fellow-traveller.

Mrs. Tantrum, having now satiated her fury, came a little to herself again: when, reflecting upon the damage she had probably done herself, if her guests should refuse to pay for the dinner, which, though they had smelt, they had not tasted; and beholding likewise the visible effects of her unbridled passion, in greasing her floor, and making unnecessary work for herself and her servant; she was going to repeat the outrage upon her innocent daughter-in-law: but the girl had wisely withdrawn till the storm was over. She therefore sent the maid, to clean the room, and set things to rights again: and the travellers, having craved the maid's assistance in cleaning their persons, desired her to bring them the loaf and cheese, and a tankard of ale; with which they endeavoured to console themselves for the loss of the savoury food, by the sight of which they had been so disagreeably tantalized.

CHAPTER VIII

The Mistress of an Inn not easily to be converted

WHEN Mrs. Tantrum was a little recovered from the violence of her resentment, the daughter-in-law ventured to assure her, 'that the stranger had not offered to take the least freedom with her; but had only talked to her about Mr. Whitfield, and our Saviour Christ, and such sort of discourse.'—'Mr. Whitfield!' quoth she: 'I'll be hang'd then,' (says Mrs. Tantrum) 'if it is not one of these Methodists, that go about the country. Run, and take away the silver spoon and pepper-box! A pack of canting toads! I thought he looked like one of those *hypothetical* rascals. There was one of them at Salisbury, not long ago, married two wives; and another was hanged for sheep-stealing—Run, I say, and take away the pepper-box.'

The poor girl said, 'She did not think the gentleman would *steal* any thing neither, *for all* he talked about *religion*. He did not look like that sort of man, she imagined.'—Whilst they were thus debating the matter, Wildgoose and his friend came into the kitchen, to pay their reckoning; and Mrs. Tantrum, surveying them more calmly, could not discover any thing very thievish in their physiognomy. So, to make some little amends for the rough usage with which she had treated her guests, she dismissed them with a tolerably decent welcome,[1] and wished them a good journey. Wildgoose returned her compliment with a prayer for her conversion: and told her, 'that, unless God would give her grace to subdue her boisterous passions, she could no more relish the joys of Heaven, than an hog or a sow could a clean parlour.'—'Ay! ay! (added Tugwell) thou art a *vessel of wrath*, doomed to perdition.' —'I a *vessel of broth!* you pot-gutted rascal! no more than yourself! marry come up! what does the fool mean? Sure I know my own business best,' says Mrs. Tantrum; then concluded, in her own way, that 'every tub must stand upon its own bottom.'

CHAPTER IX

The Travellers pursue their Journey

POOR Wildgoose was a little chagrined at being suspected of carnal intentions; but comforted himself with recollecting several of the chosen Saints, who had been thus buffeted by Satan, and lain under the same groundless suspicions. But he would probably have been more shocked, if he had known that he was judged capable of stealing a silver spoon. These were consequences of his extravagance, which he could not foresee, and of which he had hitherto no conception. I have often thought, however, it is happy for us, that we do not know the half which is thought or said of us behind our backs, by the smiling Hostess or the surly Hostler, who attends us on our arrival at, or departure from, an inn upon the road.

Our sturdy Pilgrims, having sufficiently refreshed themselves, proceeded on their journey with great alacrity; and, as it was not yet past mid-day, pushed on to reach Bath that night. They travelled the whole afternoon without any incident worthy the notice of a grave Historian. But reaching Lansdown, within a few miles of Bath, towards sun-set, they spied a poor horse, which, being over-loaded, was fallen down, and struggling under his burthen: and very near him two men, instead of assisting the wretched animal, were scuffling and pummeling each other without mercy. One of them was a slender, gentleman-like man, and the other appeared to be a Butcher's servant, or something in that style. Wildgoose and his fellow-traveller having interposed, and parted the combatants, the Butcher began to vent his wrath upon his antagonist, 'D-mn your blood,' says he, 'who the devil are you? What, can't a man be in a passion, and beat his own horse, for *all* you, and be pox'd to you?'

Wildgoose, having rebuked him for his insolence and profaneness, applied his hand to the stern of the horse; who after some further efforts, being rouzed, the Butcher remounted him, rode off, and, instead of thanking Wildgoose for his assistance, calls out, 'D-mn you all together, for a pack of whores-birds as you are!' The gentleman, who had fought the Butcher, surveyed him for a moment with great indignation and contempt: then, refreshing himself with a pinch of snuff, 'There,' says he, 'there goes a true picture of English Liberty!'—'Pray, Sir,' says Wildgoose, 'if I may make so free, what was the subject of your altercation?' To which he replied in the following manner.

CHAPTER X

A Knight-errant of a peculiar Kind.
Compassion for dumb Creatures

'YOU see, Sir,' says the gentleman, 'how hard that poor beast is loaded. Now that brute of a fellow, instead of driving the horse before him (as he was probably ordered by his Master to do), had galloped him, loaded as he was, for near a mile along the road, in my sight; when the poor creature happened to trip, and come down with his rider, who began to bang him with that stick about the head with so much fury, that, if I had not interposed, he might probably have killed him upon the spot. My officiousness, however, only made the fellow change the object of his wrath: for he fell upon me with the same weapon; which however I wrested from his hands, and banged him with to some purpose; till, he running in to me, we came to that close engagement, from which you parted us.'

Wildgoose staring at the gentleman with marks of surprize,— 'My compassion for dumb animals' (continued he) 'is so excessive, that it often makes me quite miserable. Our sympathy and assistance is certainly due, in the first place, to our fellow-creatures of the human species, as they stand in a nearer relation to us, and as they hold a superior rank in the works of the creation. But, I own, the incapacity of a poor brute creature to utter his distress, and his want of reason to find out the means of relieving it, often plead more powerfully with me, than all the rhetoric of a beggar, practised in the art of moving compassion.'

'Yes,' replies Wildgoose; 'and I think, Sir, you have suggested the reason of this; because, in the latter case, there is often a suspicion of insincerity in the petitioner; whereas, in the former instances, undisguised nature, though void of speech, expresses herself in the most emphatical manner. For the same reason, the silent rhetoric of tears, or of bashfulness, is often more pathetic than all the oratorical flourishes in the world. And I dare say, Sir, the helpless condition of an *infant* in distress must affect you still more sensibly, than that of any of those dumb creatures for which you express so much concern.'

'I don't know,' replies the gentleman; 'it certainly ought to do so: but I cannot reason myself out of this strange effeminacy—nor do I recollect any instance of *human* distress, that has given me more pain, than the sight of a poor hare, for instance, almost *run down*, as they call it; to see her squatting behind an hedge; panting and listening, with her ears erect, to the cries of her pursuers, from whom her natural scent, augmented by the perspiration she is thrown into, makes it almost impossible for her to escape.

'I entirely agree with Mr. Addison, in applauding the humanity of the Sultan, who chose rather to cut off the sleeve of his robe, than awake his favourite Cat, which was asleep upon it. And I myself, in my walks, have often gone a furlong out of my way, rather than disturb a poor unwieldy Ox, that has been lying down

and chewing the cud; or than interrupt an innocent Lamb, that
was sucking its anxious dam.

'Nay; I have gone so far, as to erect an urn in my garden, as
a testimony of my compassion for dumb animals, with the inscription from Ovid's speech of Pythagoras,

> Quid meruistis, oves, placidum pecus—&c.
> Quid meruere boves, animal sine fraude dolisque,
> Innocuum?[1]
>
> What have ye done, ye flocks, a peaceful race!
> Or what the harmless ox, so void of guile,
> To merit death?'

'Why, as for those animals, which are fairly slaughtered, without
torture, for the support of human life,' (says Wildgoose) 'I can
easily reconcile myself to their fate: as the pain of death consists,
I believe, chiefly in the apprehension. And when it is instantaneous
(as in those cases it is or ought to be) they enjoy themselves, and
feel nothing till the stroke arrives; and the moment it does so, the
violence of it either deprives them of life, or at least of the sense of
pain. Mr. Pope has finely described this in his ethic epistles:

> The lamb, thy riot dooms to bleed to-day,
> Had he thy reason, would he skip and play?
> Pleas'd to the last, he crops the flow'ry food;
> And licks the hand, just rais'd to shed his blood.
> Oh! blindness to the future! kindly given,
> That each might fill the circle mark'd by heaven.'[2]

'Why, doubtless,' (returns the gentleman) 'one feels the most for
those animals that are tortured and abused. But, I think, none are
more so, than the generality of horses and beasts of burthen, from
a want of sensibility in the reasoning brutes to whose care they are
usually intrusted. You saw how little compassion that Butcher's lad
has shewn to his loaded Steed. And to see a noble creature start and
tremble at the passionate exclamation of a mere Yahoo of a stable-
boy; who, if he knew his own strength, could drive a dozen men
before him; I own, equally excites my pity and my indignation. I
never meet a string of Pack-horses, bending under their loads, but
my heart bleeds for the mute sufferers: and I make it a point of conscience to give them the road. Nay, I have, in my own mind, added
one more to the curses denounced by Moses against the unmerciful,
"Cursed be he that maketh the Pack-horse to go out of his way!" '

Here Tugwell could not forbear putting in his verdict. 'Well,' (says Jerry) 'the Taylor of our town is the best man for that. He keeps a horse to lett; but then he'll never lett him to any one, till he has made him promise faithfully, that the poor horse shall stand still to *do his needs*.'—The gentleman laughed at Tugwell's instance of compassion. But Wildgoose, silencing him with a significant look, observed, 'that the good man, to be sure, was merciful, even to his beast. And it is pity,' continued he, 'that cruelty to those animals cannot be provided against by our laws, as it was in a great measure by the laws of Moses.'

'Very true, Sir,' replies the gentleman; 'and as that cannot well be done in this land of *liberty*, I wish every gentleman would endeavour to supply that defect, by discouraging all cruelty of that kind, as far as his power or influence extends; and certainly, every parent should be particularly careful to instill principles of mercy and tenderness, to birds, beasts, and insects, into the tender minds of children. For my part, I profess myself a sort of Knight-errant in the cause: and assure you, have met with many such skirmishes as this which you found me engaged in, by interfering where I had no other motive but humanity and compassion.'

CHAPTER XI

The polite Philosopher

THE frank disposition of this gentleman (who called himself Graham) encouraged Wildgoose, as they walked along, to communicate something of his own pretensions: and he informed the gentleman, 'that he himself was a volunteer in the service of his fellow-creatures; and professed to regulate their opinions in a matter of much greater importance than any thing which regarded this life, even the salvation of their immortal souls.'

'I presume then' (says Mr. Graham) 'you are one of these Methodists, which have made such a noise in the world.' Wildgoose replied, 'that he might call him by what name he pleased; but what he professed was, to preach up true Christianity and the genuine doctrines of the Reformation.'

'Why,' returns Mr. Graham, 'though I have formerly conversed

much in the world, I have of late confined myself a great deal to
books and meditation, and the investigation of truth; the result of
which is, that I cannot reflect with patience upon the many absurd
practices and opinions which prevail in the world, and have often
been tempted to turn itinerant myself; and sally forth in order to
reform mankind, and set them right in various particulars.

'When I hear of a father's marrying his daughter against her
inclinations, and sacrificing her happiness to her grandeur; I am
ready, like the Spanish Don, to challenge him to mortal combat,
and rescue the unhappy victim from the power which he abuses.

'Though I am not in Parliament, nor am fond of politics, I could
not forbear giving the public my advice, in a pamphlet, upon the
Militia Act, Triennial Parliaments, and the necessity of *Sumptuary
Laws*.

'I have by me also a manuscript, which I call, *Literæ Hotten-
toticæ*; or Letters from a beautiful young Hottentot to her friends at
the Cape; giving an account of the many barbarous customs and
preposterous opinions which she had observed in our metropolis
during her three years abode amongst us.'

'But, Sir, you will pardon my freedom, when I declare, that of all
the opinions which have been the subject of my contemplation,
none appears more absurd to me, than that all Religion should be
made to consist in *thinking* rightly upon a few abstruse points;
which have been controverted ever since the Reformation, and
about which hardly any two persons think exactly alike. I really
believe, when the Methodists first set out (as Providence often
brings about salutary ends by irregular means) they did some good,
and contributed to rouse the negligent clergy, and to revive practical Christianity amongst us. But, I am afraid, they have since
done no small prejudice to Religion, by reviving the cobweb
disputes of the last century; and by calling off the minds of men
from practice, to mere speculation. For, by all the accounts I have
heard of late, if a man does but frequent their meetings regularly,
express himself properly upon Justification, and a few more of their
favourite topicks, he is immediately ranked amongst the Elect,
and may live as carelessly as he pleases in other respects; nay, may
be guilty of drunkenness, fornication, luxury, and what not: in
short, if a man does but *talk* and *look* like a Saint, he may, without
any reproach, live like a Sinner.'

'Sir,' says Wildgoose, 'whatever the case may be with a few

individuals who *call* themselves Methodists; you cannot say, that
any of those irregularities are the *necessary* consequence of their
principles.'

'No, Sir,' replies the gentleman; 'but they are the *probable* consequences of their practices; for, by being thus distinguished from
their brethren, they begin to look upon themselves as a sort of
privileged persons: and finding so much stress laid upon *thinking*
rightly, they begin to be more careless about *acting* properly;
and the original depravity of their nature returning upon them
thus unguarded, they are but too prone to relapse into the greatest
enormities; which reflection, I am afraid, might be confirmed by
too frequent experience: not to mention the tendency which their
particular doctrines of *Assurance* and *inward Feelings* have to make
men presumptuous, and to delude them to their own destruction.'

Wildgoose was not inclined to continue the dispute with a person who appeared so much prejudiced against his doctrines; and
who indeed was so full of reflections, made in his solitude, that he
would hardly give him leave to put in a word.

As their road, however, lay near a mile the same way, they talked
upon various subjects; and Wildgoose found, in the course of their
conversation, that Mr. Graham was quite a polite Philosopher, had
a competent knowledge of almost every science, had travelled over
most parts of Europe, and made many delicate and curious remarks
upon the manners and customs of the several people with whom he
had conversed.

But what gave a peculiar beauty to his conversation, was the
delicacy of his taste, which selected the most agreeable or the most
striking circumstances, on every subject; so that his descriptions
and narrations never became languid, by too minute a detail of
uninteresting particulars.

He now lived a very retired life; went sometimes to Bath, as a
mere spectator: but, having sequestered himself from the world
on a particular occasion, and having had sufficient experience of the
selfishness, malignity, and insincerity of the vulgar part of mankind, he confined himself to a few select friends; and by exercise
and temperance contrived to pass through the autumn of life, with
health, chearfulness, and tranquillity.

Mr. Graham was a man of that natural benevolence, that he
rather affected the misanthrope, than was really such. He invited
Wildgoose and his friend, therefore, with great cordiality, to refresh

themselves at his Hermitage (as he called it), which he pointed out to them amidst a tuft of lofty oaks, at a little distance, on the descent of the hill. Mr. Wildgoose, being impatient to join his Christian friends at Bath, would have waved the accepting this invitation: but Tugwell, having an habitual thirst upon him at this time of the year, said, 'he should be obliged to the gentleman for a draught of small-beer, or a cup of cyder.'

They therefore accompanied him to his habitation.

CHAPTER XII

A singular Mansion

Mr. Graham's house was almost concealed from the road by trees, and was literally 'founded upon a rock,' some craggy parts of which appeared rising upon each side of the house: a clear spring, which rose from the bottom of one of them, almost covered with moss, hart's-tongue, and other fountain-plants, determined the situation.

They entered, by a strong door, into a sort of porch or vestibule; on one side of which Mr. Graham shewed them a neat bed-room, about seven feet square; on the other side, a beaufet, and other conveniences about the same dimensions. He then took them into a parlour, elegantly furnished, of about twelve feet square, exclusive of a bow-window, which commanded an extensive prospect over a beautiful valley, terminated by a distant view of the city of Bath and its environs: and this was apparently the whole house.

Mr. Graham, however, took them down a few winding steps, cut out of the rock, to another room under the former; which served him for a kitchen, cellar, and all other accommodations for himself and his maid. She was a middle-aged woman, and was sitting there at work with her needle. But, to prevent all suspicion of her serving him in any other capacity than that of a servant, Mr. Graham had pitched upon a deserving person, with one eye, a protuberant shoulder, and one or two more accidental deformities, sufficient to stop the mouth of that infernal fury, Scandal herself. Besides his crooked Maid, Mr. Graham had an old cat with one ear, and a dog with one eye; who seemed originally to have had no other

merit than their *animality* to recommend them. A garden, proportioned to the house and its inhabitants, was laid out in a simple
taste, and stored with those fruits, flowers, herbs, and plants, which
were natural to the climate in which they were to grow.

Mr. Graham left Tugwell to drink some cyder, with his maid
Maritornes,[1] and took Mr. Wildgoose into his parlour, and offered
him a glass of something better—which it is not recorded that
Wildgoose refused.

As Mr. Graham opened the door of a little closet, or rather niche
in the wall, which contained his books and his cordials, Wildgoose
could not forbear fixing his eyes upon a small oval picture, of a
young lady, in a gilt frame, that was fixed in a panel, within-side
of the door; which Mr. Graham observing, shook his head with
a sigh, and said, 'the lady whom that picture represented, had
influenced the whole tenour of his life, and was the original cause
of his present retreat from the world.' Wildgoose expressing some
curiosity on that subject, and himself fetching a sympathetic sigh
on having the idea of Miss Townsend revived by the sight of that
picture; Mr. Graham said, 'his story could not be very interesting
to a stranger. But, Sir,' says he, 'as I take a sort of melancholy
pleasure in recollecting the occurrences of my youth; if you have
patience to hear me, I will relate the particulars.'—He therefore
began, without more ceremony, in the following manner.

CHAPTER XIII

Mr. Graham's Story [2]

'I AM a younger brother, of a younger branch, of a noble family;
but, partly by my own bad œconomy in the former part of life, and
partly by that of my father, I have at present but a slender income;
yet sufficient to live very comfortably in my present situation.
I was bred at the University, and after that was sent to the Temple:
and when a young man there, went to make a visit to my sister,
who was married to a Baronet in the northern part of this county.'
(Here Wildgoose listened with a more earnest attention). 'During
my stay here, we were invited to a supper and a ball at a neighbouring gentleman's, where was a great deal of genteel company.

L

Amongst the rest, there was a Clergyman's daughter, whom I will call Ophelia, who had the character of a learned lady and a great wit. She was tolerably handsome, but had a very melancholy air: which, upon enquiry, I found to be the effect of a disappointment in her first love, by the sudden death of a man of fortune, to whom she was upon the verge of being united in marriage. As she thought it a kind of indecorum to mix in the gaiety of the company (though she had been invited with a good-natured intention to divert her melancholy), Ophelia sat by in a bow-window in the room; and, as I was always of a studious turn, and not fond of dancing, I chose to keep her company.

'We two were of course engaged in a separate conversation. But, instead of what is usually meant by a Wit, a pert girl that values herself upon saying smart things with a saucy petulance; I found her a young woman of great good sense and delicacy of sentiment, and thoroughly versed in all the best writers in the English language; and even the translations from the classicks; upon whose several beauties and defects she passed sentence, with a penetration and judgment, superior to any one I had ever conversed with.

'In short, I was quite charmed with this young lady's conversation, which of course brought on a personal attachment; and I made an errand to her father's the very next day, under a pretence of enquiring after his daughter's health, and how she got home. He was a very learned and a very sensible man, but had very small preferment: and, as he had exerted all his abilities in instructing his daughter; so he had gone to the utmost limits of prudence, in dressing her out rather above her rank. However, in other respects, they lived in a frugal, though genteel manner; and I was so pleased with my quarters, that I stayed all night, with my servant and two horses; and repeated my visits very frequently.

'You will imagine, from this account, that I met with a very cordial reception from the young lady. But this was by no means the case. I found her affections still so much attached to their first object, that it was near half a year, before I appeared to have made any impression upon her heart. After this, however, we continued an intimacy for above two years: during which time we lived in all the innocent endearments of a mutual fondness; and I was determined to make her my wife.'

CHAPTER XIV

Mr. Graham's Story continued

'YOU will wonder, no doubt,' says Mr. Graham, 'what prevented my marrying Ophelia immediately. Why, nothing but my absolute dependance on my mother for my future support. She had a large jointure; and, as I was a favourite, she promised to increase my younger brother's fortune by what she could save out of her annual income. I had a considerable legacy left me by a relation. But, as I had lived very expensively, I was obliged to make free with the principal, and had almost run through it: so that I had reason to fear my mother's resentment, who, you may suppose, was not at all pleased with this indiscreet engagement; as it not only disappointed her in her hopes of my marrying advantageously in point of fortune, but involved me in a life of indolence, quite inconsistent with my study of the Law, and making any figure in my profession. She therefore made use of every prudent stratagem to break off my attachment to this young creature: in which alas! she at length succeeded.

'While I was in London for a month, at my mother's earnest request, who had a house in town; I received an anonymous letter, full of invectives against the Clergyman, his daughter, and in short against the whole family. As I was convinced many of them were without foundation, so I had good reason to believe the principal aspersion upon the young lady herself, was entirely so; which was, "that she had got a habit of drinking spirituous liquors, for her private amusement."

'I was greatly shocked at the contents of this letter; but thought it unjust and ungenerous to be influenced, in an affair of such importance, by a letter of that kind, which was evidently written with a malicious intent.

'I immediately, therefore, went down to my sister's, with a design to come to an eclaircissement with poor Ophelia; or at least to inspect her conduct more narrowly in the particular alleged; though, I confess, I was shocked at the want of generosity in such a proceeding, with regard to a person, with whom I had had so long an intimacy, without the least reason for such a suspicion. I recollected indeed, that she would drink two or sometimes three glasses of wine after dinner, without those squeemish airs, which some ladies affect. But I have always thought it a good rule in these cases, "that a woman, who, upon proper occasions, refuses *one* glass in public, will drink *two* or *three* in private."

'When I came to Lady ——'s, (my sister); I found there a young lady of the neighbourhood upon a weeks visit to my sister. She was a young woman of good fortune; and a smart sprightly girl; and one that I might probably have liked well enough, if my affections had not been pre-engaged.

'I shewed my sister the letter which I had received; at which she affected a great surprise: but added, "that she was afraid most of the facts alleged, had too good a foundation." And with regard to the principal accusation with which the young lady was charged, she used so many plausible arguments to convince me of the reality of it, with so many artful insinuations, that I began to waver in my opinion of the matter: and, in short, instead of waiting on Ophelia, as I ought to have done, and as I at first intended, I was prevailed upon only to write her a letter; in which, after some excuses from the imprudence of such an engagement, as my entire dependance on my mother would probably involve us both in indigence and distress, I desired the affair might proceed no farther.

'This bare-faced declaration produced such an answer as I had reason to expect from a girl of Ophelia's spirit; whom I had quite teazed into a return of affection, and now very unhandsomely, not to say basely, deserted; so that her resentment, though so well founded, contributed to abate my fondness: and I now thought myself at liberty to attend to the coquetry of Miss —— (whom I shall call Lavinia), upon whom my sister had prevailed to act a part; and to play off her artillery, on purpose to draw me off from my former engagement.

'I proceeded so far, as frequently to ride out with her alone (attended only by a servant); and she (very maliciously) made me accompany her one day, to dine at a gentleman's house in the village where poor Ophelia lived, and by whose very door we must necessarily pass.

'This behaviour, though it probably extinguished the love, yet it so far wrought upon the *honest* pride of Ophelia, that, in a few days, it brought on a fit of distraction; which in a few months terminated in her death.

'This shocking event of my perfidy awakened my fondness,

and alarmed my conscience; and I immediately quitted my sister's house (where the artful Lavinia was still detained), and returned to London. I had been there but a few days, when I received, inclosed in a frank, a large packet; which I found sealed with Ophelia's seal, and the direction in her hand-writing. My mother and a younger sister were in the room; the moment I saw the seal and superscription, the letter dropt out of my hand, and I almost fainted away in my chair. My mother and sister ran to my assistance, reasoned with me upon my folly; and, by my permission, my sister opened and perused the letter.

'The case was this. The cause of my deserting the celebrated Ophelia was not long a secret; and coming to her ears, though she disdained to vindicate herself to a man who could treat her so ungenerously, yet she had written a long defence of her conduct, and pointed out, almost to a demonstration, from what quarter the malicious tale had sprung; and this she had ordered to be delivered to me after her decease.

'The person hinted at, as the conductor of this wicked artifice, was Lady ——— my sister; against whom I vented my indignation; and could hardly preserve the decency due to my mother, for opposing a match, upon which my happiness depended. However, instead of settling again to the study of the Law, I found myself incapable of applying to any thing.

'I determined, therefore, by way of diverting my melancholy, immediately to go abroad, and rambled all over Europe for four or five years; at the end of which, I was recalled by the death of my mother; which event was rather seasonable, as I was almost reduced to the last hundred pounds of my own fortune.

'I took possession of five thousand pounds, which she left me, and which brings me in about two hundred pounds a year. I left the north of England, where I was born; changed my name; and came and built this Cottage near Bath; where I have lived these ten years, and where I intend to pass the remainder of my days.'

CHAPTER XV

Mr. Graham's Way of Life

WHEN Mr. Graham had finished his story, Mr. Wildgoose said, 'he was unwilling to interrupt him in his narration;' but added, 'that an event of this kind had happened, when he was a boy, in almost the next village to that where he was born; but (as he had often heard the story) the gentleman's name was ———.'

Mr. Graham changed colour, and said, 'that was his real name; and that he was the guilty person.'—'Well,' says Wildgoose, 'the poor old gentleman (Ophelia's father) is now very infirm, and, by various unlucky accidents, in great distress.'—'Good God!' cries Mr. Graham, 'is he still alive? Why, before I went abroad, I had begged leave to erect an Urn to poor Ophelia's memory; and by the person whom I employed for that purpose, was then informed that her unhappy father was at the point of death, of a broken heart.

'But my meeting with you, Sir, is very providential; and it will be the greatest pleasure to me, to make some atonement for my wickedness, and even the expence I put the family to, by relieving his distress; which I will take the first opportunity of putting in execution.'

Wildgoose observed, 'that Mr. Graham's expression of "making an atonement for his wickedness," was somewhat exceptionable; as our Saviour had made a sufficient atonement and satisfaction for the sins of the whole world; and that we should be cautious in ascribing any *merit* to our own good works.'

'Zounds! Sir,' says Mr. Graham (who had no patience with such nice distinctions), 'you don't think there is any sin in relieving the distressed, upon whatever motive it is done? As for placing any merit in such an action, I should think myself a rogue if I did not do it, in the present case: but if so much caution is necessary upon such occasions, a man, that happens to tumble into a river or a ditch, may be drowned or suffocated, whilst we are deliberating about the proper motive or state of mind, with which we are to pull him out again.'

Mr. Wildgoose did not think proper to reply to a man of so warm a temper; but observed (by way of changing the discourse) 'that Mr. Graham seemed under a necessity almost of living the life of an Hermit; as the dimensions of his habitation would not admit of much company.'

'Why,' says Mr. Graham, 'a life of absolute solitude is a visionary and unnatural state, and can only subsist in poetry and romance. I don't pretend to live upon roots and rock-water; though I can feast upon mutton and potatoes, and a bread pudding. And though I don't love mobs and routs, I would not have you imagine I never entertain any company in my cell; I have two or three friends, of the same simple taste with myself; who (for the sake of varying the scene) frequently eat their morsel with me, when we wait upon ourselves, and limit each other as to the number and variety of the particulars that are to constitute the entertainment.

'As to your paltry little Esquires, or those who have not sense enough to dispense with the forms of life, or come without a servant to wait behind their chair; puppies, who will drink a bottle or two with you in private, and perhaps not know you in public; I affront them, if ever an impertinent curiosity brings them to my cottage— so that I am seldom troubled with any visitors of that kind.

'Neither am I very fond of the company of Ladies, out of regard to the memory of poor Ophelia; the recollection of whose excellencies makes the generality of female conversation truly insipid— *Deleo omnes dehinc ex animo mulieres*[1]—I blot from my memory every other woman; those every-day beauties (as Terence calls them) who have nothing but their sex to recommend them.'

Mr. Wildgoose was a little scandalized at the warmth of temper and appearance of uncharitableness in Mr. Graham; though (as was observed before) this misanthropy was rather in speculation, than in practice; as he could not treat any one, that came to his house, without the highest politeness.

Wildgoose now looking at his watch, Mr. Graham said, 'if he was impatient to get to Bath, he would shew him a shorter road over the hill;' which he accordingly did: and having pointed out the great road to them again, he left the two pilgrims to pursue their journey.

BOOK V

CHAPTER I

The two Pilgrims arrive at Bath

'SOME people,' (says an Italian writer upon politeness) 'in the midst of an agreeable conversation, are apt to fall asleep. This' (says he with great solemnity) 'is by no means a *genteel* custom, as it shews a contempt of our company.'[1]

Now, if I might differ from so profound an Author, I should rather impute the infirmity of such drowsy people to want of taste, than to a contempt of their company: and if the Reader should have taken a nap in the midst of the last Chapter; for my own credit, I would willingly impute his drowsiness to the same principle. But to proceed.

The setting sun now gilded the summit of the mountains and the tops of the highest towers, when the two pilgrims came within sight of Bath. Upon the first view of that elegant city, Tugwell, who had received all his ideas of grandeur from his Bible, and whose head always ran upon what he had read of the Holy Land, observed, 'that Bath seemed to be situated like Jerusalem, according to David's description of it:

> As mighty mountains huge and large
> Jerusalem about do close.'[2]

'According to Sternhold and Hopkins' description of it, you mean,' says Wildgoose.—'Well, well, Master; that's as our Clerk sings it. But I suppose your Worship likes the *new diversion* better.' —'No,' says Wildgoose, 'I like neither of the poetical Versions so well as the plain prose.

'But' (continues Wildgoose) 'Bath seems huddled so close together, that I should compare it to Jerusalem in another respect, "Jerusalem is built as a city that is at unity in itself."[3] And yet perhaps this little place may be divided into as many parties, and abound as much in scandal, envy, and malice, as London itself.'

Wildgoose, however, being vastly struck with the richness of the valley, and the elegance of the buildings, especially of the villas dispersed on the surrounding hills, remarkable for the beauty of their verdure, observed, 'that, however fruitful the Land of Canaan might be formerly, when inhabited by a populous nation and properly cultivated; yet, by all accounts of modern travellers, the present face of the country about Jerusalem was not to be compared to the environs of Bath. Though I cannot but wonder,' continued he, 'that any one should doubt the veracity of the sacred writers in their encomiums upon the ancient fertility of that country, which is confirmed by the concurrent testimony of several Pagan authors: yet I am inclined to think, it was called "a land flowing with milk and honey," partly in opposition to the arable lands of Egypt, and partly in preference to the sandy deserts through which they were to pass in their retreat from thence; neither of which were to be compared to the rich pastures or vine-clad hills of Palestine.'

Wildgoose and his friend Tugwell, who were now come into the town, cut but a dusty figure, in comparison with the spruce inhabitants of Bath; which made them desirous of getting under cover as soon as possible: and Tugwell, espying a sign whose device struck his fancy, exhorted his Master to set up his staff there, especially as the house seemed suitable to Mr. Wildgoose's appearance in his present voluntary humiliation.

Tugwell was no sooner entered, than he almost mechanically called for 'a cup of the best.' 'Ay! my Lad,' (says mine Host, who was a facetious sort of fellow) 'thou shalt have it in the turning of a pork griskin. But let's see; what hast thou got in thy wallet? some *Run*[1] *Tea*, or some *Welsh Stockings?* what dost thou deal in? Cry thy trade.'—'No, no,' says Jerry, 'we don't deal in *stockings* nor shoes neither; though, for that matter, as good shoes as ever trod the ground have gone through my hands. But no matter for that. I hope God has called me and my Master here to a better occupation.'

My Landlord, not being willing to throw away any longer conversation on such guests, without any further reply, stept to the tap, drew some ale, and, having blown off the froth, which occupied a third part of the cup, and drunk the Traveller's health in another third, he presented the remainder to Tugwell, who had called for it. Whilst Jerry was drinking, my Landlord surveyed Wildgoose with more attention: and observing in him an air rather above a common Pedlar, asked 'if the gentleman would not please to walk into another room.'—Tugwell replied, 'that, to be sure, his Worship had not been used to sit in a kitchen; but *howsomever*, my Master (says he) *scorns* to despise a poor *parson*; and is not above keeping company with any good Christian.'—'Hey-day! good Christian!' quoth my Landlord; 'why, we are all good Christians, I hope; but, I fancy, thou hast left off *mending* of shoes, and art set up for a *mender* of *souls*. I suppose, thou art one of these *Methodites*, or *Mithridates*, or what the devil do you call 'em? Why, sure a gentleman may be a good Christian, without keeping company with all the Tag-rags and Scrubs in the country.'

Then, turning to Wildgoose, having heard Tugwell call him his Worship, my Landlord went a step further; and, to make amends for his first neglect, 'Won't your *Honour* walk into the parlour?' says he. 'What shall I get your *Honour* to eat?' This was language which mine Host had learned from the Footmen, who greatly frequented his house; and who, I have observed, rather than not discover that they have been used to wait upon people of fashion, will bestow those honourable appellations on the lowest of their acquaintance, and even on persons whom they despise.

And here, by the way, I cannot but lament the ridiculous prostitution of titles of distinction amongst the inferior part of mankind in this age. In the glorious days of Queen Elizabeth, *Master* was esteemed a very respectful address to any one beneath the dignity of a Peer. And even in James the First's reign, *your Worship* was the highest degree of adulation or respect with which a Servant or a Vassal approached his Lord, or the Master whom he served. From the French, I believe, in the last century, we learned to apply the monosyllable *Sir* to any one, whom we considered as greatly our superior. But now, *your Honour* is the title universally given, to every one that appears in a clean shirt and powdered wig, by the Drawer, the Chair-man, or the Shoe-black; who are unwilling to hazard the loss of a customer, by addressing him in a style beneath his real or fancied importance.

In higher life indeed, where particular titles are appropriated to particular ranks or offices, this confusion has been hitherto avoided. Our Sovereign, the fountain of honour, is at present content with that of *Sacred Majesty*, one of the lowest attributes of Divinity; as our Religion does not admit of downright Deification. Neither has any one, as yet, been guilty of so presumptuous a piece of flattery, as to bestow the title of *Majesty* on any subject whatsoever.

And, as the several orders of our Nobility are created by Patent, and their titles purchased either by money or merit; it is not usual, amongst that *right honourable* fraternity, to invade each other's property in that respect, or to give the superior titles to those of inferior quality. But amongst the aforesaid lower race of mortals, as the love of false honours increases in proportion to the decrease of real worth; and as the base multitude pay that respect to money which is properly due to merit, it is not easy to say to what a ridiculous extreme this humour may at length be extended: and I should not be surprized, in process of time, to hear an Haberdasher saluted, with, 'A coach, your *Grace!*' or to see a Shoe-black importune a walking Taylor with, 'Black your shoes, your *Majesty!*' But to return to our Pilgrims.

CHAPTER II

Popular Reports sometimes a little erroneous

MR. WILDGOOSE did not chuse to accept of my Landlord's invitation of going into a room at present; but asked him, 'whether there were any of those Methodists' (as he meant to call them) 'in Bath.'—'Are there?' says mine Host. 'Yes, I believe there are; enough to turn the heads of all the Prentices and Journeymen in the nation. I am sure, I cannot keep a Chambermaid, or a Tapster; but the toads must be singing Psalms, or preaching to my Customers, and be pox'd to 'em, from morning to night.'—'Well, but you should not blame the poor creatures for being too good,' says Wildgoose.—'Too good!' replies my Landlord: 'I don't know that they are any better than other folks. I *loves* a Psalm at church, as well as a merry Catch over a glass of liquor; but to be singing *Sol Fa's* all day long, in such a house as ours is, I *does not* approve of it, it's *perphane*; it's quite *perphane!*

'Besides!' continues my Landlord, (without giving Wildgoose room to reply) 'they are some of the worst people *that is*; there is nothing but whoring and rogueing amongst them. There was one of 'em, at Gloucester, (as a gentleman's servant told me that[1] very

morning) caught in bed with a Millener's prentice but last week;
nay, and one of them is in Gloucester Gaol at this time, for setting
fire to the Cathedral.'—'Not to the Cathedral,' (says a Footman
who was drinking in the house) 'but to some other Church, as this
gentleman here told me.'—'D--n thee,' (says another Footman)
'I did not say, set fire to a Church; but to the *little* Church, as they
call the Methodists' meeting.' Wildgoose and Jerry stared at this
intelligence; and, after his astonishment would give him leave,
Wildgoose assured him, 'that he came from Gloucester but yesterday morning; and that there was not a word of truth in what he had
heard.' He told him, however, the probable foundation of the latter
report, and the story of the gun-powder plot: but concluded with
reprimanding him for his credulity; and made some reflections
upon the malignity of the world, and the absurdity of those popular
stories, which are so freely propagated by the vulgar part of
mankind.

CHAPTER III

Landlord alters his Tone. A Female Saint

M Y Landlord now began to smell a rat; and, as it was his business
to adapt himself to the taste and principles of his customers, he
suddenly changed his tone, and said, 'that, to be sure, some of the
Methodists were good sort of people, for that matter; and did a
great deal of good in the world; and were very charitable to the
poor. And they *preaches* main well (as they do say); but for my
part,' continues he, 'I never was at their Meeting.'

'What part of the town do they meet in then?' says Wildgoose.—
'Why, I don't know; but, here! Deborah,' (says he to a woman that
had been washing in the back kitchen) 'give the Gentleman an
account of your little Tabernacle in Avon-street, or where the
deuce is it?'—'Good lack-a-day!' (quoth Deborah, wiping her
hands upon her apron) 'What! has the gentleman a mind to go and
hear our Preaching then? Why, to be sure, we have some fine men
come amongst us. I am a *'Scriber*; I can introduce the Gentleman
any night; I *'scribes* three-pence a week. Ah! Sir, we have such
soul-searching teachers! Such *ravishing* ministers! They come *so*

close to the point; and does so *grapple* with the sinner! They probe his sores to the very quick; and *pour in such comfortable balsam!* And (as Mr. Twangdillo told us last night) though it may pain; yet, like physic in the bowels, it pains us to some purpose;—and, to be sure, as he said, Conversion follows Conviction, as naturally as Thread does the Needle.'[1]—Whilst the good woman was thus retailing her panegyric, she leaned over the chair of a Journeyman Taylor, who was drinking a penny pot, and breathed in his face such blasts, so strongly tinctured with gin and Scotch snuff, that the Taylor cried out, 'Why, Dame, thou savourest strongly of the *Spirit* truly. I fancy thou art a little intoxicated to-night.'— '*Tosticated! Tosticated!* I scorn your words,' cries Deborah. 'I defy the best man in Bath, to say, Black is my eye; or that I was ever *consarned* in liquor, since my name was Deborah. *Tosticated!* No; God help me! I have drunk nothing to-day, but a little tea for breakfast, and half a pint of ale at my dinner, except a little still'd water, that my Mistress gave me in the morning to keep out the wind; and I am sure there is no harm in that: is there now, Mr. Alcock?'

Mr. Alcock (which was my Landlord's name) put a stop to the torrent of her eloquence, by enquiring again the place of their meeting: which when he had learned, he sent his Tapster to shew Wildgoose the house, where he was directed to some of the most considerable of the Fraternity.

CHAPTER IV

Wildgoose attends a Bath Meeting

WHEN Mr. Wildgoose had made himself known, he was surprised to find that his fame had reached Bath before him: for during his residence at Gloucester, several passengers, who had come that road, hearing that a young man of some fortune was commenced Methodist Preacher, had brought the news to Bath, not without enlarging his fortune from four to seven or eight hundred pounds a year; so that Wildgoose came with the prepossession in his favour, 'that he was the famous Preacher, who made so much noise at Gloucester.' The Brethren, therefore, were not a little pleased

with a convert of so much supposed consequence; and accordingly
received him with great cordiality and distinction.

At their next meeting, Wildgoose attended as one of the audience;
and both he and Tugwell were greatly delighted with their spiritual
hymns (which Deborah had assured them were very melodious.)
But when the Preacher, who, that night, was neither better nor
worse than a Journeyman Stay-maker, began to display his
eloquence; Mr. Wildgoose, who had had something of an academical education, could hardly digest the homeliness of his
language, or the meanness of his comparisons; and was a little
mortified with the apprehension that he himself probably should
make no better figure in the Rostrum. But being encouraged by
some of his friends, who reminded him of the salubrious effects of
his preaching at Gloucester, and also of the heinous sin of 'wrapping
up his talent in a napkin;' he was prevailed upon to promise, 'that he
would exhibit himself the next evening:' which accordingly he did;
and displayed his oratory before a crowded audience, with no small
approbation and applause.

CHAPTER V

He harangues on the Parade

WILDGOOSE's fame began now to be trumpeted forth amongst
all ranks of people. And, as he had naturally a good elocution, an
harmonious voice, and an agreeable person; he was considered
by the Society at Bath, as a proper instrument to represent their
doctrines to advantage, in an harangue to the company that resorted
thither.

Accordingly it was given out, 'that a young gentleman from
Oxford, who had renounced the ease and affluence of a good
fortune for the sake of religion, was to preach on the grand Parade
the next morning.'

The greatest charity we can bestow on people of fashion, at a
public place, is the furnishing them something new, to talk of. A
new Singer, a new Philosopher, a new Rope-dancer, or a new
Preacher, are objects equally amusing to the idle and indolent that
frequent Bath. The company therefore adjourned, from the Pump-

room to the Parade, in eager expectation of seeing and hearing this youthful adventurer.

But Mr. Nash,[1] though he himself had greatly reformed and regulated the manners and behaviour of his subjects in the public room; yet, being orthodox in his tenets, and very well content with the present state of religion amongst them, he did not desire any reformation in that article. Having notice, therefore, of this intended preachment, he got ready his band of music, with the addition of two or three French-horns and kettle-drums: and as soon as the Orator had exhibited his person on the Parade, stretched forth his hand, and (like Paul in the Cartoon) was *in act to speak*, Nash gave the signal for the grand chorus of 'God save the king.' The music struck up; and playing so loyal a piece of music, no one had the hardiness to interrupt them. Nay, a majority of the company were probably pleased with Nash's humour; and, it being now breakfast-time, the mob was easily dispersed.

Mr. Wildgoose's friends, however, would not tamely give up a point of this importance; but took an opportunity that very evening, when the company were going to the rooms, to produce their champion on a sudden; and met with better success.

As Mr. Nash had given out that Wildgoose was mad, he made use of St. Paul's words for his text; 'I am not mad, most noble Festus, but do speak forth the words of soberness and truth.' Wildgoose did not confine himself, however, to the words of the text; but (as he had been instructed by the Brethren) inveighed with great severity against luxury in dress, cards, dancing, and all the fashionable diversions of the place; and even against frequenting the rooms with the most innocent intentions of recreation and amusement.

As soon as Wildgoose had finished his harangue, which was almost of an hour's duration, a jolly[2] Footman (about the size of one of the gentlemen in the horse-guards) bustling through the crowd, stretched out a gigantic fist, and presented the Orator a single card. Wildgoose, who had not, of late, been much in genteel life,[3] could not guess at the meaning of this ceremony; but imagined it was some joke upon his invective against *gaming*. The Footman, however, with a surly air, cried out, 'Read it, friend! read it; my Lady desires to see you at her lodgings here on the Parade.' Wildgoose then, perusing his billet, read as follows:

'A Lady, who is disgusted with the world, desires half an hour's conversation with Mr. Wildgoose, as soon as he is at leisure.'

Wildgoose, after a short pause, told the Footman, 'he would wait on the Lady immediately.' So, as soon as he had given a short answer to two people (one a Fan-painter, the other a Butterfly-catcher) who had consulted him about the lawfulness of their several professions, he followed the Footman to his Lady's place of abode.

CHAPTER VI

A Digression on Message-Cards

THERE are few customs generally prevailing in the world, how absurd soever they may appear, which had not some real propriety or convenience for their original: but when the fashion is once established amongst the polite, it descends of course amongst the vulgar; who blindly imitate it, as such, without any regard to its primitive institution. Thus, for instance, the conveying messages by a Card, was introduced into the fashionable world, as the readiest expedient against the blunders and stupidity of ignorant servants. And, it must be confessed, that in some characters, and on some occasions, this practice has not only no impropriety, but carries with it a genteel air of ease and negligence; and really saves a great deal of unnecessary trouble, both to the person that sends, and him that receives the message.

The Man of pleasure, who transacts his most important concerns in a coffee-house or a tavern; or the modern Lady, the whole sphere of whose existence is a drawing-room, can never be supposed without a Card in readiness on every emergency: and therefore parties at Whist can no way be more aptly formed, nor messages of compliment more elegantly conveyed, than by these diminutive tablets; which are generally suited to the subject, to the genius, and laconic style of the parties concerned.

But, on the other hand, what can be more absurd than this practice in more serious characters, and on occasions of more solemnity? How remote from probability is it, that a grave Divine, who is continually inveighing against the vices and follies of the age, should have a pack of soiled Cards in his pocket, ready for his engagements of business or pleasure? or that a venerable

Counsellor, who is continually surrounded with Briefs, Leases, or Acts of Parliament, should prefer a trifling Card, in transacting business with his Client, before a shred of parchment, or even a scrap of common paper? And I should have kicked my Taylor the other day, for minuting down the dimensions of my sleeves and pocket-holes upon a Card—if I had not luckily recollected that his last bill was unpaid.

Neither are Message Cards proper on *all occasions*, any more than in persons of all characters or professions. It is a known impropriety in a French Marquis, who, coming to pay his devotions at the shrine of a Saint, whilst his image was gone to the Silver-smith to be repaired, left a Card for his Godship, to acquaint him with his intended visit. And though a certain Lady, near St. James's, very innocently invited a woman of quality to her rout, by a *whisper* at the Communion-table; yet, (in my humble opinion) she could not so decently have slipped a *Card* into her Ladyship's hand, at so sacred a place as the Altar.

Granting, however, the general and unlimited use of this pasteboard correspondence; there is yet a propriety to be observed, and many absurdities to be avoided, in the choice of the Cards; according to the persons addressed, or the occasions on which we address them.

It is too obvious an hint, and, I suppose, too trite a piece of adulation to a fine woman, to convey our compliments to her on the 'Queen of Hearts:' as, on the contrary, it would have been an affront to a late East-India Governour[1] (though he laboured under so groundless a slander) to have enquired after his health by sending him the 'Knave of Diamonds.' The Deuce or two of Clubs, I think, should be appropriated to challenges and duels. And the Black Aces should be entirely *discarded* in our correspondence with Ladies of character; as the Nines and Tens are at Ombre or Quadrille.[2] But these hints are left to be improved by the facetious Mr. ——.

My intention was chiefly to observe, that the disgusted Lady (mentioned in the last chapter) should have made use of paper with black edges, in a message to Mr. Wildgoose, rather than a profane Card; which he could not but consider as a diabolical invention, and consequently as intended for an affront to so pious a man. However, he obeyed the summons (as has been related), and attended the Lady in her own apartment.

M

CHAPTER VII

Tête à Tête

MR. WILDGOOSE was introduced by the Footman into an handsome dining-room, elegantly furnished. The Lady received him in a genteel dishabille; sitting, or rather leaning, on a rich sofa, in such a posture as necessarily displayed an handsome foot, somewhat above the instep. She was an agreeable woman, about six and twenty. And though her face was not so exquisitely beautiful as it seemed to have been in her earlier days, yet, being shaded by a chip hat, and receiving a gloss from a white sattin night-gown in which she was dressed, she made upon the whole no unpalatable figure.

I would not insinuate, that she had any intention to captivate our Hero. Yet thus much, I believe, is certain: that a woman who has once been handsome, and experienced the power of her charms, seldom lays aside the hopes of making conquests; but contracts an habitual fondness for admiration, and would be disappointed in not receiving that incense even from a man whom she despised.

Mr. Wildgoose, however, was at present no despicable object. He was now in his twenty-fifth year. He was well made, and had an agreeable countenance, which his late abstemious way of life had improved, by giving quite a delicacy to his complection. His hair was of a dark brown; and though it had not received the fashionable frizure, it was grown thick enough to shade his face, and long enough to curl. And his dress, though plain, was tolerably neat and becoming.

In short, though Mrs. Booby[1] (which was the name of this Lady) really fancied she had occasion for some ghostly advice; yet probably she might not have thought of this ceremony, if she had not liked the person of her Casuist; whom she viewed, as he was declaiming, from the window of her apartment.

After bowing to Mr. Wildgoose, and desiring him to sit down, she pulled out her fan; and having played it a little, in a negligent manner, said, 'she should make no apology for giving him this trouble, as she was convinced, from his character, he would not refuse his advice to any one in affliction.'

Wildgoose bowed, and made a proper speech upon the occasion, and she proceeded.

'In short, Sir,' says she, 'I am sick of the world. But, that you may be a better judge of my situation, I will beg leave to trouble you with a short history of my past life; which will let you into the nature of my present uneasiness.'

Wildgoose expressed his earnest desire to give her some spiritual consolation; and Mrs. Booby thus began.

CHAPTER VIII

Mrs. Booby's Story

'WHEN I was about nineteen, I came with my mother for the first time to Bath: and, whether there was a scarcity of beauty there that season; or whether, in my bloom, I might not be reckoned tolerably handsome; I don't know.' Here Wildgoose bowed again; and muttering a complaisant speech, Mrs. Booby blushed, and went on. 'Well, Sir, as I was going to say, I found myself in great vogue; much caressed by the gentlemen, and in possession of a great number of admirers. Amongst the rest, there was a very sober youth, of a good person and a genteel fortune, who was particular in his attachment to me; and, as my mother seemed to have no objection, I encouraged his addresses: and, I own, he had made some progress towards gaining my affections. But, after about a month's intimate correspondence with Mr. Clayton (which was this young man's name), application was made to my old Lady by another gentleman, of a much larger fortune, but much older than myself; who offered me a settlement of eight hundred pounds a year; and, if required, two hundred pounds a year for what is called Pin-money.

'My mother was charmed with this proposal, and hoped "I would not hesitate a moment, in preferring so advantageous an offer to that of the young fellow who had been dangling after me for some time."

'I was startled at this speech, and told her, "I should certainly pay a proper deference to her opinion in an affair of that importance; but, Madam," says I, "you know I have encouraged Mr. Clayton's addresses, and cannot, in honour, listen to any other proposals.—" "In honour!" cries she, "a fiddlestick! well," continues she, "you may do as you please; I shall not force your inclinations: but, whether you accept of Mr. Booby's offer or not, I shall insist upon your not admitting that fellow's visits (meaning Mr. Clayton's) any more."

'This stern prohibition, though it obliged me to alter my external behaviour, could make no alteration in my affection for Mr. Clayton. I was denied to him indeed the next time he came; but we contrived two or three short interviews at the rooms: and I told him, "that although I could not think of disobeying my mother's express commands; I would vow eternal constancy to him, and promise faithfully never to give my hand, much less my heart, to any other." '

CHAPTER IX

Mrs. Booby's Story continued

'MR. CLAYTON was now obliged, by some business of consequence, to leave Bath for some time, and was detained near two months in the country. We contrived, however, to carry on a correspondence by letters; in which he lamented, "how much he suffered by this separation; and how impossible it was for him ever to be happy in my absence." I answered his letters, at first, with more fondness perhaps than it was prudent, or even decent, for any young woman to express, whatever her real sentiments may be; and made the most romantic declarations, of preferring retirement and a competence with the person I loved, to the most splendid circumstances with one whom I detested.

'The most ardent love, however, may grow cool, by a long separation from its object; for, though a short absence increases, too long a one frequently extinguishes a passion. In short, I am convinced, that time and a variety of amusements must weaken the force even of the sincerest affection.

'As my Mama, without mentioning a word of Mr. Booby's proposals, was continually representing to my fancy the dazzling images of a splendid equipage, a numerous attendance, and the deference and respect which are usually paid to wealth and affluence: and the like topics, which those parents who prefer the grandeur of alliances to the happiness of their children are fond of inculcating: I must own my weakness; and confess, that I began to feel my excessive tenderness for the absent Clayton gradually wearing off; and in short, I determined, at length, to find out some pretence for breaking off all correspondence with him.

'The engagements of Lovers are like treaties between Princes. The party that is desirous of coming to a rupture, is never at a loss for a pretence. In one of his letters, poor Clayton, out of his great fondness perhaps, had expressed his concern, as naturally he might, lest the constant solicitations, to which every woman, who is not absolutely ugly, is exposed in this place, might prove prejudicial to his love; and had even hinted, how happy it would make him, if I would not appear in publick, more than was necessary to oblige my Mama: who, he knew, was more fond of the rooms, at that time, than I myself was.

'This modest request, the consequence probably of the most tender regard, furnished me with the opportunity, which I wanted, of breaking with Clayton. I told him, in my answer, "that a woman could never be happy with a man of his suspicious temper; and, if I was to be abridged of the most innocent amusements by a person who could claim not the least right to that power, what must I expect from the authority of an husband of so jealous a disposition? In short," I added, "as this engagement was entirely inconsistent with the obedience due to a parent, and the correspondence carried on in defiance of my mother's express prohibition, I desired the affair might proceed no further."

'Instead of answering this letter, which greatly alarmed him, Mr. Clayton came post to Bath: the news of which, I must confess, staggered my resolution. And meeting him the next day, by accident, at the house where, by agreement, our letters had been left, I found all my fondness revive at the sight of him; and instead of exchanging our letters (which, after the receipt of so unaccountable a one from me, he said, was the utmost of his expectation), we seemed to have established our correspondence upon a more lasting foundation than ever.

'After two or three clandestine interviews, Mr. Clayton was again obliged to leave Bath; and we again renewed our literary correspondence. But oh! how little do we know our own hearts! Whether the continual incense of flattery, which I received from a number of admirers, revived my ambition, or whether mere absence weaned my affections from their object, I began, a second time, to feel a great indifference in regard to Mr. Clayton. In short, Sir, not to trouble you with too tedious a detail of particulars, I again found a pretence for dropping all further intercourse with him. And Clayton himself, instead of coming again in person, (or perhaps thinking me now beneath his regard) only wrote me a defence of his conduct. Such, at least, I guessed to be the contents of his letter; for, with unparalleled insolence, I sent it back un-opened. And thus ended our connexion.'

CHAPTER X

Mrs. Booby's Story concluded. Wildgoose's Opinion of the Marriage-Contract. Description of a Bath Life

'MY Mother, perceiving the gloom which appeared in my coun-tenance on Mr. Clayton's departure begin now to wear off, and my usual chearfulness return, gave Mr. Booby an hint to renew his addresses. These, at first, I again rejected with great indignation. But, when I perceived, that although my Mama declared against forcing my inclinations, yet that her constant frowns, and perhaps her lasting displeasure, and all the negative discouragements in her power, would be the consequence of my refusal, I began to listen to Mr. Booby's proposals: and, after stipulating for a decent time to consider of it, and insisting upon his first offer of two hundred pounds a year, pin-money; I condescended to accept his terms: and in short, our persons were joined together in wedlock, though two such *hearts* could never be united.

'Mr. Booby indeed was not disagreeable in his appearance: and though he was near twenty years older than me; yet, by his manner of dress, in a public place, he concealed what little depredation Time had made on his person. But when we had been married near three years, without the consequence which he expected from our union (for he was very desirous of an heir to his estate), he began to lay aside the very desire of pleasing me. And, as he became a sloven, I began to neglect my dress; so that, from being merely indifferent, we soon became thoroughly disagreeable to each other. Every trifle was now made matter of dispute; and we frequently quarrelled *one day*, about what had been the subject of our dispute the day before.

'But what rendered Mr. Booby completely odious to me, was the high opinion he had conceived of the superiority of his sex; and the arbitrary notions he entertained of the authority of the husband over us poor domestic animals, called wives. In short, Mr. Wild-goose, this was a constant subject of debate; and in fine, the real cause of our separation.'

'Is Mr. Booby then alive? and do you live separate from him?'— 'Why, Sir, you shall hear. It was a thing utterly unavoidable; and nothing but an absolute necessity should have forced me to take so imprudent a step. I was driven to it by the most brutal behaviour, as you shall hear.

'Mr. Booby's family-seat is in the North of England; but being so remote from Bath (which waters were thought necessary for his health), and a bad sporting country, which is his whole delight, he had taken a hunting seat near the Wiltshire Downs; whither I was banished soon after our marriage; or rather where I was im-prisoned, and confined to the conversation of dogs and horses; or, what is worse, mere Country Squires, Parsons, and Fox-hunters: for there was not above one conversible neighbour within ten miles of us; and that family we rarely saw above once in a quarter.

'One day, when Mr. Booby returned from hunting, he brought home with him, according to custom, the Parson of the parish, and a neighbouring Attorney; though he knew that I had invited the only genteel family, which (as I told you) we had in the neighbour-hood, to spend the evening with me. As those politer meetings were but rarely indulged me, I usually made an handsome supper; and as our house was a mere box, though I had a dining-room to receive my company in on those occasions, yet we were always obliged to sup in the common parlour. As soon, therefore, as we had dined, I desired Mr. Booby and his rustic companions to adjourn into a little smoking-room, to take their pipes and their bottles; which he absolutely refused. Upon my pleading a right to the parlour, to entertain my company in, he insisted upon his prerogative of being master in his own house. In short, after many aggravations, I pro-ceeded so far as to tell him, "I would rather live in a cottage, than with such a brute as he was;" to which he replied, "that he would sooner live in a wind-mill, than with such a vixen as I was; and, that he never desired to see my face again." Upon which I threw my hoop-ring¹ in his face; and, having dispatched a card to put off my company, ordered the chariot, and drove immediately to Bath: where I have lived ever since last October.

'Now, Sir, I should be glad of your opinion; whether I have done any thing inconsistent with my duty, or contrary to my marriage-vow, upon this occasion. For you must observe, Mr. Wildgoose, nothing but the most *brutal usage* could have forced me to take this step; and you see I was under an *absolute necessity* of acting as I have done. You must mind *that*, Mr. Wildgoose: and then, I am sure, you must pass sentence in my favour, and acquit me of any thing wrong in this affair.'

Wildgoose was at first struck dumb with astonishment, and could not tell what answer to make: but, after recovering a little from his confusion; 'Madam,' says he, 'as you ask my opinion, I am persuaded you expect me to give it you with the utmost sincerity; and my conscience will not permit me to speak what I do not really think: and a good Christian should rather run the risque of appearing unpolite, than insincere.

'I would by no means, Madam, cast the blame entirely upon you: for, I think, there was no probability that such an alliance as you have described, could be productive of any lasting felicity; as it was not founded on a mutual affection; nor (I am afraid) entered into on a religious principle, or in the fear of God. Your affections, you own, were pre-engaged; or, at least, having been disappointed in their first object, could not exert their natural force on a second.

'Then, I am afraid, Madam, you have not sufficiently considered your obligation to *obey* the person, to whom you have, by the marriage-contract, given up, in some measure, your natural freedom.'—'Given up my *freedom!*' (cries Mrs. Booby) 'I'd sooner resign my life.'—'Give me leave, Madam, to explain myself,' says Wildgoose. 'I do not speak of this obligation, as founded on the mere words of the marriage-ceremony (for all human ordinances are vain and frivolous); but as evidently enjoined by the holy Scripture, and to be deduced from that superiority which Nature seems to have given the man over the more delicate sex.'

'Ay, that's so like my husband now!' cries Mrs. Booby, turning red, and playing her fan with some vivacity: 'but you must excuse me, Sir, if I cannot allow the *superiority* you plead for.'—'Well, Madam,' replies Mr. Wildgoose, 'I will not enter into the dispute about the natural equality of the sexes; which has of late been brought frequently upon the carpet; though the *novelty* of the Ladies claim is, I think, a strong presumption in our favour. But be that as it will; I am clearly of opinion, that in domestic, as well as civil government, to prevent continual dissensions and struggles for superiority, there must somewhere be lodged a *dernier resort*, an *arbitrary*, or (to use a softer name) a *sovereign* power. And I am certain, that Religion, as well as Reason, has placed this power in the husband.'—('Very well,' says Mrs. Booby with a contemptuous sneer.)—'For a proper use of this power, however,' continues Wildgoose, 'the husband is accountable both to the laws of God and of man. And I am convinced, Madam, if you could have acknowledged this superior authority in Mr. Booby, and had thought it your duty to submit in such trifles as that which was the immediate cause of your separation, you would have been much happier than by your own account you now are. For, I believe, as depraved as our nature is, there is no man so brutish, that could bear to tyrannize over a poor helpless creature; who (instead of displaying that masculine ferocity which is too common in the sex) acknowledged her entire dependence upon him for support and protection.'—

'*Support* and *protection*, indeed!' exclaims Mrs. Booby: 'my pin-money will *support* me, and I scorn his *protection*.'—'Give me leave, Madam, to conclude my argument,' says Wildgoose. 'The very circumstance which you mention, has, I am afraid, contributed not a little to bring on that separation, which you seem now to repent of: I mean, that monstrous article of modern refinement called pin-money; which, I perceive, is always uppermost in your thoughts. The allowing a woman a maintenance, independent of her husband, is not only destroying that mutual affection which arises from a sense of their interest being inseparably united; but is also a continual temptation to a woman to fly out on the slightest dispute: and to despise the authority of an husband, without whose assistance or support she has it in her power to live in affluence and splendor. Separate purses between man and wife are as unnatural as separate beds: which indeed one often hears of amongst people of fashion; where there is no more difficulty in making up *two* beds, than one. But the surest way of preventing such a separation, is to have but one bed to go to; which is most commonly the case with the happier couples in lower life.

'In short, Madam, I am inclined to think, the great facility which you found in exchanging the solitude you complain of, for the gaieties and *pleasures* of Bath, was a principal motive of your deserting Mr. Booby, and precipitating yourself into this misfortune: which rash conduct, I find, now sits so heavy upon your conscience.'

'Indeed, Sir,' replied Mrs. Booby (starting from a kind of reverie), 'you are vastly mistaken. I am more sick of a public place, if possible, than of my own home:—whither indeed I have lately had some thoughts of returning; as I have received several overtures from Mr. Booby to that purpose. The *pleasures* of *Bath* indeed! No; I detest the place; and could wish to be banished from it for ever! It is a tedious circle of unmeaning hurry, anxiety, and fatigue: of fancied enjoyments and real chagrins:—to-day one is in vogue, the Lord knows why; to-morrow deserted, and equally without reason. In the former case, one is pestered and distracted with variety of engagements; in the latter, left a prey to melancholy, and the disagreeable reflections on the slights we meet with. Such indeed is the spirit of public places. Every one is aspiring after the company of his superiors; while he despises his equals, and sacrifices the real enjoyment of friendly conversation to the foolish ambition of being seen in, what is called, *good company*. In short, nothing can be more trifling than the life of a Lady, nor more insipid than that of a Gentleman, at Bath: the one is a constant series of flirting and gadding about; the other of sauntering from place to place, without any scheme or pursuit. Scandal or fashions engross the conversation of the former; the news of the day, the price of fish, the history of the preceding night at the tavern, or savoury anticipations of their next debauch, furnish out the morning entertainment of the latter.'

'Well, Madam, I am glad to hear you speak with so much disgust of this scene of dissipation; which, by all accounts, it highly deserves: and I hope it is a good symptom of the New-Birth. If you are once properly sensible of your own misery, you will soon be glad to take refuge, where only true joys are to be found.'

'Oh Sir, you do not know half the follies and impertinences of this place. There are some indeed who appear more seriously employed; and who pore whole mornings over a game at Whist, with the attention and solemnity of Mathematicians or Privy-counsellors. But one might as well affect tranquillity in a storm or a whirl-wind, as enjoyment at a gaming-table. It is exposing one's self continually to the caprice and sport of Fortune, and to every boisterous, unsociable, and selfish passion. For my part, though, I confess, I have been fond of cards, yet they are now my utter aversion; I renounce them for ever; and (if I know my own mind) am determined never to touch a card again as long as I live.'

Whilst Mrs. Booby was making this declaration, and Wildgoose highly applauding her resolution, the Footman opened the door, and announced the arrival of Lady Fanny Flurry, who rushed in, tossing her hoop three yards before her. But, seeing so unfashionable a figure as Wildgoose, she started back, and taking him for a Shoe-maker or something in that style, she cried out, 'Oh! Booby, you are engaged, I see.' But Mrs. Booby winking upon her, and assuring her she was not; 'Well, my dear Booby,' says Lady Fanny, 'I only came to bespeak you for a party at Quadrille to-night, and shall depend upon your company at the Rooms.'— 'Oh! Lady Fanny! name it not,' cries Mrs. Booby; 'I have just made a *firm* resolution never to touch another card—after the bad run I had last night. But—your *La'ship* is so obliging, there's *no* resisting *you*—yet, I hate the Rooms; and positively I cannot be of your party *there*.'—'Oh! ho! my Dear,' replies her Ladyship, 'have you betrayed yourself? What! you are piqued then at not being invited to poor Clayton's public breakfast this morning? Come, come! you had the refusal of him; and how can you blame the creature for seeking consolation elsewhere? And, really, thirty thousand pounds, with a pretty woman, is no unpromising prospect of consolation.'

And now the secret was out. The true cause of Mrs. Booby's disgust with the world, and of her desiring this conference with a Quack-preacher, was the arrival of her former lover, Mr. Clayton; who, a few years after she had sacrificed him, either to her Mother's importunity or to her own ambition, had married a very agreeable heiress with thirty thousand pounds, whom he had now, for the first time, brought to Bath, where she made a very brilliant appearance. And Mrs. Booby not having been particularly invited to a public breakfast which Mr. Clayton gave that morning; this slight, together with a bad run at cards, had made her *sick of the world*: and, to *amuse* herself chiefly, she had had recourse to this spiritual

Knight-errant. However, she was so well pleased with our Hero's company (for, where the peculiarities of his religious system were not concerned, Wildgoose was really very agreeable), that notwithstanding his offer to take his leave, Mrs. Booby insisted upon his company to tea and coffee, which now made its appearance.

CHAPTER XI

A Scene in genteel Life. Enter Mrs. Bardolph,
Miss Trufle, and Mr. Rouvell. Their Characters

'THE most material difference between keeping good company and bad, is, the hearing the same things said before a dozen waxlights at the court-end of the town, or before a couple of mold candles in the city.' This, or something to the same purpose, was remarked by a celebrated Genius of the last age. But I am inclined to think, that the honest Citizens of our times would suffer by such a comparison: for in that serious part of the metropolis, there are still some remains of the British plainness of speech and manliness of conversation. There, Business, Politics, News, History, or even Religion, are, in their turn, sometimes admitted as interesting subjects of discourse or argumentation. But amongst those choice spirits who have monopolized and appropriated to themselves the style and title of *good company*, one rarely hears any other topics introduced than annals of the Whist-table or anecdotes of the Turf, Operas, Routs, and Masquerades; the most trifling relations of the most trifling transactions. And, as Lord Shaftesbury observes of his times, 'If any thing of Learning is introduced, it is Pedantry; if any thing of Morality, it is called Preaching.'[1]

In these reflections, however, the good company now introduced is not particularly concerned.

Mrs. Booby, not having appeared in public that day, was visited by most of the idle and impertinent part of her acquaintance. Amongst the rest there now arrived those two amiable persons, Mrs. Bardolph and the well-known[2] Miss Trufle; the latter with a black spaniel under her arm and a squirrel in her pocket. These ladies were immediately followed by Mr. Rouvell, or (as he was aptly called) Beau Rueful.

Mrs. Bardolph was the wife of a very worthy man: which circumstance, together with the good table which she kept, and her readiness to make one at a party at Quadrille, introduced her into a numerous acquaintance amongst people of fashion. Of which privilege, however, she made no other use, than that of passing away the time less tediously; of dining and supping agreeably, and of transmitting the insipid occurrences of one family into that of another; the particulars of which her memory enabled her to retain longer than people of more reflection. So that she was a living Chronicle of every incident, good, bad, or indifferent, that had befallen her acquaintance for twenty years together.

Of much the same importance was the character of Miss Trufle. She was a woman of family; but had neither fortune, beauty, wit, or even good-nature, to recommend her. Indeed her person was not only despicably small, but deformed likewise; her understanding of the same dimensions, and her temper as deformed as her person. Yet, under all these disadvantages, her rank and the good company she always appeared in might haply have captivated some Country Esquire, who would have thought himself honoured by the alliance; but for, that eternal bane to every thing that is amiable, her affectation.

Miss Trufle had two or three sisters who were admired; and from two or three occasional compliments which she had met with on their account, she flattered herself (in downright contradiction to her looking-glass) that she herself had some pretensions to the family features. In consequence of this, she noddled her head, was saucy, and said rude things to one's face, and gave herself all the coquettish airs of a celebrated toast; the natural result of which was, that, having lived a virgin to the age of thirty, and now despaired of becoming a mistress of any other sort of family, she had settled her affections on squirrels, monkeys, and lap-dogs, with which, for want of other gallants, she was constantly attended; though they frequently supplied the wags with personal comparisons, not much to Miss Trufle's advantage.

Mr. Rouvell, or Beau Rueful, was a young fellow, who, by a strange concurrence of lucky circumstances, with the help of a convenient assurance and a laced coat, had wriggled himself into tolerable company: and, what is more strange, by boldly criticising every new pamphlet, laughing at every thing serious, and by putting modest people out of countenance, was by some people esteemed a formidable Wit. Nay, what is most strange of all, his profuse expences having almost dissipated a genteel fortune left him by a relation, he was now commenced fortune-hunter; without any kind of merit, either of person (which corresponded with his nickname *Rueful*); or of understanding, which was of the lowest standard; or even of birth, which was very mean, he being the son of a Grocer, in the ancient city of Coventry.

As straws and feathers attract each other on the surface of the water, these three worthy persons, as if linked together by a mutual sympathy, came in a train to Mrs. Booby's apartment.

Rouvell bowed to Mrs. Booby and to Lady Fanny; nodded to Mrs. Bardolph, and patted Miss Trufle upon her bare shoulders; but took no more notice of Wildgoose, than of the Footman that waited, or of the Dutch Mastiff which lay sleeping on a cushion in the corner of a room. Being seated, however, he lolled over the settee; and, with the corner of his hat held up to his face, asked Mrs. Booby, in an audible whisper, 'Who, the Devil, she had got there?' Mrs. Bardolph's curiosity likewise being raised, she asked the same question, in the same tone, but concealing her face with her fan. Miss Trufle stared in Wildgoose's face; burst into a laugh; then, turning to Rouvell, asked him, 'Why he did not wear his own hair, which, she heard, was coming much into fashion?'

In answer to Rouvell's and Mrs. Bardolph's questions, Mrs. Booby said aloud, 'that the gentleman was Mr. Wildgoose; and she hoped would make them all as good Christians as he was himself.' On hearing Wildgoose's name, Mrs. Bardolph asked, 'if he was any relation to the Wildgooses of Wiltshire?'—'Wildgooses of Wiltshire!' says Mrs. Booby, 'I know no such family.'—'What! not Miss Wildgoose, that ran away with her father's Butler?'—'Lord! you mean Miss Gosling.'—'Bless me!' says Mrs. Bardolph, 'so I do: but I am the worst person in the world to remember *names*' (which however was no inconsiderable part of her erudition). 'Well; Wild-goose or Gosling; they are not much unlike.'—'No;' says Rouvell, 'I suppose they are of the same family, and bear the same arms— a Grey-goose, *cankant*, *regardant*.' Rouvell's blazonry was un-intelligible to all but himself; and consequently received no applause, but from an affected laugh of his own.

Wildgoose had no very pleasant time of it, whilst the affair of his name and family was adjusting. But his attention was diverted from this conversation, by the Footman's treading on his toe, as he was handing the coffee to him. Wildgoose begged Mr. John's pardon for putting his foot in the way; and moved his chair with no small trepidation. But Mr. John, far from being mollified by his submissive behaviour, owed him another good turn; and, in handing his tea to him, did it with so scornful an air, that it flashed[1] plentifully over Wildgoose's plush breeches. Mrs. Booby, however, observed the insolence of her servant, and very properly reprimanded him for it: upon which, Mr. John vouchsafed to wait with a little more dexterity.

Nothing would have kept Lady Fanny so long silent, but the sublime contempt which she had conceived of her company. She had been trifling with her spoon, and cooling her tea, with an absent air; and now drank half a dish, emptied the rest into the slop-bason; then, starting up, 'Lord!' says she, 'what am I about! I am engaged to tea at the rooms this evening; and have a myriad of visits to make before I go thither.'—'Sir,' says she to the Footman, 'please to order my chair.'—Then pulling out her pocket-book, 'Let me see,' says she, 'Lady Loiter, old Lady Shockingphyz, Sir Arthur Lurch;—yes, our Whist-parties are full for Thursday, Friday, and Saturday evenings. But on Sunday-night, Booby, we will expect you, for a party at Quadrille.'—Here Wildgoose erected his eye-brows; and fetched a deep sigh, or rather groaned in spirit. But Lady Fanny correcting herself, 'bless me!' cries she, 'what do I talk of Sunday? I forget that I am at Bath. That superannuated old creature, Nash, will not let us play on Sunday-night—in public. Well, to-night however, at eight o'clock, I shall depend upon you.' Then rising up, and tossing her hoop over Wildgoose's head as she rushed by him, she took her leave, with '*Adieu! ma chere Booby; je vous attend, tout à l'heure!*'

CHAPTER XII

Various Chit-chat

AFTER Lady Fanny was gone, Mrs. Booby, with no other view than to give Mr. Wildgoose an opportunity of saying something, asked him, 'what his opinion was of frequenting the rooms at Bath, or other public places?' Wildgoose replied, 'that he had had no opportunity of forming any opinion upon that head from his own experience. But, Madam,' continues he, 'as, by all accounts, the chief intent of those assemblies is either gaming, intriguing, or unmeaning dissipation; in short, to prevent our being left a prey to our own thoughts, and seeing our own misery and corruption; I cannot think it adviseable, even for people with the best intentions, to countenance, by their example, meetings of this kind.'

'Well, Sir,' says Rouvell, 'you may preach as long as you please; but, I believe, you will hardly prevail upon people of fashion to give up so agreeable an amusement.'

'Why, Sir,' replies Wildgoose, 'from the description which Mrs. Booby has just now been giving me of a Bath life, I am so far from thinking it even *agreeable*; that it appears to me a mere scene of vanity and folly. Pray, Madam,' continues Wildgoose, 'did you ever read the Pilgrim's Progress.'—'Ha! ha! ha!' cries Rouvell, in a horse-laugh; 'I believe we may all have read that, and Jack the Giant-killer too, in the nursery.'—'Well, Sir, you may laugh; I now only mention that original author upon a ludicrous occasion, as I think his account of "Vanity-Fair" seems to be no bad description of the insipid intercourse (to say no worse of it) that usually passes between the thoughtless creatures, at most of those public assemblies.'

'Well,' says Rouvell, 'granting it to be as *insipid* as you please; yet wherever people of distinction agree to assemble, those that would not be out of the world must follow them. Even those that set up for reformers of mankind must frequent those assemblies, if they would do any good amongst them. I will answer for it, St. Paul himself, who *became all things to all men*, if he had come to Bath, would have gone to the Rooms; and St. Luke, like other Physicians, would have frequented the coffee-house.'—'Very fine!' (says Miss Trufle) 'and I suppose you think the Four Evangelists would have made a party at Quadrille! you will make a fine Parson indeed!'

Wildgoose was struck with horror at this prophane raillery: but Mrs. Bardolph, by way of changing the subject, asked Mrs. Booby, 'if she had heard how old Lady Shockingphyz was mortified at the Ball last night; or rather at the Pump-Room this morning?'—'No;' says Mrs. Booby, 'I have not had a soul come near me to-day, except the present company and Lady Fanny.'—'Why,' says Mrs. Bardolph, 'you know her Ladyship's family pride.'—'Yes,' says Mrs. Booby; 'as she has no merit of her own to plead, her Ladyship is forced to subsist upon the family fund; and that is pretty well exhausted. She has only one daughter, I think, to keep up the honour of it.'—'Well, it was for that daughter' (says Mrs. Bardolph) 'that she desired Nash to get a partner: who recommended a very genteel young man, and very well dressed; and Miss jigged it down, the whole evening, with great alacrity and satisfaction. But this morning, at the Pump-room, the busy Mrs. Marrall came out of breath to Lady Shockingphyz, and told her, "that the young man her daughter danced with, was a Linen-draper in Cheapside." "Indeed!" says her Ladyship, "what does that saucy fellow Nash mean, by using me thus?" And away she trudges, to reprimand him for it. Mr. Nash, after some enquiries into the affair, told her Ladyship, "that (to be sure) the Gentleman did deal in linen; but that it was in the *wholesale* way; and that he never *cut* a piece of cloth in his life."—"Are you sure of that?" cries her Ladyship: "Are you sure he never *cut*, Mr. Nash? If the Gentleman never *cut*, why certainly there is no such great matter in it."

'Thus her Ladyship ran on, till the whole company burst into a loud laugh, both at her Ladyship's ridiculous pride, and at the mortification it had deservedly met with.'

'Well,' says Rouvell, 'as Mrs. Bardolph has told you how lady Shockingphyz was mortified this morning, I will tell you how Lord —— was terrified yesterday in the afternoon.

'An honest Tradesman, who has an handsome wife, was busy in his shop (which is much frequented by the company some parts of the day); but having occasion to go up into his bed-chamber, to his bureau, he saw a very fine *Point d'Espagne* laced hat, lying upon his wife's toilette; and, upon casting his eye round the room, he espied a man's foot, with a fine stone buckle, peep out from under the bed-curtain; behind which Lord ——, who lodged in the house, was endeavouring to conceal himself. From the confusion his Lordship was in, and from several other circumstances, the honest Tradesman had now no doubt that an amorous correspondence was carrying on between his Lordship and his wife; a glimpse of whom he had just seen, as she slipped down the back-stairs, from a closet of communication.

'The Tradesman, though a man of a tame disposition and mitigated resentment, yet, upon such an occasion, burst forth into a most vehement rage; venting his indignation in a menacing tone,

N

and in the following manner. "My Lord! as sure as you are now alive, if ever I catch you in my bed-chamber again, with my wife—depend upon it, as sure as I have a head upon my body, I will—I will—certainly—throw your laced hat out of the window!"

'His Lordship, though not greatly dismayed at this terrible denunciation, yet determined, for the future, to prosecute his intrigue with greater precaution.'

CHAPTER XIII

Story of Calomel and Lady Riot

MRS. BOOBY now observed, 'that Lady Fanny had looked very grave to-day; one would think' (says she) 'her Ladyship had met with some mortification.' Rouvell remarked, 'that people of rank were always so in mixt company; though for my part,' continues he, 'I have always found persons of quality the most affable creatures in the world. I remember, the first time I spent a week at Lord Grandison's, there was Sir Peter Pierpoint, Jack North, and half a dozen more of us. And I remember I was as free with the young Peer the first hour, as I am at this day.'—'Who suspects you of any *mauvaise honte*, or bashfulness?' says Miss Trufle.—'I shall never forget a droll accident that happened there,' continues Rouvell, undaunted by Miss Trufle's hint.—'His Lordship had a Swiss servant, who pretended to have discovered a new japan, or liquid blacking; and the fellow must needs make the experiment upon our shoes. But, would you believe it? the composition, whatever it was, had contracted the pores of the leather to *such* a degree, that the next morning we all came hobbling into the room, like so many old gouty fellows.—Lord Grandison was so diverted with the scene, that I thought his Lordship would have split his *diaphragm* with laughing.'—'Why, this was an incident worth recording, truly!' says Mrs. Booby.

'Oh! now you talk of people of quality,' cries Mrs. Bardolph, 'there is Lady Sherwood wants much to have some conversation with this gentleman. She has heard a great character of his piety; and, I believe, her Ladyship is well inclined towards the Methodists. And I can take upon me to assure you, Sir, that she would be very glad if you would call on her at her lodgings.'—Wildgoose replied, 'he should be very happy in contributing to the conversion of the lowest of his fellow creatures: and should certainly esteem it an honour to wait on her Ladyship, if she desired it.'

But here Rouvell again interposed, by observing, 'that persons of distinction often diverted themselves at Bath, with odd characters; and that people who did not know the world might easily be drawn in, to make themselves thoroughly ridiculous. Did you never hear how Lady Riot served poor Calomel, an eminent Apothecary of this place?' Upon the company's answering in the negative, 'I will tell it you,' says Rouvell.

'Mr. Calomel is a very honest man, and an experienced Apothecary; but highly absurd in his conversation and manner of address: Lady Riot, who is a woman of humour, has often detained him at her lodgings for her amusement, when his patients wanted his lenient hand for more salutary applications. Calomel was so elated by this distinction, that, though he was turned of fifty, he entertained some faint suspicions that his person, as well as his conversation, might have pleased Lady Riot.

'Having therefore some business in London, last winter, he took it into his head to *call upon* her Ladyship, at her house in town; and not finding her at home, he left her Ladyship a card, with "Mr. Calomel's compliments to Lady Riot; lets her Ladyship know, that he did himself the honour to wait on her Ladyship; and that he is to be spoken with at The White Bear, in Piccadilly."

'When her Ladyship came home to dinner, at five o'clock, she was highly diverted with Calomel's style of politeness: and it being her assembly-night, she produced his card before the whole company; who, being let into the character of Calomel, voted to send for *him* thither; and *bets* were laid, *pro* and *con*—come or not come—for fifty guineas.

'But Lady Riot, to make sure of her point, ordered her coach, and slipping slily out of the room, took Lady Rattle with her, drove to the White Bear, and enquired for Mr. Calomel. Calomel, being a sober man, and having a *reverend regard* to his health, had retired to his bed-chamber, got into his night-gown and slippers, tied his night-cap under his chin, and was just going to his repose; when the Drawer brought up the message. Calomel at first said, "he supposed they were some naughty women of the town, and he would have nothing to say to them." But upon the Drawer's assuring him, it was some Lady of quality in her own carriage, with a couple of flambeaux; Calomel came down to the door in his dishabille, to reconnoitre them. The moment Lady Riot beheld him, she cries out, "My dear Calomel, how do you do? Come, I must have some chat with you; do not stand in the street in your night-cap; step into the coach a moment." Which having done, the Footman (as he had been instructed) clapped to the door; the coach drove immediately to her Ladyship's house; where Calomel was produced before thirty card-tables, in his night-cap and slippers.

'The brilliancy of the assembly, and the wax-lights, a little disconcerted poor Calomel at first; but his vanity soon prevailing over his bashfulness, he mixed with the society, and greatly diverted them with his absurd buffoonries.

'To complete the farce, the Butler had his cue, to mix a soporific with whatever he gave him to drink. And upon Calomel's desiring some Madeira negus, a bason was brought him, properly medicated; which soon began to operate; and before eleven o'clock, Calomel was fast asleep in an elbow-chair. They then rolled him up in his night-gown, like a collar of brawn; and swathing down his arms with his sash, laid him safely to bed by a fat Scullion, where Calomel slept as sweetly as probably he would have done in her Ladyship's own bed-chamber.'

'Well, and how did the poor man get back to his Inn, in the morning?' (says Mrs. Bardolph). 'Nay,' says Rouvell, 'I have put him fairly to bed; let him get back in a chair or hackney-coach, or how the devil he pleases. Further this Deponent saith not.'

CHAPTER XIV

Universities defended, &c.

'WELL,' says Mrs. Booby, 'to be sure, a mere Citizen of Bath is as pedantic a creature, as a mere Fellow of a College: is often as proud, has as absurd notions of life; and is as much out of his element, when he gets out of his shop or his lodging-house, as the other is out of his own common room.'

'Yes, rot them,' says Rouvell; 'and they get rich by the money we spend here, before they know how to carry their heads, or come into a room.'

'And yet I know a great many sensible, polite people,' says Mrs. Booby, 'amongst the inhabitants of this place.'

'Why, it would be strange indeed,' replies Rouvell, 'if the great resort of the politest company in Europe did not polish the creatures a little: for I take Bath, as a public place, to be a better school for any young fellow, than all the Universities or Colleges in the world. And I do not see, but those who have had no other education, appear as well in company, as people who have been plodding at the sciences in a College for seven years together.'

Here Wildgoose could not forbear interposing; and observed, 'that although Religion was, he believed, at as low an ebb in the Universities as in other parts of the kingdom, notwithstanding the excellence of its institution for that purpose, yet he could not but think them still the chief fountains of erudition.

'There is indeed' (says he) 'a slight tincture of learning, a superficial knowledge, diffused amongst all ranks in this generation. But if there were not some *repositories* for the sciences, and some encouragements, such as those for our Professors, to search more deeply into them, than the generality of the world seem disposed to do; I am of opinion the very principles of them would, in time, be lost; and we should again relapse into Gothic ignorance and barbarism.

'There may be men of courage, that do not wear a red coat; and a gentleman may know how to use a sword, without going into the army; or to stand fire, though not educated in the navy. But still there is a kind of military spirit, peculiar to gentlemen of those professions; a set of traditionary maxims of honour and courage'— Just at this instant Wildgoose started up with the utmost surprize and trepidation, and alarmed the whole company. Rouvell burst out into an horse-laugh—Mrs. Booby cried out, 'Lord! Miss Trufle, what are you about?'—The case was, Miss Trufle (who for some time had sat in silent contemplation of her own importance, and playing with her lap-dog) whilst Wildgoose was in the midst of his harangue, had put her Squirrel upon his shoulder: the little animal began dancing about; and, fixing his claws in Wildgoose's neck, gave him so smart a pinch, that if he had had the insensibility of a Stoic, or even a Spartan education, he could not have borne it without some emotion of terror or surprize.

When the company had sufficiently laughed at Miss Trufle's wit, and were again composed; Mr. Rouvell, resuming the discourse, said, 'he did not undervalue an University education, as an old maid rails at matrimony, because he had been denied the sweets of it. Only I say,' (continues he, casting a look of complacency on his own person) 'that I am more indebted to Bath, and the company of the ladies, for being what I am; than to all the lectures of Tutors and Professors, which I attended in the University.'—'I dare say you are, Mr. Rouvell,' replies Mrs. Booby; and I am sure the figure you make does credit to your education, whatever place had the honour of it.'

Upon hearing Rouvell's name for the first time, Wildgoose observed his features more narrowly; and asked him, 'if he was not of such a College in Oxford, some years ago; because I remember a person of your name of our College,' continues Wildgoose.— 'That may be, Sir,' replies Rouvell; 'but I am a Cambridge man.— Well, Ladies,' continues Rouvell, 'we are very rude in troubling you with our pedantic disputes.'—Then, pulling out his watch, 'Pox take it!' says he, 'I was engaged to meet Sir James Townly, at seven o'clock, at the Coffee-house.' Having said this, he started up, and, somewhat abruptly, took his leave.

The truth was, Rouvell had actually been of the same College with Wildgoose, and now very well remembered him: though the alteration which his own hair had made in the one, and the high frizure and laced coat in the other, prevented them at first from recollecting each other's person, especially as there had not been the least acquaintance between them: for, notwithstanding the airs which Rouvell now gave himself, he had worn a Servitor's gown at Oxford, which, upon an accession of fortune, he had exchanged for a Fellow-commoner's at Cambridge.

As soon as Rouvell was gone, the Ladies, without the least reserve, spoke of him in such a manner, as convinced Wildgoose that he was the jest of the place. And the evening now drawing on, it was almost time for Wildgoose to attend their religious assembly. He therefore took his leave, after Mrs. Bardolph had acquainted him with Lady Sherwood's lodgings; whom she desired him to wait upon the next morning, notwithstanding Mr. Rouvell's discouraging insinuations to the contrary.

When Wildgoose was come down, he saw Rouvell walking upon the parade, not with Sir James Townly, whom he was to meet at the Coffee-house; but with two elderly virgins, of that homely stamp, who, to view them in a *public place*, seem formed for no other end, than to make a variety in the works of creation; but who, if they would confine themselves within their proper sphere, their own families in the country, might make tender nurses to their aged parents, exemplary aunts to their young nieces, or charitable assistants to their indigent neighbours; or even shining objects at a country assembly in a remote province: whilst at Bath, or Tunbridge, they expose themselves to the insolent contempt of youth and beauty; are almost shoved out of polite company, as useless lumber; and are glad to take up with such fellows as Rouvell, who was but one remove from the man described by Shakespear, as 'fancifully carved out of a cheese-paring after dinner.'[1]

CHAPTER XV

Tricks among Servants. News from Mrs. Sarsenet

WILDGOOSE, having been sufficiently exhausted with haranguing on the Parade, as well as by sitting in form at a ceremonious visit, made part of the audience this evening at the Tabernacle, where a Tallow-chandler held forth, and *melted* his flock by the *pathetic force*, and promoted a plentiful consumption of candles by the tedious *prolixity* of his discourse.

During Mr. Wildgoose's visits to Mrs. Booby, poor Tugwell had been left to amuse himself at the Inn; he met his Master however at the Tabernacle, from whence they adjourned to their quarters.

As they were going along, Jerry informed his Master what a reprobate place they were in—'That there was nothing but card-playing, gaming, and swearing, from morning to night, amongst the servants and apprentices that resorted thither. That he heard a Footman bragging how cleverly a friend of his had imposed upon his Mistress—That, having had the misfortune to break his leg, he had been confined to the house for three months: at last, his Mistress told him "it would do him good, to lay up his leg upon a stool, and ride behind her coach, as she went out for an airing;"

which accordingly he did. The next morning he goes to his Lady's Maid, with a sorrowful countenance, and told her, "that he had had a sad misfortune by going behind the coach; that as he was forced to lay up his leg, the motion of the coach had shaken six guineas, all the money he had saved in service, out of his pocket." Upon the Maid's telling the case to her Mistress, she, very good-naturedly, gave him the money again out of her own pocket. But it happened a little unluckily, that, a few days after, as the Maid was in the Butcher's-shambles, she heard another servant tell the Butcher, "that such a Footman, which was her fellow-servant, had lost six guineas, such a night, at the gaming-table;" which coming to the Mistress's ears, the fellow lost his place by his trick, and was forced to march off to London.'

Wildgoose was shocked at this instance of baseness and villainy, and at the idle character of the house they were in: but said, 'they should lie only that night at Bath; for that he had observed the two Brethren, who had preached there those two nights, had *preached* almost contradictory doctrines; and each of them different from that of his own: that he was determined, therefore, to go to Bristol the next day, and consult Mr. Whitfield; who, he did not doubt, would resolve all his scruples, and put him in the true road to salvation.'

When they came to their quarters, my Landlord asked our Hero, 'if his name was not Wildgoose?' To which when he had answered in the affirmative, my Landlord gave him a letter, 'which' (he said) 'a gentleman's servant had brought that afternoon from the Bell at Gloucester, having been desired to find such a gentleman out. And, upon my describing your Honour, and telling him that you lodged here, he left it with me.'

Wildgoose took the letter, which, he found, was from Mrs. Sarsenet, and read it with great eagerness, in hopes of hearing some news of Miss Townsend; who, he found, engrossed a considerable share of his thoughts, and whose sprightly idea none of the fine-dressed Ladies at Bath had power to efface.

Mrs. Sarsenet informed him of the state of their little Church under hers and Mr. Keen the Barber's auspices and inspection: 'that she already foresaw, from one or two instances, some temporal inconveniences to herself, in regard to her trade, from so strict an adherence to her duty: but that she counted all things as dross, in comparison with the love of Christ.' She concluded with observing, 'that there was something mysterious in Miss Townsend's be-haviour; that she could not persuade her to attend their Meeting since his departure: and that though she seemed seriously enough disposed, and even talked respectfully of Mr. Wildgoose, yet she seemed inclined to ridicule his notions of Religion. In short,' (says Mrs. Sarsenet) 'I believe, she is rather an enemy to your principles, than to your person.'

But the most extraordinary part of her letter was the postscript; in which she informed him, 'that Miss Townsend's father had come to Gloucester two days after *he* left it; that he had sent for Miss Townsend to the Inn, and received her with a mixture of fondness and resentment; that he was angry with her for being with Mrs. Sarsenet, and yet had determined nothing about removing her from thence.'

This letter, upon the whole, gave Wildgoose rather more pleasure than pain; and he sat down and answered it before he went to bed. He gave them some account of his success at Bath, and of his intention however of going to Bristol the next day. He con-cluded with the warmest expressions of respect to Miss Townsend; 'whose conversion,' he said, 'he should not cease earnestly to pray for.'

CHAPTER XVI

A serious Conversation with Mr. Rouvell

WILDGOOSE, having been kept awake with reflecting on the transactions of the day past, and by the hurry of spirits into which the news of Miss Townsend had thrown him, was but just drest, when a Footman brought him a card, with Lady Sherwood's compliments, who begged the favour of his company to breakfast; for Mrs. Bardolph had not failed to visit her Ladyship the pre-ceding evening, and to give her a faithful account of what had passed at Mrs. Booby's lodgings; and had greatly extolled Mr. Wildgoose's person, modest behaviour, and agreeable conversa-tion. Wildgoose, therefore, taking a direction from the Footman, promised to wait on her Ladyship at the hour appointed.

As he was going a back way into Orange-grove, where Lady

Sherwood lodged, he accidentally met with Mr. Rouvell, in a genteel dishabille. He saluted Mr. Wildgoose with a more familiar air
than he had assumed at Mrs. Booby's; and asked him immediately,
'whether he was not of such a College in Oxford?'—'Yes,' says
Wildgoose.—'Why, look you, Sir,' continues Rouvell, 'you must
know I was of that College too. But I thought you asked me, last
night, whether I was at *this time* of Oxford: for you must know,
I had a considerable fortune left me by a relation, which enabled
me to enter myself a Fellow-commoner at Cambridge; and, to be
sure, one would not chuse to have it mentioned amongst people of
fashion, that one had worn a Servitor's gown in the University.'—
'I don't imagine,' replies Wildgoose, 'that people of fashion, out
of the University, trouble themselves about those things. However,
I don't see why a man should be ashamed to have appeared in a
situation which was agreeable to his circumstances. There is
nothing ridiculous in a small fortune, or even a low birth. But there
is in the discovery that we are too anxious to conceal them, and
even give the lye to them by our dress and appearance.'—'Sir,'
says Rouvell, 'if you knew the honour and happiness of being upon
an agreeable footing with people of distinction, you would not
scruple a little artifice, to conceal any trifling circumstance that
might disgust them; or grudge an expence a little beyond one's
income, to enable one to appear in some measure upon a level
with them.'—'Sir,' replies Wildgoose, 'I apprehend, it is neither
dress, birth, nor fortune, but *education* and *behaviour*, that puts all
gentlemen upon a *level*, even in the opinion of the world.

'But, Mr. Rouvell, let me take the freedom to return the hint
which you gave me yesterday; that we may be easily deceived in the
civilities which people of distinction shew us, and mistake mere
politeness for a particular attachment; and by presuming too much
upon their plausible behaviour to our faces, expose ourselves to
their ridicule behind our backs. And I really believe, Mr. Rouvell,
you would meet with more real respect amongst people of distinction by a more serious, or even religious behaviour, and if you
were to turn Methodist (as it is called), than you do now.'

'Well, I am obliged to you, my dear Sir, for your frank advice:
and 'faith, betwixt you and me, though I detest the solemnity of
the sacerdotal character, I have at this time some thoughts of
exchanging my laced coat for a black one. For, by a Parliamentary
interest, I have now the offer of a very good living in my own

country: which (if I do not succeed in picking up a good fortune this season) I may probably accept of; for, you must know, that is another reason for my appearing rather above what I can at present afford: and I had actually almost carried off a Merchant's daughter of Bristol, who will be worth twenty thousand pounds. But old Square-toes would not part with cash enough down upon the nail. And the Devil take me, if I would marry an Angel upon the footing of a mere Smithfield bargain.'

Wildgoose, though shocked at the libertine airs which Rouvell gave himself, could not but smile at the opinion which he entertained of his own person: but said, 'he was obliged to attend Lady Sherwood at ten o'clock.' He therefore took his leave, and went to her Ladyship's lodgings, as he had been directed.

CHAPTER XVII

Lady Sherwood's Character and present Situation

LADY SHERWOOD was of an ancient and noble family, and wife to a Peer of the realm. She was a woman of fine understanding, though her judgment appeared sometimes almost eclipsed by the brilliancy of her imagination. Her Ladyship was now past her bloom; yet in her youth she had been tolerably handsome, and made a splendid appearance in the great world. But her Lord, either from some disgust, or from a fondness for retirement, having early in life withdrawn from the Court, Lady Sherwood had entirely conformed to his humour; and, to amuse herself in her solitary situation, she had formerly indulged the suggestions of her fancy, and turned my Lord's Park into a poetical Arcadia: where her Ladyship and a female companion or two lived almost the whole summer a mere pastoral life; and ranged about, with their crooks in their hands, like so many Grecian shepherdesses. Garlands of flowers, or baskets of fruit, were seen suspended on every beautiful oak, with rustic pipes, rakes, pitch-forks, and other rural implements, disposed in a picturesque manner, in different parts of the Park. Nay, the poor Chaplain was forced to leave his bottle and his pipe, and back-gammon table, with my Lord; and even neglect his *pastoral* function assigned him by the Bishop, to attend her Ladyship and her bleating lambkins; and to sit whole afternoons under a spreading tree, to entertain them with his flute: for the Steward had actually bought her Ladyship 'a score of sheep at Banbury-fair'[1] (according to Justice Shallow's expression) for this romantic purpose.

The inclemency of the weather, however, in this Northern climate was by no means favourable to these lovely Bœotians; neither did many of the pastoral functions suit with the delicacy of a modern woman of quality: for her Ladyship frequently caught the tooth-ach, and was forced to have recourse to a neighbouring Apothecary (a character seldom introduced in the ancient Buco-licks); and one of her companions met with a terrible accident in the discharge of her office: for having seized the leg of a large bell-weather with her crook, which was fastened to her wrist by a blue ribband, the rude unclassical brute struggled with such force to disengage himself, that he pulled down the poor Pastora, dragged her some yards, and disfigured her face to such a degree, that she could not appear again for six weeks; and this put an end to this extravagant scene in pastoral life.

Lady Sherwood was now grown tired of the country. But, as she could not decently go to town against her Lord's inclination, considering the complaisant terms upon which they lived together; the Physician therefore had an hint given him, to order her Lady-ship to Bath for her health. Not finding that relish, however, in public places, which she had formerly done (when every passion was agreeably flattered by her appearance in them), she grew sick of the world; and began to see, *in a true light*, the emptiness and unsatisfactory nature of all secular enjoyments.

In such a situation it is evident, that nothing but Religion could yield any solid consolation. But, as the plain rational scheme of the established Religion, which prescribes nothing more than our duty to God, our neighbour, and ourselves, under the sanction of future rewards and punishments, could not satisfy the uncommon genius and lively fancy of Lady Sherwood; she listened with the same attention to the enthusiastic doctrines of these itinerant Preachers, as a person labouring under an hypochondriacal dis-temper does to the extravagant pretensions of a Mountebank: and was glad of this opportunity of conversing with so agreeable an Enthusiast as Mrs. Bardolph had represented Wildgoose to be.

CHAPTER XVIII

A learned Conversation, not essential to the Story

WHEN Mr. Wildgoose arrived at the Countess's lodgings, he found her attended only by Mrs. Bardolph; whose principal plan being to amuse the time between breakfast and dinner, she preferred every place to her own house; and assisted with equal satisfaction at making a convert; or making a match, at a religious conversation, or at a pool at Quadrille.

Lady Sherwood, after a little preliminary chat, opened the congress, by observing the great indifference of the world with regard to Religion; and asked Wildgoose, 'how he could reconcile the present state of Christianity with the pompous descriptions given by the Prophets of the kingdom of the Messiah?' Our Hero was a little surprized at so learned an attack. But, after pausing a moment, answered, 'that the dispensations of Providence were very mysterious: that, however, God might be supposed to have given the Prophets a general view of the kingdom of Christ, from its first establishment, to the end of the world; for which reason, they generally represent it as in its full lustre.'

'Well,' replies Lady Sherwood, 'I can only say, that, as far as I have observed, the lives of the generality of Christians are so little better than those of Heathens or Mahometans; that, I confess, it a little puzzles me to account for so strange a phænomenon: and how it comes to pass, that a *divine* institution should answer its end no better.'

'Why,' says Wildgoose, 'as your Ladyship, I dare say, is very well acquainted with ancient history; if you would compare the state of Religion and Morality in the world for several generations before the coming of Christ, and that of the unconverted Heathens afterwards, with the three or four first centuries of the Christian æra, you would find a remarkable difference between them.'

'I don't imagine the world was worse than it is now,' says Lady Sherwood.

'I am convinced it was,' replies Wildgoose. 'The Heathens were so utterly void of proper principles, that impurities of every sort were scarce accounted faults among them; nay, most kinds of debauchery were defensible, and even sanctified by their religious system. Exposing of infants, cruelty to slaves, and the sanguinary diversions of gladiators, were permitted, and even applauded, by the wisest and politest nations of the world.

'But how different a scene of things does Christianity present to us in its primitive state! Its votaries were pious, humble, chaste, and temperate; and their lives were a just comment upon the precepts of their Master. If our religion therefore must be judged by its effects, we ought to take it at its first institution; as its earliest were probably its most genuine fruits.'

'That is but reasonable, to be sure,' says Mrs. Bardolph, who affected to be very attentive to this learned dissertation.

'But,' proceeds Wildgoose, 'such is the degeneracy of our nature, that every effort of Providence for our recovery, in time, loses its force, and becomes ineffectual. It seems necessary, therefore, that the divine Power should, at different periods, interpose in an extraordinary manner, and give fresh vigour to his own institutions. And, accordingly, I am persuaded, that, in the present age, he has poured out an uncommon measure of grace upon his chosen servants Mr. Whitfield and Mr. Wesley, and their associates: which empowers them to break through the cobweb restraints of human ordinances, and, by seemingly irregular proceedings, to rouse men from their dangerous lethargy, and engage their attention to the pure and genuine doctrines of Primitive Christianity.'

'Sir,' says Lady Sherwood, 'I have a great opinion of Mr. Wesley and Mr. Whitfield; and, as I hear you are a follower of them, have taken the liberty of desiring this conference with you. But give me leave to ask you, Sir, whether those doctrines are not taught in our own Church?'

'Madam,' replies Wildgoose, 'the Articles and Homilies of our Church, as drawn up by our pious Reformers, certainly contain those doctrines in their proper sense. But, I am afraid, the present Clergy are departed from the most essential of those doctrines, as particularly that of Justification by Faith alone; and depend more upon their own works, than on the merits of Christ, for their Salvation.'

'I do not know,' says Mrs. Bardolph. 'I have often heard that said of late. I own, I am a very bad judge of those things: but all the Clergy, whom I have happened to hear treat of that subject, have taught me, not to rely on my best performances, but to confess myself still an unprofitable servant. In short,' continued she, 'I cannot but think, that, if we practised what we hear at Church, we should have a tolerable chance for going to Heaven.'

Lady Sherwood observed, 'that she had attended the public worship very regularly for some time, and with a sincere endeavour to know the will of God; but found herself little edified by such formal devotions.'

Wildgoose replied, 'he could not but own, that there were several noble strains of true devotion in our Liturgy: and though people, who went to church with an intention to criticise, might perhaps find out some trifling imperfections; yet that, upon the whole, it was an admirable performance. But,' continues he, 'I am afraid, the fault is not in the service, but in those who perform it. The most pious sentiments will affect us but little, when delivered by the lips of those who appear to have no religion in their hearts; and loll on their elbows, and stare about for objects of amusement; as if their devotions were a fatigue and confinement to them, and they were impatient to return to the pleasures or vanities of the world.

'In short, my Lady, as things are at present, we must look else-where than at Church for the means of salvation. For my own part, I must confess myself as yet only in search of the right way; and intend this very day to pay a visit to Mr. Whitfield at Bristol; to whom, with your Ladyship's permission, I shall communicate your good disposition; whose present uneasiness is, I hope, a promising symptom of the New-birth.'

Lady Sherwood was going to inform Wildgoose, 'that she had already frequently conversed both with Mr. Whitfield and Mr. Wesley;' when the Servant came and whispered to her Ladyship, 'that Mr. —— was below, and desired to know if her Ladyship had any commands to London.'—'Lord!' says she, 'that man teazes me to death; he calls himself my Cousin, merely because his grand-father married my great grand-father's second-wife's daughter by a former husband. I wish we could make a convert of him; for, I believe, he is of no religion at all, and neither loves nor cares for any body but himself. Well,' says she to the Footman, 'desire the Gentleman to walk up.'

When he came, he told Lady Sherwood 'that he was tired of Bath, and was going the next day to London.'—She said, 'she had no commands;' but told him, 'he had interrupted them in a very agreeable conversation upon Religion; and wished he had been there to have heard it.'—'Religion!' says he, 'I do not want to hear any thing about Religion. It serves people to talk and dispute about; but I do not see that any body regulates their actions by their religious principles.'—'That is,' replies Lady Sherwood, because they do not really believe them: they have not a true practical faith in those principles.'—'Faith!' cries the Gentleman; 'for my part, I am of Mr. Pope's way of thinking in that respect,

> For modes of Faith let senseless bigots fight:
> His can't be wrong, whose Life is in the right.[1]

I live as well as I can; pay my taxes, and pay my tradesmen: and if I meet with an object of charity, that really moves my compassion, I relieve him. I go to the tavern indeed sometimes; but I never drink or eat more than does me good. And though I have no wife of my own, I never invade another's property. In short, I do not see what the best Christian can do more than I do.'

Wildgoose was going to interrupt him in his career; but Lady Sherwood calling him by his name, Wildgoose found himself disagreeably affected: though he could not at first recollect upon what occasion he had heard it before. But, after some time, he remembered that was the name of the very Gentleman who had endeavoured to seduce Miss Townsend; and, comparing it with his dress (which was the same individual blue and gold she had described), his square person, his manner of life, but (above all) his system of religion; he had not the least doubt that it was the same man.

Wildgoose was at first inclined to lead him, by some means, to the subject: but reflecting, that it could not possibly answer any good end; and being likewise impatient to set out for Bristol; and Mrs. Bardolph beginning to gape, and to consult her watch; he took his leave of Lady Sherwood; who charged him with her compliments to Mr. Whitfield; and said, 'she should be glad to see him again, if he returned through Bath.'

CHAPTER XIX

*Learned Account of the Bath Waters. Mr. Wildgoose
and his Friend take their Leave of that City*

WHEN Wildgoose returned to the Inn, he found Tugwell just
come from visiting the hot baths; the cause of which surprizing
phænomenon my Landlord, in conjunction with a journeyman
Apothecary, was endeavouring to explain to honest Jerry. My
Landlord said, 'he had heard say (though he did not know it to be
certainly so) that the heat of the bath was caused by a constant
fire in the bowels of the earth; which had been burning ever since
Noah's flood, and would in time burn up the whole world, which
was to be destroyed by fire.'

'Fire in the bowels of the earth!' says Opifer, the Apothecary,
with a sneer: 'thou mayest as well tell me, the boiling of thy pot
is caused by a fire in the bowels of the earth. No, no; such a constant,
regular *ebullition* can never be the effect of a gross *culinary* fire;
but is produced by a more latent cause; which we can explain by
the operations of *chemistry*. By a chemical process, we can analyze
the Bath waters, and reduce them to their simple elements, or
constituent particles, which are nothing but sulphur and a small
quantity of steel.

'And that the heat of these waters is caused by their running over
strata, or beds of steel and sulphur, we can demonstrate by an easy
experiment: for if you take an equal quantity of the filings of steel
and flowers of sulphur (or what the vulgar call brimstone), and
form these into a paste with water, it will produce that fermentation
to which the heat of the Bath waters is *indubitably* to be ascribed.'

'Yes, yes,' says Tugwell, 'the Gentleman talks main well; and
has made it as plain as the nose in one's face, if one did but understand him.'

Wildgoose, who had been present during part of this learned
discourse, observed, 'that the Philosophers of this age were not
content to make all useful experiments, but had a strange fancy
to be creators; and to find out the secret *art*, by which Nature
performs all her operations. They would not admit any such thing
as mysteries in Philosophy, any more than in Religion: and seemed
almost to dispute with Providence his peculiar attributes of omni-
potence or unlimited power, as well as unlimited knowledge.'

o

Mr. Wildgoose now called for his bill, and was preparing to set out. But though he had been but an indifferent customer, yet there was a secret charm in his serious and religious deportment, which made my Landlord desirous of obliging him: he therefore gave him an hearty invitation to a fillet of veal, which was roasting at the fire: and, as Tugwell seemed unwilling to travel upon an empty stomach, they made an hearty dinner, paid their reckoning, and set out for Bristol.

VOLUME TWO

... multi
Nomine DIVORUM thalamos iniêre pudicos.

OV.[1]

... venit & Crispi jucunda senectus.

JUV.[2]

S Wale del.   C. Grignion Sc.

BOOK VI

CHAPTER I

Mr. Wildgoose meets an old Friend

WHEN the two pilgrims were now come into the suburbs of Bath,
Tugwell very civilly enquired which was the Bristol road. 'Follow
your nose, and your a-se will tag after,' says a taylor's 'prentice.—
'You might learn to be more civil to strangers,' says Tugwell, 'for,
I am sure, you live by them.'—'Not by such strangers as you,'
replies the 'prentice; 'who preach against fine cloaths and innocent pastimes.'—'Come, come, Master,' says Jerry, 'come along;
let us shake off the dust of our feet, for a testimony against
them.'[1]

An elderly man, however, called out to them, that the way to
Bristol was 'straight forwards at the first turning on the right
hand.' Though this direction was a little ambiguous, Tugwell was
unwilling to hazard a more minute enquiry: they trudged straight
along therefore, without asking any further questions.

Tugwell, being highly disgusted with the insolent behaviour of
the Bath people, and expressing himself with some bitterness
against them; Wildgoose observed, 'that the mob of all places were
alike; and that he ought not to reflect upon a whole body of people,
for the wanton petulance of a few ignorant wretches.'

Jerry then asked what my landlord had charged for his supper
at Bath. 'Why, only eight-pence a night,' says Wildgoose. 'Eight-
pence a night!' says Jerry; 'an unconscionable, *dis*torting rascal!
Why, I will be hanged if I have eat three pennyworth of bread and
cheese for supper the three nights that we have been there. I have
a good mind to go and make the rogue give me back your Worship's
money.'—'No, no, Jerry, these things are customary; and it is best
to pay it without making a disturbance. At these houses, one pays
for lodging, and house-room, and attendance, as well as merely for
what one eats and drinks; and I think, upon the whole, we came off
very reasonably.'

Thus they went on talking near two miles; and, having reached the summit of the hills when it drew towards evening, they came to a place where the roads divided. Mr. Wildgoose was inclined to turn to the right, and Tugwell to the left hand; which created a little debate upon the probability of each opinion. But Tugwell, having learnt to decide dubious points by lot, threw up an half-penny, crying out, 'that heads should determine him to the right, and tails to the left hand road.' Fortune declared for the former; which Jerry, then changing his note, said *must* be the road to Bristol, by the *course* of the country.

While they were yet debating the affair, Tugwell, spying a man in a plain drap coat walking soberly at a small distance from the road, calls out, 'Holloo! Master! Master! which is the road to Bristol?' Whether the gentleman was immersed in thought, or whether he disliked the familiarity of Jerry's compellation, he made no answer. Wildgoose therefore, advancing a little towards him, repeated the question in a more civilized manner, and asked which of those two was the road to Bristol. 'Why, neither of them,' replied the gentleman; 'the road you are in would lead you to Wells.' Wildgoose was going to crave his assistance, to put him in the right way; when he and the stranger surveying each other with an air of surprise, 'What! Mr. Rivers!' cries Wildgoose.—'Bless my soul! my friend Wildgoose!' replies he; 'what expedition can you possibly be upon in this part of the world?' They then embraced (in the language of Romance) or, in plain English, took each other by the hand with great cordiality, expressing great joy at this unexpected rencounter: for they had been very intimate in the university, though no sort of intercourse had past between them for six or seven years.

Wildgoose enquired how long he had been in this country, and whether he was settled any where in the neighbourhood, as he knew him to be originally a north-country man. Mr. Rivers told him, he had an house within a mile of that place; whither he insisted upon Wildgoose's accompanying him for that night at least, as it was now too late to go to Bristol on foot, if they had not been some miles out of their road. Wildgoose and his companion were well enough pleased with the invitation, in their present circumstances: besides, as Wildgoose recollected that Mr. Rivers had in his youth a very religious turn, and that was always uppermost in his thoughts, he immediately conceived some hopes of converting his old friend to his own opinions. As they went along, Mr. Wildgoose, at Rivers's request, let him into the nature of his present undertaking; at which his friend expressed some concern, as well as the greatest astonishment; but politely added, 'that he was glad even of this opportunity of renewing their friendship.'

CHAPTER II

Description of Mr. Rivers's House, and some Account of his present Situation

MR. RIVERS had now brought his friend Wildgoose, with Tugwell, to the brow of the hill, which overlooked one of those rich vallies in which that part of the country abounds. A gate opened into a wood, through which they descended, by a rough, unfrequented road,

Where the gilt chariot never mark'd the way,[1]

almost to the bottom of the hill. There an old Gothic mansion presented itself, surrounded towards the road by a lofty stone-wall, covered with moss, maiden-hair, and other wild plants, enough to puzzle the whole Royal Society, and the indefatigable Dr. Hill into the bargain.[2] The house seemed to have been built during the civil wars between the houses of York and Lancaster; but had been *modernized* in Queen Elizabeth's reign, and new-glazed and painted for the reception of Mr. Rivers.

Rivers knocked at the gate; which being opened by a servant in a russet coat, they now came into an elegant court, where they were regaled with the sight and fragrance of all the flowers of the season. From thence they entered a gloomy old-fashioned hall, but neatly fitted up; the wall covered with maps and chronological tables, above which were a number of cheap prints, representing the customs and habits of the various nations of the world.

Mr. Rivers then, shewing Tugwell with his wallet the way towards the kitchen, took his friend Wildgoose into a large wainscotted parlour, adorned with some fine prints, a few good paintings, and a bust or two over the chimney: but all his attention was immediately fixed upon Mrs. Rivers, to whom his friend introduced him. She was sitting (like the divinity of the place) at the upper end of the room, at her needle, attended by a boy, and a fine girl about five or six years old. Mrs. Rivers received Wildgoose, as her husband's friend, with a sweet smile; which, like the sun-shine so much admired in the landscapes of Claude Lorraine, diffused an additional chearfulness over every other object.

Mrs. Rivers was about five and twenty, tall, and well-shaped; and though the pleasing cares of a young family had taken off a little of her first bloom, yet had it given such a languishing air to her eyes, and such a delicacy to her complexion, as rather improved than diminished her charms.

Mr. Rivers informed her who Mr. Wildgoose was, and how accidentally they had met. She made some obliging speech upon the occasion, and then rang the bell for tea; which being over, Mr. and Mrs. Rivers attended Mr. Wildgoose into a garden, which commanded a beautiful, though confined, prospect. It was laid out in a romantic taste, with a proper mixture of the allegro and the penseroso, the chearful and the gloomy: tufts of roses, jasmines, and the most fragrant flowering shrubs, with a serpentine walk of cypresses and laurels, here and there an urn, with suitable inscriptions, and terminated by a rough arch of rock-work that covered a dripping fountain, were its principal beauties.

After a few turns, Mrs. Rivers being summoned by her maid to a consultation about supper, Wildgoose, notwithstanding his religious severity, made some encomiums upon her person and behaviour, and said, 'he was less surprised at his friend's marrying so early in life, than at his good fortune in meeting with so agreeable a woman.' He expressed some desire, therefore, to be informed of the particular incidents of Mr. Rivers's life since he left the university. 'Why,' says he, 'though my story has nothing very uncommon in it, yet, as I flatter myself that I have escaped into one of the fortunate islands, from that rock on which the happiness of many a young fellow is totally ship-wrecked, I think, as an experienced voyager, I ought to satisfy the curiosity of a friend, and give him all the intelligence in my power, that he may steer the like course with equal success.' Then, taking Wildgoose into an alcove, shaded with honey-suckles and sweet-briars, Rivers thus began his narration.

CHAPTER III

The History of Mr. Rivers and Charlotte Woodville[1]

'SOON after you left the university,' says Mr. Rivers, 'I was elected fellow of a very worthy society,[2] where I pursued my studies with some regularity, and spent near two years greatly to my satisfaction: but, whether the way of life was too sedentary, or too sociable, (for I usually spent the day in reading, and the evening in company) whatever was the cause, I found myself after some time in a very indifferent state of health. I determined therefore, during the long vacation, to retire into the country. But, as I had neither father nor mother living, and my fellowship obliged me to an occasional residence, I did not care to travel into ——shire, which, you know, is my native country, and where I had an elder brother and some near relations residing; but was recommended by an acquaintance to a pleasant village in ——shire, about twenty miles from Oxford; who also prevailed upon a gentleman farmer, of whom he had some knowledge, to take me as a boarder.

'Mr. Woodville, which was the farmer's name, was a very worthy, honest man, and had a spirit of generosity far above his situation. He was, indeed, quite a gentleman, in his appearance, behaviour, and way of thinking. He was about fifty, and had married for his first wife a young lady of a genteel family, by whom he had one son and two daughters: but, being afterwards almost a cripple with a rheumatic gout, he had been persuaded to marry a good motherly sort of woman, beneath his own circumstances; who was glad of the match, (though sure to be a nurse) for the sake of providing better for her children by a former husband.

'I had here a tolerable apartment, entirely distinct from the rest of the family; which suited with my scheme of prosecuting my studies, and of giving a particular attention to my health, which was the principal end of my retiring from college; having, as you know, little taste for the more robust diversions of the country. But, in this retreat, remote as I was from the intrusion of my former jovial associates, I did not long enjoy an absolute tranquillity.

'There are few persons of so phlegmatic a constitution as to content themselves with merely rational pursuits. The passions, the appetites, and the imagination, all lay claim to their respective gratifications. Love particularly is a plant which springs up so naturally in the breasts of young people, that, when I hear one in the heat of youth affect to talk with a stoical indifference of that tender passion, I generally suspect him of indulging it privately, either for an *unworthy*, or at least for an *improper* object. The latter only was my case; for though an engagement of that kind was highly *improper* in my circumstances, yet the object itself was worthy the love, I might say the ambition, of a prince.

'Mr. Woodville, as I have said, had two daughters. The elder was about nineteen; and though she had nothing remarkably defective in her featutes, yet the sour and selfish passions had taken such absolute possession of her countenance, as to render her almost ugly. The younger daughter was hardly fifteen, and as different from the elder as a Grace from a Fury.

'Descriptions of a beloved object are generally heightened, and usually embellished with all the charms which the enraptured imagination is able to give them. Charlotte Woodville however was, I think, so near perfection in that respect, that, although a severe critic might possibly spy out some trifling defect, yet, upon the whole, she had so striking an appearance, that few people could behold her without admiration.

'She was rather tall than of a middling stature, but every way finely proportioned, and of a natural, easy shape. Her features were neither too large, nor too small; the extremes in either respect being, I think, less agreeable. Her eyes had always such a brilliant lustre, that I never knew their real colour. But her hair (which she had in great abundance) was of a bright brown, and gave an inimitably fine shade to her complexion. Her complection had, at that time, rather the glossy bloom of high health, than that transparent delicacy which is generally the concomitant of too tender a constitution.

'But, what gave the greatest spirit and force to her external charms, was the beauty of her mind, which was every thing that can be conceived of sweet and amiable. Good-nature and good sense, sprightliness and an artless freedom, the emanations of her charming soul, distinguished themselves in her eyes, and in every feature of her face.

'Such was this young creature in her native simplicity, without the least assistance of art, or indeed of any other education, than what was to be met with in a country place; and which the loss of a genteel mother, when she was very young, had not suffered to be applied to the utmost advantage.'

'Sir,' says Wildgoose smiling, 'you might have spared yourself the trouble, or rather denied yourself the pleasure, of this description; for, in the picture you have drawn, I can easily discover the features of Mrs. Rivers, though a few years may have abated, or rather softened, the glaring lustre of the colouring. But proceed, my friend, in your narration.'

'Well,' says Rivers, 'you may suppose a young fellow, though of more philosophy than ever I pretended to, could not be long in the same family, without taking particular notice of so lovely an object. But, as any sort of love-engagement would have been highly improper in my circumstances, a discreet person would certainly have checked any tender sentiments, and not have thought of trifling with so young a creature, who, considering my education and future prospects in life, was, in a *prudential* view, beneath my consideration. For, according to the maxims of the world,

> Love's but the frailty of the mind,
> When 'tis not with ambition join'd.'[1]

'Ah!' says Wildgoose, 'nothing but the love of God can satisfy the *reasonable ambition* of an immortal soul.'—'Very true,' replies Rivers. 'But to proceed in my story.'

CHAPTER IV

Mr. Rivers's Story continued

'As I was at that time quite a valetudinarian, and willing also to lose as little time as possible from my studies, I desired to eat at my own hours, and avoided all intercourse with the family as much as I decently could without the appearance of pride or moroseness. Mrs. Woodville kept one maid to do the work within doors; and whose business it was to wait upon me: but, as she was often otherwise engaged, the daughters would frequently by turns supply her place. After some time, however, I could not but observe, that the younger was more assiduous in her attendance on me than the elder; which yet I looked upon as accidental, and imputed it either to the good-nature of the one, or the churlish temper of the other.

Charlotte Woodville did every thing in so pretty a manner, that
although it gave me no small pleasure, yet was it a somewhat
painful tax upon my complaisance, which would not suffer me to
receive any thing from so fair a hand without some little gallant
acknowledgement. The more civility I shewed, the more obliging
was this fair nymph; and, by degrees, as I seemed disappointed
whenever any other part of the family attended me, so she grew
more kindly officious in her attendance, and,

> Tho' I call'd another, Charlotte came.[1]

'I am convinced, however, that she was utterly void of any design in
this, and at present only followed the dictates of her native benevolence and freedom of disposition: though a more powerful motive,
I believe, soon took place in her little breast; and *my* indiscretion
put matters upon a different footing.

'There happened to be a wedding in the village one morning; and
curiosity had drawn to church the whole family except the younger
daughter, who staid to attend on her father, who was confined to his
bed by a fit of the gout. Charlotte came into the parlour, upon some
occasion or other, while the bells were ringing upon this jocund
occasion. A wedding in a country place sets every girl in the parish
to simpering; and, matrimony being an inexhaustible topick of
raillery, I happened to joke with Charlotte upon the happiness of
the state. She made me some very innocent reply; which however
tempted me to chuck her under the chin, the lowest degree of
dalliance with an inferior. She blushed, and retired with some
precipitation, and with such a sweet confusion, that I longed to
repeat the freedom; and begging her to return for a moment, as
soon as she came within the door, I caught her round the neck,
and snatched a kiss. This increased her surprize, and she again
retired with a glow upon her cheeks, which I fancied expressed
some indignation; at least it so alarmed her virgin innocence, that
I saw her no more that day.

'I had now passed the rubicon of discretion.'—'Yes,' says Wildgoose, 'you had tasted the forbidden fruit. "The poison of asps is
under the lips"[2] of the most innocent of the sex. There is no
security against the encroachments of love, but by checking its
first motions in the soul. "Whoso looketh upon a woman, to lust
after her, has committed adultery already with her in his heart."'[3]

'You are too severe upon me,' replied Rivers; 'but I will proceed
in my narration.'

CHAPTER V

Mr. Rivers's Story continued

'I TOOK a walk before dinner; and, upon my return through the hall, where the family generally sate, Charlotte, instead of meeting my eyes with an open, chearful countenance, looked down with a bashful consciousness, and almost hid her face in her bosom.

'My mind was now in such a situation, that, if I had believed the freedom which I took had really offended this innocent maid, I should probably have entirely desisted, and have pursued the affair no further: but, as a little coldness would easily have nipped my passion in the bud, so the slightest encouragement sufficed to keep alive the flame. I cannot omit a trifling circumstance, which I considered in that light.

'Being under a kind of regimen as to my diet, I usually supped upon a bason of milk. This the servant brought me that evening, accompanied with a plate of wood-strawberries. It being early in the year, I asked her whence they came. She said, they were a present to one of her young mistresses. As I had met with so little complaisance from the elder, I easily guessed to whom I was obliged for this favour. This slight instance of her forgiveness, expressed in so pretty a manner, tended but little to the cure of my growing passion.

'The next day, in the absence of the maid, Charlotte ventured again into my apartment. I gave her a significant smile, in allusion to what had passed the day before; and, taking her hand, pressed it with some eagerness. She repulsed me in such a manner, as seemed rather to return the compliment, than to express any displeasure at my freedom. In short, though I had no great opinion of my own person, yet I began to flatter myself that I had made some little impression upon Charlotte's tender heart: and, as nothing is a stronger incentive to love than an opinion of its being mutual, this naturally endeared her to me, and made her appear more amiable every time I saw her. In reality, I began to love her extravagantly.

And she more lovely grew, as more belov'd.

'Jealousy is often a sign of a little mind and a meanness of spirit; and a jealous *husband* is certainly a ridiculous animal: but a jealous *lover*, I think, deserves the compassion, rather than the contempt, of his mistress. Suspicion after marriage betrays a want of confidence in her of whose fidelity we are supposed to have received sufficient assurance. But it is excusable in a lover to be a little apprehensive of the success of his rival, when it would be esteemed a degree of presumption to be too confident of his own preference in her affection and esteem. In short, whatever a woman may think of a jealous lover in other respects, she can have no reason to doubt of the sincerity of his passion.

'For my part, I began to be so fond of my little mistress, that I could hardly suffer her to be out of my sight; and, as I thought I had condescended a little in settling my affections, I could not bear with patience the thoughts of a rival; nor, indeed, had I any reason to fear one in her present situation. However, I one evening saw her engaged in so sprightly a conversation, and laughing with so coquettish an air (as I fancied) with a young fellow of the neighbourhood, who was talking to her brother at the door, that it immediately alarmed my jealousy, and I could not forbear discovering it. I rang the bell with some vehemence, intending only to put her in mind of me. Instead of sending the maid, as I expected, she immediately left her company, and came herself. I bid her send in a glass of water, which, with great good-nature, she brought with her own hands. I had seated myself, sultan-like, in a great chair; and, lolling in an insolent posture, affected to be engaged in reading, and with a haughty nod bad her set it down. She was sensible of the insult, and, immediately assuming the dignity of her sex, drew herself up, and flung out of the room with the air of a countess.

'It appeared afterwards, indeed, that the young man, whom I feared as a rival, was at this time engaged, and upon the brink of being married, to another girl in the neighbourhood; and I was convinced, that my suspicions with regard to Charlotte were entirely without the least foundation. The little quarrels of lovers generally conclude in more tender reconciliations. Miss Woodville's spirited behaviour on this occasion, and the explanation which it produced, greatly augmented our fondness for each other; and this tender intercourse was continued for some time, without being suspected by any one. I was so happy in my amour, that I never considered the probable consequences of so improper an engagement, but rather shut my eyes against any disagreeable reflections.

'As a French writer[1] observes, "The most common view that people have, when they commit imprudent actions, is the *possibility* of finding out always some resource or other:" so I flattered myself with the notion of being able to recall my affections when I thought it proper; and imagined I might amuse myself for some time, innocently enough, in so retired a place, without subjecting myself to the censure or remarks of any one, whose opinion I much regarded.'

CHAPTER VI

Mr. Rivers's Story continued

'ABOUT this time I thought it necessary to visit my friends in Staffordshire, being particularly invited by an old relation, whom you have heard me mention, the little fat clergyman, from whom I have always had some considerable expectations. Though I found myself at present but little inclined to take such a journey; yet I had fixed the day, which was now at hand.

'As my interviews with Miss Woodville had hitherto been very transient, and there was no probability of our ever being long together without subjecting ourselves to observation, I made a request to her, in which I was afraid she could not oblige me; and that was, to give me an hour of her company in the evening, after the family were in bed. As Miss Woodville was very young and innocent, and entirely ignorant of the arts of our sex, having never had any female friend to caution her against them, she made no scruple of promising me her company, if she could get her sister (who was drowsily enough inclined) to sleep without her; in order to which, she would sit up in her chamber, she said, under pretence of finishing some piece of needle-work, which she was very intent upon.

'When night came, and the family were retired, I sate myself down, with great composure, to wait the event of our assignation: I even took a book, and read, (to amuse my impatience) but with as little attention as our candidates for a degree read their wall-lectures,[2] when they expect the beadle every moment with the joyful news that their time is expired. Thus I waited for near two hours, and now quite despaired of my promised happiness; when, unexpectedly, the stillness of the night was agreeably interrupted by a gentle rap at the parlour-door. I started up, and opened it with great alacrity. In she came, but with a down-cast look, and sweet blush upon her countenance, and with an apology for the rashness of her conduct, which her native modesty now represented to her in the strongest light.

'I told her, "I had begun to despair of being favoured with her company, and asked her if her sister had any suspicion of her intention."—"I believe not," says Charlotte, "for she was asleep in five minutes after she was in bed."—"Why then did you delay my happiness so long?" said I. She replied, "That, upon thinking better of it, she was afraid she had done wrong in promising me, and had more than once resolved not to come down; nay, that she had actually been in bed, but as I talked of going early in the morning, she had not the heart to disappoint me."—I acknowledged her goodness, and assured her, "she should never repent of the confidence she reposed in me."

'I could not but take notice of one particularity in Miss Woodville's conduct on this occasion; which was, that she had taken the pains to put on a clean apron, handkerchief, and ruffles, and adjusted every part of her dress with the nicest exactness; which trifling circumstance convinced me both of the delicacy of her taste, and the purity of her imagination, or rather that she was absolutely void of the least apprehension of any thing contrary to the strictest decency in my behaviour to her.

'Nothing can be more insipid, upon repetition, than the conversation of two fond lovers; and it is a sort of prophanation to repeat any thing that passes upon those occasions: but, as something very serious ensued from this interview, I cannot forbear mentioning a few trifling particulars. I kept her up pretty late. My journey and the month's absence were the principal subjects of our conversation; in the course of which she expressed her apprehension, "that there were probably more ladies which I was fond of in other places."—"Oh! what is life without love?" said I. "To be sure, I must have a mistress at every place I go to; half a *dozen* at Oxford, you may suppose." She affected a sort of laugh at the humour of my descriptions, and, I imagined, took it, as I designed it, merely as unmeaning chit-chat. "But my favourite girl, continued I, is a ——shire lass, the very picture of yourself, a tall, brown beauty, and the best-tempered creature in the world. O! how happy shall I be next Thursday night!"

'Nothing can equal my astonishment at what now happened. Whilst I was running on in this coxcomical strain, I found her sunk back in her chair, pale as death, without breath or motion, or the least appearance of life. I was shocked, and distressed to the last degree how to proceed. I could not bring myself to alarm the family, and yet had the most terrible apprehensions of what might be the event of this affair.

'There was a decanter of water stood on the table, some of which I sprinkled in her face; and having some spirit of lavender in my pocket, I rubbed her temples with that, and applied some to her nostrils; which, after a few minutes, very happily brought her to herself again.

'I cursed my own folly, and assured her, "that what I had said was a mere jest, and that there was not a girl in the world for whom I had the least fondness, but herself."

'This proof of Miss Woodville's affection for me, you may be sure, endeared her to me extremely; and I parted from her the next morning with the greatest reluctance.'

CHAPTER VII

Mr. Rivers's Story continued

'I HAD proposed being out a month on my journey; but my eager desire to see my fair villager made me shorten my absence, and I returned in less than three weeks.

'As I had written to Mr. Woodville, and given him notice of my intention, I found every thing in great order for my reception; but was disappointed in not finding Charlotte Woodville ready to welcome me on my arrival: the rest of the family were sitting in their usual apartment. After making my compliments to them, I *affected* to look round, and enquired if some part of the family were not wanting. Mr. Woodville looked down with some confusion; but Mrs. Woodville, putting on a smile, answered, "that their daughter Charlotte was gone to school again for a little time; that, as she discovered a tolerable hand at her needle, they were willing to improve her as much as possible: she will be at home again in the evening," continued she, and then turned the discourse.

P

'I immediately suspected there was some mystery in this, as I had often heard her extolled for her extraordinary skill in needle-work, and was convinced she could not learn much at the place they mentioned, which was at the next village, whither I found she was forced to walk every morning, and return in the evening: besides, I knew it must be a great mortification to a girl of Charlotte's spirit (who was near fifteen, and very tall of her age) to be sent to such a paltry school amongst a parcel of children.

'I waited with great impatience for the evening and Charlotte Woodville's return. At last I heard her voice in the next room; which was musick to my ears. I immediately ran towards the door, where I could hear every thing that passed. Poor Charlotte, seeing some unusual preparations for supper, enquired into the occasion of them. "Oh!" says the step-mother, "I believe you can give a shrewd guess. It is for you and your gentleman, I suppose, after we *are in bed*." This spiteful speech of the old lady let me a little into the secret, and soon convinced me that our intimacy was discovered.

'As I imagined therefore I should have no other opportunity of seeing or speaking to her that evening, I immediately went out into the room where the family was, under pretence of enquiring how long it was to supper. The moment Charlotte saw me, a blush overspread her cheeks; which was succeeded by a total want of colour. She just courtesied, and welcomed me home; when she was dispatched by the old lady, upon some frivolous pretence or other, into another room; and I saw her no more that evening.

'The next morning, however, we found an opportunity of being alone together for a few minutes; when Miss Charlotte informed me of the true situation of our affairs. She said, "That her sister, having some suspicion of my affection for her, had feigned herself asleep the night when she came down to me, and had discovered it to her father and mother; that her father had given her a very serious lecture upon the occasion; but that her mother-in-law[1] had been outrageous about it, had talked at first of desiring me to quit my lodgings immediately, to which her father would not consent, he having expressed a great opinion of my honour and of my innocent intentions; in short, that at last they had come to a determination to send her out to school for the present, till they could think of some other way of disposing of her."

'Any one might imagine from this, that Mrs. Woodville was a

very careful step-mother, and had the true interest of her husband's children greatly at heart. But the reverse of this was really the case. She was what might be called, on the whole, a good sort of woman: but in all second marriages, if there are children on both sides, there must necessarily be separate interests; and a woman, who had changed her state with that view, could not be much blamed for consulting chiefly the good of her own offspring. But, in order to do that effectually, another point must be secured; I mean, an absolute sovereignty over her husband's affections; which Mrs. Woodville seemed to have gained, and of which she was excessively jealous. As Charlotte Woodville then was deservedly a favourite with her father, no wonder that the mother-in-law took every opportunity of lessening her in his esteem, and even desired to wean his affection from the darling of his age. She was pleased therefore with this instance of her indiscretion, which she aggravated to the highest degree. She said, "it confirmed what she had often insinuated to him, that Charlotte was a proud and forward hussey;" and insulted him with the prudent behaviour of her elder sister, who, for an obvious reason, had never been guilty of any thing of this kind. Mrs. Woodville had really no more regard for the elder daughter than the other: but, as Miss Betsy's unhappy temper made her no great favourite with the rest of the family, Mrs. Woodville, by a very slender shew of kindness, had bribed her to her interest, and employed her as a sort of spy upon her sister; which office she executed with an ill-natured fidelity, not scrupling sometimes to exceed the bounds of veracity, in order to ingratiate herself with her constituent.

'For old Mrs. Woodville not only considered her daughter Charlotte as a rival in her husband's affections; but also envied her the probability of so advantageous a match as mine was considered to be, and could not bear the thoughts of her being treated by me with such distinction. She therefore took every opportunity of mortifying her; and, in order to lessen her consequence in my eyes, put her upon any servile employment in the family for which she could find a decent excuse. In short, though she contrived to make poor Charlotte's situation (and mine upon her account) as disagreeable as an excessive spleen, joined with absolute power, could do, yet her behaviour had a contrary effect from what she expected, and only the more endeared to me the innocent object of her persecution.

'Accordingly, I found my passion for this young creature daily increase; and we continued our intimacy for some time. I had, indeed, indulged my fondness the more freely, as I fancied myself entirely retired from, and unnoticed by, the world; but in this I was greatly mistaken.'

CHAPTER VIII

Mr. Rivers's Story continued

'IT is more difficult for a man to live *incognito* in a country village than in the most populous city. The very precautions he takes to conceal himself alarm the curiosity of the neighbourhood; and as, in a retired place, small matters serve for amusement, the most trifling incidents soon become the subject of general conversation.

'As my regard for Miss Woodville was now no longer a secret in the family, it soon spread through the neighbourhood; and by some means or other the news had been conveyed to my friends in the university. Accordingly, the next time I went thither, I was attacked on all sides, and raillied with great freedom, upon the subject of my amour: nay, one of my more intimate friends, when we were alone together, took upon him with great seriousness to expostulate with me about the imprudence of it. He represented the ill consequences of such early engagements, and the inconveniences of settling in life without a proper competency, in such glowing colours, and set the cruelty of involving a young girl, that I had an affection for, in the distress of narrow circumstances, in so strong a light; and, in short, he harangued upon these topics so long, that at last I told him, "I was resolved to break off all correspondence with her, and, in order to that, to quit my situation in Buckinghamshire as soon as I conveniently could."—"Well, then," says my friend, taking me at my word, "I will ride over, and settle your affairs there to-morrow morning, and make some excuse for your sudden decampment."—Here I found my resolution begin to stagger. Charlotte had taken such possession of my heart, that I could not bear the thoughts of being banished from her for ever. I hastily interrupted my officious counsellor, and told him, "that my affairs were in such a situation there, that I must necessarily go over *once more* myself; but, however, that I would (if possible) take some opportunity of breaking off my imprudent engagement." He flew into a violent passion, and immediately gave me up for lost. "Then" says he, "will this little slut, with one false tear, [*unâ falsâ lacrymulâ quam vix vi expresserit*][1] undo all that I have been labouring;" and, having said this, he left me with an emphatical shake of the head, and a smile, which expressed both indignation and contempt.

'However, I returned into Buckinghamshire the next day, full of philosophical reflections, and absolutely determined (as I flattered myself) to regulate with prudence at least, if not to put an end to, this imprudent amour. But it is very difficult to know one's own heart; and, whenever reason prevails over passion, it is more frequently, I believe, to be attributed to the weakness of the one, than to the strength of the other. The moment I saw Miss Woodville, I found my resolution begin to fail me; and though I was weak enough to inform her of what had passed at Oxford, and even of the design I had formed of leaving her for some time, till I had finished my studies, and was in such circumstances as might make it more prudent for us to come together, yet I found my project so inconsistent with the present situation of my heart, and the professions I had hitherto made, that I was heartily ashamed of the figure I must make in this young creature's eyes. And, as an unsuccessful rebellion strengthens the hands of the government, so this temporary defection from my duty helped to rivet my chains: and our interview ended, on my part, with more earnest protestations of future fidelity, and a solemn promise never to forsake her.'

CHAPTER IX

Mr. Rivers's Story continued

'THOUGH Miss Woodville and I behaved with great caution and reserve to each other in the family, so as not to give Mrs. Woodville an opportunity of any open expostulation with us upon the subject; yet she was so provoked at the success (as she esteemed it) of her daughter-in-law's charms, that, with pretended concern for her daughter's reputation, she privately insisted upon Mr. Woodville's talking to me upon it, and bringing me to an explanation. He took an occasion, one day when I was alone with him, to ask me, with great good-nature, what my friends would say to my love-affair; and added, "that, as he could not give his daughter any considerable fortune, it must be an imprudent match for me, and that she would probably be happier with one in her own station; and therefore he begged I would not trifle with so young a girl, nor perplex her with fruitless expectations."

'I replied, "that though I was certain I could not be happy without her, yet I was sensible, that, as I had only a younger brother's fortune, I must make both myself and Miss Woodville unhappy, if we should marry before I was settled in any profession; that, however, as I had a very honourable passion and sincere regard for her, I hoped he would not be uneasy at my continuing the present correspondence with her, till something should happen in my favour, or I should be settled in some way of increasing my fortune; and that then I should prefer his daughter to all the women in the world."

'As Mr. Woodville was a good-natured, easy man, and I believe had forced himself to make this remonstrance only in compliance with his wife, he was soon answered; and our conversation ended without any peremptory stipulation as to my future behaviour to Charlotte Woodville. Accordingly, we took every opportunity of being alone together, as usual; which so much increased Mrs. Woodville's animosity against us both, that I soon found it would be impossible for Charlotte to continue long under the same roof with her step-mother.

'Besides, though Miss Woodville had something naturally polite and genteel in her manner, yet I thought it would be highly necessary for her to receive some better instructions, in the common accomplishments of the sex, than were to be met with in that very retired situation. After consulting her therefore, though I found her delicacy a little shocked at the thoughts of being obliged to me for any part of her education; yet, upon setting the affair in a proper light, and representing to her, how unlikely it was that her step-mother would suffer her father to be at any extraordinary expence, with a view to forward a match which she seemed so much averse to, Miss Woodville at last submitted to the necessity: and, with her permission, I at first proposed to her father to send her to a boarding-school, at a large country town, some distance from home: but after reflecting that London was the fountain-head of politeness, and that she would be there further removed from the speculation of her impertinent neighbours, I determined (with his approbation) to send her thither. He said, "that, for his part, he had an entire confidence in my honourable intentions, and should not scruple to trust his daughter wholly to my care. But," says he, "the world will be apt to censure both your conduct and mine, if I suffer her to go from home before I have some security for your marrying her. Besides," continued he, "I am certain my wife will not consent to her daughter's taking such an imprudent step upon any other conditions." In this, however, Mr. Woodville was mistaken. It had always been his wife's policy, to work her own children as much as possible into her husband's favour; and, in order to that, she was continually filling his head with comparisons between their behaviour and that of his own children, which were always injurious to the latter; and had a particular pique (as I have observed) against his daughter Charlotte, as her rival in Mr. Woodville's affections. She therefore was not at all displeased with the prospect of getting rid of so dangerous a competitor, by her engaging in an adventure of this kind, which she foresaw would probably bring some reflections on her prudence at least, if not entirely ruin her reputation: for that reason therefore, as also because she found it in vain to oppose an affair in which she saw me now so seriously embarked, she on a sudden altered her behaviour both to me and to her daughter-in-law.

'As to my marrying Miss Woodville immediately, I told her father, "that, as I was fellow of a college, though we did not absolutely forswear matrimony (as was a vulgar opinion) when we accepted of a fellowship, yet that a forfeiture of the preferment was the penalty annexed; which I must necessarily submit to, as soon as my marriage became public. As I had therefore some particularly prudential reasons for continuing at college for some time longer, I desired him to dispense with our performing the ceremony; and I would give him any security he should require for fulfilling my engagements as soon as we arrived in London. As he was of an honourable temper himself, he was not apt to be suspicious of others; but, however, could not be brought to acquiesce in such an ambiguous declaration.'

CHAPTER X

Mr. Rivers's Story continued

'ABOUT this time we had an invitation from Mr. Woodville's brother, (who farmed a little estate of his own at a few miles distance) to spend the day with him. The house he lived in was situated in the midst of woods, in a very solitary part of the country. It was a large old mansion-house, and had a chapel contiguous to it, in which service was performed once a month. As Mrs. Woodville was now upon better terms with me and her daughter, she graciously condescended to accompany us in this little expedition. As the road lay through two or three villages where we were known, this caused some speculation; and it was generally believed in the neighbourhood, that we went thither to be married. And whether Mrs. Woodville endeavoured to persuade her husband that we really were so, in order to facilitate our removal, or whatever else was the cause; soon after this, I found him disposed to consent to his daughter's going with me to London.

'Accordingly, after a few days preparation, (but without any previous provision for lodgings, or for a place of education to settle my charge in, for I had no friend in town to whom I could communicate a scheme of this kind) I sent to a large town, at some distance from Mr. Woodville's, and took places in the stage-coach, which set out every day from thence to London.

'As poor Charlotte had never been two days together from her father before, who was excessively fond of her, and also in a precarious state of health from very frequent returns of the gout, the parting between them was very affecting; and I believe there was not a servant, or any one in the family, that did not shed tears at her departure: even Mrs. Woodville herself behaved with a very decent dissimulation.'

Mr. Rivers was going on with his story, when the servant let them know that supper was upon the table. Mrs. Rivers had furnished out a plain, but elegant, supper; and Wildgoose, being happy in the company and friendly conversation of an old acquaintance, forgot a little his usual austerity, and seemed to enjoy himself like a man of this world.

After supper, however, upon Mr. Rivers's drinking an health to his *friends* in Gloucestershire, Wildgoose fetching a deep sigh,

'Ah!' says he, 'the friendship of this world is enmity with God.'—
'Well, my good friend,' says Rivers, 'not to dispute the propriety of
your application, I hope you do not think natural affection, or the
regard which one feels for one's relations, is sinful: for my part,
I am so far of a different opinion,' continued Rivers, 'that, however
unsociable I may appear, or however I may renounce the common
friendship, or rather impertinence, of the world; yet I think the
chief happiness of this life was intended by Providence to arise
from the exercise of the social affections. In this our present limited
state, indeed, it must necessarily be confined within narrow bounds.
The pride, malice, and perverseness, of too great a part of mankind,
arising from the opposition of their several interests, may make it
prudent to restrain our connections to a few friends, and almost
within one's own family: yet hereafter our benevolence, and consequently our happiness, will be greatly enlarged: and the whole
universe will probably converse with the same mutual love and
harmony as a single family.'

Wildgoose was going to reply; when a little boy, about five years
old, with the face of a cherubim, ran into the room, and, leaping up
into Mrs. Rivers's lap, ran his head into her bosom, by way of
asking *her* blessing. She looked down upon him with inexpressible
sweetness, and the air of a Madonna by Raphael or Corregio; and,
having squeezed him to her breast, dismissed him with a thousand
kisses. Wildgoose smiled; and owned, 'that was an unanswerable
proof of the happiness arising from natural affection.' And Mrs.
Rivers retiring soon after, Mr. Rivers proceeded with his story.

CHAPTER XI

Mr. Rivers's Story continued

'Upon our setting out for London, as I told you, Mr. Woodville
sent a trusty domestic with us, to meet the coach at ——, where we
lay the first night at an inn which the family always made use of.
I committed my charge to the care of the mistress of the house,
who, being a widow woman, let Charlotte sleep in her own chamber,
and in the morning saw her safe in the stage-coach. I need not
trouble you with the particulars of our journey: but suppose us

arrived in town about the dusk of the evening, and set down at the "Bolt and Tun" in Fleet-street. Whoever has seen that ancient gloomy hotel (which, however, may have been a magnificent palace before the Reformation) will easily imagine with what horror it must strike a young person, who was never before from her father's house in the country. We were taken, by a tall masculine creature in petticoats, into a dark back-parlour, with one window in it; which, instead of green fields and blooming hedge-rows, which she had been always used to, had no other prospect but into a dusky court, just large enough to contain an old bottle-rack, which faced the window, and bounded our view.

'The moment we came into this apartment, "O, Heavens!" cries Miss Woodville, "is this London? Well, Mr. Rivers, I am entirely under your protection. O, my poor father!" and almost fainted away in my arms. I endeavoured to sooth her, by assuring her she should stay but one night in that house, and that the next morning I would look out for some agreeable lodging; and that she would soon have a different opinion of that grand metropolis.

'We were now interrupted by the entrance of a drawer, to know if we called. He surveyed us both with some accuracy; and immediately sent in the chamber-maid, to ask if we must have separate beds. As soon as I had answered her in the affirmative, in comes the mistress of the house, and, after viewing Miss Woodville with an affected indifference, desired to know what we would have for supper. In short, I now began to reflect, which I had hardly suffered myself to do before, in what light the dear object of my sincerest affection must necessarily appear, and was not a little shocked at the reflection. However, I again requested the mistress of the house to get the young lady a safe bed-chamber, which she did in a closet within her own apartment.

'The next morning, as soon as we had breakfasted, I sallied forth in quest of lodgings. The most retired part of the town, that first occurred to me, was St. Martin's-lane, where, upon the pavement, I saw a bill up, with a second floor to be lett. Upon my rapping at the door, there came out a small middle-aged woman, with a tolerable aspect, who, upon my mentioning my business, entered at once into my schemes, and, with apparent benevolence, and great volubility of tongue, told me "she had lately had a clergyman's wife, out of ——shire, in just the same circumstances which I had

mentioned, and who loved her as if she had been her own mother;
that she had two daughters of her own, who would be good companions for the young lady, and went to a dancing school in the
neighbourhood, which would answer my purpose."

'In short, we soon came to terms for lodging and boarding;
and I brought Miss Woodville thither before dinner, who appeared
much pleased with the chearfulness of the apartment, and I did not
doubt but she would be here very agreeably situated.'

CHAPTER XII

Mr. Rivers's Story continued

'WELL, I had now this young creature entirely in my power;
and you might imagine, that nothing was wanting to compleat my
happiness. But, alas! I was conscious to myself, that all was not
right; and was greatly at a loss how to proceed. There was evidently
but one path which I could honourably pursue; and that appeared,
upon a superficial view, incompatible with prudence. I had no
friend in town, that I could consult upon this occasion; nor, indeed,
did I care to communicate an affair of this kind to any of my
acquaintance.

'The next morning, happening to stroll into the Park, by a great
accident, or rather, by the particular care of Providence, (for upon
this incident, in a great measure, depended the future ease and
comfort of my life) I met an old friend, whom I had not seen for
many years. Mr. Hammond (which was his name) enquired what
brought me to town. To which I made him some evasive answer.
But during our walk, as I knew him to be a man of uncommon
sense, a great knowledge of the world, and also of impenetrable
secrecy, I soon determined to make him a confident. I desired him
therefore to drink tea with me at my lodgings that very afternoon;
which he complied with: and as soon as he came, I opened to him
my adventure, and prepared him for the appearance of Miss Woodville.

'As he knew I was fellow of a college, and had only a younger
brother's fortune, and that such a scheme must be in every light
highly imprudent, he began, with great earnestness, to conjure me

by all means to put an end to it; begging me to reflect "what a concern it would be to my relations, and how probably terminate in my own infelicity." I granted all he suggested; but desired him, "to consider how far the affair had proceeded; that I had brought a young creature from her friends and from her father, who either believed that we were really married, or at least depended upon my honour to make her my wife."

'Miss Woodville now made her appearance; and, I observed, Mr. Hammond seemed vastly struck with her person and figure. However, he spoke very little; but seemed entirely wrapt in thought the whole time she was in the room. When she had made tea for us, and was again retired, Mr. Hammond made some short en-comiums upon her sweet appearance, her easy and unaffected behaviour (which was so natural to her); then took his leave, and said, "he would call upon me again the next day."

'When he came, after some little pause, "Mr. Rivers," says he, "I have been considering your affair with great deliberation; and, though I could have wished you had not engaged in it at all, yet, as things are circumstanced, and as I do not doubt but you really intend to marry Miss Woodville, I do not see how you can possibly avoid the performing your engagements imme-diately."

'Though this was what I earnestly wished, and was sensible it was what I ought in honour to do; yet, I own, the thoughts of resigning my little preferment, and embarking in the wide world with so young a consort, a little embarrassed me: yet, now I had so prudent and faithful a pilot to direct me, I was glad not to defer my happiness any longer; and he telling me, "that he knew a person who was a curate in a remote part of the city, and who would per-form the ceremony with great secrecy," we determined, with Miss Woodville's leave, to have it done as soon as possible.

'Though poor Charlotte had consented, under the sanction of her father's approbation, to put herself entirely under my protection; yet I could not but observe, by an air of dissatisfaction, and several hints that dropped from her, that she was very uneasy in her present situation. You must suppose, therefore, that in such cir-cumstances she could make no objection to my proposal. After some decent scruples, then, she consented to my request, to com-plete my felicity the very next morning; which was accordingly put in execution. And, it being necessary to acquaint the people of the house with the alteration of our condition, I ordered a hand-some dinner, and invited them to a participation: though, by their behaviour afterwards, they affected to believe this no more than a sham wedding; at least, they treated Mrs. Rivers as if they con-sidered her in no very honourable light.'

CHAPTER XIII

Mr. Rivers's Story continued

'AFTER staying a week in town, completely happy in the possession of all that was dear to me, I was obliged to leave my wife, and go down to Oxford.

'Whether Mr. Hammond considered me in the character of a Spanish husband, or whatever was his motive, he did not offer (nor did I think of asking him) to visit Mrs. Rivers in my absence: nor did I acquaint her where he lodged, or give her (as I ought to have done) any direction where to find him, in case of an emer-gency. Such a precaution, however, (as it proved) would have been no more than necessary. I had often been in London before for some months together, and fancied I knew the town tolerably well; but I had no suspicion, that about one house in ten, near that part of it, was inhabited by people whose principles, if they had any, were quite abandoned.

'I had not been ten days in the country, before I received a most terrible letter from my wife, informing me, "that she was in very bad hands;" and conjuring me "to come up to town immediately." I set out, with post-horses, the very next morning; and arrived at her lodgings early in the evening. The woman of the house came to the door; and, upon my enquiry for Mrs. Rivers, "Why," says she, "your lady is gone to bed already. Poor creature!" continued she, "she is very whimsical, and fancies she is not well." As I knew how healthy Charlotte had always been, I was greatly alarmed. I flew up to her chamber; and, to my great concern, found her in a high fever. Upon enquiring into the cause of her illness, I found it to be as follows.

'There lodged in the same house a young gentleman, of a very sober, modest appearance, with whom we spent one or two evenings before I went into the country. He told me, "he had commanded a man of war in the Mediterranean;" and I believe, by several circumstances, that this account of himself was true. Soon after I was gone down, the woman of the house came to Mrs. Rivers; and, after some general insinuations, told her, "that this Oxford scholar, who had brought her to town, would leave her there, and never return any more; that it was a common trick among them; and that she would advise her to make herself as easy as she could." Mrs. Rivers (you may be sure) was greatly startled; but her youth and inexperience was, in this case, her consolation: for it could not enter into her imagination, that there was any one in the world so base, or that what this woman told her was true. She proceeded, however, by degrees, to assure my wife, "that the young Captain was violently in love with her; and, if she would consent to live with him, he would keep her a maid and a footman, buy her much richer cloaths, and, in short, take much better care of her than ever I had done:" and a great deal more to the same purpose.

'The Captain himself had frequent opportunities given him of being in company with Mrs. Rivers; but, as he always behaved with great modesty and politeness, she was not very uneasy at what the good woman had said to her.

'One evening, however, the Captain came in to them, and, pretending some particular occasion of rejoicing, said, "he would treat them with a bowl of arrack-punch." At this the landlady of the house affected to be (and probably was) greatly rejoiced, promised how merry they would be, and talked with great glee of the approaching evening.

'Mrs. Rivers had no suspicion of any design; but was not much disposed to be chearful, as she began to have a very bad opinion of her company, and of course to be impatient for my return.

'The glass went merrily round, with my landlady, her daughters, and two or three neighbours of her own stamp, whom she had invited to partake of their jollity. Mrs. Rivers could hardly be prevailed upon to swallow one or two half-glasses: but, whether it was owing to her not being used to any thing strong, or whether they had contrived to convey any thing intoxicating into her glass, she soon found her head begin to grow giddy; so, without taking leave of her company, she slipped out of the room, and retired to her own apartment. Being apprehensive that they might pursue her, she locked her door; and observing that the bed ran upon castors, she exerted her strength, and placed that against it. She had hardly taken this precaution, when she heard the whole company (like Comus and his Bacchanals) come laughing and shouting, rather than singing, up the stairs, and protesting, "that they would pluck her out of bed." She was not undressed; but the timidity of her sex, and the particular cause she had to be apprehensive in her situation, almost threw her into hystericks, especially when she heard them thundering at the door, and declaring, "they would break it open." But her greatest danger was from the abandoned part of her own sex; for, when the Captain perceived, from the tone of her voice, and other circumstances, the excessive fright she was in, he very honourably forced them to desist from their frolick, as mine hostess affected afterwards to call it.

'Mrs. Rivers was so much alarmed, that she could not close her eyes the whole night; which, together with the pernicious liquor they had forced upon her, made her very ill all the next day.

'On Sunday, which was the day following, she was a little recovered; and the two girls, towards the evening, made her take a walk with them into the Park; where she had never been but once before, with me and Mr. Hammond.

'After walking once round, they came to the canal; and stood some time to observe several people who were feeding the ducks there. This rural amusement attracted Mrs. Rivers's attention, and, by recalling to her mind the ease and happiness of her life in the country, soothed her melancholy; and she stood fixed in a sort of reverie: but, on a sudden looking round, she missed her companions, and with great terror and surprize found herself amongst a crowd of strangers. I do not believe she knew so much as the name of the street where she lodged, nor one step of the way that led towards it. She looked wildly round on every side; and her apprehension almost took away her senses: but, in the midst of her distress, she saw a gentleman come bowing and smiling up towards her; and who should this be but the Captain! His first appearance (you may suppose) gave her some comfort in her distress: but it immediately occurred to her, that this was a premeditated contrivance between him and the people of the house. The captain conducted her towards the Bird-cage walk, and began to enquire seriously into the truth of her story, and whether she was really married to me or not. She told him so many particular circumstances, and with an air of so much simplicity, that he seemed convinced of her sincerity. He then brought her towards the gate at Spring-gardens, which, to Mrs. Rivers's great terror, they found to be shut: the Captain, however, led her through at the Horse-guards, conducted her safe home, and never tendered her any gallantries afterwards.

'These several frights and alarms, however, worked so much upon Mrs. Rivers's sensibility, that they brought a return of her indisposition; and she, the next day, wrote the letter which hurried me to town.

'I found her in a high fever, as I have related; but the calmness which my return brought to her spirits, and the excellence of her constitution, soon restored her to her usual health: and, after a little fruitless expostulation with the good lady of the house, we immediately shifted our quarters.

'I had now fixed upon an elegant lodging in a neat court, near —— square; which I was not the less pleased with, when I found the people of the house were rigid Dissenters: for, though the characters and conduct of people have seldom much connexion with their religious systems; yet, as most of those that dissent from the established church are supposed to do it upon principle, they have an additional check upon their behaviour, that they may not discredit the sect to which they belong; and, as their teachers usually take more particular care of them on that account, they have generally more appearance of religion amongst them than the common people who call themselves of the established church.'

'Ah!' (says Wildgoose, with a sigh) 'it is of little consequence what church, or what sect, we belong to, if we want a true vital faith, and are not born again of the Spirit.'

'Well, Sir,' continued Mr. Rivers, 'I stayed a week with my wife at her new lodging; when I was again obliged to go into the country: but, though the family she was now in had a very sober appearance, yet, as she had had such bad luck before, I was determined at my return to fix her as a parlour boarder in a genteel school, not far from the square, whither she now went every day, for the sake of improving herself under the several masters that attended there: and I had also given her directions where to apply to Mr. Hammond, in case of any disagreeable contingency.

'I had not been a fortnight in the country, before I received a letter (to my no small surprize) that she had again been obliged to quit her lodgings, after being again greatly alarmed, though she did not mention the particulars. When I came to town, I found, to my astonishment, the case to be as follows.

'The mistress of the house went very regularly every *Sabbath-day* to the meeting. She had not been gone long, the Sunday after I left them, when Mrs. Rivers rang the bell for the maid, to assist her in altering her dress. After waiting a few minutes, she heard her (as she thought) come tripping up the stairs: but, to her great amazement, the moment she opened the door, in came the master of the house. He was a little, middle-aged man, of a Jewish complexion, with one leg considerably shorter than the other; and being of a dirty, though one of the genteeler kind of mechanick trades, gave one no bad idea of the poetical Vulcan. His wife, however, being no Venus, (like that of the Lemnian God) he was greatly inclined to violate the matrimonial contract.

'He told Mrs. Rivers, then, "that he had a very good hand at lacing stays;" and, seeing her without a handkerchief, he offered to take great liberties. She was more provoked than terrified at this despicable gallant; and, bursting from him, ran immediately to the sash, and called out to one Mrs. Thomas, (a woman of good family, but small fortune) who lodged upon the first floor across the court, and who, seeing so agreeable a young person left in such indifferent hands, had contrived to get acquainted with her the day after I left her. This spirited proceeding in Mrs. Rivers soon put to flight her limping lover: and, upon telling the affair to Mrs. Thomas, she assisted her in packing up her things, slipped out, and, calling a coach, conveyed her immediately to the boarding-school which I had fixed upon before I went down.

'Upon my expostulating with her gallant upon this affair, he said "that, happening to go by the dining-room as Mrs. Rivers was dressing, he owned it was a great temptation; and, if *God had not given him grace*, confessed he might have yielded to the force of it; but vowed he had not offered the least incivility." As this wretch was beneath my resentment, and I was desirous of causing as little speculation as possible, I thought it best to pocket the insult, as well as the money, which he voluntarily returned, having a little unconscionably extorted it, for the ensuing week's lodging, though Mrs. Rivers was obliged to quit it on account of his ill usage.

'You may be apt to wonder what there could be in Mrs. Rivers's person or behaviour, that could expose her to so many insults of this kind. You may guess (by what you now see of her) that she

Q

must have been a very desirable object, in the bloom of fifteen, which received no small addition by a very chearful though innocent behaviour. But, I believe, it was chiefly owing to the light she must appear in, as my peculiar situation in life required me to affect a privacy; and her prudence and knowledge of my fortune would not permit me to keep her a servant: so that these low people, presuming upon the criminal appearance of our connection, made those attempts, which they would probably have been afraid to have done upon a more favourable supposition.'

CHAPTER XIV

Mr. Rivers's Story continued

'MRS. RIVERS was now settled in a tolerably agreeable family, where she had an opportunity of improving herself in every polite accomplishment from the best masters, under whose care, in a very short time, she made an incredible progress. And having now equipped herself in a more fashionable manner, and being somewhat improved in her carriage (though she wanted but little addition to her natural gracefulness), she attracted great regard wherever she made her appearance. If she happened to walk the streets, no one passed by her without particular notice; and every young fellow thought her an object worth a second view, and generally pursued her with his eyes till she was out of sight.

'Upon her appearing once or twice in the side-boxes, she had several glasses leveled at her from different parts of the theatre; and though two or three fashionable ladies of quality endeavoured to stare her out of countenance, as one *that nobody knew*, yet her conscious innocence, and her natural good sense, which immediately penetrated through the frippery of the millener and the tinsel of dress, and saw nothing in those insolent fair-ones which gave them any real superiority over herself, prevented her discovering any *mauvaise honte*, or rustic bashfulness. And she was distinguished by nothing, but by her attention to the interesting scenes on the stage, from one that had been all her lifetime in public places.

'I cannot forbear mentioning an odd kind of distress, which was occasioned by her appearing once in an improper part of the theatre. She went, with the rest of the young ladies, to their dancing-master's benefit, who was very eminent in his way, and the chief dancer on the stage at Drury-lane. Having a very full house, he was obliged to place his scholars in one of the balconies, which, you know, on common nights, are generally occupied by kept-mistresses, and people of dubious characters. Her striking figure immediately drew the eyes of all the gentlemen in the pit. Amongst the rest, a young man of fortune, one Mr. Fitz-Thomas, whose seat was in her father's neighbourhood in the country, and who had frequently dined with me at his house, immediately knew her; and, as he had heard of her leaving the country with me, and was sensible that those sort of elopements too frequently ended in the ruin of such young creatures, it immediately occurred to him, that this was the case with poor Miss Woodville, especially when he saw her in that ignominious part of the play-house. He was a man of uncommon humanity, and began to be excessively concerned, on account of the worthy man her father, and the rest of the family. However, that he might not too rashly take up with such a surmise, he resolved to go round and speak to her; when he was agreeably undeceived, and found, to his great satisfaction, the true cause of her improper situation.'

'Ah!' (says Wildgoose, with a sigh) 'I cannot but think every situation *improper* in that temple of Satan, the play-house:¹ but please to proceed with your story.'

'Well,' continued Mr. Rivers, 'you will think I dwell too much upon Mrs. Rivers's personal charms. But, matrimony being usually considered as making a purchase at the expence of our liberty, nothing is more natural than the pride we take in finding our choice approved by the suffrages of the world. I will only trouble you with one instance more.

'There was a lady, who had a little daughter in the school, and who was herself a parlour-boarder in the absence of her husband. She and one of the teachers (I know not with what view) dressed themselves out one day, and took Mrs. Rivers to the Chapel-Royal at St. James's, where, they assured me, a young hero of the highest rank eyed her with his glass the whole time. And, upon their meeting with some difficulty in getting to their chairs, an officer in his regimentals, under pretence of extricating them, enquired very minutely in what part of the town they lodged; in which this lady fancied he had some mysterious view: but, as she was a woman of intrigue herself, she was apt to suspect some deep design in the most indifferent transactions.

'The character and behaviour of this lady, indeed, whose name was Mrs. Birdlime, rendered Mrs. Rivers's situation far less agreeable than it would have been, and was one cause of my removing her sooner than perhaps I should otherwise have done. Mrs. Birdlime (as I told you) was a parlour-boarder; and, as it is usual in that situation to find their own wine, &c. and this lady was very fond of her bottle, she was teazing Mrs. Rivers every evening to join with her for a bottle of port, or a bowl of punch; and, because she had not politeness enough to trifle away her money for what was disgustful to her, Mrs. Birdlime had often reproached her with her *low birth* and country education.

'I had an opportunity one afternoon of drinking tea with this *high-bred* lady; and, after being informed that she was an Oxford woman, and having studied her features with some attention, I soon discovered her to be our old toast, Sally Burrage, an inn-keeper's daughter, who had so long powdered her red locks, and prostituted her face to her father's customers: and, by a judicious mixture of freedom and reserve, had drawn in a genteel young fellow with a pretty fortune to marry her, who, partly with a view of improving his income, and partly perhaps of being more frequently absent from his doxy, had purchased a commission in a marching regiment, and was now recruiting in the north. Mrs. Birdlime, however, contrived to console herself, in her occasional widowhood, sometimes with a chearful bowl, and sometimes, I am afraid, with less innocent amusements, if one might judge by her conversation and appearance. In short, though I found Mrs. Rivers had, at present, almost an aversion to this woman and her way of life; yet, as it is very unsafe for the best-disposed young persons to be too familiar with vice, I was determined to remove her from hence as soon as possible.

'Upon my mentioning this to the governess, who was a very genteel woman, though elderly and very infirm, she expressed great concern at the thoughts of parting with her; for, she assured me, "that, since Mrs. Rivers had been with her, she had not had the least care upon her hands, having found her so prudent and faithful, that, young as she was, she had left the chief management of her domestic affairs to her discretion."

'This account of my wife's œconomy gave me as much pleasure as the vast encomiums she bestowed upon her improvement in dancing, musick, and the other superficial accomplishments; since I had now no reason to doubt but she would appear to as much advantage in the capacity of a mistress of a family, as she had hitherto done in every other situation.'

CHAPTER XV

Mr. Rivers's Story continued

'MRS. RIVERS had, by this time, been near a twelvemonth in town; when I received a message one day from a gentleman of distinction, who was then in London, requesting me to bring *Miss Woodville* to spend the day with his lady. This was one Mr. Wylmot, whose seat in the country was not many miles distant from Miss Woodville's father's, and who, though much older than myself, from some accidental circumstances, had honoured me with a particular friendship and esteem. Accordingly, I took my wife (in the character of Miss Woodville) to dine with them at their lodgings; where she was received with great complacency and politeness.

'Upon my being left alone with Mr. Wylmot, after complimenting me upon my good choice, he, in a very friendly manner, enquired "in what manner I intended to settle in the world, if I should marry before I was engaged in some profession, as he apprehended (he said) I should be tempted to do." Upon finding myself thus closely attacked by a man whom I knew to be my friend, and with whom I should have been ashamed to trifle; after some hesitation, I told him, "that we had been already married for some time; and, what was more, that Mrs. Rivers, I believed, was pregnant." "Why, then," (says he, with some quickness) "do you not own your marriage, and resign your fellowship?"—I hardly knew what reply to make to this question; but told him, however, "that I intended it very soon, as the time allowed by the college was already expired."—"Well," says he, "I have nothing to do with your conduct in regard to the college; but, for God's sake! do not run the hazard of exposing yourself to the censure of the world, by keeping your marriage private any longer. Bring Mrs. Rivers immediately into the country, and acknowledge her publickly as your wife."—Observing me struck silent at this proposal, he very generously proceeded: "I see," said he, "you are under some difficulty what scheme to pursue."—He then told me, "that he had such a particular house at my service, and that he would assist me in furnishing it; and that we should not only be welcome to live there till we could determine upon some better situation, but that he should be very happy in having us for his neighbours."

'I was quite oppressed with the generosity of Mr. Wylmot's behaviour, not only in offering me so elegant an habitation in so polite a manner, but also his patronage and countenance against the malevolence of the world; for he was a man of such a strict regard to decency, that no one in the neighbourhood would presume to question the rectitude of our conduct, when we were under his protection. I therefore gratefully accepted of his proposal, told him "I would go to ——, and settle my affairs, resign my fellowship, and bring down Mrs. Rivers as soon as possible."—Mr. Wylmot said, "he should go into the country the next day; and, when we came, would send his chariot to meet the stage-coach, and convey us *in a more decent manner* to the place of our abode."

'Upon my communicating my intentions to Mrs. Rivers, she almost shed tears of joy at the thoughts of returning into the country: for, though she patiently acquiesced in continuing so long in town, as she thought it necessary for her improvement, yet she had often sighed to herself, and sent forth ardent wishes to see her father, her friends, and even her native place again; from which she had never before been absent a week together.

'As to her father, old Mrs. Woodville (you may suppose) had soon undeceived him with regard to our being married before we left the country; and had taken occasion, from thence, to aggravate his favourite daughter's imprudence, in consenting to go off in such a manner with an Oxford scholar. Upon my having visited him therefore, after I had settled Mrs. Rivers in London, he had discovered great anxiety on her account, and, with tears in his eyes, desired to know, "when he should have the pleasure of seeing his daughter again, and when I intended to fulfill my engagements to her." As I found what made him uneasy, I gave him sufficient proofs of my having done it already; and assured him, "that she was my wife; and that he should see her again, as soon as was consistent with the end proposed in taking her from home." On his account, therefore, Mrs. Rivers was particularly happy in the thoughts of returning into that part of the country.

'After preparing for our journey, and furnishing ourselves with several elegant, though trifling, articles of furniture, which are apt to occur to young housekeepers before things of real use or convenience; we set out from London, accompanied also by our good friend Mr. Hammond, and arrived safe at the place where Mr. Wylmot's chariot, with two servants, met us, and conveyed us with no small state to his seat. As I was known to be a friend of Mr. Wylmot's, and considered as a young man, who, though of small fortune at present, had considerable expectations, we were received with as much staring and speculation as if we had been people of more consequence. We stayed a few days in Mr. Wylmot's house; and when we were settled in our elegant little mansion, partly out of respect to him, and partly, I suppose, out of curiosity, we received the compliments of the neighbouring gentry; and for some time, I believe, were the subject of no small speculation.'

CHAPTER XVI

Mr. Rivers's Story continued

'As every particular of this part of my life is very interesting to me,' continued Mr. Rivers, 'I may probably have been a little tedious in my narration. I will therefore hasten to a conclusion.

'As soon as we were a little settled in our place of residence, Mrs. Rivers was impatient to pay her duty to her father; whither Mr. Wylmot sent a servant to attend us. You can more easily conceive, than I can describe, the tenderness of a meeting between a parent, who doated upon his daughter, and had some reason to fear the event of the journey she had taken, and a daughter, who had never before been absent from so indulgent a father.

'Though Mrs. Rivers was greatly improved since she left the country, both in her carriage, in her manner, and in the delicacy of her complexion; yet her travelling dress a little obscured her appearance the first night. But, the next day, (being Sunday) when she came down dressed for church, the whole family were

struck dumb with admiration. Mrs. Rivers, indeed, wanted no
ornaments to set her off; but a full-dress always became her: and
she dressed in so good a taste, that it greatly heightened her
natural charms.

'The fame of Mrs. Rivers's beauty and appearance soon spread
amongst the neighbouring villages; and some of the young swains,
of the best substance, who had formerly looked upon themselves as
Miss Woodville's equals, began now to curse their folly, in suffering such a prize to be carried off by a mere stranger; nay, some of
the most vain and sanguine began to enquire, "whether she were
yet really married;" boasting, "that they could yet rescue her from
the clutches of such a mere milk-sop," as, I found, they esteemed
me. But these conceited rustics had no conception, that the
improvements in Mrs. Rivers's mind would have been a greater
obstacle to their ambition than those in her mere outward appearance; for, besides her having read a great deal, and conversed with
people above their rank, Mr. Hammond, as well as myself, had
taken particular pains to cultivate Mrs. Rivers's understanding:
and, by letting her into the real characters of the several persons
into whose company she had been introduced, and by giving her
a few general maxims for her conduct in life, a girl of her penetration and natural good sense soon became furnished with a sufficient
knowledge of the world. And Mrs. Rivers was as quick-sighted in
discovering a fool, or a coxcomb, as if she had conversed her whole
life with (what is called) *the best company*.

'We spent a few days with Mrs. Rivers's father, in that complete
felicity which sincere friends enjoy after a tedious absence. I soon
perceived, however, that the pleasure, which Mr. Woodville took
in his daughter's company, was fatal to Mrs. Woodville's peace of
mind; and that she had been insinuating to her husband, "how
proud his daughter was got; that she almost disdained to set her
foot to the ground; and that nothing in *their* house seemed good
enough for so fine a lady." Though nothing could be further from
the truth than this representation, and though Mrs. Rivers behaved
with that sweetness and affability as to gain almost the adoration
of the whole family, except her step-mother; yet I thought it best
to shorten our visit: and we returned to what we at present considered as our home, and where for some time we lived extremely
happy.

'Mr. Wylmot indeed took every opportunity of shewing us

marks of his esteem, and endeavoured to make every thing as agreeable to us as possible. Mrs. Rivers was invited to partake in every party of pleasure; and Mr. Wylmot and I went frequently whole mornings a simpling, which botanical taste was what I alluded to, as the original of our intimacy; and, in short, Mr. and Mrs. Wylmot did every thing with so much delicacy and politeness, that we were not sensible of any sort of dependance. But yet, you may be sure, so precarious a situation could not be entirely satis-factory to any man, that was not void of all consideration or fore-sight.

'I could not bear to reflect upon the light we must probably appear in to the neighbourhood (who would not long be ignorant of my slender fortune), to the servants, and perhaps (though I do not know that it was so) to some distant relations of that worthy man: for I have observed, that, when a man of fortune has no children (which was the case with Mr. Wylmot), as soon as ever he begins to decline from the meridian of life, he is marked out, by his most remote collateral kindred, as one that exists merely for their emolument; as a steward, who is to manage and improve his fortune for them or their offspring; that he is generally beset by mercenary people of that kind, to whom he is accountable for every act of friendship or generosity; and that they often contrive to supplant every one, who seems to have the least share in his favour or affection.

'But though Mr. Wylmot was continually shewing us little marks of his kindness (as has been before mentioned); yet it was in such instances as were rather convenient to us, than very expensive to himself; and he had too high a sense of justice to his relations, to suffer his generosity to strangers to be any real prejudice to them.

'Another reason for our living less agreeably in this situation was (what, perhaps, you would not have imagined) its not being very distant from Mrs. Rivers's native place: for, though I am con-vinced no woman of the noblest birth or highest education could behave with more true politeness or propriety (as was acknowledged by every one that visited us when we first came into the country, and whilst they were pleased with the novelty of the affair); yet I soon found that the humble station of some part of her family, and Mrs. Rivers's former situation amongst them, were uppermost in the thoughts of many trifling people of fashion; and that those circum-stances were made a pretence, at least, for censuring that behaviour in *her*, which would have been applauded in any other woman. If she dressed genteely, it was called "giving herself airs which did not become *her* of all people; surely a woman of *her* rank had a very good excuse for not following the fashions so very scrupulously." If she happened to omit, or to be mistaken in, the minutest particular of ceremony (which was very seldom the case); then, "what could be expected from a person of *her* education? her behaviour shews what she *was*! one may always distinguish the *true* gentlewoman in the most trifling particular!" In short, as no people are so sensible of any little slights or indignities as those who find themselves sunk, either by misfortunes or their own misconduct, below the rank which they were born to (and for that reason people of the best breeding are usually more careful not to omit the usual marks of respect to persons in that situation); perhaps I was more jealous of my little rights in this respect than many people would be, and was less happy in my present situation on that account than I should otherwise have been. Notwithstanding my friend's great goodness and generosity, therefore, I was determined to get into some more independent state of life as soon as possible.'

CHAPTER XVII

Mr. Rivers's Story continued

'YOU will be surprized, perhaps, my friend Wildgoose,' (continued Mr. Rivers) 'that, after taking my degrees, and residing so many years in the university, and having had what is called a learned education, I had not pursued one of the learned professions, Law, Physic, or Divinity. But, in the first place, in each of those professions, as well as in higher life, "Ambition should be made of sterner stuff,"[1] as Shakespear says, than what my constitution consisted of; and I fancied I had substantial arguments against each of them: at least, though I had formerly some inclination to the study of Physic, and had made some progress in Botany, Anatomy, and the other preparatory sciences; yet, by marrying so early in life, I had precluded myself (as I imagined) from a sufficient application either to that profession or to the Law; for few people will care to trust, either their health to a Physician, or their fortune to the management of a Lawyer, who is not an adept in his profession: and, as to the Church, the usual sanctuary of many an idle young fellow, the little progress I afterwards made in Divinity, from a wrong plan of study, and an ill-directed application, discouraged me from engaging in so solemn a profession; for, though I might be qualified to *read* a sermon once a week to a country congregation, I think it would be much better for the community, if more persons in such circumstances would descend to a more humble sphere of life, rather than (by intruding into a province for which nature, or at least their education, never intended them) to mislead others, by their blunders and ignorance, in the discharge of that sacred function.'

'Ah!' says Wildgoose, 'it is neither nature nor education, but grace and the call of the Spirit, that can qualify a man for that sacred function.'

'Why, that may be true, in some measure,' says Rivers. 'A man should not take upon him that office without some inward call from the Holy Spirit: but the most material part of the ministerial call now-a-days seems to be the *outward call* to a good living; and, if I had not by this match disobliged my good cousin Mr. Gregory Griskin (whom you have often heard me mention), I should probably have inherited the advowson of which he is now possessed: but, as somebody has taken care to misrepresent my wife to him as a very vain extravagant woman, he will neither see me, nor hear any thing in our favour. I have therefore now no prospect of any living; and I do not chuse to go into orders, to be a curate all my life-time, and work for about fifteen-pence a day, or twenty-five pounds a year.'

CHAPTER XVIII

Mr. Rivers's Story concluded

'WELL, Sir,' continued Mr. Rivers, 'whilst I was in this uncertainty, and undetermined what scheme to pursue, I went to spend a day or two with that Mr. Fitz-Thomas whom I mentioned to you as living in the neighbourhood. I there met another Oxford acquaintance (or rather true friend), who had a good estate in this country where we are now settled. It was Mr. Grandison, whom I believe you remember; a near relation to Sir Charles Grandison[1] (who has since made so great a figure in the world), and little inferior to him in the most shining parts of his character.

'Upon talking over my precarious situation with my two friends, Mr. Grandison said, in a jesting manner, "that I must go and take his farm," which was then vacant by the death of an old tenant, and was now upon my friend's hands. Mr. Grandison had probably no serious design in this; but, though I was very ignorant of the mystery of modern Farming, yet, having been so much conversant in the classicks, I had conceived a romantic notion of Agriculture, with which my taste for Botany also had some connexion. I was therefore agreeably struck with the idea of turning Farmer, and began to think seriously of Mr. Grandison's random proposal. In short, upon talking the affair over with him more minutely, I found, that, supposing I should not make the most of things, it would yet be no difficult matter to raise the rent which Mr. Grandison expected from it; and that, with the interest of my fortune, I might live upon it very comfortably. And, when he found I was really inclined to settle in such a retired way, Mr. Grandison seemed pleased with the thoughts of having a tenant, of whom he could upon occasion make a disinterested companion in that part of the year which he usually spent in the country.

'Not to trouble you with any more uninteresting particulars, after consulting with Mrs. Rivers and Mr. Wylmot, I came down with Mr. Grandison to view the premises; which appearing every way agreeable, he gave me a proper security for an uninterrupted possession of my farm, upon paying the old rent, which was a very moderate one; and we soon after left our elegant modern cabinet in ——shire, for this Gothic dwelling where you now find us, and where, by the help of an honest old couple, who live in that cottage behind the Elms, and take the chief drudgery of managing the farm off our hands, we pass our time in a manner entirely suitable to our love of ease and retirement. The farm more than furnishes us with all the necessaries of life; and it is incredible, with Mrs. Rivers's œconomy, how small an income supplies us plentifully with all the elegancies which temperance and an unexpensive taste require.

'We are happy in a friendly intercourse with the Rector of our parish and his lady, who are sensible, worthy people. We are sometimes invited by people of higher rank in the neighbourhood; but, as I am convinced, that, as soon as they have satisfied their curiosity, and displayed their magnificence, there is an end of their civility, I give but few of them that satisfaction.

'I converse as little with the generality of my brother Farmers; yet, though many of them are people of low cunning, and never speak a word, even about the weather, without some artful design; yet I now and then meet with a great deal of good sense among them, and a plainness and simplicity which are truly valuable wherever they are found.

'But my study affords me sufficient relaxation from the business of my farm, which indeed employs a considerable part of each day, so that time never hangs heavy upon my hands; and I really take as much pleasure in the neatness of my farm, as grander folks do in their woods and lawns.

'Nay, I have reconciled myself even to the dirtiest part of my business, and can discover some sort of beauty in a dunghill; which, by reducing the most worthless things in nature into an useful compost, gives me a pleasure similar to that of an artist, who produces order out of confusion; or even that of a painter, who exhibits a pleasing landscape from contemptible materials, and from the confused jumble of various colours upon his pallet. But I begin to be tedious; and will conclude with the poet's triumphant distich,

> I've gain'd the port, and safe at anchor ride;
> Farewell, vain hopes!—let others stem the tide.'

Mr. Rivers having now brought his narrative to a conclusion; though Wildgoose thought his friend's situation favourable enough to his views of making him a proselyte, and was inclined to give a spiritual turn to the conversation: yet nature now prevailed over grace; and being exhausted with attention, as well as fatigued with his walk, he expressed his drowsiness by a very significant extension of his jaws. Rivers, therefore, waited upon his friend to his apartment; and they retired to rest.

CHAPTER XIX

Mr. Wildgoose questions Mr. Rivers on Religion

'Pox take you! I wish you were married and settled in the country!' says the Duke of Buckingham to a dog that snapped at him as he walked the street. This his Grace considered as the greatest *curse* he could wish to his greatest enemy. Yet there have been people who have found happiness in a country life, and who have thought even Matrimony a *blessing*; and poor Rivers was weak enough to rank himself in that number.

Mr. Wildgoose, being waked pretty early by the singing of the birds and the vivacity of his own imaginations, was impatient to pursue his journey to Bristol, the place of his destination; and coming down stairs, he found his friend and Mrs. Rivers with their little family already assembled in the breakfast-room, into which the sun darted his beams through an eastern window. The neatness of the tea-table, the freshness of Mrs. Rivers's complection, and the chearfulness of her countenance, attended by her little Cupids with their rosy cheeks, revived in Wildgoose for a moment his social inclinations; and he began to think but meanly of the present vagabond profession in which he had voluntarily engaged, and could not forbear the tribute of a sigh to the absent Miss Townsend.

After breakfast, however, he thought it his duty 'to put in a word for God,' as his usual expression was; and began to examine his old friend about the state of his religion.

'I remember,' says he, 'when we were acquainted at college, you were very piously disposed; and, though God had not then awakened me, I could not but admire those who were more religious than myself.'

'Why, I do not know,' replies Rivers, 'that I was any better than my neighbours. However, I am indebted to a very good, though perhaps an odd man, for what little notion I then had of religion: my good cousin I mean, Mr. Gregory Griskin, the little fat Staffordshire clergyman, whom you have often heard me mention, and with whom I lived for some time after the death of my father.

'My father, though a very learned and studious man, took but little care of our religious education. I had an old aunt, indeed, who lived with us, after the death of my mother, and who used to talk to us upon the subject once a week. But she generally came out of her closet on a Sunday night in such a peevish humour as gave us no very amiable idea of devotion; for, if we did but laugh or talk, she would fall into an outrageous passion, and reproach us with minding nothing that was good. We used to read "The Whole Duty of Man" to her;' [here Wildgoose shook his head with a contemptuous smile;] 'and I remember her often inculcating to us what some pious author says of temperance in eating and drinking; "that the only end of those natural functions is to preserve life; and that it is even unlawful to propose any pleasure in them."¹ So that I found the most temperate meal I had ever made had been highly sinful; for I always found that the satisfying one's hunger, even with bread and cheese, was necessarily attended with pleasure. Hitherto therefore the very mention of religion always damped my enjoyment.

'But at my cousin Gregory's I was inured to its severities by an agreeable mixture of mortification and indulgence. There the flesh and spirit seemed to have entered into a very amicable compromise, not to invade each other's territories. My cousin Gregory, as no man prayed more, so no man eat better. He was as hearty at his meals, as at his devotions. The bell often rang, indeed, three times a day, to summons us to prayers, either in the family, or in the church. But then we immediately adjourned, either to breakfast, to dinner, or to supper; from collects to collations, and from litanies and absolutions to hot rolls in the morning, to tythe-pigs and fat geese at noon, and to rasberries and cream and apple-custards at night: the very recollection of which, at this distance of time, is no unsavoury contemplation.

'The good books, however, with which my cousin Gregory supplied me, being better adapted to my taste and to my capacity, gave me the first notions of practical religion; such as, "Bishop Ken's Manual, the Great Importance of a Religious Life, Nelson's Devotions, Burkit," and the like plain and sensible writers.²

'Yet I cannot but confess, that, after I came to the university, by reading the writings of Free-thinkers, and conversing with dissolute people, I became quite a sceptic in religion, and had hardly any settled opinions at all: but, upon having recourse to my Bible, (though I found several things there, which, from the nature of those writings, must necessarily be obscure, yet) the essential duties of religion are so strongly delineated, that, I am convinced, nothing is wanting, but an humble mind and an honest heart, to make us understand our duty; and the ordinary assistance of God's Spirit, to enable us to practise it.'

Wildgoose began to controvert his friend's opinions: but, finding him rather obstinate, he was unwilling to push matters too far at present. He began therefore to think of proceeding in his travels, and setting out for Bristol, according to his first intentions.

He had addressed himself once or twice to Mrs. Rivers. But Mr. Rivers interposing, 'My good friend,' says he, 'my wife says her prayers, and takes care of her family, and does all the good in her power amongst her poor neighbours: but women, whose affections are employed upon their children, and their attention taken up with domestic concerns, have not time for these nice speculations, in which, I find, you have of late been so deeply engaged, and which seem to have taken entire possession of your imagination. We will therefore drop the subject, if you please, and take a walk in the garden, or try to catch some fish for our dinner.' Wildgoose thanked his old friend; but said, 'he could not possibly accept of his invitation, as he was determined to get to Bristol that evening.' He therefore took his leave of Mrs. Rivers; and, with his fellow-traveller Tugwell, set out upon his expedition, Mr. Rivers going with them to direct them into the great road.

CHAPTER XX

Comforts of Matrimony

MR. RIVERS walked a mile or two with his old friend, to direct him, as I observed, into the great road. Wildgoose could not forbear complimenting him upon the apparent happiness of his situation; and said, 'he only wanted "the one thing needful" to complete his felicity.'

Mr. Rivers replied, 'that he flattered himself with the notion of being as happy as any one can be in this world. I consider every man,' says he, 'before marriage, as climbing the hill of life. Every step presents him with some new prospect, and flatters him with the hopes of more complete enjoyment. I am now arrived at the summit of the hill, and, I believe, in possession of all the felicity which this world can afford.

'At the same time, I have a clear and distinct view down the whole vale of mortality; and can perceive, that there is nothing very exquisite to be expected from it: but, by making the best of every incident, whether fortunate or otherwise, I think a wise man may make the journey tolerably easy through this life, and must wait with patience for more perfect happiness in the next.'

Wildgoose made some objection to the inactivity of such a situation for so young a man. To which Rivers answered, 'that he saw, indeed, some of his acquaintance rising into Bishops, Generals, Admirals, Judges, or eminent Physicians: but,' says he, 'they have their reward in the splendor and the applause of the world; I have mine in the ease and tranquillity of my life.'

Before they parted, Rivers took the liberty, in his turn, to expostulate with his friend on his present romantic undertaking; and said, 'that although he did not doubt his intention was good, and that the world stood in need of some reformation; yet he could not think that any private person could be justified in disturbing the peace of society, without some divine commission for that purpose.' But reasoning with a man under the influence of any passion is like endeavouring to stop a wild horse, who becomes more violent from being pursued. The two friends, however, took leave with mutual good wishes. Wildgoose said, 'he should pray for Mr. Rivers's conversion:'—and Rivers, 'that it would be a great pleasure to him, to hear that Mr. Wildgoose was returned to his friends and usual residence.'

CHAPTER XXI

They arrive at Bristol

It was now past the middle of the day, and the weather extremely hot. Tugwell, therefore, interceded with his master, 'to stop and refresh themselves at a small inn, a few miles short of Bristol;' with which request, though impatient to get to his journey's end, Mr. Wildgoose thought it expedient to comply. He took himself a very slight refreshment; but desired Jerry, 'to call for what he chose;' which having done, and taken his pipe according to custom, Jerry sate down upon a bench, between a Bath postilion and the

R

tapster, and took a comfortable nap. But Wildgoose soon rouzed him from his tranquil state, and again set out with hasty strides for the great commercial city of Bristol; which he considered, however, in no other light than as the Capernaum, the present residence of that great apostle Mr. Whitfield. Here they arrived about six o'clock in the evening.

As soon as they were got through the city-gate into Temple-street, (which gives one no very favourable idea of that opulent city) some boys called after Tugwell, who was a few yards behind his master, 'Ha! Jerry! your humble servant, Master Jerry.' Before he could express his surprize, another cries out, 'God ha' mercy, Jerry!' A third hollows out, 'Jerry for ever!'

As soon as Tugwell could come up to Wildgoose, 'Odsbobs,' cries he, 'why, Master, our name is up; we may lie abed; I suppose they have heard of our preaching all over England by this time; the very boys in the street seem to know us, and call us by our names.'—'Why,' replies Wildgoose, 'I do not suppose it is altogether the fame of our preaching that makes us known here; but I do not doubt that God will send his angel before us, as he did before Mr. Whitfield in Wales;[1] and where-ever we come, prepare people for our reception.'

Wildgoose was going on in his observations; when Jerry now getting before him, he saw his name, in capital letters, written upon his back, with chalk; which was a piece of waggery of the tapster's at their last stage, who, having heard his master call him Jerry, while Tugwell took a nap between him and the postilion, as was related, had put that joke upon him. Wildgoose rubbed out the chalk as well as he could, to prevent them from being exposed to unnecessary speculation; and they trudged on towards the heart of the city.

Upon enquiring after a lodging of a sober sort of a tradesman at his door, they were directed down to the Quay: where they met with a tolerably decent apartment at a Gingerbread-baker's, on reasonable terms; though they were obliged, by a prudent precaution of their landlady, to pay a week's rent on their taking possession of the premises.

Wildgoose, thinking it now too late to wait on Mr. Whitfield that evening, employed it in making proper enquiries after his lodgings, and in giving good advice to the people where he himself lodged; and, after eating a slight supper, retired early to his repose.

BOOK VII

CHAPTER I

Mr. Wildgoose's Interview with Mr. Whitfield

ALL the civilized nations of the world had now —— boiled their tea-kettles; and all the inhabitants of Great-Britain (except those of the court-end of the metropolis) were at this instant recruiting their spirits with a comfortable breakfast; when Mr. Wildgoose, ever attentive to the great object of his peregrination, summoned his fellow-traveller, Jeremiah Tugwell, from the kitchen chimney-corner, where he had got leave to smoke his morning pipe. 'Come, Jerry,' says Wildgoose, 'up, and be doing; lay aside your pipe, and follow me.'

When they were come into the street, Wildgoose told Jerry, 'that he had found out Mr. Whitfield's lodgings, which,' says he, 'are but a short walk from this place. But,' continued he, 'that tobacco of thine has a most ungodly savour; thy smell is as the smell of a tippling-house, and will be highly offensive to that holy man, who, I am persuaded, has been watching and praying for some hours, or, perhaps, has been feeding his *five thousands* with the heavenly manna of his eloquence: for my part, I was determined neither to eat nor drink till I had been admitted to commune with him; that I might be the more fit to receive the divine instructions of so great a master.'

As Wildgoose was thus expostulating with his friend, they arrived at Mr. Whitfield's lodgings; and, upon enquiring for him, they were shewn up one pair of stairs by the maid of the house, who tapping at the door, the two pilgrims were immediately admitted to Mr. Whitfield's presence.

Mr. Whitfield was sitting in an elbow chair (in an handsome dining room), dressed in a purple night-gown and velvet cap; and, instead of a Bible or Prayerbook (as Wildgoose expected), he had a good bason of chocolate, and a plate of muffins well-buttered, before him.

Wildgoose made a pause at the door, being a little dubious whether they had not mistaken the room; and Tugwell drew back, quite struck with awe at so episcopal a figure. But Mr. Whitfield hailed them with a cordial condescension: 'Come, come in, my dear friends; I am always at leisure to receive my Christian brethren. I breakfasted early this morning with some prisoners in Newgate, upon some tea and sea-biscuit; but found my stomach a little empty, and was refreshing myself with a dish of chocolate.[1]

'Well, my good friends,' continued Mr. Whitfield, 'has God made use of the *foolishness* of my preaching, to convince you of sin, and to bring you to a sense of your fallen condition? Come, my brethren, sit down; and let me know, when you were converted, and what symptoms of the New Birth you have experienced in your souls.'

'Ah! Sir,' replied Wildgoose, 'we have not yet had the happiness of hearing you preach; but I hope God has, by some other means, vouchsafed to give us some little sense of religion: and we have taken a pretty long journey, to learn from your mouth a more perfect knowledge of this way.'

'Yes, yes,' (quoth Tugwell, a little encouraged by Mr. Whitfield's condescension) 'his Worship is no novice in these matters himself: he can preach like any Bishop, upon occasion, if that were all; but he is come to know how your Reverence will please to employ him, and to get a little more of your Gospel *lingo*, and such like.'

This discovery of Wildgoose's intentions was by no means agreeable to Mr. Whitfield; for, whether he gloried in the number of his followers, and began to taste the sweets of such distinction, or whether he thought that too great a number of labourers in the vineyard might render the soil less fruitful to himself; however it was, he did not seem inclined to admit any more sharers in the labour;[2] but began to complain of the great number of divisions already among them; 'that one was of Paul, and another of Apollos; that brother Wesley had preached another Gospel, entirely contrary to his; and in short, that, from that source, "strife, envy, wrath, reviling, back-biting, drunkenness, and every evil work," began already to prevail amongst them.'[3]

'Well, well,' (says Tugwell, before Wildgoose could reply) 'his Worship does it only out of love and good-will (as a body may say); we have travelled pretty near an hundred miles *a foot* upon this errand; though, for that matter, Master *Wildgoose* has as good a gelding in his stable as any gentleman in the county; and can afford to spend his own money, if need be, and does not do it for the lucre of gain.'

When Mr. Whitfield heard the name of *Wildgoose*, he immediately recollected the accounts he had received, by letters from Bath and Gloucester, of this opulent convert; and immediately found himself inclined to receive more favourably Mr. Wildgoose's proposals. He thought he might advantageously employ, in some remote province, so creditable a Missionary, of whose abilities he had heard no common encomiums. He now, therefore, began to enquire more particularly into the circumstances of his conversion, and what proofs he could give of a ministerial call and qualifications.

'Well, brother Wildgoose,' says Mr. Whitfield, 'when and where were you converted? when did you first begin to feel the motions of God's Spirit? in what year, what month, what day, and in what manner, did you receive the secret call of the Spirit to undertake the work of the Ministry? what work of grace has God wrought upon your soul? and what symptoms have you felt of the New Birth?'[1]

Wildgoose, not being prepared for a scrutiny of this kind, began to stare, and could not readily give an answer to these questions. After a little recollection, however, he said, 'that several circumstances had contributed to wean him from the vanities of the world; which disposition was confirmed,' he said, 'by hearing one or two Gospel-preachers, but chiefly by reading several good books, and particularly his and Mr. Wesley's Journals; whence, from observing the great success God had given to their labours, he found himself inclined to attempt something in the same way.'

Here Tugwell could not forbear putting in his verdict. 'Odsbobs!' says he, 'I believe I understand what the gentleman means by the *New Birth*. It is no longer ago than last October, we had been grinding apples, and making cyder, for Madam Wildgoose, your Worship's mother; and all the next day I was mortal sick, and troubled with the gripes and the belly-ach; and I thought I should have *sounded away*. Old Madam gave me some *Higry-pigry*;[2] and our Dorothy, who is the best wife in England, would have had me eat some bacon and eggs: but I could not bear the smell of victuals; and I thought I should have died. But at night, as soon as ever your Worship began to preach in our chimney-corner, I found comfort;

and, from that time to this, I have never drunk a drop of cyder, nor been at an ale-house, till we came this journey, nor at any merry-making, nor *sich* like; as your Worship very well knows.'

Wildgoose endeavoured more than once, by winks and nods, to give a check to Tugwell's volubility. But, though Jerry probably mistook the colic for the symptoms of the New Birth, yet Mr. Whitfield desired to hear the particulars, and endeavoured to give the most religious turn that he could to his impertinence. Then addressing himself again to Mr. Wildgoose:

'Well, Sir,' says Mr. Whitfield, 'I would have you consider before you put your *hand* to the *plough*, and *compute the costs*; that is, how you can bear the persecutions, the insults, and mockeries, which you must expect to meet with in this arduous undertaking. You must submit to the lowest offices in this *labour of love*; you must pass through *evil report* and *good report*, converse with publicans and sinners, and even with harlots, if there be any prospect of their conversion. And I will consider,' continues Mr. Whitfield, 'of the properest method of employing your talents. But, I believe, I shall send you to preach the Gospel to the poor Colliers in Stafford and Shropshire, or to the subterraneous inhabitants of the lead-mines in the Peak of Derbyshire, who are as sheep without a shepherd:[1] though I hope my brother Wesley has, by this time, been amongst them.'

Wildgoose replied, 'he should dispose of him as he thought proper.' And Tugwell, who (though he fancied himself another Timothy, yet) considered amusement chiefly in his travels, cried out, 'Odsbobs! I shall like to travel into Derbyshire, and see the wonders of the Peak. There is a hole in the earth without any bottom to it, as they do say; and a passage into the other world, which they call, the Devil's a-se o' Peak.—'[2] 'I do not know what they call it,' replies Mr. Whitfield; 'but, by all accounts, the Devil has an extensive property, and great power, over the whole world at present, especially amongst those poor people, whose subterraneous employment cuts them off from all chance of spiritual instruction. But I hope, by the help of my good brother here, and other friends, we shall soon make the Devil's kingdom shake to its very centre.[3]

'I am to preach this afternoon,' continues Mr. Whitfield, 'to the poor Colliers of Kingswood (where, my greatest enemies must confess, I have done considerable service); and in the evening to one of our Societies in Bristol: to both which places I hope you will accompany me, and behold the wonderful works of God.'

Wildgoose said, 'he would with pleasure attend him;' but added, 'as God had so far prospered his journey as to bring him to the sight of Mr. Whitfield, he would trespass no longer upon his time at present than to deliver Lady Sherwood's compliments, as he had promised her Ladyship, whom he saw at Bath.' Mr. Whitfield replied, 'that that was an Elect Lady, a Star of the first magnitude; and he did not doubt but she would be an instrument, by the influence which her rank and fortune gave her, of promoting the great work which was going to be wrought upon the earth.'

Mr. Wildgoose then took his leave, promising, 'to attend him with great punctuality, both at his afternoon's and evening's engagement.'

CHAPTER II

Hears Mr. Whitfield at Kingswood

A s soon as they were come into the street, 'Odsbodikins!' cries Tugwell, 'this is a desperate *familler* gentleman. Methinks he and I could be as good company together as if we had been acquainted these twenty years. But I think he might have offered us a bit of his oven-cake, and a drop of his buttered-ale, or whatever it was. But come, Master, let us go and get something to eat; you will never be able to hold out as Mr. Whitfield does. He seems to like a bit of the good *cretur* as well as other folks.'

'Ah! Jerry,' says Wildgoose, 'thy thoughts still run upon thy belly and the flesh-pots of Egypt. However, our Master does not deny us the use, but the abuse, of his good creatures. "Thou shalt not muzzle thy ox, or thy ass, that treadeth out thy corn."[1] Those, that labour most in spiritual things, have the best right to these carnal things; though they do not place their happiness in them.'

By the time they came to their lodging, however, their hostess had got a good warm dinner of homely food; the savoury smell of which revived Wildgoose's appetite: so that, the natural man getting the better of the spiritual, he sate down with Tugwell and the family, and ate as heartily as the best of them.

The time was now come when they were to attend Mr. Whitfield to Kingswood; where, when they arrived after a sultry walk, they found about ten thousand people assembled; the trees and hedges being lined with spectators. There had been a violent storm of thunder and lightning; but this was dispelled by a single ejaculation: and Providence was pleased so visibly to interpose, in causing the weather to clear up just as he began, that Mr. Whitfield could not avoid taking notice of it in his discourse to the people, and to hint, 'that the course of nature had been altered in favour of his harangue.' The sun now shone, and all was hushed; and, notwithstanding the distance of some part of the audience, they all heard distinctly; for, indeed, the wind was extremely favourable.[1]

Whilst all was thus in a profound calm for near an hour, every one being attentive to the voice of the preacher, on a sudden the skies again grew black; and the assembly was alarmed a second time, by a most tremendous volley of thunder and lightning, and a storm of rain.

A remarkable difference now appeared between the Saints and the Sinners. Those whom curiosity, or perhaps some less justifiable motive, had brought thither, scampered away with the utmost precipitation to trees or hedges, or some occasional sheds which had been erected amongst the coal-works, to avoid the impending storm; whilst those, who either were, or fancied they were, possessed of true faith, scorned to flinch, or to discover the least regard to their bodies, whilst they were thus refreshing their souls with the heavenly dew of Mr. Whitfield's eloquence.

Mr. Whitfield now very dextrously shifted his discourse to the present occasion; and observed, 'that although Providence had, at their first meeting, so miraculously put a stop to the rain; yet he had now, with the same gracious intention, permitted it to rain again, to try the zeal of his audience, and to distinguish his sincere votaries from pretenders and hypocrites: and he did not doubt, but, together with the rain, God would shower down upon them "the gracious dew of his blessing," and refresh them with his spirit.' And this compliment many of them thought a sufficient consolation for their being wet to the skin.

The service being now ended, though the storm was over, and the sun shone out; yet a good part of the audience were in such a dripping condition, that it furnished many a pious soul with a good pretence for taking a cordial; and the brandy-bottle and ginger-bread were plentifully distributed by the suttlers, that always attended on these occasions.

CHAPTER III

Evening's Entertainment

MR. WILDGOOSE and his friend Tugwell had hardly dried and refreshed themselves after their return from Kingswood, when they were again summoned to attend Mr. Whitfield to the nightly meeting at the Tabernacle; where he harangued to a less numerous, yet not a less crowded, audience than that at Kingswood. He usually made choice of a different text at each meeting; but, whatever the subject was, it always ended, like Cato's speeches in the senate-house, with, *Delenda est Carthago*, '*Down with your good works!*' with a denunciation against self-righteousness, and a recommendation of Faith alone in its stead, as if Virtue were *inconsistent* with the belief of the Gospel; though (as a great Divine[1] observes) 'this doctrine of renouncing their own righteousness has been generally found most agreeable to those who have no righteousness of their own to renounce.'

And now Wildgoose discovered the true secret of making converts. He had often himself had the satisfaction of being followed and applauded for his eloquence; but had reason to suspect that he rather entertained his audience, than made them real converts to his opinions. His mistake was, that he began at the wrong end. He went the old-fashioned way to work, and was for persuading people to repent of their sins, and reform their lives; to practise the precepts, as well as believe the doctrines, of the Gospel; which kind of preaching, though inforced in the most pathetic manner, was not so generally palatable as might be expected.

Mr. Whitfield, on the contrary, said little about Repentance, but laid all the stress upon Faith alone; so that, if a man was, or fancied, or even said, that he was, possessed of true Faith, he was immediately pronounced a convert, and, whether he *reformed his life or not*, became a Saint upon easy terms. By this means chiefly such crowds of Colliers and Chimney-sweepers were transformed into Angels of light, and became entitled to many a comfortable breakfast of buttered-toast and tea with the more wealthy devotees, and helped to increase the fame and popularity of these itinerant Reformers: not to mention the many facetious tales with which Mr. Whitfield amused his hearers from Joe Miller,[2] and other authors of facetious memory; and the attractions which were found in their Psalms and Hymns; which, being chiefly set to popular tunes, had the same effect in recommending their doctrines, as the like cause had formerly in establishing the fame of the Beggar's Opera.

The meeting being ended, and Mr. Whitfield somewhat fatigued, he took his leave of Mr. Wildgoose for that evening, but desired his company to breakfast the next morning; with which Mr. Wildgoose punctually complied. Mr. Whitfield then told him, 'he had it revealed to him by the Spirit, that Mr. Wildgoose should go towards the North in a few days, and preach to the Colliers and Lead-miners in those parts; but that he should first give the word of exhortation to their brethren at the several meetings in Bristol, that he might judge of the soundness of his doctrine, and give him any necessary instructions for his future conduct.'

Though this was but a proper compliment to so distinguished a convert, and Mr. Whitfield was willing to treat his followers with a little variety; yet, as he found some few sparks of jealousy in his own breast, he was desirous of dismissing Wildgoose as soon as he decently could. Mr. Whitfield, indeed, had the advantage of him in complexion, and the solemnity of his periwig (and a good periwig, as the Barber observed, contributes not a little to the conversion of Sinners); yet Wildgoose excelled Whitfield in an expressive countenance, and a more gentleman-like air; not to mention the weight which an opinion of Wildgoose's superior fortune would probably give to his eloquence.

Mr. Whitfield therefore proposed, 'that Wildgoose should hold forth that very evening at one of their meetings;' to which, with a decent reluctance, he consented; which point being settled, Wildgoose took his leave for the rest of the day.

CHAPTER IV

Wildgoose mounts the Rostrum. An unexpected Incident

IN the evening, at the usual hour, the two Brethren met at the Tabernacle; and Wildgoose was conducted to the desk by Mr. Whitfield himself, where several ladies were already seated (which is a compliment usually paid to persons of any fashion); and they seemed particularly pleased with the genteel, though plain, appearance of this youthful orator.

Mere novelty gives a Preacher no small advantage, if there is nothing very dull or ungracious in his manner. Wildgoose, however, having several other recommendations, was heard with particular attention and applause; and his fame soon spread universally amongst the Saints of Bristol; and he preached almost every evening to more crowded audiences than Mr. Whitfield himself.

But his fame was accompanied also with more solid advantages, and introduced him to the acquaintance of two or three wealthy dowagers, and as many handsome wives. Among the rest, he was particularly intimate with Mrs. Cullpepper, the young wife of a wealthy Alderman of the city of Bristol; who, having no children to amuse her, and finding but few of the comforts of Matrimony in the society of an elderly husband, chose to pass two or three evenings in a week at these Religious Assemblies; in which innocent amusement her spouse gladly indulged her. These pious ladies then thought nothing too good for such good and holy men; so that, with chocolate and rolls for breakfast in the morning, biscuits and sack at noon, with turbot, ducks, and marrow-puddings, for dinner, and roasted fowls or partridges for supper at night, Wildgoose passed his time in no unpleasant manner.

After he had been haranguing one evening, with the pretty Mrs. Cullpepper (like the Angel usually painted at the back of St. Matthew) leering over his shoulder; when the meeting was ended, and the crowd began to disperse, he handed her out of the desk; and, when they came to the door of the Tabernacle, they found a crowd gathered round two genteel sort of women in travelling dresses, one of whom, they said, was fallen into an hysteric fit. As this was no uncommon symptom of the New Birth, Wildgoose approached to administer some spiritual comfort, when the lady should come to herself again; but, when that happened, how great was his astonishment to find, that the lady in a swoon was no other than Miss Townsend, for whom Wildgoose had conceived so tender a regard when he was acquainted with her at Gloucester.

Mrs. Sarsenet, it seems, under whose protection Miss Townsend had placed herself after her imprudent elopement from her father, had some business at Bristol-fair, which began about that time; and Miss Townsend, having a desire to see Bristol (and perhaps from some more tender motive), had desired to accompany her in the stage-coach; and, having been awaked early in the morning, fatigued with her journey, and perhaps somewhat affected at the sight of Mr. Wildgoose's gallantry to Mrs. Cullpepper, it was more than her delicate constitution could well support.

Wildgoose, having acknowledged them as his acquaintance, and made a proper apology to Mrs. Cullpepper, begged leave to accompany Mrs. Sarsenet and Miss Townsend to their inn; where they spent the evening together, in talking over the state of affairs at Gloucester, the adventures of their journey, and such other chit-chat, which, though insipid enough to others, is very interesting to friends who have been any time absent from each other. In short, the evening passed away very agreeably to Wild-goose and to Mrs. Sarsenet; and probably, if the truth were known, no less so to the sprightly and amiable Miss Townsend.

CHAPTER V

Gloucester Journal

As Mrs. Sarsenet and Miss Townsend stayed the next day in Bristol, Wildgoose passed most of the time with them. Mrs. Sarsenet informed him, amongst other things, of 'the persecution which poor Keen, the Barber, had undergone from his neighbour at the pot-house, who, to be revenged on the Barber for taking him before the Mayor, had gone privately and paid off a year's rent which he owed his landlord, and arrested him for the money; by which means the poor Barber was reduced to the utmost distress.' She told him likewise, 'that she herself had made some enemies, by telling people, in the way of her business, some disagreeable truths; but that she was happy in the slightest persecution for the Gospel's sake.'

Miss Townsend also, at Wildgoose's request, related what had passed at her interview with her father, who, he soon found, was the same curious gentleman whom he had accidentally met at Lord Bathurst's house in the wood. 'My father,' says Miss Town-send, 'sent for me to the Bell-inn; and, upon my falling upon my knees before him, raised me up, and with great tenderness clasped me in his arms, the involuntary tears trickling down his cheeks: he soon began to chide me, however, as he had too much reason to do, for my unparalleled imprudence; but said, "he could more easily have forgiven me, if I had not aggravated my crime by taking refuge with my good friend here, Mrs. Sarsenet, who, he alledged, had been guilty of so many deliberate affronts to him and Mrs. Townsend in her letters."

'Upon my attempting to justify this part of my conduct (as Mrs. Sarsenet had been a friend of my mother's, and as I was afraid to return home, where I had been so ill-used by Mrs. Townsend); he flew into a violent rage, and said, "that, under the pretence of a great regard for my mother, I shewed a great disregard for him; and that it was very saucy and undutiful in me, to take upon me to censure his conduct, or to behave with disrespect to a person who was so useful to him in the management of his family; and, in short, that he could not desire to see me at home again, till I could bring myself to behave with more civility and complaisance to the widow Townsend; but," says he, "I will think of some method of disposing of you; for you shall not continue with this woman here," meaning my good Mrs. Sarsenet.

'He then sent the servant with me to Mrs. Sarsenet's, after taking a very cool leave, and bidding me "consider of it, and behave better for the future." The servant told me, as we went along, "that he believed his master was going into Warwickshire before he returned home;" so that, I imagine, my dear father intends to send me to a very worthy Clergyman's, who married a near relation of ours; which, as things now are, would be a situation the most agreeable to my wishes.'

Miss Townsend then asked Wildgoose, in her turn, 'whether he had heard any thing further of his poor mother, who, she was persuaded, must be greatly concerned at his absence; and when he thought of returning into that part of the country?' Wildgoose replied, 'that he was soon to go towards the North, and intended to call upon Mrs. Sarsenet and his friends at Gloucester; but was afraid it would be too much out of the road to visit his native place; though in this,' he added, 'the dictates of the Spirit must be his guide.'

As Mrs. Sarsenet and Miss Townsend were to return the following day, Wildgoose took them in the evening to hear Mr. Whitfield; though much against Miss Townsend's inclination, who also absolutely refused to go into the desk (whither she was invited), because she saw the same Mrs. Cullpepper there, whom we before mentioned as a constant attendant of Mr. Wildgoose, and whom she had seen him gallanting out of the desk the night before at the Tabernacle.

Wildgoose took his leave of his two friends that evening, who were to return the next morning in the stage-coach. Yet, when the morning came, he could not forbear another visit to their inn, to take a second leave of the amiable Miss Townsend; which was done with no small degree of tenderness on either side.

CHAPTER VI

Triumphs of Faith

AFTER his two friends were gone, Mr. Wildgoose went to have another conference with Mr. Whitfield, who took him to visit the prisoners in Newgate, and to several other objects of charity; to whom Wildgoose was more liberal than it was prudent for him to be, considering how soon his stock might be exhausted, and how difficult it would be, in his present situation, to recruit it.

Amongst other objects of distress, Wildgoose released from his confinement a journeyman Sugar-baker, who had been thrown into prison by his master out of spite, for being a follower of Mr. Whitfield, and for—a trifling mistake in his accounts.

Another young fellow was confined (as he assured them) only for writing the name of a Country Justice to a petition, out of mere charity to a poor Farmer, who had suffered great losses by fire.

Mr. Wildgoose also bestowed an handsome gratuity upon a poor woman, who had been used to retail Gin about the streets, but who pretended to have lost her trade, and to be reduced to poverty, by so many of her customers having been converted by Mr. Whitfield. This complaint strongly recommended her to Mr. Whitfield's attention, and to Wildgoose's benevolence and liberality.

Mr. Whitfield then conducted Wildgoose (by way of curiosity) to several different people, who were great advocates for the right of Private Judgement, and for the liberty of interpreting Scripture their own way; who looked upon all Creeds and Confessions of Faith as unjust impositions, and as insults upon the Freedom of

Human Nature; who were for the Independence, not only of each Congregation on other Churches, but of every Individual on each other.

In order to pursue their plan the better, these people had given up all secular employment, and did nothing but study the Scriptures from morning till night, the precise literal sense of which they strictly adhered to. There were half a dozen of them, who lived together in one house, and had 'all things in common' (in which was included a community of wives); so that they lay *higgledy-piggledy*, just as it pleased their fancies: they wore each other's shirts and shifts; and it sometimes happened, that the men wore petticoats, and the women wore the breeches; so strictly did they adhere to the letter of the law.

There was one man who had 'sold all that he had,' even his very cloaths (which, indeed, was only a coat and breeches), and had 'given it to the poor;' so that he himself was become one of that number; for he was quite naked, and forced to subsist upon the charity of his Christian brethren:[1] this, however, he might easily do; for, according to another precept of the Gospel, he thought it necessary to become as a little child, and, like a new-born babe, fed upon nothing but milk, or pap made of the mouldy crusts which were sent him for that purpose. Similar to this was the error of another poor man, who made it a rule to 'give to every one that asked him;' so that, having given away all his own money in charity, he now did the same by all that he could extort by begging from good Christians in more affluent circumstances.

These people also shared the benevolence of Mr. Wildgoose; though he and Mr. Whitfield endeavoured to shew them the absurdity of their principles, and the ridiculous consequences which, amongst ignorant people, might arise from thus realizing the metaphors of the Oriental languages. 'Thus,' says Wildgoose, 'the Painter (in Mr. Wesley's History of the Bible) has drawn one man with a long beam sticking out of his eye, and endeavouring to pull a little straw, or mote, out of his brother's eye.[2] And, although we are commanded "to build up one another in the Faith," it would make but an odd sort of a picture, to see a parcel of Christians turned Masons and Carpenters, and piling up one another like so many stocks and stones.'

Mr. Whitfield said, 'their principles were too absurd to be criticised. However, as God had once opened their eyes to see part of the truth, he did not doubt but he would perfect his own work, and bring them at last to the true faith.'

Mr. Whitfield then took Wildgoose into a very dark street, where the houses in the upper story almost met. Out of the middle of this street they went into a little court, then up a winding stair-case, where Mr. Whitfield knocked at a chamber-door, which was opened by a little thin man, who desired them to walk in. His apartment was small, but neat enough, having a print of the Crucifixion over the chimney. There were no signs or implements of any art or trade; nor any books but a Quarto Bible, which lay open on a table under the window.

'Mr. Wildgoose,' says Whitfield, 'give me leave to introduce you to a Religious Curiosity; or, rather, if he does not deceive himself, to a Miracle of Divine Grace! Our Brother Slender here is a man, that has not committed sin these five years.'—'Hem!' (cries Slender, lifting up his eyes, and laying his hands upon his breast) 'nor ever will again, whilst in the body, by the grace of God.' —'What way of life is Master Slender in, then?' says Wildgoose.— 'I am a Stay-maker by trade,' quoth Slender.—'Do not you work at your trade, then?' says Wildgoose.—'No, by the grace of God,' answered Slender; 'for, though I was bred to it, I think it an unlawful calling.'—'Why so?' says Wildgoose.—'Because it administers to sin, and to the works of the flesh,' replies Slender.— 'I do not see how so necessary a part of the female dress as a pair of stays can contribute to sin,' says Wildgoose. 'I should rather think it had a contrary tendency, and might sometimes secure the virtue of the fair sex; at least, as it does not *directly* administer to vice, I can by no means think that of a Stay-maker an unlawful calling.

'But how does Master Slender live, then?' continues Wildgoose. —'Upon the charity of my friends and the good Providence of God,' answered Slender.—'I am afraid, then,' replies Wildgoose, 'your whole tenour of life is sinful; as no man has a right to be supported, without contributing something to the public stock.'

'Why, Mr. Wildgoose,' says Whitfield, 'I have shewn you our Brother Slender, rather as a poor soul under the dominion of Satan, than as one whose sentiments I entirely approve of. Our friend has a good heart, but a weak head; for certainly, "if we say that we have no sin, we deceive ourselves."'—'Sir,' says Slender, 'Mr. Wesley has given a different interpretation to those words, and applied them to man only in his unregenerate state.'—'That may be,' replies Mr. Whitfield; 'but yet I am afraid, my friend, your present contemplative way of life is really not to be defended, either by Reason or Scripture, as it renders you entirely useless to the world, and a burthen (though but a *slender* one) to society.'

As Slender, however, had told them that he subsisted upon the charitable contributions of his friends, Wildgoose thought proper (to prevent any suspicion of opposing his opinions from selfish motives) to shew him a specimen of his liberality; so gave him something handsome, and took his leave.

CHAPTER VII

Theatrical Entertainments. A new Project for their Regulation

MR. WILDGOOSE, during his stay at Bristol, saw instances enough of the infectious nature of Enthusiasm, and what absurdities people frequently run into who have once forsaken the guidance of Reason, to have restored a man of his natural good sense to the use of his understanding; but he was so far intoxicated with zeal, as well as with the applause which he gained by his eloquence, that he proceeded with great alacrity and perseverance.

He held forth again in the evening to a crowded audience; and, after the meeting was ended, again supped with Alderman Cullpepper, his fair spouse, and some other company.

The Alderman was a good sort of man, who, by his care and frugality in the earlier part of his life, had amassed a considerable fortune. He was much older than his wife; and, having no children (as was observed), could not find sufficient amusement for her at home: he was not displeased, therefore, with her spending two or three evenings in a week in so innocent a way; though he himself was too fond of the pomp of Cathedral service, and of appearing at Church in his Fur-gown, to frequent the Tabernacle of the Methodists.

There supped with them that evening a Scotch Officer, one Captain Gordon, who commanded a Frigate of war, which lay at that time in King-road, and was soon to sail and join the fleet in the West-Indies. Just as they were sitting down to supper, there came in also a Welsh Grocer, who had long been supplied with

S

goods by Mr. Cullpepper; and, having been two or three days at Bristol during the Fair, had gone that evening, for the first time in his life, to see a Play. Being asked, 'how he came to return so soon, and whether he did not like the Play?' he said, 'It was fery goot Plaa; they plaad three bouts upon the fiddles, and the harps, and the pipes; but there were some Great Shentlemen came in, who had some private business to talk of together, and hur thought it was not goot manners to stay any longer.'

The case was, poor Taffy (as it has probably happened to other country gentlemen) had mistaken the Music *before* the Play for the Play itself, and so came away as soon as the Actors made their first entry.

This incident, however, introduced a conversation upon that subject, and gave Mr. Wildgoose an opportunity of inveighing with great vehemence against Plays and Theatrical Entertainments. He said, 'the Stage was a nursery of lewdness and debauchery, and wondered that any Play-houses were tolerated in a Christian country.'—'Come, come,' says the Alderman, 'I will warrant you, you have been at a Play before now. I cannot think there is any great harm in an innocent Play.'—'Why, I cannot deny,' says Wildgoose, 'that I have been too often at those entertainments in my youth; but then I deny that there is any such thing as an innocent Play. Every Play, that I have ever read, or seen acted, is a representation of some love-intrigue, or of some base and villainous action, filled with blasphemous rants, prophane imprecations, lewd descriptions, or obscene and filthy jests. In short, I look upon the Play-house to be as much the house of the Devil, as the Church is the house of God; and that it is absolutely unlawful for a Christian to frequent it.'[1]

'Why,' says Captain Gordon, 'I am afraid there is but too much foundation for what the Gentleman says; yet, I imagine, his inference from it, "that all Plays are unlawful," is unjust, and proves too much: for, if a mere representation of vicious or immoral actions (though with a design to expose them, or to deter others from imitating them) be unlawful, how shall we defend the practice of the Sacred Writers themselves, both of the Old and New Testament, who have recorded many cruel, unjust, and some lewd actions, even of God's peculiar people?'—'Sir,' (says Wildgoose, with some warmth) 'I hope you do not compare the inspired authors of the Holy Bible with our modern scribblers of Tragedy or Comedy?'—'No, by no means,' replies the Captain: 'I only say, that the Sacred Writers relate many *tragical*, and, with reverence be it spoken, some *comical* events; but then it is always with a moral or religious intention: whereas, I confess, too many of our modern Plays have a very immoral and irreligious tendency; which is a strong argument in favour of what I was going to propose, and what I have often thought would be a very proper regulation.'— 'What is that?' says Wildgoose.—'Why,' says Captain Gordon, 'as all Plays are already subject to the inspection of the Lord Chamberlain, to prevent any thing offensive to the Government from being brought upon the Stage; so, to prevent any thing from being exhibited offensive to Religion or contrary to Good-manners, they should likewise be inspected by the Bishop of the Diocese.'—'By the Bishop!' (cries Mrs. Cullpepper, with some surprize)—'By the Bishop!' (quoth Wildgoose, with a significant sneer)—'They ought to be entirely prohibited and suppressed.'—'Why,' continues the Captain, 'to be sure, those things are at present upon an odd footing in this country. Players, I believe, are considered by your laws as vagabonds; and, I have been told, are excommunicated by some antient Canons of the Church, and yet are permitted to stroll about, and corrupt the morals, and introduce an habit of dissipation, in almost every little borough and market town in England.'

'Well, well,' says the benevolent Alderman, 'all trades must live. I believe, indeed, these Plays fill the heads of our prentices and young girls with wanton fancies sometimes; but, perhaps, they might spend their time less innocently elsewhere: and young people will have amusements of some kind or other.'—Wildgoose was going to reply; but Captain Gordon was now saying gallant things to Mrs. Cullpepper, and rallying her taste in preferring the amusements of the Tabernacle to that of the Play-house and other more fashionable places of dissipation. It must be observed, however, that Mrs. Cullpepper seemed more inclined to listen to Wildgoose than to Gordon; which occasioned some little jealousy in the latter (who for some time had been a sort of *cecisbeo* to Mrs. Cullpepper) which was attended with consequences that precipitated Wildgoose's departure from Bristol.

CHAPTER VIII

A ridiculous Distress. Advantages of the Sacerdotal Habit

THE next day, in a conference, Mr. Whitfield told Wildgoose, 'that he would have him be prepared to set out for the North; for that he had frequent invitations, by letter, to visit the Brethren amongst the Coal-mines in Staffordshire and Shropshire: though he was in hopes that Mr. Wesley would take them in his way from that part of England.

'But,' continues Whitfield, 'to prepare you for the persecutions which you may expect to meet with from the Prince of this world, I would have you undergo some voluntary trials before you leave this city.' He then told Wildgoose, he should visit the Criminals in the Condemned-hole in Newgate there, and also bear his testimony against one or two places where Mr. Whitfield could not go often without giving offence to weak Brethren; that is, to a noted Gin-shop, which he considered as an emblem of Hell; as also against an house of ill fame, or Bawdy-house as it is called, 'the Mistress of which,' he said, 'had felt some pangs of the New Birth, and was not far from the Kingdom of Heaven. And, indeed,' continues Mr. Whitfield, 'I have more hopes of converting Publicans and Harlots, or, in modern language, Whores and Rogues, than those self-righteous Christians, who are usually called *good sort of people*.'[1]

Wildgoose was so zealous to execute any of Mr. Whitfield's commands, and had now so much confidence in the force of his own rhetoric, that he would have gone immediately, and have attacked, not only Mrs. Toddy in her Gin-shop, or Mother Placket in her Bagnio, but even Satan himself, if required, in his Infernal abodes. Whitfield, however, advised him to defer it till another day, and to reserve himself for the evening; because he had heard, that several profligate young fellows, drawn by the fame of Wildgoose's eloquence, were to attend the Tabernacle that night. And 'Providence,' he said, 'often made use of the Curiosity, and even the Malice, of such poor creatures for their own conversion. And he could easily imagine, without any shock to his own vanity, that a *new* Preacher might effect what he himself had not been able to do.' Wildgoose, therefore, took his leave at present, and went to his own lodgings, to adjust his dress a little, and to wait for the time of assembling in the evening at the Tabernacle.

When Wildgoose came home to his lodging, he was struck with astonishment, to see his friend Tugwell decked out with an immense grizzled periwig, instead of his own shock-hair and jelly-bag cap; and, in the place of his short jerkin, dressed in a long, full-trimmed, old, black coat. Alderman Cullpepper, it seems, finding how fond his wife was of Wildgoose's company, and seeing Tugwell frequently about the house, thought there was something more decent and creditable in the second-hand finery of a Town Plebeian, than in the rustic coarseness of a simple Clown. He had, therefore, broken through the habitual reluctance which he felt to *parting* with any thing, and equipped Tugwell in that droll manner out of his magazine of old cloaths, of above twenty years standing.

Wildgoose could not forbear smiling at his friend's paradoxical appearance; but, having been used of late to allegorize every event, he was going to make some practical inference from Tugwell's strange metamorphosis: when Jerry cut short his master, by pointing out a monstrous chasm which he had spied in Wildgoose's plush breeches, from which two or three inches of his shirt hung dangling down in a most facetious manner. This was a misfortune which Wildgoose could not have forseen; and, as he had no change of raiment, was greatly distressed how to remedy. It could not have happened at a more critical or unfortunate juncture: as, in half an hour's time, he was to mount the rostrum. What must be done? There was no precedent of any thing like this recorded in the Journals of our modern Apostles. Wildgoose could not bear the indecency either of sitting without his breeches, or of admitting a female hand so near his person, in a part so liable to inflammation.

From this aukward distress, however, he was quickly relieved by his trusty squire Jeremiah Tugwell; who, amongst the other furniture of his wallet, had had the precaution to pack up a large stocking-needle, and some strong worsted, with which he generously undertook to deliver his Master from his perplexity, and with great dexterity leveled his needle at the schism in his Master's trowsers.

Tugwell, however, could not forbear, during the operation, to make an obvious reflection in favour of the clerical habit and sacerdotal accoutrements. 'Ah! Master,' (says he), 'if your Worship now had but a gown and cassock, or could but put on a surplice, like our Parson, you might have gone to the Tabernacle without any breeches at all. Adzooks! methinks I almost long to go to our Parish-church again, to hear the bells chime on a Sunday, and see the Parson walk up to the desk an' it were any Bishop; and then turn over the great Bible with such a smack, it does one's heart good to hear him.'—'Ah! Jerry,' says Wildgoose, 'these are only the outside ornaments, the mere husks of Religion, and fit only to be cast before swine; that is, merely to amuse the senses of the vulgar; but afford no real nourishment to the soul.' Wildgoose would probably have said a great deal more upon the subject, if, in the midst of his harangue, Tugwell's needle had not slipt a little too deep, and made him cry out with some vehemence, which put a stop to their dialogue.

CHAPTER IX

Modern Prophecies. Effects of Wildgoose's Eloquence

IT was now time for Mr. Wildgoose to be at the Tabernacle. When he came thither, and was going to begin his sermon; Mr. Whitfield himself cried out, 'Let us *wrestle* in prayer for our dear Brother Alderman Pennywise, who lieth at the point of death. He is a Chosen Vessel; he loveth our Nation, and has contributed largely towards building us a Synagogue.'

As soon as Mr. Whitfield's prayer was ended, a Journeyman Shoemaker, who was a zealous Christian, and himself an occasional Preacher, cries out, 'Hallelujah! we have prevailed; God has given us the Alderman's life: it is revealed to me, that the fever has left our Brother Pennywise, and he liveth.' They then began an Hymn of Thanksgiving, for the recovery of Alderman Pennywise; but, before they had done, one came in, and told them (to their great disappointment), 'that their Brother Pennywise was *fallen asleep.*'[1]

Wildgoose now began to harangue with great vehemence; and, as they expected some young fellows to come and make a riot that evening, Wildgoose was determined to exert himself, and, if possible, gain their attention.

In order to this, he resolved to imitate Mr. Whitfield's lively manner and facetious similitudes.

He took his Text from the Book of Ecclesiastes, chapter xi.

'Rejoice, O young man, in thy youth, and walk in the ways of thy heart, and in the sight of thine eyes: but know, that for all these things God will bring thee to judgement.'

' "Rejoice in thy youth—" As if he had said, "Go on, young man, and take your swing; go to the tavern, and call for your bottle, and your pipe, and your Welsh-rabbit; entertain yourself with cards and dice, or with a play; then away to Mother Douglas's, and regale yourself with a mistress; and, in short, indulge every appetite and passion to the utmost: but, take this along with you, if you do, you will be damned."

' "Damned! for what?" you will say.—Why, not for whoring, or drinking, or gaming; not for cheating, lying, or swearing: no; God Almighty is not so captious, as to quarrel with his creatures for such trifles as these: no; it is for your want of *Faith*; it is your Infidelity, that you will be damned for.

'I will tell you a story. A Roman Catholic Gentleman went a Partridge-shooting along with a Protestant neighbour of his on a Fast-day: they were driven, about noon, by a thunder-storm, to a little public-house, where they could get nothing to eat but some bacon and eggs. The good Catholic had a tender conscience, and would eat nothing but eggs; the Protestant, his companion, who was one of your *good sort* of people, said, "there could be no harm in his eating a bit of bacon with his eggs; that bacon could not be called flesh; that it was no more than a red-herring; it is fish, as one may say." So the Catholic took a bit of bacon with his eggs.

'But just as he had put it in his mouth, there came a most tremendous clap of thunder. Upon which, the poor Catholic slipped it down upon his plate again, muttering to himself, "What a noise here is about a bit of bacon!" He foolishly fancied now the sin was in his eating the bacon. No such matter. It was his want of Faith. He had not a proper Faith in his own superstitious principles.

'I remember, when I was at Oxford, I used to pray seven times a day, and fasted myself to a skeleton. I powdered my wig, and went every month to the sacrament, with the "Companion to the altar" in my pocket.[1] I might as well have had Ovid's Epistles in my pocket. The Devil stood laughing behind the church door. The Devil loves these formalities. I fancied myself a good Christian:

and had no conception, that I was as dead as a door-nail; that I must be born again to a new life; and that I had no more saving Faith than a Jew or a Mahometan.'

Thus Wildgoose went on for some time, in the style of Mr. Whitfield: but what was natural in the one, was rather ridiculous in the other, and had a contrary effect from what he had apprehended; for there were some youthful scoffers, who at first were a little riotous; yet they were soon overpowered by Wildgoose's eloquence, when he insensibly resumed his own stile; and for near a quarter of an hour all was hushed in silence. But, on a sudden, a little girl, who did not seem to be above thirteen years old, cried out from the midst of the croud, 'that she was pricked through and through by the power of the word.'[1] This occasioned some confusion; but the people about her checked her zeal, and stopped the poor girl's outcries; when a young fellow near the door, who was half fuddled, cried out, 'Damn such nonsense! these fellows ought to be whipped at the cart's tail, by G—d!' He then threw a piece of an apple at the Preacher; and he and his companions, setting up a laugh, rushed out at the door, hollowing and singing, 'Down with the roundheads! damn all preaching and praying, say I.

> A fig for the Parson, and a fart for the Clerk;
> Let's put out our candles, and kiss in the dark.
>   Derry down.'

Their rude behaviour, however, rouzed the fury of the Lambs without doors, who began to pelt them with stones and dirt, and soon drove them off the stage.

Wildgoose was now proceeding: when a poor Collier entered the room; who, as soon as he had done his day's work, had hurried away, without his dinner, to attend the Tabernacle. A woman selling black-puddings at the door, and the poor fellow being very hungry, he buys one; gnaws off one end of it; and, not being able to reach his pocket for the throng, buttons up the remainder in his bosom.

As every orator seems to direct his discourse to some particular object, or, at least, towards some one part of his audience; the Collier, being the head and shoulders taller than the rest of the congregation, Wildgoose fixed his eyes upon him; and, as his subject now led him, went on thus:—

'Let a man be exalted ever so much in the opinion of the world;

let his outward appearance be ever so fair and honest; yet every one has some darling vice; some dark and secret sin; or perhaps some *black* and *bloody* design, which he carefully conceals, and wraps up in his own bosom'—

The poor Collier thought some part of his *black* pudding might appear, and looking confused, buttoned it up still closer; whilst Wildgoose, imagining he had made some impression upon the man, still directing his discourse to that part of the room, and even pointing his hand toward the Collier, proceeded thus—

'And the more he is cautioned against it, the closer he hugs this favourite vice; he keeps it concealed in his bosom, like a delicious morsel; and flatters himself that no one can perceive it; but the eye of Providence can pierce the thickest folds of hypocrisy, and penetrate the very inmost parts of our breasts'—

The Collier still persisting in his mistake, began to sweat, and to wipe his face, and to pull his coat still closer together. Wildgoose, observing his confusion, proceeds with greater vehemence—

'But let us not, through false shame, still harbour this black and poisonous serpent in our breasts; which will sting us to the very soul:—Let us confess our sins to one another—let us drag the accursed thing from our bosom—before the congregation; and spread it before the Lord, as Hezekiah did the letters'—

The poor Collier wriggled about in great agonies, and the Preacher was more urgent—

'Out with it! Cast it from thee! and trample under foot every vile lust and carnal appetite that thou hast harboured in thy bosom!—'

The poor fellow, now convinced that he was discovered, and yet vexed at the importunity of the Preacher, cries out, 'The devil take the hog's-pudding!'—threw it amongst the crowd; and made his escape from this imaginary persecution.

As the preaching was a little interrupted by these incidents, Whitfield took the opportunity to comfort his brother Wildgoose; and observed, 'that Satan envied their happiness: but, courage! my friend; we shall make his kingdom shake before we have done with him, I will warrant you.'[1] Wildgoose then continued his discourse; and after he had done, he and Mr. Whitfield were again invited, by Mrs. Cullpepper, to partake of a comfortable supper.

CHAPTER X

Effusions of Self-importance. Wildgoose meets
with a Repulse

MR. WHITFIELD, having some other engagement upon his hands, withdrew soon after supper; and, Mrs. Cullpepper retiring to her closet for an hour, the Alderman and Mr. Wildgoose were left alone, *tête à tête*.

Alderman Cullpepper, as was observed, by his industry and his frugality, had made a considerable fortune. And though his ideas were very low, and his soul excessively narrow, yet he had some ambition to get the character of a generous man, if he could obtain it without much expence, or any sensible diminution of his finances.

As the Alderman therefore was obliged to keep something of a table, he was glad of that sort of submissive companions, who would express some glee at a parsimonious treat, and, content with a glass of wine now and then, would connive at his keeping the bottle on his right hand, and other stratagems of frugality, which he had learned in his less affluent circumstances.

With the same view, he was always recounting acts of munificence, which he had formerly performed; though, like the Traveller who boasted of the extraordinary leap which he had taken at Rhodes, he chose rather to refer you to witnesses who could attest his generous actions, than repeat them.

The Alderman and Wildgoose being now alone, then, partly to prevent too quick a circulation of the glass, and partly to give Wildgoose an idea of his consequence, and to convince a person of his *liberality*, who, he imagined, would never put it to the trial; Cullpepper filled up the intervals of each whiff of tobacco with the following ebullitions of vanity and self-importance.

'Why, to be sure, there is not a man in the Corporation (though I say it) that has a better interest in both the Members than I have; though I make no other use of my power than to serve my friends. As for Sir Harry Plausible, he has a particular personal regard for me. (Sir Harry is certainly one of the *most agreeablest* men in the world.) It is not because I have a little interest in the Corporation. No, no; it is not for that.'—'I dare say it is not,' says Wildgoose.— 'No; I was acquainted with Sir Harry long before he had any thoughts of representing the city. The Baronet is reckoned a proud man, indeed; but, I am sure, I never found him so. To be sure, the Senator is a little reserved, when he does not like his company (and you know, Sir, men that know the world are so): but, when I and He are alone together, I can talk as freely to him as you can to your fellow-traveller here, Mr. What-d'ye-call-him.'—'Ah!' says Wildgoose, 'nothing is more vain than the petty distinctions which the children of this world are so fond of. Though we are not all Members of Parliament; yet all true Christians are *Members* of Christ, and one of another.'—'Why, that is true, to be sure, Sir, as you observe,' says the Alderman.

'But did I never tell you how I got a Living for our Curate the other day?'—'I cannot say you did,' replies Wildgoose.—'I will tell you how cleverly I managed it. It was at the last treat Sir Harry gave the Corporation. I sate next to the Member. The glass went pretty briskly about.'—'Ah!' says Wildgoose, 'I do not doubt it. Corporation Feasts are the Devil's Festivals.'—'Well,' (continued Cullpepper, without vouchsafing Wildgoose the least degree of attention) 'as I was saying, the glass went briskly about; and we had drunk pretty freely, but in a moderate way. *Howsomever*, the Senator, who is a sober man too, began to wax mellow. Now, as I have pretty good intelligence, I had heard, that very morning, that the Living of Ganderhill was become vacant. So, *says* I to the Senator, "Yonder is our poor Curate, *says* I, at the bottom of the table. He is a very worthy man, *says* I. He has been Curate here these eighteen years. I have a great regard for him. I wish it were in my power to get him some little addition to his income. Indeed, he married a relation of mine: it was a distant relation. But the man is a very worthy man."—"Sir," says the Member, "if it ever lies in my power to oblige you, you may command me upon any occasion."

'I believe the Senator said this as words of course. However, I clinched him immediately. "Well, well, Sir," *says* I, "remember your promise. I have a thing in my eye, if it should happen to fall: it is in the Chancellor's gift; but a word from you would do the business at once."

'In short, having broken the ice, I said no more at that time. But, the very next morning, away *goes* I to the Member's house, told him how lucky it was; that the very thing I had in my eye, was become vacant; and by his interest got it for my friend.'

As soon as the Alderman had finished this narration, and received

the incense of a complaisant speech from Wildgoose, he began
another, about his lending money to set up a young tradesman:
neither of which was very interesting to Mr. Wildgoose; yet, as his
liberality had quite exhausted his stock of cash, he thought this
a fair opportunity of trying the force of his host's generosity in
regard to himself.——'Well, Sir, this was very good in you, to be
sure. I shall never want to ask any favour of that kind. However,
Sir, your generosity encourages me (as I have this opportunity)
to beg your assistance in a trifling affair; in which, I know, it will
give you pleasure to oblige me.'—'Aye, aye, Mr. Wildgoose, anything that is in my way to serve you, I shall be very glad to do it, if
it is not any thing very much out of the way.'—'Why, Sir,' says
Wildgoose, 'since I have been in Bristol, I have met with several
objects of charity; and, as I brought but little money with me from
home, my stock is almost exhausted.' [Here Cullpepper took his
pipe from his mouth.] 'I do not know,' continues Wildgoose, 'that
I shall want any money on my own account (for I trust to Providence for my own necessities); but if you could spare me nine or
ten guineas, to assist any poor brother in distress'—'Nine or ten
guineas!' (says Cullpepper, laying down his pipe) 'and how can
you be sure of returning it again?'—'Sir,' says Wildgoose, 'I hope
I shall have some opportunity or other of doing it; but, if I should
not, as you will lend it in the support of so good a cause, you will be
sure of being rewarded an hundred fold at the great day of Re-
tribution.'

'Mr. Wildgoose,' says Cullpepper, 'I have nothing to say against
the cause you are engaged in; but I assure you, Sir, the Merchants
of Bristol understand business better than to lend their money upon
so precarious a security. In short, Sir, I must take the liberty to tell
you, that, from what I have heard, you are very indiscreet in the
management of your money, and squander it away amongst a pack
of idle rascals, who, instead of working at their trades, run about
from one Meeting to another, and take no care of their wives and
families at home.'

Whilst the Alderman was haranguing in this lofty strain, and
giving Wildgoose advice, instead of lending him money, Mrs. Cullpepper came into the room, and, finding the cause of her husband's
displeasure, soon pacified him with a smile, and assured Wildgoose,
with a nod and a wink, 'that any little distress, which his charitable
disposition might have occasioned, would be relieved by their

Society; that nobody was more generous than Mr. Cullpepper; but that he did not quite approve of one or two acts of liberality, which, he had heard, Mr. Wildgoose had performed'—and the like.

Wildgoose said, 'it was no great matter; he could make very good shift for the present.' And it being now near ten o'clock, the alderman's bed-time, he took his leave for that night; but at the door met Captain Gordon, who was coming to take a final leave of the Alderman and his wife, having received an order to sail the very next morning for the West-Indies.

Alderman Cullpepper was so full of this unexpected attack upon his generosity, that he could not forbear mentioning it to Captain Gordon; and Mrs. Cullpepper, taking Wildgoose's part more warmly than was prudent, irritated her husband, and raised the jealousy of Captain Gordon; which produced an event which she could not have expected.

CHAPTER XI

Mr. Wildgoose becomes a great Casuist

MR. WILDGOOSE had promised Mr. Whitfield to attend him to Kingswood the next morning, and to give a word of exhortation to the poor Colliers there. For which purpose, he was got up before six o'clock, that he might give his advice, in imitation of Mr. Whitfield, to any poor people that came to consult him. Tugwell also was ready at the door, with his inseparable companions, his oaken staff in his hand, and his wallet on his shoulders, stuffed with two or three stale rolls and cold meat (which the Alderman's servant had given him), for fear of accidents. Jerry had also put on his grizzled wig (to look more solemn); but had left his full-trimmed coat in his bed-chamber, that he might not be incumbered in his walk.

Just as Wildgoose was coming out of his chamber, a fat elderly woman, tolerably well dressed, came to the door, grunting most bitterly, and casting up her eyes with now and then a pious ejaculation, and enquired whether Mr. Wildgoose was stirring. Upon Tugwell's answering her in the affirmative, and shewing her into his room, she begged leave to sit down a little; and, after a few more groans and ejaculations, she opened her case. She said, 'her name was *Placket*; that she kept a little Coffee-house, where gentlemen and ladies sometimes met to drink a dish of tea together, in a harmless way, for what she knew to the contrary; but that she had censorious neighbours, who had given her house a bad name.'— 'Why,' says Wildgoose, 'the world is very censorious, without doubt: but we should take care, not to give room for any *just* reflections upon our conduct.'—'Ah! Sir,' says she, 'why that is my business with you. God forgive me! I am afraid there may have been some little frolicks now and then carried on at my house. When young people get together, you know, Sir, they will be kissing and toying; and one does not always know where those things may end.'—'Why, by your account, Mrs. Placket, you do not keep so good an house as you should do.'—'Dear Sir!' says she, 'that is what pricks my conscience; for, I must confess, I have sometimes taken money to bring young gentlemen and ladies together; and, indeed, always keep some young women in my house, to assist a friend or so.'¹—'Oh! Mrs Placket, I find then you keep a downright Bawdy-house.'—'Why, to be sure, Sir,' says she, 'that is what ill-natured people call it; and I would willingly know, Sir, whether it is a lawful employment or not: for you must observe, Sir, I keep as good orders in my house as any woman in England; and though (I thank God!) I have always had good custom, and have had twenty couple at a time, taking their recreation, in my house, yet (I bless God!) I never had any murder, or riot, or daggers-drawing, since I have been in business. Then I make my poor Lambs read the Bible every Sunday, and go to church in their turn; and, in short, though their bodies may be polluted, I take great care of their souls: and I hope God will wink at my poor Lambs that *sport themselves together*.'—'Why,' says Wildgoose, 'without doubt, our outward actions are indifferent in themselves; and it is the heart that God chiefly regards. God *sees* no sin in the *Elect*. If we have true Faith, that will sanctify our works. Thus Rahab the harlot, you know, was accepted through Faith. But, as yours is an uncommon case, I will consult Mr. Whitfield upon it.'—'Ah! God help me!' says Mrs. Placket: 'I am afraid I am not long for this world; and what will become of my poor Lambs, when I am gone to my dear Redeemer?'

Whilst Wildgoose was engaged in this conference, in comes the poor girl that was pricked through and through, by the power of the

Word, at his last preachment, attended by her mother. The girl
looked very pale, and, upon coming before Wildgoose, was taken
with an hysteric fit. Wildgoose bad the mother, 'not be frightened;
for, as Mr. Whitfield had assured him, these were common symptoms of the New Birth.'—'Lack-a-day! Sir,' says the mother,
'I wish it may be nothing more than the New Birth. But I have been
very much terrified; and am sadly afraid my poor girl is with child.'
—'With child!' says Wildgoose; 'why, she is a mere child herself.'
'Ah! Sir,' says the mother, 'so she is indeed; for though she is a
fine-grown girl, yet, if she lives to Lammas-day next, she will be but
fourteen years old, as sure as eggs *is* eggs. But a wicked rogue of
a Sailor, who promised her marriage, I am afraid, has had *cardinal
knowledge* of her, and has now left her; and I shall never be able to
maintain her and her child: times are so hard, and money so scarce,
I can hardly maintain myself.'—The case was, the poor woman had
heard of Wildgoose's generosity, and was in hopes of partaking of
his bounty, and therefore brought her daughter under pretence of
consulting him as a Casuist. But he, having at present neither silver
nor gold, gave her only some spiritual comfort; and told her, 'that
this accident was probably a very providential thing for her
daughter, as it was a maxim with Mr. Whitfield, "The greater
the Sinner, the greater the Saint;" that she had nothing to do but
to lay *hold* on Christ, as Mary Magdalen did, by an active Faith;
and she would enter into the Kingdom of Heaven, before those
self-righteous, good sort of women, who fancy they need no repentance.'

These customers were hardly retired, when a dirty-looking
fellow was introduced by Tugwell, who, peeping round the room
and shutting the door, spoke in a low voice to Wildgoose, and said,
'his was a scruple of a particular kind, upon which a friend had
desired him to consult Mr. Wildgoose.'—'Well, what is it?' says
Wildgoose.—'Why, Sir, whether it is not fighting against God,
for a man in gaol to use means for making his escape.'[1]—Wildgoose, after a short pause, answered, 'that, doubtless, self-preservation was the first law of Nature; and a man in prison, it should seem,
might use all lawful means to gain his liberty; but Nature is one
thing, and Grace another. A good Christian must submit to every
ordinance of man, as the dispensation of Providence; and if he is
committed to prison by legal authority, I question whether any
other authority can innocently set him free. But, as this is a dubious

point, Mr. Whitfield and I will determine it by lot.'¹—'Ah!' says
the fellow, 'it is too late to cast lots about the matter; for I made my
escape from Salisbury gaol last spring, and am now going on ship-
board, but should be glad to go with a quiet conscience.'

Before this man had done, a tall lanthern-jawed fellow, whose
features seemed lengthened by a long weather-beaten wig, which
hung below his cheek-bones, desired to lay his case before Mr.
Wildgoose, when the other was dismissed. He said, 'he was bred
a Dissenter, and a Button-maker by trade; and in his apprenticeship
had married an elderly woman, with a little money; but she was so
bad-tempered a woman,' (continued he) 'that I could not possibly
live with her: so I went and worked in London, where, upon hearing Mr. Wesley, I became a new man; and, meeting with a very
sober young woman of my own trade at the Tabernacle, to whom
I honestly told my situation, we agreed to live together for some
years, and have had several children: but she is lately dead; and
now my conscience pricks me, and I cannot be easy day nor night:
but still, I hope, Sir, *God will sanctify every dispensation.*'²

'What became of the old woman, then?' says Mr. Wildgoose.—
'Why, Sir,' says he, 'as I had got me another wife, I believe she
got herself another husband, more agreeable to her own age.'—
'And so,' says Wildgoose, 'by putting away your wife without
a sufficient cause, you have caused her to commit adultery.'—
'Why,' says the Button-maker, 'I am afraid I have; but I hope *God
will sanctify every dispensation.*'—'Friend,' replies Wildgoose, 'God
cannot sanctify adultery. You must confess yourself a vile sinner,
and *lay hold* on Christ by Faith; for you can have no hopes but in
him, who came into the world to save sinners.'

CHAPTER XII

Some unexpected Incidents

WILDGOOSE, though not displeased with observing the good he
was likely to do by awakening so many wicked sinners, was almost
tired of his company; when in came Mrs. Cullpepper's maid,
curtseying and simpering, with her Lady's compliments: and,
before Wildgoose could ask how she did, produced a little packet,

carefully sealed up; which being opened, to his surprize he found it contained five guineas, with the following billet:

'My dear Brother,

'Give me leave to contribute my mite towards the great work which is going to be wrought upon the earth; but do not come any more to our house, till you hear further from your sister in the Lord,

RACHAEL CULLPEPPER.'

Wildgoose could not recollect any precedent in Mr. Wesley's or Mr. Whitfield's Journals of their having received money for their private occasions: as he was conscious, however, that his intentions were charitable, he did not refuse so seasonable a supply. He therefore returned his compliments to Mrs. Cullpepper, with thanks for the contents of her packet; but was less pleased with the present which he had received, than shocked with the hint that accompanied it, not to repeat his visits to Mrs. Cullpepper.

Wildgoose was now come out into the passage, and was observing to Tugwell, 'that the Spirit testified he should do great things in Bristol; and that he had a Call to tarry in that city many days.' To which Tugwell seemed to have no manner of objection.

But, while they were yet speaking, another ill-looking Irish Sailor, with one eye, and several scars on his cheek, came to consult Wildgoose. He said, 'he had been the vilest of sinners' (to which confession his appearance bore sufficient testimony); 'that he had been guilty of every kind of uncleanness; nay, that, when on shipboard, he had an intrigue with a cat.'—'Aye,' says Tugwell, 'and she has left some tokens of her kindness upon thy cheeks.'—'But,' says the Sailor, 'notwithstanding my sins are so numerous, I am so far from any sorrow, or contrition, that my greatest affliction is the being violently addicted to *laughing*, which, I am afraid, is a token of Reprobation. Now, I should be glad to know, whether Laughing be any sin or not; for I have heard, that Adam never *laughed* before the Fall.'[1]

Wildgoose stared with astonishment at this strange Penitent: but Tugwell, who was impatient to get to breakfast, used this gentleman with less politeness. 'Come, come, friend,' says he, 'this is no time for *laughing*; we have more serious matters upon our hands; you had better be going about your business.' He then thrust him towards the door. Upon which the Sailor gave the signal with a Boatswain's whistle, and in rushed four or five stout fellows,

T

amongst whom was the man that had escaped from Salisbury gaol. He immediately thrust an handkerchief into Tugwell's mouth; pulled his long wig over his eyes; twisted the wallet, which hung over his shoulder, round his neck; and muffled him up in such a manner, that he could not make any sort of resistance. Some of the rest secured Wildgoose, who never offered to interrupt them; and led them both to a covered boat, which lay ready on the Quay, and rowed away immediately for Kingroad; where when they arrived, they put the two Pilgrims aboard a large ship, which was riding at anchor, and which set sail the moment they were on board.

CHAPTER XIII

Event of their Voyage

WILDGOOSE was so well prepared to submit to the various dispensations of Providence, that he appeared quite calm upon the occasion, and let the Sailors dispose of him as they pleased. But Tugwell, being less passive, struggled, and hung an a-se, and laid about him as well as he could; for which refractory behaviour, he got three or four hearty knocks on the pate: but, as soon as he was restored to the use of his tongue, he expressed the transports of his grief and rage in a most vociferous manner. Sometimes he lamented the forlorn condition of his poor wife Dorothy; then fell foul upon Mr. Wildgoose, for seducing him from home; then cursed himself, for leaving his Cobler's stall, and his own chimney-corner, to go rambling about the country: in short, though Jerry had read books of travels with so much pleasure, and often wished to accompany the adventurer in his voyages as he perused them in his own stall; yet he found, in fact, the company of Sailors, upon this occasion, not so agreeable as he expected.

Wildgoose endeavoured to comfort his fellow-sufferer, and desired him, 'to trust to Providence, who would bring them,' he said, 'to the haven where they *should* be.' And, notwithstanding Wildgoose so lately felt a Call to remain in Bristol; yet he was now convinced, that he was chosen for some more important service, and was to 'preach the Gospel in other *cities also*.'[1]

Whilst they were thus engaged in lamentations on one side, and consolations on the other, the ship was falling gently down the channel; when who should come into the cabin, where the two Pilgrims were stowed, but their old acquaintance Captain Gordon? The Captain started back; and, affecting some little surprize, 'Ha!' cries he, 'what, Mr. Wildgoose! what, was it for this, then, that our friend Cullpepper sent my rascals a guinea to drink this morning? I was surprized at his generosity. Well, Sir, he has played you a comical trick; for I am going a pretty long voyage.'—Wildgoose, after expressing his surprize, answered, 'that he did not know how he had offended the Alderman: but, however,' continues he, 'I am convinced, that Providence has some important end to serve by this dispensation, to whatever part of the world I shall be transported.'—'Why, Sir,' says the Captain, 'I am bound for North-America, and am to join the fleet in the gulph of St. Lawrence. But, as I am to touch at Corke or Kinsale, to lay in more provisions, if you chuse it, I can set you on shore in that part of Ireland.'—Wildgoose thanked the Captain for his civility, not suspecting that this had been a scheme concerted between him and the Alderman; the Captain being jealous of him, as a rival in Mrs. Cullpepper's good graces; and the Alderman being suspicious, that his wife might supply him with *that* money which *he* had refused him.

When Tugwell heard of being set on shore in Ireland, he renewed his lamentations, and made sure of 'having his throat cut by *Papishes* and wild Irish: and, if they should be carried into America, he did not doubt,' he said, 'but they should be left upon some desolate island, as Robinson Crusoe was, amongst the wild Indians; and perhaps roasted alive, and have their bones picked by *Hannibals* and *Scavengers*' (so Jerry called the Cannibals and Savages), 'as he feared his poor son Joseph was.' The Captain bad him, 'not be afraid, for that they should not be used ill in any respect.' He advised them therefore 'to come out of their cabin, and take a walk upon deck;' where, the weather being fine, the water calm, and the vessel now in the midst of the Channel, between the two opposite coasts, they had no unpleasant voyage for some hours.

Towards the evening, being got near the mouth of the Channel, the afternoon having been excessively hot, some black clouds began to rise towards the South-East, and a most violent thunderstorm soon after ensued, which lasted for several hours. Those who

delight in descriptions of this kind may have recourse to any of the
Epic Poets, ancient or modern. I shall only observe, that, after
being driven from their course, and tossed about a good part of the
night, they found themselves, at break of day, near the Glamorgan-
shire coast; and found it convenient (as their tackling had suffered
a little) to come to an anchor in the Bay of Cardiff, where the
Captain, having carried the jest far enough, gave Wildgoose and
his friend leave to be set on shore; which favour, when he heard
they were on the coast of Wales, Wildgoose gladly accepted of.
After giving them the word of exhortation, therefore, Wildgoose
took his leave of Captain Gordon, thanked him for bringing them
to the haven where he wished to be; and he and his fellow-traveller
were safely set on shore.

BOOK VIII

CHAPTER I

The Pilgrims arrive at Cardiff

Mr. Wildgoose now thought himself a second St. Paul; and that, in the late storm, God had given the lives of all those that sailed with him to the force of his prayers; though every common Sailor knew there had been no real danger.

As for Tugwell, he was so sick at the coming on of the storm, that he had not been very attentive to what had passed; and was so rejoiced at reaching land again, that he dropped all resentment against the authors of this calamity. He had thrown off his great wig; but, grasping his oaken staff, and securing his wallet, he sprang eagerly upon the shore, without looking behind him; and, desirous as he had formerly been of travelling, made a solemn vow, 'never to forsake the *terra firma* again as long as he lived.'

The place where they landed was about three miles from Cardiff; and, it being early in the morning, and no living creature to be seen, Tugwell began again to wish himself at home, in his own chimney-corner, with a mess of onion-pottage, or a dish of Madam Wildgoose's pot-liquor, for his breakfast; for, having eaten nothing the whole preceding day but a sea-biscuit, he began to complain of hunger and fatigue. By good luck, however, upon searching his wallet, he found a couple of rolls and a piece of mutton-pye, which he had laid in at Bristol: he prevailed upon his master, therefore, without much difficulty, to sit down at the foot of a rock, and partake with him of what he had so providentially provided.

But, during this short repast, Wildgoose began to blame himself, for having lived too luxuriously at Bristol; observing, 'that regular dinners and hot suppers were by no means expedient for those that were called to preach the Gospel.'—'Odzooks!' cries Tugwell; 'why, I did not see but Mr. Whitfield, and other good Christians, eat and drank as well as we; and much good may it do them! I

would have every one have a belly-full. To be sure, Madam Cullpepper keeps a good house, and gave me many a good meal, and
money besides, for that matter.'

Wildgoose, upon hearing that Mrs. Cullpepper's generosity had
extended to his companion also, condemned himself for discovering
his necessity to the Alderman; and began to suspect, that some
jealousy of this kind (for he had no idea of any other) might be the
cause of his getting them kidnapped, and sent on ship-board. He
comforted himself, however, with the uprightness of his intentions,
and with the conviction that the money would be spent in a good
cause; and that he should make a better use of the unrighteous
Mammon than those to whom it properly belonged.

Though the sun was risen above the horizon, it was not yet four
o'clock; and the two Pilgrims having had little rest in the night,
Wildgoose leaned against the rock, and took a short nap; and
Tugwell, being now at ease, laid himself down on his wallet; and,
according to custom, snored most profoundly.

Wildgoose, however, having paid a slight compliment to nature,
and having in his sleep dreamed of nothing but spiritual conquests,
starts up, and rouses his fellow traveller. 'Come, Jerry,' cries he,
'this is no time for sleep; up, and be doing: the whole land of
Canaan lies before us; we must subdue the idolatrous nations, the
Hivites, the Perizzites, and the Jebusites. God has called us into
Wales; and I make no doubt but he will send his angel before us
(as he did before Mr. Whitfield);[1] and we shall go on from city to
city (like Joshua); and the Devil's strong holds will fall down at our
preaching, as the walls of Jericho did at the sound of the Rams-
horns.'[2]

Notwithstanding this spiritual rant, Tugwell grumbled at being
waked so soon, and said, 'he did not find the conquering of cities
was so easy a matter. You know, Master,' says he, 'you talked of
conquering the city of Bristol; but, I think, they have *conquered*
us, and have transported us into this heathenish country, without
our own consent, where there is nothing to be got, as I can see, for
love or money.'

The truth was, Jerry liked travelling well enough in a country
where they could meet with refreshment at every ale-house;
but, having been very sick in his voyage, and being a little chagrined
at the desolate appearance of the sea-coast, compared with the
pleasures of Alderman Cullpepper's kitchen, he could not forbear

venting his spleen against Wildgoose, for seducing him so far from home.

But the same cause, which damped Tugwell's spirits, roused Wildgoose's zeal. He languished for a little persecution (as Mr. Whitfield had often done); and thought things were not right, whilst they went on so smoothly at Bristol. He said, 'the primitive Saints were made perfect by sufferings; and, I dare say, Jerry, you yourself will be the better for this slight persecution for the Gospel's sake.'—'Yes, to be sure,' says Tugwell; 'I suppose, Master, you would be glad to see me ducked in an horse-pond, or tossed in a blanket, for the Gospel's sake: but I do not see what occasion I have to run my head against a wall, when I can get my living very well by mending shoes; and I wish I were at home again in my own stall, or in my chimney-corner with our Dorothy.'

Wildgoose said, 'he would not prevent his returning home, if he desired it; and would pay him for the time which he had lost in attending him: and then,' continues he, 'as you have been at no expence, you can have no reason to complain. Besides, you own that Mrs. Cullpepper gave you some money; and, perhaps, other good Christians may have been as liberal: and much good may it do you!' Mr. Wildgoose, however, said, 'he did not want to call him to an account; but only to make him submit with patience to the accidents which might befall them in the Pilgrimage in which he had voluntarily engaged to accompany him. But come, Jerry,' says he, 'I believe we are not far from Cardiff, where we shall meet with better accommodations, and (what is of more consequence) with a Society of true Christians, which, I believe, Mr. Whitfield established there, when he visited the Principality of Wales.'

Accordingly, in less than half an hour more, they came within sight of that handsome town; which revived Tugwell's spirits, who wished for nothing so much as a cup of good ale and a slice of toasted cheese, which, now he was in Wales, he hoped to have in perfection.

CHAPTER II

Adventures in the Inn at Cardiff

THE first public-house, which the two Pilgrims came to, was one of those old, unsightly mansions, which, having been a well-accustomed inn time out of mind, had had different conveniences added to it by different possessors; so that it made, upon the whole, a comfortable, though very irregular, appearance. The house was at present very full; yet Tugwell contrived to get a nook in the kitchen-chimney, to smoke his pipe and drink his ale (which was his principal concern); and Mr. Wildgoose had a little parlour, near the stable, for his breakfast and his meditations.

As the Cambro-Britons are a nation of gentlemen, jealous of their honour, and impatient of affronts, they are engaged in frequent litigations: and there happened at this time to be some Lawyers upon a commission at that inn. Among the rest, there was an eminent Attorney from Bristol, who came post the day before, and whose Clerk came into the kitchen, whilst Tugwell was eating a rasher of bacon, instead of toasted cheese, for his breakfast. As Jerry, by his Master's order, had been slily enquiring, 'whether there were any Methodists at Cardiff;' the Lawyer's Clerk, interposing, said, 'they had too many of them in Bristol; but, thank God!' says he, 'two of them were shipped off for North-America yesterday morning, just as my Master and I set out.'—'For what?' says one of the company.—'Why, one of the rascals,' says the young Lawyer, 'had been tampering with one of our Aldermen's wives; and, by his cursed, canting tricks, choused the poor Alderman out of an hundred pounds, or pretty near it, to my certain knowledge.'—'What was the Alderman's name, then?' says Tugwell, interrupting him, with an eager look.—'Why, Alderman Cullpepper,' says the young Clerk.—'The Devil is a lyar, and so are you,' says Tugwell; 'for I know Alderman Cullpepper better than you do; and I came from Bristol but yesterday morning, as well as you.'—'You know Alderman Cullpepper!' returns the Lawyer. 'What! thou hast been carried before him for a petty-larceny, I suppose.'—'I do not care a t—d for your *pretty lasses,*' says Tugwell; 'but I know, that what you say is a cursed lye.'—'Is it?' says the Lawyer; 'I had it from his own servant: and I will pull thee by the nose, if thou givest me the lye again,' says he. 'One of them pretended to be a man of fortune, forsooth, but wanted to borrow money of the Alderman; and the other was a broken Cobler.'—'How do you know I was a broken Cobler?' quoth Tugwell. 'If I was a Cobler, thank God, I never was broke.'— 'I will be hanged' (cries the Lawyer, staring in his face), 'if thou art not one of them; I have seen thy face in Bristol. And the Alderman's servant told me one of them was a damned guttling fellow; that he caught him in an intrigue with a pigeon-pye, behind the pantry-door, one morning before dinner; and that he had ravished above a dozen bottles of strong beer in less than a week's time.'—'I *trigue* with a pigeon-pye!' says Jerry; 'it was nothing but a piece of pye-crust that the Cook gave me, and a little best drink to stay my stomach, gentlefolks dine so plaguy late. What! must not a man, that preaches the Gospel, eat and drink as well as other folks?'— 'Thou preach the Gospel!' says the Clerk; 'thou art more fit to sweep chimneys, or black shoes, than to preach the Gospel.'——

As Jerry was going to retort with some vehemence, this dispute might probably have proceeded to an assault and battery, if the young Lawyer had not been called away by his Master. And Mr. Wildgoose, having now dispatched his short breakfast, summoned Tugwell into his little parlour, to know what intelligence he had got about any Religious Society at Cardiff. Jerry related to him, with some indignation, the report which the young Lawyer had brought from Bristol: but Wildgoose was less surprized at the exaggerations of vulgar fame, than shocked at the scandal which he and his friend Tugwell had given, by accepting of Mrs. Cull-pepper's favours. And again expressing his suspicion, 'that Tug-well might have tasted more largely of her bounty than he cared to own,' Tugwell wished 'the Devil might fetch him, if he had had above half a guinea or *sich a matter*, of any body's money, since he came from home.' Wildgoose reproved him for his passionate exclamation; but his manner of expressing himself, and his being so touchy upon the occasion, only confirmed Wildgoose in his suspicions.

CHAPTER III

Mr. Wildgoose holds forth to a Welsh Audience

WHILST the two Pilgrims were debating what course to take; as people at an inn want to get rid of guests when nothing is going forwards for the good of the house; the Drawer (or rather the Tapster) came into the room, to know whether *the gentleman called*. Wildgoose desired to pay for what they had had; and, whilst he was doing that, enquired of the Waiter, 'whether there were any Methodists, as they called them, in the town.'—'Yes, I believe there are,' says he, 'more than are welcome: and we have got the famous Preacher Howel Harris in town at this time.'¹—'Pray, who is he?' says Wildgoose.—'Why, he is a young fellow' (replies the Waiter) 'that goes all over the country to revels and fairs, and preaches two or three times a day. He does a great deal of mischief amongst the country people; but I hope somebody or other will beat his brains out one of these days.'

'What, I suppose, he spoils your trade, and would not have people get drunk, nor spend their time and money in wicked and idle diversions?'—'I do not know,' says the Tapster; 'I have nothing to say against the young fellow; I never saw any harm by him, not I: if you have a mind to hear him, I believe he preaches again to-night; and he lodges at a widow woman's, not far from our house.'

As Wildgoose had heard Mr. Whitfield make honourable mention of Brother Howel Harris, he desired the Tapster to give them directions, and went immediately and found him out. As soon as they met, like true Free-masons, they discovered each other's occupations, almost by instinct; and, in the apostolical phrase, Wildgoose gave Howel the *right hand* of fellowship.

When Howel Harris discovered Wildgoose's inclination to harangue publicly, and that he had already been employed by Mr. Whitfield, he engaged to procure the Town-hall for him that very afternoon; where, by trumpeting the fame of this new Preacher, he assembled above four hundred people. Wildgoose held forth from the Judgement-seat; where he took occasion, without Judge or Jury, to *arraign* and *condemn* the whole race of Mankind. Many were very attentive; but some mocked: and some jolly fellows, who had been drinking at the inn, one of whom kept

a pack of hounds in the neighbourhood, having had intelligence of
Wildgoose's intention by the Drawer, got a dead fox, and trailed
him round the Town-hall, and laid on his dogs to the scent.[1] The
music of the hounds, and the noise of the sportsmen, were so
loud and vociferous, that they almost drowned the voice of the
Orator: and the chearfulness of the sound had such a mechanical
effect upon the minds of many of the Cambrians, that they ran out
to join them; nay, Tugwell himself, in the midst of the preachment,
could hardly refrain from giving them a *tallio*; but the recollection
of the jeopardy he had been in, when he mistook the jack-ass for
a stag, checked his spirit, and prevented him from deserting his
station near his master, and joining the cry.

The Fox-hunters, however, were tired before the Preacher, who
harangued for above an hour to a very attentive audience; and,
what is remarkable, that part of the congregation seemed most
affected, and bestowed the most hearty benedictions on the
Preacher, who did not understand a word of English. This, however, we ought not to attribute merely to affectation, but to the
vehemence and apparent sincerity of the Orator, and the mechanical
and infectious operation of an enthusiastic energy.

It was towards evening before they dismissed the assembly; and
Wildgoose, having been disturbed by the storm the preceding
night, invited Howel Harris to sit an hour with him at his inn,
where they settled their plan for the next morning: and the two Pilgrims retired early to their repose, highly satisfied with the adventures of the day; which Wildgoose said (in the style of the Journals),
'was a day of *fat things*;' to which Tugwell (applying it in a literal
sense to his rashers of bacon and Welsh ale) heartily assented.

CHAPTER IV

An unlucky Mistake

THE house being very full (as was observed), our adventurers,
being only foot-passengers, met with but scurvy lodgings. There
was a room up five or six stairs, near the stable, with two miserable
beds in it; in one of which the Hostler usually lay; and the other was
reserved for the Drawer or Tapster, or any of the other servants,

who might happen to be turned out of their own beds upon any extraordinary conflux of company; which was so much the present case, that the Hostler himself was turned out by Mr. Wildgoose, and forced to lie in the hay-loft; and Tugwell took up the other bed contiguous to his master.

The two travellers were but just got into their first sleep, when Nan the Cook, who happened to have a nocturnal intrigue with the Hostler, slipped up to Wildgoose's bed-side, and, calling the Hostler two or three times in a low voice, disturbed Wildgoose, who began to mutter some rapturous ejaculation in his sleep; which Nan mistaking for the amorous expostulation of an impatient lover, she began to disrobe herself with great expedition; when, as ill luck would have it, one of the Waiters, being driven from his bed to make room for a Lawyer's Clerk, came into the room with a candle, and discovered poor Cooky half undressed. She was an handsome, plump girl, of about twenty-five; but, from the constant heat and unctuous steams of the kitchen, her complexion had more of the ruddy bronze of an Italian peasant than the pale delicacy of a Northern beauty. However, she was agreeable enough to the gross appetite of an Hostler, and, as the Waiter imagined, to that of a Modern Saint; for Wildgoose, being now awaked (notwithstanding the surprize which he expressed at seeing such company at his bed-side, and the angry rebukes which he made use of for this intrusion), the Waiter formed conjectures by no means favourable to his virtue. Poor Nan, pretending some mistake, collected her loose robes, and hurried down stairs as fast as she could; and the Waiter with her. At the bottom of the stairs, they met the Hostler, who, having heard somebody go up into his usual apartment, suspected the mistake. The Waiter told him, 'that he had caught Nan in bed with the Methodist Preacher;' which though he did not entirely believe, yet it so far rouzed his jealousy, that he heartily joined with the Waiter in publishing the story the next morning.

CHAPTER V

An Apparition

TUGWELL, being thoroughly fatigued, and pretty well steeped in Welsh ale, never waked during the above transaction: but, about one o'clock, when the whole house was quiet, and he had a little satisfied the importunate demands of Nature, he was disturbed by something at the feet of his bed; when, opening his eyes, he discovered by the twilight a most diabolical figure standing upright before him. It was about five feet high, of a grim aspect, with eyes that glared like fire, a long beard, and a monstrous pair of horns. 'In the name of the Father, the Son, and the Holy Ghost,' cries Tugwell, 'what art thou?'—The Spectre made no other answer; but in an hollow tone cried, 'whare? whare?' Jerry, who made no doubt but it was the Devil, and charitably supposing that his business was with the gentlemen of the Law, replied, 'that, if he wanted the Lawyers, they lay in the best bed-chambers.'—The apparition, as if he wanted no other intelligence, took his cloven feet immediately off the bed, and, like the Devil upon Two Sticks, went stumping down stairs again, and disappeared.[1]—Tugwell, however, awaked his companion in a great fright. 'Master Wildgoose! Master Wildgoose!' says he; 'for God's sake awake: Lord have mercy upon us!' says he; 'the house is haunted; the Devil has just appeared to me, and is this moment gone down stairs.'—Wildgoose, though in his discourses he frequently talked of the Devil and the power of Satan, yet did not really believe his visible appearance to mankind. He took this opportunity, however, of reminding Jerry, 'how free he had made with the Devil's name about so trifling an affair as his receiving money upon the road!'— 'Lord have mercy upon us!' says Tugwell; 'to be sure, that is the reason of his appearance. Talk of the Devil, and he will appear. I wished the Devil might fetch me, if I had taken above half a guinea since we came from *home*; and, to be sure, I have received three times as much from different people. But God forgive me, and defend me from the power of Satan, who is the father of lies.'

Though Wildgoose did not trouble himself about Jerry's perquisites, he was sorry to find, that, after so much good instruction, he had made no greater progress towards perfection. He desired him, however, 'to take another nap; for that the Apparition was only a dream, or a phantom of his imagination.'—'The *Fancy* of a *Magic Lanthern!*' says Jerry; 'no, no; I have seen a Magic Lanthern at Evesham fair. It was no Magic Lanthern,' says Tugwell; 'for I felt him, as well as saw him. He patted my legs with his cloven-feet; and he grew taller and taller, as I looked at him, till his head reached the ceiling; and I heard him walk down stairs: and, I am sure, the house is haunted by Evil Spirits; and I am for leaving this place as soon as it is day-light.'

Mr. Wildgoose, who had been haunted by the Flesh (in the shape of a fat Cook), as Tugwell had by the Spirit (in the shape of a Devil as he thought), and not knowing what use the Drawer might make of such an incident; being also impatient to get back to Gloucester, for reasons which the Reader may probably guess at; took Jerry's hint, and promised to set out by five o'clock, but desired Tugwell to compose himself till that time; which Jerry promised to do: and Mr. Wildgoose, being still much fatigued, took another nap.

Tugwell, however, could not sleep soundly; but, being waked again by the clock's striking four, and still haunted by the terrors of his fancy, he calls out again to his fellow-traveller, 'Master Wildgoose! Master Wildgoose!' says he.—'What is the matter now?' says Wildgoose.—'O, nothing,' says Jerry; 'I had only a mind to let you know, that you have but an hour longer to sleep.'—— 'Pugh!' says Wildgoose; 'but you need not have waked me to tell me so.'

The sun, however, began now to dart his first rays through the lattice, and discovered the ballads on the walls of their bed-chamber. People also began to move about the inn. Wildgoose therefore, and his friend Tugwell, thought it best to quit their beds, and decamp before the family were all stirring. Jerry, seeing his Master kneel down to his devotions, just cast up a short ejaculation; but thought it more to his purpose to examine the state of his wallet; which being pretty well exhausted, he resolved to replenish it with what he could get before they set out.

As they came down into the stable-yard, a great shaggy he-goat, drawn by the smell of Jerry's wallet, came running towards them; which Mr. Wildgoose espying, immediately observed to his friend, 'that was the Ghost which had appeared to him in the night.'— Tugwell said, 'the Apparition had horns, and a beard, like the goat; but that he was as tall as the house, and walked upright upon two

legs; and, he was sure, it could be nothing but the Devil himself.'
——Wildgoose did not stay to convince him; but, meeting with the
Tapster, who had waited on them the preceding night, paid him
for what they had had; yet not before Tugwell had drunk a pot of
ale, and furnished his wallet with some provision for their journey.

CHAPTER VI

Their Reception by the Parson of Newport

THOUGH Wildgoose was not very solicitous about the ludicrous
turn which the servants at the inn might give to his adventure
with the fat Cook; yet, as he had promised Howel Harris to hold
forth again that day at Cardiff, and was unwilling to leave room for
any suspicion in the mind of his friend, he thought it proper to call
upon him at his lodgings; and, though it was not yet five o'clock,
he found him already up, and at his meditations.

As people who are good themselves are not apt to suspect ill of
others, Mr. Wildgoose found no difficulty in convincing his
Brother Howel of his innocence. He would have persuaded Wildgoose, however, not to quit Cardiff so abruptly: but, when he
found him determined, he immediately took his staff, and set out
with the two Pilgrims towards Newport, a considerable town on the
great road; where he promised to introduce Mr. Wildgoose to the
Parson of the parish, 'who,' he said, 'was a friend to their cause,
and had lent Mr. Whitfield his pulpit, when he lately visited the
principality of Wales.'

They arrived at Newport before ten o'clock, and accordingly
waited upon the Doctor, who received them in a polite manner, and
told them, 'as he was persuaded of Mr. Whitfield's good intentions,
and knew also how fond people are of a new Preacher, and what an
impression that very circumstance often made upon careless
Christians, he had indulged his parishioners, for once, in hearing
so famous a man; but that, in general, he did not at all approve of
such irregular proceedings.

'I have already,' continued the Doctor, 'found the ill effects of
my complaisance to Mr. Whitfield. My own people, who are very
well disposed, and who were before entirely satisfied with my plain

doctrine, now, forsooth, give out, that I do not preach the Gospel, because I do not always harp upon the same string, of the New Birth, Faith without Works, and the like. They also expect me to have private meetings two or three nights in the week, and compliment them with private expositions of Scripture, extempore prayer, psalm-singing, and what not; though, I really believe, if I were to give them the very same sermons in a private room, lighted up with candles like a play-house, the very novelty of the thing would content them for a while, as well as the best of your itinerant preachers.'

Though the Doctor was not disposed to enter into the views of our Spiritual Adventurers; yet, as he kept an hospitable house, he entertained them with a good breakfast of coffee and hot rolls; after which, Mr. Wildgoose and Howel Harris parting with each other, the latter returned to Cardiff; and Wildgoose, with his fellow traveller, pursued their journey to Gloucester.

CHAPTER VII

An agreeable Solitude. An Holy Family, in the
Flemish Style

THOUGH Mr. Wildgoose's principal view was to make the best of his way into the North, agreeably to Mr. Whitfield's destination; yet his more immediate object was, to reach Gloucester as soon as possible, both to confirm the distressed Brethren there, and perhaps (in a subordinate degree) in hopes of another interview with Miss Townsend before she left that place, as she daily expected to do. However, as both Mr. Whitfield in his Journals, and also Howel Harris, had represented the inhabitants of Wales as sweetly prepared to receive the Gospel (going frequently twenty miles to hear a sermon);[1] and as Howel had also informed him that there was a considerable Society established at Monmouth, and had given him a letter to a substantial Tradesman, who was the Chief Ruler of the Synagogue there; for these reasons, Mr. Wildgoose determined to take his route by the way of Monmouth.

Though Monmouthshire is now in some respects an English

county, and is not so mountainous as many parts of Wales; yet, to those whose travels have never extended farther than Hammersmith or Brentford, or a few miles round the Metropolis, the roads in this county would not appear quite so level as a Kidderminster carpet.

Accordingly, the two Pilgrims, after two hours travelling, had now just surmounted a Monmouthshire mole-hill, and were come down into a romantic valley, on the banks of the Uske, the coolness of which, as the sun was near its meridian, was extremely refreshing. After winding along the river's side for about half a mile, they came in sight of a pleasant village, at the foot of another hill, covered with hanging woods, which formed a beautiful amphitheatre; in the centre of which the Parish-church, with its little spire, rose amongst some old pine-trees; and the ruins of a Monastery, near which the river formed a natural cascade, shewed that the place had formerly been dedicated to devotion and solitude. Wildgoose could not but admire the sequestered situation; and observed, 'that, if a true primitive spirit reigned amongst those people, they must be the happiest of mortals.'

The first cottage they came to was a tolerably neat one, and appeared the constant residence of peace and tranquillity. A little wicket, painted white, led through a small court to the house, which was covered with honey-suckles and sweet-briar: the windows were glazed; and the chimney rose, with a truly ancient British magnificence, two feet above the thatch.

As the road divided at the end of the village, Tugwell marched boldly up to the door, to enquire the way. On so near an approach, however, they found, that Peace does not always reside in a cottage; for their ears were saluted with the confused noise and squalling of children; and a female voice, with a Welsh accent (which is alway expressive of anger), answered Jerry, and bid him, 'go about his business; that there was nothing for him; and that they had beggars enough in their own parish.'—Jerry replied, 'that they did not come to beg, but to enquire the road to Monmouth.'

A little curled-headed boy, with shoes and stockings on, now opened the door; when they heard the foresaid female exclaiming, 'Why do not you make haste, and scrape the bacon? I wish those books were all in the fire.' Then, seeing Jerry's wallet on his shoulder, she cries out, 'that they never bought any thing of Pedlars; that her own father, who was a gentleman born, kept a

U

creditable shop at Newport; and she would not encourage people who travelled about to the prejudice of the fair trader.'

During this angry exclamation, Tugwell and Wildgoose had a full view into the kitchen; where, besides the boy that opened the door, they saw four or five more, and the poor woman far advanced in her pregnancy. The Master of the house, who was no other than the Vicar of the parish, was sitting down in his band and night-gown; but so far from being idle, that his eyes, his hands, and his feet, every limb of his body, and every faculty of his soul, were fully employed: for he was reading a folio, that lay on a table to the right; was hearing his little boy read, who stood by him on the left; he was rocking the cradle with his foot; and was paring turnips.

As soon as he could disengage his attention from this variety of employments, he rose up, and with a stern air asked the travellers, 'what they wanted?'—Wildgoose repeated Tugwell's question, and desired to know, 'which was the road to Monmouth?'—The Vicar told them, 'they were come near a mile out of their way; but that, with proper directions, they might easily recover the right road.'

Observing Wildgoose, however, upon a nearer view, not to have the appearance of a common tramper, he asked them, 'if they would sit down *at the door*, and refresh themselves a little in the heat of the day? I cannot desire you to walk into the house,' says the Vicar; 'for, amongst the other comforts of matrimony, I have that of sitting my whole life in a wet room. My wife, as you may perceive, is a very good housewife; but (unfortunately for me!) she has taken it into her head, that a *wet* house and a *clean* house are the same thing: so that, having only one room to sit in, and that being washed every morning, it is consequently as you now see it all the year round.'

Mr. Wildgoose said, 'he was sorry to have given him the trouble of this apology, as he could not accept of his invitation.'——Tugwell, however, who seldom slighted an offer of this kind, said, 'he would be obliged to the gentleman for a draught of small-beer.'—The Vicar, therefore, himself took a cup, stepped to the barrel, which stood in a little shed, or *enclitical* pent-house, and brought Jerry, in a literal sense, some *small*-beer, the refreshing liquor which he asked for.

CHAPTER VIII

Ecclesiastical Pride in the Diocese of Landaff

WHILST Tugwell was regaling himself with the foresaid potation, Wildgoose reposed himself upon the bench at the door; and, pointing to the ruins of the Monastery, observed to the Vicar, by way of chit-chat, 'that there had been a Religious House in his parish.'—'Yes,' says the Vicar, 'there *has been* a *Religious* House in the parish, I believe; but, I am sorry to say, it was long before my time; for, I am afraid, at present we have not one truly religious house in the parish.'——'God forbid!' says Wildgoose; 'for, I dare say, Sir, you do your duty amongst them.'—'Why,' says the Vicar, 'I hope I do my duty as well as the generality of my brethren; but am afraid, from particular circumstances, it is not in my power to do much good in my parish.'——'How so, Sir?' replies Wild-goose.—'You know, Sir,' replies the Vicar, 'that, at the Reformation, in Harry the Eighth's time, when the revenues of these Religious Houses, by the Act of Dissolution, were granted to the Crown, how slender a reserve was made in general for serving the Parish-churches. Now, you must observe, Sir, that, after spending seven years in the University, and taking a Master of Arts degree, I am possessed of a little Rectory, of about thirty pounds a year; and of this Vicarage, which, if I could make the most of it, might bring me in near twenty more: now, each of these preferments these poor people consider as a *noble benefice*; and, though you see, Sir, in what way I live, yet, because I am possessed of half a dozen spoons and a silver tankard, they envy me, as living in a princely state, and lording it over God's heritage; and, what is worse, as my whole income in this parish arises from the small tythes, be-cause I cannot afford to let them cheat me out of half my dues, they represent me as carnal and worldly-minded, and as one who regards nothing but the good things of this life, and who is always making disturbances in the parish. And this prejudice against me prevents my doing that good amongst them which I sincerely wish to do. One man has left his church, and walks three miles to a Methodist-meeting, because I took one pig out of seven, as the Law directs; another has complained to the Bishop of my extortion, because I would not take three shillings and six pence, in lieu of tythes for a large orchard, as my predecessor had done. In short, Sir, here are two or three Dissenters in the parish, who give out that all tythes are remnants of Popery; and would have the Clergy consider meat and drink as types and shadows, which ought to have been abolished with the Levitical Law.'

'Well, Sir,' says Wildgoose, 'I cannot but think the situation of a poor Vicar particularly disagreeable, and that of the Clergy in general very much so, in a temporal view. And, since "all malice (as a polite writer observes) arises from an opposition of interests," I think it is pity, even upon that account, that things could not be put upon some different footing between the Pastors and their flocks.'—'Why,' says the Vicar, 'if it could be done without too great a confusion of property, I am sure, I should have no objection to it. And I have often thought, as things now are, to prevent that odium which every Incumbent must bring upon himself, who is under a necessity of disputing with his parish the rights of the Church, a method might be contrived, to throw the burthen upon the Church itself, instead of any particular Incumbent.'—'As how?' says Wildgoose.—'Why,' says the Vicar, 'that the Bishop should be empowered, by a fund levied in some manner on the Clergy of the Diocese (in proportion to their income), to defend the rights of any particular parish; which, by reference to some neighbouring gentlemen, or other lenient methods, I should think might generally be done without much expence, and without involving a poor, miserable Incumbent in continual squabbles with his parish, and preventing him from doing that good which probably he might otherwise do. But,' continued the Vicar, 'there is no perfection to be hoped for in any human institutions; and, perhaps, an attempt to remedy the present might be attended with still greater inconveniences.'

'I think,' says Wildgoose, 'there can be no greater misfortune than a misunderstanding between a Minister and his congregation; as it prevents all probability of the people's receiving any spiritual improvement, if the Clergy were to take ten times the pains which they generally do.

'But pray, Sir,' continues Wildgoose, 'where is that Methodist-meeting, which you mentioned? Is it in our road to Monmouth?'— This enquiry confirmed the Vicar in what he had before suspected from Wildgoose's conversation, that he was a favourer at least of the Methodists. He told him, therefore, 'that, if he wanted information of that kind, any of his parishioners would give him ample satisfaction; and would, upon occasion, leave the most necessary business, and walk twenty miles, to hear the extempore effusions of an illiterate Mechanic.'

CHAPTER IX

Mr. Wildgoose collects an Audience

TUGWELL had by this time dispatched his small-beer, with a piece of bread and cheese and a pint of ale into the bargain; for the Vicar's wife, having (through her mistake) treated him at first with undeserved asperity, was willing to atone for her rudeness by a superfluous civility, especially as, during her husband's conference with Mr. Wildgoose, Jerry had supplied his place, in rocking the cradle, paring the turnips, and blowing the fire.

He was now, however, forced to leave the smell of the pot, being summoned to attend his Master, and proceed on their journey. In return for the Vicar's civility, Mr. Wildgoose took the liberty to exhort him, 'to endeavour the regaining his people's good-will, by some little popular acts of beneficence, by relieving the distressed, giving physic to the sick, or, where he was obliged to exact his Easter groats from any very poor families, to give them a six-penny loaf in the place of it; and the like innocent stratagems: but above all, Sir,' adds Wildgoose, 'if the poor people had the *true* Gospel earnestly and affectionately inculcated into them, I am convinced, all these worldly considerations would entirely vanish; and you would dwell together in unity and love.'—The Vicar thanked Wildgoose for his good advice; but said, 'he had already used his utmost endeavours to regain the good-will of his parishioners; but was afraid nothing would succeed with people, who, to save a groat, would risque their eternal salvation.'—The Vicar and the travellers then parted, with mutual good wishes.

When the two Pilgrims came towards the end of the village, they observed an old Taylor sitting on his board, with spectacles on his nose, and with more devotion than harmony quavering one of Mr. Wesley's hymns. This was hint sufficient for Wildgoose to make further enquiry about the Society of Methodists, which the Vicar had mentioned. The Taylor told them, 'there was a weekly meeting at a village about three miles farther; but that this was not the night on which the Preacher came.'—Tugwell soon let him know, 'that his Master could supply that defect; and that, if it lay in their road to Monmouth, he would give them a word of exhortation that evening.' Upon this, the old Taylor leaped nimbly off his board; and, leaving a suit of cloaths which he had promised to finish that evening, said, 'he would accompany them, if it were as far again;' and immediately ran and communicated this intelligence to a Blacksmith, his next neighbour, who leaves the Farmer's horses half-shoed, and with like speed acquaints the Farmer's wife, who was a zealous disciple of theirs. She, slipping on her shoes and stockings, leaves her cows unmilked, and her child dangerously ill in the cradle; and, with half a dozen more, who, upon spreading the alarm, had left their several employments, joined the devout cavalcade.[1]

After many questions, who the gentleman was, and whence he came, they set forwards, and now marched chearfully along the valley; Wildgoose making enquiry into the state of their souls; and Tugwell entertaining them with some account of their adventures, and what he called persecutions, which they had undergone since they entered upon their Ministry.

The village whither they were bound, and where they soon arrived, was a considerable thorough-fare to Monmouth, and a populous place. The arrival of a new Preacher was soon spread about the neighbourhood; and there assembled, in half an hour's time, above two hundred people: when Wildgoose (being always desirous of attacking the Devil in his strong holds), having first refreshed himself with what the house afforded, held forth at the door of a little inn, being mounted on an horse-block, under a shady elm, which had long been sacred to rustic jollity and tippling, and thoroughly perfumed with the incense of ale and tobacco.

CHAPTER X

Miracles and slight Persecutions

As soon as Mr. Wildgoose began to harangue from the horse-block, some servants belonging to the Squire of the village, who was a very orthodox man, and no friend to these superfluous acts of piety, began to make some disturbance, and to beat a drum (that formerly belonged to the Militia); which at first a little embarrassed the Orator: but he appearing much in earnest, and a majority of the company being more inclined to be attentive, they soon silenced these scoffers; and Wildgoose proceeded in his harangue.

A considerable part of the congregation were seated on an orchard-wall, which faced the public-house; and, whilst Wildgoose was declaiming with great vehemence, to an attentive audience, in praise of humility and self-denial, and had just assured them, 'that he who humbled himself should be exalted,' the whole wall on which they sat, being built of loose stones, fell flat to the ground, not one of them crying out, or altering his posture; nor was there the least interruption, either in the vehemence of the Orator, or in the attention of the audience.[1]

But their tranquillity was soon after disturbed by a phænomenon of another kind. A poor fellow of a neighbouring hamlet (who used to be always quarreling with his neighbours, but who had been greatly affected by hearing Mr. Wesley preach two or three times), came galloping through the street, upon a little poney, about the size of a jack-ass, hallooing and shouting, and driving men, women, pigs, and children, before him. He was without an hat, with his long red hair hanging about his ears; and, staring wildly, he rides up to Wildgoose, crying out, '*Got* bless you! Master Wesley; hur is convinced of sin; and Got has given hur revelations, and visions, and prophecies; and has foretold, that hur shall be a king, and tread all hur enemies under hur feet.'[2]

As the preaching was interrupted by this poor man, some of the company told Wildgoose, 'that he had been almost mad ever since he had heard Mr. Wesley preach.'—'Mad!' quoth Wildgoose; 'I wish all that hear me this day were not only *almost*, but altogether as mad as this poor countryman. No,' says he, 'these are the true symptoms of the New Birth; and he only wants the obstetric hand of some Spiritual Physician, to relieve him from his pangs, from these struggles between the Flesh and the Spirit.' He then desired those who were strong in Faith to *wrestle* in prayer for the poor Enthusiast: but he left them to wrestle by themselves; and, without waiting for the event of their application, galloped off again upon his Welsh tit, hallooing and whooping, and as frantic as before.

The preachment being ended, Tugwell, who had been vastly taken with the singing of hymns, which he had heard at Bristol, thought he might venture, in a country place, to exhibit a specimen of his own talent at Psalmody, and give out the Psalm; though Jerry's voice was as unharmonious as the falling of a fire-shovel upon a marble slab. Both his music and appearance, therefore, were so far from any thing of devotion or solemnity, that the Squire's servants, who had been awed to silence by the vehemence of Wild-goose's eloquence, could now hold out no longer. But one of them began again to beat on the drum; and another discharged two or three addled-eggs, which he had brought for the purpose, at Tugwell's head; one of which flying directly into the aperture of Jerry's extended jaws, the unsavoury odour of the rotten eggs, and Jerry's resentment of the indignity offered to a man of his fancied importance, threw the whole congregation into confusion, and soon after dispersed the assembly.

Wildgoose now began to reflect upon the escape his audience had had from the tumbling wall, and to bless God for what he fancied so miraculous an attestation to the truth of his Mission. But the Farmer, who owned the orchard, considered the affair in a different light; and, being no friend to the cause, insisted upon an indemnification; and made poor Wildgoose pay five shillings and six pence for dilapidations.

As the evening now came on, and the two Pilgrims were much fatigued with their early rising and long walk, they thought it best to set up their staff at the public-house where they had preached. Tugwell, indeed, complained likewise of his having been pelted with addled-eggs. But his Master exhorted him, 'to count it all joy, that he met with these divers temptations.'—'Yes! great joy, indeed,' (quoth Jerry, in a pettish mood) 'to have rotten eggs in one's mouth, besides spoiling one's cloaths, which I shall not get sweet again this half-year.'——Tugwell, however, having got a rasher of bacon with his eggs, and smoked his pipe, was tolerably well pacified; whilst Wildgoose went about, giving spiritual advice to different parts of the family: and then the two friends retired to their repose.

CHAPTER XI

Reception at Monmouth

THE sun had been risen about an hour, when Wildgoose sprang from his bed; and, it being likely to prove a very hot day, soon rouzed his fellow-traveller, and set out for Monmouth. Tugwell, however, could not leave an house of entertainment without laying in some provision for the journey of the day.

In all his travels, indeed, Jerry never wanted a substantial reason for making a good meal, and filling his belly. In the morning, it was a maxim with him, to make sure of a good breakfast, for fear they should not meet with a dinner. When dinner-time came, he pretended to be more hungry than *ordinary* that day, because they had breakfasted before their time; and at night he would observe, that his journey had got him an appetite, and he never was *so hungry* in his life before: though, if Wildgoose had attended to his impertinence, he had probably made the like apologies every day since they came from home.

As their road lay through shady lanes or green meadows, they made pretty good speed; and, without any thing worth recording, arrived at Monmouth early in the afternoon.

When Mr. Wildgoose had found out the Tradesman, who was one of the Fraternity, to whom Howell Harris had given him letters of recommendation, he delivered his credentials. The man, casting his eye over the letter, and finding Wildgoose's business, received him at first with some little coolness; and said, 'they had of late had so many *strange* Preachers, that the credit of their Society had suffered greatly by their indiscretions.' But, perusing the letter more carefully, and finding that Mr. Wildgoose was no common itinerant, but a man of some fortune, and particularly delegated by Mr. Whitfield, he altered his style, and, by way of apology for the suspicions he had expressed, related the following incident, which, he said, had lately happened in that neighbourhood.

'A genteel young man,' says he, 'came down from London, who pretended to have been a Preacher at one of Mr. Wesley's Societies. He preached frequently at Monmouth; and was well received in a gentleman's family in the neighbourhood, who were religiously disposed. The gentleman had a daughter, whom he was upon the point of marrying, to great advantage, to a person of superior fortune; and the alliance would have made two families extremely happy.

'This Itinerant, however, finding the young lady rather indifferent in her affections for this gentleman, who was, indeed, fourteen or fifteen years older than herself, persuaded her, "that she could not in conscience give her hand without her heart; and that it was a kind of legal prostitution, to dispose of her person merely for the sake of a genteel settlement in the world, and the like; especially to a man, whom he represented as *no Christian*, because he did not frequent their Religious Society."

'In short, to prevent her yielding to the importunity of her friends, and even to the commands of her father, he persuaded the young lady to march off with him into Ireland, which was his native country, and where he had been a Journeyman-barber, and came to London in that capacity. But, by frequenting Mr. Wesley's Tabernacle for a few months, he had learned a few Scripture-phrases, which, by virtue of a modest assurance, he retailed to us in the country with great applause; though, it is to be feared, he had no true Faith, nor, indeed, any Religion at all in his heart. And this affair has brought a great scandal upon our Society, and given too just occasion for our adversaries to blaspheme.

'However, Sir,' continues the Tradesman, 'I hope a gentleman so well recommended will contribute to retrieve our credit; and I will acquaint the Brethren with your arrival, and hope you will this evening give a word of exhortation at my house.'

Wildgoose said, 'he would do his best, as God should give him utterance; but would go to the inn for an hour or two, to rest and refresh himself, and about seven o'clock would meet the Society.'

CHAPTER XII

A Stranger introduced to our Hero

OUR two Pilgrims went to a second-rate inn; where, whilst Wildgoose was eating some dinner in the parlour, Tugwell had published the good qualities and present occupation of his Master (over a pipe) in the kitchen. This my Landlord had communicated to a young Officer, who was quartered there, and was lounging in the bar, and whom mine Host, for the good of the house, contrived, as often as he could, to introduce to his company, to make one at a bottle of wine, or a bowl of punch.

This young man, however, had reasons of a more serious nature, for wishing to converse with a man of Mr. Wildgoose's character and pretensions; and willingly consented to the Landlord's proposal, of being introduced to this devout Itinerant. As soon, therefore, as Wildgoose had finished his slight repast, the Landlord told him, 'that a young Officer, who was quartered there, would be glad to drink a glass of wine with him.'—Wildgoose replied, 'if the gentleman desired it, he should be very glad of his company; though he could not promise to drink much wine with him.'

Accordingly, there was introduced a tall, genteel young man, in his regimentals, who, throwing himself into a chair, and laying down his hat, with a smart cockade, upon the table, unbuckled his sword-belt, and hurled his sword, with some indignation, across the room, crying out, 'Thus let the weapons of war perish!'

Wildgoose was a little dismayed at this frantic behaviour, and stared at him with silent astonishment; when the Man of war, looking wildly in his face, exclaimed again, with an air of distraction, 'Zounds! Sir, can you give any relief to a soul that is haunted by Furies?'—'Come, Sir,' says Wildgoose, 'do not despair of God's mercy, whatever your case may be: *Nil desperandum, Christo duce.* Never be cast down, whilst you have Christ for your guide. I hope these are favourable symptoms of the New Birth.'—'New Birth! Sir: God forbid! What! be born again! It is my misfortune that I ever was born at all.

> Why was I born with such a sense of Virtue,
> So great abhorrence of the smallest Guilt;
> And yet a slave to such impetuous Passion!'[1]

As he was thus ranting in Heroics, Wildgoose endeavoured to comfort him. 'Come, Sir,' says he, 'the first step to conversion is, to be convinced of sin, as I hope you are: but, that I may be able to administer a proper remedy, let me know the nature of your disease.'

'Well, Sir, if you have patience to listen to a long series of irregularity and guilty pleasures, I will give the best account of myself that I can; as it is always some relief to the miserable, to

lay open their griefs, where they can do it with safety, as I am convinced I may to a man of your character, though you are a stranger
to me, and I have been guilty of murder; nay, parricide, I believe;
adultery, and what not.'—'Well, well, so much the better,' says
Wildgoose; 'the more wicked and abandoned you have been, the
more likely you are to be convinced of sin. But please to favour me
with the particulars of your transgression.'—The stranger then
began the following narration.

CHAPTER XIII

The Adventures of Captain Johnson

'MY father,' says the Captain, 'was a Merchant in London;
where for some years he carried on a considerable trade: but, his
health declining, and having only one hopeful son (the wretch
whom you here behold), he early in life retired from business. I was
bred up at Westminster; and passed through the school, I believe,
with some degree of credit; and was sent to the University with the
character of an excellent Classick.

'My father, hearing that my parts and sprightly genius had introduced me to the *best*, that is, the most *expensive* company in the
place, gave me very liberal appointments; of which I made a very
ungenerous use: for, instead of improving myself in learning, or any
valuable accomplishment, the only science, in which I made any
progress, was that of a refined luxury and extravagance. And, in
short, I was guilty of so many irregularities, that although the
Governors of the University were unwilling to expel me, yet they
privately admonished my father to remove me from a situation, of
which I was so far from making any proper use, that it must soon
prove equally destructive to my health and to my fortune.

'My father, who was too fond of me, thought it prudent to appear
ignorant of my bad conduct; and wrote me word, "that, as I had
probably, by this time, made a tolerable proficiency in polite learning and philosophy, he was willing to finish my education by letting
me make the tour of Europe."

'Accordingly, with no other Governor than an honest Swiss, who
served me in the double capacity of a Tutor and a Valet, I set out

upon my travels; to make my observations upon the laws and customs, that is, to learn the vices and follies, of all the nations in Europe.

'During my stay at Paris, I became intimate with an English gentleman of some distinction, who was settled with his family at R——, in Normandy; whither, in consequence of a pressing invitation, I accompanied him to spend part of the summer. As both he and his Lady were fond of company, I was soon introduced to people of the best fashion, of both sexes, in that province.

'There was a young Lady of great beauty, the wife of one of the Members of the Parliament of R——, who was the most frequently of our party. She had a gaiety in her temper, and a coquetry in her behaviour; but not more than is common in the married women of that nation.'—'Ah!' cries Wildgoose, 'I am afraid, what you call by the soft names of gaiety and coquetry, are the lusts of the flesh, under a specious disguise; and that the French are an adulterous and sinful generation.'—'I am afraid they are,' says the Captain; 'and yet I question whether the inhabitants of this island are in that respect much inferior to their neighbours on the Continent.— But to proceed in my story.'

CHAPTER XIV

The Adventures of Captain Johnson continued

'LADY RUELLE (which was this Lady's name) had been something particular, as I fancied, in her behaviour to me. One evening, as we were walking in the gardens of my friend's house, with a large party of polite people, we found ourselves insensibly got into a private walk, detached from the rest of the company. "Monsieur Anglais," says Lady Ruelle, "I long to see Londres, and wish I could meet with an opportunity of going over into England."— As I thought this nothing more than unmeaning chit-chat, I imagined the most proper answer I could make her Ladyship was, "that I should be very happy in shewing her our Metropolis; and wished I might, some time or other, have that honour."—She replied, with a sigh and languishing air, "Ah! I wish, Monsieur, you were sincere in those professions."—The manner in which she spoke this surprized me a little; yet, as a man of gallantry, I could not but repeat my acknowledgments of the honour she did me, and offer to conduct so fair a Lady through the world, if she would permit me. She then declared, "that she was serious in her intentions;" but (as some company now walked towards us) said, "she would explain herself more at large when she had an opportunity."

'Lady Ruelle spoke no more to me that night: but, the next time we met, she took occasion to let me know, "that her husband used her extremely ill; that she had taken a fancy to me the first time she saw me; and would put herself, and ten thousand pounds sterling, in money and jewels, into my hands, if I would accept of the offer."

'Though I was startled at such a proposal, it flattered my vanity so agreeably, that, without reflecting on the consequences, I affected to receive with rapture and gratitude so charming an overture.

'Not to be too minute in this detail, she had laid her plan; and was determined, I found, to make her escape from a Masquerade-ball, to which we were invited, near the suburbs of R——, the next night but one; when she knew also, that her husband would be engaged the whole evening from home. I had time enough to deliberate upon the wickedness and the danger of this expedition; the injury I was going to do the gentleman her husband; and the dishonour I should bring upon my English friend, who had introduced me to them: but, fired with the glory and gallantry of the action (as things then appeared to me), I was blind to every other consideration.

'The next morning, therefore, I sent my trusty Swiss to Dieppe, with orders to get a vessel ready to sail at a minute's notice.

'On the night appointed for the Masquerade, about ten o'clock, Lady Ruelle appeared, dressed like a young gentleman, in a sort of hunting suit of green and gold, and adorned with not less than five thousand pounds-worth of diamonds, which she had contrived to borrow of her husband's relations, under the pretence of this Masquerade-ball.

'My servant had got the post-chaise ready, under a mount at the corner of the garden-wall: and, after supper, when the company were separated into parties, Lady Ruelle and I easily contrived to give them the slip. I let myself down; and the Lady, with great courage and alacrity, threw herself into my arms. I put her immediately into the carriage; and we drove off, attended only by the Postilion, and by my Swiss armed with a carbine, with great expedition, for Dieppe.'

CHAPTER XV

The Adventures of Captain Johnson continued

'As the distance, I believe, is not above ten leagues, or about thirty miles, we should probably have reached Dieppe without any interruption: but, upon our coming into a forest, where the road divided, our Postilion drove us some miles out of the way, before he pretended to have discovered his mistake. We had just recovered our route, when we were overtaken by three men, well armed, who charged us to stop, in the King's name. I had time to cock both my pistols: and my servant, who was a bold fellow, bid them produce their credentials; which he received upon the end of his carbine, but shot the poor fellow dead upon the spot: the other two, like cowards as they were, fled with great precipitation; and we proceeded without any further molestation to Dieppe. I there dismissed the Postilion, after presenting him with the post-chaise, which I had bought, for his faithful service; though it appeared afterwards that he had betrayed us.

'When we came to the harbour of Dieppe, we found the ship, which my servant had bespoken, riding at her cable's length, ready to sail. When we came on board, the Master of the vessel demanded our pass-ports. I produced one for myself and for my servant: but, when he found I had none for the young gentleman in green and gold, he shook his head, and refused to sail. I immediately cocked my pistol, and threatened to shoot him through the head, if he persisted in his refusal. He said, "I might do as I pleased; but, if he carried off that young gentleman, whom he suspected to be a person of consequence, he should be hanged the moment he returned to France." I was not yet so abandoned as to take away the life of an honest man, upon so slight a provocation. After trying him again, therefore, with a round sum of money, to no purpose, we were forced to hire another chaise, and resuming our journey by land, proceeded to Boulogne.

'Being come the next day within a few miles of that city, we were again overtaken by a man, whom, from his particular dress, I knew to be an emissary of the Police. He made a pause, surveyed us all with an eager attention, and then made on, post-haste, towards Boulogne. As I guessed his intention was to apply to the Magistrates of that place, and to take us into custody; I therefore ordered the chaise to halt a little, and with Lady Rouelle's permission, got out, mounted my servant's horse, changed part of my dress with him, and rode on full-speed, to reconnoitre how matters were likely to go in the city.

'When I came thither, I found the guards drawn out, and, with drums beating, patrolling the streets. I enquired for one of the principal inns; at the door of which I met by accident a young Englishman, whom I knew to have been a school-fellow at Westminster, though he did not recollect me. He immediately told me, by way of news, "that the town was in an uproar, in expectation of seizing an English gentleman, who had carried off a Lady of the first quality from R——; and that he would be secured the moment the chaise came within the gates of the city."

'Upon this intelligence, I immediately rode back as fast as I came; and, holding a council with my Swiss and the Postilion, we resolved to turn back out of the great road, and go to a small fishing town, where, the Postilion told us, we had a better chance for hiring a vessel than at any of the more considerable sea-ports.

'When we came thither, I soon met with a petty commander of a fishing-boat, who, for a small sum of money, readily agreed to convey us the next day to Brighthelmstone. But I, foolishly enough, pulling out a purse of fifty louis-d'ors, which I offered him if he would sail immediately, at the sight of so extraordinary a sum, the fellow began to be alarmed; and then demanded our passports, which he had never thought of before. I again produced those for myself and my servant; and shewed him a written paper, as a passport for the Lady. As the man could not read, he said, "he would go with us to the Curé, or Minister of the parish, to have the passports examined."

'The Curé had a gentleman-like appearance. I took him aside, and told him, "I would express my gratitude to him, in any manner he should name, if he would assure the Master of the vessel, that the pass-port was good, and prevail upon him to sail immediately." The Curé replied, with a very serious air, "that he would not, for the whole world, abuse the confidence which his Parishioners placed in him, by deceiving them in a matter of such importance;" but very politely offered us an asylum in his house for that evening. As we had no alternative, we gladly accepted the Curé's offer, that we might have time to consider what step was next to be taken.'

CHAPTER XVI

The Adventures of Captain Johnson concluded

'It was now the third night since Lady Ruelle had been in bed; and, though she had slept a little in the post-chaise, she could not but be very much fatigued: with much difficulty, therefore, I prevailed on her Ladyship to go to bed. And having myself sat up till about twelve o'clock with the honest Curé, I lay down, and had just composed myself, on a settee in the parlour, when I was awaked by an alarm, that the house was beset by the Officers of the Police.

'As we had reason to apprehend this, we had taken care to barricade the approach, and were determined to stand a siege. There was no way that they could attack us, but from a little garden near the parlour-window. I had armed my servant with his carbine, and myself with a pistol in each hand; and ordered him to keep his fire as long as possible: but he, having a fair mark at one of them by the light of the moon, let fly, and killed him upon the spot. But four more immediately marched up to the window, armed with blunderbusses. I fired one pistol without effect. Upon which, they rushing in upon us immediately, and threatening to fire if we did not surrender, it would have been madness to make any further resistance.

'Lady Ruelle and I were seized, and put under a guard till near the morning; when we were placed back to back, and our hands bound behind us, in a sort of covered waggon; and in this manner conveyed to R——.

'Lady Ruelle, however, had the generosity, at my request, to slip her watch and a pearl necklace of considerable value into my Swiss's hands; with which, by my orders, he contrived to make his escape into his own country; and this circumstance was of great weight upon my tryal.

'I could not but remark one particular in Lady Ruelle, quite in the French style. In the midst of her distress, her eyes swimming in tears, and when she could not but dread the consequence of this adventure, she ran up to the glass, adjusted her head-dress, and put some *rouge*, or red paint, upon her cheeks.'

'Ah!' says Wildgoose, 'those are the works of the Devil, the father of lies, and of every kind of deceit.'

'Well,' continues Captain Johnson, 'upon our arrival at R——, I was sent a close prisoner to the castle. From thence I was soon brought to my tryal before the Parliament of R——; and, as one of their Members was the injured party, should have been severely dealt with, if they could have proved either the murders, or the robbery, directly upon me: but, as my servant was principal in the former, and also the only witness of the latter, and he had made his escape; and as the Lady appeared rather more culpable than my-self, having really seduced me; the chief party concerned seemed willing to drop the further prosecution of the affair, especially as my good friend at R—— had made a very powerful application, by means of our Ambassador, at the Court of Versailles. So, after some little confinement, I was dismissed, with orders to quit the kingdom in three days time; with which I chearfully complied: and the poor Lady was immediately dispatched to a convent.

'Upon further enquiry into the cause of this Lady's violent resolution, I found she had a suspicion of the most horrid kind, that her husband, who was much older than herself, had an intrigue with her own mother.'

Wildgoose stared with tokens of horror. But, after some pause,— 'Nay,' says he, 'I wonder at nothing of this kind; for we are all by nature in the same state with the Gentiles of old, "given up to vile affections, unnatural lusts, and a reprobate mind, and to work all uncleanness with greediness."'[1]

'Well,' says the Captain, 'I am not yet come to the most material part of my story, especially so far as my own temporal interest is concerned: for, on my arrival in England, I found my wicked course of life had contributed to shorten my father's days, and my extravagance greatly diminished his fortune: for he was dead; and, instead of the affluence which I had always depended upon, he left but about two thousand pounds, to support me and a mother, who is now but a middle-aged woman, though, from grief and vexation, become very sickly and infirm.

'Not to be tedious, I found myself in immediate possession of no more than five hundred pounds; with which I purchased a Lieutenancy, and am now doing penance in country quarters, strutting about in my red coat and cockade, but really a prey to melancholy, and tortured with reflecting upon those vices which have brought me so early in life to this wretched situation.'

CHAPTER XVII

A Temporary Conversion

CAPTAIN JOHNSON having finished his narration, Mr. Wildgoose bid him, 'not despond; that Providence often brought about our conversion by severe trials; and that it was a maxim with them, "The blacker the Sinner, the brighter the Saint." But,' says he, 'I am going to meet a Society of true Christians; where, I make no doubt, you will find those, who have been as wicked as yourself, now full of peace and joy. And, I assure you, Sir, I have heard Mr. Whitfield often say, "that he had rather preach to a congregation of Publicans and Harlots, or what the world may call Whores and Rogues, than to a set of mere nominal Christians, or good sort of people as they are called, who flatter themselves that they need no repentance."'[1]

The Captain said, 'that, although he should be called a Methodist, and was really invited to dance at a sort of Welsh assembly, he would accompany Mr. Wildgoose, by his leave, to their Society.'

Accordingly, having sitten together till near seven o'clock, Mr. Wildgoose took Captain Johnson with him, attended by his friend Tugwell, to the Tradesman's house; where he found a pretty large congregation, assembled in an upper room, over his warehouse in the garden.

Wildgoose harangued upon the usual topics with great pathos; and, as several people round him sighed and groaned, and even wept, the Captain found himself variously affected, sometimes inclined to laugh, at other times to cry: but what he found most contagious were, the tears of a very pretty girl, a Grocer's daughter, who sat near him, with whom the Captain would have been glad to have compared his *feelings* and *experiences*; for, though he was probably sincere in the compunctions which he discovered in conversing with Mr. Wildgoose, yet, when the passions have got strength by long indulgence, they are not immediately to be subdued, but are apt again to take fire upon approaching a tempting object: nay, as twenty or thirty of the most zealous of them were desirous (according to a common practice) of spending the night in the Society-room, the Captain stayed amongst them for some time, and was thought to have been made a complete convert by this young female disciple.

As Mr. Wildgoose, however, had been up early in the morning, and was fatigued with the toils of the day; he himself, about eleven o'clock, lay down upon a bed that was offered him by the pious Tradesman; and Tugwell's devotion was so far from being enthusiastic this evening, that, before Wildgoose had done preaching, he was fallen asleep in the corner of the room.

But, about two in the morning, Mr. Wildgoose was waked by a confused noise, as if a number of men were putting to the sword.[1] He went up into the Society-room, where the people had worked themselves up to such a pitch of religious phrenzy, that some were fallen prostrate upon the floor, screaming, and roaring, and beating their breasts, in agonies of remorse for their former wicked lives; others were singing hymns, leaping and exulting in extasies of joy, that their sins were forgiven them. Amongst the rest, there was a little boy, of three years old, who had caught the infection, and acted the Sinner with as much appearance of contrition as the best of them.[2] The uproar increased when Wildgoose came into the room, and began to pray with them: but Nature, having now been strained to its height for some hours, subsided into a calm. Wildgoose, therefore, dismissed them with a short exhortation, and lay down again till the morning, leaving Tugwell to finish his night's rest, where he had begun, upon some hop-sacks in the corner of the assembly-room.

The Captain (he found upon enquiry) about eleven o'clock had conducted home the Grocer's daughter, whose father and mother had sent for her; for, although they indulged her in going (with some other young people) to the Meeting, they did not approve of those late nocturnal vigils, which were frequently solemnized by the warmer devotees.

Amongst others in this devout assembly, there was a substantial Miller's wife, who lived about a mile out of town, that was more zealous than any of them. She intreated Mr. Wildgoose, 'if possible, to come home to her, and give her some private consolation; as Mr. Whitfield, Mr. Wesley, and other gentlemen,' she said, 'had sometimes done.'—When Wildgoose found she lived partly in the road towards Gloucester (whither he intended to direct his course in the morning), he promised the good woman to call and take a breakfast with her about seven o'clock.

CHAPTER XVIII

A warm Breakfast, followed by a cold Collation

JERRY TUGWELL, having been disturbed by the uproar in the night, no sooner met his Master in the morning, than he began to vent his indignation with some warmth against the good people of Monmouth. 'Gad-zookers!' says he, 'these Welsh people are all mad, I think; I never heard such rantipole doings since I was born; a body cannot sleep o' nights for 'em.'

'Ah! Jerry,' replies Wildgoose, 'this is a glorious time! these are the triumphs of Faith! these are the true symptoms of the New Birth! People are never nearer to the Kingdom of Heaven than when they are *mad*, as you call it; and have never better reason to hope for Salvation, than when they are ready to hang and drown themselves.

'But come, Jerry,' says he, 'a poor sister is labouring under the pangs of the New Birth, and wants our assistance. We must walk a mile or two before breakfast.'—'Walk a mile or two before breakfast!' says Tugwell; 'why, I had no supper last night; and my stomach is so empty, that I can hardly walk at all without my breakfast. If the young woman is in *labour*, she has more need of a midwife than our assistance.'

As Wildgoose, therefore, was taking leave of the Tradesman, Tugwell got a piece of bread and cheese, and a cup of ale; and then they went to the inn, to call upon the Captain: but, hearing that, notwithstanding his fancied conversion, he had gone from the Religious Meeting to the profane dancing assembly, and had not

been come to bed above two hours, the two Pilgrims set out upon
their expedition.

When they came to the mill, which was not above a mile out of
town, they found a good breakfast prepared for them by their kind
hostess, the Miller's wife; for, the Miller having set out early in
the morning to a fair in Herefordshire, the good woman, who
thought she could not do too much for such pious people, had got
some cakes baked and buttered, and all other requisites for a
comfortable *dejeuné*. And in this manner, with the addition of some
godly conversation, the poor woman frequently regaled herself;
and always found herself more happy, than in the surly society of
her morose husband; which happiness she ascribed to the power
of religion, rather than to, its more probable cause, the variety it
introduced, and the comfortable soothing doctrine of being saved
by Faith without Works.

And, indeed, the Miller, though fond of his wife (who was much
younger than himself, and a tolerably handsome woman), and
unwilling absolutely to forbid her frequenting these pious Meetings; yet, as he was often, by this means, deprived of his conjugal
claims, and the company of his spouse, who (according to the old
Liturgy), ought to have been *buxome both at bed and at board*, he
was generally out of humour upon these occasions; and could not
forbear expressing his disapprobation of the many Itinerants which
came to the house, amongst his workmen and servants. These
fellows, therefore, who were more in their Master's interest than
in that of their Mistress, laid a plot, which they knew would not
displease their Master, but which, if he had been at home, he
probably, out of regard to his wife, would not have suffered them to
execute.

The nearest way, for the two Pilgrims to return into the great
road, was through a meadow, into which they must pass over the
Mill-stream, by a narrow plank, which was laid across it. This
plank the fellows contrived to saw almost in two, on the under-side.
When, therefore, the travellers had taken their leave of the Miller's
wife, Wildgoose, leading the way, marched foremost nimbly over
the bridge; which, though it cracked, did not entirely break down
till he was landed; and Tugwell came upon the middle of it, who,
being a heavy-a—d Christian, and moreover encumbered with his
loaded wallet, fell plump into the stream, bawling out for help, to
the no small diversion of the spectators. The men ran, however, to

Jerry's assistance with a feigned concern, and dragged him out of the water; but took care that he should first be dipped into it considerably above the waist.

The fright and the surprize at first took away Jerry's voice, that he could not vent his indignation. One of the fellows handing him up his wallet, ' 'Sblood! Honesty,' (says the man) 'thou hast but just *saved thy bacon*.'—'What the Devil do you mean by saving my bacon?' says Tugwell. 'It is nothing but my Master's Bible and some good books in my wallet.' The fellow, indeed, by that proverbial expression, only alluded to the narrow escape Jerry had had; but spoke the literal truth by chance: for the Miller's wife, it seems, out of her great regard to the godly, had offered Tugwell a piece of bacon, of about five or six pounds, which, for fear of accidents, Jerry (unknown to his Master) had accepted of, and stowed in his wallet; and the consciousness of his greediness now made a discovery, which the Miller's men perhaps would not otherwise have suspected.

One of the fellows asked Tugwell, with a sneer, 'if he would go back and dry himself, and have another dish of tea.' But Tugwell, muttering some threats, trudged after his Master as fast as he could, equally ashamed to be thus out-witted, and vexed to be wetted to the skin. And, upon Wildgoose's exhorting him 'to suffer tribulation with patience;' Jerry replied, in great wrath, 'that he did not care who suffered tribulation, so that he was got safe home again in his chimney corner.'

CHAPTER XIX

A seasonable Relief

THEY had now proceeded about three miles on their journey from Monmouth; when they came to a considerable brook, which ran at the foot of a steep hill, covered with extensive woods. There was a foot-bridge to pass over; but, the rivulet being swelled by a violent thunder-storm which had fallen in the night, they could not possibly approach the bridge. Being obliged, therefore, to halt, they sat down upon the bank, and were deliberating what course to pursue; when Tugwell began to complain of being very chill, and of the head-ach, and said, 'he was certainly going to have a fit of the ague, and should not be able to go any further.' He then heavily bemoaned himself, and said, 'if he were at home, Dorothy should carry his water to the *Cunning Man*, who would cast a spell, or send him a bottle of *stuff*, which would cure him after the third fit; or else Madam Wildgoose would send him some *Higry-pigry*,[1] which would stop it at once.'

Whilst they were thus engaged, Tugwell complaining, and Wild-goose endeavouring to encourage him by the examples of Martyrs, Saints, and Confessors; they observed a horse grazing at some distance by the wood-side, with a sort of pack-saddle upon his back, and the bridle hanging loosely between his legs. Having now waited near a quarter of an hour, and nobody appearing to whom the horse might probably belong; Mr. Wildgoose observed to his friend, 'that Providence had certainly delivered this horse into their hands, to promote the great work in which they were embarked.'—Tug-well, however, for more reasons than one, objected to taking an horse, which certainly did not belong to them.—Wildgoose owned, 'it was not lawful to steal, or even to covet our neighbour's ox, or his ass, or any thing that does not belong to us. But,' says he, again 'we are commanded to use all diligence in our power; which must signify, the using all the means, to compass any end, which falls in our way. Now, we shall certainly make more speed on horse-back than on foot; and, therefore, we may lawfully, I think, make use of this horse, which is thus providentially ready bridled and saddled for our use.'[2]

To this Tugwell made two objections; first, 'that, perhaps, the water was too high for them to ride through;' and, secondly, 'that he could not ride, having never been on horse-back since he was ten years old.'

Wildgoose replied, 'that, as Jerry was afraid, he himself would first ride through, and, if it were safe, would return and take Jerry behind him, and convey him to the next inn; and, by putting him into a warm bed, he did not doubt but he would soon be as well as ever.

'But,' continues Wildgoose, 'to make sure of the lawfulness of what we are about, we will have recourse to our Bible, as Mr. Wesley and Mr. Whitfield have often done.'[3] Upon opening it, therefore, they dipped upon that passage where the disciples were ordered to bring the ass's colt, for their Master's triumphant entry into Jerusalem. This Wildgoose considered as a case in point, and decisive in their favour. He went therefore to catch the horse, when he spied also an old blue great coat thrown into the ditch; which it puzzled him yet more to account for. But, as he intended to leave the horse at the first inn they came to, he thought it best to take the coat also, and wrap up his companion, who was still shivering with cold.

Upon searching the pocket of the great coat, they found in it an old crape hat-band, a pocket knife, and an iron tobacco-box.

Wildgoose now leaped upon Rosinante;[1] and, riding boldly into the brook, found it barely fordable (as the flood was abating), which it probably had not been in the morning, when it was at the highest. He, therefore, returned, and with some difficulty dragged Jerry up behind him, wrapped in the great coat; and, thus crossing the brook, they marched slowly up the hill, through a deep and rough hollow way. They descended the hill again; and, after riding about a mile further, came to a little village, where meeting with a public-house, they stopped, hung the horse at the door with the great coat upon the pad, and put Jerry into a warm bed, who desired a little treacle-posset, which threw him into a perspiration, by which he soon recovered his usual vivacity.

CHAPTER XX

The Pilgrims taken up upon Suspicion

WHILST Wildgoose was waiting in a sort of little parlour for his fellow-traveller's recovery, my Landlord had prevailed upon him, as his beard was near a week's growth, to submit to the operation of a Barber, who had just shaved my Landlord. The operator had just finished one side of Wildgoose's face, when five or six men rushed into the house, armed with clubs, pitch-forks, and an old gun; which was part of the hue-and-cry raised by a Farmer, who had been robbed that morning, in his way to the fair above-mentioned, by a man upon the very horse which Wildgoose and his friend had made use of.

They enquired where the person was, to whom the horse at the door and the blue great coat belonged. My Landlord pointed to Wildgoose, as he was shaving in the next room with his back towards him. The fellows surveying him pretty narrowly, one of them cried out, 'Aye, that is he; I can answer to him; he was a tall, thinnish man, just his size.' They then began disputing, who should go first into the room, and seize the villain. The Farmer that had been robbed said, 'it was the Constable's duty to apprehend the criminal.'—The Constable said, 'he would take him before the Magistrate, but would not venture his life upon other people's business.'—A Butcher, who was amongst them, made signs to the Barber, to cut his throat without any more ceremony. But, the honest Barber either not understanding their hints, or having more sense than to comply with them, the Farmer's son who had been robbed, a young man about seventeen, snatched the gun out of the hands of one of them, and immediately seized Wildgoose, in the King's name, for *villoneously* robbing an honest Farmer that morning upon the King's highway. And, without suffering Wildgoose to make any defence, or the Barber to finish the other side of his face, they were hurrying him immediately before a Justice of Peace; when my Landlord informed them, 'that there was another of them, who came with the horse, and who wore the blue great coat which was left upon the pack-saddle.'

At that instant, Tugwell finding himself pretty well recovered, and his returning appetite putting him in mind that he had acted the sick man long enough, he was just come down into the kitchen. And the Landlord tipping the wink, the Constable seized him also by the collar, in the King's name. 'What the pox is the matter now?' says Tugwell; 'what do you collar me for, and be hanged?'—'Only for stealing an horse, and robbing upon the high-way,' says the Constable. The man who had been robbed seeing Jerry seized, and hearing his voice, cried out again; 'Aye; that is the very rogue that robbed me; I can swear to his voice.' And he now said, 'it was a short thick-set fellow;' though he had before given just the contrary description of him.

The gentlemen of the hue-and-cry were going to tie the culprit's hands behind them, and their legs under the horse's belly, in order to carry them before the Justice; but mine Host observing, 'that there were enough to guard them without that precaution,' they set them both upon the horse as they had been before: and thus they marched with them near four miles, to one Mr. Aldworth's, on the borders of Herefordshire; Tugwell (according to custom) bewailing his misfortune; and Wildgoose administring his usual topics of consolation.

CHAPTER XXI

A Justice, and a Justice of the Peace

MR. ALDWORTH was an opulent country gentleman, and a very worthy Magistrate. His way of living gave one the truest idea of that hospitality for which the English nation was formerly distinguished. I mean not in the days of Queen Elizabeth, when even the Ladies breakfasted upon toast and metheglin, or cold beef (which days I consider, in that respect, as semi-barbarous and uncivilized);[1] but of that hospitality which subsisted amongst our gentry till the Revolution, and continued in some measure to the days of Queen Anne and George the First: when, instead of being tantalized with a dozen of French dishes (which no Frenchman, however, would ever taste), and stared at by as many French servants, dressed better than yourself or their own Master; instead of being dragged out, the moment you have dined, to take a walk in the shrubbery, and wonder at his Lordship's *bad* taste, and then frightened away with the appearance of cards and wax candles; instead of this refined luxury, I say, you were sure to find at Mr. Aldworth's, a ham and fowls, a piece of roast beef, or a pigeon-pye, and a bottle of port-wine, every day in the week; and, if you chose to spend the night at his house, a warm bed, and an hearty welcome.

This hospitable temper and friendly reception generally filled Mr. Aldworth's table; and none of his old acquaintance, who came within ten miles of him, ever thought of lying at an inn, when he was in the country; which, indeed, unless any extraordinary business called him to London, was usually the whole year.

The reader will pardon this tribute to such primitive merit; which, indeed, serves also to render more probable an incident in the sequel.

Mr. Aldworth was at dinner, with some company, when the culprits and their cavalcade arrived at the door: they were, therefore, ordered into a little summer-house, at the corner of the garden; where the Squire used both to take a sober glass with a particular friend, and to distribute justice amongst his neighbours with equal wisdom and impartiality;

> And sometimes counsel take, and sometimes wine.[2]

Amongst other company now at Mr. Aldworth's, there was one

Mr. Newland, a young man of fortune; who, instead of going to
the University, to Paris, or even to the Temple, to study the Laws
of England, had been educated under an eminent Attorney in the
country, and consequently was a rigid observer of the letter of the
Law; and, having but lately been put into the Commission, he was
impatient to act the Magistrate, and flourish his name at the side
of a Mittimus.

Mr. Newland, therefore, having paid a proper compliment to
the second course, by swallowing a leg and wing of a duckling, and
a plate of green pease; and having drunk hob-or-nob with a young
Lady, in whose eyes he wished to appear a man of consequence; he
hurried out into the summer-house, where he made the Clerk
immediately swear the evidence, and take the depositions; over
which as soon as young Newland had cast his eye, and had surveyed
Wildgoose's face, half-shaved (which he took for a disguise);
'Well, you rascal,' says he to Wildgoose, 'what have you to say
for yourself, guilty or not guilty?'—'Ah!' says Wildgoose, shaking
his head, 'I am but too *guilty:* God forgive me! and am laden with
iniquities.'—'There,' says the young Magistrate to the Clerk, 'you
hear he confesses it.' He then bid the Clerk fill up the Mittimus;
and he would sign it, without giving Mr. Aldworth the trouble of
leaving the company.

CHAPTER XXII

A Friend in Need is a Friend indeed

WHILE this was transacting, however, the good old Gentleman,
being aware of his young Colleague's precipitate temper, came out,
with the napkin tucked in his button-hole, and began to enquire
a little into the circumstances of the affair. It appeared from the
deposition, 'that the Farmer had been robbed of seven guineas
that morning about five o'clock, by a man upon that very horse,
and in that blue great coat, with a black crape over his face, and
armed with that very long pocket-knife;' all which were found in
Tugwell's and his Master's possession.

Mr. Aldworth, however, notwithstanding these particulars, and
the suspicious circumstance of Wildgoose's double-face (which,
indeed, the Landlord soon cleared up), saw an appearance of

honesty in Wildgoose, and even in his friend Tugwell; which inclined him to think more favourably of them than Mr. Newland had done. He, therefore, asked Wildgoose, 'what account they could give of themselves, whence they came, and whither they were going?'——Wildgoose replied, 'that they had come from Gloucester, and had been at Bristol upon a business of consequence; but, for some particular reasons, had been obliged to return through Wales and Monmouthshire.'

This account appearing somewhat incoherent, Mr. Aldworth asked, 'how they came by that horse and the great coat?' Which Wildgoose explained to him; and added, 'that probably the person, who committed the robbery, finding the brook not fordable in the morning, on account of the flood, had made his escape into the woods on foot. But, however that might be, though he owned himself guilty of many other crimes in the sight of God, yet he was never guilty of robbery; and that he himself and his fellow-traveller were at breakfast at a Miller's, near Monmouth, at seven o'clock that morning; and that he could bring an hundred people to witness, that he had preached at a Religious Society at Monmouth the preceding night.'

'O, ho!' says Justice Newland, 'are you at that sport? Your preaching at Monmouth last night does not prove, that you did not rob upon the highway this morning. Many of these Itinerant Preachers have done the same.'

'Well, well,' says Mr. Aldworth, 'let us suspend our judgment till we have enquired more into this affair. Where is your proper place of residence?' says he to Wildgoose; 'and what trade or profession are you of?'—Upon Wildgoose's answering, 'that he lived in the North part of Gloucestershire;'—Mr. Aldworth said, 'they should then probably get some light into his character, and give him an opportunity of clearing himself, by a Gentleman who was then in the house. Here!' says he to a servant, 'desire Mr. Powell to step hither a moment.'

Wildgoose, finding himself oddly affected at the name of Powell, though he did not immediately know why, changed colour; which Justice Newland observing, winked upon Mr. Aldworth with a sagacious nod. 'But,' says he, 'this old rascal is the principal; and I suspect he is returned from transportation, for I remember his face at Monmouth assizes seven years ago, when I was first Clerk to Mr. Traverse.'

Tugwell was going to clear himself of that aspersion, when Mr.
Powell appeared, who was no other than the Parson of the parish
where Mr. Wildgoose lived, and whom we mentioned as the
accidental cause of Wildgoose's disgust with the world. Mr. Powell
was returning from a visit to his friends in Wales; and had made
Mr. Aldworth's house a convenient stage by the way.

The mutual astonishment of Mr. Powell and the two Pilgrims,
at meeting each other in this place, and on such an occasion, was
proportionable to the improbability of such a rencounter.

Mr. Powell expressed his concern at seeing his old neighbours in
such a situation; but could hardly forbear laughing, to see one
side of Wildgoose's face close-shaven, and the other with a beard
half an inch long.

Mr. Wildgoose was in some confusion at this unexpected meeting with Mr. Powell, as he did not like to be obliged to a man,
against whom he had conceived so violent a prejudice; and also
was afraid of being disappointed, in what he really wished for, the
being persecuted for the Gospel's sake, as he esteemed it, and (like
honest John Bunyan) the singing of Psalms in a Gaol.

Upon Mr. Powell's telling him, however, 'that his mother had
been greatly affected with his absence, and had had a dangerous
fit of sickness,' he found some symptoms of humanity revive in his
breast; an involuntary tear rose into the orbit of his eye; and he even
expressed some hope, that she was quite recovered.

But, as for Tugwell, his joy was excessive, and quite sincere, at
meeting the Vicar of his parish, for whom he had always a thorough
reverence and esteem.——'God in Heaven bless you, Master
Powell!' cries Jerry: 'how does our Dorothy do, and my poor dog
Snap, and Madam Powell? Ah! Master, we have been all the world
over, by sea and by land, over mountains, desarts, and quicksands,
since we went from home; and, after preaching the Gospel all over
England and Wales for pure love, here they have taken us up for
horse-stealing, only for riding a horse (that we found grazing by
a wood-side) about a mile or two, when I was ready to perish with
the ague.'

'Why, my good friend Jerry,' (says Mr. Powell) 'I think you
might as well have been in your own stall, repairing old shoes, as
rambling about the country to reform the world: but I will answer
for it, Jerry, neither you, nor Mr. Wildgoose, had any hand in
stealing this horse.'—'I find, then,' says Mr. Aldworth, 'Mr.

Powell does really know these men. Appearances are by no means in their favour; but what can you say for them, Mr. Powell?'—'Why,' replies Mr. Powell, 'I will be answerable for their honesty; and that neither of them is concerned in the fact of which they are accused.'

'I do not dispute Mr. Powell's knowledge of the criminals,' says young Newland; 'but the circumstances are so strong against them, that, I think, we have nothing to do but to make their Mittimus.'

'Sir,' replies Mr. Aldworth, 'many an innocent man has been condemned and executed upon circumstantial evidence; we cannot, therefore, be too cautious in this affair.'

'I am not going to condemn or to try them' (rejoins Newland with some quickness); 'that is the Judge's business. I shall only commit them to a Gaol till the assizes; when, I hope, their innocence will appear to the gentlemen of the Jury.'—Mr. Powell observed, however, 'that it would be a great hardship for innocent men to lie in Gaol for three months upon so slight a suspicion.' To which Newland answered, 'that the Law did not consult the ease of individuals, but the good of the whole.' Mr. Aldworth was going to reply; when a great bustle at the summer-house door interrupted him.

CHAPTER XXIII

The real Highwayman produced. Tugwell escapes a Gaol, and gets a Dinner

THE noise at the summer-house door was occasioned by another party of the hue-and-cry, who had gone a different way, that morning, in pursuit of the robber, and had actually taken the real culprit, who, having left his horse by the river's side, where Wildgoose and his friend found him, had escaped through the wood into a different road, where these people had seized him, from his guilty appearance; and had actually found upon him, not only the exact sum of money, with two Portugal pieces, to which the Farmer immediately swore, but also an old pocket-book, containing a regular account between the Farmer and his Landlord; which, with other circumstances, appeared so evident, that the Justices had nothing more to do, but to commit him without further examination.

Mr. Aldworth, having now turned over the rest of this ragamuffin assembly to the care of his Butler (who never suffered any one, that came about business, to leave the house without some refreshment), desired Mr. Powell to conduct his two countrymen into a little breakfast-room, as he thought it in vain to ask Wildgoose, in his present trim, to go into the parlour where his company had dined. But Mr. Aldworth himself, after making an apology to his other friends, returned, attended by a servant with a napkin and tray, and some remains of a plentiful treat; which was no unsavoury prospect to people in Wildgoose's and Tugwell's situation.

When the two Pilgrims had now refreshed themselves, and Mr. Powell had recounted most of the occurrences in the neighbourhood during their absence; he began to persuade them, with all the rhetoric in his power, to return to their respective homes. Tugwell listened with great complacency to this exhortation: but Wildgoose, with a religious obstinacy, persisting in his first resolution, said, 'he was not at his own disposal, but should fulfill the engagements he was under to his friends;' though he did not think fit to explain to Mr. Powell the particulars.

Mr. Aldworth, when he found that Wildgoose's elopement was contrary to his mother's approbation, shook his head with a melancholy air, and said, 'he heartily sympathized with every parent in that situation: and that he could not but join with Mr. Powell in advising Mr. Wildgoose to return to his mother. As I have suffered myself by the imprudence of an only son, I would endeavour to rescue any parent from the like distress; and, I flatter myself, that, on my late journey to town, I was instrumental in restoring a young Lady to her friends, who, from some unaccountable whim, had eloped, entirely alone, in the stage-coach to London, and by my earnest persuasions prevailed on her to return, the very next day, in the same stage, to her father: and I cannot but intreat you, Sir, though a stranger, to restore your distressed mother to her tranquillity, by accompanying Mr. Powell to your native place.'

As the imprudence which Mr. Aldworth lamented in his son was the pursuing his own inclinations, and marrying a young woman with less fortune than Mr. Aldworth had destined him for:

so the reader will probably guess, that the young Lady, whom he had rescued from destruction, was no other than Miss Townsend; in whose story Mr. Wildgoose was so much interested.

Wildgoose's colour came immediately into his cheeks; and he could hardly forbear discovering the acquaintance he had with that young Lady, and also informing Mr. Aldworth of the accident that had frustrated his benevolent intentions; which, if Miss Townsend had been indifferent to him, he would most certainly have done: but, as the delicacy of his passion made him reserved in speaking of her, so his surprize passed off without being remarked by the company.

As the afternoon was now far advanced, Mr. Aldworth invited Wildgoose (with his fellow traveller) to take a bed there; and told Wildgoose, 'that his Butler should finish what the Barber had been prevented from doing by the insolence of the hue-and-cry.'— Wildgoose thanked the old Squire for his civility; but, not feeling himself quite happy in Mr. Powell's company, and finding a stronger attraction towards Gloucester the nearer he approached to it, he chose to proceed on his journey.

Wildgoose, however, sent his dutiful respects to his mother; and Tugwell took an opportunity of whispering to Mr. Powell, 'that he did not half like this vagabond way of life; and wished the Spirit would give Mr. Wildgoose leave to return home again. But, Master,' says he, 'tell our Dorothy we shall be no losers by it. And here, Master, please to give her this crooked sixpence for a token.' Mr. Powell smiled at Jerry's instance of generosity; but advised him to carry it himself.

The young Magistrate, Mr. Newland, on his return to his company, had acquainted them with all the particulars of Wildgoose's story; which raised the curiosity of the Ladies: and, when they were informed of their marching off, they all ran to the window which looked towards the lawn, where the two Pilgrims passed in review before them.

Tugwell's spirits being quite elevated by his good cheer, he took the lead, in his short jerkin, his jelly-bag cap (which he had kept on since the morning), and his wallet on his shoulder; which, by a kind of instinct, he secured amidst all adventures; and which, like

> His oaken staff, which he could ne'er forsake,
> Hung half before, and half behind his back. [1]

Y

Mr. Wildgoose, however, exhibiting only that side of his face which had undergone the Barber's operation, made no despicable appearance; but raised a concern in the Ladies, that so handsome a young man should have taken so odd a turn, and travel about the country like a Scotch Pedlar.

CHAPTER XXIV

Man of Ross

WHEN the two friends were got clear of Mr. Aldworth's premises, and were now alone in the road to Gloucester; whilst Mr. Wildgoose was wrapped in meditation, Tugwell interrupted him, by commenting upon the adventures of the day, and observing what a narrow escape they had had from being sent to gaol. He said, 'he would take care how he got on horse-back again, especially upon other folk's horses. What a fine story our Parson will have to carry home! that I and your Worship were taken up for horse-stealing!' —'Ah! Jerry,' replies Wildgoose; 'how often must I remind thee of the blessing promised to those who are unjustly persecuted, and falsely accused? "Happy are ye, when men shall say all manner of evil of you, falsely, for my name's sake." '[1]—'Yes, yes, that is true,' says Jerry; 'but a man does not like to be counted a thief, for all that, when a body does not deserve it. One's good name is one's livelihood; and I never was counted a night-walker, or a sheep-stealer, before I kept company with your Worship (as I may say): and I had rather have been ducked in a horse-pond, or pelted with cow-turd, than have had the disgrace of such a scandalous thing.

'But come, hang it! we did get a good dinner at the Squire's, *howsomever*; and I believe he is a very honest gentleman.'

Thus Tugwell went on, grumbling and consoling himself alternately, without much conversation from his Master, till they came, towards the evening, to a tolerable public-house; where they thought it best to repose themselves, after the fatigues and distresses of the past day.

The first thing Wildgoose did was, by Tugwell's admonition, to finish what the Barber had begun; after which, according to his usual custom, he went to impart some spiritual exhortations to the family that received him. There was in the kitchen an old Gentle-man-farmer, with locks as white as wool, and a face as red as a red-streak:[1] he was smoking his pipe, and drinking cyder, with my Landlord. Wildgoose, perceiving by his discourse that he came from the neighbourhood of Ross, in Herefordshire, took that opportunity of making some enquiries after the famous Man of Ross, so justly celebrated by Mr. Pope for his public spirit and unbounded generosity.[2] 'What! old Kyrle!' says the Farmer; 'yes, I knew him well: he was an honest old cock, and loved his pipe and a tankard of cyder as well as the best of us.'—'Well,' says Mr. Wildgoose, 'if he used these with moderation, there was no great harm in either of them: and though a man may endow hospitals without charity, and build Churches without Religion; and though I am afraid the Man of Ross relied too much upon his good works; yet he was certainly a very useful man, and a great benefactor to your country.'

'Yes,' says the old Farmer; 'he certainly made good roads, and raised causeys, and brought conduits of water to the town: but it was not *all* at his own expence; he made the country pay for it, by pretty handsome levies, and a tax upon the public.'

Wildgoose was not a little shocked at the malignity of the vulgar part of mankind, in detracting from the merit of the most heroic characters, and bringing every one down, as near as possible, to their own level; which seemed to be the principle on which this jolly old fellow proceeded in his character of the benevolent and worthy Man of Ross.

CHAPTER XXV

Forest of Dean. Equality of Mankind

As Wildgoose was impatient to proceed on his journey to Glou-cester, he had gone early to bed, and awoke soon in the morning. But Tugwell having been thoroughly harrassed and fatigued the preceding day, it was not in his master's power to rouse him from his bed till near eight o'clock; when, as soon as Jerry had taken a short breakfast (which he made a conscience of not omitting), they set forwards on their journey.

Their road lay through the romantic Forest of Dean; and the very name of a Forest filled Tugwell's imagination with ideas of wild beasts, robbers, and out-laws: and, though Jerry had no great matter to lose, all the stories which he had ever heard in the chimney-corner, or read in his penny-farthing histories, now occurred to his memory. But, upon Wildgoose's assuring him, 'there was no danger to be apprehended now-a-days, either from wild beasts, giants, or out-laws,' they jogged on pretty peaceably all the fore part of the day; and about dinner-time, coming to a fine tuft of oaks, upon a bank by the side of a crystal brook, the coolness of the scene invited them to rest a little in the heat of the day, and to regale themselves with the contents of Jerry's wallet, which Mr. Aldworth's Butler had liberally furnished with provisions the preceding day.

While they were thus employed, Jerry began to make comparisons between the different situation of some poor fellows whom they had just passed by (who, in the dog-days, were sweating at the forge belonging to a great iron-work in the Forest), and the company which they had seen the day before at Mr. Aldworth's. Jerry observed, 'how hard it was that some people should be forced to toil like slaves, whilst others lived in ease and plenty, and the fat of the land!'—'Ah! Jerry,' says Wildgoose; 'true happiness does not consist in meat and drink, but in "Peace and joy in the Holy Ghost:" and, I am convinced, there is not that difference in the real enjoyment of men, which you imagine. You only see the outside of the wealthier part of mankind; and know nothing of the care and anxiety they suffer, which is frequently more insupportable than any bodily labour which poor people undergo.'

'Odsbobs!' says Tugwell; 'if I had but as good a dinner every day, as I had yesterday at the Justice's, I would not value of a straw all the care and *hangciety* in the world.'

'Well,' replies Wildgoose; 'but these distinctions amongst mankind are absolutely necessary; and, whilst men have the liberty of doing as they please, it cannot be otherwise.

'I suppose,' continues Wildgoose, 'you would have every body provided for alike; so that no one should be, either very rich, or very poor.'—'Why,' says Jerry, 'methinks it is very hard, that one man should have five or six hundred pounds a-year, when another mayhap has not fifty.'

'Well, then,' (replies Wildgoose) 'we will suppose, that you and

I, Jerry, and all the people of our parish, and in the next parish, and in the next market-town, and so on, had each an hundred pounds a-year, and no more.'—'Aye, that I should like now, well enough.'—'Well, then, but where should I get my shoes made?' says Mr. Wildgoose.—'Troth, Master, you must even make them yourself; for I should work for nobody, but for myself and our Dorothy.'—'Well,' says Wildgoose, 'and where would you buy your leather?'—'Why, of Mr. Jones, the Currier, at Evesham.'— 'Where would you get awls, hammers, and cutting-knives?'— 'Why, from Birmingham.'—'Very well; and where would you get your cloaths made?'—'Oh! Isaac, our Taylor, should work for me; he is a very honest fellow.'

'Ah! Jerry,' says Mr. Wildgoose, 'thou dost not consider, that all these people would be fully employed in working for themselves; so that, for all thy hundred a-year, thou must not only make thy own cloaths, but raise thy own corn, build thy own house, make thy own chairs and tables, thy own linen, stockings, shoes, and buckles; and, in short, either every man must work ten times harder than the poorest man now does, or, if he were idle or extravagant, those that were more frugal and industrious would again grow rich, and the others poor: which shews the unavoidable necessity of that inequality amongst mankind, with which your complaint began.'

'Odzookers! Master, why, I do not know but it may be true enough, as you say; and perhaps I may be as happy as Squire Pelican himself, though we brew nothing but small beer: for, though the Squire can afford to get drunk every day in the week, yet he is laid up with the gout half the year; and, thank God! I have seldom any thing the matter with me, except the cramp now and then; and that I can cure by a cramp ring, made of the hinge of an old Coffin.'

CHAPTER XXVI

Perils amongst false Brethren

THE two Pilgrims having reposed themselves for a considerable time in the heat of the day, it grew almost dark before they approached the city of Gloucester. Tugwell again began to renew the subject of thieves and robbers; but, as his Master had before raillied him for his cowardly apprehensions, Jerry affected to talk of High-waymen in a jocular strain. He said, 'the cleverest book he ever met with was, The Exploits of Captain James Hind,[1] who lived in Oliver's days;' and though, to Jerry's surprize, his Master had never heard of him, 'he was born,' he said, 'but at Chipping-Norton. Did you never hear how he served the Parson?' continues Jerry.—'Not I, indeed,' says Wildgoose.—'It is a comical fancy enough,' says Tugwell. 'Captain Hind had just robbed a gentleman of two hundred pounds; but, more company being just behind, he thought they would pursue him: and so, meeting a poor Parson, who was a little pot-valiant, the Captain pretended he himself was pursued by some highwaymen, and desired the Parson to take one of his pistols, and fire it in the face of the first man he met; whilst Hind rode down to the next village, to get more help. And so, in short, the Parson did; but was taken by the gentleman, and had like to have been hanged for it.

'Another time, the Captain was enchanted for three years by an old Hag. But the cleverest trick is what he served the old Miser.'—'Well, well,' says Wildgoose, 'I shall listen no longer to thy stories: I do not wonder that such foolish tales delighted thee in thy unregenerate state; but, I am afraid, nonsensical books such as these have brought many a poor wretch to the gallows; as they always interest one in favour of their heroes, and represent vice in too agreeable a light.'

The road now lay through a dark lane, shaded with elms: and, Wildgoose being equally happy in the thoughts of seeing Miss Townsend, and in beholding the flourishing state of his little Church, which he had planted under the care of the Barber and Mrs. Sarsenet, they moved along with profound silence; when out leaps a man from the edge, and, with a thundering oath, snapped a pistol full in the face of Tugwell, who happened to be foremost, which, however, only flashed in the pan. Tugwell, though not deficient in courage, as we have observed, yet was extremely terrified at the sight of fire-arms, to which he had not been accustomed. He, therefore, bawled out, 'Murder! Murder!' and, running back, knocked Wildgoose down, and himself tumbled, a—se-over-head, souse upon him. The Footpad, holding the pistol to Tugwell's head, bid him and his Master, 'deliver their money, or they were dead men.'—Wildgoose, who had more presence of mind, begged him, 'to take away his pistol, and he would give him money enough to relieve his present *necessity*; as nothing,' he observed, 'but the *utmost necessity* could possibly drive a man to such desperate acts of violence.'

As Wildgoose was proceeding in his unseasonable exhortation, the Robber, who knew his voice, cries out, 'God forgive me! Master Wildgoose! Is it possible, that I should be so unfortunate, as to make my very first attack upon you! Do not you know me?' proceeds he.—'Who are you, then?' says Wildgoose.—'Ah! Sir! I am Tom Keen the Barber, where your Worship lodged at Gloucester.'—The two Pilgrims now recovered from their fright, but not from their surprize; and enquiring, 'what could possibly tempt him to hazard both his life and his soul, by robbing upon the highway?'—'Oh! Sir!' says the Barber, 'nothing but the most urgent necessity, as you rightly observe. You yourself, however, (without intending it) have been the principal cause of bringing me to this distress. My neighbour Fillpot, at the public-house, out of spite, paid off a year and a half's rent, which I owed my Landlord, seized upon my goods, turned me out of my house; and now my wife, who has just lain-in, is destitute of the necessaries for a woman in her condition; and my children are, at this instant, crying for bread.'

'Well,' says Tugwell, 'I pity any one that wants a meal of victuals. But, 'sblood! that is no reason why you should take away my life, and fire a pistol in my face.'—'Ah!' cries the Barber, 'you were in no danger of your life from my pistol; for you may see (if it were light enough) that it is nothing but a pistol tinder-box, which I took out of Mr. Pasty's (the fat Prebend's) bed-room, who has made no use of it these ten years.'

Wildgoose then said, 'he was sorry to find that any degree of necessity could suggest to him this method of relieving his distress: but, as his first attempt had been providentially made upon himself,' Wildgoose observed, 'it would be attended with no ill consequences; and, as he had been the cause of his calamity, he hoped it would be in his power, some time or other, to make him some amends for his temporal sufferings.—But he hoped no distress would ever prevail upon the Barber to be guilty of such another desperate attempt to relieve it.'

CHAPTER XXVII

At Gloucester

As this worthy Triumvirate were now travelling amicably together towards Gloucester, Wildgoose enquired, 'how Mrs. Sarsenet went on?'—The Barber replied, 'he did not know that her business declined at all; and Mrs. Sarsenet was a very good woman. But' (says he) 'charity begins at home. She has got an old infirm mother and a lame sister to support; and yet, she has of late so many spiritual Bargemen and pious Colliers, that come up from Bristol, whom she entertains at breakfast with tea and coffee, and buttered rolls, that, I am afraid, it is more than she can well afford.

'And then the young woman that lodged with her is gone away; and, I suppose, she paid handsomely for her board (for I find her father is a rich Squire); and she was a clever, notable young body, and of great use to her in her business.'

This piece of news was a great disappointment to Mr. Wildgoose; which, with the shock he received from hearing the ill consequences of his preaching (to the temporal interests of his disciples), threw him into a fit of musing, and put a stop to their conversation till they arrived at Gloucester.

It was near ten o'clock when Wildgoose and his fellow-travellers reached the town. Having, however, supplied the poor Barber with half a guinea for his immediate necessities, which was full as much as he could prudently spare out of his present stock; he and Tugwell went to Mrs. Sarsenet's, whom they found at supper, with her mother and sister, upon a bunch of radishes and some dry bread.

Mrs. Sarsenet was greatly rejoiced to see Mr. Wildgoose, to whom she was a most sincere convert. She offered to get the travellers something for supper, and also told Wildgoose, 'that, as he was deprived of his old lodging, he should be welcome to the bed in which Miss Townsend had lain.'

Though Mr. Wildgoose probably thought (what David said of Goliath's sword), that there was none like it; yet Mrs. Whitfield (after she became acquainted with his merit when last at Gloucester) having pressed him to leave his lodgings at the Barber's, and come to the Bell; he now thought it would be very convenient, at least for that night, to accept of her kindness, and improve the favourable opinion which she seemed now to entertain of him.

Having made all proper enquiries, therefore, after Miss Townsend, and being informed of all the particulars—'that Mr. Townsend had sent a carriage, and conveyed her to a relation's in Warwickshire;' and having read three or four times over a direction, written with her own hand, 'To Miss Julia Townsend, at Dr. Greville's, at ——, near Warwick;' he sighed, and took his leave of Mrs. Sarsenet for that evening, and went to Mrs. Whitfield's, at the Bell, to the no small joy of Tugwell; who infinitely preferred the smoak and savoury smell of a greasy kitchen to the meagre neatness of Mrs. Sarsenet's parlour, notwithstanding it was adorned with a glass-door, to peep into the shop, and the Ten Commandments, worked at the boarding-school, in a gilt frame; with King William and Queen Mary, and several other Metzotintos painted on glass, which had been in the family ever since the Revolution.

CHAPTER XXVIII

The Pilgrims kindly treated by Mrs. Whitfield

MRS. WHITFIELD received Mr. Wildgoose with great cordiality, notwithstanding he brought no letters of recommendation from her brother-in-law, as the reader may suppose, on account of his precipitate departure from Bristol. Mrs. Whitfield's husband, being fatigued with *too close attention* to the *proper business* of his calling, was retired to rest: so that she was at supper alone, upon a brace of partridges, with a large China *bason* of warm punch; which was no disagreeable contrast to the mortified repast of poor Mrs. Sarsenet. And, as the relation she stood in to Mr. Whitfield sanctified whatever she did in the eyes of Mr. Wildgoose, he made no scruple in partaking with her of the good things which were set before him. Mrs. Whitfield laid Wildgoose in one of her bettermost rooms, the only good bed he had met with since he came from home; and Tugwell also shared the same kindness: which made ample amends for the contumelious reception they had met with on their first arrival at Gloucester.

Though the little Church, which Wildgoose had planted, was partly dissolved by the poor Barber's calamity; yet, the next morning, he collected as many of the Brethren together as could be suddenly assembled, and gave the word of exhortation to them in a field belonging to Mr. Whitfield at the Bell.

Before he departed, he recommended to them the Barber's distressed condition; and, by consulting also with Mrs. Sarsenet and Mrs. Whitfield, they put him in a method of recovering part of his old customers; and Mrs. Whitfield promised to get him the occasional custom at the Bell, as the Barber who used to attend was going to settle at Bath.

CHAPTER XXIX

They set out for the North

THE two Pilgrims being now within a day's journey, or a little more, of their native place; Tugwell was impatient to return home, partly to see his good wife Dorothy, and partly to recount his adventures amongst his neighbours, and exhibit the fancied improvements he had made in his travels. Wildgoose, indeed, was principally bent on pursuing the great object which had taken possession of his imagination: yet the impression, which Miss Townsend had made on his heart, a little distracted his thoughts, and made him deliberate, whether he should go the nearest way into Stafford and Shropshire (which was through Worcester); or go round by Warwick, where he had some prospect of seeing Miss Townsend. As in the latter case, however, he could not well avoid passing through his own village, where he might meet with some obstruction to his project from Mrs. Wildgoose, he determined upon the former. Accordingly, after taking leave of his friends at Gloucester, and writing a tender epistle to Miss Townsend, and exhorting Mrs. Sarsenet to join a little of the prudence of the serpent with the innocence of the dove, Mr. Wildgoose and his friend Tugwell set out for Worcester.

VOLUME THREE

. . . pudet hæc opprobria nobis
Et *dici* potuisse. . . .
HOR.[1]

Humour without a moral is buffoonry.
HUGHES[2]

S.Wale del.   C.Grignion Sc,

BOOK IX

CHAPTER I

Good Effects of Mr. Wildgoose's Labours

BOTH Wildgoose and his friend Jeremiah, having each of them been somewhat disappointed (the former in his expectation of meeting Miss Townsend at Gloucester, and the latter in his hopes of returning home to his Dame Dorothy), travelled on for some time with a kind of solemn taciturnity. Tugwell, at length, ventured first to break silence, by observing, 'that they might now have got home in one day's time, if so be *as how* his Worship had been so disposed.'—Wildgoose replied, with some degree of peevishness, 'Why, Jerry, to be sure, you are not my hired servant; and I cannot oblige you to attend me against your will: but how can you think so meanly of me, as to imagine I will desert my post, and not execute the commission which Mr. Whitfield has given me; especially as Heaven has inclined the hearts of such numbers to listen to my instructions, and I have so fair a prospect of *converting* so many poor souls from the error of their ways?'

'*Convart* them!' says Tugwell. 'Odhang it! Master, why, to be sure, your Worship does preach main well, that is certain; but, as for *convarting*, methinks some of them are only *converted* from bad to worse. There is the Barber now: he was poor enough, I believe, when we first went to his house; but he is now *convarted*, from a poor, honest Shaver, to a wicked Robber, and, from *scarifying* men's faces, to *terrifying* folks upon the highway.'—Wildgoose was not pleased with being reminded of this unlucky instance; but said, 'the Barber's was a particular case; that he was persecuted by his neighbours, and driven by necessity to one wicked attempt; and that, he made no doubt, the Barber was still in a state of Grace, though appearances were against him.'

'Then there is Madam Sarsenet,' says Tugwell; 'to my thinking, she was a very good sort of woman before she was *convarted*, and maintained her mother and her sister; and I saw them at dinner upon some good roast mutton and baked pudding; and now, since she has been *convarted*, it seems to be but poor with them; or else, methinks, they would have had a bit of soft cheese, or butter, with their bunch of radishes last night.'

Wildgoose not thinking it worth while to make any answer to his friend's observation, silence again ensued for some time; and, in short, nothing material befell the two travellers before they reached Tewksbury, about twelve o'clock; where they halted for an hour or two, to refresh themselves in the heat of the day.

CHAPTER II

The Hotel at Tewksbury

MR. WILDGOOSE, enquiring of my Landlord where they stopped, 'what he could have to eat;' was answered, 'Whatever you please, Sir; but,' continues mine Host, 'you may dine with us, if you chuse it. We have a fine leg of veal, an excellent gammon of bacon, and a couple of charming fowls roasted; and only two very civil Gentlemen and a Lady, that quarter in the house, dine with us.'—Though Wildgoose was not very hungry, yet the bill of fare, and my Landlord's account of the company, inclined him to accept of his invitation.

When dinner came in, there appeared, besides my Landlord and his wife, an old Lady about fifty, one Gentleman about the same age, and the other seemed to be about twenty-five.

The leg of veal, which my Landlord had mentioned, was only the knuckle, cut pretty close; and the bacon, the most bony part of the fore-gammon; the veal was *red*; and the bacon *white*, the lean part I mean; for the fat, being thoroughly tinged with smoak, was of a different complexion.

As Wildgoose was not very fond of boiled veal, he would not rob the company of this part of their short commons, but reserved himself for the second course.

When the fowls appeared, they were full-grown, nicely roasted, and frothed up,[1] and looked tempting enough; but, when they were to be carved, my Landlord laid hold on one leg, and his wife on the other, and with some difficulty dismembered them. As the

rest of the company were less complaisant than Wildgoose, the
wings were soon disposed of; so that he and my Landlord took each
of them a drum-stick, which, Wildgoose said, 'he always chose;'—
and my Landlord said, 'it was the best part of the fowl.'

But now came the difficult part of the atchievement. The muscles
of the leg were so hard, that no human jaw could possibly make any
impression upon them. The Gentlemen, indeed, observed, 'that
even the wings were a little tough.'—'Yes,' says my Landlord, 'the
flesh is *firm*; they were well fed; Jemmy Cockspur is one of the best
feeders in the country.'

And now the secret was out. They had had a cock-fighting the
day before; and these fine, plump fowls had died in the field of
battle, after having triumphed victoriously for five or six years
successively. In short, poor Wildgoose, after sucking the drum-
stick, and licking up his parsley and butter, concluded his dinner
with a good slice of Gloucestershire cheese and a crust of bread.

Tugwell, however, who regarded more the quantity than the
quality of his food, fared better in the kitchen, where was a good
pan-full of cow-heel fryed with onions; on which Jerry made a very
comfortable meal.

CHAPTER III

The Life of a Stroller. Criticisms on Shakespear

As Wildgoose had leisure enough, during his repast, to make
observations upon the company; he was studying their several
characters, in order to suit his spiritual advice accordingly. He was
at first a little puzzled to guess at their several professions. There
was a sort of shabby smartness in their dress, that suited neither
with the rank of a Gentleman, nor that of a Tradesman. The
young man had on a faded, green cloth, which discovered the marks
of a gold lace, that had probably been ripped off, to answer some
particular exigency. Wildgoose observed, that his companion
called him—your Highness. The elderly man had a black crape
about his neck, a ramillee wig,[1] and a pair of half jack-boots, with
the tops of some old thread stockings pinned on; which riding-
dress seemed to be no otherwise necessary, than to supply the

want of shoes and stockings. The old Lady had a long black cardinal, and something like a cambrick handkerchief pinned round her head.

The old man happened to assert some trifling matter upon his *honour*: to which the young man replied, in heroics,

> 'Honour's a sacred tie, the law of kings:
> It is not to be sported with.——
> Syphax! thou art a false old traitor.'[1]

This speech convinced Wildgoose (of what he had before suspected), that they were part of a Company of Strollers. The Company were on their route from the West of England to Birmingham; and were to perform Cato that night in a barn, to defray their expences upon the road.

The old man was to play Syphax; and was the very character he intended to act. He had a most villainous physiognomy, and seemed, by his conversation, to have been a Street-robber. The old Lady was to appear in the character of Marcia, though she had lost one eye; and instead of an even 'two-fold *hedge* of teeth,'[2] as Homer expresses it, her broken snags were more like park-pales, or what school-boys in Latin verse call a Dactyl, that is, a foot of three syllables, the first long, and the two last short; yet the old Lady resembled Marcia in one respect;

> The virtuous Marcia tow'rs above her sex;

for she was near six feet high, and (I will answer for it) had lived a most *virtuous* life for many years.

Juba had a swelled face, yet was really a genteel young fellow, and had had a good education; but, as he confessed to Wildgoose, had been ruined by his vanity, and a humour for spouting tragedy, which he had learned at school; for he had spent near two thousand pounds, which his father left him; and, though bred to a genteel profession, could never settle to business.

'Then, I was quite an idolater of Shakespear,' quoth the Player; 'and having seen Mr. Garrick play Hamlet and Othello two or three times, (he acts with so much *ease* as well as propriety, that) I imagined it no difficult matter to succeed in the same parts; which determined me to go upon the stage.'

'Why,' says Wildgoose, 'I have seen a few Plays some years ago; and must own, Mr. Garrick is almost the only Actor I have met with, who keeps sight of Nature in his action, and has brought her back upon the stage, whence, by all accounts, indiscriminate rant and unmeaning rhodomontade had banished all truth and propriety time out of mind. But, Sir, I profess myself an enemy to all Theatrical entertainments; and even to Shakespear himself, in some respects.'

'Oh! Sir,' (cries the young Player, stretching out his hand) 'I must not hear a word against our venerable Patriarch and great founder of the English Drama.

'I will allow every objection that you can imagine against him. I will forgive Ben Jonson his malignant wish, "that, instead of one line, he had blotted out a thousand."¹ I will not pull Voltaire by the nose (though he deserves it), for calling his Tragedies *monstrous Farces*.² I will grant the Frenchman, he has offended against the laws of Aristotle and Boileau, and slighted the unities of action, time, and place; that, upon some occasions, he abounds in mixt metaphors, and uses some harsh expressions, which the age he lived in might *tolerate*, and which are become venerable only by their antiquity. But read one act, or even one scene, in Hamlet, Othello, or Macbeth, and all these trifling criticisms disperse like mists before the orient sun.'

Wildgoose began to explain himself, and to give the conversation a spiritual turn. In order to which, he first observed to the Players, 'that their situation was very unfavourable to the practice of Religion.'—'Religion!' (cries the Prince of Mauritania) 'I only wish we had any morality, or even common honesty, amongst us. No, we are Heroes, Kings, or Sultanas, upon the stage; but Beggars, Sots, or Prostitutes, in our private lodgings. There is the lovely Marcia,' (says he, whispering to Wildgoose) 'would drink you two quarts of ale now, if you would give it her; and, if she had six-pence in her pocket, Cato's daughter would get drunk with gin, before she came upon the stage. In short,' (continues the young Player) 'I intend to take my leave of them very soon.'

Old Syphax, hearing part of this declamation against the life of a Stroller, said, 'there was one agreeable circumstance attending it, that they frequently fell into company with some Gentleman of fortune, who would treat them with a bottle of wine, or a bowl of punch.'—This the wily African said in consequence of the intelligence he had gained from Tugwell in the kitchen, 'that his master had four or five hundred pounds a year.'—But Wildgoose not taking the hint, my Landlord, perceiving there was no more liquor called for, began to grudge such company the use of his parlour. He, therefore, bid the Waiter bring a bill; and Wildgoose soon after took his leave, and with his trusty Squire set out for Worcester.

CHAPTER IV

State of Religion at Worcester

MR. WILDGOOSE, impatient to execute the commission which Mr. Whitfield had given him, traversed with hasty strides the spacious streets of Tewksbury; and, getting clear of the town, the two Pilgrims now ascended a little hill; when Wildgoose looking round him, 'I wonder' (says he) 'how many miles it is to Warwick.' —Then, without waiting for Jerry's reply, he trudged on again at a round rate.

Tugwell's inclinations still pointing homewards, he likewise made a soliloquy in his turn. 'Odzookers! one might almost see our steeple, now, from this hill, and the smoak of my cottage. I wonder what our Dorothy is doing at home; and our poor dog!'

The travellers now proceeded without any interruption, and arrived at Worcester about eight o'clock in the evening.

Mr. Wildgoose made immediate enquiry, 'whether there was any religious Society in that city;' and found that only a few of the lower sort of people met once a week at a private house, whose zeal was kept alive by now and then an occasional Preacher that came amongst them; that a considerable part of the town had their attention taken up by their China-work, lately established there, under the auspices of the ingenious and excellent Dr. Wall;[1] that the learned Prebends were immersed in profound studies, or engaged in the care of their health; as their wives and daughters were at Whist or Quadrille. The two Pilgrims, therefore, set out again early in the morning, and took the road towards Wednesbury, Dudley, and Walsal; which are the chief collieries and manufactories in that part of the country.

CHAPTER V

An unexpected Rencounter

TOWARDS the middle of the day, our travellers came into the gravelly bottom of a deep valley, through which a silver stream ran winding along, shaded with alders, and inviting them to repose a little in so cool a retreat. Wildgoose, according to custom, pulled out a little godly Manual, and began to read; as Tugwell, by a kind of instinct, began to rummage his wallet, for something to eat; whose example having stronger attractions for the former, than his amusement had for the latter, Tugwell soon brought over Wildgoose to his party; and they took a comfortable noonchine[1] together.

Whilst they were thus employed, two more travellers came, the contrary road, to the same spot; and, without much ceremony, sate down to partake of so agreeable a shade. One of them looked like some mechanical handicraft; but the other (though his long hair was somewhat in the style of Ralpho in Hudibras) had a gentleman-like appearance, both in his dress and his address.

Wildgoose making some overtures by a few general topicks and introductory preludes, they soon entered into further conversation.

Two or three small birds coming to drink and bathe themselves, with great boldness and security, as the travellers were sitting in a calm repose; Wildgoose said, 'that he could never sufficiently admire the beauty, elegance, and harmless innocence, of those little animals of the winged creation; and that he had often thought the familiar, friendly, and almost conversible air, with which some birds and other animals approached mankind, till they were alarmed and frightened away by some violent motion or menacing attitude, seemed to give credit to the doctrine of Transmigration, as if some of our own species were doing penance in those animals, and wanted to express their sufferings or complaints, or to renew their intimacy with some old friend, or former acquaintance. At least,' continues Wildgoose, 'one is puzzled, without some supposition of this kind, to account for the *final* cause of their creation; many animals being frequently persecuted and tortured in such a manner, as to make their being rather a curse than a blessing.'

The stranger replied, 'that, when we come to talk of final causes, or the ends proposed by Providence in any part of the creation,

we soon get out of the depth of our shallow understandings; though
I am convinced,' says he, 'that God has formed all his creatures
with a capacity of being happy, if they do not forfeit it by their own
fault.'

This discourse on Pre-existence brought on the subject of
Predestination, Election, and Reprobation; which his Puritanical
library, and his conversing with Mr. Whitfield, had taught Wildgoose to maintain in its strictest sense.

The stranger opposed his opinions with great vehemence; and
said, 'he would sooner renounce his Bible, than believe those
doctrines, as Calvin of old, or Mr. Whitfield had of late, taught
them.'—'Sir,' says Wildgoose, 'I suppose then you are a follower
of John Wesley's.'—'No,' replies the stranger; 'I am John Wesley
himself.'[1]

Wildgoose started up with the utmost surprize, and accosted him
with the most profound reverence and respect; and, by way of
apology, said, 'that, although he had lately become personally
acquainted with Mr. Whitfield, and confessed himself a convert
to most of his opinions, yet he had so great a regard for all those
who were embarked in the same general cause, that he was extremely happy in this opportunity of conversing with a man, whose
character he had so long admired.'

He then acquainted Mr. Wesley who he himself was; when he
found Mr. Wesley was no stranger to his character or conversion.
Mr. Wesley returned the compliment with a pious wish, 'that he
might be able to give him any spiritual assistance.' After which,
Wildgoose let him know his present situation, and his intentions
of visiting the poor Colliers at Wednesbury, Walsal, and so forth.
But Mr. Wesley began immediately to dissuade him from pursuing
his scheme at present; 'for that he himself was, at this instant,
escaped from a most violent persecution; that a large and enraged
mob, stirred up by some interested people, were now in arms, and
in search of every Preacher of their denomination; and that it
would be tempting Providence to run into the very jaws of that
many-headed monster, a drunken multitude, who knew not what
they did.'

An Enthusiast, like a man of courage, is so far from being dismayed by an appearance of danger, that he generally becomes more
resolute. Wildgoose, therefore, was still more inclined to try the
strength of his eloquence, and to proceed to Wednesbury; till

Mr. Wesley assured him, 'it would be injuring the cause, to attempt to convince them, whilst their passions and prejudices were so strongly engaged on the other side.'—Wildgoose, therefore, stood corrected: and a man now coming up with Mr. Wesley's horses, which he had been obliged to leave behind, Wildgoose took his leave; and, instead of pursuing the intended road, turned off towards Birmingham, in order to make the best of his way to the Lead-mines in the Peak of Derbyshire.

CHAPTER VI

A just Character of Lady L—n, from a discarded Servant

OUR two Pilgrims being a little fatigued with travelling in so hot a day, they halted in the afternoon at a publick-house, in the neighbourhood of Hagley. Wildgoose seeing a number of people drinking under a tree at the door, observed to my Landlord, 'that *his* seemed to be a well-accustomed house.'—'Yes,' says mine Host, with an air of piety (taking Wildgoose for a Clergyman), 'blessed be God! I have my share of custom, at this time of the year, please God to send fine weather, as every body comes to see Hagley Park here.'—Wildgoose replied, 'that his house seemed to stand well for the refreshment of travellers; but that he did not understand how he could bless God for some of his idle customers, who spent the money, which ought to support their families, in getting drunk, and making brutes of themselves.'—Mine Host replied, 'that (to be sure) poor men who worked hard, and had no beer at home, would now and then have a little good drink; but then' (says he) 'I never suffer them to have more at my house, than they have money to pay for.'

Wildgoose then said, 'he supposed Sir George L——n's house was worth seeing, as so many people came thither for that purpose.'[1] —'Yes,' (says a young man in a livery frock) 'Hagley is a noble seat; and *abundance* of *quality resort* thither at this time of the year.'— 'Ah!' says my Landlord, 'and Sir George has something at Hagley better worth seeing than his fine seat. He has, for his wife, the finest woman, and the best Christian, in England. But,' says he, 'my son here knows all about it; he was Under-butler at Sir George's; and

Sir, as you seem to be a Gentleman, please to step into this parlour, and I will tell you more (coming! Sir, coming!)' My Landlord then shewed Wildgoose into a little nook, divided from the kitchen by a partition of deal-boards, which prevented you from being seen, but not from being overheard by any one that was disposed to listen. 'Now,' (says my Landlord) 'as I was telling you, Sir, my son was Under-butler at Hagley. But, Sir, betwixt you and I, the house-keeper is the d—mdest b—tch in England.'—'Well, well,' says Wildgoose, 'I do not want to be let into family secrets. But my Lady, you say, is a very good woman.'—'That she is' (says mine Host); 'and, if she had had her way, my son would never have lost his place.'—Though my Landlord was very full of this subject, he and his son did great justice to Lady L——n's character: 'that there was not a poor person, a sick person, or a wicked person, within five miles of the place, but she found them out, and gave them money, physick, or good advice; and, what is more' (says he) 'there is not an *idle* person, but she contrives to employ them, and keep them out of harm's way; and they mind what my Lady says, more than all the Parson preaches, or the Doctor can say to them when they are sick. Then' (continues he) 'my son says, my Lady has wit at will, and will *hold discourse* with any Lord or Bishop that comes to Sir George's table; and knows every thing that happened in former days, or in foreign parts, as well as the best of them.'[1]

Mr. Wildgoose said, 'he did not in the least doubt the justness of my Landlord's panegyric; for that he had known Lady L——n from a child (she being his country-woman); though he had not seen her for some years.' He was then going to give mine Host some spiritual instructions; when Tugwell came to the door, to remind his Master, 'that it was very dusty travelling, and that he seemed to have forgotten their intention of calling at a public-house.'—My Landlord then asked, 'what they would please to drink?' But, there being no great variety of liquors or provisions at this hotel, they refreshed themselves with some fresh ale, and some new cheese; and then proceeded in their journey towards Birmingham.

CHAPTER VII

*A Sketch of the Leasowes, and of the Character of
the worthy Possessor of that Place*

THE sun was now far upon the decline towards the West, when the
two Pilgrims had passed a little market-town, on the Birmingham
road, called Hales-Owen. As they walked on, they saw an object,
amidst the woods, on the edge of the hill; which, upon enquiry,
they were told was called, Shenstone's Folly. This is a name, which,
with some sort of propriety, the common people give to any work
of taste, the utility of which exceeds the level of their comprehension.

As they ascended the hill, through a shady lane, they observed a
Gentleman, in his own hair, giving directions to some labourers,
who were working beyond the usual hour, in order to finish a
receptacle for a cataract of water, a glimpse of which appeared
through the trees on the side of the road.[1] As Wildgoose and his
friend, partly out of curiosity, and partly to take breath, made
a little pause, the Gentleman turned his face towards them; when
Wildgoose immediately discovered him to be no other than his old
acquaintance, the now celebrated Mr. Shenstone, whose place
began to be frequented by people of distinction from all parts of
England, on account of its natural beauties, which, by the mere
force of genius and good taste, Mr. Shenstone had improved and
exhibited to so much advantage. And this had discovered to the
world his own fine poetical talents and polite learning, which, from
his modesty, would otherwise probably have been buried in
solitude and obscurity.

Mr. Shenstone soon recollected his old academical friend and
associate; and, with that warmth of benevolence for which he is
distinguished amongst those that know him, insisted upon his
staying, that night at least, with him at the Leasowes; which
invitation Mr. Wildgoose was sufficiently inclined to accept of,
though he had not been prompted to it by his fellow-traveller, who
never was so cynical as to slight the least overture towards an
hospitable reception.

As they passed towards the house, Mr. Shenstone pointed out
to his friend many of the beauties of his place. He shewed him his
cascades, which are so deservedly admired, and the reservoirs

that supplied them; the prospects of the country from various points of view; his grove, dedicated to Virgil; his urns, statues, and his admirable inscriptions. He mentioned several people of the first quality, and, what Mr. Shenstone valued more, of the first taste, who had done him the honour to visit his place. And particularly he informed him, 'that he expected Lord D—tm—th,[1] and some other company, the very next day; on which account, he had been inspecting his reservoirs, got his walks cleaned out, and made the men work so late, in order to finish the cataract, where his friend had first seen him.'

As Wildgoose knew the elegance of Mr. Shenstone's taste, he could not but add his suffrage to those of the rest of the world, in admiring his place; and observed, 'that, doubtless, the pleasures we receive from gardens, woods, and lawns, and other rural embellishments, were the most innocent of any *amusements*; but then we should consider them as *amusements* only, and not let them engross too much of our attention; that we ought to spiritualize our ideas as much as possible; and that it was worth while to enquire, how far too violent a fondness for these merely inanimate beauties might interfere with our love of God, and attach us too strongly to the things of this world.'

This gave Mr. Shenstone an opportunity in his turn, of combating his friend's enthusiastic notions; who (he found by his own account) had deserted the station in which his own choice and his Mother's approbation had fixed him, to sally forth and preach the Gospel, without any other call to that office than what a warm imagination had suggested, and which a romantic view of converting sinners *at large* had prompted him to undertake.

The two friends, however, supped together very amicably; and, after drinking a cool-tankard, and spending a pretty late evening in talking over the incidents of their youth, which they had spent together in the University, Mr. Shenstone shewed his friend into an elegant bed-chamber, fitted up in a Gothic taste; to which the bed itself, the rest of the furniture, and the painted glass in the window, all corresponded. And contiguous to this, he lodged Tugwell, his trusty Squire and fellow-traveller, and wished them a good night.

CHAPTER VIII

A Practical Lecture against the Vanities of this World

As soon as Mr. Shenstone rose in the morning (which was not always at a very early hour), he went up to his friend's apartment, to summon him to breakfast; when, to his surprize, he found both him and his companion departed, without taking leave of him; and upon Wildgoose's table was left the following letter:

'My good Friend,

'I am called hence by the Spirit: in the visions of the night, it was revealed unto me. I must own, that, like the good Publius, you have received and lodged us courteously; and my bowels yearn for your salvation. But, my dear friend, I am afraid you have set up idols in your heart. You seem to pay a greater regard to Pan and Sylvanus, than to Paul or Silas. You have forsaken the fountains of the living Lord; and hewn you out cisterns, broken cisterns, that will hold no water. But my conscience beareth testimony against this Idolatry. Bel boweth down; Nebo stoopeth.[1] I have delivered my own soul; and will pray for your conversion. I am,

'Your brother in the Lord,
'GEOFFRY WILDGOOSE.'

This extraordinary letter, and his friend's abrupt departure, greatly alarmed Mr. Shenstone: but, going out to view his principal cascade, he soon discovered the mystery; that his friend, imagining he was too much affected with the applauses which were bestowed on his good taste in laying out his place, had forced open his sluices, and emptied his reservoirs, so that, in a literal sense, his *cisterns could hold no water*, nor his cascades make any great figure that day. And, what was more distressful, he had thrown down a leaden statue of the Piping Fawn from its pedestal; which was a damage that could not easily be repaired before the arrival of his illustrious guests.

Mr. Shenstone was a little provoked at the first discovery of this incident; but, upon reflection, could not forbear laughing at his old friend's frantic proceedings; and thought the singularity of the adventure would afford his guests as much entertainment, as a greater flash from his cascades, or as viewing his place in more exact order.

CHAPTER IX

A Discourse on Idolatry

WHEN the travellers were got into the Birmingham road again; Tugwell, who did not rightly comprehend nor approve of his Master's conduct on this occasion, nor understand what he meant by saying, 'that Mr. Shenstone quite idolized or worshipped those lifeless objects:'—Jerry, I say, began now to express his apprehensions of the consequences of what they had done. 'Odzooks!' says he, 'it is well if the Gentleman does not get a warrant for us, and *trouble* us, for robbing his fish-ponds (as he may think we have), or for damaging his images.'—He observed, moreover, 'that, as he seemed to be a sensible Gentleman, he could not think he would be so foolish as to *worship* images, as the *Papishes* do. Why,' (continues Jerry) 'there is our Squire has got a naked *thing-em-bob* stands up in the middle of the grove (it is either the Virgin Mary, or Fair Rosamond, or Dinah[1] that was ravished by the Jacobites); and yet I never heard that the Squire, or any of the family, ever said their prayers to it, or worshipped it.'

'Why, Jerry,' (says Wildgoose) 'a person may be guilty of Idolatry by setting his affections too much upon any thing; upon riches or pleasures, a fine house or a fine child; and, in those cases, it is an act of friendship in any one, to take some method (as I have done with Mr. Shenstone) to wean them from those objects. And Providence, out of mere kindness, often deprives us of those things which we have so entirely fixed our hearts upon.'

'Why, to be sure,' (says Tugwell) 'God Almighty may do what he pleases, for that matter: but then, if one *man* was at liberty to take away from another, whatever he had *set his heart* upon, they might take away one's wife, or one's cow, or one's dog, or one's cat; and then there would be no living at peace in the world. Now, there is my dog Snap; I *loves* him almost as well as I do my wife; and, if the best man in Gloucestershire were to steal my dog, I would take *the law on him*, if there was any law to be had in the kingdom.'

Wildgoose did not think it material to continue the dispute; but it occurred to him, in the course of this conversation, how much his affections were attached to Miss Townsend. This, however, he considered as a spiritual attachment; he intending only the good of Miss Townsend's soul by an union, which, from the little encouragment she seemed to have given him, he had some slight hopes of effecting. This project engaged his thoughts in an agreeable reverie; which prevented any further conversation till they arrived, about eight o'clock in the morning, at Birmingham.

CHAPTER X

Slight Persecutions

As Mr. Wildgoose intended, if nothing very extraordinary prevented it, to visit the Colliers at Wednesbury on his return; he made no longer stay in Birmingham than whilst he himself took some slight refreshment, and Tugwell an hearty breakfast, at the first inn they came to; and then proceeded towards Litchfield, in their way to the Peak of Derbyshire.

As they walked through Birmingham streets, they heard two or three fellows in a workshop, up two pair of stairs, quarrelling, swearing, and cursing, in a most tremendous manner. Wildgoose, thinking it incumbent upon him to reprove their profaneness, made an halt; and, beckoning with his hand, called out to the vociferous garretteers, 'to hold their blasphemous tongues.'—The litigants, observing a man of a tolerable appearance addressing himself to them, were silent for a moment; but, when they heard Wildgoose, with an air of authority, charging them, in the name of the King of kings, 'not to take the name of God in vain,' with a mixture of mirth, indignation, and contempt, they redoubled their oaths and imprecations upon the Preacher; and one of them emptied the stale contents of an unscowered piss-pot full upon the heads of him and his companion. As Mr. Wildgoose was got almost into the middle of the street, in order to direct his voice to them more commodiously, he received only a slight sprinkling of their intended kindness; but, as Tugwell stood just under the window, with his mouth open, waiting the event of his Master's exhortation, he received a more liberal portion, part of which came full into his mouth, and penetrated pretty deeply into the cavity of his throat.

Wildgoose, observing the inefficacy of his rebuke, cried out, in the Apostolical style; 'Well, my brethren; I have delivered my own soul; look you to it; your *blood* be upon your own heads.'

Tugwell, being less patient (at this ill return of their intended favour), spitting and rubbing his face, and shaking his cloaths, exclaimed with some indignation against his Master for this unseasonable interposition; 'Pock-i-cat take it, for me! the *blood*, and guts, and the Devil, and all, I think, is upon *our* heads: and it was no otherwise likely; what, the *dickins*! had we to do, with folks that were quarreling up in a garret, and never troubled their heads about us?'

'Well,' quoth Wildgoose, 'as the Roman Emperor said, when he laid a tax upon urine, "the smell of money is sweet whencesoever it comes;" so, I can say, persecution is sweet and wholesome in any shape whatsoever.'—'Yes,' says Tugwell, 'even in the shape of a piss-pot, I suppose. The smell of money may be sweet; but, I am sure, neither the smell, nor the taste, of what was thrown upon our heads was either sweet or wholesome; at least, I had rather your Worship should have it than I, if you think it so very sweet and so wholesome.'

The hapless Pilgrims now passed on through Birmingham; Wildgoose leading the way, and Tugwell at some little distance behind him. Wildgoose, reflecting upon what had just happened, said, 'he began to wonder what they had done, that the world was so civil to them.'

'Odsbobs!' cried Jerry (looking up to the window of a little shop), 'there is fine plumb-pudding!'

'The friendship of the world is enmity with God,' continues Wildgoose.

'It is smoking hot, just out of the oven,' says Tugwell.

'My zeal began to cool; and I grew quite remiss in my duty,' proceeds the Master.

'I have a great mind to have a penny-worth of it,' says the man.

'But, come, let us make the best of our way, to rescue the poor Miners from the power of Satan,' says Wildgoose.

'I must and will go back, and have a slice of that pudding,' says Tugwell.

Thus the Master and Man proceeded in a kind of soliloquy, entirely inattentive to each other. But, when Wildgoose discovered his fellow-traveller's gluttonous intention, and saw him return with a good slice of pudding in his hand, 'Ah! Jerry, Jerry,' (cries he) 'swallow thy spittle, and subdue thy appetite. I thought thou hadst just satisfied the demands of Nature with an hearty breakfast; and now thou art at it again: if thou hadst but a grain of true Faith, thy mind would not be thus continually hankering after these carnal indulgences.'

'Odsbodikins!' (cries Tugwell, as soon as he could empty his mouth) 'cannot a man have true Faith, that loves plumb-pudding? Why, Master, I was very hungry to-day;—and then I wanted to get the taste of the *persecution* out of my mouth, which, your Worship says, was so sweet and so wholesome.' Wildgoose smiled to himself, but made no reply, and trudged on.

CHAPTER XI

A Glimpse of Miss Townsend

BEING now got clear of the town, the travellers came to a direction-post, where the roads divided. On one of the hands was written, 'the road to Litchfield;' on the other, 'to Warwick.'—As Wildgoose had as strong an hankering after the place of Miss Townsend's residence, as Tugwell had after his own fire-side, they kept their eyes for some time fixed on the hand which pointed toward the object of their respective inclinations; and, as a string of Coventry pack-horses had raised a cloud of dust, they did not perceive a chariot and pair, bowling along on a brisk trot, till it had almost passed by them.

There seemed to be in it an elderly Gentleman and his wife; and a young Lady sate side-ways on the stool, with a very white arm resting upon the window of the chariot. The young Lady, with a female curiosity, thrusting herself out to have a view of the travellers, dropped a cambrick handkerchief (probably without perceiving it), which Wildgoose immediately picked up; and was going to return it, when, casting his eyes upon the mark, he instantly knew it to be Miss Townsend's cypher. This occasioned such a surprize, as fixed him motionless for a moment, and would have prevented him from overtaking the chariot, if (upon recollection) he had thought it either prudent or adviseable to endeavour it. Though Wildgoose had hardly a glance of Miss Townsend's face; yet, as imagination magnifies every object beyond its real dimensions, this incident, and the initial letters of 'Julia Townsend,' contributed more perhaps to keep alive Mr. Wildgoose's passion, than the most tender Epistle, or a complete view of her, might have done.

Wildgoose was deliberating with himself, whether he should not return to Birmingham, and find out Miss Townsend, especially when he had so good a pretence as that of returning her handkerchief; when Tugwell came up to him (with his jaws yet in motion from masticating his baked pudding), and cries out, 'Well, Master, as God sends good luck, let us be thankful, and spend it at the next public-house. This white handkerchief will buy us a quart of best drink, I will warrant you; though, mayhap, it is only cut out of the tail of an old smock.'

Wildgoose was so provoked at Jerry's gross ideas, that he could hardly forbear striking him.—'Best drink!' (cries Wildgoose, pressing the handkerchief, which breathed the fragrance of lavender and eau-de-luce, with rapture to his breast) 'I would not part with it for the richest wines of Canary or Cyprus, nor for all the wealth of the Indies.'

'Odsbobs! Master,' (says Tugwell) 'you seem to be as fond of the young woman's handkerchief, as I am of plumb-pudding. One would think it was a love-toy; and that it was given you by your sweet-heart. And, for that matter, it seemed to be a good plump young woman that dropped it out of the coach, and drest like a Queen. I suppose, she was daughter to some Squire, or some topping Button-maker here in Birmingham at least.'

'Ah! Jerry,' (replies Wildgoose) 'I value this handkerchief, because it belongs to a very good girl. That young Lady in the chariot was no other than the Miss Townsend, whom we saw at Mrs. Sarsenet's at Gloucester.'

'What! the young woman that came after us to Bristol,' (says Jerry) 'and was taken with *compulsion* fits at the Tabernacle? I thought I had seen her face before' (continues he); 'but then she is got fatter than she was. I suppose, she has her belly-full now; which, belike, she had not at poor Madam Sarsenet's, at Gloucester.'

Wildgoose did not like to have the object of his affection treated with so much familiarity; and was also afraid of discovering to Jerry the situation of his heart. Neither was he yet determined, whether he should return to Birmingham or not, and endeavour to get an interview with Miss Townsend. But, recollecting that the races at Warwick would be within a fortnight, which being the nearest meeting to his own native place, and fancying he had a particular call to bear his testimony against the lawfulness of those diversions, he was determined in himself (as soon as he had opened his commission in the Peak) to attend them. He therefore dropped the subject at present, and trudged on (at a good rate) towards Litchfield.

CHAPTER XII

Meet with a seasonable Invitation

THE two Pilgrims having pursued their journey above three hours, and the turnpike road being very hot and dusty; Tugwell proposed, where they could commodiously do it, to walk through the fields within the hedge. This insensibly led them too far from the great road, and brought them where two foot-paths led different ways; and they were puzzled which to pursue. Tugwell, therefore, went to make enquiries of a fellow that was at plow, in the adjacent field. At the end of the furrow, they saw an odd figure of a man, standing upright, with his eyes shut, and his mouth open, his neck stretched out, and his hands hanging strait down, in the attitude of the Pierro in a Pantomime. Though the sun was burning hot, he had a green surtout coat on, with the cape over his head, and buttoned round the neck.

Wildgoose, as his ideas ran constantly upon religious objects, thought immediately it was some poor soul under the agonies of the New Birth, and waiting for the influx of the Spirit. He accosts him, therefore, in his own way, 'God comfort your soul! my good friend,' says Wildgoose.—The Gentleman, starting from his Swiss meditation or reverie (in which he had been unexpectedly surprized) and throwing himself into a tolerably genteel attitude; 'Sir,' says he, 'I do not know you; but am obliged to you for your good wishes: though my body has more need of comfort than my soul, at present.'—'What is the matter then,' says Wildgoose, 'if I may make so free? What is your complaint, Sir?'—'Ah!' says the

Gentleman, 'if I could tell you that, I should tell you more than all
the Physicians in England have been able to tell me.'—'Where does
your chief disorder lie, then?' says Wildgoose.—'Why, Sir, I have
a complication of disorders,' replies the Gentleman. 'I have the
gout, the rheumatism, the scurvy, a dropsy, and an asthma; and
what not? I have a *cachexy*, or bad habit of body, which has brought
on a nervous *atrophy*; so that nothing I eat or drink will *nourish*
me. And what plagues me more than all these, is, a disorder which,
perhaps, you never heard of.'—'Pray, what is that?' says Wildgoose.—'Why, a sort of convulsion, or hiccup in the ear. In short,
Sir, I believe mine is a total decay of nature; and I do not expect
to live a month to an end.'

'Ha!' says Wildgoose, 'that is very surprizing. Why, Sir, you
look extremely well in the face.'—'Ah! Sir,' says the Stranger,
shaking his head, 'that is the very thing that alarms me. I eat, drink,
and sleep well. And so did a friend of mine look; and ate, drank,
and slept well, to the very last; and yet died suddenly this last
winter.

'I have, as you see, Sir, rather a ruddy complexion. But, then,
if you observe, there is an odd sort of bluish cast mixt with it;
which is a sure sign of an apoplectic habit.'

'Come, Sir,' says Wildgoose; 'I fancy you are a little hippish;[1]
and, I hope, you fright yourself without any reason. But, pray,
Sir, what crop are you plowing for at this time of the year?'—
'Why,' says the Gentleman, 'I have had no other crop, than what
you see, from this field these five years; and yet these three acres
pay me better than any land I have.'—'In what respect?' replies
Wildgoose.—'In saving my Doctor's fees, and Apothecary's bills,'
answered the Gentleman. 'You know, I suppose,' continues he,
'that nothing is so wholesome as the smell of new-plowed earth.
I keep this little field, therefore, in my hands for no other purpose;
and make my servant, every day before dinner, turn up two or three
furrows, and follow the plough, as I have been now doing; which
gives me an appetite to my dinner, and, I am convinced, has kept
me alive these five years.'

Wildgoose thought this Gentleman somewhat whimsical; but
having listened with a more serious attention to the detail of his
maladies than many people would have done, the Gentleman was
prepossessed in his favour: and when Tugwell came up, with his intelligence, 'that it was still three miles to Litchfield,' the Gentleman

said, 'as Wildgoose, he supposed, had not dined, he should be very welcome to take pot-luck with him; that his house was but at the end of that avenue of firs; and he was just going to dinner.'— 'Why, yes,' (says Tugwell, before his Master could speak) 'as Providence has directed us to so good an house, you had best accept of the Gentleman's good-will.'—As Wildgoose always flattered himself with the hopes of doing good, or, what he esteemed the same thing, of making converts to his opinions, he was easily prevailed upon to accompany the Gentleman to his house, to which he was so hospitably invited.

CHAPTER XIII

Some Account of this Stranger

As they went along, Mr. Slicer (which was the Gentleman's name) made some efforts towards gratifying his own curiosity, and discovering Wildgoose's profession, and what expedition he was bent upon. This Wildgoose evaded, by enquiring of Mr. Slicer, 'what first brought him into this low-spirited way; or, as he called it, this indifferent state of health?'—To which Mr. Slicer answered, 'that he had formerly been in considerable practice as a Solicitor in London; where he underwent great fatigue, yet never knew what it was to be sick: but, a relation leaving him an estate in that country, and having no family, he retired from business, in hopes of finding in retirement a more complete felicity than what he enjoyed in the hurry of business, and in the noise and smoak of the town. However, I was soon convinced' (continued Mr. Slicer) 'that happiness is not the product of any particular place, or way of life; much less is it to be found in a state of absolute inactivity: that some employment was necessary, to divert the mind from preying upon itself. And, whereas I enjoyed good health, ate with an appetite, and slept soundly, when fatigued with business; I now found every thing reversed: my sleep went from me; my appetite was palled; even venison lost its relish; and though, by constant attention, and the use of several excellent medicines, I have a little recovered my strength and spirits, yet I am convinced it is all forced and unnatural; for, though I am not sensible of any particular complaint,

A a

yet, as I said before, I am daily apprehensive of a sudden dissolution.'

Wildgoose was going to observe, 'that he had not yet found the
true road to happiness; that there was no real cordial for the
miseries of life, but an assurance that our sins are pardoned, and
the witness of the Spirit of our souls, that we are the children of
adoption:' but they were now arrived at the door of the Gentleman's house; which prevented any further conversation for the
present.

CHAPTER XIV

The Life of a dying Man

THE moment they had entered the hall, Mr. Slicer's old house-
keeper, Mrs. Quick, met him with consternation in her looks.
'Good-lack-a-day! Sir,' (says she) 'we have had a most terrible
accident. You would not let the chimney be swept; I told you how
it would be.'—'What! is the chimney on fire, then?' says Mr.
Slicer.—'Oh! no,' says she; 'but a whole heap of soot has fallen
down into the fish-kettle, and entirely spoiled the carps. I very
providentially caught up the loin of veal upon the spit; or else that
would have been covered with dust and ashes.' 'Well, well,' (says
Mr. Slicer) 'accidents will happen; it is well it is no worse; we must
dine without the carp, then.'—'But, lack-a-day! Sir,' (continues
Mrs. Quick) 'why did you stay so long? the fowls are boiled to a
rag; and the veal is roasted to powder; and there is not a drop of
gravy left; and the Parson and Mr. Selkirk have been here, waiting
for their dinner, this half-hour.'—'Well, well,' (says Slicer) 'if that
be all, there is no great harm done.——But—

'Let me see; I took my Bostock's Cordial this morning. Come,
bring my Stomachic Tincture: I will just take a few drops of that,
to strengthen my stomach; and a little Balsam of Life, and one or
two of my Pilulæ Salutariæ; and then you may send up dinner as
soon as you will.'

'But,' (says Mrs. Quick) 'if I had known you would have brought
any strangers, I would have made a custard-pudding. However, I
can just beat up two or three eggs, and a spoon-full of cream, and

a little orange flower-water, and make a little pudding, in the catching up of a sausepan.'

Mr. Slicer said, 'she might do as she would.' Then, bidding her shew Tugwell into the kitchen, he took Mr. Wildgoose into an handsome parlour; where they found Mr. Slicer's niece (who was come on a visit), with her little boy and girl; Mr. Selkirk, above-mentioned, who was a School-master in the village; and a little sleek Divine, whose spruce wig, short cassock, his japanned shoes, and silver buckles (worn smooth with the daily strokes of the brush), gave him rather the appearance of an Arch-deacon, than (what he was) the Parson of the parish.

After an apology for making his company wait, Mr. Slicer introduced Wildgoose to them; and then took his Stomachic Tincture, his Balsam of Life, and his *Pilulæ Salutiferæ*, one after another; strongly recommending a dose of the Stomachic Tincture to Mr. Wildgoose, as 'an excellent medicine to fortify the stomach, and create an appetite.' Wildgoose waived the offer; and said, 'he thanked God, he had a very good appetite, without any assistance of that kind.'

Slicer then bid the servant, 'bring him Mrs. Stephens's Medicine for the Stone and Gravel; which he never omitted,' he said, 'since it was first discovered.'—'What! are you afflicted with the Stone and Gravel, then?' says Mr. Selkirk.—'*Afflicted!*' says Slicer; 'no, Sir, God forbid! nor ever was *afflicted* with it; but, I suppose, I should have been *afflicted* with it before this time, if I had not taken this admirable medicine. And, as every one is subject, more or less, to gravel and sabulous concretions, it is madness to neglect so easy a precaution, as this noble Lithonthriptic; which Providence has permitted to be discovered, and for which the Parliament has granted so handsome a reward.'[1]

The servant having brought the preparation, with a large bason of veal-broth, Slicer swallowed the nauseous prescription with great alacrity; though the virtues, or even the safety, of that medicine have justly been questioned, notwithstanding the decision of our wise Legislators in its favour.

Wildgoose could not but express his astonishment at Mr. Slicer's credulity in this respect; and said, 'he was afraid he might injure his health, by mixing together too many of those *excellent* medicines, with which the world now abounded.'

'Sir,' (says Slicer) 'I despise the common quack medicines, as much as you can do; and never take any but what perform their operations in a rational manner, and whose effects I can in some measure account for (for I know something of Physic myself, by experience at least); such, I mean, as either *brace* up the *relaxed fibres* of the stomach, and assist the concoction; or such as *cut, divide,* and *attenuate,* the *tough* and viscid *humours,* and prepare them to be thrown off by insensible *perspiration*; or such as *strengthen* the *nerves, comfort* the *brain,* and revive the spirits; or' (as an ingenious Writer expresses it) 'such as, *ambitious* of *immortal fame,* fly *immediately* to the *part* affected, and *enter into contest* with the *peccant* humours, and either expel or subdue them.'[1]

Wildgoose and the rest of the company could with difficulty suppress their mirth, to hear poor Slicer thus retail the studied panegyricks of interested Empirics in favour of their own nostrums. But the little fat Rector of the parish, who was a good-natured and polite man, turned the conversation to some general topicks; and dinner soon made its appearance.

CHAPTER XV

A Remedy for Want of Appetite

WHEN dinner came in, Wildgoose found that the old housekeeper's apology was only words of course; for there were three fine full-grown pullets; an excellent Yorkshire ham; a loin of veal; and the custard-pudding, which Mrs. Quick had tossed up, adorned with currant-jelly; a gooseberry-tart; with other ornamental expletives of the same kind.

Wildgoose observed, 'that, although Mr. Slicer was careful enough about the *quality* of his food, yet he was less scrupulous about the *quantity* of what he eat.' He would not touch a morsel of skin, or fat, nor eat any butter with his veal or his boiled fowl, 'because it *eluded* the *concoctive*[2] *powers,*' as he said; but he made shift to pick the very bones of a pretty large pullet, with two good large *vertebræ,* and half the kidney of the loin of veal; not to mention a good quantity of supplemental pudding, gooseberry-tart, and apple-custard: so that it appeared probable, Mr. Slicer palled his appetite by over-loading his stomach; that he destroyed his health by too great a quantity of *wholesome* food; and made work for the Doctor, by an unnecessary use of quack medicines; by infallible Nostrums, Restoratives, Cordials, Balsams of Life, Tinctures, Elixirs, and the like. For he could never read an advertisement of that kind, but he longed to make the experiment; taking it for granted, that every medicine had all the virtues it pretended to, and really performed all that its vender engaged for in his feeling recommendation of it to the public.

CHAPTER XVI

History of a Long-liver, and other Chit-chat

AFTER dinner, Mr. Slicer put round the bottle of port, but bid the servant bring *him* his *Scorzonera*-water. Mr. Selkirk asked him, 'What the virtues of that Scorzonera-water were, which he observed he drank every day after dinner.'—'I do not know what the particular virtues are,' says Slicer; 'I only know, that it has contributed to prolong life to above an hundred years.

'Did you never meet with the History of Francis Hongo, sur-named Hyppazoli, who died at an hundred and fourteen (the beginning of this century) at Smyrna, where he was Consul for the Venetians?

'Hongo never was sick; his sight, hearing, and intellectual faculties, continued entire to the last. He would walk seven or eight miles every day. At an hundred, his white hairs are said to have turned black again; and, what is equally surprizing, having lost all his teeth, at an hundred and ten he cut two large ones in his upper jaw.

'This Gentleman drank no other liquor than a water distilled from Scorzonera, or Vipergrass; no wine, strong liquors, coffee, or tea; nor used tobacco. Towards the last, he lived chiefly upon broths and ripe fruits, which he always eat with bread.

'He was a man of great merit, wit, and honour; his only failing was too great an attachment to the fair sex. He had, by his wife and two or three concubines, nine and forty children.'[1]

As soon as Mr. Slicer had finished his little history, all on a sudden he bent down his body, and learned his elbows upon his knees, distorting his face into a variety of wrinkles. 'Bless me! Uncle,' says the Lady, 'what is the matter? I am afraid you are ill.'—'Oh! nothing at all,' says Slicer, smiling; 'only a little touch of the colic, which my pills have given me. I love to have the colic sometimes; it is the best symptom in the world; it is a sign the peccant humours, instead of entering the mass of blood, are spending their force on the *primæ viæ*, or intestines, where they will soon find themselves a passage; and then the pleasure of being at ease again is greater than the pain one suffers from the complaint.'

Slicer now fell into a musing posture for near a minute, with his eyes fixed upon the Lady. 'Niece,' says he, 'your husband's father lived to above ninety, merely by walking; and *I will walk.*' He had no sooner formed his resolution, than, forgetting for a moment that there was any company in the room, he started up, and put it in execution. After a turn round the garden, recollecting that some of the company were strangers, he returned to them again, with an apology, 'that he found, by experience, his dinner never began to digest till he had taken a little turn or two in the garden.'

The little Divine told him, with a smile, 'it was well he was not born at Sparta.'—'At Sparta! Why so?' says Slicer.—'Why, the Spartans, you know, were a military establishment, and spent most of their time in athletic exercises; they thought it an idle thing, therefore, to *walk* merely for walking's sake; and, being informed that the inhabitants of a certain city, under their jurisdiction, used to take *evening walks*, merely for recreation, instead of making a decree, with a long preamble like a modern Act of Parliament, the Magistrates sent them this laconic message, Μὴ περιπαλεῖτε, *do not walk!* which immediately put a stop to that unnecessary consumption of time, as they esteemed it.'[1]

'Well,' says Slicer, 'I should be sorry, on account of my brethren of the quill, to have that *laconic* stile introduced into our law-proceedings. But you put me in mind of another instance of Spartan severity, not foreign to our purpose, on the subject of health.

'Lysander going upon public business into Ionia, amongst other presents sent him upon his landing, there was some ox-beef and a large cheese-cake. He surveyed the latter with some curiosity; and, in the modern phrase, enquired, "what the Devil it was?" Those that brought it told him, "it was a composition of honey, cheese, and other ingredients."—"Oh! very well," says he; "give that to my servants; for I am sure it is not fit for a Gentleman to eat." He then ordered the beef to be dressed in the Spartan way, and on that made an excellent meal.'

'Why, to be sure, the only way to preserve health, is to eat plain food,' says the Scotchman; 'and the only way to destroy it, is to cram in such mixtures as you do in England, since French Cooks have been in vogue.'

CHAPTER XVII

Rules for Health

THE little Rector observed, 'they had had a long dissertation upon the subject; and, doubtless, a good state of health was an inestimable blessing, as it was the foundation of all other enjoyments. But,' continues he, 'too great a solicitude on that account is not only unworthy a man of sense and a good Christian, but is really destructive of what we are so anxious to preserve. I know, with regard to myself,' says he, 'that, having gone through a course of Anatomy in the University, and observed how fearfully and wonderfully we are made, and having dabbled a little in books of Physic, I brought myself, by my whims and apprehensions, and by tampering with my own constitution, into a very bad state of health. I have read a treatise upon sleep, that has kept me awake all night; and I studied Dr. Cheyne upon *Health* and *Long Life*, till I brought myself to the brink of *Death*.'[1]

'Why,' says Wildgoose, 'I have heard of a young man at Oxford, who, going through a course of Anatomy, and hearing the Doctor expatiate upon the beautiful contrivance of Nature in guarding the *Ductus Thoracicus* (or the tube that conveys the whole chyle of the body into the arteries), by the ribs on one side, and the backbone on the other, and being told that the least touch almost on that part would be immediate death; the young fellow was met, the next day, leaning forwards, with one hand held up to guard his breast, or thorax; and the other stretched out, and desiring every one he saw to stand off; "for, (says he) if you do but touch my *Ductus Thoracicus*, I am a dead man." '

'Yes,' says Slicer; 'and I have heard an addition to that story, which, I suppose, you do not care to mention.—Sir John Shadwell, Physician to George the First, was telling this very story at court to Lady D——, who laughed heartily at it; and, meeting the Doctor the next day, she put herself in the same attitude, and desired him to stand off; "for, (says she) if you do but touch my— *what do you call it?*—I am a dead woman." '

'Well,' says the little Rector, 'it is certainly better to be really ill sometimes, than to be so hippish, and perpetually anxious about one's health. A friend of mine, a jolly fellow, finding me in my room with Cheyne's book upon Health and Long Life before me, threw it into the fire; partly to cure me of my whims, and partly, I believe, for the sake of a distich, which he pretended to repeat extempore:

> I'd scorn the health, such rigid rules must give;
> Nor sacrifice the ends of life, to live.'

As this conversation seemed obliquely to glance at Mr. Slicer, Selkirk said, by way of countenancing his friend, 'Why, to be sure, my countryman might carry the matter too far; yet, I think, no man can be too careful of his health, nor be blamed for studying the rules which have been laid down by Physicians for that purpose.'—'Why,' says Wildgoose, 'as most diseases incident to the human body are generally allowed to proceed from indolence and repletion, I should think there can no rules be wanting, to preserve, or even to restore it, but exercise and temperance; and, in many cases, even *fasting*, or an entire abstinence from all kinds of food; this, at least, if made use of at the beginning of a disease, I have always found sufficient to check its progress, or put a stop to most complaints.'

'As you all seem to be proposing compendious rules or laconic precepts for health,' says the little Rector, 'I think, there can be none better, or more comprehensive, than those which Dr. Scarborough, Physician to Charles II. gave to the Dutchess of Portsmouth; "Madam, (says he) you must either eat less, or use more exercise, or take physic, or—be sick."''

CHAPTER XVIII

A new System of Education

MR. SLICER now (by way of shifting the conversation) asked Selkirk, 'how his Pupil went on?' which was Slicer's little Cousin Johnny, and who was in the room, with his black string, and blue silk waistcoat.

Mr. Selkirk (as we have already observed) was the School-master of the village. He had formerly been a travelling Scotchman; but, marrying a Farmer's daughter with four or five hundred pounds, had opened a shop, and set up a little school, and professed to teach, not only Reading, Writing, and Accompts, but Latin and Greek, Algebra, Logarithms, and Trigonometry, and all the most abstruse parts of the Mathematics. He had really had the rudiments of a learned education, and was intended for the University and some learned profession; but, being of a rambling disposition (like many of his ingenious countrymen), chose to travel southwards, and carry a pack for his amusement; as he would sometimes humorously confess.

Mr. Slicer then informed the company of Selkirk's excellent plan of education; 'that, instead of the rigid severity of the usual method in our public schools, he taught his boys all the rudiments of the Latin tongue, amidst their childish sports, by way of diversion.'—'What! in Locke's method, I suppose?' says Wildgoose.—'What! *Johnny Loke?*—No,' says Selkirk, 'I hope I have improved upon *Johnny Loke*, and Milton too.'—'In what manner, Sir?' says Wildgoose.—'Here, *Jockey!*' replies Selkirk: 'let the Gentleman *see* you decline the pronoun article, *hic, hæc, hoc.*'—Master Jacky immediately began hopping round the room, repeating, *hic, hæc, hoc*; Gen. *hujus*; Dat. *huic*; Acc. *hunc, hanc, hoc*; Voc. caret; Abl. *hoc, hâc, hoc*, &c.

'There, now,' says Selkirk, 'in this manner I teach them the whole Grammar. I make eight boys represent the eight parts of Speech. The Noun Substantive stands by himself; the Adjective has another boy to support him; the Nominative case carries a little wand before the Verb; the Accusative case walks after, and supports his train: I let the four conjugations make a party at Whist, and the three concords dance the Hay together, and so on.'

The company laughed at Selkirk's project; but the little fat Doctor, who had been bred at a public school, observed, 'that it was very pretty in theory (and so was Milton's and Locke's method), and might please fond mothers; but, he imagined, the great men in Queen Elizabeth's time had studied this affair more deeply than has been ever done since; yet they thought some *coercive* power in the Teacher was very necessary; and, if boys were suffered to lay by the pursuit of dead languages as soon as it ceased to be *agreeable* to them, he was of opinion they would make but a very slender progress in Greek and Latin.'

Instead of continuing the dispute, Mr. Slicer observed, 'that Mr. Selkirk, though a Scotchman, taught the true pronunciation of the English language much better than the generality of school-masters;' and, as a proof of his assertion, took up a Common Prayer book, that lay in the parlour-window, and made little Johnny give a specimen of his abilities in that respect.—'Mamma,' says Jacky, 'I am to have a new hat, next Sunday.'—'Yes, my Jacky; mind your book, and you shall.'

Jacky then, by Selkirk's direction, began to read, with an audible voice, the exhortation in the Morning Service, where the words *humble* and *acknowledge* come two or three times over. He pro-nounced the *h* in *humble* very strong; and *ac-know-ledge* as it is written. 'There, Doctor,' says Mr. Slicer, 'you Gentlemen of the Clergy never read that right. You leave out the asper in *humble*; and pronounce *knowledge* as if it were written *knolledge*; which is absurd.'

'Why,' says the Doctor, 'as languages were not originally formed by a Committee of Philosophers, but arrived gradually at per-fection, and were established by *custom*, I think *custom* ought to regulate the pronunciation;[1] and I cannot but think it a good rule in this case, as well as the rest of our conversation, to think with the wise, but to talk and pronounce with the vulgar. The rules of Grammar cannot, in any language, be reduced to a strict analogy; but all general rules have some exceptions.' 'True, Sir,' (says Selkirk) 'but we ought to come as near to perfection in every thing as possible.'—'According to that rule,' says the Doctor, 'why do not you pronounce the *h* in *honest* and *honour?*[2] why do not you pronounce the word people, *pe-ople*, as it is written? and why does not every body say, *bu-rial*, as my Clerk and the Grave-diggers in Hamlet do? In short,' says the Doctor, 'there is something so dis-agreeable to me in pronouncing the word *humble* with an aspirate, that I could as soon chew tobacco (which I mortally hate) as bring myself to pronounce it so.'

CHAPTER XIX

Account of the little fat Rector

THE company smiled at the little Rector's delicacy on that point; and Mr. Slicer said, 'that, to be sure, there was some truth in what Mr. *Griskin* observed.'—Upon hearing the little Doctor called Griskin (for the first time), Wildgoose looked at him with some attention; and enquired, 'whether he had not a near relation, one Mr. Rivers, near Bath, in Somersetshire?' After a few questions, Wildgoose was soon convinced, that this was no other than Mr. Gregory Griskin (whom he had so often heard of), kinsman to the Mr. Rivers, whose adventures were related in the former part of this history.

Mr. Griskin lamented, 'the disappointment he had met with in Rivers's imprudent match; that he had flattered himself with the hopes of his Nephew's making some figure in life, and even distinguishing himself in the learned world; and had intended to have done something handsome for him at his death;' and the like.

Wildgoose began to make some excuse for his friend's imprudent conduct, by encomiums on Mrs. Rivers's personal accomplishments and behaviour: to which Griskin (looking down with a reserved air) made no reply.

When Mr. Griskin found, however, (by several circumstances) that Wildgoose had been intimate with his Nephew in the University; and also that he had only come accidentally to Mr. Slicer's house for refreshment on his journey; he said, 'he should be glad to have more conversation with him upon the subject;' and invited him, 'to go and drink coffee at his house, and even to take a bed there, if consistent with his engagements.'

As Wildgoose was in hopes of doing his old friend Rivers some service, and also knew the little Doctor to be piously disposed, he accepted of his invitation, having first provided for the reception also of his fellow-traveller; and, taking leave of his benevolent host Mr. Slicer and his company, went to the Rectory with Mr. Griskin.

The Parsonage-house was a modern building, and neatly furnished; and the gardens (instead of being laid out, in the present taste, with sunburnt lawns and barren shrubs) were comfortably inclosed with fruit-walls, filberd-hedges, and codlin trees; with a good pigeon-house, poultry-yard, and fish-ponds; and, in short, with every thing that could contribute to the comfort and convenience of this life.

Griskin was a man of the old-fashioned piety, that shewed his Faith by his Good Works. He gave much in charity, prayed often, and fasted now and then. Having the tithes in his own hands, it enabled him to keep a plentiful table, to which every sober honest man was welcome. He every Sunday invited by turns some of his Parishioners to dine with him; one or two of the most substantial in the parlour, and as many of the oldest and poorest in the kitchen. This made them pay their tithes and dues chearfully; which Griskin exacted of them punctually, but not with *rigour*. If a Farmer had any loss, or remarkably bad year, he made him some little allowance; and, if a Cottager paid him a groat at Easter, which he could ill spare, perhaps he would give his family a six-penny loaf the Sunday following. By this means he kept up his dignity, and secured his right and the love of his parish at the same time.

CHAPTER XX

Further Account of the little fat Rector

WHEN Mr. Griskin was alone with Wildgoose, he told him, 'that he should not have been so much displeased with his Nephew Rivers, for pleasing himself in marrying, if he had stayed till he had finished his studies, and had married a prudent woman: but that he found his wife was a proud minx, who regarded nothing but dressing, visiting, and going to the public rooms and balls at Bath; and that, by what he had heard of her extravagance, his Nephew would soon be in a gaol.'

Wildgoose was very much surprized at this complaint of Mr. Griskin; and said, 'he would venture to assure him, he had been misinformed with regard to Mrs. Rivers's character and turn of mind; for, from what he himself had seen of her, he was certain, the very contrary was the truth of the case, and that she had not the least taste for that sort of gaieties; and, from the unreserved friendship which had subsisted between himself and Mr. Rivers, he could depend upon the account he had given him of Mrs. Rivers's conduct, and their retired way of life; especially as he had given him that account, as a matter of course, to satisfy his friend's curiosity, when there was not the least probability that he could ever have the present opportunity of doing that justice to their character which he now was favoured with.'

Mr. Griskin replied, 'that he had very good authority for what he had asserted;' which Wildgoose found was that of a splenetic old Dowager, who went sometimes to Bath, and who had seen Mrs. Rivers at the only ball she had appeared at, when they first went into the country; and that she had picked up two or three malicious gossiping stories, with which Bath as much abounds as any country-town in the three kingdoms.

Wildgoose then proceeded to describe the amiable qualities of Mrs. Rivers, and the manner in which she seemed to pass her time, in the care of her children and family; which, though it did not immediately convince, yet it gave great satisfaction to Mr. Griskin; and he seemed to wish it might be true.

The conversation then took a different turn; and Mr. Griskin (as his Nephew had informed Wildgoose) being very piously disposed, Wildgoose made no scruple of letting him into the secret of his present undertaking; and they soon fell upon the subject of Religion. Their sentiments did not correspond, indeed, with regard to some speculative points; but Griskin was much pleased with Wildgoose's zeal for the conversion of Sinners. He lamented the great decay of Christian piety; and informed Wildgoose of the methods he himself had taken to revive it in his own parish, 'by reading prayers publicly every Wednesday and Friday, and privately every morning and evening in his own family.'

He told him likewise, 'that, having a public-house belonging to him in Litchfield, in order to sanctify in some measure the unrighteous mammon, he had endowed a little charity-school with the annual rents of it.'

Though Wildgoose had rather a contempt of these formal devotions and good works, he was too polite to shock his kind Host with any reflection of that kind; and, in short, by his simplicity and sincerity, he gained so much upon the good opinion of Mr. Griskin, that he insisted upon keeping him and his fellow-traveller all night: and, the next morning, before they parted, he gave

Wildgoose a commission to write to his old friend Rivers, 'that a visit from him and Mrs. Rivers would be no ways disagreeable to their relation Mr. Griskin.' This commission Wildgoose executed immediately; and it was attended with the desired effects on both sides.

Wildgoose now took his leave of Mr. Griskin, being rejoined by his friend Tugwell, who had spent the evening as much to his satisfaction in the kitchen, as his Master had done in the parlour.

CHAPTER XXI

Set out for Ashbourn, near the Peak

WHEN the two friends were now alone in the Litchfield road again, Tugwell began to express his approbation of 'the hospitable way of life which Mr. Griskin lived in; and that he thought him a true Christian; and that, if any body went to Heaven, Mr. Griskin certainly would.'

Wildgoose, without mentioning Mr. Griskin's name, endeavoured to regulate Jerry's opinions by his own standard; and said, 'a man might fast and pray, and give all his goods to feed the poor; and yet not have true Christian *charity*, or what Saint Paul calls Faith working by Love.'—Tugwell clinched his observation, by echoing back some of his own expressions; yet still remained a convert in his heart to Griskin's more comfortable system of Christianity.

Having made an hearty breakfast at Mr. Griskin's, our travellers stayed no longer in Litchfield, than whilst Wildgoose found out the post-office, and put in his letter to his friend Rivers; and then trudged on, with great alacrity, without halting, till they came to Uttoxeter, in their way to Ashbourn, the first town of any note in Derbyshire.

There was a nearer way through the Forest of Nedwood, but more difficult to find; and Tugwell could not yet separate the ideas of Robbers, Outlaws, and Wild-beasts, from that of a Forest; notwithstanding his Master assured him, 'there were no Wild-beasts to be found, except herds of Deer, in any of our Royal Forests; nor so many Robbers as there were upon the great roads, or in the streets of London.'

They kept the great road, however, and, without any damage to their persons or property, and without any adventure worth recording, arrived at Ashbourn-in-the-Peak, as it is usually called, about six o'clock in the evening.

BOOK X

CHAPTER I

A Phænomenon

THE town of Ashbourn, being a great thorough-fare to Buxton Wells, to the High-peak, and many parts of the North; and being inhabited by many substantial people, concerned in the mines; and having also three or four of the greatest horse-fairs in that part of England, every year, is a very populous town.

There had appeared at Ashbourn, for some market-days past, a very extraordinary person; in a character, and with an equipage, somewhat singular and paradoxical: this was one Dr. Stubbs, a *Physician* of the itinerant kind. The Doctor came to town on horseback; yet drest in a plaid night-gown and red velvet cap. He had a small reading-desk fixed upon the pummel of his saddle, that supported a large folio; in which, by the help of a monstrous pair of spectacles, the Doctor seemed to read (as the horse moved slowly on) with a profound attention. A portmanteau behind him contained his cargo of sovereign medicines; which, as brick-dust was probably the principal ingredient, must be no small burthen to his lean steed.

The Squire, or Assistant, led the Doctor's horse slowly along, in a dress less solemn, but not less remarkable, than that of his Master.

The Doctor, from his Rosinante,[1] attended by his Merry Andrew (mounted on an horse-block before the principal Inn) had just begun to harangue the multitude, when Mr. Wildgoose and his fellow-traveller arrived; and the speech with which he introduced himself each market-day was to this effect—

CHAPTER II

A modest Plea

'My friends and countrymen! you have frequently been imposed upon (no doubt) by Quacks and ignorant pretenders to the noble art of Physic: who, in order to gain your attention, have boasted of their many years travels into foreign parts, and even the most remote regions of the habitable globe. One has been Physician to the Sophi of Persia, to the Great Mogul, or the Empress of Russia; and displayed his skill at Moscow, Constantinople, Delhi, or Ispahan. Another perhaps has been Tooth-drawer to the King of Morocco, or Corn-cutter to the Sultan of Egypt, or to the Grand Turk; or has administered a clyster to the Queen of Trebasond, or to Prester John, or the Lord knows who—as if the wandering about from place to place (supposing it to be true) could make a man a jot the wiser. No, Gentlemen, don't be imposed upon by pompous words and magnificent pretensions. He that goes abroad a fool, will come home a coxcomb.

'Gentlemen! I am no High-German or unborn Doctor—But here I am—your own countryman—your fellow-subject—your neighbour—as I may say.—Why, Gentlemen, (eminent as I am now become,) I was born but at Coventry, where my mother now lives—Mary Stubbs by name.

'One thing indeed I *must* boast of; without which I would not presume to practise the sublime art and mystery of Physic. I am the *seventh son* of a *seventh son*. *Seven* days was I before I sucked the breast. *Seven* months before I was seen to laugh or cry. *Seven* years before I was heard to utter *seven* words; and twice *seven* years have I studied, night and day, for the benefit of you, my friends and countrymen. And now here I am—ready to assist the afflicted, and to cure all manner of diseases, past, present, and to come; and that out of *pure love* to my country and fellow-creatures, without fee or reward—except a trifling gratuity, the prime cost of my medicines; or what you may chuse voluntarily to contribute here-after, out of gratitude for the great benefit, which, I am convinced, you will receive from the use of them.

'But come, Gentlemen, here is my famous *Anti-febri-fuge*[1] Tincture; that cures all internal disorders whatsoever; the whole bottle for one poor shilling.

B b

'Here's my *Cataplasma Diabolicum*, or my Diabolical Cataplasm; that will cure all external disorders, cuts, bruises, contusions, excoriations, and dislocations; and all for sixpence.

'But here, Gentlemen, here's my famous *Balsamum Stubbianum*, or Dr. Stubbs's Sovereign Balsam; renowned over the whole Christian world, as an universal remedy, which no family ought to be without: it will keep seven years, and—be as good as it is now. Here's this large bottle, Gentlemen, for the trifling sum of eighteen-pence.

'I am aware, that your Physical gentlemen here have called me Quack, and ignorant Pretender, and the like. But here I am.—Let Dr. Pestle or Dr. Clyster come forth. I challenge the whole faculty of the town of Ashbourn, to appear before this good company; and dispute with me in *seven* languages, ancient or modern: in Latin, Greek, or Hebrew—in High-Dutch, French, Italian, or Portuguese—Let them ask me any question in Hebrew or Arabic; and then it will appear, who are men of solid learning, and who are Quacks and ignorant pretenders.

'You see, Gentlemen, I challenge them to a fair trial of skill; but not one of them dares shew his face: they confess their ignorance, by their silence.

'But come, Gentlemen: who buys my *Elixir Cephalicum, Asthmaticum, Arthriticum, Diureticum, Emeticum, Diaphoreticum, Nephriticum, Catharticum.*—Come, Gentlemen, seize the golden opportunity, whilst health is so cheaply to be purchased!'

CHAPTER III

The Generosity of a Quack

AFTER having disposed of a few packets, the Doctor told the company, 'that, as this was the last time of his appearing at Ashbourn (other parts of the kingdom claiming a part in his patriotic labours), he was determined to make a present, to all those who had been his patients, of a shilling a-piece. He therefore called upon all those who could produce any one of Dr. Stubbs's bottles, pill-boxes, plaisters, or even his hand-bills, to make their appearance, and partake of his generosity.'

This produced no small degree of expectation amongst those that had been the Doctor's customers, who gathered round him, with their hands stretched out, and with wishful looks. 'Here, Gentlemen!' says the Doctor. 'Stand forth! hold up your hands. I promised to give you a shilling a-piece. I will immediately perform my promise. Here's my *Balsamum Stubbianum*; which I have hitherto sold at *eighteen-pence* the bottle. You shall now have it for *six-pence*.'

'Come! *Gemmen*;' (says the Merry Andrew) 'where are you? Be quick! Don't stand in your own light. You'll never have such another opportunity—as long as you live.'

The people looked upon each other with an air of disappointment. Some shook their heads, some grinned at the conceit, and others uttered their execrations—some few, however, who had been unwilling to throw away *eighteen-pence* upon the experiment, ventured to give a single *six-pence*; and the Doctor picked up eight or nine shillings more by this stratagem, which was more than the intrinsic value of his horse-load of Medicines. He then took his leave; and was retiring to his inn, to enjoy the fruits of his public-spirited labours; when Wildgoose, seeing an audience ready to his hands, immediately mounted the horse-block, which the Merry Andrew had quitted; and, in order to draw their attention, bid Tugwell give out the hundredth Psalm. Many of the people were greatly surprized; but, two or three itinerant Preachers having of late passed through the town, some of the company understood the signal, and even joined the two Pilgrims in their oddly-timed melody.

CHAPTER IV

Ecce autem alterum!

AFTER singing a couple of stanzas, Wildgoose began his address to the mob, by observing 'how anxious they were about the health of their *bodies*; when they could listen with patience to every itinerant pretender to the art of Physic; who, without any previous instruction or experience, boasted of that complete knowledge of diseases, which Physicians of a regular education (after many years study) find it so difficult to obtain; and, without any regard to different cases or constitutions, often sell the same remedies for contradictory complaints.'

Wildgoose then (by an easy transition) proceeded to direct them to the true Physician of their *souls*: and recommended *Faith alone*, as the infallible catholicon for all their maladies.

'Yes, yes,' cries Tugwell; 'here is the true spiritual Mountebank, Gentlemen: here is the Quack Doctor of your souls.'

'Yes,' says the Merry-Andrew, 'and thou art the true spiritual Tom Fool.'

Doctor Stubbs himself also (having stopped on his horse at the gate-way of the Inn, to hear and see the event of Wildgoose's mounting the rostrum), observing the obvious parallel between Wildgoose's irregular practice in the Theological way, and that of a Mountebank in the Medical, could not forbear appealing to the mob; 'whether an itinerant Preacher (such as these Methodists) were not more of the Quack than he was, who pretended to have discovered a more compendious way to Heaven; and to prescribe *Faith* alone, as the universal cure for all diseases. Let the Parson keep to his church; the Farmer to his plough; and the Cobler to his stall'—says the Doctor.

Tugwell, thinking the Doctor had discovered something of their profession, now took up the cudgel; and said, 'he was no Cobler; but *made* shoes, as well as *mended* them: that his Master was no *Farmer*; but as good a Gentleman as the Doctor, for all his red cap! and kept as good an horse, if he had a mind to make use of him.'

The Merry Andrew, hearing his Master treated with such familiarity by a fellow of Tugwell's mean appearance, laid hold on his wallet, which hung over his shoulder, and almost pulled him backwards; telling him, at the same time, 'that he supposed it was filled with old shoes.' Tugwell, who was afraid of nothing (but ghosts and fire-arms), began to retort upon Pill-garlic with the arm of flesh; but he, having more wit and agility than courage, gave Jerry a swinging blow on the face with his sword of lath; and then made his escape amongst the croud. This raised Tugwell's choler, together with a loud laugh and hubbub; and, the mob being by this time pretty well tired, the assembly was soon dissolved: each party, the Doctor with his Merry Andrew, and Mr. Wildgoose with Tugwell, retiring to their respective apartments, in the same hotel.

CHAPTER V

An affecting Scene. Tugwell in Jeopardy

MR. WILDGOOSE, before he went to rest, having made proper enquiries which was the most unfrequented part of the Peak, yet abounded with the greatest number of mines, arose pretty early; and having, at Tugwell's request, taken a slight breakfast, he was preparing to sally forth; when a woman, who (as she returned from the Doctor) had heard Wildgoose hold forth the preceding night, came and intreated him 'to go and pray with her husband; who (she said) had been in a languishing condition for some time, and was now (she feared) near his end.'

Wildgoose was pleased with the opportunity of doing a charitable action, as well as with the compliment paid to his eloquence and his piety. He therefore immediately complied with the woman's request.

When he came, he saw a very affecting, though, at the same time, a somewhat ridiculous scene. The poor man had one son, who was a great *schollard*; that is, he could read without spelling: and, by way of comforting his father, the young man had got an old folio Common Prayer book; and was reading the *act of uniformity* to the sick man, with a very *audible* voice: to which the poor man listened with great attention; and said, 'it was very comfortable doctrine.' Wildgoose asked him (as he seemed so well disposed) 'why he had not sent for the Minister of his parish?' The sick man said, 'he had done so, when he was first taken ill; but that the Minister had given him no comfort; for,' the poor man confessed, 'he had lived a very wicked life, and had gained a livelihood by very dishonest means; and had it not in his power, if he were inclined to do it, to make restitution, as the Minister would have him do.' Wildgoose bid him, 'not despair; for that he and all mankind were equally sinners; and that he had nothing to do but to lay *hold* upon Christ by faith; and all would be well.' The poor man *said*, 'he did so, and trusted only to *his* mercy.' Wildgoose then assured him, 'his sins were forgiven;' and they parted entirely satisfied with each other.

When Wildgoose returned to the inn, he found, to his great surprize, his friend Tugwell taken into custody by a Constable; who was hurrying him away before a Justice of the Quorum, that lived very near the town; for Jerry, though far advanced in life, had had but little experience of the ways of men. Being therefore in his political principles (as we have already observed) rather attached to the Stuart family; and the town of Ashbourn, since the late march of the Rebels through that place, being divided into two parties (who persecuted each other with great violence); Tugwell, it seems, had somewhat imprudently taken the part of an honest Barber; who, as he was drinking his morning cup in the kitchen, had fallen into a dispute, about the Rebellion, with a dissenting Baker, who was very zealous for the Government, and, upon Jerry's interfering, had charged the Constable with him, as a disaffected subject.[1]

Upon Mr. Wildgoose's interposing in his friend's behalf; Doctor Stubbs (who had joined the crowd assembled in the gateway of the inn) whispered the Constable, 'that, to his knowledge, Wildgoose was a Jesuit in disguise; that he had seen him in York gaol, during the Rebellion; that he had let his hair grow, to conceal the clerical tonsure; and that several Jesuits had of late appeared, in the character of Methodist Preachers, in several parts of the kingdom.' The Constable, therefore, charged some of the company, in the King's name, to assist him in carrying them both before a Magistrate; and the Doctor pretended to follow them, and make good his allegations.

CHAPTER VI

A judicious Magistrate

WHEN they came before the Justice, all that could be proved against Tugwell was, that he *seemed* to *favour* the rebels; that he said, 'he loved to read about battles and massacres; and that he should have been very *glad* to have seen the young Pretender.' The Justice (who was a sensible man, and endeavoured, as much as possible, to restore and preserve the peace amongst his neighbours) observed, if that were all, he could find nothing treasonable in what the prisoner had said; especially as he spoke of the *Pretender* as such, and not as having the least shadow of right to the crown of England. In short, it appeared to him, that all he had said, seemed to proceed from *curiosity*, rather than from *disloyalty* to King George.'

The Justice then asked, 'what they had to say against the other prisoner, Mr. Geoffry Wildgoose by name?' The Constable said, 'there was a Gentleman present, who knew him to be a Jesuit, and had seen him in York gaol during the Rebellion; and would take his oath of it.' Doctor Stubbs was then called upon, to make good his charge. But the Doctor, who only owed Wildgoose a grudge for speaking disrespectfully of his profession, and was conscious all he had said was an impudent lye, had given them the slip; and had taken this opportunity of marching out of town, without being pelted by the mob as he richly deserved.

An old man, however, whose wife was a favourer of the Methodists, said, 'such fellows as Wildgoose and his companion ought to be punished, for making a disturbance, and hindering people from their work; that they had *converted* his wife in particular, who used to mind her knitting, and bustle about, and *scold* at him all the day long. But, since these Methodists had come about, and *converted* her, she minded nothing but reading and praying, and singing Psalms, from morning to night.' The good Justice said, 'if the *convarting* his wife was all the mischief they had done, he wished they would *convart* all the *scolds* in the parish.' And so, after asking Wildgoose a few questions, he ordered the Constable to release them, and dismissed the company from his presence.

The Jacobite Barber, whose cause (as we observed) Tugwell had espoused, as soon as his Worship was out of sight, clapped Jerry on the shoulder, by way of triumph; and said, 'as he himself was acquainted with the Butler; and Tugwell, he found, was a curious man; he would shew him a curiosity.—The *Prince* is in this house now,' (says he, whispering in Tugwell's ear). Jerry starting with surprize, the Barber got his friend the Butler to take him up the back stairs, into a long gallery, which led to the principal bed-chambers; on the doors of which had been written by the Quartermaster with chalk (and afterwards traced over with whitelead by way of curiosity) the names of *the Prince*, Lord Ogilvy, Pitsligo, and other Rebel-chiefs; who, in their way to Derby, having halted one night in Ashbourn, had been quartered in this Gentleman's house.

Tugwell expressed great surprize at seeing the very place where so renowned a personage had lately lodged; whose name he had often heard read in the Gloucester Journal; which Mrs. Wildgoose had lent the Vicar, the Vicar had smuggled to his Clerk, who had frequently retailed it to the whole parish, under the great elm, at Tugwell's cottage-gate.

Wildgoose returning to the inn before his fellow-traveller, and finding a number of people, who had been assembled on the report of Tugwell's being taken into custody, still loitering about, took the opportunity of mounting the *suggestum* or horse-block once more, though without much effect; people's passions being rather calm in a morning, and not so well disposed to catch the fire of enthusiasm in open day-light, as amidst the dazzling lustre of sconces and chandeliers at the evening tabernacle. Some of those who had taken a cup in the morning were a little riotous; some few, however, seemed affected, and consulted with Wildgoose what further was to be done towards their conversion; and also informed him, which were the most uncultivated parts of the Peak, and stood most in need of the labours of his mission.

CHAPTER VII

They set forth towards the High-Peak

OUR Spiritual Quixote was now impatient to sally forth, in quest of more spiritual adventures. But Tugwell, hearing so romantic an account of the mountainous country they were going to traverse, intreated his Master not to do any thing rashly, nor set out upon an empty stomach; and, it being now past the middle of the day, they made a pretty hearty meal upon some cold mutton-pye; a good segment of which, for fear of accidents, Jerry stowed in his wallet: and about three o'clock they set out on the Buxton road for the High-Peak.

After travelling about an hour and a half, our two Pilgrims imagined they had climbed to the summit of the mountains: but they still found 'Alps on Alps arise!'[1] At length, however, they came upon an extensive plain, to the extremity of which their sight could not reach. Jerry, after reading so many books of travels, and having been near two months on foot, now lifting up his hands with astonishment, cried out, 'he did not think the world had been half so wide.'

As the sun had now journeyed far towards the west; and they

could see neither village, hut, nor even a single tree to shelter them from the dews of the night; Jerry's heart began to fail him: and he could not forbear again to wish himself at home with Dorothy, in his own chimney-corner; or at least at the inn at Ashbourn, which they had quitted so late in the day.

As the road led them by degrees towards the extremity of the moor; they heard, at a distance on the left hand, the sound of a French-horn; which a little revived Tugwell's spirits, though it revived at the same time the jeopardy he had been in amongst the stag-hunters, as related in the beginning of this history.

Jerry, however, intreated his Master (as the evening was coming on) 'to turn aside, and try whether they could find any place to lodge at; especially as there was nothing to preach to, but a few sheep and some black cattle, which were feeding amongst the rocks.'

Though Wildgoose was unwilling to listen to any overtures of indulgence, he thought it prudent enough to comply with his friend's proposal. Proceeding, therefore, towards the edge of the plain, they came to a precipice of an astonishing height; from which was a stupendous view into a deep valley; the hill rising on the opposite side, covered with woods, near half a mile perpendicularly. The river Dove ran winding at the bottom, amidst pyramidical rocks, that rise detached from the hill, with shrubs growing from their tops, and the roots hanging down in a grotesque manner. In some places, they almost meet, and intercept the view; in others they open, and discover rocks beyond rocks, in long perspective up the valley, in a most beautiful profusion.

CHAPTER VIII

Fall in with a musical Party

THE French-horns, which were blown by two servants, placed in the opposite woods, now ceased; and upon their approaching, out of curiosity, to the edge of the precipice, the two Pilgrims were surprized to hear (seemingly about half way down the hill) an angelic voice, accompanied by two German-flutes, singing a song from the Masque of Comus:

On ev'ry hill, in ev'ry grove,
   Along the margin of each stream;
Dear, conscious scenes of former love!
   I moan; and Damon is my theme.
The hills, the groves, the rocks remain;
   But Damon there I seek in vain.[1]

Wildgoose was filled with rapture at the sound: and, when the song was finished, could not forbear repeating to himself (yet loud enough for his fellow-traveller to hear) these beautiful lines from Shakespear, with whom (as we observed) he had formerly been conversant,

I thought that all things had been savage here——
——But, whate'er you are
That, in this desert inaccessible,
Lose and neglect the creeping hours of time;
If ever you have liv'd in better days;
If ever been where bells have knoll'd to Church—'[2]

'Ah!' says Tugwell, 'I wish I could hear our *Bells knoll to Church* this very moment: I would soon be at home again in my own stall. I am quite tired with this *vaggibond* life. But, come, Master, let us go and enquire our way to the next town, and not wander about this wilderness country all night.'

Jerry then looked about, and found a sheep-track, that led winding down the hill; but they were forced to descend above a quarter of a mile, before they could discover the place from whence the music proceeded; when they beheld a lofty arch, or natural cavity, in the side of the rocks, to which there was an artificial ascent by near an hundred steps, guarded by a slight rail: at the mouth of this grotto, there was a broad space, like a balcony; from which there appeared a genteel party of nine or ten people well-dressed; some with musical instruments; others with books in their hands; and one or two with bottles and glasses before them; amusing themselves as was most suitable to their several tastes and inclinations.

Upon Tugwell's appearing in sight, a servant came to him; and, in a surly tone, demanded, 'what he wanted there?'—Jerry answered, 'that they did not come to beg or to steal; that (he thanked God) his wallet was well stored, and his Master had money in his purse: but that they had lost their way upon the moors; and desired him to direct them to the nearest town, or place of entertainment for travellers.'

The servant asked him, 'who, and what the Devil, he and his Master were?'—'Why,' says he, 'my Master is a Gentleman of four or five hundred pounds a-year (but no matter for that); he is a good Christian, and travels about the country, to *convart* people from their wicked ways, and *sich* like.'

'Well,' says the servant, 'I can tell thee, for thy comfort, there is no town, nor hardly an house, within these five miles; except the village which we live at: but, if thou wilt stay till we go home (which will not be long), I will direct thee to a public-house, where there are good quarters and good liquor: and what would'st have more?'

When the servant had given Jerry his answer, and was returning, a young Lady (whose curiosity was very impetuous) ran down a few steps, to enquire what those men wanted; and, having satisfied herself, ran and told the company, 'that there were two droll *creachers*, who had lost their way; and one of them pretended to be a Gentleman of fortune; but (she supposed, by the servant's account) was a Methodist Preacher.'

This company consisted of Sir William and Lady Forester (who lived in the neighbourhood), and some friends that were with them in the house; who came to enjoy a fine evening in this romantic scene, which Sir William had a little decorated, as above described.

CHAPTER IX

Characters of Sir William and Lady Forester

SIR WILLIAM FORESTER[1] was a Gentleman of fine sense; and (what is not always a consequence) of fine taste, not only in the polite arts, Music, Painting, Architecture, and the like; but in life and manners. He had the art of making every company happy; and the greater art of making himself happy in every company. Some of his wise neighbours, indeed, were a little scandalized at his admitting people of inferior rank so frequently to his table: but Sir William (like Swift's Virtuoso, who could extract sun-beams from cucumbers)[2] had the skill of extracting entertainment from the most insipid companions; of discovering humour in the most

phlegmatic Divine; or solid sense in (the most trifling of all characters) a country Dancing-master.

Lady Forester was a woman of uncommon merit, considering
the peculiar circumstances attending her education. She was the
daughter of Lord ———, who was a profest Infidel, and absolutely
forbid those who were about his children to instill any religious
prejudices (as he called them) into their tender minds, by teaching
them their Catechism, or by suffering them to read any books on
religious subjects. Nay, he severely punished his favourite child,
of ten years old, for presuming to look into a Bible.

He was of Lord Shaftsbury's opinion, 'that there is no necessary
connexion between Religion and Virtue; and even that people may
be good moral men, and good members of society, without the
belief of a God.'[1] And he considered himself as an instance of his
assertions; as he lived a tolerably sober life, and performed several
generous and charitable actions, without the pretence of any religious motive; though it is well known that, for want of an uniform
principle, he was frequently guilty of the most flagrant instances of
vice and immorality.

Lady Forester's mother, however, (who was a very pious and a
very sensible woman) had taken care to instill some short principles
of Religion into her daughter; but, dying whilst Lady Forester was
very young, she underwent a tryal of a different kind from the
capricious indulgence of her father; who settled her, when she was
just sixteen, in a house in town, with an equipage and suitable
domestics and attendants, entirely at her own command. Her
Ladyship's good sense, however, supported her, without the least
censure, in this critical situation; and the utmost indiscretion,
which the severest critic could ever charge her with, was of a
romantic kind; the rambling once or twice into Hyde-park, at a
distance from her equipage and attendants; and reading under
a tree (accompanied only with a female friend) with all the security
of rural innocence.

Lady Forester was now, however, the mother of several children;
whom she bred up in the strictest principles of Religion and Virtue,
which will probably make them ornaments to the rising generation; though her Ladyship herself was a little inclined to the
mystic, or rather the seraphic, Theology; being a great admirer of
Fenelon's, Norris's, and other works of the same kind.[2]—But to
return to our Story.

CHAPTER X

Character of Colonel Rappee

MISS KITTY FORESTER (who, though much younger, was sister to Sir William, and the Lady whose voice they had heard), having made her report, 'that the travellers had lost their way;' the company voted, by way of fun, 'to send for them up to *Reynard's hall*;' which was the name given to this natural grotto, or cavity in the rock, where the company was sitting.

As Wildgoose, though in his travelling dishabille, had a gentleman-like appearance, he was desired to sit down amidst this *belle assemblée*; and Tugwell, with his wallet, was turned over to the care of the servants. After some little conversation with Wildgoose upon his journey, and the like, the company sate down to (what in romance would be called) a cold collation; which, in plain English, was a good quantity of cold ham and fowls, cold tongue, orange cheese-cakes, and other portable provisions of the best kinds.

Wildgoose, having made an hearty meal at Ashbourn, eat little; but drank two or three glasses of Rhenish wine. The evening was now extremely fine; the heat of the day being succeeded by an agreeable *fraicheur*: the parting sun gilded the summit of the mountains; and the river Dove ran murmuring at their base. The French-horns, at proper intervals, enlivened the scene; and, in short, by the politeness of Sir William and Lady Forester, Wildgoose found himself much at ease and very happy, notwithstanding the sneers and stifled titterings of some of the company.

Among the rest, there was a Colonel Rappee, an Officer in the Guards, who was upon a visit at Sir William Forester's. The Colonel had made a very *shining* figure in the army, during a thirty years peace; and had behaved with the greatest courage and magnanimity, in above twenty engagements and reviews—on Hounslow-heath, or Hyde-park.——But, at the battle of Preston-pans (in the year forty-five) he was one of those Gentlemen who retreated with so much precipitation, as to outride the Express, and bring to London the first news of their own defeat.[1]

The Colonel, however, appeared by no means deficient in personal valour; for, though he had never fought any duel in form, he had frequently given the look of defiance; and kicked two or three impertinent fellows, who were dismayed at the ferocity of his countenance and his military dress.

The Colonel's person, indeed, gave him the advantage over any common antagonist; and also recommended him to the notice of people of rank; for he was near six feet high. And,

> Tho' lambent dullness play'd about his head,[1]

he had an air of sagacity and importance, which commanded respect from the less discerning part of mankind; nay, and having 'a little kind of an odd sort of a small wit' (as Congreve says),[2] and uttering now and then a tolerable thing with a decisive air, he even passed for a man of sense; and, by a discreet management, was received upon a decent footing in many families of distinction.

Upon being much in company also, the Colonel had picked up a few common-place maxims and topics of ridicule, upon Matrimony, Religion, Scotch-men, Parsons, and Old Maids; which he applied indiscriminately upon all occasions: but frequently with so little propriety, as could not but shock the delicacy of Sir William and Lady Forester; who accordingly rather *endured*, than *enjoyed* his company, and considered his *visits*, or rather his *visitations*, as afflictions from Heaven, to which they were in duty obliged patiently to submit.

CHAPTER XI

A Conversation on Religion and other Subjects

THE Colonel then looked a little sour upon Mr. Wildgoose; and having too much pride, or rather too little penetration, to discover what was really valuable in his character, considered him as a common stroller; and was quite affronted at Sir William's presuming to introduce such company to a man of his consequence. He began, therefore, to say rude things upon Impostors and Hypocrites, and to give hints 'how much Sir William was the dupe of Parsons and Buffoons.'

Lady Forester, however, contrived to change the discourse, and to introduce some religious topic: upon which she gave Wildgoose an opportunity of displaying his knowledge of the subject in such a manner, that Rappee was afraid to interpose, for fear of discovering his own ignorance.

By way of venting his spleen, however, the Colonel began throwing out common-place invectives against Religion in general, and Christianity in particular, from the constant feuds and animosities it had accidentally occasioned amongst the different sects, and the like; and said, 'if people would but live according to Nature and Reason, it would be better if there were no such thing as Religion in the world.'

Sir William said, 'he was glad that was only Rappee's private opinion, unsupported by any reasons:' but begged the Colonel, 'if he had discovered any new arguments against Religion, which he thought of any force, he would keep them a secret from his wife, his children, and his servants; as he was convinced it was for the good of mankind, that they should not be undeceived in that particular, supposing Religion to be all a cheat or a political invention.

'But, Colonel,' (continues he) 'you are frequently uttering complaints of this kind; notwithstanding the King your Master is the Defender of the Faith; and Christianity is at present the Religion of your country, by Law established. If you find yourself aggrieved by it, why do not you, or some of your wise associates, draw up the heads of a bill, and join in a petition to the Parliament? And I will undertake to present it to the house, for the redress of those grievances which this oppressive institution has brought upon mankind.'

The Colonel saw the absurdity of his usual complaints against Religion, when set in so strong a light; and was struck silent for a few minutes. But soon rallying his spirits, he shifted the discourse in his turn; and (with a more placid air) contrived to bring another subject upon the carpet, and, at the same time, to display his own importance, by mentioning 'a magnificent entertainment, to which he had lately been invited by a noble Lord.'

Bob Tench, a sporting companion of Sir William's, and a near relation of the famous Will Wimble, who was waiting till the first sickle was put into the corn, in order to go a partridge-shooting— Bob said, 'he never desired to be entertained better than he was this morning at Sir Harry Hotspur's; where was a cold venison-pasty, and some excellent strong beer, which he was sorry to see banished, to make way for tea and chocolate, and other hot liquors, unknown to our sporting ancestors.'

The conversation now turned upon genteel or on magnificent entertainments in general, which any of the company had either been present at, or had read of in history.

Miss Forester said, 'she could never sufficiently admire Cleopatra's gallantry, in her entertainment of Mark Anthony; and was particularly pleased with her dissolving a pearl of immense value, and presenting it in a golden cup of rich wine.' Colonel Rappee ridiculed this, by mentioning some modern wh—re, who had been suffered by her fond keeper to swallow an hundred pound banknote, between two slices of bread and butter, at breakfast. Somebody mentioned the Roman Emperor (I think) who presented each of his guests with the gold cup, which they drank out of.

But Sir William Forester said, 'he never read of a more polite reception, than what Vokeèr, the rich Augsburgh Merchant, gave the Emperor Charles V. He had lent the Emperor a very considerable sum of money, for which his Majesty had given him a promissory note, or order upon his exchequer, or some written security of that kind. Soon after, the Emperor on his march (by way of doing honour to his friend) lay at his house in Augsburgh. The Merchant gave him a most magnificent supper; and, when the Emperor retired to his chamber, there was a fire laid of cinnamon wood; which Vokeèr himself set fire to, with the Emperor's note of hand, or order for the money; and then wished his Majesty a good night.'

'Well, Sir William, (says a young Templar, who was of the party[1]); you have told us how a subject entertained an Emperor of Germany: I will tell you an entertainment, or rather a family dinner, that was given by the Emperor of Morocco to an English subject, Dr. Shaw, who has lately published his travels into Africa and Egypt.[2]

'At the top, there was a dish of fish, consisting of a young whale boiled, and a few sturgeons and porpuses fryed round it. At the bottom, was the hind-quarter of an elephant. On one side, a brace of lions, fricasseed: on the other, the neck of a camel, made *kabab* (as the Doctor calls it), or, in plain English, *cabob'd*.

'The second course, a brace of ostriches roasted, at the upper end, with the ropes on a toast; at the lower end, a griffin: on one side, a dish of cranes and storks; on the other, a potted crocodile.

'There was no Butcher's meat, but a roasted buffalo at the side-table.

'The Doctor says, he only picked the short ribs of a lion; which (to use his own expression) was *a delicious morsel*.

'His Majesty asked the Doctor, whether he should help him to the *leg* or to the *wing* of the griffin? which being half bird and half beast, his Majesty thought facetious.

'You must observe, griffins are looked upon as great rarities, even in Africa.'

'I suppose,' says Sir William, 'this is some piece of humour upon the *marvellous* in the Doctor's Travels; though I have heard them spoken of as very learned, as well as entertaining; and that the Doctor has rectified several errors in the geography of the countries which he passed through.'

'I have heard' (says the young Templar), 'when the Doctor was introduced to the King, on his return from his travels, that he told his Majesty, amongst other things, he had really eat the short ribs of a lion, and that it was a *delicious morsel*.'

'Well,' (says Wildgoose, smiling, and looking round upon the prospect, and pointing to the French-horns, which were placed in the woods, at some distance from them,) 'I have no idea of a more agreeable entertainment, than that to which Sir William has done me the honour to admit me.'

The company having finished their collation, Miss Forester was desired to favour them with another song; which Sir William and the young Gentleman from the Temple again accompanied with their German-flutes. After which, the sun being now setting, the Ladies were taken up in a carriage, which came to the edge of the hill; and the Gentlemen walked to Sir William Forester's, which was not above a mile across the plain; only, the noble Colonel thought it beneath his dignity to march with the infantry: he had, therefore, ordered his servant to bring his horses; and, mounting his iron-grey, with his *demi-pique* and furniture, flanked the coach upon the *grand pàs*; and Wildgoose, with his fellow-traveller, (at Sir William's request) joined the cavalcade.

CHAPTER XII

A Scene in the Nursery

SIR WILLIAM had by this time fully discovered Mr. Wildgoose's intention of preaching to the subterraneous race of Lead-miners in the High-peak; and, as he was sensible, from their situation and constant employment, they could have but slender means of instruction, either in the principles of Religion or Morality, he by no means discouraged Wildgoose from pursuing so disinterested a project. He desired him, however, 'to halt a day or two at his house; and he would make some proper enquiries where his instructions might be applied to the best advantage.' He told Wildgoose, moreover, 'that Lady Forester was herself very religiously disposed, and would be pleased to have him talk to her children and her domestics upon that subject.'

When they came to Sir William's house, which was a venerable pile of Gothic building, fitted up in an elegant modern taste; Lady Forester, who paid great attention to Wildgoose, told him, 'she always went into the nursery as soon as she came home (especially in an evening), to visit her little folks, and hear them their prayers.' She likewise invited Wildgoose to attend her thither. At the nursery-door, Mrs. Molly, her Ladyship's maid, met her, with a little boy of about a year old in her arms, as the most agreeable service she could perform to her Lady; for he, being the least, and the most helpless, possessed of course the largest share in Lady Forester's affection. She clasped him in her arms, kissed him, and gave him her blessing; and then went round to three or four more, heard them their prayers, and made them ask a blessing; and then, wishing them a good night, returned to the company.

Wildgoose was struck with Lady Forester's affectionate care of her amiable progeny; which she observing, 'You see, Sir,' said she, 'where my treasure is, there will my heart be also. I am afraid, indeed,' continues her Ladyship, 'you will think these dear children engross too much of my affection. But, I assure you, Sir, they are the most infallible pledges of my devotion to Heaven. Their health is so dear to me, and I have so constant a sense of their depending for every pulse of life upon the good-will of Providence, that my whole life almost is one continued prayer for their preservation.'

Wildgoose answered, 'nothing could be more amiable than the

tenderness her Ladyship expressed for the welfare of her offspring. He only wished (in his way), that she did not love that little child in the Nurse's arms more than the *holy child* Jesus; through whose mediation alone' (says he) 'we are entitled to the favour and protection of Providence.'

CHAPTER XIII

Family Prayers; followed by Repartees

THEY now came into the great hall; and Wildgoose was not a little surprized to find the whole company (except the Colonel) assembled; and Sir William waiting for Lady Forester, with a large quarto Common Prayer book on the table, in order to read prayers to the family.

This would have appeared more extraordinary, if he had known that Sir William, before his marriage, had lived a remarkably gay life, and had even been tainted with many of the fashionable opinions of the age; but his regard for Lady Forester, and a sense of the importance of religious principles to every individual of society, had made Sir William so much a domestic man, as (even when in town) to read prayers every evening (unless any thing very extraordinary prevented it), and a sermon every Sunday night, to his family.

As soon as prayers were ended, Colonel Rappee again made his appearance; but was raillied by Miss Sainthill (a very sensible maiden Lady, a friend and companion of Lady Forester's), on 'his fondness for private meditation, and the care he took to avoid all appearance of hypocrisy.'—Rappee said, he knew no reason, why a man could not say his prayers as well in private as in public, in a walk upon the terrace as well as in a closet; that Religion was a mere personal affair, and the like.' He hinted, however, 'that he might have as much true devotion, as those who were always canting about Religion, and pretended to set up for Reformers.'

Miss Sainthill replied, 'that, to be sure, people might say their prayers in any place, or in any posture, and even in a warm bed; but she could not but think, there was a natural decency of behaviour due to the Supreme Being, as well as to our fellow-creatures; and she was afraid' (she said) 'those who deferred their prayers till they lay down upon their pillows (as she fancied the Colonel did), very frequently fell asleep without saying them at all.'

'Well,' says the Colonel, 'there is one part of my devotions, which I never forget; and that is, thanksgiving. I have always thanked God for three things.'—'Pray let me hear those curious particulars,' says Miss Sainthill. 'I suppose the first is, that you are not an old maid.'—'No,' says Rappee; 'The first is, that I was not born in Russia.'—'What! because you are afraid of the cold? I suppose!' says Miss Sainthill.—'No,' says the Colonel, 'because I am afraid of the knout, and do not like arbitrary Governments.'—'Well, and what is the second particular?'—'Why, that I was not bred a Cheese-monger.'—'What! because you do not love the smell of cheese?' says Miss Sainthill; 'but, for a like reason, you should not have been bred a Soldier,' continued she.—'Why so?' (says the Colonel.)—'Why, because you do not love the smell of gun-powder.'

Rappee bowed, and smiled; but said, 'he was most thankful for the third particular.'—'And, pray, what may that be?' says Miss Sainthill.—'Why, that I have not a very *long nose*,' cries the Colonel.

——Miss Sainthill courtesied, and took a long pinch of snuff, being conscious how liberal Nature had been to *her* in that respect; and being willing to give Rappee a short triumph, by inviting a laugh in his favour at her own expence; of which he was not a little conceited. Miss Sainthill, however, retorted, and said, 'a long nose would certainly be very inconvenient to the Colonel in the day of battle, especially if he should ever *face* the Highlanders again; as it would be more exposed to the stroke of a broad-sword.'—'Well fought, Miss Sainthill,' says Sir William. 'Colonel, leave off, whilst you are well. *Cedant arma togæ*: Let Heroes to the Gown give place.'

There was now a side-board laid, with some anchovies, olives, and a few trifling things, for those that chose to eat again, after their collation amongst the rocks in Dove-dale.

The company now appearing disposed to retire to their several apartments, candles were brought in by the Butler, attended by Mrs. Molly with a wax-light for her Lady. Molly was a very pretty girl; and had a pair of eyes most perniciously piercing, which she played off upon Mr. Wildgoose, as thinking him a guest not much above her own level. As the eyes are known to have a fascinating power, Wildgoose could hardly avoid returning Mrs. Molly's amorous glances; which was perceived by the jealous eyes of Mr. George, the Butler, who was her admirer.

Mr. George was ordered to wait on Mr. Wildgoose to his apartment; which office he performed with tolerable civility. But Mrs. Molly officiously enquiring, 'whether there was a bottle and bason carried into the Gentleman's room,' Mr. George (with a surly air) bid her, 'mind her own business.' He then proceeded with his charge up the grand stair-case, and wished him a good night.

CHAPTER XIV

A Morning Conversation on the Back Stairs

IT was now eight o'clock in the morning, when Betty, the housemaid, was sweeping the back-stairs; but suspended the motion of her brush, and leaned against the rails, to make way for Mrs. Molly, who now made her first appearance, with a ruffle half-hemmed in one hand, and a volume of Pamela in the other.

'So, Mrs. Molly, you were up late again last night, I suppose!'—'Yes, pretty late,' says Mrs. Molly.—'Ah! Mrs. Molly,' (cries Betty) '*I wou'dn't not* do it, no, not for the best Mistress that ever trod upon shoe-leather.'—'Why, Betty,' (replies she) 'to be sure, my Lady is a very good Lady; and we are so fond of each other's company, that we never know when to part. We were talking till after twelve o'clock about this strange Gentleman. To be sure, the Gentleman is very much of a Gentleman, for that matter, if he did not travel about on foot, like a Scotch Pedlar.'—'Why what trade is the Gentleman then?'—'What trade! you fool! Why, he is a Gentleman, I tell you; and has got a good estate of his own; but he is going to preach to the poor Miners in the High-Peak.'—'Why, I thought nobody could preach but Parsons,' quoth Betty.—'No more they could in former times,' says Mrs. Molly; but people are more *cute* and *cleverer* now-a-days, than they were formerly. Why there is our George, the Butler, can read a play, or a sermon, better than our Curate.'—'Oh,' says Betty, 'I thought you and George would have *fit* last night about this Gentleman.'—'George indeed!' (says Molly) 'a jealous-headed *cretur!* if *any body* does but speak to *a body*, *a body* must be called to an account by him, forsooth! What is the Gentleman to me? The Gentleman never spoke a word to me, nor I to him; only wished me a good night.'—'Well,' (says Betty) 'Mr. George swears he will be a match for him and the Cobler his fellow-traveller, if my Mistress keeps them here another night.'

Here the Lady's bell rang, and put a stop to the dialogue; and Mrs. Molly and Betty hastened to their several departments.

CHAPTER XV

On the Expediency of a regular Ordination

THOUGH Mr. Wildgoose had of late been very neligent of his person, yet, being now in a genteel family, by the time the bell rung for breakfast, he had got himself shaved, his hair rubbed up with pomatum, and had supplied himself with clean linen from Tugwell's wallet; so that, when he joined the company in the bow-window, he made no despicable appearance.

After the usual compliments of the morning, Lady Forester again introduced the subject of Wildgoose's preaching to the Miners; and said, 'his intention was certainly very laudable; but wondered, as she found he had had an University education, that he did not get into regular orders, before he engaged in an undertaking of that kind.'—'Yes,' says the Colonel; 'Don Quixote himself (mad as he was) would not enter the lists, nor undertake any atchievement of consequence, before he was dubbed a Knight: and, though I hate all preaching, I am for a proper subordination, and would have people keep to their *ranks* in life. A Commissary, or a Quarter-master, might as well pretend to rule an army, or to give the word of command in an engagement, as a Layman to interpose in the Parson's trade, and mount the rostrum.'—'Why,' says Wildgoose, 'if the Commanding Officers neglected their duty, it were better sure that a Quarter-master, or any body else, should give the word of command, than that a whole army should be cut to pieces.'

'I should think' (says Sir William, interposing) 'the cases are by

no means similar; for, though the life of a Christian be justly compared to that of a Soldier, yet, to make the cases parallel in the
present view, you must suppose that the Officers neglect their duty,
not merely in a single engagement, but during a whole campaign;
in which case, there would be room for complaint to be made to
the superior powers, and get them punished, or removed from their
commands. So, if a Clergyman is negligent of his duty, not in one
or two single instances, but in the general conduct of his life, the
Officers of a parish are bound, by oath, to present and make complaint of him to the Bishop of the diocese; but the Church-warden,
for that reason, has no *right*, suppose he had *abilities*, to exercise
the sacerdotal function, mount the pulpit, and harangue the people.
Such a conduct would necessarily be productive of disorder and
confusion.'

Wildgoose replied, 'that, in a political view, those regulations
might be of some consequence; and that (in general) he did not
think it right to break through the restraints of society; but
that, upon extraordinary occasions, those formalities were to be
dispensed with: and I cannot but think' (continues he) 'that
Providence approves of the proceeding of Mr. Wesley and Mr.
Whitfield, by the extraordinary success he has given to their
labours.'

'That is a very fallacious way of arguing' (cries the young
Templar), 'because Providence often brings about good ends by
very bad means.'

'Well,' says Sir William, 'if such irregular proceedings can be
proper upon any occasion, they are so in the present instance,
which Mr. Wildgoose has determined upon, that of preaching to
our poor Miners in the Peak, who are properly as sheep without a
shepherd.' Sir William then said, 'they intended, the next day, to
go upon a scheme of pleasure to Matlock, and to shew some young
people the wonders of the Peak (as they are called); and that, if he
chose it, Mr. Wildgoose might accompany them in their expedition.'—Wildgoose promised to attend them; but it proved otherwise in the event.

CHAPTER XVI

A Lecture in the Servants Hall

AFTER breakfast, the company began to separate, and amuse themselves as suited their inclinations. As Bob Tench and his party proposed to angle upon the river Dove, they asked Wildgoose to accompany them. But Lady Forester said, 'she would be glad of his company, to attend her and Miss Sainthill in their walk into the Park, after she had visited her young people in the nursery, and dispatched some domestic affairs which required her attendance.'

Whilst his Master was thus entertained in the parlour, Tugwell was entertaining the second-rate gentry in the servants hall. The Butler had given Jerry an horn of strong-beer with his breakfast, which opened his heart, and loosened his tongue. Jerry, therefore, diverted the company with the adventures they had met with in their travels; how well they had fared at Alderman Cullpepper's, Justice Aldworth's, and Parson Griskin's; and also what perils they had gone through, by land and by sea. He gave them likewise a sketch of his Master's private life; the credit he had lived in at home, and the converts he had made in his travels; but gave hints, at the same time, 'that he thought him a little crack-brained sometimes; and that he himself was fool enough to leave his wife and a good trade, and ramble about the country upon such a *wildgoose* chace.'

Whilst Tugwell was yet speaking, Mr. Wildgoose was come (at Lady Forester's request) to the servants hall, to examine and instruct her domestics in the principles of Religion; and, hearing Tugwell prating full-speed about himself and his adventures, he shook his head: 'Ah! Jerry,' says he, 'I was in hopes you were edifying these good people with some religious discourse, instead of entertaining them with your carnal buffoonries. I find, thou hast not yet put off *the old man*, with his affections and lusts.'—'Well, well, Master,' (says Jerry, being a little pot-valiant) 'if I am an *old man*, that is my misfortune, rather than my fault; we shall all be old men (or old women), if it please God we live long enough.'

Mr. Wildgoose then addressed himself to the servants (who had not quite finished their breakfast), and said, 'he was sure, they had a very good Master and Mistress.'—'That we have' (cried all of them with one voice), 'the best in England.'—The Butler, however, said, 'he had one complaint against Sir William; that, if he should dismiss him from his service, he had spoilt him for any other place; as he could never submit to the arbitrary and capricious treatment which servants met with from too many masters.'—Mrs. Molly, who stood at the door with her work in her hand, said, 'she had a complaint of the same kind against her Lady.'—Wildgoose replied, 'if that was all their complaint, he hoped they would not, like too many servants, make it their whole business, when they got together in their hall, to abuse their Master and Mistress, to waste their victuals, damage the furniture, notch the tables, and do all the little mischief in their power.

'But,' continued Wildgoose, 'we have all one greater Master, of whose favour we ought to be more ambitious; and with a view to whose approbation, we ought to serve our earthly masters with fidelity and care.'

Wildgoose then proceeded to ask each of them some questions about the principles of Religion; and found Lady Forester had taken great pains in instructing them: but, as he thought them yet ignorant of the true Faith, and the doctrine of the New Birth (as he and Mr. Whitfield understood it), he began to talk to them a little mysteriously on that subject; when, some of his expressions being necessarily capable of a *double* meaning, Mrs. Molly cast down her eyes, but gave Mr. George a side-look, with a wanton archness; who, being apprehensive that the same tender glances might be directed where he would not wish them to be, told her, with a jealous surliness, 'that she had better go to her Lady's dressing-room, or to the nursery, which was her proper sphere.'

Lady Forester, indeed, now rang the bell; on which the servants all dispersed to their several stations: and, after her Ladyship had given the house-keeper her necessary orders, she summoned Mr. Wildgoose to attend her and Miss Sainthill in their morning walk.

CHAPTER XVII

Lady Forester's Morning Engagement

LADY FORESTER always made it a rule to answer every demand of *duty*, before she indulged herself in any kind of amusement; and accordingly went her circuit, almost every morning, amongst the poor people in the village, however she might be engaged the remaining part of the day. Having made up some linen for a poor woman that was near her time, her Ladyship's first visit was made to *her*, to whom she delivered the bundle. As the woman had generally a child every year, Lady Forester had got the linen made of a strong new cloth, that it might serve for more than one child. The poor woman turned it about, and surveyed it with some attention; and, upon Lady Forester's asking her, 'how she liked it?' she said, 'it was pretty coarse, but she believed it *might* do.'

Miss Sainthill asked the woman, 'if she did not thank her Ladyship for her trouble?'—The woman replied, 'Ah! my Lady has so many maidens to work for her, it is no great trouble to *she*.'

Wildgoose shook his head; and Lady Forester smiled, and proceeded to another cottage, where lived a poor woman with seven or eight small children, almost naked, and who appeared to be half-starved.

Lady Forester enquired, 'why she had not sent for some broth for her children, as she used to do?'—The woman replied, 'Why, to tell you the truth, my Lady, the broth is not so good as it used to be, since this new Cook came.'—'I am sorry for that,' (says my Lady); 'but what is the matter with it now?'—'Ah!' (cries the woman) 'Mrs. Filch, the old Cook, used to give a poor body a bit of meat now and then with one's broth. Mrs. Filch had some charity, and was very good to the poor.'

'I am afraid not,' (says my Lady): 'she was good to some of them (when she was in the humour for it), and bad to others: she would give what was very improper to those that were her favourites, and send others away with reproaches and empty pitchers, just as the whim seized her: and that was a principal reason for my parting with her.'

In the next house which they came to lived a poor man, that had had an ague for some time; to whom Lady Forester had sent a cordial infusion of the Bark. She enquired, 'how it agreed with him, and whether he had yet got rid of his ague?'—The man replied, 'the stuff had done him no good at all.'—'Perhaps you did not take it regularly?' says my Lady.—'Ah! no,' replied the man; 'it was so *bitter*, I could not bear the taste of it.'—Lady Forester told him, 'all the virtue of it consisted in its bitterness; and, if he would not take that, there was no other remedy for an ague.'—The man said, 'then it must be as it pleased God; for he could not take *Doctor's stuff*, if he died for it.'—And so they left him.

They now met a poor miserable-looking old fellow, who seemed to be just slipped out of an ale-house, which stood by the road-side, near the end of the village. 'Well, John,' cried Lady Forester, 'I am glad to see you abroad again; I thought your lameness had still confined you. How do you like the book which I sent you to read in your confinement?'—'I don't know, my Lady; to be sure, it is a very good book; but I have been so busy, I have not had time to read a word of it.'

Wildgoose could not but observe, 'that her Ladyship had been rather unsuccessful in her endeavours to do good amongst her poor neighbours;' but added, 'that she would not lose her reward.'

Lady Forester replied, 'she was sufficiently rewarded, in the consciousness of having discharged her duty.'—Wildgoose added, 'if her Ladyship could but bring them to have a true Faith, she would see the effects of it, in bringing forth the fruits of the Spirit, Meekness, Humility, Sobriety, and every Christian virtue.'

'Well,' replied Lady Forester, 'that you may not think all my efforts entirely fruitless, I will take you to one of my more promising institutions.'

CHAPTER XVIII

A Scene more agreeable than the last

LADY FORESTER now took Wildgoose to a more neat, or rather an elegant, habitation, on a little eminence near the Park-wall. There was a small court before it, planted with sweet herbs, shrubs, and flowers. On their approach, the door immediately opened to them, and discovered near twenty little girls and boys, working or reading; and a genteel elderly woman in the midst of them, instructing them in their needle-work, or in their books.

The moment Lady Forester entered, one of the little girls threw herself upon her knees before her, and begged her Ladyship, 'not to send her home; and she would never be guilty of stubbornness any more.' This, it seems, was a piece of discipline observed by the Matron of the school, that, when any of the children were refractory, and a slight punishment proved ineffectual, she turned them over to her Ladyship's visitatorial authority; which kept them more in awe, than the severest corporal chastisement would probably have done.

The children were all clean and neat; and their dress was reduced to a kind of uniform, by a sort of band, or handkerchief, with which they were presented when they came to the school: and, as the children were employed part of the day in weeding the garden, or other necessary business about the house, several useful servants had been sent out from this seminary, within the nine or ten years that Lady Forester had been in the neighbourhood.

Wildgoose asked the School-mistress, 'what religious books she taught the children; and whether she had met with any of Mr. Wesley's excellent tracts for that purpose?'—She replied, 'that she had taught them the Church-Catechism and a short Exposition of it; and endeavoured, from thence, to inculcate into them their duty to God, their neighbour, and themselves: but did not think children of that age capable of any speculative notions, or any of the mysterious doctrines of Christianity.'

Wildgoose replied, 'that there had been of late many instances of children at five or six, nay, even at three years old, who had had great *experiences*, and had *assurance* of their sins being pardoned, and had also been favoured with visions and revelations of an extraordinary nature;[1] and that we had no reason to doubt, that even now, as well as in times of old, God could make even babes and sucklings instruments of his glory.'

The School-mistress expressed some surprize at this discourse; as being ignorant of Wildgoose's peculiar character. But Lady Forester said, 'they were going to take a walk in the Park;' and so put a stop to the dialogue.

CHAPTER XIX

A slight Alarm

THEY were now come to one of the Park-gates, to which Lady Forester had a key. The Park had a fine sylvan appearance; and they were beginning to admire the prospect, when they heard at some distance a most dismal outcry, of 'Help! help! Murder! murder! I shall be murdered.' Wildgoose desired Lady Forester and Miss Sainthill to retreat back again to the Park-gate, and ran full speed to the assistance of the person in distress. Passing round a thicket of oaks, he saw, with astonishment, his friend Tugwell lying upon the ground, rolled up as round as a wood-louse, with his head between his knees, and guarding himself with his elbows; but could discover no visible cause of this terrible vociferation. At the same instant Mr. Bob Tench, who (not getting any body to angle with him) had been poaching about the Park with his gun, was running also to Jerry's assistance. Upon their calling to him once or twice, Jerry ventured to look up, and began to give an account of what had befallen him.

The case was, Tugwell being so little versed in the natural history of animals, as not to distinguish a Stag from a Jack-ass (which sufficiently appeared at his first setting out on his travels) he had rambled into the Park, to see the deer; where meeting with a large herd, one of them (which had been bred up as a tame fawn) advanced before the rest, and offered his forehead to be scratched; with which instance of familiarity Tugwell was at first highly delighted. But the young deer, who was now above a year old, waxing wanton, began by degrees to be more familiar than Jerry approved of; who therefore poking him off with his staff, the deer began to be in earnest, and, drawing himself up, attacked Tugwell in front with great vehemence, and soon overset him; and when down, battered him with his young horns so furiously, that Jerry had good reason to cry out for assistance. The young pricket, however, at sight of Bob Tench, had made off, and joined the herd; so that Wildgoose thought his friend had again been alarmed (as he was at Cardiff) by the vain terrors of imagination.

Wildgoose now returned to find out the Ladies, and acquaint them with the cause of the outcry they had heard: but they were so terrified, that they had run home and alarmed the whole family, many of whom were by this time come to the Park-gate; and, being informed of the truth of the affair, were greatly diverted with the bastinado Jerry had received from the tame deer; and only lamented, that they had not come soon enough to be witness to the ludicrous operation.

But though Tugwell was not much damaged in his person by this accident; Sir William, for fear of the stag's becoming more mischievous as his horns became more capable of doing mischief, ordered the poor animal to be shot the first opportunity.

CHAPTER XX

The Lawfulness of eating a good Dinner

IT being now dinner-time, most of the company were assembled in the dining-parlour; where (as Sir William kept a constant table) the cloth was laid, and the side-board set out with some degree of splendor. Wildgoose could not forbear making a comparison between the elegance with which Sir William lived, and the scenes of misery which they had just been viewing amongst the poor people in the village: and, addressing himself to Lady Forester, said, 'he ought not to indulge himself in *faring sumptuously*, whilst the poor Miners were perishing for want of that spiritual food with which he had undertaken to supply them.'—'Well,' says Lady Forester, 'but there is a time for all things; we will not detain you when you have fixed upon a plan of operation.'—'Why, I think,' (says the young Templar) 'it would be a proper act of mortification, for the Gentleman to set out upon his mission immediately, now dinner is coming upon the table: as I have heard Mr. Wesley and his friends (when they first set up this scheme of reformation in the university) used frequently to bespeak an handsome dinner, and as soon as it was brought in, send it immediately to the prisoners in the castle; and dined themselves upon dry bread and green tea.'[1] —'Yes,' says the Colonel, 'but they know better, I believe, by this time; and are not often guilty of those Popish austerities. They love feasting, as far as I can see, as well as other people.'

'Why,' says Sir William, 'I do not apprehend it at all unlawful for the best Christians to frequent, occasionally, the festival entertainments of their friends and acquaintance. If that were the case, our Saviour, instead of giving us prudential rules for our behaviour on those occasions ("when thou art bidden to a wedding, go and sit down in the lowest room") would probably have said, "when thou art bidden to a wedding, do not go!"'

'Pray,' says Lady Forester, 'now you are talking divinity, what is become of our Chaplain to-day, the Parson of the parish?' '—Oh!' says Mr. Tench, 'I can tell your Ladyship; he is gone to the Bowling-green club. I promised to attend the Doctor thither; but forgot it till it was too late.'—'Ah! Mr. Wildgoose,' (says Lady Forester) 'those are things that I disapprove of as well as you.'— —'Madam,' replies Wildgoose, 'I disapprove of those things, because I have really no relish for them; and it would be as great a penance to me, if I were obliged to play a whole afternoon at bowls, cards, or back-gammon, as it was to the primitive Saint, to stand all night upon a pillar forty feet high.[1] And I suppose your Chaplain has no more taste for books or spiritual joys, than I have for those carnal amusements.'

'Sir,' says Bob Tench, 'the Doctor is a very learned man, and *publishes* something almost every month.'—'In the Magazine, I presume?' says Wildgoose.—'No, in the Church,' replies Mr. Tench; 'he *publishes* the banns of marriage between the lads and lasses, who want to be joined together in holy matrimony.'

As dinner was now upon table, all conversation began to grow insipid. Wildgoose indeed still kept harping upon the same string for some time, and said, 'that no one, who had *tasted* the pleasures of a divine life, could any longer relish such trash as the amusements of this world generally were.'—'Mr. Wildgoose,' says Lady Forester, 'let me help you to some of this hashed calve's head.'— The savoury smell of this dish soon put to flight Mr. Wildgoose's spiritual ideas. He accepted the calve's head; and began to fancy himself in the land of promise; and, with a true patriarchal appetite, he feasted most devoutly.

CHAPTER XXI

Protestant Nunneries. The disconsolate Widow

DINNER being ended, Lady Forester's favourite topic, Religion, was again brought upon the carpet; upon which subject, she and Miss Sainthill talked with pleasure. The Colonel, however, could not bear with patience the compliment which he thought was paid to a mere vagabond in this respect; and, at last, said with some wrath, 'that he was of the same opinion, in regard to the Methodists, which Charles the Second was in regard to the Presbyterians—that there never was a *Gentleman* of that Religion, since the first pro-pagation of it.'

Sir William Forester replied, 'that he had always considered that observation of King Charles (if he really made it) as a compliment to the Dissenters of that reign; when the word *Gentleman* meant a fellow of a *genteel* address perhaps, and polite accomplishments; but who would drink, whore, or debauch the wife of his friend or companion; and, when called to an account for it, run him through the body without any more ceremony.'

Miss Sainthill, out of opposition to the Colonel, took the part of the Methodists with some spirit—to all which the man of war only replied in the words of Hamlet—

'Get thee to a Nunnery, Ophelia; get thee to a Nunnery.'[1]

'So I would,' (says Miss Sainthill) 'if there were in England any such thing as a Protestant Nunnery: and I could spend my life, in such a situation, with great satisfaction.'

'Why,' says Rappee, 'I should think it a very proper way of dis-posing of some part of your sex—of the old and the ugly; of old maids, and of young women who were too homely to get them-selves husbands.'—'And, I assure you,' says Miss Sainthill, 'I should think it a very happy refuge from the impertinence of fools and coxcombs, with which the world abounds.'[2]

'Why,' says Lady Forster, 'jesting apart, Miss Sainthill and I have often been laying a plan for an asylum of this kind: and I can-not think, if there were such an institution in every county, under proper regulations, it would be attended with any bad effects. I do not mean to draw in young thoughtless creatures upon every disappointment in love; or young women, who might be useful in the world, as servants, milleners, or mantua-makers, and other necessary employments: but as a refuge for young ladies of good families and small fortunes, who are now forced to live in a dependant state, or perhaps to take up with matches of mere convenience, which make them miserable their whole lives.

'There should be a proper succession of working, reading, and amusement. They should enter voluntarily into them, and not before a certain age; as thirty or forty, suppose: yet, to guard against the caprice and inconstancy of human nature, they should be under some little restraint; and not be released from their engagement, without some considerable forfeit for the good of the society. The number should be limited: and, to make it an honourable situation, the Queen perhaps for the time being, or some of the royal family, would vouchsafe to patronize these institutions; who should also have a power of visiting them, and be the judges of the qualifications of persons to be admitted, and of the causes for which they might plead to be released.'

'Well,' says the young Templar; 'but, by a Statute of the 27th year of Harry the Eighth, all Monasteries, Nunneries, and religious houses, are for ever dissolved; and I do not imagine any thing of this kind could be established without an act of Parliament.'

'Ah!' (says the Colonel in his common-place way) 'and besides,

> Vows of virginity should well be weigh'd;
> Too oft they're broke, tho' in a *convent* made.

'There was a Widow in ——shire, the other day; who was so disconsolate upon the loss of her good man, that she made a *vow*, not only to live single, but absolutely to renounce the world, and never to behold the face of a man again.

'To soothe her melancholy, she sate constantly in her dressing-room, with her curtains half-drawn; and, with folded hands, kept contemplating a miniature picture of her husband, fixed in the pedestal of a little pyramid, or mausoleum, formed of her jewels (which she had gotten worked up into that form, and placed upon her toilette) from morning to night.

'After carrying on this farce for near three months, some affairs respecting her jointure, which was very large, made it absolutely necessary for her to go to London. When she took coach for that purpose, her men servants were ordered to be out of sight; and she was handed in, veiled, by her own maid.

D d

'A friend of mine, in the Guards, who, though not personally known to her, was (by means of a servant who had lived in the family) acquainted with every circumstance of her fortune and the present state of her mind, (by a few half-crowns properly applied) got intelligence of her intended journey, and of all her motions. My friend therefore contrived to meet her equipage at the first stage: and taking his station in the bar, as soon as the Dowager's maid stepped out of the coach, he flies to the step; thrusts the Abigail aside; and, with a gallant yet submissive air, seized the Lady's hand; and offered to conduct her to the parlour.

'At the sight of a man, even through her veil, she gave a faint scream, and affected to be extremely angry with her maid for deserting her in such a manner. She felt something contagious, however, in the touch of an handsome young fellow in his regimentals; and, though she charged her servant to be more careful for the future, her curiosity prompted her to enquire, "whether she knew who the Gentleman was?" then repeated her charge, "to make sure that the coast was clear, at the next inn they came to, before she got out of the coach."

'My friend stayed and dined at the inn, as the Lady also did; and suffered the carriage to set out before him; but ordered his servant (by means of a bowl of punch with which he treated the Lady's coachman) to get strict information, where and at what inn they were to lie that evening.

'Nay, as her servants had no idea of the Lady's delicate distress on the loss of her spouse, they considered her behaviour as mere affectation: and as that sort of gentry are always pleased with such chearful events as promote feasting and jollity, they were much inclined to facilitate a good understanding between their Lady and so generous a lover. They contrived, therefore, a stratagem to overcome the Dowager's reserve, and to lay her under a necessity of another interview with the Captain, by loosening some of the traces of the carriage, and, when my friend overtook them, by alarming the poor Lady with an outcry of danger; which forced her to get out of the coach, whilst they pretended to set matters to rights. At this instant the Captain made his appearance, leaped off his horse, and again handed the Lady out of her carriage. She could not avoid admitting him to converse with her, whilst they stood waiting for her equipage in the public road. The Captain made the best use of his time; ogled, sighed, and played all the artillery of love so effectually, that the Lady condescended at length to thank him for his civilities; and added, "if he *happened* to go to the same inn, she would be glad of his company to sup with her."

'In short, there was so close an intimacy commenced from that evening, that, when the poor Dowager came to town, she found her affairs so perplexed, and herself (a poor helpless woman) so little able to conduct them, that she began to consult with her maid, whom she had best call in to her assistance. Mrs. Abigail had seen too much of the rapid progress of her Lady's passion, to hesitate on the choice, and immediately determined, "that the Captain was the only man in the world for her purpose."

'In short, the exigence of her affairs was such, and her *distress* so urgent, that she thought any longer delay would be quite imprudent. So that, in less than six months, she laid aside her weeds, had her *jewels new set*, married the Captain, and was as fond of her second spouse as she had been of her first.'

CHAPTER XXII

Frailty not confined to Females

'WELL,' says Lady Forester, 'and what do you infer from this gossiping tale? That women are poor frail creatures, and do not thoroughly know their own hearts; but frequently act contrary to their best-formed resolutions?'

'Yes,' says Wildgoose, 'and we are all equally frail and impotent, without the assistance of the Divine Spirit. This Lady indeed seemed sensible of her own weakness, by her first resolution to avoid the very sight of a man for the future; for there is no security, but by guarding every avenue of the soul against the approach of our spiritual adversary!'

'I am afraid, however,' (says Sir William) 'there are as many instances of frailty to be met with in ours, as in that which is called the *softer* sex. The Lady, whom the Colonel has mentioned, was guilty of a very common, and, I suppose, a very innocent frailty. She buried one husband, and married another. But there has lately happened a very shocking instance of frailty, or rather of an irregular indulgence of the passions, in one of our sex; the particulars of which (as I believe it was in his neighbourhood) Mr. Wildgoose perhaps may be able to inform us of: I mean, the dreadful story of Sir W. K.[1] who, in a fit of jealousy, (as I have heard) burnt himself and a magnificent house, which he had built to please the fancy of an imperious Mistress, whom he kept; though he had really been as fond of his own Lady, as the Dowager (Colonel Rappee talks of) was of her husband.'

Wildgoose replied, 'that the particulars of that affair were known to all the neighbourhood in which *he* lived. But the catastrophe was too tragical to entertain so chearful a company. Yet,' says he, 'if Sir William desires it, I will take some opportunity of relating the whole progress of that affair.'

The Ladies, according to a laudable custom, now leaving the Gentleman at liberty to enjoy a more licentious conversation, and to drink bumpers; and neither Sir William nor his company being disposed to make use of that indulgence; they also soon after dispersed. And Sir William invited Mr. Wildgoose to accompany them to a very romantic place (which he was going to shew to the young Templar) being the seat of a Gentleman in the neighbourhood; where the river Manifold, after running three or four miles under ground, bursts forth from a hollow rock in the garden, which is laid out with grottoes and cascades, suitable to so grotesque a scene.[2]

Wildgoose would have declined this gratification of his curiosity, but for the sake of a small lead-mine, which Sir William told him they should pass near in their walk thither; where, he thought, he might reconnoitre the ground, in order to begin his operations the first opportunity.

The Colonel, conscious of the advantageous figure he made on horse-back, chose to ride, attended only by his servant. But Bob Tench accompanied them, for the sake of throwing his fly by the way, and angling for trout in the river Dove. And one or two of the servants took Tugwell as far as the lead-work, notwithstanding his bruises from the tame deer in the morning, in hopes of having some sport with him when they came thither.

CHAPTER XXIII

Wonders of the Peak

ONE of the servants that attended Tugwell in his walk was the old Gardener, who was a man of some humour; and had read many books of Travels and of Natural History, as well as those which more immediately related to his own profession. He entertained Jerry, as they went along, with some account of the wonders of the Peak; 'which,' he said, 'they would see, if he and his Master went with the company to-morrow, as he found his Lady intended they should.'

The Gardener told him, 'there was an hill called Mam-torre (as big as any of the Welsh mountains which he had been talking of), that was continually mouldering and shivering down earth and parts of the rock; and yet neither was the hill visibly diminished, nor the valley beneath raised up, in the memory of man.[1]

'There is also a perpendicular chasm, or opening into the very bowels of the earth, called Elden-hole, above fifty feet wide; and which has been fathomed above eight hundred yards, and no bottom discovered.[2]

'Then there is Chatsworth, the finest house in England, belonging to the Duke of Devonshire. The frames of the windows are all gilded with gold; and the gardens are the most beautiful that can be conceived.'

'Well! but where is the D-vil's A-se o'Peak, which they talk so much of?' says Tugwell.—[3]'Why that is the greatest curiosity of all,' says the Gardener. 'It is a monstrous cavern, as high as the inside of a cathedral church, at the bottom of a prodigious mountain. In the mouth of the cavern are several cottages, where the poor people make pack-thread, &c. And across it run three different streams, which are lost under ground. Two of them you may pass over in a flat-bottomed boat. But the rock closes almost entirely over the third; so that it is generally thought to be impassable. This, however, a man of great curiosity once ventured to pass over, laying himself flat on his face in the boat, and being shoved over by his companions; but he was near a whole day before he returned.'

'And what, *the dickins!* did he see,' says Tugwell, 'when he got thither?'

'Why,' says the Gardener, 'as soon as he landed, he came into a fine *green* meadow, not covered with grass, but paved with green Emeralds; at the extremity of which was a large city, inhabited by people about a span long. Upon enquiring the name of the country, he found they understood his language, and did not seem much surprized at his appearance; having often seen and conversed with the inhabitants of this outward surface of the globe, in the remoter parts of their dominions. For, you must know, the place where he landed was the Mineral Kingdom; and the town which he saw, the capital city of the King of Diamonds. They are a race of Fairies, that preside over the different productions of the Mines: not only Gold, Silver, Copper, Lead, and all the useful metallic ores; but also the precious stones which mortals are so fond of, Diamonds, Rubies, Emeralds, Sapphires, and the like: which they crystallize, ripen, purify, and refine, by incessant chemical operations, in the bowels of the earth. Their city was surrounded with walls of common Agate or Cornelian; the gates were either Brass or Iron; their houses were built of different-coloured precious stones; regard being chiefly had to their several ranks or professions. The Royal Palace was of Rubies and Garnets, the doors of Gold and Silver. The Bishops houses were of purple Amethysts, the inferior Clergy of blue or Sapphires, and so on: though most of them were lined with Cornelian, or some stone that was not transparent, to keep out the scorching rays of the sun, and to prevent the inspection of their impertinent neighbours. They set no great value upon Diamonds, on account of their want of colour; but prepared them chiefly for traffic. They had plenty of the finest liquors: their conduits ran with a liquor called Nectar, Honey-water, and Eau-de-luce; and their springs with the most spirited mineral waters, such as Spa or Pyrmont produce. But, it being very hot weather, our poor adventurer would rather have had one quart of small beer, than all the gold and precious stones in the universe.'

'Well,' says Tugwell, 'but how, the Deuce! did he get back again?'

'You shall hear,' says the Gardener. 'He was going to pocket a few loose Diamonds, with which the high-ways were mended, and to pluck up an old Silver gate-post, when he found himself pinched all over his body, and received a great blow upon his back with a stone; and the boat was driven down the stream to a good landing-place, where he returned to his companions: being uncertain, whether he had not fallen asleep in his passage; and whether what he saw, was a dream, or a reality.'

This strange description put Jerry in mind of the Utopia of school-boys; who said, 'he had rather have gone into the country which he had heard of, where the houses are built with plumb-cake or ginger-bread, and thatched with pancakes; the streets paved with apple-dumplins; and where the roast pigs ran about with knives and forks stuck in their buttocks, crying, "Come, eat me! Come, eat me!" Though I should like to see the *Mineral Kingdom* too,' says Jerry, 'if I could see it without crossing the water.'

CHAPTER XXIV

View of a Lead-mine

THEY were now come to the Lead-mine, at the bottom of an high hill; where they saw only three Miners, who were winding up a basket of ore: but the Gardener told Jerry, 'There were probably twenty more under ground; and that he had better go down and preach to them; or at least prepare them a little for what his Master had to say to them when he came. And then you will see something of the Mineral Kingdom into the bargain.'

As Jerry had heard Wildgoose harangue so often on the same subject, he was a little conceited of his own proficiency, and really fancied he could almost equal his Master; and seemed at first well enough pleased with the compliment that was paid him. But, when he approached the shaft or mouth of the Mine, he was greatly terrified at the appearance; and said, 'For his part, he did not pretend to preach: that God had not bestowed upon him the gift of utterance, and of understanding hard words; but that he only went with Mr. Wildgoose for company's sake; who, he did not doubt, would some time or other pay him for his trouble.'

'Well,' says the old Gardener, 'but, as your Master may not come in time, you would not suffer so many poor souls to perish, for want perhaps of what little instruction you can give them?'— Tugwell replied, 'He was nothing but a poor Cobler; and it was not his business to *save souls*.'—'That's true,' says the Gardener, 'as you are a Cobler; but, as you pretend to be a Methodist, you ought to preach, "in season and out of season," above ground or under ground, wherever you have an opportunity.'

''Sblood!' cries Jerry, with a licentious air, 'I am no Methodist, I tell you; and would not go down into such a hole as this, to save all the souls in Purgatory.'

The servants, however, as soon as the Miners had emptied their load, winked upon them, and made signs to put Tugwell into the basket; which two of them very dextrously performed (notwithstanding Jerry laid about him, and made great resistance); and the third got into the basket with him, and held him fast; whilst the other two, by means of the windlass, let them several fathoms down the shaft; Tugwell roaring out like a mad bull, as he descended into the horrid chasm.

Just at that instant Mr. Wildgoose, attended by Bob Tench, (having left the company as soon as they had taken a slight view of the romantic gardens at Ilam) came to the Lead-mine: and, hearing the out-cry, enquired with some eagerness, 'What was the matter?'—The Gardener told them, 'that they had persuaded Mr. Tugwell to go down and preach to the Miners; but that now he was got into the shaft, he seemed a little frightened at the manner of going down.'

Wildgoose, being no stranger to Jerry's want of courage in adventures of that unusual kind, was apprehensive of some bad consequences: he therefore desired them to wind him up again; which, upon Bob Tench's likewise insisting upon it, they immediately performed: so that Jerry saw but little of the Mineral Kingdom.

As soon as Tugwell was safely landed again, he began rubbing his fists and spitting in his hands, and challenged to fight any two of the Miners who had treated him in that treacherous manner; when, perceiving his Master (who attempted to moderate his resentment), Jerry fell foul upon him with bitter complaints; and said, 'If Mr. Wildgoose had a mind to preach to the Miners, he should go by himself: for he would not be buried alive upon other people's business; and I am sure,' (adds Jerry) 'if I had gone much lower, the cold damps would have taken away my breath.'— 'Well,' (says Wildgoose) 'I don't desire you to run any risque; but I myself will immediately go down amongst these poor people, and open my commission; and they shall not remain one night longer under the dominion of Satan.'

Wildgoose then desired the Miners 'to let him down the shaft, as he understood there were several more of their, fellow-labourers under ground.'—But the Miners then told him, 'that there were no more than themselves there; and that the Mine had been under water for this week past; and that they had been employed to bring away some ore, that was left in a cavity about half way down the shaft; and that they only took the other honest man' (meaning Tugwell) 'to frighten him a little, by way of diversion.' Wildgoose, therefore, having asked them some few questions more; he, Mr. Tench, and the rest of the company, returned towards Sir William Forester's.

Tugwell, by not submitting to his fate with Christian patience, had got a broken head in the scuffle; which, though he did not perceive it at first, bled pretty freely. But, as Bob Tench was never at a loss for expedients; and had always a little phial of Fryars Balsam in his pocket, some gold-beaters skin and court-plaister, as well as his cork-screw and mohock;[1] he soon set Jerry's skull to rights, and stopped the bleeding.

Upon Wildgoose's lamenting his disappointment in not finding any number of people at the Lead-mine, the old Gardener told him how precarious those operations were: 'that a great Copper-mine in that neighbourhood, which had brought in six thousand pounds a-year, was now under water, and would probably be the ruin of a very worthy family:[2] that one gentleman had spent eight or nine hundred pounds in quest of a vein of ore; and was then obliged (for want of money) to desist: another gentleman pursues the same work—and, within two feet of the spot where the former adventurer had left off, discovers a rich vein, and makes a fortune of ten thousand pounds.'—'Ah!' says Wildgoose, 'I wish people would seek after righteousness, as they do after silver; and search after true religion, as they do after hidden treasures.'—'Troth!' (says Tugwell) 'I had rather work for eight-pence a-day above ground; than venture down into a Mine, for all the hidden treasure in the world.'

As they went along, Bob Tench left them for an hour, to angle upon the Dove for trout; and it being a fine calm evening, he soon caught a brace and a half, which he brought home in triumph; and said, 'that was the finest prospect he had seen to-day.'

CHAPTER XXV

Beauties of Nature

SIR WILLIAM and the young Templar, and the other parties, all came to the rendezvous pretty near the same time. When they were come into the parlour and sat down, Mr. Wildgoose appearing rather more serious than usual; Lady Forester said, 'He seemed tired with his walk;' and asked him, 'how he liked Ilam?' Wildgoose answered, 'it was certainly a most romantic place; and he enjoyed prospects of that kind as much as any one, formerly. But—' —'But what?' says Miss Sainthill, with some quickness. 'Why, to be sure,' replies Wildgoose, 'the natural man cannot but be delighted with these terrestrial beauties; yet, considered in a religious light, these stupendous rocks and mountains appear to me as the ruins of a noble palace, designed for man in a state of innocence; and, I own, it makes me serious, when I reflect on the fallen state of mankind; and that the whole creation suffers for our guilt, and groaneth for redemption.'

'Well,' says Lady Forester, 'all this may be true; but you don't think it any sin to be charmed with the beauties of Nature? You say; the *natural man* is delighted with them; that is, every thing great, beautiful, or uncommon, is *naturally* agreeable to the imagination: and I can never think it unlawful to enjoy (under proper restrictions) what Providence has formed us for enjoying.'

'No,' says Miss Sainthill, 'if it were, David must have been a very wicked man: who always speaks with rapture of the beauties of Nature; of the magnificence of the heavenly bodies; the Moon and Stars, which thou hast created; the variety of seasons thou hast made, Summer and Winter; the sweet approach of even and morn! Thou that makest the out-goings of the morning and evening to praise thee. O! Lord, how manifold are thy works! (says he)—in wisdom hast thou made them all.'

'Well prayed! Miss Sainthill,' cries the Colonel. 'Why Lady Forester has no occasion for a Chaplain; you quote chapter and verse as well as the best Divine in Christendom.'

Supper now appeared; and the *natural man* again resuming his place in Mr. Wildgoose, he eat as heartily as the best of them. After supper, when they had taken a glass or two round, Sir William put Mr. Wildgoose in mind of the promise he had made, to give them the particulars of Sir William K———'s[1] unhappy affair.

Wildgoose replied, 'that he could not, without some reluctance, recollect so tragical a story, which concerned a family for whom he had a great regard. But,' says he, 'as the thing is public, and shews in a striking light the dreadful consequences of irregular indulgences, and also how corrupt the *natural man* is when destitute of divine grace, I will relate the particulars, with as much brevity as I can.'

CHAPTER XXVI

Narrative of a licentious Amour

'Sir William K———te was a Baronet of very considerable fortune, and of an ancient family: and, on his return from his travels, had so amiable a character, and was reckoned (what the world calls) so fine a gentleman; that he was thought a very desirable match for a worthy Nobleman's daughter in the neighbourhood, of great beauty, merit, and a suitable fortune.

'Sir W. and his Lady lived very happily together for some years, and had four or five fine children; when he was unfortunately nominated (at a contested Election) to represent the Borough of W—r—k; in which county the bulk of his estate lay, and where he at that time resided. After the Election, as some sort of recompence to a zealous partizan of Sir W.'s, Lady K———te took an Innkeeper's daughter for her own maid. She was a tall, genteel girl, with a fine complexion, and an appearance of great modesty and innocence.

'Molly I———n (which was her name) had waited on Lady K———te for some time, before Sir W. appeared to take the least notice of her; though Lady K———te (perhaps from some sparks of jealousy, and to try how Sir W. stood affected) would frequently observe, "what a fine girl Molly I———n was grown!" To which Sir W.'s usual reply was, "That he saw nothing extraordinary in the girl:" and even affected to speak slightingly of her person, and to censure her aukwardness and her vanity: for which as there was not the least foundation, Sir W. probably intended it to conceal his real sentiments.

'After some time, however, the servants in the family began to entertain some suspicions, that Molly I——n was too highly in her Master's favour. The House-keeper in particular (who in the course of forty years had been actually engaged in at least forty intrigues) soon perceived there was too much foundation for these suspicions. Knowing, therefore, that the Butler had himself made overtures to Molly, she set him to work, whose jealousy made him so vigilant, that he soon discovered the whole of the affair: and that it had proceeded much further, than was at first apprehended. The House-keeper (as that sort of gentry are apt to triumph in the indiscretions of young people) made use of the Butler's *name*, as well as his intelligence, to her Lady: and this threw every thing into confusion.'

'Lady K——te's passion soon got the better of her discretion. For if, instead of reproaching Sir W. with his infidelity, she had dissembled her resentment, till his first fondness for this new object had abated (which, for her own sake as well as that of her children, she ought to have done), she might probably have reclaimed her husband; who, notwithstanding this temporary defection, was known to have a sincere regard and esteem for his Lady.

'The Butler's officious sedulity, however, had like to have been fatal to the poor fellow. For his name being mentioned, as having made the discovery; and Molly I——n having told Sir W. "that he was only piqued at her rejecting his addresses"; Sir W. went up into the servants apartment the very next night, and ran his sword several times through the bed where the Butler used to lie; who had (for some reason or other) changed his lodging, and happily escaped his destruction. And this rash proceeding of Sir W. shews how true it is, that whoever offends against the laws of God in one point, is often (in a literal sense) guilty of violating the whole law.'

CHAPTER XXVII

The Narrative continued

'THE affair being now publicly known in the family; and all restraints of shame, or fear of discovery, being quite removed; things were soon carried to extremity between Sir W. and his Lady, and a separation became unavoidable: Sir W. left Lady K——te, with the two younger children, in possession of the mansion-house in W—shire; and retired himself, with his Mistress (and his two eldest sons), to a large farm-house on the side of the Cots-wold-hills. The situation was fine; plenty of wood and water; and commanded an extensive view of the vale of Evesham. This tempted him to build an handsome box there, with very extensive gardens, planted and laid out in the expensive taste of the age. And, not content with this, before the body of the house was quite finished, Sir W. added two large side-fronts (if I may so express it) for no better a reason (as I could hear) but that his Mistress happened to say, "What is a kite without wings?"

'I mention these particulars, because, I believe, the expence of finishing this place (which was at least ten thousand pounds) was the first cause of Sir W.'s encumbering his estate: and the diffi-culties in which he was involved making him uneasy, he (as is too' natural) had recourse to the bottle for relief. Sir W. kept, what is called, an hospitable house; and too many people being fond of the freedom and jollity which is usually found at a table where no Lady presides,[1] he was seldom without company; which brought on a constant course of dissipation and want of œconomy: by which means Sir W.'s affairs, in a few years, became almost desperate: though, it must be confessed, Mrs. I—n, in her situation, behaved with great care and frugality.

'Well; Sir W. was now turned of fifty; and his eldest son (the present Sir J—s) being grown up and returned from the university; Sir W. instead of sending him abroad, or giving him the advantages which a young man of his rank might have expected; kept him at home, and made him a witness, and (in some measure) a partaker, of his debaucheries: and, what is most to be lamented (in a temporal view), drew him in (by some plausible pretence or wrong indul-gence) to part with his reversionary right to his mother's jointure; which was very considerable, and almost the only part of the estate which had not been already mortgaged for its full value.'

CHAPTER XXVIII

Its fatal Event

'BUT to hasten to the catastrophe of my tale. There was taken into the family, about this time, a fresh-coloured country girl, in the capacity of a Dairy-maid, with no other beauty than what arises from the bloom of youth: and, as people who once give way to their passions (and are unrestrained by grace) know no bounds; Sir W. (in the decline of life) conceived an amorous regard for this girl, who was scarce twenty. This event produced still further confusion in the family. Mrs. I—n soon observed this growing passion; and, either from resentment, or from the apprehension, or perhaps the real experience, of ill usage, thought proper to retire to a little market town in the neighbourhood: where she was reduced to keep a little sewing-school for bread.'—'Aye, and good enough too for such hussies!' cried some of the Ladies.

'Well,' continued Wildgoose, 'young Mr. K—te, whether shocked at this unparalleled infatuation of his father; or (as was commonly said) finding himself considered as a rival in the affections of this poor creature; sought an asylum, and spent most of his time with Lord L——, a friend of his, in W—shire.

'Sir W. though he had now a prospect of being successul in this humble amour, and of indulging it without molestation; yet began at length to see the delusive nature of all vicious pursuits: and though he endeavoured to keep up his spirits, or rather to drown all thought by constant intoxication, yet in his sober intervals he became a victim to gloomy reflections. He had injured a valuable wife; which he could not even now reflect upon without some remorse: he had wronged his innocent children; whom he could not think upon without the tenderest sentiments of compassion. His son, who had been a sort of companion to him for some years, had now left him, through his ill usage. And, as she had been for some time useful to him, he was shocked at being deserted even by the woman for whose sake he had brought this distress upon his family: and he found himself almost alone, in that magnificent but fatal mansion, the erecting and adorning of which had been the principal cause of ruining his fortune.

'Tormented by these contending passions, he had, for a week past, raised himself, by constant inebriation, to a degree of frenzy;

and had behaved in so frantic a manner, that even his new favourite, the poor Blowselinda, could bear it no longer, and had eloped from him.

'On the morning of the day on which he executed his fatal resolution, Sir W. sent for his son, and for his new mistress; with what intention can only be conjectured: but luckily neither of them obeyed the summons. Early in the evening (it being in the month of October, I think) the Butler had lighted two candles (as usual) and set them upon the marble table in the hall. Sir W. came down, and took them up himself, as he frequently did. After some time, however, one of the House-maids ran down stairs in a great fright, and said, "the lobby was all in a cloud of smoke." The servants, and a Tradesman that was in the house upon business, ran immediately up, and, forcing open the door whence the smoke seemed to proceed, they found Sir W. had set fire to a large heap of fine linen (piled up in the middle of the room), which had been given by some old Lady, a relation, as a legacy to his eldest son. Whilst the attention of the servants was entirely taken up with extinguishing the flames in this room, Sir W. had made his escape into an adjoining chamber, where was a cotton bed, and which was wainscoted with deal, as most finished rooms then were. When they had broken open this door, the flames burst out upon them with such fury, that they were all glad to make their escape out of the house: the principal part of which sumptuous pile was, in a few hours, burnt to the ground; and no other remains of Sir W. were found the next morning, than the hip-bone, and the *vertebræ*, or bones of the back; with two or three keys, and a gold watch, which he had in his pocket.

'This was the dreadful consequence of a licentious passion, not checked in its infancy: or rather, thus may every unregenerate man expect to be drawn on from one degree of wickedness to another, when deserted by the Spirit, and given up to his own imaginations.'

CHAPTER XXIX

A Remedy against Suicide

'WELL,' says Colonel Rappee; 'we are obliged to the Gentleman for his story—and for a sermon into the bargain.'—'Why, it is a very serious affair,' says Sir William, 'for a man to destroy himself; and rush into the presence of his offended Judge, with all his sins and follies unrepented of about him.'—The Colonel replied, 'if life was given as a blessing; when it ceased to be such, he thought a man might resign it again, without offence to any one.'—'Yes, yes,' says Sir William, 'if he were under no obligations to any law, either of Nature, or Reason, or Society: not to mention the Revealed Will of God, by which all murder is forbidden.—But, I would desire no other argument against self-murther' (continues Sir William) 'than its being contrary to the very first law of nature, self-preservation; and its shocking the natural feelings, and common apprehensions of all mankind.'

The young Templar said, 'that, as suicide was the most horrid of all murders, a friend of his proposed to have the offender punished as other heinous murderers are.'—'How is that?' (says the Colonel.)—'Why, by being hanged in chains,' (says the Templar.) —'Oh!' says Sir William; 'but that would be rather a punishment to his surviving family, than to the deceased offender.'—'Yes,' says the Templar; 'and that is the very thing proposed; as the thoughts of bringing such a reproach upon his innocent wife and children would probably restrain many a man from so rash an action, who was deaf to every other consideration.'—'Well,' says Miss Sainthill, 'but this penalty would be no restraint upon you and me, Colonel—upon old Maids and old Batchelors. And a man that *burns* himself (like Sir W. K.) would evade the law.'

The Colonel was going to make some reply, when the attention of the company was attracted by a burst of loud laughter from the servants hall; and a sort of riotous mirth, not usual in Sir William's family. Miss Forester, attended by Mr. Bob Tench, took upon her to go and enquire into the cause of this boisterous merriment. When they came to the door of the servants apartment, they found it was Tugwell who had 'set the table on a roar,' by getting up on the end of it, and holding forth in imitation of his Master and Mr. Whitfield.

The truth was, Jerry being pretty thirsty, after his long walk and the numerous perils he had undergone that day, the Butler plied him with strong beer, till he began to wax mellow; in which state of things, Jerry thought proper to mount the table, and harangue in praise of *temperance*; and, in short, proceeded so long in recommending *sobriety*, and in tossing off horns of ale, till he became as drunk as a piper. This inconsistency of conduct exposed our Orator (as it has done more respectable characters) to the ridicule of his audience: so that the Cook had made so free with the Preacher, as to pin a dish-clout to his rump; and the other servants, in their different ways, had offered Jerry many indignities. Nay, they proceeded so far at last, as to give him the strappado, or ancient discipline of the boot, with no feeble arm, upon his posteriors; and then conveyed him hand and foot (like a dead pig) decently to bed.

When Miss Forester returned into the parlour, she laughed to herself, and whispered Lady Forester in the ear.—Sir William asked Bob Tench, 'what was the cause of all that noise below stairs?'—Bob cast a sneering look at Wildgoose (as if he were answerable for the absurdities of his comrade); and said, 'Mr. Wildgoose's friend was entertaining the company with a dissertation upon *sobriety*; but his long walk, and an horn or two of ale, were a little too much for him.'

Wildgoose could not forbear blushing at the indiscretion of his fellow-traveller; being sensible that he must rather injure the cause than promote it, as his zeal was probably much greater than his knowledge or his abilities.

CHAPTER XXX

Love triumphant over Sensuality

IT being now bed-time, Mrs. Molly brought candles for the Ladies; and, in allusion to what had passed in the servants hall, simpered upon Wildgoose. But there was something so lascivious in her smiles, that he considered it as almost an act of sensuality to return them; which yet it was almost impossible to avoid.

The Gentlemen sate talking near half an hour after the Ladies

E e

were gone; and then retired to their several apartments. When Wildgoose was got to his chamber, had shut the door, and was going to his devotions by the bed-side; he was surprized with the sight of a pink petticoat, a cotton gown, a pair of white stockings, and some green stuff-shoes, thrown carelessly upon the floor; and, upon looking within the curtains, saw a girl, as he thought, in a laced night-cap, her face turned from him, and (as he supposed) fast asleep. Wildgoose was struck silent with astonishment at first: but imagining that Mrs. Molly, who had ogled him so frequently since he came, had laid this snare for his virtue, he broke out into this kind of soliloquy: 'Ah! wretch that I am! I have brought this poor creature to the very brink of destruction, by my own carnal concupiscence. I have encouraged her amorous wishes, by return-ing her wanton glances; instead of nipping her hopes in the bud, by a severity of countenance, as I ought to have done. But how shall I resist such a temptation? The spirit is willing; but the flesh is weak. I can renounce the world, and defy the devil.—But the flesh—Oh! the flesh is weak.—Heaven protect me!'—Whilst he was utter-ing this rhapsody, he, by an almost involuntary motion, pulled Miss Townsend's cambrick handkerchief out of his pocket; the ambrosial scent of which immediately revived her agreeable idea, and the tender sentiments which Mr. Wildgoose entertained for that Lady; and gave a new turn to his thoughts. 'But oh! wretch that I am!' (continues he) 'how can I forget the kind looks and modest blushes of the incomparable Miss Townsend; and be guilty of any act of infidelity to so amiable a Lady?—Avaunt, Beelzebub! Get thee behind me, Satan!' says he, with a vehement emphasis; which threw the counterfeit Mrs. Molly into a fit of laughter: and out leaped Tom the Stable-boy (whom the Butler had got to act this farce), and, running to the chamber-door, joined Mr. George and some others of the servants who were in the secret, and who were waiting in the lobby for the event of their stratagem.

Mr. Wildgoose stared with surprize; and was at first a little angry at the joke which was put upon him. But, immediately recollecting that he had invited this insult by his own indiscretion, he thought it best to take no further notice of it. He therefore went to bed; but was kept awake an hour or two, by his vexation at this incident, and other meditations of various kinds.

CHAPTER XXXI

More nocturnal Perils

MR. WILDGOOSE was just composing himself to sleep, however, when he heard his door open again, and was afraid of some real attack upon his chastity; when, to his astonishment, he heard the lamentable voice of his friend Tugwell. 'Master Wildgoose! Master Wildgoose!' says he, 'for God's sake, awake: I will not stay a moment longer in the house.'—'Why; what is the matter?' says Wildgoose.—'Why,' quoth Jerry, 'the house is haunted, and the bed-cloaths are bewitched; and I would not go to bed again for an hundred pounds.'—'I am afraid' (replies Wildgoose) 'thou art not sober yet, Jerry; for I hear thou gottest fuddled to-night in a most ungodly manner.'—'Ah! Master,' (cries Jerry) 'I am as sober now as ever I was in my life, and have had two or three hours good sleep. But, I am sure, the bed is bewitched: for there was not a soul in the room besides myself; and a witch, or a spirit, kept pulling the bed-cloaths off me, twenty times, as fast as I could pull them on me again. And I am certain it could be nothing but witchcraft.'

The case was, the Cook and the House-maid (by a common contrivance amongst girls who love to be playing tricks with young fellows) had tacked the bed-cloaths together; and, by a long pack-thread fixed under the quilt and brought under the door, as they went up to bed, had played off this piece of fun, to the terror and annoyance of poor Tugwell.

Mr. Wildgoose desired Jerry 'to go to bed again till the morning; when he himself' (he said) 'intended to depart: as he found the servants, instead of minding the things which belonged to their salvation, were all in a conspiracy to put tricks upon them, and to defeat their pious intentions.'

'Yes,' says Jerry, 'and so are the Miners too, as far as I can see; and I am for getting out of this heathenish country as fast as we can.'

'Why,' says Wildgoose, 'Sir William and Lady Forester are very good people; but we have done wrong, to entangle ourselves in the pleasures of this world: and, though I had promised to accompany them into the Peak to-morrow; yet the servants perhaps may prejudice the Miners against us. In short,' (says he) 'I am afraid, the hour is not yet come for their conversion. Therefore, Jerry, go you and lie down for an hour or two longer; and, at dawn of day, we will leave this place.'

Tugwell, however, could not be prevailed upon to return to his own bed (which he considered as haunted by some invisible being or evil spirit); but, putting on his cloaths, and laying his wallet under his head, slept upon the carpet in his Master's room.

As for Wildgoose, he composed himself for a few hours; but awaking between three and four o'clock, he roused his fellow-traveller, and they set out before any of the family was stirring.

Wildgoose left a note upon the table, expressing his obligations to Sir William and Lady Forester, and making an apology for his abrupt departure: but said, 'God had called him elsewhere; and, the end for which he had come into the Peak being (as he thought) frustrated by some unexpected incidents, he would defer his visitation of the Miners to some more favourable opportunity; when he hoped again to pay his respects to his worthy friends Sir William and Lady Forester.'

BOOK XI

CHAPTER I

The two Pilgrims decamp without Beat of Drum

THE two Pilgrims set out from Sir William Forester's (as was related) about four o'clock in the morning; and, as Tugwell did not know what his Master's intentions were, he was much pleased to see him turn his face towards the South. He was suprized, however, to find him so easily give up his project of preaching to the Miners in the Peak; with which view they had travelled so many tedious miles.

But the truth was, that, besides his apprehensions lest the servants might make a ludicrous use of the adventure of the Stable-boy whom the Butler had put into his bed, Mr. Wildgoose had a more powerful motive for hastening his departure towards the South. Mr. Bob Tench, in their walk from Ilam, had told him (by way of conversation), 'that he had promised to attend Sir Harry Hotspur to Warwick races, which' (he said) 'were within two or three days at furthest.'—Mr. Wildgoose, therefore, having determined (as a *coup d'eclât*) to bear his testimony against those ungodly meetings, thought no opportunity could be more proper than the present; when he could have a good chance for an interview with Miss Townsend, for which he so eagerly longed.

Mr. Wildgoose now travelled on for two or three hours in profound silence; reflecting on the disgrace he should probably bring upon himself and the cause in which he was embarked, if the servants should maliciously misrepresent the ridiculous adventure above-mentioned.

At length, however, Jerry ventured to ask his Master, 'What o'clock it was?'—Wildgoose, looking at him with a serious air, answered, 'Ah! Jerry, do not be so anxious to know the times and the seasons: for my part,' continues he, 'I am resolved, for the future, *to know nothing but Christ crucified*; nor, as far as I can answer for myself, ever to laugh again as long as I live, that I may not, by any levity of behaviour, inspire any weak Christian with wanton thoughts, nor give occasion for any suspicions to the prejudice of my own character.'[1]

'I will tell you what, then, Master; if you are resolved never to *laugh again*, you must never do two things more—you must never read Scoggan's Jests,[2] nor ever hear the Merry Andrew at Evesham fair—for they will make you burst your belly with laughter, in spite of your resolution.'—Wildgoose had almost broken his vow at first setting out; and could not but *smile*, at least, at Jerry's idea of wit and humour.

About eight o'clock, our travellers came to a public-house, at a small distance from a Nobleman's seat; where they thought it proper to halt and refresh themselves. There were two smart servants, with guns and pointers, in the kitchen, who, as well as the neighbouring seat, they found, belonged to Lord B——, Lady Forester's father. The servants were going a partridge-shooting; and, as soon as they marched out of the house, my Landlord shook his head, and said, 'it was a shame, to turn their pointers into the corn, before the Farmers had begun harvest.'—'Yes,' says my Landlady, 'they are a sad pack of them; they have debauched the whole country: there is hardly a sober man, or an honest woman, within ten miles of my Lord's house. I do not desire their company here; for I know they only want to ruin my daughter, if they could have their will of her.'

Wildgoose thought this a melancholy contrast to the character of Lady Forester; the force of whose good example had diffused a spirit of Religion and Virtue as widely round, as her Father's vicious principles had extended their baleful influence.

Wildgoose answered mine Hostess, 'that he imagined my Lord B—— was a good moral man; though he knew he was no great friend to Religion.'—'Yes,' says she, 'my Lord does some generous things, to be sure, but then there is no depending upon him: he will be very charitable to a poor man one day; and, if he happens to affront him, send him to gaol the next.

'He almost starved our whole market-town last winter, to be revenged upon them for an affront which they had put upon his Lordship.'—'How was that?' says Wildgoose.—'Why,' says my Landlady, 'he went and bought up three or four thousand pounds-worth of coals (for my Lord is very rich, you know); so that there was not a bit of coal to be got at any of the pits for ten miles round

the place.'—This account confirmed Wildgoose in his opinion of
the precarious nature of mere human virtues, when unsupported
by principles of Religion, or (as he called it) when void of Faith or
Divine Grace.

CHAPTER II

A learned Inn-keeper. Wildgoose meets an old Acquaintance

MR. WILDGOOSE and his fellow-traveller having had but little
rest the preceding night, they made a short stage that day, lodging
at a small public-house on the edge of the forest of Nedwood; and
the next morning reached Litchfield again about eleven o'clock.
They observed upon a sign there a *Greek* motto,[1] to this purpose,
Either drink, or depart about your business; which they imagined
to have been supplied by some learned Prebend, who either
frequented or patronized the house. They complied with the first
part of the precept, and *were drinking* a pint of ale upon a bench in
the yard; when my Landlord, who was a genteel sort of man, vouchsafed to speak to them; and, soon finding that Wildgoose had had
a liberal education, sate down by them, and began to inform them,
'that he himself had been bred at Cambridge as a Physician, and
had actually practised at Litchfield; but, finding the fees but small,
and that (such as they were) they came in but slowly, he had
married a young widow, who kept the inn. And here' (says he) 'I
see a good deal of genteel company; I am *Master* of a good house;
have the most amiable woman in the world for my wife; and live
as happy as a King.'

Whilst my Landlord was thus displaying the felicity of his situation, the amiable Mrs. Brewer (his wife) rang the bar-bell with some
vivacity; and, with no very melodious voice, cried out, 'Dr.
Brewer, where are you? what the Devil are you about? why *don't-
chee* come, and shell some pease? Here's a Family coming in; and
you sit prating to your Foot-passengers, who are drinking three-
halfpenny-worth of mild-ale—forsooth!'

The Doctor moved like clock-work at the sound of the bell and
Mrs. Brewer's voice; and told the travellers, 'he would wait upon
them again immediately.'

The case was—just at that instant, there rode in, at the back-gate, a young man in a silver-laced hat and a blue great-coat, and called the Hostler with great authority.—'Here, Master; here am I,' says the Hostler; 'who's a coming?'—'Who's a coming! why, I am coming, you puppy,' says the young man.—'Yes, Master, I see you be,' returns Robin: 'but what Family, what equipage have you got? and how many stands shall you want for your horses?'

My Landlady, hearing the Hostler ask these questions, took it for granted some grand Family was at hand. But the Gentleman, who caused all this uproar, turned his horse into the stable, bade the Hostler bring in his *saddle-bags*, and ordered a mutton-chop for his dinner.

As he passed by our two Pilgrims upon the bench, Mr. Wildgoose thought it was a face which he had seen before (and, indeed, it was a pretty remarkable one); yet, being engaged with his own thoughts, he did not on a sudden glance recollect him. But, the young man having got rid of his great-coat (which, though in the midst of the dog-days, he had chiefly worn to conceal his saddle-bags on the road), he again exhibited himself at the door; when Wildgoose immediately knew him to be Mr. Rouvell (or Beau Rueful), whom he had remembered at College, and met with at Bath.

As there were now no *persons of distinction* in the case, Rouvell did not disdain to recognize his old acquaintance. Wildgoose being now an Itinerant by profession, Rouvell expressed no surprize at meeting him there. But Wildgoose asked Rouvell, 'what had brought *him* to Litchfield?'—'Why, business of consequence,' replies Rouvell; 'and, if you will dine with me here, I will explain the affair to you; and, indeed, should be glad to consult with you upon the subject.'

Though Wildgoose was rather impatient to get into Warwick-shire; yet, as the races did not begin till the day following, he had time enough upon his hands. He therefore accepted of Mr. Rouvell's invitation.

CHAPTER III

The last Efforts of expiring Vanity

WHEN Mr. Wildgoose and Rouvell were alone together, Rouvell acquainted him with his present situation; 'that, having been jilted by a woman of fortune, whom he thought himself upon the brink of marrying, he had, in a fit of disappointment, married an agreeable woman, with a few hundreds, who was really the widow who kept the house where he had lodged at Bath; that he was now determined to live a more retired and regular life; and, in order to that, had accepted of a presentation to a living, given him by one of the Members for Coventry; and that he was now going to the Bishop for orders.'

'To the Bishop for orders!' cries Wildgoose; 'what! in a laced hat!'—'Oh,' says Rouvell, 'that is only to gain a little respect upon the road, as I could not conveniently bring my servant with me; but I shall immediately get that piece of finery ripped off before I wait upon the Bishop. I must confess, however,' continues he, 'I have been so long accustomed to the gaiety of the world, and to dress like a Gentleman, that I do not at all relish the peculiarity of the Clerical habit. Indeed, I can see no reason why a Clergyman should be distinguished from the rest of the world by such a funereal appearance, nor what connexion there is between Religion and a black coat; as if Christianity were such a gloomy affair, and so fatal an enemy to all kind of enjoyment.'

'Why,' says Wildgoose, 'I do not imagine there is any virtue in a black coat; but it seems proper, by some external mark, to put the Clergy in mind of the gravity and importance of their function: as also, to prevent their following the vain fashions of the world, and changing their dress according to the caprice of mankind, it seems adviseable to confine them to some one particular habit; which, I have heard, was the common dress about the time of the Reformation.'

'Well,' (says Rouvell) 'I can assure you, I think it a great act of mortification for a young fellow of eight and twenty to give up so material an article as that of dress; and could not forbear expressing my sense of this hardship, t'other day, in a ludicrous advertisement, which I will shew you.' Rouvell then pulled out a smart Morocco-leather pocket-book, and read the following advertisement:

'Whereas, on Sunday last (being Trinity-Sunday), between the hours of ten and twelve, two or three ill-looking fellows, disguised in *crape* (expressly contrary to the *black* act), did lay violent hands on a poor young Gentleman near the Bishop's palace at B—d—n; putting him in *bodily fear*, by bidding him *stand*, and *answer* them several odd out-of-the-way questions; and did insist upon his taking several horrible oaths, and extort from him several unreasonable concessions; particularly, that they, and all the Gentlemen of their profession, were very honest, civil Gentlemen, (contrary to his real sentiments and their known practices,) and had a right to treat in that manner, and impose their opinions upon, all that fell under their clutches; and, moreover, did rob him of twelve and six-pence in money; and did strip him of all his wearing apparel, namely, a smart coat with a red silk lining, a laced waistcoat, and a pair of red breeches, with about half-a-dozen ruffled shirts, and as many pair of white stockings; and did even rip the silver button and loop off his hat:—Now, this is to give notice, that whoever will bring any of the said offenders to the two-faced pump in Oxford, or to any of the pumps, or horse-ponds, in Oxford or Cambridge, so that they may be brought to condign punishment, shall receive an handsome reward.

'*N.B.* The Head of this gang is an old offender, and has followed these practices for many years; and has brought up several of his sons in the same *idle* way, who desired to follow some genteel trade, and to get their bread in some honest gentleman-like way of life.'

'Well, Sir,' says Wildgoose, 'there is no great harm in this piece of humour; I only think it a sort of *jesting*, which (as St. Paul says) is not quite so *convenient* or *decent*, especially in a man that is going to the Bishop for Holy Orders. Many a man has paid dearly for his jest. A Candidate for the Consulship at Rome, you know, lost his election, by jesting upon a poor Mechanic for the roughness of his hand. However, I should think, the change of character, which is expected in a Clergyman, a more weighty consideration than the mere change of dress; and that it is a greater sacrifice in a young man, to give up the gay amusements of life, than to lay aside his laced waistcoat or white stockings.'

'Why,' says Rouvell, 'I should imagine it would be no disadvantage to Religion, or to the Clergy in particular, if they were to remit a little of that solemnity of character, which has exposed

them to the imputation of hypocrisy, and the ridicule of the world;
and to mix a little more of the Gentleman, both in their dress and
in their deportment, which frequently prejudices people against
very worthy and ingenious men. And, now my pocket-book is out,
I will shew you another ludicrous composition, which a friend of
mine gave me, when I first talked of taking the gown.'—Wildgoose
said, 'he did not approve of that sort of buffoonry;' but, as he
would hear all the objections Rouvell had to the profession he was
now engaging in, Rouvell read the following parody on Shakespear's celebrated description of the seven stages of human life.

CHAPTER IV

A Parody on the Speech of Jaques, in Shakespear's As you like it

'As this parody is put into the mouth of a fop,' (says Rouvell) 'it is
rather a compliment to the Clergy, than any reflection upon them.

```
————Sir Plume,
————————Religion's all a farce;
And Parsons are but men, like you or me.
They have their foibles, and their fopperies:
And one sees amongst them sundry characters.
To mention only seven.——And first,—the Curate,
Humming and hawing to his drowsy herd.—
And then the Pedagogue, with formal wig,
His night-gown and his cane; ruling, like Turk,
All in his dusty school.—Then the smart Priest,
Writing extempore (forsooth!) a sonnet
Quaint, to his Mistress' shoe-string.—Then the Vicar,
Full of fees custom'ry, with his burying gloves;
Jealous of his rights, and apt to quarrel;
Claiming his paltry penny-farthing tithes,
E'en at the Lawyer's price.—Then the Rector,
In sleek surcingle with good tithe-pig stuff'd;
With eyes up-swoln, and shining double-chin;
Full of wise nods and orthodox distinctions:
And so he gains respect.—Proceed we next
Unto the old Incumbent at his gate,
With silken scull-cap tied beneath his chin;
```

> His banyan, with silver clasp, wrapt round
> His shrinking paunch; and his fam'd, thund'ring voice,
> Now whistling like the wind, his audience sleeps
> And snores to th' lulling sound.—Best scene of all,
> With which I close this reverend description,
> Is your Welsh Parson, with his *noble living*,
> *Sans* shoes, *sans* hose, *sans* breeches, *sans* every thing.'[1]

'Why,' says Wildgoose, 'this parody might be characteristic of the Clergy of the last age: but, I am apt to think, the descriptions are now obsolete; and the Clergy of these times are rather too polite than too aukward, and have more of the Gentleman than either of the Christian or the Pedant, in their characters. They read more plays and pamphlets, than sermons or commentaries on the Bible; they are rather witty in conversation, than wise unto salvation;

> Polite apostates from God's Grace to Wit.[2]

'But I am most sincerely of opinion' (continues Wildgoose), 'that the only way for the Clergy to escape the ridicule of the gay world, and to keep up their credit, is, not to join in its fopperies, but to revive the primitive manners, and to preach up the genuine doctrines of the Reformation. And I cannot but hope, Mr. Rouvell, that, whatever levities you may have hitherto indulged yourself in, you will lay them aside, with your ruffles and your laced hat.'

Rouvell replied, 'that he had seriously resolved to do every thing in his power to redeem his lost time; and that, although he might not be able to do much *good* by his learning or eloquence, he was determined not to do any mischief by an immoral or indecent behaviour.'

This serious conversation was now interrupted by the appearance of a leg of lamb and cauliflowers, and a custard-pudding, which Rouvell had ordered for dinner; and, though they differed something in their theological opinions, the two travellers were unanimous in their approbation of Mrs. Brewer's cookery, and eat very heartily.

After dinner, Rouvell called for a bottle of port, and said, 'he would take a decent leave of the Laity;' but, as Wildgoose did not chuse to drink his share, they proposed inviting Dr. Brewer, in the character of mine Host, to partake with them; who graciously condescended to honour them with his company, and assist them in the arduous task of dispatching a bottle of his own manufacture;

as pleasant a revenge, as making a Physician swallow his own prescription.

Wildgoose having resumed the subject of Rouvell's taking orders, and having earnestly exhorted him 'to consider the importance of the office which he was going to take upon him;' the afternoon was far advanced, before they parted; Rouvell setting off for the Bishop's palace at Eccleshall; and Wildgoose, attended by his trusty friend, pursuing his journey towards the borders of Warwickshire.

CHAPTER V

Trifling Difficulties

OUR spiritual adventurers, having sufficiently refreshed themselves, travelled at a good rate; Wildgoose being desirous to reach Sutton-Cofield, in his way to Warwick, that night; so that little conversation passed between them: Tugwell, however, could not but express his surprize, that the Gentleman, whom he had seen to-day in a laced hat (and whom he had taken for a Gentleman's servant), was to be a Parson to-morrow.

As it was now some time past the summer-solstice, night overtook them sooner than they expected; and, when they came into the forest, or chace, near Sutton, it was quite dark, and they had wandered considerably out of the great road. At length, however, they came to what they took for a direction-post; when Wildgoose told Jerry, 'if he could but climb up the post, and trace out with his finger the first letter upon either of the hands, he could tell which way to turn; as, he took it for granted, one road led to Birmingham, and the other to Warwick.'—'That I can do then, Master,' (says Jerry); 'for, when I was a young fellow, there was not a boy in the parish could climb a crow's nest so well as myself.' Tugwell, therefore, desiring his Master to take care of his staff and his wallet, ran up the post like a cat; but, when he was got about seven or eight feet high, he made a sudden pause; and squelch he came down again, bawling out, with great consternation, 'Lord have mercy upon us! as sure as I am alive, there is a dead man hanging up.'—which, indeed, was partly true; for a highwayman, who had committed a murder, was hanged in chains there two or three years before; but, the body being decayed, only part of the skeleton remained, for a terror to these honest men, rather than to those hardened wretches for whose edification it was intended.

They now travelled on, therefore, under the direction of Providence; and in half an hour more saw some lights at a distance; which proved to be Sutton-Cofield, whither they were bound.

The two Pilgrims, coming in late, soon retired to rest, without meeting with any incident worth recording: only, finding a drunken Blacksmith in the house, whom mine Host pretended he wanted to get rid of, Wildgoose began preaching to him about the New-birth; which soon put him to flight, and sent him home to his wife and family.

CHAPTER VI

Tugwell is under a Necessity of drinking Strong-beer instead of Small

WILDGOOSE having been assured, by my Landlord, 'that the races did not begin at Warwick till the next day;' notwithstanding the strong attraction which he felt in his heart towards the residence of Miss Townsend, they did not set out till near nine o'clock. After travelling three or four hours in the heat of the day, about one o'clock they passed near some corn-fields; where they saw a company of Reapers, who had just begun harvest, sitting at dinner under a shady oak, and laughing and singing with great glee and alacrity.

As making converts was the game which Wildgoose had constantly in view, he fancied he had a call to give a word of exhortation to these honest people, whom he considered as indulging a culpable festivity.

When they came up to them, therefore, Jerry introduced himself, by asking, 'whether they could give a poor man a draught of small-beer, this hot weather?'—'Aye, and of strong-beer too' (says one of them), as much as thou canst drink: it costs us nothing; and we give it as freely as we receive it.'

This hospitable invitation encouraged Tugwell to sit down by

them without any more ceremony; and he began to rummage out
a crust of bread and a piece of cheese, which he had stowed in his
wallet. But a young Farmer told him, 'he should not eat bread and
cheese there;' and, taking up a basket, he cut him off a good slice
of some boiled beef, and a piece of plumb-pudding; of which, at
Tugwell's request, Mr. Wildgoose vouchsafed to partake. After
eating pretty heartily, and drinking a draught or two of strong-beer
out of a leathern-bottle; one of the company desired the young
Farmer (who appeared in a genteeler style than any of the rest) to
entertain them with a song, as he was going to do when he was
interrupted by the arrival of Tugwell and his Master. 'Mr. John,'
said one of them, 'can sing in the Playhouse fashion; for he has
lived two or three years with my Lord in London.'—'But what
must I sing?' says he.—'Why, the Harvest-home song, that your
brother made last year,' replied the other.—'Well,' says he, 'I have
got a sad cold; but I will sing it as well as I can, though we have
many a weary day to come yet before our harvest-home.'——He
then sang, with a tolerable grace, the following ballad.

THE TRIUMPH OF CERES:
OR,
THE HARVEST-HOME

To the Tune of, *What beauteous Scenes enchant my Sight!*

> What chearful sounds salute our ears,
>   And echo o'er the lawn!
> Behold! the loaded car appears,
>   In joyful triumph drawn:
> The nymphs and swains, a jovial band,
>   Still shouting as they come,
> With rustic instruments in hand,
>   Proclaim the Harvest-home.
>
> The golden sheaves, pil'd up on high,
>   Within the barn are stor'd;
> The careful hind, with secret joy
>   Exulting, views his hoard.
> His labours past, he counts his gains;
>   And, freed from anxious care,
> His casks are broach'd; the sun-burnt swains
>   His rural plenty share.

> In dance and song the night is spent;
>   All ply the spicy bowl:
> And jests and harmless merriment
>   Expand the artless soul.
> Young Colin whispers Rosalind,
>   Who still reap'd by his side;
> And plights his troth, if she prove kind,
>   To take her for his bride.
>
> For joys like these, through circling years
>   Their toilsome task they tend:
> The hind successive labours bears,
>   In prospect of the end;
> In Spring, or Winter, sows his seed,
>   Manures or tills the soil;
> In Summer various cares succeed;
>   But Harvest crowns his toil.[1]

When the young Farmer had finished his song, Wildgoose said, 'it was rather better than the common ballads;' and enquired, whether his brother really made it, as the Reapers hinted?'—The Farmer assured him, he did; for that his brother had been bred at Cambridge; and though his father would have been glad to have had him assist them in the field, when he came home in the long vacation, yet, instead of binding up the sheaves, or making hay, he would sit half the day under a tree, and make verses.'

Mr. Wildgoose was now going to exhort them 'to sanctify their labour, by singing hymns and spiritual songs, instead of those ungodly ballads;' when Tugwell, observing a company of women who were gleaning in the field, wished 'his old wife Dorothy were amongst them, for that she would make a better hand at leasing[2] than any of them.'

'She would hardly make a better hand of it,' (says the young Farmer) 'than a young woman did here last harvest, and to whom we are obliged for our good cheer today.'—'How much might she earn in a day, then, by her leasing?' says Jerry.—'Why, more than this field and the next to it will produce these ten years,' says the Farmer.—Tugwell expressing some surprize, the young Farmer said, 'the story was remarkable; and, if they would give him leave, he would tell it them.' Accordingly, he began the following narration.

CHAPTER VII

The fortunate Isabella

'THIS manor (the greatest part of which my father rents) was purchased by our Squire's father, a great Counsellor in London, who died before he had taken possession of it. The young Squire, being fond of the country, came and settled here about two years ago. He took a small part of the estate into his own hands, for his amusement; and, having a few acres in tillage, used to ride out most days in the harvest-time, to view his Reapers at their work.

'Amongst the poor people who came to glean in the field, there was a young woman, whose mother came a stranger into the parish, and had lived there for nine or ten years, with no other family than this one daughter, who was now about sixteen, and so handsome, that several young Farmers in the neighbourhood admired her; and, if she had had a little money, would probably have been glad to marry her. She dressed, like our other parish girls, in a coarse stuff-gown, straw-hat, and the like; but, somehow or other, she put on her cloaths so cleverly, that every thing became her. Her caps and her handkerchiefs, which were of her own making, were in a better taste than those of our other country girls; and, when her gown was pinned back, an under-petticoat appeared, with a border of flowers of her own work.

'The young Squire could not but take notice of her genteel shape and elegant motions; but she was so bashful, that he could hardly get a sight of her countenance. He enquired who she was; and, as nobody could give much account of her (because neither she nor her mother went out amongst their neighbours), he one evening, as she returned home, followed her at a distance, up a winding valley, to the cottage where she and her mother lived. It stands by a wood-side, at a distance from our village, near a lonely farm-house; which is the only neighbour they have.

'The Squire hung his horse to the gate, and went in; where he found the old Gentlewoman (for so we all thought her) knitting some fine stockings, and surveying with pleasure the produce of her daughter's labour. The house was very plainly furnished: but the Squire was surprized to see an handsome harpsichord, which took up half the room, and some music-books lying about, with other books proper for young Ladies to read.

'Isabella (which was the name the young woman went by) blushed up to the ears, when she saw the Squire come in; and, making a courtesy, retired into another room.

'He made a short apology to the mother for his intrusion; but said, "he was so struck with her daughter's appearance, that his curiosity would not suffer him to rest till he had made some enquiries about her; as there was something in her manner, that convinced him she must have had a different education from what usually falls to the lot of young women in that humble sphere of life."

'The mother told him, "they had lived better formerly, but had been reduced by misfortunes; that, however, by her daughter's industry and her own work, they contrived to live very comfortably in their present situation."

'As she did not seem inclined to be more communicative, the Squire took his leave, but not without offering her an handsome present of money; which, to his surprize, she absolutely refused.'

CHAPTER VIII

Further Account of Isabella

'The next day Isabella appeared again in the field, and was as intent upon her leasing as usual. The Squire could not keep his eyes off her; and, having now a pretence for enquiring after her mother, entered into some further discourse with her; and found she expressed herself so properly, and discovered so much good sense and delicacy, that her personal charms appeared to much greater advantage, by the beauty of her mind; and, in short, the Squire became quite enamoured of this rural damsel.

'After two or three days, he went again to her mother, and begged, with the most earnest importunity, "to be further informed of her story, and by what accident she had been brought to submit to her present obscure way of life; for that he was greatly interested in her's and her daughter's welfare, and hoped it might be in his power (if she would give him leave) to make their situation somewhat more agreeable to them, than it could possibly be, whilst both she and her daughter were forced to work so hard for a sub-sistence."

'There appeared so much sincerity and modesty in our young Gentleman's manner, that the mother could not avoid gratifying his curiosity. She then told him, "that her husband had enjoyed a genteel place under the government, and by his care and frugality had saved a considerable fortune; but that, not being in the secret, he had lost the whole in the iniquitous project of the South-sea; the shock of which had proved fatal to his health; and he died a few years after, leaving her and this one daughter (who was then about six years old) without any support, but what she could raise by the sale of a few jewels, which did not amount to three hundred pounds. To avoid the slights of my former acquaintance (con-tinued she), I retired into this part of the country (where I was pretty sure I should not be known), and have taken the name of Fairfax; for my real name is————.''

'The young Squire heard this short account with an eager atten-tion; but, upon hearing the name of ————, "Good heavens!" (cries he) "is it possible you should be the widow of that worthy man Mr. ————, to whom our family is under the greatest obliga-tions? as I have often heard my father declare; who always lamented, that he never could hear what was become of you and your daugh-ter; and, I am certain, would have been extremely happy in an opportunity of shewing his gratitude to the family of his worthy friend. I hope, however, that happiness is reserved for me. But," (continued the Squire) "did not you know that my father had pur-chased this manor; and that he was the friend of your late valuable husband?"—"Why," replies Mrs. Fairfax, "my time is so con-stantly taken up with the instruction of my daughter, and with the business necessary for our support, that I converse but little with our neighbours; and though I may have heard, that a Mr. ———— had purchased the manor, and know that my dear Mr. Fairfax (so I call him) had a friend of that name, yet I never thought that your father was under any further obligations to assist his friend's dis-tressed family than many others were, from whom I never received the least act of friendship, though I knew they had it in their power to alleviate our distress."

'The Squire then told Mrs. Fairfax, "that he hoped there were various ways by which he could render their situation more happy than it seemed to be at present; but that there was only one way by which he could do it with complete satisfaction to himself; which was, with her permission, by laying himself and his fortune at her daughter's feet; which he should do with the greatest pleasure."

'Mrs. Fairfax was astonished at so generous an offer; but desired the young Gentleman, "not to engage rashly in an affair of so much importance, and to consider thoroughly how he could support the raillery of his acquaintance, and perhaps the resentment of his friends; which he might reasonably expect from so *imprudent* an alliance." The young Squire replied, "that he was his own master; that he was sufficiently acquainted with Isabella's personal charms; and would rely upon Mrs. Fairfax's care of her education, for every other accomplishment; and should think himself completely happy, if the proposal proved agreeable to the young Lady's inclinations."

'In short, the fair Isabella was immediately sent for; and the Squire left the mother to propose it to her daughter; who, after a decent parley, with gratitude surrendered her charms to so generous a lover. They were married in a fortnight's time; and are now as happy as the day is long.

'The old Lady will not be prevailed upon to forsake her little cottage by the wood-side; but has enough allowed her to keep a maid-servant; and the coach is sent almost every day, to carry her to the great house.

'As a compliment to his Lady, the Squire intends every year to give us a dinner out in the field on the day we begin harvest; and another at the hall, by way of harvest-home; on which occasion last year, my brother made the song which I have now sung.'

'Well,' (says Tugwell, when the young Farmer had finished his story) 'this is right now, to take care of the old Gentlewoman; and, I dare say, she now makes three meals a day, and a supper at night. Why, this is just for all the world like a story in a history-book.'— 'Yes,' says Mr. Wildgoose, 'it is like a story in the Book of books, the story of Boaz and Ruth.'—'Well,' says Tugwell, 'the Squire is a man after my own heart; and I will drink his health in another draught of strong-beer, if you will give me leave.'

The leathern bottle then went round, and Jerry began to talk apace; when Mr. Wildgoose endeavoured to give the conversation a religious turn; and, amongst other things, observed, in allusion to their present employment, 'that the harvest, indeed, was great; but the labourers (meaning the true Ministers of the Gospel) were few.'—The Reapers, not understanding his allegory, said, 'they were enough of them to cut down that field, and as much more, in a week's time.' But, considering Wildgoose's speech as an hint that it was time for them to resume their labour, they leaped up, and fell to work with great chearfulness and alacrity, leaving the two travellers to pursue their journey at their leisure.

CHAPTER IX

A curious Inscription

ABOUT eight in the evening, Mr. Wildgoose and his humble friend came to a public-house near Meriden, on the Chester road; whose sign being suspended in a shady elm, it has obtained the name of, The George in the Tree. Wildgoose, during this peregrination, had adopted a laudable custom, though attended with some little expence, as well as trouble; which was, when he came to an inn, to read whatever he found written either on the walls or in the windows; and, where-ever there was any thing obscene or immoral, either to write under it something by way of antidote; or, if it were very shocking, he would entirely erase it, if written upon a wall; or, if in a window, break out the pane, and pay the damage.

As he was examing the parlour-windows in this little hotel (which, affording entertainment for horse as well as man, *might* be called an inn) he observed the following remarkable inscription:

J.S. D.S.P. D. HOSPES IGNOTVS,
PATRIÆ (VT NVNC EST) PLVSQVAM VELLET NOTVS,
TEMPESTATE PVLSVS,
HIC PERNOCTAVIT,
A.D. M DCC XXVI.

'Jonathan Swift, Dean of St. Patrick's, in Dublin, here a stranger unknown, but in his own country (such as it now is) better known than he would wish to be, being driven by a storm, lodged here all night, in the year of our Lord 1726.'

Mr. Wildgoose, having at present little curiosity of that kind, did not take out the pane; as he probably might have done for three

halfpence, and as was done soon after by some more curious
traveller.

He then went into the kitchen, according to custom, to give
some little spiritual instructions to the family, or to any one that he
might accidentally meet with; where he saw two travelling women,
who seemed much fatigued, as they had sufficient cause, having
travelled on foot that day above twenty miles. One of them seemed
a pretty genteel woman, but had a melancholy, dejected look; which
attracted Wildgoose's particular attention; and he addressed himself to her as a person under affliction, applying the common topics
of consolation for the evils of life. But, the poor woman making
little reply, Wildgoose soon left her, without satisfying his curiosity
for the present, and went early to rest.

CHAPTER X

Mr. Wildgoose makes a new Acquaintance

As they had but a short stage to Warwick, and the races were not
to begin till the afternoon, the two Pilgrims did not set out very
early; but, travelling a good pace, they soon overtook the two
women whom they had seen the preceding night, though they had
set out some time before them. As they were to travel half a mile
further the same road, Tugwell asked them, by way of conversation, 'whether they were going to London, or not?'—One of them
answered, 'No; but into ——shire.'—The afflicted Lady then
asked Mr. Wildgoose, 'if he knew any thing of one Squire Townsend in that county?'—'Squire Townsend!' (replies he, with some
surprize) 'yes, I know something of the family.'—She then
enquired, 'if he knew whether either of the daughters were married
lately, or likely to be married?'—Wildgoose answered, 'that he did
not know that they were; and that he could venture to assure her
to the contrary; though I have heard,' (continued he) 'that an half-
pay Irish Officer had made pretensions to one of them: but her
father, I am pretty sure, will never listen to the proposals of such
an empty coxcomb, and one who has no visible fortune to support
his daughter.'

The poor woman turned pale as Wildgoose was speaking; and

all on a sudden burst into a flood of tears. Wildgoose expressing great astonishment, the other woman (who was the Lady's maid) said, 'that Irish Officer was the vilest of men; that he was this poor Lady's husband, with whom he had had a good fortune, and by whom he had three fine children; but he had gone to England, under a pretence of soliciting better preferment in the army, and left her destitute of any other support than what she could meet with from her own friends; and, what was more base, (if their intelligence was true) he was going to draw in another young Lady of family and fortune, by a marriage which must necessarily be invalid.'

This intelligence greatly alarmed Mr. Wildgoose; as he did not know what impression this Irish hero might have made upon the object of *his* affection. But when the Lady, finding him so well acquainted with the family, produced the letter which she had received upon that subject, he was struck dumb with astonishment; for the person who gave the intelligence, and who had been a servant to the late Captain Townsend, mentioned Miss *Julia* Townsend, as the Lady to whom Captain Mahoney was going to be married: so that Wildgoose began to suspect, either that Miss Townsend had not been sincere in the contempt which she expressed of Captain Mahoney; or that, since he had seen her, some scheme of that kind might have been brought about by the widow Townsend's influence over her father.

Mr. Wildgoose, however, carefully concealed how much he was interested in the affair; and, knowing how whimsical Mr. Townsend was in giving Roman names to his children, he told Mrs. Mahoney, 'that the person, who wrote the account, must certainly have mistaken Miss Julia Townsend for Miss Lucia; as, to his knowledge, the former had been some months from her father, and was now with a relation near Warwick; and that he himself was in hopes of seeing her there, either that very night, or the next morning at furthest, after he had dispatched some business which he had upon his hands that afternoon.' He added, moreover, 'that the nearest way she could go to Mr. Townsend's was, to leave the great London road, and go through Warwick, whither he himself would conduct her.'

Mrs. Mahoney and her companion thought themselves very fortunate in meeting with a man, who seemed capable of assisting them in the affair which had brought them to England, and gladly

joined them. This droll party, therefore, united by an odd concurrence of interests, trudged on very amicably together, and about
dinner-time arrived at the borough of Warwick.

Mr. Wildgoose was at first inclined to go immediately to Dr.
Greville's, and inform Miss Townsend of the discovery he had
made: but, thinking it sinful to prefer the temporal felicity of one
family to the immortal happiness of thousands, which, he flattered
himself, depended upon his preaching, he rejected with horror
that design.

CHAPTER XI

At Warwick

MR. WILDGOOSE took his company to the first inn that presented
itself. They found every one in motion, and preparing to set out for
the course, which was some little distance from the town. They
got some dinner, however, and all sate down together: during
which, Tugwell observed, 'how comical it was, that they should
happen to meet with the Lady so cleverly;' and said, 'if he could
but meet with his son Joseph again, he should think his time well
bestowed. It was but last night,' added Jerry, 'that I dreamed about
him: I thought *as how* they were going to let me down in the Lead-
mines again; and *as how* our Joe came and drew his sword, and beat
the Miners off, and *drawed* me up again. But I shall never see poor
Joe any more; if he had been alive, we should certainly have heard
from him in five years time: but, perhaps, one reason why Joe has
never wrote to us, is, because he can neither write nor read.'

As the company had more important concerns of their own to
engage their thoughts, they paid little attention to Jerry's dis-
quisition. But, as soon as they had made a short meal, and Mr.
Wildgoose had safely deposited Mrs. Mahoney and her companion, under a promise to wait at the inn till his return, he set out
with his friend Tugwell, conducted by an intelligent lad belonging
to the inn; who, as they walked together, promised, at Mr. Wildgoose's request, to furnish him with a table, or joint-stool, from
their booth; for, the lad taking Wildgoose for a Conjurer, the poor
boy imagined he should (by that means) see his legerdemain performances, or slight of hand, for nothing.

CHAPTER XII

Olympic Honours

THE two Pilgrims approached the scene of action just as the horses were going to start. Their ears were saluted with variety of sounds: the trumpet had just given the signal to prepare for the first heat; a recruiting party, with drums and fifes, were beating up for volunteers; and, in every part of the field,

Steed answer'd steed in high and boastful neighings,[1]

as Shakespear expresses it. The whole course was in motion; the coaches and chariots whirling towards the starting-post, or other convenient stands; the horsemen scampering different ways, according as they imagined they should get the best view of the sport; in another part, the knowing ones, with great composure, though with horrid oaths and imprecations, were settling the bets, and, with profound skill, deciding the fates of the different horses.

Wildgoose was moved with compassion, or (to use his own expression) his bowels yearned for his poor brethren, to see with what thoughtless eagerness and vain curiosity they scowered across the plain, in pursuit of they knew not what; each miserable Mechanic apparently as solicitous about the contest, as if his salvation depended upon the event. Amongst other objects, he could not but take notice of a young man of fortune, an old Oxford acquaintance, exalted in the stand, or balcony, of the starting-post; who looked down with the utmost contempt upon all below him; fancying himself superior to a Roman General in his triumphant car, or even to Mr. Whitfield, when he preached from the starting-post at Northampton.[2]

Wildgoose's zeal for the cause he was engaged in was raised almost beyond controul. He thought it best, however, to defer his harangue till after the first heat; when the people would be more inclined to listen to his admonitions, than in the present tumultuous agitation of their spirits.

CHAPTER XIII

Mr. Wildgoose's Farewell Sermon

ACCORDINGLY, the heat being now over, and people a little composed from their eager attention to the sport, Mr. Wildgoose applied to his young friend at the booth that belonged to the inn where they had dined, who procured a table, which Tugwell placed upon a little eminence; by which means his Master was sufficiently exalted above the crowd; who, with several chariots and horsemen, soon gathering round him, Mr. Wildgoose, without more ceremony, began to harangue them with great vehemence, both of language and gesticulation.

Though Wildgoose insisted strenuously upon the unlawfulness and bad tendency of these Paganish diversions, and the bad effect they had upon the mind of a Christian; yet his principal intention was, to make use of this opportunity to inculcate his peculiar tenets, and to make proselytes to true Christianity, or, what he always thought equivalent, the doctrines of Mr. Wesley and Mr. Whitfield.

But, whilst Wildgoose was enumerating the evil consequences of these ungodly assemblies, and, amongst the rest, graphically describing the sad effects of drunkenness and intemperance; a young fellow on horseback, who was drinking with some more company, having a glass decanter in his hand, before it was quite empty, hurled it with great vehemence at the Preacher's head, bidding him, 'drink, and be d—mn'd!'

The decanter struck Wildgoose just above the left temple; and (being, in order to deceive the customers in the measure, fluted and crumpled into various angles) not only brought him senseless to the ground, but also cut a branch of the temporal-artery, from which the blood issued forth in great abundance, and alarmed all the company, who thought Wildgoose killed upon the spot.

Poor Tugwell, seeing his Master struck down, and, for aught he knew, mortally wounded, broke out into doleful lamentations; being equally concerned, both for his friend and for himself. He said, 'he should be hanged, for enticing Mr. Geoffry from home;— or, at least, should lose Madam Wildgoose's custom, and be forbidden the house.'

Jerry, however, thrust away and shoved off the crowd, in order to assist his Master; and was so angry with every body about him, that he gave one a blow in the face, another a punch in the guts, and another a knock on the pate with his staff; which brought three or four surly fellows upon Jerry's back; and he would probably have suffered as much in the scuffle as his Master had done, had not a young fellow in a military habit, with a knapsack on his back, and a cutlass by his side, pushed through the crowd very opportunely, and come to his assistance.

Jerry, in his hurry, could hardly forbear striking even his deliverer; but, seeing an hanger by his side, he was kept a little in awe, and made a bow to the Gentleman Soldier, for his friendly aid. The Soldier, catching hold of Tugwell with both his hands, cried out, 'Dear father! do not you know me? Give me your blessing. How does mother do?'

Tugwell stood staring for some time, before he knew his son Joseph; who (as the reader may, or perhaps may not, remember) has been mentioned more than once, as being sent for a Soldier, and supposed to have died in America. Jerry threw his arms about his son's neck, expressing the utmost joy and surprize; and said, 'Now his dream was out!' and began to ask twenty questions in a breath; which, Joseph said, 'he would answer at a proper time.'

They now therefore assisted in carrying young Wildgoose, whom Tugwell had announced to his son, into the booth, that proper care might be taken of their friend in this unhappy situation.

CHAPTER XIV

Work for the Doctor

AMONGST the horsemen whose curiosity had drawn them to hear Wildgoose, was a well-booted Grecian,[1] in a fustian frock and jockey cap, who seemed greatly affected with this accident, and rode immediately with great trepidation in quest of a Surgeon. This was no other than the benevolent Mr. Bob Tench, who (the reader may recollect) became acquainted with Mr. Wildgoose at Sir William Forester's in the Peak, and said, 'he was to attend Sir Harry Hotspur to Warwick races.' Bob was directed by some of the company to Dr. Slash, an elderly Surgeon, who was smoking his pipe over a tiff of punch, by himself, in the next booth. Bob summoned him, with great authority, 'to come immediately to the wounded Itinerant, who,' he said, 'would bleed to death.'

The Surgeon continued smoking on with great composure; and asked, 'who was to pay him for his trouble?' observing, 'that he could not work for nothing; that their education was very expensive; that, besides serving seven years apprenticeship, they were obliged to walk the hospitals, to attend anatomical and pharmaceutical lectures, and the like.'

'D—mn your *anno-domical*, *farta-shitical* lectures' (cries Bob); 'why, the man is dying, and, if you don't come immediately, will bleed to death. Come along; I myself will see you paid.'

Dr. Slash then beat out his pipe; took another glass of punch; and, with a very important air, rose up, and went to attend the wounded Orator, who by this time was carried into the other booth, and was come a little to himself again. The Doctor, however, shook his head; magnified the danger of the contusion; and took several ounces of blood from the Patient, notwithstanding what he had lost from the wound. While the Doctor was preparing his bandages and dressings, the company, according to custom, were very officiously giving their advice. Bob Tench was for applying only some Fryars Balsam, and some Gold-beaters skin; which (as we observed) he always carried in his pocket. Jerry Tugwell wished, 'that his namesake, Dr. Tugwell, the great Bonesetter of Evesham, was there; who,' he said, 'would cure his Worship in the twinkling of an eye.'—Young Tugwell said, '*if so be* the Surgeon of their regiment were there, he would cut off a leg, and tie up the arteries, and stop the blood, in the firing of a pistol.'—My Landlord belonging to the booth, putting in his verdict, said, 'a little *permacetty* and a dram of brandy was the *sovereignst* thing in the world for an inward bruise.'

Dr. Slash (you may suppose) did not look very pleasant during these wise instructions. On the contrary, he gave himself no small airs; and said, 'if they made such a noise, and the Patient could not be kept more quiet, the Devil might dress the wound; for he would have no more to do with it.'

CHAPTER XV

An old Gentleman in Black arrives

JUST as Mr. Slash had mentioned the Devil, a tall elderly Gentleman in black came into the booth; and, applying himself to Slash,
enquired, 'whether the Patient might be removed without any
danger, as he could not have proper care taken of him in such a place
as that?'—The Surgeon, bowing with great respect, answered,
'that, to be sure, there would be some danger in removing him;
for, if the artery should bleed again, he did not know how it would
be stopped; but, however, with great care,' he added, 'he *might* be
removed.'

Wildgoose himself said, 'he should be glad to be conveyed, if
possible, to the inn at Warwick; as some company waited for him
there, with whom he had business of great consequence.' He then
called Tugwell to him, and told him, 'he would have him go, that
very night, with a note which he would write to Miss Townsend, to
acquaint her with the discovery which they had made in regard to
Captain Mahoney.' He then pulled out his pen and ink, and some
paper out of his letter-case, and wrote a short note, which he sealed,
and directed it, 'To Miss Townsend, at Dr. Greville's, at ——,
near Warwick.' This direction he shewed to Mr. Slash; and asked
him, 'whether he could instruct his fellow-traveller how to find
out the place?'—'Why,' (says Slash, with surprize) 'this Gentleman in black is Dr. Greville himself.'—He then informed the
Doctor of Mr. Wildgoose's request.—Wildgoose, who was agreeably surprized at this unexpected interview, desiring to speak with
Dr. Greville in private; the Doctor replied, 'that they would get
into his chariot, and then they might converse without interruption.'—Wildgoose, therefore, taking leave of Bob Tench, and
directing Tugwell, with his son Joseph, to meet him at the inn at
Warwick, was lifted into the chariot; and he and Doctor Greville
(who gave the Surgeon orders where to see his Patient the next
day) set off together.

CHAPTER XVI

Character of Dr. Greville

DOCTOR GREVILLE was a Clergyman, in whom the sacerdotal character appeared in its genuine dignity; not in an assumed solemnity of aspect, or formal grimace, and a pompous perriwig as big as Dr. Sacheverell's;[1] but in a serious, yet affable, behaviour; the result of a sincere piety, sanctity of manners, and goodness of heart. He had a considerable independent fortune; which enabled him to obey the impulse of a generous and humane disposition. And it was a maxim with him, 'that, while a single person in his neighbourhood wanted the necessaries of life, he had no right to indulge himself in its superfluities.'

He undertook the care of a large and populous parish; but with no other motive than that of doing good, the stipend being hardly sufficient to maintain a resident Curate.

Dr. Greville really was what Mr. Wesley and his associates ought to have been, and what (I sincerely believe) they at first intended to be. He revived the practice of primitive piety in his own person, and in his own parish; and, by his examples and admonitions, excited many of the neighbouring Clergy to be more vigilant in the discharge of their duty. He had a *Faith*, which worked by *Love*; or, in modern language, his belief of the truths of the Gospel made him consider as an indispensable duty those acts of beneficence which his humanity prompted him to perform.

If Dr. Greville had seen the poor man who fell amongst thieves, he would not, like the Priest and the Levite, have passed by him on the other side; but, like the good Samaritan, would have set him upon his own horse, would have bound up his wounds, and poured in *oil* and *wine*, which (if the modern practice had adopted so excellent a balsamic), upon so good authority, I should think (by the way) at least equal to Fryars Balsam or Opodeldoc.[2]

Dr. Greville, then, would have been the first to have run to the assistance of poor Wildgoose, had not his attention been engaged by an object nearer home: I mean, a young Lady in the chariot with him, who, upon the sight of Wildgoose's accident, had fainted away, and who, the reader will easily guess, was no other than Miss Julia Townsend.

When Mr. Wildgoose first began his harangue, Miss Townsend

told Dr. Greville, 'that she had seen him at Gloucester; and that he was a young man of a pretty good fortune:' which partly induced the Doctor to drive up, and make part of the audience; though he was glad of this opportunity of seeing young Wildgoose, on account of what had happened previously to this, and which it is proper to explain.

Wildgoose had written to Miss Townsend a letter from Gloucester (as was mentioned), which she received, and carefully preserved in her Morocco-leather pocket-book; but which she had accidentally left upon her toilette, one morning, whilst she was gone with Dr. Greville to take a walk in the fields. Mrs. Greville going into Miss Townsend's room, female curiosity got the better of the point of honour, and she could not forbear examining the contents of this letter; which, indeed, was a liberty that Miss Townsend's situation, since her imprudent elopement, sufficiently warranted so good a friend to take. This letter was written in so ambiguous a style, that it was difficult to determine whether Mr. Wildgoose were more solicitous for Miss Townsend's happiness, or his own. And there was such a mixture of the amorous and the devout, that it might be taken either in a spiritual or in a carnal sense; though, to any one that knew human nature so well as Dr. Greville did, there could be no difficulty in what sense such a correspondence between two young persons of different sexes ought to be interpreted. Dr. Greville was not displeased, therefore, at this opportunity of making some observations upon Miss Townsend's behaviour on such an occasion; and the violent effect, which Wildgoose's accident had upon this young Lady, left Dr. Greville no room to doubt of the tender regard which she entertained for him.

Dr. Greville was greatly alarmed at Miss Townsend's fainting away, and sent the Footman, in a great hurry, to procure some water from the next booth; who, seeing the Lady of their manor in her coach with her two daughters, acquainted them with the accident. She immediately sent one of her daughters to Miss Townsend's assistance; and, by Dr. Greville's permission, took Miss Townsend into her coach for the rest of the afternoon; which left him at liberty to make proper enquiries after the wounded Pilgrim, and to take him into his chariot, as has been related.

CHAPTER XVII

Dr. Greville and Mr. Wildgoose

As soon as they were alone together in the chariot, Wildgoose related to Dr. Greville the circumstances of his getting acquainted with Miss Townsend at Gloucester; and then his accidental meeting with Mrs. Mahoney, and the discovery he had made of Captain Mahoney's villainous design upon some one of Mr. Townsend's daughters; which greatly alarmed Dr. Greville, though he said, 'that all Mr. Townsend's friends had a very bad opinion of the Widow Townsend, whom he had taken into his house.

'It is very lucky, however,' (added Dr. Greville) 'that Mr. Townsend will be at our house this very evening, if he is not yet arrived; in expectation of which, Mrs. Greville stayed at home to-day. And for that reason (and because, I believe, you will be better taken care of at my house than at an inn), I would have you by all means go home with me to my parsonage-house.'—Wildgoose found no great reluctance in complying with so kind a proposal; which would give him the opportunity, he so long wished for, of seeing and conversing with Miss Julia Townsend. After a decent apology, therefore, for giving so much trouble to strangers, he told the Doctor, 'he would gladly accept of his offer.'

They now arrived at the inn at Warwick; where they found Mrs. Mahoney waiting with patience for Wildgoose's return. She was not only surprized, however, to see him return in that manner; but his pale look, and the bandage about his head, disguised him so much, that she could hardly be persuaded he was the same man. But, when that point was cleared up, and she was informed of Dr. Greville's connexion with Mr. Townsend's family, she confirmed what she had said to Mr. Wildgoose; and also produced the letter which she had received upon the subject.

When Dr. Greville, however, found Miss Julia Townsend mentioned, he laid but little stress upon this intelligence. But, after talking the affair over, they concluded there would be no harm in shewing Mr. Townsend the letter, who would be able to judge what regard was to be paid to it. And then, advising Mrs. Mahoney to rest contented at the inn till the next morning, Dr. Greville and Wildgoose took their leave.

As they travelled gently along, Dr. Greville took the liberty to expostulate a little with Wildgoose about his present romantic and irregular undertaking; and his eloping from his Mother, without and even contrary to her approbation; who, he found from Miss Townsend, was greatly affected by his extravagant and enthusiastic proceedings.

Wildgoose replied, 'he was sorry for that accidental consequence of his performing his duty; but,' says he, 'whosoever loves father, or mother, more than Christ, is not worthy of him. And, in short,' (adds Wildgoose) 'a necessity is laid upon me; yea, woe unto me, if I preach not the Gospel!'

Dr. Greville smiled at Wildgoose's application to himself of what was only applicable to St. Paul and the primitive Apostles, who certainly had a *divine call*; and wondered 'that a young man, of so much good sense as he seemed to be in other particulars, should be so strangely imposed upon by a spirit of enthusiasm, that had possessed his imagination.'—Wildgoose was going to defend the *call* of the *spirit*, 'which, he was convinced, he had received in as ample a manner as any Apostle of them all.' But Dr. Greville was afraid of bringing on too violent an agitation of spirits, and of renewing the hæmorrhage, or bleeding of the artery; and therefore changed the discourse for some other topic, which lasted till they arrived at the parsonage-house.

CHAPTER XVIII

At Dr. Greville's

MR. TOWNSEND being not yet arrived, they found Mrs. Greville alone. She had been so much used to Dr. Greville's acts of humanity, that she was less surprized at seeing a person in Wildgoose's situation, than at not seeing Miss Townsend in the chariot with them. But she was more surprized to find, that this was the very person who had written to Miss Townsend from Gloucester; and a little wondered at Dr. Greville's conduct in bringing him into the house to Miss Townsend; with whom she was by no means pleased, for admitting a private correspondence with a mere stranger, and (as she found by Miss Townsend's own account he was) an enthusiastical Itinerant. She soon acquiesced, however, in Dr. Greville's

G g

private reasons; who thought he might, at the same time, perform an act of humanity, in getting Wildgoose cured; and, perhaps, a greater act of charity, in reclaiming him from his erroneous opinions; and also make proper observations upon his general character, or (if he found it worth while) make a more particular scrutiny into the circumstances of his family and fortune.

Dr. Greville would have persuaded Wildgoose immediately to lie down upon the bed; but, as he found himself very easy, and able to sit up till the evening, Mrs. Greville ordered some tea, and said, 'the maid should get a proper room in readiness for him, whenever he should be disposed to retire to rest.'

Before Mrs. Greville had finished the ceremony of the tea-table, Mr. Townsend's servant came to the gate; and brought word, 'that his Master was at the end of the village, and would be there very soon; that he had met with the old Wood-man as they came along, who told Mr. Townsend, "that he had found some other curiosity as he was digging in the old camp on the brow of the hill;" and that his Master waited whilst the old man fetched it from his cottage.'

Accordingly, in a few minutes more, Mr. Townsend arrived, and was met by Dr. Greville at the court-gate: but, not seeing Miss Townsend as he approached the hall-door, which stood open, he cried out, 'Where is Julia? what! she has not eloped again, I hope. Ah!' (continues he, shaking his head) 'I every day hear fresh instances of her imprudence. Captain Mahoney was at Gloucester last week; where he was assured, that the little slut had like to have gone off from thence with a rascally Methodist Preacher. Well, the Romans were a wise people; and, in the best ages of the Republic, they gave fathers a power of life and death over their children; which kept them under a proper subjection.'

Dr. Greville said, 'Miss Julia was very well, but was not yet come from the course; where she was in Mrs. Mowbray's coach. I am sorry, however,' (adds the Doctor) 'to find you give so much credit to Captain Mahoney's intelligence; who, I believe, is no friend to any part of the family.'

Mr. Townsend was going to reply: but, coming now into the hall, and seeing Wildgoose, he stopped short; and, paying his compliments to Mrs. Greville, 'So, Cousin,' says he, 'you have got a Patient to nurse, I see, according to custom. Pray, whom have you here?'—Dr. Greville answered, 'it was a young gentleman who had

met with an accident at the race; and whom he had brought thither
in his chariot, till he could be conveyed to his friends, who lived at
some distance.' He carefully concealed Wildgoose's name, however, and the nature of his present adventure.

Mrs. Greville made some fresh tea for Mr. Townsend; and, as
it was not thought proper to discuss family affairs before a stranger,
as Wildgoose appeared to be, the conversation became general for
some little time. 'Well, Cousin,' (says Dr. Greville) 'you have been
enquiring after Antiquities, according to custom, of our old Wood-
man?'—'Yes,' replies Mr. Townsend, 'I thought, by his account,
he had found a Roman Stylus (which they used to write with);
but, I am afraid, it is nothing more than an old iron skewer.'—
Wildgoose then observed, 'that Mr. Townsend had lost the principal day's *sport*, as it is generally *called*.'—'Why, that is the very
salvo which I should have made,' replied Mr. Townsend; 'for
what is *called sport*, I assure you, is not so to me: and though I have
been used, for some years, to make my Cousin Greville a visit at
this season, my principal pleasure is in viewing the noble castle,
and other antiquities in the neighbourhood of Warwick; which,
I am convinced, was the *præsidium*, or chief station, of the Romans
in Britain, as being seated in the very centre of the island; and I
value it more for having been the station of the Dalmatian *horse*
(as Camden assures us), than for its paltry *horse-race* here once a
year.'[1]

If Wildgoose had not recollected Mr. Townsend's person, his
conversation would immediately have convinced him that he was
the same Virtuoso whom he had met in Lord Bathurst's woods.
And Mr. Townsend likewise, after a little time, said, 'he had seen
Wildgoose somewhere before: and, though I cannot recollect your
name,' says he, 'I know your face as well as I do that of Marcus
Aurelius, or Caracalla.'—As Wildgoose did not care to discover
too much, he only said, 'as he had been rambling about pretty
much of late, that probably Mr. Townsend might have seen him
before, though, he fancied, he had never been acquainted with his
name.'

CHAPTER XIX

Mrs. Mahoney's Intelligence canvassed

WHEN the servant had removed the tea-equipage, Dr. Greville thought it best not to defer the acquainting Mr. Townsend with Mrs. Mahoney's intelligence, as he did not know how far the affair between Captain Mahoney and Miss Townsend, if there was really any truth in it, might have proceeded.

After a proper introduction, therefore, he shewed Mr. Townsend the letter that Mrs. Mahoney had received; which when he had read, and seen the name with which it was subscribed, and that Miss Julia Townsend was mentioned as the object of Captain Mahoney's affection; 'Pshaw!' says Mr. Townsend; 'this is all a contrivance of a rascally fellow, who was a servant to Captain Mahoney when he was quartered at Corke; and he having dismissed him, Captain Townsend hired him, and brought him into our neighbourhood; where he is married and settled, and, out of a pique, has been endeavouring to do Captain Mahoney some prejudice. Why, Captain Mahoney is *brother* to the Widow Townsend, and never was married in his life.'—'Sir,' says Wildgoose, 'the Lady who calls herself Mrs. Mahoney assured me, he never had any *sister*; and that very circumstance looks very suspicious.'— 'Well, I don't know,' says Mr. Townsend, 'who this pretended Mrs. Mahoney may be; but I am pretty sure, that Mrs. Townsend would not connive at Captain Mahoney's making overtures to my daughter without my approbation, as she must know, that her place depends upon her fidelity to me.'

'Well,' says Dr. Greville, 'I wish this intelligence may be without any foundation; but the Lady to whom this letter was written seems very sincere in her apprehensions, and gives a very plausible account of herself; and so you will say, when you see her, which you may do to-morrow morning.'

CHAPTER XX

Mr. Wildgoose retires to Rest

I T now began to grow dusk; and, as Wildgoose looked very pale and fatigued, Dr. Greville prevailed on him to go to rest; and himself very politely waited on him to his chamber; though he was extremely desirous of sitting up till Miss Townsend came home: for, though we have not yet taken notice of it, we may be sure, Mr. Wildgoose could not take Miss Townsend's place in the chariot (as he found by Dr. Greville he had done), nor be in the very house where she was expected every moment, without very sensible emotions of tenderness and expectation.

When Wildgoose was gone out of the room, Mr. Townsend immediately asked, 'who he was?' observing, 'that he seemed a very sober, sensible young man.'—Mrs. Greville replied, 'that he was a young Gentleman of pretty good fortune in Gloucestershire, and, she believed, an humble admirer of her Cousin Julia.'—'Is he?' (says Mr. Townsend, with some quickness) 'then, for God's sake, let him have her; for I know not who else will, after her imprudent elopement: and, I believe, the poor girl wants an husband; I am sure, at least, I don't know what to do with her, for my part.'— 'Why,' says Mrs. Greville, 'these are partly my sentiments of the matter; and I fancy (between you and me) such a scheme would be no ways disagreeable to Miss Julia: and this was Dr. Greville's chief motive, I believe, for bringing the young man to our house.'

When Wildgoose, attended by Dr. Greville and the servant with candles, came into his bed-chamber, he was making apologies for the trouble he gave; but the servant setting down one of the candles upon the toilette, Wildgoose immediately espied a miniature picture of Miss Julia Townsend hanging under the glass; which fixed his attention so entirely, that Dr. Greville wished him a good night, smiling to himself at this further discovery which he had made of Wildgoose's attachment to his Cousin Julia.

When Dr. Greville returned to the parlour, he found Mr. Townsend and Mrs. Greville in close debate on the subject above-mentioned, and added his suffrage to the scheme proposed. But, while these good people were in the midst of their deliberations, Mrs. Mowbray's carriage came to the door, to set down Miss Townsend, 'whom,' Mrs. Mowbray said, 'she had brought safe home; though she desired proper care might be taken of her, as she had been very languid and low-spirited the whole afternoon.'

Dr. Greville made an apology for leaving his Cousin to Mrs. Mowbray's care, 'as he was sensible she must have been rather a troublesome companion; but that he himself had been engaged in a charitable office, which required a more immediate attention.'

Miss Townsend flew with a sincere transport into her father's arms; in whose breast, notwithstanding his slight resentment, Nature resumed her place; and he received his favourite daughter with great tenderness and affection.

BOOK XII

The Inn at Warwick

TUGWELL, with his son Joseph, went, as Mr. Wildgoose had ordered him, to the inn at Warwick: where he found Mrs. Mahoney and her companion; who informed Tugwell, 'that Dr. Greville had taken Wildgoose to his own house.'

As Mrs. Mahoney desired to have Tugwell's company in a little parlour which she had gotten adjoining to the kitchen, Jerry desired to introduce his son also, with whose unexpected return he acquainted her.

When Joseph came into the room, he and Mrs. Mahoney's Maid expressed a mutual surprize at the sight of each other: for, though Mrs. Mahoney was too attentive to her own distress, the Maid immediately recollected, that he had come over with them from Dublin to Park-gate in the same vessel.

When young Tugwell heard Mrs. Mahoney's name, he said, 'he remembered a Captain Mahoney at Corke, when he was there two years ago; and that he was one of the gentlemen who had like to have married the woman that Captain Townsend married.'

This account startled Mrs. Mahoney; as she knew her husband had been quartered there about that time: and though she could not guess what Joseph meant, by his being likely to marry Mrs. Townsend; yet she shook her head, suspecting, with too much reason, that it was some other instance of his infidelity.

Joseph, however, alluded to what he had told his father, in the circumstantial account which he had given him of his five years adventures, as they returned together from the course. But, as a great part of them would be uninteresting to the Reader, we shall only mention, 'that Joseph, upon listing for a soldier to avoid marrying a common strumpet (as was mentioned in the beginning of this history), was put on board the transports that accompanied the grand fleet upon the ever-memorable expedition against Carthagena.

'All the world knows the disastrous event of that expedition. After sacrificing the lives of so many brave fellows in forcing the straits of Bocca-Chica castle; and when the Spaniards were ready to abandon Carthagena upon the first attack; by the unaccountable delays and strange conduct both of the Admiral and the Commander in chief of the Land-forces, the affair was protracted till the rainy season set in: when our troops became a prey to sickness; and it was thought adviseable, after a general council of war, to reimbark them aboard the transports: where, though there were several young Surgeons aboard the fleet, who longed to assist their perishing countrymen; yet, the General disdaining to ask, and the Admiral to offer any assistance, the poor people dropped off like rotten sheep.

'Young Tugwell, however, by good luck, got leave to wait on Captain Townsend; who, being reduced by sickness to a declining state of health; as soon as the fleet returned to Jamaica, got leave to return to England; and, at his request, got young Tugwell's discharge.

'They landed at Corke in Ireland; where Captain Townsend, being laid up with the gout, stayed for some time: and, amongst other Gentlemen, became very intimate with a celebrated Barmaid at a Tavern there; and, thinking a Nurse of some sort was necessary to a man in his situation, he robbed the public, and married that girl; who was the identical Widow Townsend, that has been mentioned so often in this History.

'Amongst her gallants, Captain Mahoney being at that time an handsome young fellow, was distinguished as her favourite; which made Joseph think that he had like to have married her.

'Young Tugwell, having taken the liberty to advise his Master (Captain Townsend) against this match, was of course dismissed as soon as it took place. He met, however, with another English Officer on the Irish establishment, who expected every day to return to England: but, being disappointed from time to time, Joseph at length left his service at Dublin, and happened to embark in the same ship with Mrs. Mahoney; and was now on his way home, to visit his father and mother, and his native place.'

CHAPTER II

Kitchen-stuff

As Tugwell and his company were at supper in their little parlour, which was only separated from the kitchen by a deal partition, they heard a fellow holding forth over a pot of ale; and, with the air of a Politician, abusing all the gentlemen Shoemakers[1] in the country. Jerry, thinking himself concerned in the affair, and fancying like-wise that he was not entirely unacquainted with the voice, listened to the following harangue—'I have looked into their shops, Master Crisp; and I don't approve of their knavish proceedings. I might have been fore-man to Mr. Cutwell of Coventry. But, Sir, I assure you, they are the most *roguishest* sett of people upon earth. Why, I remember when a pair of shoes was sold for two shillings; nay, for eighteen-pence, when I was 'prentice in London.'—'Why, were you 'prenticed in London?' says Mr. Crisp. 'Yes; that I was, and served seven years in White-chapel. And I have an Uncle, that is a topping Shoe-black near the Royal-Exchange. Ah! London's the place: and yet London is not half the place it was formerly—for *old shoes*.'

'Well, Cobler,' says Master Crisp, 'I hope you are a better husband than you were.'—'Yes, thank God; I hope I am. Indeed, if God Almighty gives one health and money, one ought to take a chearful glass, now-and-then, with a friend or so—But hang it, what signifies money in the country? If I had a hundred pounds, I would not spend a farthing of it in the country. In London you have something for your money. There's liquor! There you may take a glass in a genteel *discreet* manner. There is not a Land-lord in the country that knows common sense.'—'Come, come,' says the Landlord, (a little offended at this freedom) 'come, pay as you go, Cobler; you have had two pots, and have paid for none.'

The dialogue being now at an end, Tugwell went out into the kitchen, to see who this fluent Orator might be; and found (to his surprise) it was his old friend Andrew Tipple, who had worked for Jerry in his prosperity as a journeyman; but was now become quite an itinerant Cobler and peripatetic Politician. Andrew was as much surprised at the sight of his old Master; and cried out, 'Ha! Master Tugwell! why, we heard you were sent to gaol for horse-stealing.

What have you done with young Mr. Wildgoose? I was at your town but last week. Your wife Dorothy is very angry with you, for leaving her; but says, "she should not have minded it, if you had not gone in your best waistcoat." And Madam Wildgoose threatens to disinherit Mr. Geoffry; and has actually taken two of her grandchildren to live with her, since the young Squire took to these vagabond courses.'

Jerry looked a little foolish at this account of the state of affairs at home; but, clapping his hand upon his pocket, with a gallant shake of the head, said, 'they should make matters up again when they got home.'

Jerry then called for a pot of ale, with which he and his old friend drank an health to their friends in Gloucestershire, and so they parted; Tugwell returning to his company.

CHAPTER III

At Dr. Greville's

WHEN Mrs. Mowbray's coach came to the door with Miss Townsend (as was related), Mr. Wildgoose was just going to bed; but flew to the window, like an hawk at his quarry; where, by the light of the moon, he had a full view of Miss Townsend, as she ran up the court, drest, on the occasion, much more splendidly than he had ever seen her at Gloucester. This slight glance threw poor Wildgoose into such a palpitation and hurry of spirits, that it was a considerable time before he could compose himself to sleep: and Miss Townsend was the prevailing idea in his dreams for the whole night.

It was now eleven o'clock, and Dr. Greville's family were all in bed, when they were awaked by an hasty rapping at the door; and were greatly alarmed, when the servant brought up word, 'that a man was come out of ——shire, with a letter for Mr. Townsend.' This messenger proved to be the old Coachman, who was mentioned to have assisted Miss Townsend in her elopement to London; and who, partly to atone for his imprudent conduct in that affair, and partly out of regard to the family, had taken his horse, and rode thirty miles after five o'clock that evening, to bring a letter, which his wife had intercepted, addressed to Miss Lucia Town-send, from Captain Mahony. This letter being carried up to Mr. Townsend, he opened it, and found the contents to be as follows:

'To Miss TOWNSEND.

'My dear Lucia,

'Every moment is an age till my happiness is compleated; and the deferring our departure another day, is a contradiction to the impatience of a fond Lover. But I am disappointed of the phaeton which I had bespoke; and was obliged to send to Oxford, whence I have ordered one of those post-chaises which are lately come into vogue, and which will convey us with more expedition either to London or Bristol: though I now think the latter is more advise-able; as we can be conveyed from thence to Corke in eight and forty hours.

'You and Mrs. Townsend will be ready, to-morrow evening, as soon as it grows dusk, with your baggage, behind the grove of firs: till which time, my dearest Lucia, I remain

Your impatient Lover,

PATRICK MAHONEY.

P.S. Write me a line by the bearer.'

Mr. Townsend was greatly provoked at this discovery: but, upon reflection, became sensible that he had no one but himself to blame, for the confusion which his imprudent connexion with the Widow Townsend had introduced into his family.

He at first thought of setting out again immediately: but, as the time fixed by Mahoney for executing his wicked scheme was not till the following evening, he thought he might take a few hours rest, and get out very early in the morning. He therefore sent for the old Coachman up to his bed-side, and enquired how he came by that letter: in answer to which, he gave him the following account.

'Ben, the Hostler at the George,' says he, '(where Captain Mahoney quarters) is third cousin to my wife; and, having been sent by the Captain with this letter to Miss Townsend, Ben thought it proper to let my wife know what he had heard from the Hostler at the Black Bull, who told Ben, "that Captain Mahoney, having been disappointed of *their* phaeton, had sent him to Oxford for a post-chaise; which was ordered to be at the Captain's quarters the next day about ten o'clock, who was going a long journey." And as all the neighbourhood talk very freely about the Captain's designs upon Miss Townsend, my wife was willing to forward this letter to your Honour, at a venture; and sent Ben back to the Captain with an answer from Miss Townsend by word of mouth, "that it was very well."'

Mr. Townsend said, 'he was obliged to the Coachman for the trouble he had taken, bade him feed his horse, and then go to-bed; and that he himself would set out by four o'clock in the morning: which, as he found by the letter that the Captain had put off his scheme till the next night, he hoped would be soon enough to prevent it.'

Dr. Greville had slipped on his night-gown, and was come into Mr. Townsend's room, to enquire into the cause of this alarm; which being informed of, though he secretly triumphed over Mr. Townsend's credulity, yet he begged him to lose no time in an affair of that consequence; and said, 'that he himself would take the liberty to awake Mr. Townsend at three o'clock, by which time he would be a little refreshed after his day's journey: and that he would take care to convey Mrs. Mahoney by a man and double horse, if it should be thought necessary: though he did not imagine,' he said, 'that the Captain would stay to dispute the matter with Mr. Townsend.'

CHAPTER IV

At Mr. Townsend's

NOTWITHSTANDING Dr. Greville's caution, and his eager desire to hasten Mr. Townsend's departure, it was near five o'clock before he set out; and near eleven before he reached his own house in ——shire; when he found it deserted both by his daughter and the Widow Townsend; which, we may imagine, shocked him to the utmost degree.

But, upon enquiry, he found the case not quite so bad as he at first expected: for the servants who were left at home informed him, 'that Mrs. Townsend had sent a letter, by the Stable-boy, early in the morning, to Captain Mahoney; who came with a post-chaise (about half an hour before Mr. Townsend came home), and had taken away Mrs. Townsend, with all her luggage in two large trunks: but that they were both in great confusion, at not finding Miss Townsend, who had been missing all the morning; and of whom the servants could give no other intelligence.'

Whilst Mr. Townsend was deliberating what method to pursue, the Coachman's wife came very opportunely, and relieved him from his distress, by giving the following account of Miss Townsend.

'That she (the Coachman's wife) being apprehensive that Captain Mahoney might suspect his plot was discovered (by his receiving no answer to his letter), and therefore might hasten the execution of it; she had therefore consulted with Mr. Thompson (the Squire's principal Tenant, and whom, she knew, he greatly confided in upon all occasions); and he had contrived to get Miss Townsend to his house pretty early in the morning, under a pretence that somebody wanted to speak with her; and that Mrs. Thompson had locked herself up with Miss Townsend in their parlour till the Squire himself should come home, as they supposed he would do, in consequence of the letter which the Coachman had conveyed to him.'

Mr. Townsend therefore went immediately to Farmer Thompson's; where he found Miss Townsend confined, as the Coachman's wife had informed them.

Mr. Townsend gave his daughter a proper lecture upon the occasion; and explained to her, with great tenderness, the escape she had had; and the discovery which he had made (of Captain Mahoney's being already married) by means of a young Gentleman, who was now at Dr. Greville's, and had providentially met Mrs. Mahoney upon her road from Ireland.

When they returned to the Manor-house, Mr. Townsend found that the Widow Townsend had carried off not only her own property, but likewise some of his; particularly a gold repeating watch of his late wife's, a valuable ring or two, a great many fine laces, and a brocaded suit of cloaths; in all, to the value of above two hundred pounds. But, as he had placed so unlimited a confidence in her, this was to be considered rather as a breach of trust, than a robbery; and, having now sufficient proof of her infidelity and wicked designs, he was really glad to get rid of her upon any terms.

As for the two fugitives, it may be proper to have done with them here; and to inform the Reader, that they made the best of their way to Bristol; where embarking for some remote part of Ireland, they lived together for some time upon the fruits of the Widow Townsend's plunder; till, satiated with each other's person, a mutual disgust ensued; and the Captain having shared the best part of the Widow's fortune, his fickle temper soon dissolved a connexion which was built upon so precarious a foundation.

CHAPTER V

At Doctor Greville's

LET us now return to our wounded hero, Mr. Geoffry Wildgoose.

For fear of any accident in the night, Dr. Greville had ordered the Footman to lie in a closet joining to his room: who, coming down in the morning, told the Maid, 'that the Gentleman had slept very soundly all night; but that, ever since he had awaked, he had been lamenting and bemoaning himself like a child. I asked him' (says the fellow) 'whether he was in pain; but he says, he is quite well again; only I fancy he is troubled in mind. I suppose,' says the Footman, 'he has lost money by betting at the races; or perhaps he has left a sweet-heart behind him somewhere or other.'

Dr. Greville, being informed of what the Footman had said, went up to Wildgoose's bedside; and asked him, 'how he found himself.' Wildgoose took the Doctor by the hand, and thanked him for the great care he had taken of him; and said, 'he had had a fine night; and found himself quite well. And, thank God,' says he, 'I find my head much clearer than it has been for some months. But, Sir, I must confess, many things appear to me in a very different light from what they have lately done. And I am particularly shocked at having left my disconsolate Mother so long in a state of anxiety and concern on my account. For, oh! Sir, I am now convinced, that no doctrine, no religious opinion, can be true, that contradicts the tenderest feelings of human nature, the affection and duty which we owe to our parents.'

Doctor Greville replied, 'that he was glad the mist was dispelled from his mind, and that he seemed to see things in their proper light; though perhaps,' says the Doctor, 'your last assertion ought to be admitted with some little restriction: as there may be some parents so unreasonably wicked, as to expect their children to prostitute their very consciences, as well as sacrifice their reason, to *their* absurd opinions or dishonest practices; in which case, children are evidently under a prior obligation to religion and virtue: though they should be very certain of the justice of their cause, before they venture to oppose so sacred an authority as that of parents over their children. But I am afraid, Sir, indeed, that you left your unhappy mother, merely from the blind impulse of an overheated imagination; to engage in an undertaking directly opposite to the laws of the land, without any pretence of a divine commission. And therefore I cannot but conclude you were under a wrong influence.'

'I am afraid I was,' says Wildgoose; 'but yet, in times of general defection from the principles of the Gospel, and the doctrines of the Reformation; I cannot but think that every one has a divine call to stem the torrent, and endeavour to revive the practice of true Christianity.'

'I own they have,' (replied the Doctor) 'by their example and their persuasion, within the sphere of their own neighbourhood. But then nothing, I think, is so evident, as that we are commanded, "to submit to every ordinance of man, for *the Lord's* sake; to let every thing be done decently and in order:" and therefore no one has a right to break through the regulations of society, merely from the suggestions of his own fancy, and unless he can give some visible proof of a supernatural commission. I am partly of Erasmus's opinion, in regard to Reformations—*Nolo seditiosam veritatem*, I would not have even truth propagated in a seditious manner.[1]

'As to a "general defection from the truths of the gospel;" we are very apt to judge of the state of Religion, as we are of the politeness, knowledge, or learning of the age, from what we feel in our own breasts. We fancy the world is more knowing, because we ourselves know more than we did in our infancy: and we think the world less religious, because we perhaps have thrown off the restraints of religion, and are more wicked or debauched than we were in our youth or childhood.

'The most likely method of convincing any one, is to make our adversary some concessions. For a general opposition to his whole system, not only irritates his passion; but, finding you mistaken in some particulars, as you probably are, he concludes, at random, that you are wrong in all.

'I grant you' (continues Dr. Greville) 'that there may be some cause of complaint against the negligence of the Clergy; and that, if the people had plenty of wholsome food or sound doctrine, they would not be hankering after the crude trash of *some* of your itinerant Preachers. But does this warrant every ignorant Mechanic to take the staff out of the hands of the Clergy, and set up for Reformers in Religion?

'There are corruptions perhaps, or neglects at least, in every branch of the Civil administration: as no human institution can be perfectly administered. But suppose an honest Country Justice to be a little negligent in his duty, or not very accurately versed in the subtleties of the Law; would this warrant any neighbouring Attorney (who spies out his error) to take upon him to administer justice in his room? No; an appeal is open to a superior court; and his errors must be rectified in a legal manner: otherwise strange confusion would ensue.

'The Parson of your parish, suppose, neglects his duty, or is immoral in his life and conversation. Let application be made to the Bishop of the diocese: who, at his visitation, not only receives his Synodals, but sends out articles of enquiry, relative to the conduct of every individual Clergyman within his jurisdiction, "Does your Minister lead an exemplary, or, at least, a sober and regular life? Does he do his duty decently and in order? Does he catechize and instruct the children and other ignorant persons in the principles of religion, at several times of the year, as the canons direct?" If he does not, why is not he regularly presented by the officers of the parish, and complaint made to the Bishop? who will not fail, first of all, to exhort him in private; and, if he does not alter his conduct, to censure him publicly at the next visitation; and, if he continues obstinate, to suspend him entirely from the exercise of his function.

'Nothing, I think can well be contrived better, or more wise, than our Ecclesiastical polity is in itself, if properly put in execution.

'As to the particular doctrines which the Methodists pretend to have revived, and on which they lay so great a stress; I do not imagine, the advantage which they seem to have *gained* over the regular Clergy arises from those cobweb distinctions, which, I am convinced, not one in ten of their followers really comprehend: but from the seriousness of their lives, and the vehemence and earnestness of their harangues; which may have a temporary effect upon their audience whilst the impression on their fancy lasts; and have, I believe, really awakened many indolent and careless Christians to a sober and devout life.

'As to the doctrines themselves; that of Justification by Faith, for instance; I know no Clergyman that expects to be saved by the merit of his own works. We do not preach up the *merit* of *good* works, but the *necessity* of them: and unless a good man and a good Christian are inconsistent characters, I do not see how good works, which is only another name for Virtue, can be dispensed with. In short, though the negligence of too many of the Clergy may have given these Reformers some little advantage over them; yet the extravagant proceedings and monstrous tenets of many of their itinerant Preachers have given them an ample revenge. One man declaims against the lawfulness of some of the most necessary callings. Mr. H—ll, who married a near relation of Mr. Wesley's, having used the poor Lady ill by an intrigue with another woman, defended the lawfulness of polygamy.[1] One Roger Ball asserted, "that the Elect had a right to all women."[2] These are not the necessary consequences, I own, of any of their principles; but they are the probable effects of an unlimited toleration of unlicensed, or rather, such licentious Teachers.

'I would by no means undervalue the great talents and the pious labours of Mr. Wesley and many of their Leaders. They are, I am convinced, men of sound learning and true devotion: and, whilst they live, to inspire and give vigour to their new establishment, some good may probably result from it. But when they come to be succeeded by men, who, instead of a zeal for Religion, will be led by interest to prefer the ease and advantage of a Teacher to the drudgery of a mechanic trade; the same indifference and negligence will soon prevail amongst them, which they have complained of in the established Clergy, and their classes will probably be as much neglected, as some of our parishes now are: so that, after prejudicing the people against their proper Pastors, they will leave them a prey to the ignorance, and perhaps much greater immorality, of illiterate Plebeians; and so will have made another schism in our Church to very little purpose.'

'Well,' says Mr. Wildgoose, 'but suppose Mr. Wesley and his

H h

friends really convinced of the great decay of Christian Piety; and that they were obliged in conscience to use their utmost endeavours to revive the practice of it; what course were they to take?'

'Why,' (replies Dr. Greville) 'I should think, if their little Society, when it was first formed in the University, (before they had made themselves obnoxious to the Clergy by their irregular proceedings) had quietly dispersed themselves, and settled upon Curacies in different parts of England; and had there formed little associations amongst the neighbouring Clergy; the influence of their example would gradually have spread itself, and produced more real and more permanent effects than it is now likely to do; without any bad effects, which, I am afraid, must proceed (as I have observed) from such licentious proceedings.'

Dr. Greville was going on to convince Mr. Wildgoose of the mistake he himself had laboured under, in regard to his late conduct; and Wildgoose seemed to listen with great attention, and shewed signs of confusion in his countenance; when the Servant brought word, 'that Mr. Slash the Surgeon was come;' whom Mrs. Greville attended up to Wildgoose's room.

The Surgeon first of all, with the air of a Radcliffe or a Freind,[1] felt his pulse; which he pronounced to be in an healthy state. Then, taking off the bandage, he found, that, although Mr. Wildgoose had been stunned by the blow, and lost a great deal of blood, yet the wound in itself was very trifling; and, knowing that Mrs. Greville was herself a skilful practitioner in Surgery, he shewed her the wound; who was surprized to see how slight it was. Slash therefore paid her the further compliment of leaving a few dressings, which, he said, with truth enough, 'she could apply as well as he could;' adding, 'that, if the Patient did not heat or fatigue himself, he might travel whenever he pleased.' And Wildgoose, intending, at furthest, to set out the next morning, took his leave of the Surgeon, by slipping half a guinea into his hands, with which Mr. Slash (having no great expectation from a Knight-errant) was very well contented; and Wildgoose himself was obliged to limit his generosity, having but a few shillings left, to defray the expences of his journey.

CHAPTER VI

An Interview

MR. WILDGOOSE, being now left alone, that he might equip himself for breakfast; and finding his mind much more easy since his
conference with Dr. Greville, and the thoughts of seeing Miss
Townsend giving him fresh spirits; he adjusted his cravat, rubbed
up his hair with some pomatum, and, in short, made his whole
person as spruce as his present circumstances would permit: and,
his bandage being now reduced to a decent patch of black silk,
Wildgoose made no despicable appearance.

When he came into the breakfast-room, he was greatly smitten
with the sight of Miss Townsend; who was so much more elegantly
dressed than in her state of humiliation at Gloucester. Dr. Greville
introduced them to each other; observing, with a good-natured
smile, 'that they two were old acquaintance.' This speech raised a
blush in Miss Townsend's countenance, which still heightened
her charms; and, what is not common, her real appearance sur-
passed even the bright idea, which, for a month past, had glowed
in the imagination of poor Wildgoose, her absent lover.

'Well,' continued Dr. Greville, 'you have both been a sort of
fugitives, and have given your friends some uneasiness; but, as the
cause of Miss Julia's ill usage at home will, I hope, soon be removed;
so, I flatter myself, Sir, your motive for rambling abroad will also
cease. Not that I wish to see you less serious in the practice of
Religion; nor even less an Enthusiast, in some sense; as, I am convinced, nothing great can be effected without some degree of
Enthusiasm: but I would not have your zeal transport you so far,
as to hurry you into any irregularities, which only expose you to
danger and ridicule, and can never answer any really useful purpose.'

Miss Townsend, though herself in some little confusion, began
to railly Mr. Wildgoose upon the accident he had met with; and
hoped 'it would cure him for the future, of such romantic under-
takings.'—Wildgoose replied, 'that he should not be deterred from
doing what he thought his duty, from any danger which might
accrue to his person: but that Dr. Greville had almost convinced
him, that such irregular proceedings were inexpedient, if not un-
warrantable.'

Wildgoose then asked Miss Townsend, 'whether she had heard from their friend Mrs. Sarsenet at Gloucester lately;' which gave Mrs. Greville an opportunity of observing, 'that Mrs. Sarsenet was a very worthy, *good creature*; and, she believed, had judged very rightly of the Widow Townsend's character: but yet had been the accidental cause of poor Miss Julia's ill usage at home, and of her consequent elopement; though (she added) no usage which a child could be supposed to receive from a parent would justify such a violation of the duty which every child owes to its parent, or such a defiance of the authority which Nature has given a parent over his offspring.'

CHAPTER VII

Mrs. Mahoney's Story finished

DR. GREVILLE, by way of changing the subject (which could not be very agreeable to the young people), said, 'He would take his horse, as soon as they had breakfasted, and ride to Warwick; that he might acquaint Mrs. Mahoney of the further discovery which they had made of Captain Mahoney's intrigue, and consult with her about her future proceedings.' But, whilst they were talking about it, Tugwell and his son Joseph arrived from Warwick, in order to enquire how Mr. Geoffry did; and to propose their going home, and acquainting Madam Wildgoose of the accident. But to this Wildgoose would by no means consent, as, he said, 'it would be too great a shock to his Mother, and he himself was well enough to set out with them that afternoon.' Dr. Greville however said, 'that would be very wrong; and that he would run a great hazard of inflaming his wound and perhaps of renewing the hæmorrhage. But (says he) if you are determined to travel so soon, I will to-morrow morning give you a lift in my carriage, as far at least as the turn-pike road extends; which, I imagine, is within a mile or two of your village.

'And as for these honest men, they shall stay and dine here; and, then, if they chuse it, they may go part of the way to-night, and halt for us to-morrow morning at Stratford, if they can find their way thither.'

'Oh!' says Jerry, 'I know Stratford upon Avon well enough: it's the place where Shakespear, the *great Jester*, was born.[1]—Grandfather's father lived a servant with the Jester himself; and there is a mulberry-tree growing there now, which he helped Mr. William Shakespear to plant, when he was a boy.'

'Well, Master Tugwell,' (says Dr. Greville) 'you may go and visit the mulberry-tree which your great grandfather helped to plant; and meet us to-morrow morning about eleven o'clock at the White-Lion; and then we will proceed together.'

Mr. Wildgoose then enquired after Mrs. Mahoney; when Jerry cried out, 'Odsbobs! I forgot to tell you, that the Gentlewoman is very bad, and has not been able to get out of bed to-day. And her Maid says, "She does not know how she will be able to travel any further."'

This account moved Mrs. Greville's compassion, as her curiosity had been raised before; and she immediately ordered her chariot, and went alone to Warwick, that, if it should be necessary, she might bring Mrs. Mahoney with her to Dr. Greville's.

When she came to Warwick, however, she found Mrs. Mahoney just come down stairs. And upon Mrs. Greville's enquiring after her health, she answered, 'that her complaint was nothing more than excessive fatigue: that she had been so intent upon the object of her journey, as not to perceive herself in the least wearied for three or four days: but that, since she had lain still, her spirits began to flag, and she found herself unable to travel any further.'

After informing Mrs. Mahoney of the fresh discovery which had been made of Capt. Mahoney's designs upon Miss Townsend, and of the means which Mr. Townsend had used to prevent its taking effect; Mrs. Greville added, 'that she had come alone in the chariot, with an intent to take Mrs. Mahoney with her, if she approved of it.'—Mrs. Mahoney, after recovering her spirits from the hurry into which this intelligence had thrown her, thanked Mrs. Greville for her kind invitation; but said, 'she had a near relation in London, an elderly Lady of good fortune, who had often importuned her, by letter, to make her a visit; and, as she might be a friend to her children, she had made that a secondary object in taking this journey. She intended, therefore, to get a place in some stage-coach the next day, and go to London; as it seemed to no purpose, at present, to pursue her graceless husband any further.'

And here the Reader may like to be informed, that this relation (who was the widow of a rich Merchant) died soon after Mrs. Mahoney's return to Ireland; and was so well pleased with her visit, that she left her an handsome competence, vested in Trustees hands, independent of her husband: that, after Captain Mahoney was tired of the Widow Townsend, and had contributed to the squandering away her ill-got wealth, Mrs. Mahoney admitted him to share her little fortune with herself and children; and his dependence on her for a subsistence secured his respect and fidelity, and by degrees reconciled him to a life of domestic happiness and sobriety. So various are the methods of Providence, to reward the virtuous, and, if possible, to reclaim the vicious from their wicked pursuits!

CHAPTER VIII

At Dr. Greville's

WHILE Mrs. Greville was gone to Warwick, Dr. Greville, according to custom, walked out to visit some of the poor and ignorant part of his parish; so that Mr. Wildgoose was left alone for some time with Miss Townsend, which opportunity he did not throw away upon theological speculations; but employed it upon a practical subject, more to his present purpose.

He introduced a sort of amorous conversation, by producing the cambric handkerchief which Miss Townsend had dropped from the chariot-window, when Wildgoose had that transient view of her near Birmingham. Miss Townsend immediately knew the mark; but said, 'she had no idea that it had fallen into his hands: for, though from the slight glance she had of him in a cloud of dust, she at first imagined the person whom they passed was Mr. Wildgoose; yet, as she heard no more of him, she had taken it for granted that she was mistaken.'

Wildgoose replied, 'it was merely out of respect, that he had not gone to Birmingham to enquire after her;' and he declared, 'he never underwent a greater mortification. But' (says he, putting the handkerchief to his breast) 'I have preserved this pledge, with as much devotion, as the most zealous Papist does his imaginary relicks of saints and holy virgins.'

Miss Townsend endeavoured to evade an application of this intended compliment, by her sprightly raillery; and said, 'she hoped Mr. Wildgoose was now almost tired with rambling about in so strange a manner, and would settle at home with his disconsolate Mother.'

Wildgoose, still pursuing his point, said, 'he should return to his Mother, in compliance with Miss Townsend's advice; and should probably quit his present rambling way of life, in condescension to Dr. Greville's opinion: but,' says he, 'it will be impossible for me to *settle* at a distance from the object of that enthusiasm of another kind, which you have raised in my breast.'

Though the meaning of this declaration was too obvious to be misapprehended, and though Miss Townsend was by no means insensible to Mr. Wildgoose's tender expostulations, yet she affected to treat them in a ludicrous style; and, when Wildgoose came still closer to the point, she answered with a very serious air, 'that, notwithstanding she had been guilty of one imprudent and undutiful act, in eloping from her father (on account of what she thought severe treatment); yet she could not listen to a conversation of that kind, without his knowledge and approbation.'

This little repulse cast a sudden damp upon Mr. Wildgoose's spirits. But as Miss Townsend's declaration, 'that she would not listen to his overtures *without* her father's approbation,' might be interpreted to imply the contrary if his approbation were obtained; he was not entirely destitute of some pleasing hopes. But their farther conversation was soon interrupted, by Mrs. Greville's return from Warwick, and the Doctor's from his morning walk.

CHAPTER IX

An Invitation to Mr. Townsend's

AFTER dinner, Tugwell and his son Joseph, as had been agreed, set out towards Stratford; but with a strict intention to wait at the White-Lyon, till Mr. Wildgoose should come thither, which Dr. Greville promised he should, the next morning.

Wildgoose spent the afternoon very agreeably with Miss Townsend and her two worthy relations. And, as he now talked very rationally upon Religion, as well as upon common subjects, Dr. Greville and his Lady were highly entertained with his company.

About ten o'clock in the evening, when they were just retiring to rest, they were again surprized with the arrival of a servant from Mr. Townsend; who brought them the agreeable intelligence of the Widow Townsend's having withdrawn herself with Captain Mahoney: and also a letter from Mr. Townsend, earnestly requesting Dr. Greville and his Lady to conduct Miss Julia Townsend home again, and to spend a week or a fortnight with Mr. Townsend, to assist him in re-establishing the œconomy of his household: which invitation, for the sake of performing the friendly office annexed to it, they were very ready to comply with.

CHAPTER X

At Stratford upon Avon

MR. WILDGOOSE, having made a comfortable breakfast, and drunk some excellent tea from the fair hands of Miss Julia Townsend (which quite reconciled him to domestic and social life), took his leave of Mrs. Greville and Miss Townsend; not without a sigh and a languishing glance directed to the latter. Dr. Greville and he then set out in the carriage for Stratford; where they arrived about twelve o'clock, and found Tugwell and his son waiting for them; whom they again dispatched to pursue their journey.

Whilst the Coachman stopped to water his horses, my Landlord, out of civility, came to pay his compliments to Dr. Greville, who knew the man to have been a son of the learned Dr. Welchman, well known for his Illustration of the Thirty-nine Articles: which piece of history, as he had not much (literary) merit of his own to boast of, mine Host never failed to acquaint his customers with. 'Gentlemen,' (he would say) 'you have doubtless heard of my Father: he *made* the Thirty-nine Articles.'[1]

While they were talking to my Landlord, the church-bells struck up, and rang with great chearfulness: upon which, as the canonical hour was just expired, Dr. Greville supposed, 'they had had a wedding.'—'No,' says my Landlord: 'but we are going to have a funeral; and the bells ring upon that occasion.'

'How so?' says Dr. Greville.—'Why, have not you heard of old Mr. Shatterbrain's whimsical will? He was born in this town, and kept a tavern in London: and got ten-thousand pounds in the lottery; and has left it all to his Nephew, who was a tradesman in this town. But I will fetch you the news-paper, and you may see all about it.' He then brought the Gloucester Journal to Dr. Greville, in which was this clause from Mr. Shatterbrain's will:

'*Provided* also, That my said Nephew, on the day of my funeral, do distribute six pounds, six shillings, to six young women tolerably skilled in dancing; who, being dressed in white callico, with black ribbands, shall join with six young men, to be procured by the Undertaker (or the Undertaker himself to make one, if agreeable); who, being dressed in mourning cloaks, with black crape hat-bands, shall, in a grave and solemn manner, dance, to a good tabor and pipe, the ancient dance called "The Black Joke," in the church-yard (if approved of by the Minister); if not, as near to the place of my burial as conveniently may be; the church-bells ringing from twelve o'clock at noon to six o'clock in the evening.

'*Provided* also, That my said Nephew do cause to be inscribed on my tomb, the following moral distich;

> Since *dust* we are all, let us moisten our clay;
> Let us drink, let us dance, and *dust* it away'.

Dr. Greville observed, 'that Mr. Shatterbrain seemed to be actuated more by the love of fame, than by the love of mankind, when he made that will; and that he seemed more ambitious of being celebrated in a news-paper, than of being blessed by the poor, after his death: that six guineas, properly distributed, would make six poor families happy for a month, instead of making the testator ridiculous for ever. Indeed,' (added the Doctor) 'I have observed several of these ridiculous bequests of late years: but, if I were Lord Chancellor, I should make no scruple, upon the slightest application, of setting aside such absurd clauses; and applying the donations more advantageously, either to the publick, or to the distant relations of the testator.'[1]

CHAPTER XI

More Lumber yet ; a Wife and two Children

THE chariot was now going from the inn, when a two-wheel chaise drove into the yard, with a Gentleman, a Lady, and two children in it, attended by a servant on horseback. The Gentleman leaped down, and began to lift out a little boy and girl, when Wildgoose was agreeably surprized at discovering his friend Rivers and his Lady, whose long story (if he did not fall asleep in the middle of it) the Reader must recollect; and who, in consequence of Wildgoose's letter, was going to pay his respects to his kinsman, Mr. Gregory Griskin, the little Staffordshire Divine, from whom he had considerable expectations.

Mr. Wildgoose begged leave to detain Dr. Greville a few minutes, whilst he just paid his compliments to his old friends.

After explaining his present situation, Wildgoose began making a sort of apology for his travelling in so different a manner from what he had done when they met last.—'Come, come,' says Rivers; 'this is only a sneer upon my ecclesiastical equipage of a one-horse chaise. What sport would our old Oxford acquaintance make at a man packed up in this leather convenience, with a wife and two children!'

'Why, yes,' says Wildgoose; 'we laugh at these domestic concerns, in the university: but, when married and settled in the country, our elegant ideas give way to ease and convenience: and many a delicate man, I believe, has condescended to warm a clout, and many a learned one to rock the cradle.'

Mr. Rivers then thanked Wildgoose for the service he had done him with his kinsman, Mr. Griskin; and said, 'he had had a letter by the same post from Mr. Griskin himself; expressing great satisfaction in the account Mr. Wildgoose had given him of Mrs. Rivers's character and conduct; and inviting him to bring her and her children into Staffordshire, as soon as he conveniently could.'

Wildgoose then told Rivers, 'that, from hints which Mr. Griskin had dropped, he fancied his design was, to get Rivers into orders, that he might assist him in the care of his parish; and he made no doubt but that Mrs. Rivers's agreeable behaviour would soon restore Rivers to the same place which he formerly possessed in his cousin Gregory's esteem.'

Wildgoose, having now paid his compliments to Mrs. Rivers, and wished them a good journey, was unwilling to detain Dr. Greville any longer: so, after desiring Rivers to write him word of the success of his visit, they parted; and he and Dr. Greville resumed their journey.

CHAPTER XII

A Plan for Reformation

AFTER travelling about a mile beyond Stratford, they met a young man, in a shabby sort of livery, who appeared very sickly, and applied to them for alms. The Coachman, by way of favouring the suit of a brother servant in distress, stopped his horses, whistling to them, as if to give them an opportunity of staling. Dr. Greville asked, 'how so young a man came to beg upon the road?' The man said 'he had been dismissed his service, on account of a long sickness; and was travelling into Shropshire, to try his native air. That he had lived with Lord —— in London; who was a very good Master, kept a good house, and gave his servants good wages; but (in case of sickness) always dismissed them.'

Dr. Greville gave the man six-pence; observing to Wildgoose, 'that, although he did not like to encourage common beggars, he generally gave them some little matter to relieve their present distress: but not without a sharp reproof to those who appeared to be habituated to that idle practice.'

This incident again introduced the subject of a reformation. And Dr. Greville observed, 'that neither the preaching of the Clergy, nor even the many penal laws, which were daily multiplied, would avail any thing towards the end proposed, unless some alteration could be produced in the manners of the people, by the influence of their superiors: the luxury and extravagance of the great and people in high life descends, as a fashion, amongst the crowd, and has infected every rank of people. If (says he) an association were formed amongst some of our principal and most popular Nobility, to set an example of frugality and temperance, by reducing the number of their servants, and the number of dishes at their tables; and if the Prince on the throne would condescend to enforce the example, by regulating the splendor of the dress and equipages of those who appeared at Court; it would soon be established as a fashion: and that crowd of useless servants, who are now supported in idleness and luxury, and who, when dismissed from service, or married and settled in the world, propagate the vices and follies, which they have learned of their Masters, amongst the middling rank of people; these dissolute idle rascals, I say, would be left in the country, where they are wanted, to till the land; or to supply our handicraft trades or manufactures with useful and industrious hands. And we might then hope to see virtue and frugality restored amongst us.'

CHAPTER XIII

The same Subject continued

'As to the Clergy,' continued Dr. Greville, 'all I shall add upon that subject, is, that I could wish they would, in general, be a little more cautious and reserved in their conduct.

'I do not expect them to renounce the world, or to shut themselves up entirely in their closets or studies. Neither would I absolutely forbid them, in great towns, going to a Coffee-house or a Tavern, upon necessary occasions. But I would not have them make those places their constant rendezvous. I do not think there is any indecency in their playing at cards, or joining in other chearful transactions in private company: but am sorry to see them dancing or gaming at Bath or Tunbridge; and (as a Cambridge friend of mine expresses it) "*shining* in every *public* place—except the Pulpit."

'As to their Preaching,' added the Doctor, 'I could wish they would make their discourses more systematical, and connected one with another. I know, by experience, that a man may preach for seven years together in the common way, in unconnected sermons, and our people be never the wiser. But a sett of plain regular discourses, upon the principles of Natural and Revealed Religion: the Being, Attributes, and Moral Government of God; and the peculiar doctrines and duties of the Gospel: such a system, I say, repeated once or twice a year, would teach the people their duty, and make them more willing to attend the Church; and even pay their tythes more chearfully, when they were sensible, they had some equivalent for their money.'

'Well, Sir,' says Wildgoose, 'and I will venture to add, from my own experience, that I wish the Clergy would be a little more earnest in their delivery, and inforce their precepts with some little vehemence of tone and action; as I am convinced what an effect it would have upon the most rational Christians.

'I am sensible indeed, from what I felt when I first heard Mr. Whitfield, that too violent gesticulations are not agreeable to the modesty and reserve of an English audience; and there is certainly a difference between the action of the Pulpit and of the Stage. But, when a Preacher reads his sermon with as much coldness and indifference as he would read a news-paper, or an act of parliament; he must not be surprized, if his audience discover the same indifference, or even take a nap, especially if the service be after dinner.'

'Why, there is no doubt,' replies Dr. Greville, 'but an empassioned tone of voice, a suitable gesture, and a pathetic style, have more effect upon the middling and lower ranks of mankind, for whose use sermons are chiefly intended, than the most rational discourse, delivered in a dry uninteresting manner. And this certainly is one great advantage which the Methodists and other fanatical Preachers have over the regular Clergy, in rousing so many indolent drowsy Christians to a sense of Religion.

'There is a remarkable instance of the persuasive power of this enthusiastic Eloquence in a Capuchin Fryar, one Philip de Narni, a popular Preacher at Rome, near the middle of the last century: from whose sermons the people never departed without tears, many of them crying out for mercy in the streets. And, what is more extraordinary, we are told, that, preaching before Pope Gregory the Fifteenth, upon the subject of Non-residence, he struck such a terror into his audience, by the vehemence of his oratory, that no less than thirty Bishops set out, post, for their Dioceses the very next day.[1] And yet, it is added in the life of that Fryar, that when his sermons came to be printed, there was nothing very striking in them. We are told also, that the good man was so far disgusted with observing the great numbers who came to hear him out of mere curiosity, without reforming their lives, that he retired to his cell, and spent the rest of his days in writing the history of his Order.'

'Why, to be sure,' says Wildgoose, 'that will always be the case with too great a number of people; from the necessary imperfection of human nature. But we should use the most probable means of doing all the good in our power, and leave the event to Providence.'

CHAPTER XIV

Mr. Wildgoose's Reception at Home

IN this kind of discourse were Dr. Greville and Mr. Wildgoose engaged, when they came to the point where the road turned off towards the village to which Wildgoose was bound. Here Tugwell and his son Joseph had again made an halt; and, while they were waiting for Mr. Geoffry under some shady trees by a brook-side, regaled themselves with a slice of cold roast beef, which Dr. Greville's Servant had stowed in the wallet.

Mr. Wildgoose was now at a loss how to act; as he could not press Dr. Greville to convey him any farther, through a long and dirty lane, to his native place; nor yet dismiss him without an invitation to rest his horses, and to take a dinner, or at least some refreshment, at his mother's house.

But from this perplexity Dr. Greville himself delivered Mr. Wildgoose. As the long summer had made the road better than usual, and very passable for a carriage, the Doctor insisted upon carrying Mr. Wildgoose quite home.

Indeed one principal end in his taking this journey was, to make some enquiries into the circumstances of Mr. Wildgoose's fortune; and, if he should find it agreeable to his expectations, to make some overtures to Mrs. Wildgoose, for a match between her son and Miss Julia Townsend.

The carriage now proceeded, with Tugwell and his son in the rear: and, after many jolts and jumbles, in half an hour's time, brought them in sight of their village spire, which rose amidst a grove of pines, at the foot of the Cotswold hills: the sight of which, after near two months absence, rejoiced the very cockles of Jerry's heart; though not without a mixture of solicitude, about the reception he might meet with from the offended Dorothy, whose indignation his friend Andrew Tipple had announced.

As for Mr. Geoffry, he was impatient to restore his Mother's peace of mind; whose maternal fondness for him he was too well acquainted with, to fear any thing from her resentment, when once he should have returned to his duty.

It being now the midst of a very sultry day, and most of the village people out in the fields, they arrived at Mrs. Wildgoose's gates without much speculation. Mrs. Wildgoose's old hind, Stephen, was just gone into the yard with a load of wheat; and a little boy and girl, whom Mr. Geoffry was surprized to see there, ran in, crying out, 'A coach! a coach!'

These little folks were no other than Mrs. Wildgoose's grand-children, by her daughter, whom we mentioned, in the beginning of this narrative, to have married contrary to her parents approbation; and of whose children, therefore, very little notice had been taken, till since Mr. Geoffry Wildgoose's elopement.

Though Mrs. Wildgoose never dressed fine, yet, as she was always neat and clean, she was consequently always sufficiently prepared (for a woman of her time of life) to see company. By the time therefore the chariot came to the door, she was come out to receive them. Having not, for some years, seen her son in his own hair, she did not immediately know him; especially, as the black patch on his temples added to the paleness of his complexion, which his loss of blood had occasioned. But, when he stepped out of the chariot, and (agreeably to a custom now obsolete) bent one knee to receive her blessing; Mrs. Wildgoose's surprize was so great, that she almost sunk to the ground. Wildgoose supported her in his arms; till Dr. Greville also coming out of the chariot, they attended her into the hall; by which time she had recovered her spirits; and Wildgoose began to introduce the Doctor, and to inform his Mother of the great obligations which he had to him.

Mrs. Wildgoose made proper acknowledgements to the Doctor; and then, looking on her son, 'Oh! Geoffry!' says she, 'how could you desert me in such a manner; without once acquainting me with your intention, or where I might make any enquiries after you? Your unkindness might have been fatal to me; and if I had died under the first sense of your undutiful behaviour, it would have been a great misfortune to you. I find you have taken a pique against poor Mr. Powell; but, I assure you, it was entirely owing to his honesty and discretion, that I did not pursue the dictates of my resentment, and make a will greatly to your prejudice.'

Dr. Greville made answer for Mr. Geoffry; 'that he believed he had been for some time under the influence of a deluded imagination: but that the mists, which clouded his reason, seemed now to be dispelled; and he saw things in a more proper light: and that he could venture to answer for him, that he would never be guilty of the like act of unkindness for the future.'

Mrs. Wildgoose's flutter of spirits being now a little composed, she began to reflect, that it was high time to order the cloth to be laid, and to consider in what manner she should entertain Dr. Greville: which, however, as a plentiful dinner was provided for her harvest-people, gave a woman of Mrs. Wildgoose's good sense but little trouble.

CHAPTER XV

Jerry Tugwell's Reception at Home

THOUGH I have lived to speculate near half a century on the humours of mankind, I hardly remember a more remarkable instance of self-partiality, than the desiring to *perpetuate*—or of deference to fortune, than the submitting to *unite*—the poor, pitiful, and almost obscene monosyllable of *Dunk*, with the noble high-sounding polysyllable of M—ntague, Earl of H—lif—x: yet I had a personal regard for the worthy Mr. Dunk himself, and a great respect for the noble Earl;[1] and only make this remark, to shew the fascinating, or rather the omnipotent, power of accumulated riches—though not much to my present purpose, which was, to describe the interview between Jerry Tugwell and his wife Dorothy.

Dame Tugwell was infinitely exasperated against poor Jerry for presuming to elope from home, in downright defiance of her sovereign authority; and had meditated with herself, as she sate at her spinning-wheel, every variation of phrase, expressive of the most furious resentment, to attack the hapless culprit with, whenever he should make his appearance.

But, as Jerry knew Dorothy's blind side, and the only part where (on these occasions) she was vulnerable; instead of any supplicating apology, or endearing caresses, after so long an absence, Jerry approached her with a free and joyous air (as she sate at her wheel), but extending his right hand, filled with silver, two or three half-guineas being interpersed amongst it; the sight of which precious metals immediately softened Dorothy's features, from the truculent fierceness of the Fury Tisyphone, to the simpering smiles of a Galatea, an Hebe, or an Euphrosyne.

Some deep Politician might here suggest, that Jerry's wisest and most certain way to make peace would have been, to send their long-lost son Joseph into the house before him. I think otherwise; for, after the first transports of that happy meeting were over, Jerry's offence would still have remained in full force, the subject of a severe reprehension: but, by convincing Dame Dorothy at once, by so evident a proof, that he had not neglected the main chance, and that she would be no loser by his long absence, the way was smoothed for a thorough reconciliation; and nothing now remained, but to indulge their mutual congratulations on account of their son's happy return.

As for Dame Tugwell's surprize and joy on the sight of her son Joseph, I shall not pretend to describe it. Instead of any concern about Jerry's travels, she would have asked as many questions about Joseph's adventures as his father had done at their first unexpected meeting at Warwick races. But her affection was more active than her curiosity; and she immediately began puffing up the fire, and was going to set on her best scowered pot, and to cut an untouched flitch of her best bacon, to entertain her guests; when a boy from Mr. Wildgoose's came, to invite Jerry, his son Joseph, and even Dame Dorothy, to eat some beef and pudding with her harvest people in the kitchen. Which invitation, in the present gaiety of her heart, Dorothy was no more inclined to refuse, than Jerry himself was.

CHAPTER XVI

The grand Point settled

Y OUNG Wildgoose, after dinner, having gone out to pay his compliments to his fellow-travellers and Dame Tugwell, Dr. Greville took the opportunity of opening his commission to Mrs. Wildgoose. After acquainting her with the rise and progress of the

I i

intimacy between her son and Miss Julia Townsend, and informing her what fortune Mr. Townsend would probably give his
daughter at present, and her expectations in future; he desired to
know (if she approved of the match), 'what kind of settlement she
could enable her son to make?'—Mrs. Wildgoose seemed, at first,
to hint, 'it would not be in her power to settle any thing in the least
proportionable to Miss Townsend's fortune and expectations:'—
but, when Dr. Greville said, 'that, as the young people seemed to
have conceived an extraordinary affection for each other, very
rigorous terms would not be insisted upon,'—she said, 'that she
could give up three hundred pounds a year, provided a proper provision were made for herself during her life; that the whole estate
was about four hundred pounds a year, and only charged with five
hundred pounds for her daughter's fortune; but that, since her
son's undutiful elopement, she had taken two of her grand-
children, and intended to add five hundred pounds more to her
daughter's fortune.'

In short, this affair was soon settled between Mrs. Wildgoose
and Dr. Greville, who, after drinking a glass of wine, walked out
with young Wildgoose to view the place, and then first opened his
intention to him; which he received with equal rapture and surprize.

Dr. Greville then told him, 'that he should go over to Mr.
Townsend's, with Miss Julia, in a day or two, and stay there a
fortnight at least; in which time, if Mr. Wildgoose would come
over, Dr. Greville would endeavour to gain Mr. Townsend's consent to their scheme. But, Sir,' added the Doctor, 'as my principal
reason for interesting myself in this affair is, that I had rather see
my Cousin Julia married to a sober, religious young man, with
a moderate fortune, than to some of your gay men of the world,
with ten times your income: so, if I thought you intended ever to
resume your late irregular way of propagating your religious
opinions, I would by no means promote such an alliance; for, as a
true rational system of Religion contributes to the happiness of
society, and of every individual; so Enthusiasm not only tends to
the confusion of society, but to undermine the foundation of all
Religion, and to introduce, in the end, scepticism of opinion, and
licentiousness of practice.'

Mr. Wildgoose replied, 'that, whatever his opinions on some particular points were (though they were yet far from being entirely

settled), he was determined, for the future, to keep them to himself, and only endeavour to enforce the practice of Religion in his
own family, and amongst his neighbours; and that he should want
no other motive for settling at home, if he were blessed with so
agreeable a companion as Miss Townsend.'

Dr. Greville repeated again, 'that he had a very good opinion of
Mr. Wesley and Mr. Whitfield, and of their first endeavours to
revive the practice of primitive piety and devotion; but I am afraid,'
says he, 'that there have already, and will hereafter, from their
examples, start up mechanical Teachers, who will preach themselves, instead of Christ; aiming at applause and popularity, to
fill their pockets, or to fill their bellies; to please the young ladies,
or the old women; and bring Religion into contempt with all
virtuous and sensible people.'

CHAPTER XVII

Modern Taste, and that of our Ancestors

AFTER viewing the garden and orchards, which, according to the
old taste, were surrounded with high walls and quickset-hedges;
Mr. Wildgoose proposed, 'if he should be so happy as ever to bring
Miss Townsend thither, to modernize his place, and lay it out
agreeably to her fancy.'

Dr. Greville replied, 'that he would sacrifice a great deal to good
taste; and,' says he, 'as the hills rise very prettily round you, I
would endeavour to catch an opening or two from the bottom of
your garden to those grand objects.

'But, for my part, I prefer the plentiful taste of our ancestors, in
whose gardens Flora and Pomona amicably presided, to the barren
taste of the present age. Why would you destroy this south wall,
covered with peaches and plumbs; and root up these pinks and
carnations, to make way for some half-starved exoticks, or perhaps
poisonous shrubs, which nothing but mere fashion can recommend?

'I like to see a grand edifice in the middle of a lawn; and would
gladly give up old moss-grown orchards, clipt hedges, and endless
avenues, for extensive views elegantly diversified with groups of
trees, hanging woods, and sloping hills. But to think of exposing

your irregular mansion by removing walls, and aiming at a lawn no bigger than a Persian carpet, is a prostitution of taste, and a burlesque upon magnificence.'

But, the old clock now striking five, Dr. Greville recollected that he had four hours driving to his own house. After settling the plan, therefore, with young Geoffry, and taking leave of Mrs. Wildgoose, he ordered his carriage, and departed.

CHAPTER XVIII

Other Matters adjusted

SOON after Dr. Greville was gone, Mr. Powell, the Vicar of the parish, and his wife, in consequence of a private message from Mrs. Wildgoose, came to drink tea; whom Mr. Geoffry immediately received with his usual freedom and cordiality. Mr. Powell took an opportunity of telling young Wildgoose, 'that he was sensible he had taken some pique against him (though he could not guess upon what account).' But, to convince him how much he was his friend, Mr. Powell shewed him the instructions his mother had given him, in regard to a will, greatly to his prejudice, and which he had prevailed upon her not to execute.—Mr. Wildgoose thanked him for the service he had done him; 'though,' he said, 'he was glad to find his elopement had been the accidental cause of having his sister taken into favour; which was what he always desired.' He then confessed, 'that he had taken some little prejudice against the Vicar upon a very trifling occasion: but that it had pleased God lately to open his eyes; and that a weight of gloom had, he did not know how, been removed from his mind: and he hoped they should, for the future, live together in their usual friendship and good understanding.'

The news of Tugwell's return being likewise soon spread about the parish, Jerry and his son were visited, that very evening, by every man, woman, and child, in the village; except by his rival in trade, the other Shoemaker; and by Dorothy's nearest neighbour, the Blacksmith's wife. Their mutual emulation will account for the conduct of the former; and a jealousy of a particular kind in the Blacksmith's wife for that of the latter.

Mrs. Enville, it seems, valued herself upon her family; her grand-father, by her mother's side, having been a Supervisor: yet, by her extravagance and want of œconomy, she was become much inferior in her circumstances to Dorothy Tugwell; and, whilst the latter was saluted by the respectable appellation of *Dame* Tugwell, the former was dwindled down from Mrs. Enville to plain Betty. When, therefore, she was told of Jerry's return, she received the news with a sullen, contemptuous silence; and, when it was added, 'that he had brought his pocket full of silver and gold,' she only said, 'it was well if he came honestly by it.'

When Jerry came to examine the state of his shop, he found an accumulation of business upon his hands—old shoes, which wanted variety of repair, and which Dorothy had taken in, under a daily expectation of Jerry's return. But he was so full of his late journey, and so much embarrassed in answering questions put to him from every quarter, that it was in vain to think of business for that night. And Dorothy was so deeply engaged with her son Joseph, and so well satisfied with the cash that Jerry had thrown into her lap (he having only reserved a *new* shilling to himself, for *antickity's* sake, which was Jerry's word for *curiosity*); Dorothy, I say, was in such harmonious spirits, that she connived at Jerry's keeping holiday for that evening.

But the next morning, when Dorothy got up to her spinning, having locked up Jerry's best waistcoat, she sent him to his stall, with a grave rebuke, 'that it was high time to settle to business again, and leave off preaching and rambling about the country.' And, though Jerry's shop was the general rendezvous, every evening, for a week after his return, Dorothy watched him narrowly, and kept him close to his work. And Jerry himself, having satisfied his curiosity, and being handsomely rewarded by Mr. Wildgoose for his trouble, seemed very well contented to spend the rest of his days in his own shop, and in his own chimney-corner.

CONCLUSION

MR. GEOFFRY WILDGOOSE and his trusty friend having now finished their Summer's Ramble, and we having fulfilled our engagements to our Readers; we might fairly enough dismiss them without any further ceremony, especially as the Reader probably may not be very deeply interested in the affairs of an Hero, who meets with no other adventures than what any man might expect to meet with, who travels through a country that is under a regular Civil Government, and in an age which appears to be under the direction of a general Providence.

But, as this History may probably be banished from the circles of the polite, to some remote province, for the winter-evening's amusement of some artless nymph, Chloe or Rosalind, whose curiosity is not yet grown callous, by a constant intercourse with the marvellous vicissitudes which abound in modern romance; methinks I hear poor Rosalind exclaiming, 'Oh! I long to know, whether Miss Julia and young Wildgoose made a match of it at last!'

Now, as I own myself to be nothing at a temptation, and could never withstand the charms of youth and innocence—in spite of the practice of Virgil, or the precepts of ancient Critics, who are for leaving many things to be supplied by the Reader's imagination— I am determined, I say, to gratify the Ladies curiosity with a peep behind the curtain, and inform them of a few subsequent particulars.

That Mr. Wildgoose, having equipped himself, not in pea-green or pompadour, but in a plain drap-coat, with a crimson-sattin waistcoat, laced with gold, peeping modestly from under it, mounted his chesnut gelding; and, attended by young Tugwell, whose military air, and the flavour of a brass button added to his brown coat, gave him a tolerably smart appearance (though Mrs. Wildgoose would not yet consent to his having a livery)—thus equipped, young Wildgoose waited on Miss Julia Townsend at her father's house in ———shire; where, by the mediation of Dr. Greville and his Lady, a match was soon concluded upon; and, after another visit or two, solemnized at Mr. Townsend's in the Christmas holidays.

That Mrs. Wildgoose, having fitted up a sort of a neat cottage for herself, resigned the mansion-house to her son Wildgoose and his Lady; where they now live together, with as much felicity as this life is capable of: yet no more than what every contented unambitious couple may be sure of obtaining, who study to make each other happy; and whose expectations are not disappointed by the vain hopes of complete happiness in this world; or who do not fatigue themselves in the constant pursuit of violent and immoderate pleasures, in a state of existence where ease and tranquility are the highest enjoyment allotted them.

Mr. Wildgoose keeps as much of his estate in his hands as will employ a pair of horses and two servants; and heartily concurs with Mr. Powell, both by his example and persuasion, to countenance industry and sobriety in the parish; as his Lady does in visiting the sick and afflicted.

He has also prevailed upon Mr. Powell to lay aside his *argumentum baculinum*,[1] or crabtree conviction, with the lower and less docible part of his parish, and to endeavour to gain their love by the milder arts of soft persuasion; having convinced him of the truth conveyed in those beautiful lines of Dryden (alluding to the Fable of the Sun and the North-wind):

> To threats the stubborn Sinner oft is hard,
> Wrapt in his crimes, against the storm prepar'd:
> But, when the milder beams of mercy play,
> He melts; and throws his cumbrous cloak away.[2]

Soon after he was married, Mr. Wildgoose received a visit from his friend Rivers, who was just got into orders, and was going, with his family, to live with his kinsman, Mr. Gregory Griskin, and to assist him in the care of his parish (as Wildgoose had hinted), with a very handsome stipend, the presentation of the Living after his Cousin's death, and a promise of the perpetuity: so that Rivers also was now as happy as he could wish. And we may draw the same *moral* (or rather the same religious *maxim*) from each story:

'THAT, where we do not obstinately oppose its benevolent intentions, nor presumptuously persist in a wrong course of life, Providence frequently makes use of our passions, our errors, and even our youthful follies, to promote our welfare, and conduct us to happiness.'

NOTES

FOR constant help I am indebted to Professor Herbert Davis, the General Editor of this series, as well as to the following friends and scholarly acquaintances: Professor Bonamy Dobrée, Mr. L. E. S. Gutteridge, Mr. Peter Millard, Mrs. M. M. Phillips, Professor R. S. Ridgway, Dr. Lucy Sutherland, Mr. Warren H. Smith, Professor P. M. Swan, Professor Hermann Tracy, Miss Helen D. Willard, Professor Francis Wormald, and Mr. John Young. For the use of their facilities I am also grateful to the libraries of Yale, Harvard, and Chicago Universities, and to the British Museum. And I must thank the University of Saskatchewan for a generous grant made while I was a member of its faculty. In what follows all of the author's own notes have been reprinted (except mere identifications of people or books that could be replaced with fuller or more accurate ones). Whenever he has a note, it is always given first, followed by his initial, (G). The editor is responsible for whatever may follow this initial and for all unsigned notes. The author's quotations are often inaccurate, but I have not printed the correct versions unless there was a special reason for doing so.

Page 1. Edward Seymour was the eldest son of Lord Francis Seymour, Dean of Wells, and nephew of the Duke of Somerset. He died 23 June 1775 at University College, Oxford, most likely while still an undergraduate, and was lamented by Graves in an epitaph, published in his *Euphrosyne* (1776–80), i. 298.

Page 3. The Heliodorus who wrote a romance called *Aethiopica* (or *Theagenes and Chariclea*) was identified by Socrates the Historian (*Hist. Eccl.*, v. 22) with a bishop of Tricca in Thessaly.

Page 4. (1) Many of those scripture expressions are omitted in this edition (G).—This footnote and the sentence to which it refers were both added in the third edition (1783). Since these scripture expressions have been restored, the footnote is no longer relevant.

(2) William Warburton, Bishop of Gloucester, whose *Doctrine of Grace* (1750) was in no sense a work of humour but a serious polemic against Methodism. Cf. p. 72.

Page 7. A *wig* is a kind of bun or tea-cake common in the north country.

Page 8. (1) 'Lippis notum & tonsoribus.' HOR. (G).—*Serm.*, I. vii. 3.

(2) Graves's list of theological writers was probably put together from

the most obscure names that he could recall. Lorenz Codomann published *Chronographia: A Description of Time* (2nd ed., 1590) and Johann Quistorp, a *Commentary on the Epistle to the Hebrews* (1638). Rudolph Goclenius, the Elder (1547-1628), was professor of logic at Marbourg and wrote some philosophico-theological works. Stumpius may be either David Stumpfius or Ludovicus Stumphius, both of whom wrote theological theses now in the British Museum, John Burstamantius may be Joannes de Bustamente, a Catholic theologian, and Conrade may be Bernhardus Conradi who published *Tabernaculi Mosaici* in 1612. About Copenstenius nothing has been learned.

VOLUME ONE

Page 11. (1) *Night Thoughts*, ii. 59-60.

(2) *La Nouvelle Héloïse*, ii. 21. 'Les romans sont peut-être la dernière instruction qu'il reste à donner à un peuple assez corrumpu pour que toute autre lui soit inutile.' J.-J. Rousseau, *Œuvres* (Paris, 1820), vi. 390. In the first edition of the novel the last words of the translation read 'to a refined people'. In the second edition (1774) they were corrected to the reading given here. Graves was annoyed over the garbling of his translation, as one of his letters to his publisher shows. See C. J. Hill, *The Literary Career of Richard Graves* (Northampton, Massachusetts, 1943-5), p. 21.

BOOK I

Page 14. (1) James Quin (1693-1766) was in his meridian at Drury Lane 1734-41, and David Garrick (1717-79) dawned at Goodman's Fields in 1741.

(2) 'Carlesis! ah! nostris & fleta & flenda camoenis.' Meret. Brit. (G).— (Careless! Oh, how you were mourned and how worthy you were to be mourned by our muses!) Betty Careless, at one time a desirable young prostitute, is said to have been the model for the old procuress shown in the third plate of William Hogarth's 'Marriage à la Mode'. John Ireland, *Hogarth Illustrated* (1806), ii. 34-35. Graves's quotation comes from 'Ad Henricum' contained in *Latin and English Poems* by a Gentleman of Trinity College, Oxford (1738)—probably Benjamin Loveling—and not, as Graves wrote, from 'Meretrices Britannicae' (British Whores), a poem contained in the same volume, but said to be of uncertain authorship.

Page 18. (1) On the Bath road (G).—Probably Froxfield, in Wiltshire. Thomas Hill was vicar of Froxfield until 1773, when he was succeeded by Thomas Brown. See Introduction, p. xx.

(2) Milton, *Paradise Lost*, i. 56-57.

Page 19. A very good book of old Baxter's (G).—Wildgoose's library contained the following among other titles: Edward Fisher, *The Marrow of Modern Divinity* (1645); Michael Sparke, *The Crums of Comfort* (7th ed., 1628); John Price, *Honey out of the Rock* (1644); Richard Baxter, *Directions for Weak Distempered Christians to grow up to a Confirmed State of Grace* (1669) (known as 'Shoves to heavy-ars'd Christians' also to Byron [see his 'Hints from Horace']), John Foxe, *Actes and Monuments* (1563), generally known as his 'Book of Martyrs'; and Samuel Clarke, *A Collection of the Lives of Ten Eminent Divines* (1662). Among the latter is a life of Mr. John Carter (1554–1634), but Graves's memory must have played him false, because Mr. Carter was born in Kent and lived most of his life in Suffolk, and because, though something is said in it about his fastings and abstemiousness, there is no mention of dumplings.

Page 22 (1) Arthur's Chocolate House at 37–38 St. James's Street was run by Robert Arthur, son of the manager of White's Chocolate House of *Tatler* fame. The Robin Hood Society was a debating club that met at the 'Robin Hood' in Butcher Row near Temple Bar. Bryant Lillywhite, *London Coffee Houses* (1963), pp. 92 and 727.

(2) On a sign there a painter had copied Roubiliac's figure of Fame on the wing: in her right hand exalting a golden boot; with a trumpet in the left, sounding forth the praises of the illustrious boot-maker (G).

Page 23. A learned antiquary insists upon it, that Tugwell is a corruption of Toghill near Bath; and Toghill of the Oak-hill; being a wood of Oaks, where the Druids went in search of the sacred Mistleto (G).—The 'learned antiquary' was probably one of Graves's friends.

Page 24. (1) *The Famous History of the Seven Champions of Christendom* (1596–7), by Richard Johnson, was reprinted frequently. The edition of Sir John Mandeville's *Travels* referred to was probably that of 1725. '. . . of antres vast and deserts idle . . .' *Othello*, I. iii.

(2) Matthew Paris, no contemptible historian, mentions his being frequently seen in the East, about 400 years ago (G).—According to the version of the legend given by Matthew Paris in his *Historia Major* (1259), the Wandering Jew had been Pilate's doorkeeper at the time of the trial of Jesus and for striking Jesus was condemned to wait on earth for the second coming.

(3) Memorable displays of the aurora were seen after the execution of Lord Derwentwater and other rebel lords in 1716. Afterwards it was often called 'Lord Derwentwater's lights'.

(4) Possibly an allusion to the Jacobite custom of toasting 'the king over the water'.

(5) Jobson and Nell are characters in Charles Coffey's *The Devil to Pay or The Wives Metamorphosed* (Drury Lane, 1731).

Page 27. Journal, p. 108 (G).—This, the first of Graves's many quotations
of and allusions to George Whitefield's *Journals*, illustrates his light-
hearted treatment of them. Here he refers to the publication entitled *A
Continuation of the Rev. Mr. Whitefield's Journal from his Arrival in
London to his Departure thence to Georgia* (1739). On p. 108 Whitefield
wrote: 'God was pleased to give me such extraordinary assistance, that
I believe few, if any, were able to resist the power wherewith God enabled
me to speak.' (24 May 1739.) The other expressions that occur on this page
of the novel, however, do not come from the same context and are probably
Graves's parodies of Whitefield's style, though parallels might be found in
scattered places throughout.

Page 29. (1) In his *Grace Abounding to the Chief of Sinners* (1666).
   (2) Revd. Mr. George Whitefield (1714-70) the Methodist leader.
Graves regularly uses the phonetic spelling.

BOOK II

Page 30. (1) Humphrey Prideaux (1648-1724), Oxford orientalist, published his *Life of Mahomet* in 1697.
   (2) Historical Review of the Transactions of Europe (G).

Page 31. (1) Vid. God's dealings with Mr. Whitfield. There is nothing so
ridiculous (or rather profane) which pious writers will not say, for the sake
of a witty allusion. Thus the learned Bishop Taylor says, that Christ was
born at the sign of the Star in Bethlehem. 'Born at an Inn, / A Star the
Sign——' Gold. Grove (G.)—In *A Brief and General Account of the First
Part of The Life of the Reverend Mr George Whitefield* (1739), Whitefield
wrote: 'I was born in Gloucester, in the month of December 1714. My
father and mother kept the Bell-Inn . . . the circumstance of my being born
in an inn, has been often of service to me, in exciting me to . . . follow the
example of my dear saviour, who was born in a stable and laid in a manger
belonging to an inn.' The lines quoted from Jeremy Taylor occur in one
of the Christmas hymns in his collection called *The Golden Grove* (1655):
'The blessed virgin travail'd without pain / And lodged in an inn, / A
glorious star the sign——'
   (2) About the year 1730 (G).—The author's account of the rise of
Methodism agrees with that given by John Wesley in an introductory
letter to his first published journal.
   (3) *The Practice of True Devotion* (2nd ed., 1715) by Robert Nelson was
reprinted many times during the eighteenth century.
   (4) Proverbs xvii. 14.

Page 36. Thomas Coryate (1577?-1617), the traveller and author of
Coryats Crudities (1611), was born in Odcombe, Somersetshire.

Page 38. This was a meeting of great renown in the last century, for an annual celebration of games, on the hills of Cotswold, instituted by one Dover, a public-spirited Attorney of Barton on the Heath in Warwickshire, which were frequented by the Nobility and Gentry for sixty miles round. They are described in a very scarce book, entitled, *Annalia Dubrensia; Upon the yearly Celebration of Mr. Robert Dover's Olympick Games upon Cotswold Hills*, &c., *Lond.* 1636, 4to. There are recommendatory Verses prefixed, written by Drayton, Jonson, Randolph, and many others, the most eminent Wits of the times. The games, as appears by a curious frontispiece, were, chiefly, wrestling, leaping, pitching the bar, handling the pike, dancing of women, various kinds of hunting, and particularly coursing the hare with greyhounds. These games are more than once alluded to by Shakespear. See Mr. Warton's very ingenious observations on that great Poet, in the Appendix to the edition published, in 1773, by Dr. Johnson and Mr. Steevens (G).—This note, as given here, appeared for the first time in the third edition of 1783. Most likely Graves had not seen *Annalia Dubrensia*, because he does not seem to know that it is not a description of the games but a collection of poems in honour of them. His note is in fact largely borrowed from Warton's (see the appendix to vol. x of the 1773 Shakespeare), which in turn is borrowed almost verbatim from Antony à Wood's *Athenae Oxonienses* (2nd ed., 1721, ii. 812-13). The alleged allusions in Shakespeare occur in *II Henry IV*, III. ii. 23 and *The Merry Wives of Windsor*, I. i. 80.

Page 39. See HURD's Letters on Chivalry (G).—*Letters on Chivalry and Romance* (1762) by Richard Hurd.

Page 43. *Paradise Lost*, v. 153-9.

Page 44. Unaccompanied by liquor.

Page 45. Quasi, Tail-oho! (G).—Graves's derivation is not endorsed by the *Oxford English Dictionary*, which derives it instead from a French hunting cry of unknown origin.

Page 48. 'Our Dorothy' must be recalling *The Merry Wives of Windsor*, IV. ii. 231: 'To scrape the figures out of your husbands' braines.' *Figure* means phantasm.

Page 49. The fly wheel that controlled the speed of a smoke-jack used for roasting meat.

Page 50. (1) Whitefield's *Journal*, 17 May 1739, 'Preached . . . at Hampstead-heath. . . . I preached very near the horse-course, which gave me occasion to speak home to their souls concerning our spiritual race'; and 23 May 1739, 'I preached . . . on a common near the town [of Northampton], from the starting-post. . . . Oh that we may all run so as to obtain the crown of life.' (Cf. p. 427 and note 1.)

(2) Whitefield preached 'from the stairs of a wind mill' at Bedford, 24 May 1739, but his journal does not record his allegorizing the occasion in the way Graves indicates.

Page 51. (1) Whitefield's *Journal*, 6 May 1739, 'I believe there were no less than fifty thousand people, near fourscore coaches, besides great numbers of horses; and what is most remarkable, there was such an awful silence amongst them, and the word of God came with such power, that all, I believe, were pleasingly surprized.'

(2) Whitefield's *Journal*, 7 February 1739, 'My dear Christian friends waited, at my coming home, to salute me.'

Page 52. Life of C. Cibber (G).—In the Dedication to his *Apology* (1740), Cibber wrote that in the country 'moderate matters serve for amusement'.

Page 56. A character now almost forgotten in England (G).

Page 57. *II Henry IV*, i. ii. 10.

Page 59. Though they despise human Learning, those that have had a learned education are fond enough of displaying it (G).—John Wesley once used syllogistic methods of argument in order to defend extemporary prayer. *Journal*, 28 November 1740.

Page 60. Smuggled.

Page 63. By *casuistical* and *tyrannical*, Mrs. Bridget probably means *jesuitical* and *puritanical* (G).

Page 64. (1) Graves means *quixotic*. For him the word *romantic* suggested the old romances that Cervantes ridiculed, and it had not yet taken on for him its larger and more favourable implications.

(2) Mr. Locke (G).—*An Essay Concerning Human Understanding*, by John Locke (4th ed.), ii. 33, sect. 10: 'The ideas of goblins and sprites have really no more to do with darkness than light.' Locke distinguishes between sprites and spirits, ordinarily using the latter word for angels.

(3) The Jacobite rebellion of 1745. The time of the action of the novel is just after the putting down of the rebellion.

Page 65. A *trencher* cap, now called a mortar-board.

Page 66. N.B. A real fact (G).

Page 67. (1) A corruption of Morisco dance, probably introduced from Spain by John of Gaunt (G).

(2) A wig with a long plaited tail having bows at top and bottom that became fashionable in 1706 when Marlborough won the battle of Ramillies. Since the wearing of wigs went out during the sixties, Graves's references to the odd appearance Wildgoose made in his own hair had lost most of their point by 1773.

Page 68. (1) A buffoon.

(2) When John Wesley left Georgia, to avoid a prosecution, he wrote in his *Journal*, 'I shook off the dust of my feet, and left Georgia.' 2 December 1737. Cf. p. 183.

Book III

Page 69. This Mrs. Whitefield was George Whitefield's sister-in-law, wife of the brother who took over the Bell Inn after George's mother married for the second time. The author's information probably came mainly from George Whitefield's *Brief and General Account*. Cf. p. 31, note 1. The Bell Inn was made famous by Henry Fielding's *Tom Jones*.

Page 72. Graves was fond of this quotation from Whitefield. Cf. p. 232.

Page 74. (1) Cf. Alexander Pope, *Epistle to Burlington*, line 150: 'Who never mentions hell to ears polite.'

(2) Whitfield's Sermons (G).—This example of Wildgoose's eloquence is a recognizable imitation of Whitefield's sermon on 'Christ the Best Husband', preached to a Society of Young Women. E.g.: 'The Lord Jesus Christ, doth espouse himself unto the children of men, in this world, but the public solemnization of the marriage, is reserved until the last day; when his spouse shall be brought forth to him, in white robes, and a raiment of perfect righteousness, more rich and curious, my dear sisters, than any of your needle-work; and the marriage feast will be kept in his father's house, in heaven, where they shall be received into the nearest and closest embraces of his love.'

(3) Tho' these kinds of expression are used in scripture, in compliance with the carnal notions of the Jews, and have affected their common language—yet on moral subjects, I think, they have but an uncouth effect (G).

Page 75. Lady Wishfort's *mot* in William Congreve's *The Way of the World*, iv. xii.

Page 76. In the third edition of the novel (1783) these words of Jesus were replaced by 'I know no man after the flesh, nor woman neither'.

Page 81. Whitfield's Journals (G).—Whitefield's assertion about Archbishop Tillotson was made in a letter published in the *Gentleman's Magazine* (ix [1739], 238-9) and vindicated in two letters published subsequently in the *Daily Advertiser* along with another 'shewing the fundamental error of a book called *The Whole Duty of Man*'. These were reprinted in 1740 in a pamphlet. The basis of Whitefield's criticism in both cases is their failure to preach the doctrine of faith without works. Cf. p. 225, note 1.

Page 86. Deposit.

Page 87. *Clever* means *good-natured*. Cf. Oliver Goldsmith, *She Stoops to Conquer*, I. ii:

> 'Then come, put the jorum about,
> And let us be merry and clever.'

Page 91. A full wig tied back in two curls.

Page 99. (1) Wigs were generally worn at this time (G).—Cf. p. 67.
(2) This came to pass, a few years after (G).

Page 100. (1) Psalm lii. 2 (Prayer-book version).
(2) *Cyropaideia*, I. iii. 2.

Page 101. In K. James the First's reign (G).—The episode is related by Sir Henry Wotton in *A Short View of the Life and Death of George Villiers, Duke of Buckingham* (1642), p. 591.

Page 104. Both Wesley and Whitefield record more than once the use of fire-rockets and crackers by their persecutors.

BOOK IV

Page 107. Recollected (an obsolete sense of the word).

Page 109. Similar legal troubles had beset Graves in his executorship under the will of his friend William Shenstone, the poet. Cf. Hill, op. cit. pp. 54–55.

Page 110. Not England, but the locality familiar to him.

Page 112. A favourite expression of Wesley and Whitefield. For example, (Wesley's *Journal*) 20 May 1739, 'Give me where to stand, and I will shake the earth'; 13 May 1740, 'The devil knew his kingdom shook . . .'; and (Whitefield's *Journal*) 8 March 1739, 'I doubt not but Satan envied our happiness. But I hope, by the help of God, we shall make his kingdom shake.' Cf. pp. 232 and 251.

Page 114. (1) Vid. Journals (G).—No source has been found.
(2) Vigorous, able-bodied. Cf. jolly tars—able-bodied seamen. Cf. p. 145.

Page 118. Jean Foy-Vaillant (1632–1706), French numismatist, gave 'a complete series of the Syro-Macedonian Kings' in his *Seleucidarum Imperium, sive Historia Regum Syriæ ad Fidem Numismatum Accommodata* (Paris, 1681), explaining on p. 254 why Alexander I of Syria was called *Evergetes*: 'id est Beneficus, ut populos hoc cognomine sibi devinciret'. He also published *Historia Ptolemæorum Ægypti Regum* (Amsterdam, 1701).

Page 120. To froth at the mouth.

Page 121. Probably Graves alludes to Richard Yate's 'A New Theory of Comets', which came out serially in the *Gentleman's Magazine* in 1743 and caused some controversy, especially as to whether sun spots were in the sun itself or were separate bodies floating nearby.

Page 123. This use of 'welcome' to refer to a gesture at parting is odd.

Page 126. (1) *Metamorphoses*, xv. 116–21.

(2) *An Essay on Man*, i. 81–86.

Page 131. (1) The name of a chambermaid in *Don Quixote*.

(2) The story of Mr. Graham and the clergyman's daughter Ophelia is essentially autobiographical. The real Ophelia was Utrecia Smith, daughter of the Revd. William Smith, Graves's first schoolmaster, whom 'for prudential reasons' Graves jilted. After her death he erected an urn to her memory in Mickleton church in 1744, upon which Shenstone wrote his fourth elegy, dedicated to Graves. Cf. Graves's *Recollections of William Shenstone* (1788), pp. 116–17, and Hill, op. cit. pp. 61–64.

Page 137. Terence, *Eunuchus*, 296 (iii. 2).

BOOK V

Page 138. (1) Joh. Casa, de morum elegantiâ (G).—In 1774 Graves published an English translation of *Il Galateo* (1598) by Giovanni della Casa, with the title *Galateo: Or, A Treatise on Politeness and Delicacy of Manners. . . . From the Italian. . . .* His quotation is a paraphrase of a passage in section II (p. 27 of his translation). In spite of his statement on the title-page, Graves made his translation from a Latin one, a fact that accounts for the Latin form given to the author's name and the title.

(2) 'As many mountains huge and great / Jerusalem about do close. . . .' Psalm cxxv. 2, as translated in *The Whole Booke of Psalmes*, by T. Sternhold, I. Hopkins, and others (1562). Jerry's 'new diversion' was *A New Version of the Psalms of David*, by N. Tate and N. Brady (1696), who translated the line thus: 'Look how the hills on ev'ry side / Jerusalem enclose. . . .'

(3) Psalm CXXII. 3. (Prayer-book version.)

Page 139. Cf. p. 60 and note 1.

Page 141. In a direct quotation the words of mine host here would have been 'this very morning'.

Page 143. All these expressions in one sermon, on redeeming time (G).— John Wesley preached a sermon on this text (Ephesians v. 16), but none of these expressions occur in it. No sermon on this text is included among Whitefield's published ones.

Page 145. (1) John Wesley had a memorable encounter with Beau Nash, Master of Ceremonies at Bath, on 5 June 1739. See his journal for that date. Nash told Wesley that his preaching frightened people out of their wits.

(2) Cf. p. 114 and note 2.

(3) Message Cards had been lately introduced (G).—See chapter VI of this book.

Page 147. (1) This seems to allude to some piece of modern history now forgotten (G).—In 1701 Thomas Pitt (1653-1726), Governor of Fort St. George (Madras), secured the famous Pitt diamond for trade, and was accused of having acquired it dishonestly. See C. N. Dalton, *Life of Thomas Pitt* (Cambridge, 1915).

(2) A set of blank Cards have since been invented, by which the above absurdities may be avoided (G).—The 'facetious Mr. ——' referred to is probably Edmond Hoyle (1672-1769), author of *A Short Treatise on Whist* (1742).

Page 148. In Fielding's *Joseph Andrews*, the hero's sister and brother-in-law are called Booby, in derision of Richardson's Mr. B.——, hero of his *Pamela*.

Page 154. A plain gold ring, probably her wedding-ring.

Page 158. (1) Lord Shaftesbury, *Characteristics* (1711), ii. 185.

(2) Twenty years ago (G).—This note may indicate that Graves had a real person in mind. The name itself was probably borrowed from Christopher Anstey's *New Bath Guide* (1766), Book II, Letter 10.

Page 161. i.e. splashed.

Page 169. *II Henry IV*, III. ii. 332.

Page 174. An imperfect recollection of *II Henry IV*, III. ii. 40-50.

Page 178. *An Essay on Man*, iii. 305-6. Pope wrote 'graceless zealots' rather than 'senseless bigots'.

VOLUME TWO

Page 181. (1) *Met.* iii. 282.

(2) *Sat.* iv. 1.

BOOK VI

Page 183. Cf. p. 68 and note 2.

Page 185. (1) Alexander Pope, *The Rape of the Lock*, iv. 155.

(2) John Hill, M.D. (1716-75), quack doctor, botanist, and voluminous

writer on medicine and botany. See Sir John Hawkins's *Life of Johnson*,
ed. B. H. Davis (Macmillan, New York, 1961), pp. 93-94, and Oliver
Goldsmith, 'A Resverie' (in *The Bee*, 1759).

Page 187. (1) Mr. Rivers's story, which occupies most of Book VI, is
largely autobiographical. Charlotte Woodville stands for Lucy Bartholomew, the fifteen-year-old girl whom Graves secretly married after having
eloped with her to London in 1748. Most of the incidents in Rivers's
history correspond similarly with ones in this chapter of Graves's life.
His description of Charlotte (p. 188) is corroborated of Mrs. Graves by
several witnesses. Cf. Hill, op. cit., pp. 64-72.

(2) i.e. a college.

Page 189. William Congreve, *The Way of the World*, III. xii.

Page 190. (1) Prior (G).—I have been unable to find this line among
Prior's works.

(2) Romans iii. 13.

(3) Matthew v. 28.

Page 193. (1) Card. de Retz (G).—Jean-François-Paul de Gondi, Cardinal de Retz (1614-97), whose *Mémoires* were published in 1717.

(2) Among the farcical requirements for the degree of M.A. in eighteenth-century Oxford was one to deliver a lecture to an empty room.
This was called a *wall-lecture* because there were no auditors.

Page 196. i.e. stepmother.

Page 199. Terence, *Eunuchus*, i. 22: 'haec verba ea una mehercule falsa
lacrimula, / quam oculos terendo misere vix vi expresserit, / restinguet.'
(By Jove, one crocodile's tear that she can scarcely force out of her eyes
with hard scrubbing will make short work of all those big words.)

Page 213. Cf. p. 244 and note 1.

Page 220. *Julius Caesar*, III. ii. 97.

Page 222. Idealized hero of Samuel Richardson's novel of the same
name (1754).

Page 225. (1) *The Whole Duty of Man* (1658), supposed to have been
written by Richard Allestree, was often reprinted and had a great vogue
as a pious manual. The words of Mr. Rivers's aunt are a reasonably accurate
summary of the section on Temperance. Wildgoose's contemptuous
shake of the head has been accounted for already. Cf. p. 81, note 1.

(2) Gregory Griskin's good books: Thomas Ken, Bishop of Bath and
Wells (1637-1711), *A Manual of Prayers for the Use of Scholars of Win-
chester College* (1687); [William Melmouth (1666-1743)], *The Great*

Importance of a Religious Life Considered (1711); Robert Nelson (1665-1715), *The Practice of True Devotion* (2nd ed., 1715); William Burkitt (1650-1713), *Expository Notes with Practical Observations on the New Testament* (1724) and *The Poor Man's Help and the Young Man's Guide* (2nd ed., 1694).

Page 228. Vid. Journal (G).—See Whitefield's entry for 7 February 1739, when he was setting out from London to Windsor: 'Lord, send thy angel before me to prepare my way.' But most likely Graves coupled this in his mind with the entry for 7 March 1739 (misdated 8 March in early editions), when Whitefield was about to leave from the New Passage for Wales: 'Our business being in haste, God having, of his good providence, sent one to guide us, we rode all night.' Cf. p. 264.

BOOK VII

Page 230. (1) Though there is no evidence that Whitefield was especially fond of eating, in his journals he sometimes mentions having had meals and of being physically comfortable, comments that Graves perhaps felt to be beneath the dignity of a pious journal. Compare his similar dig at Thomas Carter (p. 19). Both Whitefield and Wesley often preached in prisons; on 15 February 1739 the former preached in Bristol Newgate to the poor prisoners on the subject of the penitent thief.

(2) Perceived in myself something like Envy towards brother H——. JOURN. p. 6 (G).—Whitefield's *Journal*: 5 January 1738.

(3) Journal, p. 6 (G).—Probably a careless repetition of part of the previous note. The words in quotation marks are reminiscent of Romans xiii. 13 and Galatians v. 21.

Page 231. (1) This was the usual form of examination by the Tryers in the last Century (G).—Tryers were commissioners appointed to pass on all preachers before being given benefices.

(2) Cf. p. 298 and note 1.

Page 232. (1) Cf. Whitefield's *Journal*: 17 February 1739, 'My bowels have long since yearned towards the poor colliers, who, as far as I can find, are very numerous, and yet are as sheep, having no shepherd.' A favourite phrase with Graves. Cf. p. 72 and p. 377.

(2) Cf. p. 391 and note 3.
(3) Cf. p. 112 and note 1.

Page 233. Deuteronomy xxv. 4.

Page 234. Whitefield's *Journal*: 25 February 1739, 'At four I hasted to Kingswood.—At a moderate computation, there were above ten thousand people to hear me. The trees and hedges were full. All was hush when I began; the sun shone bright....' 10 May 1739, 'Preached at Kennington;

but it rained most part of the day. There were not above ten thousand people, and thirty coaches.—However, God was pleased so visibly to interpose in causing the weather to clear up, and the sun to shine out just as I began, that I could not avoid taking notice of it to the people in my discourse. Our minute philosophers . . . laugh at the notion of a particular providence. But to suppose a general, without a particular providence, is as absurd as to imagine there can be a chain without being composed of links.'

Page 235. (1) Chillingworth (G).—Perhaps a free paraphrase of part of the sermon on Galatians v. 5, by William Chillingworth (1602–44), Oxford Royalist theologian.

(2) *Joe Miller's Jests: or, the Wit's Vade-Mecum* (1739) was a popular compendium throughout the eighteenth century.

Page 241. (1) Cf. Whitefield's *Journal*: 19 May 1739. Whitefield had Joseph Periam released from Bethlehem Hospital, where he had been confined for being 'Methodically Mad'. Among other things he 'had sold his cloaths, and given them to the poor'.

(2) See the illustration by J. Sturt to Matthew vii. 3–5 in Samuel Wesley's *History of the Old and New Testament* (1716).

Page 244. Mr. Law's Christian Perfection (G).—William Law, *A Practical Treatise upon Christian Perfection* (1726): 'So that one may with the same assurance affirm, that the play-house . . . is as certainly the house of the devil, as the church is the house of God.' (pp. 369–70.) Law also published a pamphlet entitled *The Absolute Unlawfulness of the Stage-Entertainment fully Demonstrated*. Whitefield held the same belief, remarking in his autobiography that as a boy he had been a great reader of playbooks until, one day, picking one of them up, 'God struck my heart with such power, that I was obliged to lay it down again; and, blessed be his name, I have not read any such book since.' (*God's Dealings with Mr. Whitefield*.) Cf. p. 213.

Page 246. Vid. Journals (G).—Both Whitefield and Wesley often refer contemptuously to 'the company of good sort of men', preferring to minister to the lower classes. Cf. p. 293.

Page 248. It is well known how frequently these modern Prophets have been mistaken in their predictions (G).

Page 249. [William Vickers], *A Companion to the Altar: Shewing the Nature and Necessity of a Sacramental Preparation, in Order to our worthy Receiving the Holy Communion* (1707).

Page 250. Whitefield's *Journal*: 21 February 1739, 'A little girl of thirteen years of age [came to me], who told me in great simplicity "she was pricked through and through with the power of the word".'

Page 251. Cf. p. 112 and note 1.

Page 256. Cf. Alexander Pope, *Epistle to Arbuthnot*, line 131: 'The muse but serv'd to ease some friend, not wife.'

Page 257. Whitefield's *Journal*: 19 May 1739. A correspondent wrote to ask: 'If I am in prison, whether I may not, without offence to God, make use of endeavours to be discharged. . . .' One of John Wesley's good works in Oxford was to secure the release of men who had been imprisoned for small debts and who seemed to be of good character.

Page 258. (1) i.e. by opening the Bible at random and finding guidance in the first text upon which the eye happens to fall. Cf. p. 298 and note 3.
    (2) A real Fact (G).

Page 259. John Wesley's *Journal*: 9 May 1740, 'I was a little surprized at some, who were buffetted of Satan in an unusual manner, by such a spirit of laughter as they could in no wise resist. . . .' 21 May 1740, 'In the evening, such a spirit of laughter was among us, that many were much offended.' 28 February 1738, Wesley resolved 'to labour after continual seriousness, not willingly indulging myself in any the least levity of behaviour, or in laughter,—no, not for a moment'.

Page 260. Whitefield's *Journal*: 7 February 1739, 'I perceived my heart so nearly knit to my dear friends, that was it the divine will, I should gladly continue here. But I must go into every place and city where I have been already, for therefore am I sent.'

BOOK VIII

Page 264. (1) Journal, p. 20 (G).—Cf. p. 228 and note 1.
    (2) Ibid. (G).—Whitefield's *Journal*: 18 May 1739, 'As the walls of Jericho once fell down at the sound of a few rams horns; so I hope even this foolishness of preaching, under God, will be a means of pulling down the Devil's strong holds, which are in and about the city of London.'

Page 268. Howel Harris (1714–73) was one of Whitefield's and Wesley's first Welsh lieutenants.

Page 269. Whitefield's *Journal*: 8 March 1739, 'I did not observe any scoffers within; but without, some were pleased to honour me so far, as to trail a dead fox, and hunt it about the hall.—But, blessed be God, my voice prevailed.'

Page 271. *The Devil upon Two Sticks*, a popular ballad opera by Charles Coffey, was first produced at Drury Lane in 1729.

Page 274. Whitefield's *Journal*: 9 March 1739, 'I think Wales is excellently well prepared for the gospel of Christ. . . . People make nothing of coming twenty miles to hear a sermon, and great numbers there are who have not only been hearers, but doers also of the word; so that there is a most comfortable prospect of the spreading of the gospel in Wales.' 5 April 1739, 'To me [the Welsh] seem a people sweetly disposed to receive the gospel.' Wesley's *Journal*: 20 October 1739, 'And most of the inhabitants [of Wales] are indeed ripe for the gospel.'

Page 280. Such was the active zeal of the last Century:

> 'The Oyster-woman lock'd her fish up,
> And trudg'd away, to cry, No Bishop!' HUD. (G).—
>
> Samuel Butler, *Hudibras*, I. ii. 540-1.

Page 281. (1) Mr. Wesley's Journal, 1740 (G).—Actually 5 May 1747: 'Many were seated on a long wall adjoining; which, being built of loose stones, in the middle of the sermon all fell down at once. I never saw, heard, nor read of such a thing before. The whole wall and the persons sitting upon it, sunk down together, none of them screaming out, and very few altering their posture. And not one was hurt at all; but they appeared sitting at the bottom, just as they sat at the top. Nor was there any interruption either of my speaking, or of the attention of the hearers.'

(2) John Wesley's *Journal*: 4 December 1742, 'J— B—, of Tanfield-Leigh, who had receiv'd a sense of the love of God a few days before, came riding thro' the town, hollowing and shouting and driving all the people before him, telling them, "God had told him, he should be a king, and should tread all his enemies under his feet." '

Page 285. Phædra and Hypolitus (G).—From the tragedy of that name by Edmund Smith (1707).

Page 292. Probably a garbled version of Romans i. 26-28.

Page 293. Cf. p. 246.

Page 294. (1) John Wesley's *Journal*: 11 August 1740, 'Forty or fifty of those who were seeking salvation, desired leave to spend the night together, at the society-room, in prayer and giving thanks. Before ten I left them and lay down. . . . Between two and three in the morning I was waked, and desired to come down stairs. I immediately heard such a confused noise, as if a number of men were all putting to the sword. It increased when I came into the room and began to pray. One whom I particularly observed to be roaring aloud for pain was J— W—, who had been always 'till then very sure, that "none cried out but hypocrites:" So had Mrs. S—ms also. But she too now cried to God with a loud and bitter cry. It was not long, before God heard from his holy place. He spake, and all our souls were comforted. He bruised Satan under our feet, and sorrow and sighing fled away.'

(2) Whitefield's *Journal*: 20 March 1739, 'Had the pleasure of hearing of the success of my discourse yesterday upon many souls, especially upon two little children, who were observed to come home crying, and to retire to prayers.' 2 November 1740, 'As I went down from the pulpit, a woman said, "Come and see what God has done for me to-night." I looked, and her daughter, in a great agony, was crying out, "Oh my Jesus, my Jesus!" Another, a little boy, was so concerned on the pulpit stairs, that he could scarce stand. One of my friends asked him why he cried, "Who can help it?" said he. "Mr. Whitefield's words cut me to the heart." '

Page 298. (1) Hiera Picra, or Sacred Bitter (G).—A purgative. Cf. p. 231.

(2) Journal, *passim* (G).—This is unfair to both Whitefield and Wesley. The sentiment sounds more like one of those expressed by their enemies, the Antinomians. Cf. p. 451 and note 2.

(3) John Wesley often had recourse to this Christianized form of the *Sortes Virgilianae*, which he called using 'the oracles of God' and deciding 'by lot'. Cf. his *Journal* for 28 March 1739.

Page 299. The name of Don Quixote's horse.

Page 301. (1) Graves originally wrote, 'somewhat barbarous and semi-gothic'. In the edition of 1783 he altered the reading to the one in this text. The change from 'semi-gothic' to 'uncivilized' was probably inspired by the growing popularity of the 'gothic' taste in the decade 1773–83.

(2) Alexander Pope, *The Rape of the Lock*, III. 8: 'Dost sometimes counsel take—and sometimes tea.'

Page 307. John Dryden, *Cymon and Iphigenia*, lines 82–83.

Page 308. A garbled version of Matthew v. 11.

Page 309. (1) An old variety of cider apple.

(2) John Kyrle (d. 1724), celebrated in Pope's *Epistle to Bathurst*, lines 250–82.

Page 312. *No Jest Like a True Jest: Being a Compendious Record of the Merry Life, and Mad Exploits of Capt. James Hind, The Great Robber of England* (1674). Jerry's story comes from ch. VI, and the two others alluded to are in chs. IV and IX respectively.

VOLUME THREE

Page 317. (1) Actually Ovid, *Met*. i. 758.

(2) *The Lay Monk*, No. 9 (1713).

BOOK IX

Page 320. Probably means garnished. Johnson (*Dictionary*, 1755) quotes the following couplet from Thomas Tusser's *Hundred Good Points of*

Husbandrie: 'Who eateth his veal, pig and lamb being froth, / Shall twice in a week go to bed without broth.'

Page 321. Cf. p. 67 and note 2.

Page 322. (1) Joseph Addison, *Cato*, II. v. 69, 112, 116. The quotation in the next paragraph comes from I. iv. 151, and the names used in succeeding paragraphs (Juba, Syphax, and Marcia) are of characters in it.

(2) A translation of a common Homeric phrase, ἕρκος ὀδόντων. Cf. *Iliad* iv. 350; ix. 409; *Odyssey*, i. 64; and *passim*.

Page 323. (1) In his *Timber: or Discoveries* (1641) in the section entitled 'De Shakespeare Nostrati'.

(2) In his *Lettres Philosophiques*, xviii: 'Sur la tragédie'.

Page 324. John Wall (1708–76), a practising physician and amateur artist in Worcester, was one of fifteen original partners in the Worcester Porcelain Company, and may have been the prime mover in establishing it in 1751.

Page 325. Usually spelled *nuncheon*, a light refreshment.

Page 326. John Wesley's *Journal*: 20 May 1742, 'I overtook a serious man, with whom I immediately fell into conversation. He presently gave me to know, what his opinions were; therefore I said nothing to contradict them. But that did not content him. He was quite uneasy to know, whether I held the doctrine of the decrees as he did; but I told him over and over, "we had better keep to practical things, lest we should be angry at one another". And so we did for two miles, 'till he caught me unawares, and dragg'd me into the dispute before I knew where I was. He then grew warmer and warmer: told me, I was rotten at heart, and supposed I was one of John Wesley's followers. I told him, "No, I am John Wesley himself." Upon which

> Improvisum aspris veluti qui sentibus anguem
> Pressit—

he would gladly have run away outright. But being the better mounted of the two, I kept close to his side, and endeavour'd to show him his heart, 'till we came into the street of Northampton.' Graves, of course, is alluding to the well-known dispute between Wesley and Whitefield.

Page 327. Though Sir George Lyttleton (1709–73) had become 'Lord Lyttleton' in 1756, Graves never corrected this style. Lyttleton was a statesman, poet, and patron of poets, as well as the owner of the celebrated show-place, Hagley Park, and the husband of the former Lucy Fortescue. According to the *Biographical Magazine* (1794), he lived 'with this accomplished lady . . . in the highest degree of connubial felicity for five years [1742–7]'. He was already married for a second time when Graves wrote

L l

his novel, but, as the same source puts it, he 'was not equally successful'. Graves does not appear to be aware of the second marriage.

Page 328. The vulgar definition of History and Geography (G).

Page 329. Graves described the Leasowes and its owner, William Shenstone, in his *Recollections of . . . the Life of the late William Shenstone, Esq.* (1788), writing that Shenstone 'wore his hair . . . almost in the graceful manner, which has since generally prevailed'. [p. 25.] The gardens had been more fully described by Robert Dodsley in vol. ii of Shenstone's *Works* (1764), according to whom there were several cascades, including one which was the focal centre of the whole decorative scheme, as well as images of Pan and a faun.

Page 330. William Lagge, Earl of Dartmouth (1731-1801), a personal friend of George III, who presently became Lord Privy Seal. Ironically he was thought to be sympathetic to the Methodists.

Page 331. Isaiah xlvi. 1: 'Bel is broken, Nebo is destroyed.'

Page 332. It was most probably Diana, that Jerry meant by this confused account (G).

Page 338. Slang for hypochondriac.

Page 341. Parliament passed an act offering a reward to Mrs. Joanna Stephens (d. 1774), inventor of a 'cure' for the stone and gravel, if she would disclose her recipe and if it proved to be effective. She did so in 1739; see the *Gentleman's Magazine* for that year, pp. 298-9. The following year four men who had taken her medicine were publicly examined by a panel of doctors and pronounced cured. The examiners signed a certificate and Parliament presumably gave the reward. See the *Daily Advertiser*, 28 March 1740.

Page 342. (1) All expressions taken from advertisements (G).
(2) i.e. digestive.

Page 343. Graves tells this story again in his book *The Invalid* (1804), where he says of Viper Grass (Scorzonera) that it is 'supposed to be a preservative against pestilential distempers, so frequent in the Levant'. [p. 142.]

Page 344. Ælian, Var[ia] Hist[oria] (G).—This story comes from ii. 5, and the following one from iii. 20.

Page 345. George Cheyne (1671-1743), *An Essay of Health and Long Life* (1724). He begins by recommending that his patients live on a good soil, a thought that probably suggested the opening of the Slicer episode. Graves himself said that once he reduced himself to 'a valetudinary state of health' by following Cheyne's advice. *The Invalid*, pp. 22-26.

Page 348. (1) Quem penes arbitrium est, & jus & norma loquendi. HOR. (G).—*Ars Poetica*, 72. (In whom lies the authority, the rule, and pattern of speech.)

(2) See Dr. *Johnson's* Grammar, Letter *H* (G).—'The *h* in English is scarcely ever mute at the beginning of a word.' Johnson's *Dictionary* (1755).

BOOK X

Page 354. Don Quixote's horse.

Page 355. A celebrated Quack made this blunder; that is, in plain English, a tincture that will *bring on* a Fever (G).

Page 360. About the time of the second Jacobite rebellion in 1745, the Methodists were sometimes accused of pro-Stuart sympathies. Cf. Wesley's *Journal* for 11 April 1744. In one of Hogarth's engravings, a Methodist preacher is shown trying to hide his tonsure under a wig.

Page 362. Alexander Pope, *An Essay on Criticism*, line 232.

Page 364. (1) J. Dalton, *Comus, a Mask, as Altered from Milton* (1738). The author's scene may be imaginary, but he may have had in mind the grotto at Stoney Middleton in Hathersage parish, called by John Aikin (*Description of the Country . . . round Manchester* [1795], p. 496) 'one of the curiosities of the county':—'It is a narrow, deep, and winding ravine, not so much distinguished for grandeur or beauty, as for the peculiarity of the shape of its rocks. . . . Here Mr. Longdon has raised a beautiful plantation, with a grotto in the midst of it, furnished with the most elegant fossils of the county.'

(2) *As You Like It*, II. vii. 107 ff.

Page 365. (1) According to J. W. Croker, in the notes to his edition of Boswell's *Life of Johnson*, iv. 524 (London, 1831), Sir William Forester is to be identified with William Fitzherbert, Graves's first employer, and the other personae of this episode with other members of his family and his friends. Hill (*Literary Career of Richard Graves*, Northampton (Mass.), 1935, pp. 58–61) is prepared to accept this identification, though the names mean little now except those of Mr. and Mrs. Fitzherbert, Charles Pratt (cf. p. 370, note 1), and Miss Hill Boothby (Miss Sainthill).

(2) *Gulliver's Travels*, III. v.

Page 366. (1) Graves misrepresents Shaftesbury, who, in his *Inquiry Concerning Virtue* (1699), concluded that, though an atheist might possibly love virtue for its own sake, 'the chiefest security, the perfection and the highest degree of virtue, must be owing to the belief of a God'. (p. 81.)

(2) The author does not intend the slightest reflection on the general character of these excellent writers (G).—John Norris of Bemerton (1657–1711) wrote some popular books of piety, such as *Practical Discourses* and *Letters Concerning the Love of God*. There were also many translations into English of the works of François de Salignac de la Mothe Fénelon, Archbishop of Cambrai (1651–1715), especially his *Discourse on Christian Perfection*, *Pious Thoughts Concerning the Knowledge and Love of God*, and the much-read *Instructions for the Education of a Daughter*.

Page 367. Graves tells about the historical incident upon which this anecdote is based in his book called *The Triflers* (1805): 'I dined there [i.e. at the home of Ralph Allen, Esq.] with Sir J. C[o]pe, who commanded the royal army, which was defeated at the battle of Preston-Pans; and who outrid the express, and arrived at St. James's before the courier, who was dispatched to inform his majesty of that event; upon which his majesty observed, "That he was the first general he had ever heard of, who brought the news of his own defeat," and immediately turned his back upon him. When the news of the day was mentioned at table, Sir John said, "Aye, so it is written; but you must never believe anything you read in the newspapers," in hopes of invalidating the truth of the above mentioned transaction. It was then well known, that Flora Macdonald, who attended the prince in this expedition, called a run away horse, which she rode, "Johnny Cop".' (pp. 67–68.)

Page 368. (1) John Dryden, *Mac Flecknoe*, line 111.
(2) Witwoud in *The Way of the World* describes Petulant as having 'a pretty deal of an odd sort of a small wit'. (I. vi.)

Page 370. (1) Now at the top of his profession (G).—According to Croker, the young Templar is to be identified with Charles Pratt, who by the date of publication of *The Spiritual Quixote* had become Lord Chancellor with the title Lord Camden. Cf. p. 365, note 1.
(2) Thomas Shaw (1694–1751) published *Travels or Observations Relating to Several Parts of Barbary and the Levant* (Oxford, 1738). Graves's tale is out of keeping with the sober and learned tone of the *Travels*, where for the most part the privations of the travellers are emphasized. But Shaw does say that the richer Moors and Turks have elaborate feasts: 'I have seen at some of their festivals, more than two hundred dishes, whereof forty at least were of different kinds.' (p. 297.) He also mentions the hospitality of the desert Arabs: 'Besides a bowl of milk, and a basket of figs, raisins, dates, or other dryed fruit, which were presented to us upon our arrival, the master of the tent, where we lodged, fetcht us from his flock, (according to the number of our company) a kid, or a goat; a lamb, or a sheep; half of which was immediately seethed by his wife, and served up with cuscasowe; the rest, was usually made kab-ab [i.e., cut into chops

and roasted], and reserved for our breakfast or dinner the next day.' (p. v.) His book, however, was attacked by Richard Pococke in 1745 as inaccurate, a charge that Shaw answered in a supplement published in the following year.

Page 382. Mr. Wesley's Journals, *passim* (G).—Episodes of this kind are numerous in the journals of both Whitefield and Wesley.

Page 384. There seems to be no foundation for this story.

Page 385. Simon Stylites (G).

Page 386. (1) Cf. *Hamlet*, III. i. 122.

(2) Graves felt the plight of old maids deeply, and included in his *Senilities* (1801) a long essay on 'The Consolation of Neglected Virgins'. When he wrote this passage in *The Spiritual Quixote* he probably recalled the Lay Nunnery mentioned in several of the *Lay Monks*, a periodical of 1713 (cf. the second motto to vol. iii).

Page 390. (1) In the edition of 1808, the name is given as 'Sir W. Keyte'. See below, pp. 397 ff.

(2) Ilam, the seat of Mr. Porte, now well known to people of taste in most parts of the kingdom (G).—John Port, Esq., of Ilam, five miles north-west of Ashbourn. The old Ilam Hall (torn down in 1821) had belonged to the Ports for many generations. 'At Ilam', writes William Pitt (*A Topographical History of Staffordshire* [1817], pp. 38 and 238), 'is a very pleasant seat, which, from its romantic situation, suggests the idea of a glen in the Alps : two considerable rivers, the Hamp and the Many-fold, here rush from under the limestone hills, after a subterraneous pas-sage of several miles in separate streams. . . . Behind the house, on the s.w. bank of the Manifold, a flourishing wood of oak, elm, ash, etc. rises along the side of the hill, and spreads to a considerable extent, in form of an amphitheatre, and above it the ground gradually rises in a cultivated eminence to a great height, terminated by a coppice, which is a conspicuous and pleasing object, and may be seen for several miles. The river falls in two natural cascades near the mansion, and their regular and constant sound, has a tendency to tranquillize the mind.'

Page 391. (1) 'On the noted mountain Mam Tor near Castleton are evident marks of an encampment, supposed by some to have been a Roman work. The vulgar story, that this mountain is perpetually crumbling without being diminished, is evidently false, its diminution being very visible.' John Aikin, op. cit., p. 498. One of the Wonders of the Peak, Mam Tor was called the 'Shivering Mountain'.

(2) Another of the Wonders of the Peak, Eldon Hole was known as the 'Bottomless Pit', at least until 1770 when bottom was discovered at 180 feet.

Thomas Hobbes as a boy used to roll stones into it, which dropped 'to the depths of Hell'.

(3) 'Peak's-hole.—It is situated in a deep and narrow recess of the valley in which the town [of Castleton] stands. On each side and near the end of this recess, two faces of rock are seen rising to a great height. At the foot of the rock the mouth of the cavern opens: it is about 14 yards high and 40 wide; the arch at the entrance is regularly formed, and extends nearly 300 feet in a direct line: this part is tolerably light, and is inhabited by a number of poor people who manufacture pack-thread. . . . Beyond the first turning the ground gently declines, and the path is made wet by droppings from the roof. At the distance of 130 yards from the entrance, all further progress was formerly stopped by a projection of the rock, but a passage is now opened through it. The cavern . . . appears about 20 yards from hence to be entirely closed; but on a near approach, a low passage under the rock, almost full of water, is discovered. The opening just admits a small boat, but the passenger must lie almost flat while it is pushed under the rock. On landing, he finds himself in a cavern more spacious than the former, said to be 70 yards wide, and 40 high, but totally dark. . . . The whole length of the subterranean passage is said to be 750 yards. . . . A stream of water runs through the whole length, which must be crossed several times, and after heavy rains is so much swelled as to cut off access to the further parts.' John Aikin, op. cit., p. 74. Cf. p. 232.

Page 395. (1) Presumably a surgical instrument. The *O.E.D.* says 'meaning obscure'.

(2) Gilbert Cowper, Esquire (G).—Perhaps John Gilbert Cooper (1723-69), the poet, who changed his name from Gilbert to Cooper in order to inherit an estate.

Page 397. Cf. p. 390 and note 1.

Page 399. It was a point of decency at this time, not to bring a Mistress amongst strangers. I believe the custom is now altered (G).—Cf. *The Prodigal Rake: Memoirs of William Hickey*, ed. Peter Quennell (New York, 1962), p. 311.

Book XI

Page 408. (1) Cf. p. 259 and note.

(2) *The First and Best Part of Scoggins Jests*, a piece of goliardic humour, published originally perhaps as early as the 1540s, and many times reprinted.

Page 409. Ἢ ωίθι, ἢ ἄπιθι (G).

Page 414. (1) This parody is probably by Graves himself.

(2) Edward Young, *Love of Fame*, i, line 20.

Page 418. (1) This song is by Graves and was reprinted in his poetical miscellany, *Euphrosyne: or, Amusements on the Road of Life* (1776), i. 220–2.

(2) Gleaning.

Page 427. (1) *Henry V*, Prologue to Act IV, line 10.

(2) Cf. p. 50 and note 1.

Page 429. A well turned-out young man. Graves perhaps recalled Homer, *Iliad*, i. 17.

Page 432. (1) The celebrated High-Church divine who was impeached in 1709, a time at which wigs had reached their most splendid proportions. His appearance was familiar through prints.

(2) A word used by Paracelsus to describe various plasters.

Page 437. William Camden, *Britannia*: 'this [Warwick] was the very town which the Romans call'd *Præsidium*: where . . . the Præfect of the *Dalmatian* horse was posted. . . .' English edition of 1722, i. 605.

Book XII

Page 443. According to one legend the name 'the Gentle Craft' was given to the shoemakers by St. Hugh, out of gratitude to some members of that craft who had tended him faithfully when he was in prison. It was made familiar by Thomas Dekker's play *The Shoemaker's Holiday, or a Pleasant Comedy of The Gentle Craft* (1599).

Page 449. No source has been found for this very Erasmian statement.

Page 451. (1) Westley Hall, who married Martha, John Wesley's eldest sister, after jilting Kezziah, his youngest, and who later became a polygamist.

(2) An Antinomian, whom Wesley first encountered in Dublin, and who caused a great deal of trouble to the Methodist leaders for years. He believed he was 'not under the law', might help himself to any property he wished to have, and had 'a right to all the women in the world'. See Wesley's *Journal*, 23 March 1746 and 10 April 1750.

Page 452. John Radcliffe (1652–1714) and John Freind (1675–1728), eminent physicians, the first of whom founded the Radcliffe Infirmary in Oxford and St. Bartholomew's Hospital in London.

Page 455. All the idea, which the country people have of that great Genius, is, that he excelled in smart repartees, and *selling of bargains*, as they call it.—According to the original sense of the word, however, Shakespear might properly be called a Jestour.—See WARTON's Hist. Poetry (G).—

Thomas Warton, *The History of English Poetry* (1774), p. 90, considered
jesters, actors, musicians, etc., to have been all much the same.

Page 458. Mr. Welchman probably soon quitted this station: as the White-
Lyon has been kept for some years by Mr. Peyton; who, by a secret peculiar
to publicans, of making general favours appear particular ones, has brought
the house into great vogue (G).—Edward Welchman (1665-1739) published *Articuli XXXIX Ecclesiae Anglicanae . . . Illustrati* at Oxford in
1713. One of his sons became vicar of Tamworth and another kept the inn
at Stratford-on-Avon.

Page 459. There is an estate held by a ridiculous tenure, in consequence of
a will of this kind, at Castor in Lincolnshire (G).

Page 463. So Rapin and Balzac call him; but his true name was, Jerom de
Matini, of Narni (G).—' 'Tis reported that a Capuchin, named Philip de
Narny, preached at Rome in the time of Gregory the Fifteenth, with such
power, such action and zeale, that he never appeared in publick, but he
made the people, as they went out of the church, cry out in the streets,
"Lord have mercy upon us". 'Tis said of the same person, that having one
day preach'd before the Pope concerning the residence of bishops, he
terrified so by the vehemency of his discours thirty bishops that heard him,
that they fled next day every one to his respective diocese.' [R. Rapin],
*Reflections Upon the Use of the Eloquence of these Times, Translated out of
French* (Oxford, 1672), p. 108. Cf. J.-L. G. de Balzac, *Œuvres Choisies*
(Paris, 1822), ii. 372.

Page 466. The impecunious George Montagu, second Earl of Halifax
(1716-61), married the wealthy heiress Anne Dunk in 1741, and added her
name to his own.

Page 473. (1) The argument of the walking-stick.
    (2) *The Character of a Good Parson*, lines 34-37.

A LIST OF PRINCIPAL VARIANTS

THE following readings have been incorporated from the corrections made by the author in the second and third editions of 1774 and 1783. The original readings are shown in the list of variants. The first, second, and third editions are indicated by the symbols 1, 2, 3. There are no important variants in the fourth edition, 1792.

	Reading of text	*Variant*
p. 2, *l.* 17	week	time 1, 2.
p. 3, *ll.* 28–29	they are the practices . . . of the people	they are the practices, rather than the principles, of the people 1, 2.
p. 4, *ll.* 1–5	'As for the frequent allusions to Scripture . . . the author of this history.'	*Not in* 1, 2.
p. 11, *ll.* 5–6	a refined and voluptuous People	a refined People 1.
p. 23, *l.* 13	age	time 1.
p. 28, *ll.* 10–11	and, as Jerry used to say, was 'a pretty man in a pulpit;'	*Not in* 1.
p. 30, *l.* 25	few novel opinions	no new opinions 1, 2.
p. 34, *l.* 24	corruption	construction 1.
p. 35, *ll.* 12–13	but in the evening resumed their deliberations	*Not in* 1.
p. 48, *l.* 1	intended to consult	consulted 1.
p. 49, *ll.* 32–33	as he imagined	*Not in* 1.
p. 52, *l.* 22	numerous	humorous 1, 2.
p. 52, *l.* 38	found	perceived 1.
p. 53, *l.* 4–7	shun, as you would the *plague* . . . your future expectations.	desist from these anti-christian, these more than Paganish recreations, which are poison; and listen to my words. 1.
p. 54, *l.* 21	Come, come, what's that to the purpose;	Odzounterkins! 1, 2.

Reading of text	Variant
p. 57, *l.* 25 loo	putt 1, 2.
p. 58, *l.* 29 lie [*editorial change*]	lay *all eds.*
p. 65, *l.* 31 lying	laying 1, 2.
p. 72, *l.* 35 straggling	struggling 1.
p. 75, *l.* 18 compunction	compulsion 1.
p. 82, *l.* 30 as very seldom	as we had seldom 1.
p. 83, *l.* 24 apprehension	expectation 1, 2.
p. 85, *l.* 33 I saw	saw 1, 2.
p. 87, *l.* 23 of it	of the house 1.
p. 88, *l.* 39 winter [*editorial change*]	winters *all eds.*
p. 89, *l.* 16 tenderness	fondness 1, 2.
p. 94, *ll.* 21-22 I would have you make the most of your charms	I would make the most of my charms 1.
p. 97, *l.* 20 sent	wrote 1.
p. 98, *ll.* 2-3 insisted upon it, 'that I had returned in the same coach I came up in.'	*Not in* 1.
p. 112, *l.* 10 lived	came 1.
p. 113, *l.* 30 but	so 1.
p. 123, *l.* 34 our arrival at, or departure from,	our arrival or at our departure from 1, 2.
p. 130, *ll.* 34 ff. Besides his crooked Maid ... *animality* to recommend them.	*Not in* 1.
p. 132, *l.* 27 in other respects	*Not in* 1.
p. 133, *l.* 5 large	considerable 1.
p. 149, *l.* 24 eight hundred pounds	six hundred pounds 1, 2.
p. 151, *l.* 4 wearing	to wear 1.
p. 158, *l.* 32 and the well-known Miss Trufle. ... Beau Rueful	and Mr. Rouvill, or (as he was aptly called) Beau Rueful; who were immediately followed by the well-known Miss Trufle, with a black spaniel in her arms, and a squirrel in her pocket. 1, 2.

Reading of text	Variant
p. 160, *ll.* 11 ff. Rouvell [*editorial change*]¹	Rueful *all eds.*
p. 165, *l.* 6 characters	creatures 1, 2.
p. 166, *l.* 12 prevailing	prevailed 1, 2.
p. 174, *l.* 30 consolation	conversation 1.
p. 179, *l.* 5 come	returned 1.
p. 189, *ll.* 21–22 'Very true,' replies Rivers.	'Well,' replies Rivers, 'every man to his taste.' 1, 2.
p. 190, *l.* 6 and	so that 1.
p. 190, *ll.* 37–38 its first motions in	the first motions of 1, 2.
p. 191, *ll.* 27–28 express any displeasure at my freedom	be displeased with it 1, 2.
p. 195, *l.* 31 putting on	affecting 1.
p. 196, *l.* 14 believe	suppose 1.
p. 200, *l.* 17 I should be	that I was 1.
p. 203, *l.* 29 for London	*Not in* 1, 2.
p. 207, *ll.* 20–21 whose principles . . . quite abandoned.	of none, or rather of abandoned, principles. 1.
p. 211, *ll.* 25–26 calling a coach,	called a coach; and 1.
p. 223, *l.* 13 time never hangs	they never hang 1.
p. 225, *l.* 15 cousin	uncle 1.
p. 227, *l.* 25 friends and usual residence.	disconsolate mother. 1, 2.
p. 230, *l.* 35 reviling	revelling 1.
p. 232, *ll.* 5–6 But, though Jerry probably mistook the colic for the symptoms of the New Birth, yet Mr. Whitfield	But Mr. Whitfield 1.

¹ On p. 168 Wildgoose, hearing Rouvell's name for the first time, recognizes him as a former contemporary of his at Oxford. In the first edition at this point he was called by his nickname, Rueful, but in the second the author, most likely thinking it improbable that Wildgoose, who had had no personal acquaintance with him, should recognize him under a nickname, changed it to his surname, Rouvill. (The spelling was changed to Rouvell throughout in the third edition.) He made a similar change earlier in the text, whenever the name was used, but going back only as far as p. 162. In the interest of consistency the present editor has changed it also several times on p. 160.

	Reading of text	*Variant*
p. 245, *l.* 5	tendency	intention 1.
p. 245, *l.* 36	consequences that	consequences, and 1.
p. 247, *l.* 15	inference [*editorial change*]	influence *all eds.*
p. 249, *l.* 5	Rejoice in thy youth—	*Not in* 1.
p. 250, *l.* 28 to *p.* 251, *l.* 31	Wildgoose was now proceeding . . . his escape from this imaginary persecution	*Not in* 1, 2.
p. 251, *l.* 32	these incidents	this incident 1.
p. 253, *l.* 16	Feasts	Treats 1.
p. 261, *l.* 29	roasted	be roasted 1.
p. 263, *ll.* 25-26	providentially provided	providently laid in 1.
p. 264, *l.* 24	but	that 1.
p. 264, *l.* 30	the conquering of cities	that conquering cities 1.
p. 277, *l.* 24	*benefice*	*benefit* 1.
p. 279, *l.* 30	risque	resign 1, 2.
p. 290, *ll.* 1-2	resuming our journey by land, proceeded	resume our journey by land; and proceeded 1.
p. 293, *l.* 26	sitten	sat 1.
p. 295, *l.* 11	*followed by a cold Collation*	*concluded with a cold Sauce* 1.
p. 296, *l.* 6	to a fair in Herefordshire	*Not in* 1, 2.
p. 296, *l.* 7	pious	good 1.
p. 298, *l.* 3	should	would 1.
p. 301, *ll.* 8-9	semi-barbarous and uncivilized	somewhat barbarous and semi-gothic 1, 2.
p. 304, *l.* 36	good	*Not in* 1.
p. 306, *l.* 19	persisting	persisted 1.
p. 308, *l.* 11	observing	observed 1.
p. 308, *l.* 18	and falsely accused	*Not in* 1, 2.
p. 309, *l.* 11	these	them 1.
p. 309, *l.* 30	soon	early 1.
p. 311, *ll.* 29-30	made of the hinge of an old Coffin	made of hinge of old Coffins 1.
p. 312, *ll.* 21-22	nonsensical books such as these	this sort of nonsensical books 1.

Reading of text	Variant
p. 319, *l.* 7 solemn	sullen 1.
p. 324, *l.* 1 my Landlord	and my Landlord 1.
p. 325, *l.* 5 inviting	invited 1.
p. 327, *l.* 24 who	that 1.
p. 360, *l.* 8 who	that 1.
p. 370, *l.* 22 fire to	alight 1, 2.
p. 376, *l.* 11 *Expediency*	*Necessity* 1.
p. 387, *ll.* 32–34 jewels (which . . . toilette) from	jewels; which . . . toilette from 1, 2.
p. 393, *l.* 22 of	in 1.
p. 398, *l.* 16 this	their 1, 2.
p. 402, *l.* 18 the offender	it 1, 2.
p. 402, *l.* 19 murderers [*editorial change*]	murders *all eds.*
p. 402, *ll.* 28–29 And a man . . . evade the law.	*Not in* 1.
p. 407, *l.* 20 could	should 1.
p. 408, *l.* 30 moral	moraled 1.
p. 415, *l.* 35 hanging	hanged 1.
p. 416, *l.* 15 *is under a Necessity of drinking*	*compelled to drink* 1.
p. 422, *l.* 5 rashly	*Not in* 1.
p. 422, *ll.* 24–25 Squire intends every year to give	young Squire ever year gives 1.
p. 423, *l.* 28 A.D. M DCC XXVI.	A.D. 17— 1.
p. 423, *l.* 32 1726.	17— 1.
p. 427, *ll.* 20–21 his salvation	their salvation 1.
p. 431, *l.* 10 he *might*	that he *might* 1.
p. 432, *ll.* 29–30 *wine*, which (if . . . balsamic), upon	*wine* (if . . . balsamic), which, upon 1.
p. 434, *l.* 35 regard was to be paid to	stress was to be laid upon 1.
p. 434, *ll.* 35–37 then, advising . . . morning, Dr. Greville and Wildgoose	they advised . . . morning; and then Dr. Greville with Wildgoose 1.
p. 442, *l.* 24 that	who 1.

	Reading of text	*Variant*
p. 449, *ll.* 26–29	I am partly of Erasmus's opinion . . . in a seditious manner.	*Not in* 1.
p. 452, *l.* 4	replies	says 1.
p. 455, *l.* 35	make her a visit	make a visit 1.
p. 466, *l.* 24	not much to	not to 1.
p. 4, *n.* 1	Many of those scripture expressions are omitted in this edition.	*Not in* 1, 2.
p. 18, *n.* 1	On the Bath road.	*Not in* 2, 3.
p. 38, *n.* 1	This was a meeting. . . . by Dr. Johnson and Mr. Steevens.	This was a meeting of great renown in the last century, revived by one Captain Dover, for wrestling, back-sword, and other athletic exercises; and celebrated in verse by the Pindars of Oxford and Cambridge. 1.
p. 39, *n.* 1	See HURD's Letters on Chivalry.	*Not in* 1, 2.
p. 63, *n.* 1	By *casuistical* . . . and *puritanical*.	*Not in* 1, 2.
p. 99, *n.* 1	Wigs were generally worn at this time.	*Not in* 1, 2.
p. 348, *n.* 2	See Dr. *Johnson*'s Grammar, Letter *H*.	*Not in* 1, 2.
p. 366, *n.* 2	The author . . . excellent writers.	*Not in* 1, 2.
p. 395, *n.* 2	Gilbert Cowper, Esquire.	*Not in* 1, 2.
p. 455, *n.* 1	According to the original sense. . . . See WARTON's Hist. Poetry.	*Not in* 1, 2.
p. 459, *n.* 1	There is an estate . . . in Lincolnshire.	*Not in* 1, 2.

PRINTED IN GREAT BRITAIN
AT THE UNIVERSITY PRESS, OXFORD
BY VIVIAN RIDLER
PRINTER TO THE UNIVERSITY